W.J.BURLEY

WYCLIFFE IN PAUL'S COURT

WYCLIFFE AND THE BEALES

WYCLIFFE AND THE TANGLED WEB

W.J. Burley was a schoolmaster until he retired to concentrate on his writing. His many Wycliffe books include, most recently, *Wycliffe and the House of Fear* and *Wycliffe and the Redhead*. He died in 2002.

W.J.BURLEY

WYCLIFFE IN PAUL'S COURT

WYCLIFFE AND THE BEALES

WYCLIFFE AND THE TANGLED WEB

Wycliffe in Paul's Court
First published in Great Britain by Victor Gollancz in 1980

Wycliffe and the Beales
First published in Great Britain by Victor Gollancz in 1983

Wycliffe and the Tangled Web
First published in Great Britain by Victor Gollancz in 1988

This omnibus edition published in 2010
by Orion Books Ltd
Orion House, 5 Upper St Martin's Lane
London WC2H 9EA

An Hachette UK company

A CIP catalogue record for this book is available
from the British Library.

ISBN 9781407230221

Printed in Great Britain by Clays Ltd, St Ives plc

www.orionbooks.co.uk

WYCLIFFE IN PAUL'S COURT

CHAPTER ONE

Nobody in Falcon Street asked themselves where Willy Goppel had come from or how it was that the Dolls' House Shop had become as much a part of the street as St Olave's Church or the Old Mansion House or the market which closed the street to vehicles every Saturday. Willy Goppel had established himself as an institution, accepted uncritically. He spoke precise English with a German accent for, like the Bayreuth Festival, the Passion Play, Mad King Ludwig and the Nazi Party, Willy was Bavarian born. Many people in the street remembered his English wife but she had died years ago leaving him with a six-year-old son and some house property scattered about the city. His son Frederick, now a man, had left home though he still visited his father when he needed money. The property had grown too, both in value and extent, and though few people realized it, Willy was a wealthy man.

Willy lived over his shop in part of an old house of which the other, larger part, was occupied by the Wards who ran a sub post office and sold stationery, sweets and tobacco. A broad archway sliced through the ground floor of the house giving access to three modern dwellings built round a courtyard which had a splendid oak tree in the middle. A century before, the Paul family, carriers in a fair way of business, had lived in the house and kept their horses and waggons in appropriate buildings round the courtyard; now, the carrier business forgotten, those buildings had been replaced by three rather pleasant houses, secluded, not far from the city centre, and known as Paul's Court.

It had been another day of the September heatwave and in the cool of the evening Willy was out in his railed-off backyard, weeding and watering his sink gardens. He had started with one, now he had six, each laid out in an accepted style of landscape gardening with carefully chosen plants which, as far as possible, maintained the scale. On a patch of grass, protected by chicken-wire, Willy's guinea-pigs were getting their daily ration of the out-of-doors and at a little distance his marmalade cat sprawled in the sunshine, biting its paws.

The oak tree spread its green canopy over the middle of the courtyard and above a little red sports-car parked beneath it. The car belonged to Natalie Cole. Natalie lived with her fifteen-year-old daughter and Geoff Bishop in the house on the right-hand side of the Court. The other residents rather ostentatiously put their cars in the garages provided but such hints were lost on Natalie. Willy had only to raise his head from his sink gardens to see her through the wide open window of her living-room. She was seated at the table eating something, almost certainly something out of a tin, for Natalie was not a devoted housekeeper. She had spent the afternoon sunbathing on her verandah and, as on other days during this week of unusually hot weather, she had started by wearing a bikini and finished naked on the folding bed.

Marty Fiske came ambling across the Court and leaned on the fence, watching Willy at work, his eyes unwavering and vacant. Everybody treated Marty as a child though he was eighteen and powerfully built.

'You give the flowers water, Mr Goppy?'

'Yes, Marty.'

Marty laughed, gobbling his words, 'Flowers like to drink, don't they, Mr Goppy?'

6

'They must have water, Marty.'

The same conversation, with minor variations, took place every time Marty happened to come along when Willy was tending his plants.

Mrs Fiske's voice came from the far end of the Court: 'Marty! Where are you? Your meal is on the table . . . Marty!'

She could not see them because of the tree.

'I got to go now, that was mother.'

'Good night, Marty.'

'Good night, Mr Goppy.'

Willy's part of the house comprised his shop, his workshop and a little hall on the ground floor; living-room, kitchen and bathroom on the first floor, and two bedrooms on the second. There was a square stairwell and a rather impressive staircase, relic of the original house. He went upstairs to the kitchen, washed his hands and started to prepare the evening meal – lamb chop, boiled potatoes, greens and mint sauce. His tastes in food had been wholly anglicized. The cat, too well fed to be importunate, curled up under the table.

Willy was below average height, thin, with sparse grey hair, dark eyes and sallow skin. His features were rather large for his face giving him a solemn yet clownish appearance. His kitchen was separated by only a thin partition from the Wards' and their son, Henry, was in his bedroom playing jazz records very loud. Willy whistled through his teeth in time to the beat – not that he had a taste for jazz but he liked to be reminded of the life next door. He had watched the Ward children – Henry and Alison – growing up and he was fond of them both; they called him 'Uncle'.

In the Ward's living-room Alison was laying the table for their evening meal. Her mother had just come up from the shop and was in the kitchen preparing to serve the meal she had put in the oven earlier. Alison was sixteen and still at school; she wore the regulation school summer uniform – a short-sleeved frock in a small brown-and-white check; she had straight fair hair which draped itself over her shoulders, a peaches-and-cream complexion and serious blue eyes.

'How were things at school today?' Her mother's voice came from the kitchen.

'All right, I suppose. We had a history test on our holiday work and I didn't like it much.'

'I thought history was your best subject.'

Alison paused long enough to prevent the irritation she felt being apparent in her voice. 'It was all on the seventeenth century, nothing on the eighteenth I spent so much time on.'

'Never mind dear, I expect you did as well as the others.'

Julia Ward was a well meaning woman who never tired of looking on the bright side. At nineteen she had won a beauty contest and when the interviewer asked her what she wanted most in life she had answered: 'I just want to make people happy.'

There were four places at the table; Alison's father would come up from the shop at the last minute, probably when the soup was already on the table. Her brother Henry, who was seventeen, was up in his room listening to old records of Duke Ellington, his latest craze.

Four table knives, four forks, four soup spoons, four side-plates with green and gilt edging and four table napkins ... Abruptly she experienced one of those moments when she seemed to exist outside herself, able to see herself as a stranger. She saw that girl who went to school and worked hard to learn things she did not want to know, the girl who spent two hours every night doing homework, the girl who helped her mother with household chores, the girl who next year would be in the sixth form working for 'A' levels . . . 'It's your future you've got to think of, dear.' What future? *Whose* future? What would it be like to be the real Alison Ward? What would she do?

It was the time of day when the living-room caught the sun and golden light flooded in, seeming to vibrate to the brash rhythms of the music upstairs.

'Alison! What are you thinking of, love? Your father will be up at any minute and the table not laid . . .'

'Sorry.'

Natalie Cole was taking a shower; when she had finished she dried herself and walked through into the bedroom to look at her body in a full-length mirror. There was nothing narcissistic about the minute scrutiny to which she subjected herself; her body was one of her assets and, in the nature of things, a wasting one. Though not seriously so — yet.

At thirty-two she still looked girlish, her waist measurement had stayed at twenty-two ever since she had been interested enough to remember, and she had the lithe figure of a dancer; her belly was flat, her navel perfect and the pubic hair-line was low with no tendency to creep upward. A tiny appendix scar marred her right side. She remembered that surgeon: 'You'll have to wear a bit more bikini, young lady.' Smug, leering bastard! Her breasts were firm and full . . .

Her skin was changing though, losing that velvet elasticity, especially on her legs and neck. She studied her face; she was no longer a pretty girl but was she a beautiful woman? Her jet black hair, just short of shoulder length, seemed to cling and mould itself to her head, framing her face in a classical oval. She had dark eyes which mirrored every subtle change in the light and her skin had a warm colour, as though lightly tanned, neither swarthy nor pale . . . So far so good; but there was something – something about the set of her mouth which was becoming more pronounced . . . If she had seen it in another woman she would have said, 'There goes a bitch!'

'Christ! I'm getting morbid.'

She turned to pick up her wrap from the bed and saw her daughter standing in the doorway watching her. Yvette was fifteen, slim and dark like her mother but seventeen years younger. The expression Natalie had surprised on her daughter's face annoyed her; a look of detached appraisal.

'What do you want?'

'To tell you I'm going out.'

'Have you done your homework?' The question was part of a prescribed ritual, not intended to be answered.

'Who are you going with?'

'A girl.'

'Not the Ward boy?'

'No.'

'You haven't had a meal.'

'I'll get something out.'

Natalie watched her go. Jeans and a T-shirt; no bra, of course; and across the front of the T-shirt: 'Restricted Area', stencilled in red.

'Poor little bastard!' Natalie's sympathy was not so much for her daughter as for her sex. She called out, 'Don't be late, Yvette!'

The front door slammed.

A few minutes later a car drove into the Court and she went to the window to see who it was. A Rover 2600, maroon and spotless. Martin Fiske, Marty's father, was a business consultant with a firm of his own. The Fiskes lived in the house which faced up the Court. Natalie watched him put his car away and saw him come out of the garage, carrying his briefcase. Fiske was in his early forties, an ex-rugby player going slightly to seed; thinning hair, a self-important manner and the beginnings of a paunch. He wore a dove-grey light-weight suit, silk shirt and tie and suede shoes.

'Smooth bastard!'

Fiske came downstairs from washing his hands and entered the dining-room just as his wife was bringing two bowls of soup from the kitchen. The table was laid for two.

'Where's Marty?'

'In his room; I gave him his meal early because I know how much you dislike having to eat with him.'

Joan Fiske, at forty-eight, was thin, angular and careworn. Her manner towards her husband was a curious blend of subservience and aggression, like a dog who is sporadically ill-treated.

Fiske sat down, tucked in his napkin and tasted the soup before adding pepper and salt.

'I want to talk to you, Martin.'

'You surprise me. What about?'

She was crumbling a bread-roll into tiny fragments. 'It's about that woman, she's been sunbathing on her verandah again, in the nude.'

Fiske soaked a piece of bread in his soup and chewed it.

'It's Marty I worry about. I mean, that sort of stimulation could lead to anything.'

'I don't suppose he even notices the woman.'

Mrs Fiske became irritated. 'Of course he notices! He came in this afternoon and said "That lady out there with no clothes." You know what the psychologist told us as well as I do.'

Fiske finished his soup and dabbed his lips with his napkin. His wife went on: 'What a way for the mother of a young girl to carry on! But what can you expect from a woman who earns her living in a nightclub?'

'She happens to own the club.'

'What difference does that make? Those places are no better than brothels.'

Fiske turned his cold, fishy eyes on his wife. 'Of course, you know about these things.'

Mrs Fiske shifted her ground. 'I can't imagine why you brought her here in the first place.'

Fiske cleared his throat but did not raise his voice. 'I did not bring her here; I met her in the course of business; she happened to say that she was looking for a house and I mentioned that there was one vacant in the Court.'

Joan Fiske pushed away her soup scarcely touched, collected her husband's plate and went through to the kitchen. There was no conversation while she served the second course, veal cutlets with beans and sauté potatoes, but when they were seated once more she took up where she had left off. 'That man who lives with her, what does he do?'

Fiske sighed. 'Bishop? I must have told you a dozen times, he runs a garage in Fenton Street; he sells second-hand cars and hires out cars and vans.'

'He's hardly ever home. I never see him.'

Fiske helped himself to more potatoes and gravy; his wife picked at her food then put down her knife and fork with an air of finality. 'Anyway, I went to see Mrs Ward at the post office this afternoon. I told her about the sunbathing and I asked her to back me up in a protest.'

'You did *what*?' Fiske stopped eating to glare at his wife in sudden anger. 'How many times have I told you not to get involved in gossip and squabbles in the Court? I can't afford it! These people are clients of mine. I handle all Natalie Cole's business as well as Bishop's; and Willy Goppel is one of my best accounts. They're my clients and your bread-and-butter. Do you understand?'

Mrs Fiske went over to the defensive. 'I'm sure I've never done anything to upset Willy Goppel.'

'No, but you will. You'll think of something. His cat will shit on our grass or dig up a dandelion in your bloody flower-bed.'

Joan Fiske stared down at her plate and her features crumpled on the verge of weeping.

'For God's sake don't start howling! I've had enough to put up with for one day.'

From upstairs came a low moaning sound; Marty was singing to himself as he made one of his simple jigsaws for the thousandth time.

The house on the fourth side of the Court was occupied by an elderly couple, the Hedleys. They were tall, lean and desiccated. Until four of five years back a nephew of Mrs Hedley, orphaned at the age of ten, had lived with them and they had brought him up. Now he and Willy Goppel's son, Frederick, shared a flat in another part of the city. Mr Hedley was a retired council official while his wife came of a family with pretensions in the world of the arts and music and was considered to have married beneath her. As if to make the point their radio played classical music through much of the day when Mrs Hedley was not giving *bravura* piano performances of her favourite composers. The music furnished a subdued background to the other life of the Court. The Hedleys had their main meal at mid-day and he seemed to spend a lot of time moving uneasily about the house like a caged cat. From time to time he appeared on his verandah where he would stand, staring into space for ten minutes or more, a cigarette dangling from his lower lip.

The post office Wards had reached the dessert stage of their meal.

'Mrs Fiske was in this afternoon, while you were at the bank.'

Edward Ward was eating strawberry mousse with a preoccupied air and his wife had to repeat her remark.

'What did she want?'

'She bought a few stamps but she wanted us to join her in a complaint about Mrs Cole.'

'Because she keeps her car under the tree? Seems a bit childish, doesn't it?'

'It wasn't about the car; she objects to Mrs Cole sunbathing in the nude on her verandah. She's afraid it will upset Marty.'

'I shouldn't think Marty would notice one way or the other. Anyway, what did you say to her?'

'I said that being in business we couldn't afford to get involved with disagreements.'

Ward nodded. 'Quite right too.'

'Does she sunbathe in the nude?' Alison looked across at her mother.

'Apparently. I haven't seen her.'

'Have you seen her, Henry?' Alison turned to her brother.

Henry, with sandy hair and freckles, blushed easily and he did so now to his intense annoyance. 'No.'

'You seemed to be getting on well with her the other morning.'

'I helped her to start her car, that was all. She had a dodgy contact in the distributor.'

'Was that what it was? She seemed very grateful, I was watching: she positively drooled. Yvette will be jealous.'

Henry was angry. 'Why must you always—?'

Mrs Ward laughed. 'Don't take any notice of her, Henry; you ought to know her by now.'

Henry got up from his chair. 'I'm sick of her getting at me all the time. What business is it of hers anyway?' He strode out of the room, slamming the door behind him.

14

Alison was contrite.

'You really do tease the poor boy, Alison.'

'I'm sorry, but he always rises to it, it's like putting your money in a slot machine. I'll go and say I'm sorry when he's had a chance to cool off.'

The sound of another Duke Ellington record came from upstairs.

Mrs Ward looked at her daughter. 'Is he still seeing that Yvette?'

'Every day; we all three go to the same school.'

'Don't be clever, dear; you know exactly what I mean.'

'Yes, mother, and I'm not going to spy on him and report back.'

Mrs Ward was hurt. 'As if I would want you to! It's just that I don't like the idea of him getting mixed up with those people. I've no doubt the little girl is very nice but her mother . . .'

'I don't think he goes out with her mother.'

'Alison! You really are very rude.'

Henry lay on his bed listening to the Duke Ellington version of Grieg's Peer Gynt.

'What's the matter? Can't you get it to start?'

He had been on his way to school and she was trying to start her little red car.

'I don't know what's the matter with it and Geoff has gone to work. Geoff Bishop was the man who lived with her.

'Shall I have a look?'

'Do you understand these things?'

'I'm doing a course on car maintenance at school.'

'Really?'

She was wearing a trouser suit in some silky material the colour of flame.

After a few minutes with his head under the bonnet he emerged and said, 'Now try.'

The engine started first kick. 'My! You must have oily

15

fingers or whatever it takes!' She looked up at him from the driving seat of her little car. 'You must come over sometime for a drink.'

He stood by the car door, red faced. 'I'd like that.'

She saw that he meant it and was amused. 'You've been going out with Yvette, haven't you?'

'Once or twice.'

She smiled. 'Well, come over on Sunday afternoon after you've had lunch.'

'Thanks.'

'Can I give you a lift?'

'No, thanks, I've got my moped.'

The Duke Ellington record ran out and in the ensuing silence he could hear the subdued whine of the little lathe Willy Goppel used for making his dolls' house fittings. There was a tap at the door and his sister came in. She stood by the bed, looking down at him. 'Sorry, Harry-boy.'

He picked at a loose thread in his jeans. 'It doesn't matter.'

'I was only teasing.'

'I know.'

She turned to go.

'Ali, she asked me to come over for a drink on Sunday afternoon.'

'Are you going?'

'Would you?'

'Why not? Are you afraid she'll seduce you or something? In any case, Yvette will be there, won't she?'

He did not answer at once then he said, 'I know it sounds daft but I had the impression it wasn't going to be like that.'

'You mean she really does fancy you?'

'Now you're at it again!'

'No, I'm not; from what I've heard about her you could be right.'

16

He swung his legs off the bed. 'Hell! I thought life got simpler as you got older.'

His sister grinned down at him. 'Never mind, boy, when rape is inevitable, just lie back and enjoy it.'

He chuckled despite himself. 'Where did you get that one?'

'Confucius, he say.'

'I don't believe it.'

They were silent for a moment or two while they both listened to the whirring of Willy Goppel's lathe.

Alison said, 'I'd better do some homework.'

'You make me feel lazy.'

'I've got 'O' levels in November.'

'You'll be all right, Ali; when they dished out the brains to this family you got a double ration.'

'Idiot!'

Alison's room was on the same floor. It was large and she had decorated it to her own taste. The floorboards were varnished with three or four rugs scattered about; there was an armchair with a blue-linen loose cover to match the bedspread; varnished shelves held her school books and a large number of paperbacks, and she had a table and chair by the window. A magnificent three-storied dolls' house occupied one corner of the room, a masterpiece of a dolls' house furnished exquisitely in late Victorian or Edwardian style on a scale of one-twelfth. The dolls' house had been a tenth birthday present from Uncle Willy and six years later she was still under its spell. She could lose count of time sitting on the floor, peering into the rooms and imagining the lives of the people who lived in them; people for whom time had stood still on some summer afternoon when there were still nannies and children had nurseries where there was always a giant rocking-horse and mother had leg-of-mutton sleeves to her dress and father wore tight trousers and side-whiskers.

17

She sprawled on a rug with her biology textbook.

'In the duodenum the food is mixed with secretions from the walls of the duodenum itself and from the pancreas. . . .'

She closed the book on her finger and recited the enzymes and what they did, moving her lips soundlessly.

It was all very well talking about sex equality but women still had to have babies. In a confused and inarticulate way she felt that women like Natalie Cole somehow registered a protest and she was both repelled and intrigued.

Willy Goppel switched off his lathe and gathered up the sixty or seventy little pieces of wood he had turned; they were balusters for the staircase of a commissioned dolls' house. He moved from his bench by the window to a large table which occupied most of the workshop where the house was under construction. The staircase rose in a graceful double curve from the hall to a gallery which went most of the way round the first floor. Willy started to insert the balusters into little holes already drilled to receive them; the newel posts were in place and now came the moment of truth when he would fit the handrails.

Scufflings and scratchings, whistles, little grunts and cries came from the animal cages against one wall of the workshop. In addition to his guinea-pigs Willy kept hamsters and gerbils and, in heated vivaria, geckos, skinks and a variety of small snakes. Outside the light was fading but in the workshop there were two powerful lamps with green shades. Usually when he was working Willy felt completely relaxed, totally absorbed and regardless of any other care, but tonight a nagging concern troubled him so that he could not concentrate. His hand trembled and one of the balusters slipped from his fingers.

'Verflucht!'

It was rare for him to swear at all, rarer still for him to swear in German. Nowadays he seemed to think mostly in English.

That morning, before opening the shop, he had set out as usual to buy the things he needed for the day. He had never gone in for bulk purchases nor troubled himself with refrigerators or freezers so he lived from hand to mouth. He preferred it that way; he enjoyed his morning stroll, visiting the neighbourhood shops, stopping for a yarn here and there and picking up the news of the street. As he was passing under the archway he had heard Natalie Cole's car behind him; she drew level and stopped, waiting for her chance to filter into the traffic along Falcon Street. She was beside him, looking up with an amused, faintly sardonic smile on her face.

'Guten Morgen Herr Hauptmann.'

Her pronunciation was execrable but her meaning was clear and he was so taken aback that he remained standing foolishly long after she had joined the stream of traffic. He tried to tell himself that it was a joke. After all, Englishmen sometimes addressed each other as 'Skipper' or even 'Cap'n' without meaning anything by it, but the words laboriously repeated in German . . . It was too much of a coincidence.

A month ago a thief had stolen from his workshop desk a cigar box containing eighty pounds in cash and souvenirs of his youth in Germany. He had not reported the theft to the police.

Willy picked up one of the two stair rails he had carved, a thin snake of wood worked to the right section and curved in two planes with little holes drilled to fit over the tops of the balusters. A few moments of intense concentration and it was securely in place. He reached for the second rail.

Over the years, without actually saying so, he had

19

allowed people to believe that he was a German Jew, a victim of the *Totenkopfverbande*. Many times he had been asked, 'What was it really like in the camps?' And he had always answered, 'I managed to avoid that, thank God!' But if that was not a lying answer it was certainly an evasion of the truth. Now, after more than thirty years!

He looked at the second rail in his hand as though it was something strange and unfamiliar then pulled himself together and set about fitting it to the staircase.

The street-door bell rang and he went through to the shop to answer it but he did not switch on the shop light. He opened the door and his son, Frederick, followed him in.

'I saw the light from the street so I thought I'd look in and see how you are.'

Willy led the way through to the workshop. Frederick was in his twenties, slim and small and fair – rather effeminate. He stood by the dolls' house, looking at it without interest.

'What brings you here, boy?'

'I told you, I just happened to be passing.'

Willy said nothing for a while, not until he had completed the fitting of the second handrail, then he turned to his son. 'Did you happen to be passing about a month ago?'

'I don't know what you mean, it's longer than that since I was here.'

Willy looked him straight in the eyes. 'Somebody came in here while I was out doing my shopping and stole eighty pounds in money, some papers and a few souvenirs from my desk.' He nodded towards an old-fashioned high desk with a flap-lid which stood against the wall.

The young man looked scared.

'You don't think it was me? Why should I steal from you? It could have been anybody. You go out and leave

20

the shop door unlocked. Anybody can walk in and help themselves.'

Willy nodded. 'Somebody did. I wonder how they knew where to look.'

Freddie recovered a little of his poise. 'It's obvious, dad. Anybody after valuables would look in a desk, wouldn't they?'

'The desk was locked, somebody forced the lock with a chisel.'

Willy held his son's gaze for a little longer. 'You don't have to steal from me, Frederick.'

'But I swear—'

Willy sighed. 'No need to swear, Frederick. In any case it's not so much the money as the papers I'm concerned about.'

'You should lock the shop when you go out, dad.'

'I do – now. When I remember.'

There was an interval of silence then Freddie said, 'What did the police say?'

'They did not say anything because I did not tell them.'

Willy spent a little time lightly polishing the handrail he had just fitted before turning to his son again. 'Are you in some sort of trouble?'

'No trouble – no.'

'Short of money?'

Frederick laughed uneasily. 'Who isn't?'

Willy took out his wallet and drew from it three five-pound notes. 'Will that see you through?'

'It will help; thanks, dad.'

Willy sighed. 'I only help you, boy, to keep you out of trouble. You understand?'

'Yes, dad; thanks.'

'In a few minutes I shall be going upstairs to prepare my supper; there is enough for two if you care to join me.'

'No, dad, I can't; I've got to meet somebody.'

Much later, after Willy and the other inhabitants of the Court were in bed, the little red sports-car erupted through the archway and screeched to a halt beneath the tree. There was an interval before Natalie Cole got out, swaying with tiredness.

CHAPTER TWO

Yvette came downstairs, her mother and Geoff Bishop were still in bed. She went to the kitchen, took a bottle of milk from the refrigerator and emptied half of it into a glass.

Saturday morning; no school for two whole days. All week she had looked forward to being free of the boredom of school, now the day stretched ahead – blank; at least until evening. She found a sponge cake in a tin, cut off a slice and took it with her milk to the verandah. It was another fine day. Marty Fiske was playing with Willy Goppel's cat, trying to get it to chase a piece of string, but though the cat watched, green eyed, it would not budge.

The sun, the tree, the cobbles, the grass, the houses and the blue sky had a quality of unchanging stillness; she seemed to be enveloped, smothered by a *now* which threatened to go on for evermore.

'Nothing will ever happen, nothing will ever change.'

' 'lo, 'vette.' Marty grinned foolishly; he was always embarrassed when he spoke to her.

It was absurd, a man performing the antics and adopting the postures of a shy little boy. She made no allowances and she was brusque, 'Hullo.'

'I'm playing with Mr Goppy's cat.'

'So I see.'

'I like cats.'

The window of the Wards' living-room over the archway was wide open; she could hear a radio or record player and from time to time she saw Alison pass

23

the window. The Ward family had had their breakfasts, all four of them sitting round a table together. Now Mr and Mrs Ward were in the shop and Alison was clearing away. Later she would wash up. Afterwards she would spend two or three hours on her school work, then lunch. In the afternoon she would meet a couple of other girls from school and they would go off cycling together. In the evening they might go mad and visit a coffee bar.

'God!'

All the same, the Wards were a family, they held together and counted on each other. When she was with Henry it was 'We' do this or 'We' do the other. She both resented and envied his calm assumption of belonging.

She finished her cake and drank her milk. 'If only there was something I really *wanted*!'

She left her empty glass on the verandah and went down the steps, across the Court and let herself into Willy Goppel's yard. His back door was open and she drifted into his workshop.

'Good morning, Yvette. You are early this morning. I have not started to clean out the cages.'

'I'll do it.'

'But I cannot let you do it all, child—'

She snapped, 'I'll do it! And I wish you wouldn't call me "child".'

Willy was not in the least put out. 'All right, Yvette, thank you. You are a great help to me with the animals. You have a way with them which is rare. It is only that people should not have pets unless they are prepared to look after them themselves. I think.'

'There are lots of things people shouldn't do.'

Yvette liked Willy, partly because he was a loner like herself, partly because he did not ask questions or offer advice. But she was frequently rude to him because she was afraid that unless she kept her distance she might drop her guard and talk to him – really talk.

Willy hovered while she started on the guinea-pigs who were whistling to be fed.

'Why don't you get off to the market?'

'All right, if you are quite sure . . .'

'I'm sure.'

Willy was back in a few minutes wearing cavalry-twill trousers and a linen jacket. He stood for a moment watching the lithe figure of the girl as she went about her task. As she stooped, jeans and T-shirt parted company disclosing an area of slim bare back. She seemed so vulnerable that Willy was moved to say, 'Take care of yourself, Yvette.'

'Don't worry, I always do.'

For once the market had a fine day; there were stalls on both sides from one end of Falcon Street to the other. Through traffic was banned and residents' cars had to take their chance, nudging their way along. Willy closed his shop on Saturdays and in the morning he liked to wander through the street chatting with the stallholders. They were a close-knit community and in some cases the pitches had been handed down from father to son through three or even four generations.

' 'Morning, Willy! I'm busy now but if you look in on your way back I'll keep some nice toms for you. Full of green juice – just as you like 'em.'

There was little chance to talk to the men on the fruit and vegetable stalls who were kept busy by housewives, but the others – selling books, records, fancy goods, clothes and second-hand junk of every description – were glad to chat. It took him nearly an hour to work his way a hundred yards along the street and it was mid-day before he reached his favourite stall. It belonged to a tall, scholarly-looking man who wore a black Homburg hat and was universally known as the

Professor. His stock-in-trade was well above the average and included stamps, coins, medals and a range of books some of which justified the tattered notice, 'Of Antiquarian Interest'.

While the usual, rather elaborate civilities were being exchanged, Willy looked over the display. His eye was caught by a string of German war medals and the Professor must have noticed the sudden change in his expression.

'Are you interested? I bought them only last week. He spoke in a cultured voice, enunciating each syllable distinctly.

'They are mine,' Willy said.

'Yours? You mean you sold them?'

'No, they were stolen from a desk in my workshop.'

The Professor's grey eyes widened. 'My dear fellow! I had no idea that you . . . You must allow me to make immediate restitution. I insist!' He held out the medals in a grandiloquent gesture but Willy did not take them.

'No, I do not want them back. You are welcome to them.'

'But I cannot possibly allow such a thing! They are yours, my friend.'

A gentlemanly argument ensued but Willy was adamant. 'They revive memories best forgotten. I was foolish to keep them and I do not want them back.'

'If you really mean that . . .'

'I do,' Willy said, 'I do.'

The Professor looked from the medals to Willy and back again. He was embarrassed because he had always looked upon Willy as a victim of the Nazis. 'I had no idea . . . You must have had a very distinguished war record, my friend, they did not hand out these for guard duties.'

Willy was terse. 'You do not have to earn medals to own them. You should know that; such things are bought and sold.'

The Professor adjusted his Homburg. 'Of course! How foolish of me! There was I beginning to think that at some time you and I might have tried to kill each other.'

'That,' said Willy, 'is very unlikely.' He turned his back on the medals. 'Now, I wish that you will do me a favour.'

'Anything.'

'I was interested in the medals because they were taken at the same time as some papers which I value, also a photograph. Could it be that you have these also?'

The Professor shook his head. 'I am afraid not, Willy. Only the medals came my way.'

'You know who sold them to you?'

'Unfortunately not. I had never seen him before; he came into my shop and I bought the medals over the counter for cash.' There was a pause before the Professor enquired, 'How far are the police involved?'

'They are not. I did not report the theft.'

The other looked surprised. 'That is good, it makes it easier for me to help you. Tell me what it is you wish.'

'To recover my papers, or at least, to find out what has happened to them.'

The Professor nodded. 'That is reasonable. I will see what can be done. And thank you, my friend, for not making trouble.'

'Trouble,' said Willy, 'I wish to avoid.'

Freddie Goppel and Toby 'Pongo' Lennon lived on the third floor of a near-derelict house in Telfer Street, behind the pannier market. The window of their living-room looked over the narrow street, across the roofs of the market, to an office block a couple of hundred yards away. The room was shabby and dirty, furnished out of junk shops and rarely ventilated or cleaned. Toby, who had lived there since leaving his aunt's house in Paul's

Court, was in his late twenties; he had the build of a gorilla, a thatch of coarse, black hair, a bushy beard and moustache through which his lips protruded pink and moist.

Freddie was looking out of the window at the view which even the sunshine could not redeem. 'I went to see my old man last night.'

Pongo said nothing.

'He was nattering on about his papers. What were those papers, Pongo?'

'Don't you know?'

'You know damn well I can't read German.'

Lennon laughed. 'The boy is called Frederick Goppel but he can't read German.'

'The old man was against it. He wanted me, as he put it, "to up grow into a proper little Englishman".'

'And instead you grew up into a proper little rat. You must be a sore disappointment to him, Freddie.'

'But you can read German. What are they, Pongo?'

'Something to keep us warm next winter, perhaps?'

Freddie looked scared. 'You don't mean blackmail, Pongo? What's he done? I mean, it's one thing to help ourselves to a few quid now and then but . . .'

Lennon stood up and lumbered across the room. He took Freddie's head between his huge hands and looked into his eyes. 'You want to live easy, Freddie, without soiling your dainty hands.' He spoke quietly and without heat. 'Sometimes I wonder why I don't smash that pale, appealing mug of yours once and for all. What would you say to that, pretty boy?'

Freddie's face was surprisingly untroubled. 'Kiss me, Hardy.'

Lennon roared with laughter. 'You win, Freddie, boy! I was only kidding about your old man anyway. But leave the thinking to me – okay?'

'Okay, Pongo.'

Lennon returned to his chair. Freddie's eyes followed him. 'I wish I knew what goes on in that great head of yours, Pongo.'

Lennon laughed. 'Don't worry about it, boy. Pongo will look after you.' He glanced at his watch. 'It's half-twelve, what about going along to the boozer for a pint and a snack?'

* * *

On Sunday afternoon rain fell in a continuous drizzle from leaden clouds which scarcely cleared the top of St Olave's steeple. An hour after lunch Henry crossed the Court and went up the steps to Natalie's door. It stood very slightly open. He knocked and felt that he was being watched from every direction though he knew that his parents were in the front of the house and that Alison had gone out. The Fiskes could not see him and Uncle Willy would be taking his afternoon nap. That left the Hedleys, the zombie like old couple, and Mr Hedley was there on his verandah, staring into space, standing first on one foot, then on the other.

There was no answer to his knock so he pushed the door wider and stepped inside. He felt like a nervous, amateur burglar.

'It's me, Henry Ward.'

'I'm in the living-room.'

He went through the door to his right into a room which was almost wholly white. Only the pictures on the walls offered relief in different shades of blue and green. She was seated in one of the white upholstered armchairs in front of a massive, bright steel, coal-effect electric fire. She wore an acid-green sleeveless frock and she looked at him over the rim of a glass which contained ice cubes and, presumably, whisky. There was a drinks table by her chair.

29

He stood, gauche and tongue-tied.

'So you've come.'

'You said that I might.'

'What will you drink – whisky?'

'I'd rather have a beer if I may.'

She pointed to a white cabinet. 'Help yourself.'

In this cabinet, apart from a great variety of drinks and glasses, there was a miniature refrigerator stocked with beer and minerals. He opened a can and filled a glass then went to stand near her. Her eyes were puffy and her mouth seemed slack. When she spoke she did so carefully as though it involved some slight difficulty.

'You needn't look at me like that; I'm all right, it's just that I've had too much to drink.'

'Why?'

The question seemed to surprise her. 'Do I have to have a reason for drinking too much?'

He was embarrassed. 'I'm sorry, I suppose not.'

'But I do have one – the best; I'm bored – B O R E D ! Are you ever bored, Henry?'

'Sometimes.'

She looked at her glass which was empty and returned it to the table. 'Do you have to stand there like a bloody statue? Don't you bend in the middle or something?'

'Sorry.'

He sat down and she went on: 'If you are expecting to see Yvette she's not here; she's gone off somewhere for the afternoon and Geoff is at the garage so we've got the place to ourselves. Cosy, isn't it?'

'Very nice.'

She chuckled. 'I like you, Henry. You don't have a regular girl-friend?'

'Not a regular one – no.'

'Lucky devil! Just shopping around.'

'No, it's not like that either.'

'Isn't it, Henry?' She was watching him with her large

30

dark eyes which were partly veiled by their lids. 'Why did you come this afternoon?'

'Because you said—'

'Never mind what I said; why did you come?'

'I suppose it was because I think you are a very attractive . . .' he hesitated over the choice of a word then said, 'girl.'

She laughed. 'Thank you, Henry. You'll have to watch it, you have a way with you.'

He felt himself flushing and cursed inwardly. He finished his beer. 'I suppose I'd better be getting back.'

'Why?'

'I don't know really.'

She got up and came over to his chair to stand by him, ruffling his hair. 'You're a nice boy, Henry. I'm going upstairs to lie down and you can come up in ten minutes if you want to.' She paused at the door. 'First on the left at the top of the stairs. Suit yourself.'

He sat there trying to make up his mind what to do; more accurately, trying to muster the courage not to cut and run. It was one thing to get involved with a girl at a party; quite another to go upstairs with a married woman. Without having made a conscious decision he found himself climbing the stairs. He hesitated at the door which was partly open, hoping that she would speak, but no sound came from the bedroom. He went in and stood just inside the door. In the grey afternoon light, filtered by a slatted blind, he could not see clearly at first. The furniture, the blinds, the carpet and the bedclothes were all white; she seemed to have a passion for white; but the room was untidy, littered with clothes, and there was an indefinable smell over and above that of make-up and toiletries; elusive, intimate.

She was in bed and he could see only her black hair on the pillow. He went over to the bed. She was holding the bedclothes round her shoulders, looking up at him,

31

unsmiling, her eyes solemn and questioning. He did not know what to do then, with a sudden movement, she uncovered her breasts; her body appeared dusky white, slim and infinitely supple.

'Aren't you going to undress?'

He had never before been with anyone experienced in the art of love and Natalie was a revelation. He surrendered himself in luxurious abandonment to a rising tide of sexuality, he was carried along by it, engulfed, then swept into a limbo of consciousness where there was nothing left but the rhythm of his pounding heart.

When it was over quietness possessed him like a narcotic drug, seeping through his tissues, neutralizing, quelling, calming, until he began to feel deliciously relaxed. He saw the room through half-closed lids, filled with pearly grey shadows, insubstantial, ethereal. He seemed to float in a cloudy, opalescent world: soft and sensual but not cloying and wished that it would go on for ever.

'Thank you.'

'For what?'

'For everything.'

She ruffled his hair. 'Silly boy!'

Then, suddenly, Natalie was asleep, her breasts pressed against him, his sex against her thigh; the weight of her body lay across one of his legs. Afraid to move, he became rigid. Where they touched their bodies were moist and clammy. Natalie slept with her lips parted and she breathed with a slight, tremulous snore. He could smell the whisky on her breath. Abruptly his euphoria vanished and disenchantment chased away romance. He began to feel ashamed.

With infinite caution he edged out of bed, collected his clothes and went to the bathroom where he sponged himself down and dressed. Then, with his

32

shoes in his hand, like a character in a bedroom farce, he crept out. When he was half-way down the stairs the front door opened and Yvette stood in the hall looking up at him. The situation was as hackneyed as a mother-in-law joke but none the less painful for that. Her understanding was immediate and complete.

'Don't mind me, I live here.'

That evening Geoff Bishop crossed the Court in the rain to call on Willy Goppel. Although Bishop had lived with Natalie for upwards of two years he had never exchanged half-a-dozen words with Willy.

'Mr Bishop, isn't it?'

Bishop was uncharacteristically anxious to do the right thing. 'I came to the back door, seeing it's Sunday and the shop is shut . . . '

'Back door or front, they both lead to the same place,' Willy said. 'You want to see me, Mr Bishop?'

'About my garage.'

'Ah! You'd better come in.'

Bishop followed him through the workshop, looking curiously at the dolls' house under construction. 'Funny sort of job, yours.'

'You think so?' Willy did not seem anxious to be sociable.

They went upstairs to Willy's living-room, a large room elegantly proportioned, a remnant of the old house, with double doors, a marble mantelpiece and ornamental plaster ceiling. Willy's furniture was lost in it and a good deal of the space was taken up with trestle tables on which he had built a scale model of the Court. The houses, the verandahs, the yards and even the tree were all there. And the people. Outside each house the inhabitants were posed as if for a photograph. Bishop was intrigued.

'Christ! Is that me?'

'That was my intention.'

'Well, I'm damned! It's bloody marvellous. And there's Natalie sunbathing. What d'you do it for?'

'Fun,' Willy said. 'Now, Mr Bishop . . .'

Bishop fished in his wallet and came out with a letter. 'I had this from Crowther, the lawyer. It's a formal notice to quit when my lease on the Fenton Street property expires next year.'

He held out the letter to Willy but Willy did not take it. 'That is correct, Mr Bishop. I bought the property when your lease still had five years to run with an option of renewal for two. That period expires next year and I wish to put the premises to another use.'

'The hell you do!' Bishop sat down without being invited.

'Mr Crowther drew your attention to that possibility when you renewed, so it cannot have come as a surprise.'

Bishop fingered the sleek black hairs of his moustache. 'Of course, we are talking about money. Well, I don't mind admitting that the place suits me very well and while I have no intention of being a bloody milch cow for anybody, I'm willing to consider renewal at a fifteen per cent increase in rental.'

Willy shook his head.

'Fifteen per cent seems reasonable to me.'

'But as I do not intend to renew the lease, the question of rental does not arise.'

Bishop grinned. 'You're a hard man, Mr Goppel. All right, I might be prepared to stretch it a bit but twenty would be my absolute limit. Beyond that it would pay me to look somewhere else.'

'Which is what you will have to do in any case, Mr Bishop, if you wish to carry on your business.'

Bishop looked at him in astonishment. 'You bloody mean it, don't you?'

Willy did not answer.

'What have you got against me?'

'Against you? Nothing. I'm a business man, Mr Bishop, and I want to put that property to another use. Now you understand the position you will be able to make plans. I am sorry that Mr Crowther seems to have left you in some doubt.'

Bishop stood up. 'I don't give in that easy, Goppel. I've built up a business there and you aren't going to snatch the mat from under my bloody feet; don't you think it.'

Willy did not reply and after a moment, Bishop went on, 'What are you going to do with the place anyway?'

'That is my affair but you have my word that I shall not carry on a business similar to yours so you do not have to worry about competition.'

'Thank you for bloody nothing.'

'I'll see you out.'

* * *

The rainy windy weather continued through most of the week so that Natalie was not able to sunbathe on her verandah in the nude or otherwise, and Joan Fiske had no cause for complaint. But she had other worries and, on Thursday morning, seeking consolation and reassurance, she made an unprecedented visit to her neighbour, Mrs Hedley, who, it was said, was an initiate in the mysteries of the Tarot.

It was raining so hard that she had to take an umbrella even to go next door. Mrs Hedley received her with suspicion and kept her on the doorstep. Mrs Fiske was a little scared of the aristocratic and over-bearing old lady who, it was rumoured, had been to Roedean and Oxford in her day.

'I came because I happened to hear that you were an expert in the Tarot ... the Tarot, yes.' She had to

35

repeat it twice before Mrs Hedley condescended to understand.

'Who told you that?'

'Actually I heard it in the greengrocer's but I can't remember who said it.'

Mrs Hedley yielded a point. 'I've done very little recently; what do you want?'

'I wondered if you would do a Reading for me?'

She received a shrewd, appraising look. 'I do not do it for money.'

'No, of course not.'

'And I do not do it for foolish women who merely want an idle pastime.'

Mrs Fiske flushed. 'No, I—'

'But if you have a problem, something which worries you, I don't mind seeing what the cards have to say about it.' Still she continued to block the door. 'You understand that I do not guarantee anything, sometimes it is necessary to undertake two or three Readings before a clear picture is achieved.'

'Of course.'

'Very well. You had better come in. Leave that umbrella outside, I don't want it dripping all over the place.'

In the living-room Mr Hedley was standing by the mantelpiece, a cigarette attached to his lower lip. He made a move to be hospitable but his wife cut him short.

'Mrs Fiske wants me to do a Reading for her, Herbert, so you had better go upstairs and lie down for a while.' She turned to her guest. 'You sit there, opposite me.' She pointed to a chair by the table then she went to a drawer in a mahogany chest and came back with a black silk square and a pack of cards. She placed the silk square in the middle of the table and carefully sorted the cards into two unequal piles. 'These are the Major and

Minor Arcana; if you don't know what that means, it doesn't matter. When is your birthday?'

'January the twenty-fifth.'

Now that Mrs Hedley was getting down to business her manner became more relaxed if not actually friendly.

'That means Aquarius; you should choose a court card from the Minor Arcana, suit of Swords.'

Joan Fiske fumbled inexpertly through the cards and came up with the Queen of Swords; the old lady smiled. She placed the card in the middle of the silk square. 'That is you; we call it the Significator.' She showed the other woman how to shuffle the cards in a special manner then, taking them from her, she laid down three of the Major Arcana above the Significator and followed with three rows of the Minor Arcana below the Significator.

There was silence in the room except for the sound of the downpour outside. The light was dim but Mrs Hedley did not switch on the lamp. Joan Fiske looked with dull curiosity at the colourful cards which, in some fashion, were supposed to hold something of herself and her problems. The old lady studied the cards, touching them, brooding over them and muttering to herself. Her grey eyes bulged slightly and with her sparse frizzled hair, her hooked nose and long bony hands, she would have made a good stand-in for a pantomime witch.

'You don't have to tell me what it is you want to know but it saves time.'

Joan Fiske's voice trembled. 'It's difficult.'

'It usually is.'

She hesitated a little longer then plunged. 'What with Marty and one thing and another I hardly know which way to turn . . . My husband has changed. He was never

37

what you would call an easy man but lately I don't know where I am with him. He complains about what I spend on housekeeping then, in the very next breath, he grumbles that we haven't got this or that . . . ' She added after a moment with a certain coyness, 'We haven't slept in the same room for years.'

Mrs Hedley's silence seemed to encourage her.

'Last week when I had to go to Bristol for Marty's treatment I was away three days and he turned out the box-room and put a lot of things out for the dustman. Things you accumulate over the years – things which belonged to his father and to him as well as little things of mine. It seemed so cruel . . . I'm sure he *meant* to hurt me.'

Joan Fiske was near the end of her tether; several times her face moulded into a pathetic grimace, prelude to tears, but she controlled herself. 'Of course, he's six years younger than me.'

The old lady did not look up from the cards but said in a dry voice: 'So you haven't really got a specific question, my dear. Never mind, the cards may still help you. Forget about your husband for the moment. So many of our troubles come from within ourselves and can only be met with inner strength. This first line says something about you. Look – the Star, reversed . . . '

'Reversed?'

'Upside down, it alters the Reading. And on one side Force and on the other, the Hermit reversed.' Mrs Hedley pondered again. 'You lack confidence, confidence in others but especially in yourself. You are too pessimistic and you are disinclined to accept well meant advice and help . . . Against all that you have a great deal of moral courage and you are willing to suffer for what you believe to be right . . . You have the strength *to win through*.'

Joan Fiske listened as though she were hearing the

secrets of immortality and the old lady warmed to her work. 'You need to beware of judging by appearances; try to be more charitable. Bitterness harms you more than those against whom it is directed. Open your mind to fresh ideas . . .'

The Reading took half-an-hour and when it was over Joan Fiske, having achieved her catharis, was pathetically grateful. 'You've helped me enormously, Mrs Hedley. I would very much like to come again if I may.'

Mrs Hedley unbent. 'You will be welcome, my dear. You are an earnest Seeker. But do remember, so many of our problems are of our own making.'

The Wards had planned a rare break for the following week-end; they had arranged with the post office authorities for a Saturday stand-in and they were off to London for a hectic two days.

Henry had backed out.

On the Thursday they had their evening meal as usual and afterwards Henry took himself off to his room but Alison remained at the table with her parents. It was one of those evenings when the present seems curiously unreal and it is easy to sit doing nothing in a state of suspended animation.

'What *is* the matter with Henry, Alison?' Mrs Ward, unable to stay idle for long, shuffled plates together.

Alison was evasive. 'I don't know why you make such a fuss about him, mother; he gets spells when he's sorry for himself and that's all there is to it.'

'It's ever since he went to that woman's place; he goes round looking more miserable than I've ever seen him. I don't think he's doing his homework and he's not eating enough to keep a cat alive. Now he won't come with us to London.' She stopped rattling plates and looked at her daughter with great seriousness. 'I'm worried, Alison, really worried.'

Alison, because she too was a little concerned, pretended to an exasperation she did not feel. 'For goodness sake, mother, he's seventeen!'

'And she's well past thirty *and* she couldn't keep her husband so she's living with another man. I know her sort! What do you think, Edward?'

'Me? Oh, I agree with Alison; he's nearly a man and we've got to let him stand on his own feet.'

Henry's record player was churning out continuous jazz. Willy Goppel rarely suffered from nerves but this evening the insistent rhythm seemed to bite into his brain so that everything he did acquired a jerkiness like the movements of an automaton.

'The boy must be depressed,' Willy said, 'like me.'

Sergeant Kersey was planning an early night; he would spend a couple of hours watching television with the wife and kids or play Scrabble, or put a new catch on the bathroom door or bath the dog . . . A constable dropped a packet on his desk.

'What's that?'

'Just handed in at the desk, Sarge, addressed to you.'

It was an ordinary large-foolscap envelope addressed in neatly printed capitals, 'Detective Sergeant Kersey, Mallet Street Police Station'.

'Do you think it'll go bang if I open it?'

'I shouldn't think so, Sarge; everybody loves you.'

Kersey slit open the envelope and pulled out a thin wad of official looking papers, yellowing with age and creased through at the folds. He spread them out on his desk.

'They're all in German!' There was a photograph pasted on one of the documents impressed with an official stamp. 'Some poor kraut's papers from the last war. A captain by the look of it. Walter Pieck. Who the hell sent me this stuff? Who handed it in?'

'Dunno, Sarge. I just found it on the desk a few minutes ago.'

Kersey looked in the envelope once more and came up with a slip of paper on which there was a message printed in the same manner as the address on the envelope: 'These belong to Willy Goppel at Paul's Court.'

'Curiouser and curiouser.'

'Sarge?'

'I know this Willy Goppel, he makes dolls' houses and furniture for them. I wanted one for my girls when they were young but I couldn't afford it.' He gathered up the papers and stuffed them back in the envelope, 'I'll look in on Goppel on my way home.'

Kersey liked Falcon Street; it was a real city street, not one of those brash caverns stinking of exhaust fumes which often pass for streets in these days. There was more than a remnant of dignity about Falcon Street which, God knows why, had escaped the notice of planners and developers. Paul's Court was next to St Olave's Church which still had its graveyard with a few trees and shrubs, not too well cared for but none the worse for that.

'If I ever win the pools or get made up to chief D.I., I'll go for one of those houses in Paul's Court.'

Willy Goppel was fitting a gallery round the main landing of the dolls' house when Kersey came to the back door. Willy knew him by sight and felt uneasy.

'You remember me, Mr Goppel? Detective Sergeant Kersey.'

'Yes, I remember you.' Willy resumed work on the gallery, not as a discourtesy but when his hands were busy he felt more at ease.

Kersey lit a cigarette and watched. When the fitting was complete he sighed. 'I wish I could do work like that.'

Willy allowed his apprehension to peep through. 'Something has happened?'

41

But the policeman had moved over to the animal cages and was standing by them, his back to Willy. 'Look at that!' He was pointing to one of the geckos walking upside down on the glass roof of its cage. 'Clever, that.'

'He has adhesive pads on his feet. Now, Sergeant, you wish to ask me something?'

'Nothing much. Some anonymous joker sent me these with a note saying they belong to you.' Kersey spread the papers on Willy's work bench.

Although he had known what was coming Willy felt a hollowness inside. 'That is correct, they are mine.'

'This chap, Walter Pieck – was he a friend of yours?'

'I was Walter Pieck, Sergeant.' Willy had made up his mind that he would not lie.

'Was?'

'I *am* Walter Pieck, if you prefer it.' Willy spoke with dignity.

'Me? I don't care one way or the other. All I want to do is to get home to my supper. You lost these?'

'Yes.'

'Dropped them in the street?'

'No, they were taken from that desk over there while I was out.'

'Don't you lock up when you go out?'

'I do now.'

'Did you report it to the police?'

'No.'

'Anything else taken?'

'Some money and a string of medals. They were all together in a cigar box.'

'Why should whoever took them send this stuff to me?'

'I have no idea, Sergeant.'

Willy was by no means reassured by the policeman's easy, almost indifferent manner. He knew all about the soft sell.

'Sounds a bit screwy to me.' Kersey was picking up

42

fittings for the dolls' house, looking at them and putting them down again. 'I suppose you thought it would be easier to get British citizenship if you didn't apply as an ex-infantry captain. I expect you were right at that. Now you probably wish you'd stayed a Deutscher.'

Willy said, 'I took the identity of a dead man – Willy Goppel.'

'It must have been a hell of a long time ago.'

'Spring 1945.'

Kersey shrugged. 'I should think they'd look on you as a paid-up member by now.' He folded the papers and replaced them in the envelope. 'You've got no record?'

'With the police? No.'

'I don't suppose you killed this chap Goppel?'

'I did not. He was a *Sklavenarbeiter* – what you call a slave worker, a German Jew, and he died in an accident. He must have had some skill they valued or he would not have lived so long . . .'

Willy broke off. He had a sudden clear vision of a sunny country road, a sandy bank gouged out by a truck which must have careered down the hill out of control. The truck lay on its side and strewn about like rag dolls were four bodies. One of them, Willy thought, looked vaguely like him . . . What he remembered most clearly was the stillness, the sunlit silence which was almost tangible. Yet there was enemy armour across the river.

'I took a dead man's clothes and papers.'

'Have you still got his papers?'

'No, I destroyed them years ago.'

'But kept your own.'

Willy was silent. What was the use of trying to explain?

Kersey sighed. 'I shall have to send these to the Home Office but unless there's somebody there tired of sitting on his arse I doubt if you'll hear any more.'

The sergeant's words were probably meant kindly but they brought Willy no consolation. He felt that he had been stripped naked – more, that he had lost a protective skin.

'Where did your wife come into all this?'

Willy took his time. 'This was Germany in the spring of nineteen forty-five. Even before I changed my clothes with a dead man I was a deserter. I had failed to rejoin my regiment in the east after convalescent leave . . . I was making my way west with just what I could carry in a haversack.

'Just before the war I had moved with my parents and sister to Essen and all three were killed in the bombing of the Ruhr . . . ' He broke off and wiped his forehead with a red handkerchief. 'I am not excusing myself; I do not feel the need to do so to anyone who did not share the experiences of those last days . . . Anyway, within a few hours of changing clothes with the man, Goppel, I was wounded while trying to cross the river – hit by a stray bullet. I was picked up, unconscious, by a British patrol and taken to a British field hospital where my future wife was a nurse . . . I had on my person only the papers of the dead man but foolishly, perhaps with the cowardly notion of not committing myself, I had kept my own papers in the haversack with a few souvenirs. When I recovered consciousness in hospital I hoped and believed that the haversack had been lost in the river.'

Willy resumed work on the landing of the dolls' house, fitting more balusters into their tiny drilled holes. 'It was long afterwards, when we were married and settled here, that my wife returned to me my haversack and its contents which she had kept along with my secret.'

Kersey said, 'It's all a long time ago.' He glanced at his watch. 'I must be off. *Viel Glück!*'

Willy did not smile.

44

CHAPTER THREE

By Saturday the rain had gone, it was a sunny warm day and the weathermen had promised a fine week-end. Henry Ward got out of bed after a troubled, restless night. Alone in the house for two whole days he had no idea what he would do with himself. His parents and Alison had taken the night train to London and he thought of them now, breakfasting in their hotel, and wished that he was with them. He had stayed home in order to make his peace with Yvette – not that he felt deeply drawn to her but he had treated her badly and he wanted to salve his conscience. Henry hated to hurt people, but more than that he hated loose ends; he had a tidy mind.

He put on his dressing-gown, switched on the radio, made some instant coffee and took it into the living-room where he stood by the window, gazing down into the Court. Marty Fiske was there, going round and round the oak tree, lost in some vague, mysterious private world. Natalie Cole's red sports-car was parked nearby.

'If she crooked her finger I should still go running.'

He ground his teeth, hating himself.

Yvette was coming down the verandah steps from her house, wearing the eternal T-shirt and jeans. He would have gone down to her but he wasn't dressed. He watched her cross the Court and go into Willy Goppel's, presumably to help him with his animals. Perhaps he could catch her when she came out.

But he missed her. The day wore on. Out of the

mounds of food his mother had left him he heated a small meat pie and had it for lunch. After lunch he played records, keeping an eye on the Court in case Yvette should go out again.

At about half-past three he heard the engine of the little sports-car roar into life and he hurried to the window. Natalie was in the car alone. She looked up and saw him, grinned and waved. It meant less than nothing to her. He wondered how she thought of it – if she thought of it at all . . . 'A bit of fun with the Ward boy . . . Teaching the Ward boy a few tricks . . .' Or perhaps she expressed herself more crudely. He squirmed.

He supposed that Yvette would be in the house alone and he had almost made up his mind to go there when it occurred to him that Bishop might be home on a Saturday afternoon. He was still trying to decide whether or not to risk it when he saw Yvette coming out of the house. She had her shoulder bag so, presumably, she was going out. He ran down the two flights of stairs. Locking up delayed him and by the time he got to Falcon Street Yvette was nowhere to be seen. It was not surprising for the market people were packing up their cars and vans and the skeletons of their stalls were everywhere. He decided that Yvette would make for the city centre and hared off up the street to the bus stop but he was too late; he saw her get on the bus but he was too far away. He set out on foot.

He was in a strange mood; it was suddenly imperative that he should find her and talk to her. He thought that it should not be too difficult if he made the rounds of the coffee bars and discos.

As he arrived in the centre the clock over the town hall was chiming a quarter past four. Too early for the discos, so he wandered around more or less aimlessly peering into every coffee bar he came to and entering those he could not see into from the outside. In consequence he got involved with some of his school friends.

'Have you seen Yvette?'

'Oi! Oi! What's going on, then? Somebody looking for something they shouldn't. That's for sure.'

It was strange; whenever Yvette's name was mentioned somebody was sure to insinuate that she was easy. In fact, when he had been out with her she had not been like that at all. They had never got further than mild petting and whenever he had shown signs of doing more it was, 'Give it a rest, Henry . . . Lay off! What do you think I am?'

By six o'clock he had drunk several cups of coffee and got nowhere and he was beginning to feel ridiculous. The discos were opening and he promised himself that he would try one or two before giving up and going home. He had been walking more or less at random, making wide circuits round the city centre, and it happened that he was now in Hilary Street, a quiet backwater where former warehouses had been converted into antique shops, picture galleries, book shops and offices for architects and surveyors. There was only one other person in the street and it was Yvette. She was walking along the pavement ahead of him with short quick steps, her bag slung from her shoulder. He had started to hurry when she turned down a flight of steps to some basement; a door opened and she was gone.

The building was the Hilary Street Arts Centre but a neon sign with a downwardly pointing arrow indicated that the basement was The Catacombs, a restaurant. He went down the steps to a white enamelled door with a glass panel and polished brass fittings. A notice read, 'Closed. Open from six-thirty for dinners.' A brass-framed menu was fastened to the wall by the door. Expensive.

*

Willy had been feeling unwell all day, now his skin was dry and hot, his face burned, his throat was constricted and prickly and his arms and legs felt incredibly heavy.

'I must have a temperature.'

Like hundreds of others in the city Willy had contracted summer influenza. The newspapers spoke of a new and more virulent form which was especially dangerous to the old and those in late middle-age. He sat in his chair, staring into the empty fireplace, sometimes drifting off into a doze then waking with a start. When he dozed he seemed to be Walter Pieck again, twenty seven years old, re-living those last traumatic days in Germany. But things went differently. When, for example, he bent over the corpse of Willy Goppel he saw not a face but a skull, and when he started to unbutton the man's tunic to exchange clothes, hundreds of fat, pale-yellow maggots swarmed and writhed in an unspeakable cavity where the chest should have been.

The musical chimes of the black marble clock on the mantelpiece brought him back; it chimed the hour and struck eight, he counted the strokes. He rarely drank spirits but he kept a bottle of whisky in the house and he wondered if a glass might do him good. He was still wondering when the shop doorbell rang. His first reaction was to let it ring but the visitor was persistent and in the end he went slowly downstairs and opened the door. It was the Professor, come to tell him of his enquiries into the theft of Willy's papers and medals. They went upstairs together and Willy fetched the whisky from a cupboard in the kitchen. The effort of moving about made him feel better for a time but when he was back in his chair the feverish symptoms returned and now his heart seemed to be beating much faster than usual.

'You are ill, my friend.'

The Professor sat talking away but Willy scarcely

heard what he had to say though he gathered that the enquiries had met with little success.

'In the circumstances I should try to forget about your loss, my dear Willy, I doubt whether you will see your papers again.'

Willy hadn't the strength to tell him that they were already in the hands of the police. He only wished that the Professor would go.

'You need medicine, my friend. Can I get you anything? Don't you think I should telephone for the doctor?'

Willy put him off. 'The girl from next door is getting a prescription made up for me; she will be bringing it in later this evening.'

In the end, when the Professor was leaving, Willy asked him to let himself out through the back. 'The door is unlocked and it will save me coming down.'

'You wish the door to remain unlocked – is that wise?'

'Until Yvette comes with my medicine. I usually lock up when I go to bed.'

The Professor was gone at last. Willy looked at the black marble clock, it was ten minutes past nine. His friend had meant well but he had stayed too long and the whisky had made Willy's head worse. Yvette had promised to have the medicine made up for him at a chemist's; it was a prescription he had had by him for years and he used it whenever he had influenza or a heavy cold.

'I shan't be back until late but I'll be sure to get it made up before they close.'

He wondered vaguely what she had meant by 'late'. It was very quiet, no traffic in Falcon Street and the Wards were away except for Henry. Henry must be out or he would be playing his record player or listening to the radio. It was so silent that he felt muffled in cottonwool and wondered if his hearing was affected . . .

He must have dozed again for he was back in Germany, this time as a boy. He was in bed, lying prone, and he could see the high wooden foot of the bed. It was of some dark wood, elaborately carved with fruit and flowers. He was aware of his mother, a vague figure standing by the bed and she was saying something which, try as he would, he could not hear.

* * *

On Sunday morning the city looked as though it had been desolated by the plague. On what would probably be the last summer Sunday of the year half the population had joined an exodus to coast and moor.

Joan Fiske was giving Marty his breakfast; her husband was still in bed. Marty sat at the plastic-topped table in the kitchen shovelling cornflakes into his mouth with a spoon held in his fist. The kitchen window was open to the yard and a shaft of sunlight just reached the stainless steel sink making it shine like polished silver. The air was warm and fresh and balmy with the promise of a glorious day. But Joan Fiske was uneasy, her visit to Mrs Hedley and the Tarot had calmed her and she was making a determined effort to come to terms with her problems but on this sunny morning melancholy had stolen up on her unawares. She who had resolutely refused to remember the past was assailed by nostalgia; for a time before marriage; before Marty.

She looked at her son and sighed then immediately felt guilty. Marty triumphantly scooped up the last drop of milk and pushed his bowl away, then he reached into his pocket and began to take things out and put them on the table. A piece of string, an oddly shaped stone, a clothes peg, a dirty handkerchief and then a lady's watch, on a bracelet made up of lucky charms.

'Marty! Where did you get that?'

Marty looked at his mother in blank incomprehension.

'The watch, Marty – where did you get it? Tell me, Marty, it's important. . . '

It was one of her nightmares that Marty might take up to steal.

Marty merely lifted the watch to his ear, shook it and listened. His mother snatched it from him. 'Marty—' She broke off, hearing heavy footsteps on the stairs. 'There's your father. It doesn't matter now.' She slipped the watch into the pocket of her housecoat. 'Put all that stuff away, Marty! Do you hear me?'

The door opened and Martin Fiske came in looking sullen and heavy eyed. He wore a mauve dressing-gown over his pyjamas. 'Hasn't he had his breakfast yet? What's all that rubbish?'

'Collect up your things, Marty. You can go out into the Court, it's a lovely day.'

The Hedleys had been up for hours and had reached the stage of morning coffee which they drank from pottery mugs. Mrs Hedley said, 'I shall make a ginger cake.'

'But we don't eat ginger cake.'

'Toby does.'

'What's that got to do with it? He hasn't been near us for months.'

'All the same, I have a feeling. I shall make that cake . . . '

Henry Ward got out of bed at the start of another day on his own.

Willy Goppel was not around.

Natalie Cole rolled over to face the man who shared her bed. She slid one arm round his neck and pressed her body against his. 'Come on, Geoff, for Christ's sake.'

Bishop remained supine and unresponsive. 'Not this morning, I'm not up to it.'

'What's the matter? Are you ill or something? It's that bloody garage, worrying about the lease. There are other premises for God's sake!'

Bishop made an angry movement. 'Lay off, Natalie!'

Natalie whisked back the bedclothes and put her feet over the side; she was naked. ' "La Cass" isn't exactly a bloody picnic these days but I don't bring my troubles home with me. Anyway, it's half-ten, do you want any coffee?'

'If you like.'

'I don't care a damn one way or the other. It isn't exactly a privilege to wait on you.'

Bishop sat up in bed and grabbed her by the wrist. 'I told you to lay off!'

She squirmed round to face him in a sudden rage, 'And if I don't?'

He let go of her wrist and mumbled something.

'What was that?'

'I said, I feel lousy this morning. I was pissed last night.'

'Poor you! You should give up screwing that slut in your office then you might manage to be a man for me when I need one.'

She got off the bed and, still naked, went into the bathroom leaving the door open.

He heard her turn on the shower.

'What time did you get home last night, Geoff?'

'About midnight. Why?'

'Did you see Yvette?'

'No, she must've been in bed.'

When she had finished in the bathroom Natalie put on a wrap and went down to the kitchen. She put coffee in the percolator and switched it on. There was no milk in the refrigerator so she went to the front door to bring in the morning delivery. To her surprise the door was still bolted; usually Yvette would have been out long before. She called from the bottom of the stairs, 'Yvette! Are you still in bed?'

There was no answer so she went up to the girl's room; the bed was empty and unmade. Natalie was concerned. There was a sideway out of the house through the yard and into the Court but it was never used, and in any case the kitchen door was still bolted from the inside.

She shouted, 'Geoff! Yvette didn't come home last night.'

There was an incomprehensible reply and she called again but it was some time before Bishop came downstairs in his dressing-gown. He was a big man, in his late thirties, with a black moustache which drooped at the ends.

'I'm going to phone the police, Geoff.'

'I shouldn't be in too much of a hurry. Yvette can take care of herself.'

'When did you last see her?'

Bishop frowned. 'I don't think I saw her all day yesterday.'

Natalie said, 'She was with me about lunchtime, we had something together out of a tin. I left her here around three and went into town for a hair appointment; after that it was straight on to La Cass.'

'She's probably spent the night with one of her mates; she'll ring up directly.'

'To hell with that!' Natalie went to the telephone and made a 999 call. She sounded rattled, which was unusual. 'They're going to send somebody.' She went into the kitchen and poured coffee. 'She's been bloody-minded this past few days.'

'You think she might have taken herself off somewhere?'

'It's possible.' An idea occurred to her. 'If she has she'll have taken her clothes.' Natalie went upstairs and was gone some time; when she came down she looked more worried. 'As far as I can tell she only had what she stood up in, jeans and a T-shirt – what she was wearing yesterday morning.'

Bishop stood by the sink, his bottom propped against the drainer. Once or twice he started to say something but changed his mind.

She paused in front of him. 'You haven't been trying it on again with her?'

Bishop raised his eyes ceilingwards. 'God! You aren't going to let me forget that! It was just that once. I was drunk, and anyway I didn't do anything to the kid.'

Natalie shrugged.

Bishop said, 'When the cops come they'll ask a hell of a lot of questions.'

'So?'

'I shouldn't say anything to them about that. It was months ago.'

'I don't suppose you're the first bastard to try it on with a fifteen-year-old girl living in the same house.'

'All the same, better not say anything. I've got form remember.'

Natalie rounded on him. 'You make me sick!'

'But you won't say anything?'

'No, I'll draw a picture.'

They heard a car in the Court and Natalie went to the door. 'Oh, it's you.' Sergeant Kersey followed her in.

'What's all this, then? I happened to be this way and they got me on my car radio.'

'Yvette has been missing since sometime yesterday.'

'So they said. What will she be now – fourteen? Fifteen?'

'Fifteen.'

'Same age as my eldest.' Kersey took a packet of

cigarettes from his pocket and lit one absently, eyeing the decor. 'I heard you were living in one of these.'

He was no stranger to Bishop or Natalie. Banger Bishop's Car Mart and Vehicle Hire had been the scene of one or two punch-ups and Bishop himself had been convicted on a wounding charge. By the same token nightclubs are regarded as high-risk places and the police make it their business to know who runs them.

Kersey asked obvious questions and got obvious answers. He could have written the scenario himself.

'Would you say that she had any reason to run away?'

'No.'

'No rows? No tantrums? You know what kids are when they get upset.'

'No rows or tantrums.'

'Boy-friend?'

'Nobody special.'

'Have you noticed anything different about her lately?'

'No, nothing.'

'Have you enquired from the neighbours?'

'What's it got to do with them?'

Kersey dropped ash into an eviscerated glass swan which happened to be handy. 'You haven't seen Yvette since yesterday afternoon, they might have.'

'I hadn't thought of that. I'll have a word.'

'Better leave it to us now.'

Natalie was uncomfortable. Without saying much Kersey was making her feel guilty of something.

'I shall want a list of people she might visit – relatives, friends, school pals . . . ' He stood in front of one of the green and blue pictures, scowling at it. 'Are there any other kids in the Court?'

'Only the Wards at the post office; they have a boy and a girl but I think they're away for the weekend.'

'How old?'

'The girl is about the same age as Yvette but the boy is older.'

'Have you got a recent photograph?'

'She had one taken at school last term.'

'I expect that will do. Now, one more question – is it possible that Yvette has gone off with or to her father?'

Natalie looked surprised. 'I never even thought of it! They wouldn't know each other if they met in the street. It's ten or twelve years—'

'All the same, can you help us to locate him?'

'I'm not sure; the last I heard he was living in Lincoln but that must have been four or five years back.'

'Right! Now I'd like to see her room.'

Bishop said with apparent relief, 'You don't want me?'

'I shouldn't think so; not at the moment anyway.'

'I'll get along then, I'm due at the garage . . .'

Natalie led the way upstairs to a bedroom at the back of the house. It was a pleasant enough room with built-in units – wardrobe, dressing-table, desk and wash-basin. There was a divan bed which was unmade. A transistor radio on a ledge above the bed rubbed shoulders with a china cat and a framed photograph of some pop-star.

'You can't go by the bed,' Natalie said, 'she often doesn't make it until she's going to get in it again and sometimes not then.'

A shelf above the desk held a few school books, textbooks and exercise books all jumbled together. Kersey flicked through one of the exercise books and found it liberally annotated in red ink with critical comments.

'She hates school,' Natalie said.

In the wardrobe there were several pairs of jeans, a drawer full of T-shirts, and another of a random collection of briefs, bras, and stockings all stuffed in together; three or four dresses, a couple of school blazers and skirts were draped on hangers.

Kersey looked in the drawers of the desk but there seemed to be nothing of interest – two or three ball-point pens, a writing pad and some envelopes. In the deeper, bottom drawer there was a bundle of magazines of the sort that are published for not very bright teen-aged girls. He lifted them out and underneath there was a shallow tin box that had once held shortbread biscuits. In it there was a little diary of the engagement type and eighteen five-pound notes.

Natalie said, 'Good God! Where did she get all that money? Not from me, that's for sure!'

Kersey flicked through the pages of the diary, most of which were blank. Where there was an entry it consisted of initials, a cabalistic sign or a single word. Kersey passed it to Natalie.

'Do the initials mean anything to you?'

Natalie looked at the book and shook her head. 'I don't really know any of her friends, she never brings anybody home and she's the secretive type.' After a pause she added, 'I wish I knew where she got that money. You don't think she's been going with men?'

Irritation got the better of Kersey, 'How the hell should I know?' Then in his usual manner he went on, 'I'll take the diary, the initials might give us a lead.'

They went downstairs together. 'I'll make a few enquiries round the Court before I go back to the nick so if you get any messages for me, or if you hear from Yvette . . . Before I go you'd better give me some idea of who's who in the Court.'

She did so.

'What can I do?'

'Not much, I'm afraid; just be around in case she comes back or gets in touch.'

He left with a school photograph of Yvette and a description dictated by her mother.

Kersey had two daughters of his own – one thirteen,

the other fifteen. They were good kids but you could never be sure. He put in a good deal of time worrying about them. Occasionally, though not often, he wished that they were boys. You knew where you were with boys. As a cop he knew it all from the inside, the young tart who high-tails it off to London to sell her wares in a better market; the starry eyed innocent who, hand in hand with her soppy boy-friend, steals away into the sunset to find it dark, cold and wet; and the poor little devil who is just unlucky enough to catch the eye of some pervert and end up in a ditch, very dead.

Growing up in New Guinea, Coming of Age in Samoa, Male and Female . . . Kersey knew his Margaret Mead, and he'd dipped into Malinowski, Linton and Coon before coming to the conclusion that there are few so-called primitive societies where the business of growing up is so hazardous and cruel as is our own, where there is so little order and less discipline but an unrestricted freedom to go to the devil.

And it was a bad start to have Natalie as a mother. Her most engaging attributes did not make her apt for motherhood. Of course, the kid might turn up at any minute saying the boyfriend's bike had run out of petrol. Or she might not. The real question was whether she had gone away of her own accord or been per-suaded. There was an even better question, whether she was alive or dead.

Coming up for Sunday lunchtime; nobody would be pleased to see him but it couldn't be helped. He stood by his car, taking in the lay-out. Goppel's place was to the left of the archway coming in, the Wards' and their post office to the right. Natalie's house on the right and the Fiskes' at the far end were separated by a corner garden plot, shared between the two houses. The Hedleys', on the left of the Court, had no garden because the garages were on that side. Between the

58

garages and Goppel's yard there was a small iron gate which gave access to Church Lane, a pedestrian path which linked Falcon Street with parallel Church Street. The oak tree, which Kersey greatly admired, stood in the middle of the Court.

In the Fiskes' garden a man was burning rubbish in a patent incinerator. He was tall, fortyish, and his cardigan bulged slightly with a developing paunch. He worked with meticulous detachment in the manner of a man unused to such menial tasks. A column of grey-brown smoke rose in the still air, well clear of the houses, before it was caught by cross currents and whisked away.

Mr Hedley answered the door after Kersey had been ringing for some time. If it had not been for the sound of the radio he would have assumed that they were out. Hedley was very tall, very lean and pale as though he had been grown in semi-darkness, and he had a ragged, grey moustache stained with nicotine.

'What's it all about?'

'If I could come in . . . '

He was taken into the living-room where Mrs Hedley, a female counterpart of her husband though cast in a more aristocratic mould, was seated at the table in the dining alcove. He was impressed by an air of cultured if somewhat tarnished and dusty elegance; the Bechstein grand, shelves of musical scores, hundreds of books, two or three pieces of good furniture and a faded carpet of Chinese silk. Though the meal of stew he was interrupting looked unappetizing, the silver, china and glass on the table had never seen the inside of a chain-store.

'Don't let me interrupt your meal.'

Hedley took his seat opposite his wife while the radio continued to blare out Sibelius's fifth. He jerked a fork in the direction of the radio. 'That's Sibelius. Do you know, the Finnish Government passed a special law so that he could get his booze.' The old man chuckled. Clearly this was his favourite music story.

Kersey asked if the volume might be turned down.

'What does he want?' Mrs Hedley demanded of her husband.

'He wants the radio turned down.'

'Turn it off, then. I can't hear with all this going on anyway.'

Hedley switched off the set.

'Yvette Cole is missing. Her mother hasn't seen her since yesterday lunchtime.'

Mrs Hedley made a disdainful sound. 'That comes as no surprise, I doubt if she knows where the child is half the time.'

'She didn't come home last night.'

'She's a whore.'

'The child?'

'I was referring to the mother, I know nothing of the child.'

'Can either of you remember when you last saw Yvette?'

Mr Hedley said, 'I saw her yesterday afternoon.'

'At what time, approximately?'

'I was having a smoke on the verandah, it must have been between three and four.'

Mrs Hedley put in, 'My husband's memory is unreliable.'

'Was she alone?'

'I didn't see anybody with her. She came out of the house and crossed the Court. I think she went through the arch out into Falcon Street.'

'Can you say how she was dressed?'

'Of course he can't!'

Mr Hedley ignored his wife.

'She had on those tight trouser things young people

wear and a white jumper with letters on it – she always dresses like that except when she's going to school.'

'Was there anybody in the Court at the time?'

'Only Marty Fiske and he's retarded.'

Mrs Hedley said, 'In my day we should have called him an idiot and he'd have been none the worse for that. He's harmless.'

'So neither of you saw anything unusual on Saturday?'

They agreed that they had not.

'I understand that the people from the post office are away?'

'Not the boy, he didn't go.'

Hedley looked at his wife in surprise. 'Are you sure?'

'Of course I'm sure, I saw him in their yard this morning.' She turned to Kersey, 'He's another of that woman's conquests and she almost old enough to be his mother.'

Her husband was mildly shocked. 'You've no reason to say that, Emmie; the boy is a friend of Yvette's . . . '

The old lady laughed. 'You said yourself that he was there for two hours last Sunday afternoon when the man she lives with was out and so was Yvette.'

'Yes, but that doesn't mean—'

'It does with her.'

Kersey thought that he had got all that he could hope for so, apologizing once more, he left them to their lunch and the radio.

When he had gone Hedley paused with his fork half-way to his mouth.

'What's the matter now?'

'I've just remembered what I saw on Saturday night – I told you—'

'You imagined it.'

'But I tell you—'

'You said he was coming out of Willy Goppel's.'

'I said I thought he was.'

61

'You *thought*!'

They ate in silence for a while then Hedley said, 'Do you think we ought to have a word with Toby about this?'

'Why?'

'Well, the police might go to see him.'

'Why should they? In any case we can tell him when he comes over this afternoon.'

For the first time Hedley betrayed impatience. 'You know damn well he isn't coming this afternoon. You just imagine these things.'

'And I'm usually right.'

The old man sighed and resumed his meal. After a little while Mrs Hedley said, 'Turn on the radio, we are missing the concert.'

Natalie called across to Kersey as he left the Hedleys. 'They want you to telephone the nick.'

He telephoned from a box outside the post office and spoke to his immediate superior, Inspector Ware.

'What's happening, Doug?'

'I don't know yet; the girl's been missing since yesterday afternoon but whether she went off on her tod or was picked up I haven't a clue.'

Ware was young with every intention of rising fast. 'She's under age, we can't afford to pussy-foot around on this one.'

'Nobody's pussy-footing. I'm making enquiries among the people who know her. I've got a photo and description so if you like to send a patrol car to pick 'em up you can have 'em on the telex straight away.'

'I'll do that but I think we might have to off-load this one, Doug. Twenty-four hours is a long time for a kid to be missing before anybody gets a finger out.'

'That's up to you.'

'It's Natalie's girl, isn't it?'

'It is.'

'And Natalie is living with Banger Bishop – right?'

'You've been doing your homework – sir.'

'You know Bishop was sent down for G.B.H. three years ago?'

'Yes, Bishop is a dyed-in-the-wool villain and we'll trip him up one of these days but that doesn't mean he's after young girls.'

'He drew a knife on a chap.'

'I know he did, it was me who nicked him but what's that got to do with it?'

'I don't trust him. I'm going to have a word with the super.'

'No skin off my nose.'

'Okay, Doug, keep in touch.'

After a troubled night, when it was already daylight, Henry had fallen into a deep sleep and he did not wake until well past eleven. As soon as he regained consciousness he was aware of an underlying uneasiness, then he recalled his encounter with Yvette the night before. He felt that he had made matters worse. He got out of bed and drew the curtains. There was a strange car parked outside the Coles', an Escort which had seen better days. Why hadn't he gone to London with the family? He put on his dressing-gown and went downstairs. It was a beautiful day but he could think of nothing that he wanted to do. Somebody was ringing the back-door bell.

He went down to the ground floor and unlocked the door.

'Henry Ward?'

The man was not as tall as Henry but more heavily built and he wore a grey suit which looked as though it had been around for a long time. 'I'm Detective Sergeant Kersey. I want to talk to you. Can I come in?'

Henry had reached the age of seventeen without ever

being questioned by a policeman and he was apprehensive. He led the way through the office-store behind the shop and upstairs to the living-room.

'Haven't you got a room of your own?'

'Yes, of course, but what do you want to talk to me about?'

'Yvette Cole. So you didn't go to London with your parents?'

Henry was shaken by this evidence of inside knowledge. 'What about Yvette? Has something happened to her?'

'Why didn't you go to London?'

Henry, on edge, nervous, and exasperated by the sergeant's manner, burst out: 'What the hell does that matter? I'm asking you about Yvette?'

The policeman's face became wooden. 'Correction! I'm asking you about Yvette. Now, what about this room of yours?'

He would have liked to refuse but he hadn't the nerve. On the next landing he said, 'That is my sister's room, this is mine. Do you want to search it?'

Henry had meant to be sarcastic and he was shocked when the policeman started looking through his books and shuffling through his records. 'I see you've got some seventy-eights.'

'I collect jazz records. What's happened to Yvette?'

'That's what we'd all like to know. When did you last see her?'

He compromised with the truth. 'I saw her on Friday at school.'

'When did you last go out together?'

'It must be more than a week ago.'

'A quarrel?'

Now the sergeant was opening drawers and glancing through their contents as though it was the most natural thing in the world.

64

'I don't think you have any right to pry into my things like that.'

Kersey looked at him as though mildly surprised. 'No right at all. Do you object? Got something to hide? I was told that you are fairly close to Yvette and, naturally, I want to know what sort of bloke you are.'

He went on snapping laconic questions and at the same time conducting a fairly comprehensive search of the room.

'Does Yvette go round with other boys?'

'She has done; one or two, but she isn't a tart if that's what you mean.'

Kersey said, 'You went to her house last Sunday afternoon and spent a couple of hours there but Yvette was out and so, incidentally, was Geoff Bishop. Just you and Natalie. You said that it's more than a week since you went out with Yvette, did you go there in the hope of meeting her?'

Henry felt himself flushing and looked away. 'Mrs Cole invited me over for a drink because I'd helped her one morning when she couldn't start her car.'

'She was grateful?'

'I suppose so.'

'How grateful? Did she let you take her to bed?'

Henry felt outclassed; the policeman seemed to be playing with him and at any moment . . . '

'Come on, lad; you're not talking to your maiden aunt and I know Natalie.'

'All right, she did. Is it illegal?'

'No, and it might do you more good than harm if you don't try to make a habit of it. The point is, did Yvette find out?'

Henry could not find words.

'Did she? Out with it!'

He nodded. 'She came in just as I was coming downstairs.'

The sergeant whistled. 'That's bad! You had a row?'

'No, she wouldn't talk.' He paused for a moment, trying to fathom the policeman's mind. 'You are not saying that's why she's gone away?'

'How should I know?'

At that point Henry would gladly have told the sergeant all he knew, but he had promised. He perched himself on the arm of a chair trying to appear relaxed but looking instead like a sullen schoolboy in trouble. The policeman stood over him.

'I suppose you want her found?'

'Of course I do!'

'Then I'll tell you what you're going to do; you're going to make a list of every boy, girl, man and woman who meant anything to Yvette. I mean, by that, anybody who was more than just an acquaintance. Try to remember the people she talked about; it doesn't matter whether you know them or not.'

'I'll try.' He began to feel better at the prospect of having something to do.

Kersey seemed to lose interest in him. 'I'm going to talk to Willy Goppel.'

'I think he's away. I haven't seen him or heard him and he often does go away overnight at week-ends.'

'Relatives?'

'I don't think so. As far as I know his only relative is his son who lives close by – somewhere near the pannier market. He shares a flat with Toby Lennon.'

'Who's he?'

'He's Mrs Hedley's nephew, he used to live with them here in the Court.'

Kersey left the Wards' house and went out into Falcon Street. A police car was parked down the street and two uniformed men were ringing doorbells: Inspector Ware leaving no stone unturned; but it was an unprofitable occupation for a Sunday afternoon for most people were out in their cars. He decided to talk to the Fiskes.

The promptitude with which Mrs Fiske answered the door suggested that she must have been watching for him. He was shown into the living-room where Mr Fiske, the man he had seen burning rubbish in the garden, was reading the *Sunday Telegraph*.

'Come in, Sergeant! Can I offer you something?' Expansive and pompous.

'You know why I'm here?'

Fiske said, 'We saw the commotion and I stepped across the Court to enquire.'

Joan Fiske sat on the edge of her chair, her hands gripping each other in her lap. She was the pale, lean, nervous complement of her husband's suave pomposity. 'It's not that we are inquisitive but it seemed only neighbourly.'

Fiske adopted a man-to-man approach. 'I doubt if we can be of much help, but if there is anything we can tell you, needless to say . . . ' He shifted in his chair. 'You see, Sergeant, one doesn't want to gossip but if Yvette has run away it's not altogether surprising. I doubt if she even remembers her father, and her mother is fully occupied with her business. I'm not suggesting that she was in any way ill-treated but she probably felt to some extent neglected – overlooked.'

'When did you last see Yvette?'

Mrs Fiske frowned. 'We don't really take a lot of interest in our neighbours; I really couldn't tell you the last time I saw her.'

Kersey was puzzled, not by this suburban housewife line but by why, in this instance, it was accompanied by such evident tension. Mrs Fiske was making a great effort to control herself but when she spoke her voice trembled and even her husband looked at her in surprise.

Fiske said, 'I don't know when she went missing but it occurs to me that I saw her yesterday afternoon.'

'You weren't home yesterday afternoon, so how could you have seen her?'

Fiske went on as though his wife had not spoken. 'Although it was Saturday I went back to the office after lunch. I am an accountant with offices in King Street and it happened that I saw Yvette from my office window, walking along the other side of the street.'

'Alone?'

'Yes.'

'Carrying anything?'

'Nothing obvious, she might have had a handbag or something of the sort.'

'How was she dressed?'

'The usual T-shirt and jeans.'

'Going towards or away from the city centre?'

'Oh, towards the centre.'

'Any idea of time?'

Fiske considered. 'It must have been about four o'clock, give or take fifteen minutes.'

Kersey stood up. 'Thank you, Mr Fiske, that could be useful; it shows that she went into town after her mother left.'

Mrs Fiske was on her feet, ready to see him out. 'And it means that whatever happened to her didn't happen here. That centre is becoming a jungle!' Pleased with the phrase, she repeated it, 'A jungle!' She edged him towards the door. 'It's not safe to go through there in the evenings and I blame those West Indians, it wasn't like it before they came.'

Kersey was on the point of leaving when the door opened and Marty shambled in. He looked from one to another, grinned, and mumbled something about his watch.

'Not now, Marty!' His mother's voice was sharp. 'You can see we've got a visitor.' She turned to Kersey,

'This is our son, Marty, Mr Kersey. He's a little . . . You understand.'

Before leaving the Court Kersey rang Willy Goppel's doorbell but there was no response. He drove back to Mallet Street station in his little Escort which had already clocked up eighty thousand miles of hard driving and was beginning to sound like it. He had his paper-work to do, then it was almost certain that the big boys would take over and after that all he would hear of the case would be from station gossip and what he read in the newspapers. He sat at his desk, manipulated paper and carbons, cursed, lit a cigarette and started to type.

Inspector Ware put his head round the door. 'Oh, there you are, Doug! The old man's on his way and he wants a word before you push off home.'

Kersey had a considerable respect for Detective Chief Superintendent Wycliffe, the boss of CID. But it was based on hearsay, he had never worked with the chief though he admitted that he would have liked the chance. He had almost completed his report when Wycliffe came in. The chief superintendent had an unassuming presence, he was of medium height, slim, with a severe cast of countenance – monkish, in fact. For some time after his appointment he had been known as 'The Monk' but the nickname had been forgotten and he had become like a long line of predecessors, 'the old man'.

Wycliffe pulled up a chair to Kersey's desk, lit his pipe and settled down as though he had all the time in the world. 'In a hurry, Sergeant?'

'Not really, sir. Just the paper-work to finish, then I'm through.'

Wycliffe's manner was relaxed and conversational. 'You never know where you are when a young girl goes missing. You can involve half the force, run up hundreds of hours overtime, cost the tax-payer thousands, neglect everything else and then find that the little devil has just gone off to get herself noticed.'

Kersey nodded. 'But that's better than finding her body under a bush on the common.'

Wycliffe was involved in relighting his pipe but he glanced shrewdly at the sergeant. 'I agree; unfortunately, deploying an army doesn't stop that.'

They chatted about the case for twenty minutes, by which time Wycliffe knew what would be in Kersey's report without having to read it and he had, as a bonus, the benefit of Kersey's asides, his vivid thumb-nail sketches of the inhabitants of Paul's Court and a few Kerseyisms on life in general.

By the same token, Kersey had tentatively sized up his chief. He saw a man with a clear view of right and wrong who was not a bigot; he recognized a close-grained moral toughness with a hint of old-fashioned puritan zeal, but no sign of any wish to burn heretics. A man of compassion but no sentimentalist, a reformer but not a do-gooder.

Both men were well pleased. Wycliffe sat back in his chair. 'All right, what does it amount to?'

Kersey scratched a bristly chin. 'It seems to me that there are three possibilities. First, the girl could have cleared out on her own – angry, disgusted, jealous – she might be any or all of these depending on her temperament – because her mother went to bed with her boyfriend. Second, it's possible that she's gone off, again voluntarily, with some boy or man we haven't heard of yet. Third, some nutter has got hold of her, in which case she's almost certainly dead.'

Wycliffe nodded. 'But if she's gone off voluntarily, isn't it odd that she didn't take her clothes? Then there's the money; surely ninety pounds would have been useful.'

Kersey grimaced. 'As far as the clothes are concerned she might have left them deliberately to worry her mother more. You'd be surprised how spiteful some of these girls can be to their mums. But the money is more of a problem, her mother didn't even know she had it and it would be very interesting to know where she got it.'

Wycliffe tilted his chair at an alarming angle. 'One thing we must do is to find out whether anybody else is missing from among her acquaintances. The diary might help there. Can't her mother identify any of the initials?'

'Seems not.'

'Then I'll get somebody on to it. Now about your third possibility – the nutter theme?'

'That's where the big battalions come in. Saturation coverage, and even then you need more than average copper's luck.'

Wycliffe brought his chair back on an even keel. 'I think I've got the picture. In the morning, if she still hasn't turned up, we'll lay on a limited operation. Inspector Ware has already checked with the hospitals and circulated her description so I shall put a few chaps on visiting coffee bars and discos, checking with bus crews and at stations. I want you to carry on with the girl's background and contacts.'

'You want me to stay on the case, sir?' Kersey was surprised.

'Of course. As investigating officer you must be in whatever team there is.'

Kersey watched the superintendent leave and reflected that this was one of few encounters with top brass when he did not feel that he had been scarred in battle. He grinned to himself. 'Perhaps we're both on the same side.'

Kersey arrived home at his semi-detached in the early darkness. People along the road were returning from

71

their excursions, unpacking picnic gear and children, carrying tired, whimpering toddlers indoors to bath and bed.

'Have you had a meal?'

Kersey's wife, Esther, believed that the greatest risk to any policeman comes, not from a well directed brick, bottle or even bullet, but from unsuitable meals eaten at unsuitable times.

'I've got some cold meat and I can do you a salad.'

'Where are the girls?'

'Over at Kathy's.'

When he had finished in the bathroom he pushed open the door of the girls' room. Books overflowed everywhere, there were aquarium tanks containing God knows what, a cheap microscope, a record player, records not in their sleeves, clothes on the floor and all manner of prints and pictures stuck to the walls. A sight which usually dismayed him but tonight he looked at it with approval.

Toby Pongo Lennon arrived late for his ginger cake. It was evening and the Hedleys had settled down to their nightly routine; the old lady seated at the piano while her husband paced round the house a cigarette dangling from his lips. If it had not been for one of his periodic visits to the verandah it is unlikely that Toby would have made himself heard.

'Hullo, my boy, it's you! Your aunt said you would be here and she's right for once.'

Toby behaved like a dutiful nephew, thoughtfully deferential. 'How is aunt? I'm afraid it's a long time since I've been over, but you know how it is . . . '

The sound of the piano ceased abruptly and Mrs Hedley's bitonal bleat came from the living-room. 'Who is it? Who have you got out there? Is that you, Toby?'

'Yes, it's me, aunt Emmie; come to see you at last.' He

went through to the living-room and kissed his aunt.
'Things don't change here – just the same as when I was
home.'

'It's where you should be now, my boy,' his aunt said,
'But we won't talk about that. I knew you would come; I
said so to your uncle but, as usual, he didn't believe me. I
even baked one of your ginger cakes.' She got up. 'I'll
make some coffee.'

Hedley waited for his wife to disappear into the
kitchen: 'If it isn't the piano it's the radio and it goes on
from morning to night; I get classical music running out
of my ears.'

'You're looking well, uncle.'

'Oh, I keep pretty well; pretty well. What are you
doing with yourself? Got a job?'

Lennon sat down. 'Not exactly a regular job, uncle,
but a bit here and a bit there; I manage.'

'Still living with the Goppel boy?'

'Freddie is still sharing with me, yes.'

'You should find yourself a nice girl. I don't like this
business of two cockerels sharing the same roost.'

'Ask him if he's heard the news,' Mrs Hedley called
from the kitchen.

'News, aunt?'

Hedley said, 'She means about the Cole girl – you
remember the Coles.'

'You mean Natalie.'

'Not Natalie, her daughter – she's disappeared.'

'But she's only a kid.'

'She's fifteen, old enough to meet and make trouble
these days. Anyway, we've had the police here questioning everybody.'

'What do they think has happened to her?'

Hedley shook his head. 'God knows what they think;
I suppose she's gone off with some man.'

Mrs Hedley came in with a tray. 'Now you just tuck in

73

to that, Toby. I'm sure you don't feed yourself properly. I expected you earlier.'

Lennon said, 'Did you, aunt? As a matter of fact I would have been here earlier but I had a late night and I stopped in bed until lunchtime.'

'Late night?'

'Oh, just a party – a chap who lives in Grenville Road. You may remember me speaking of Jeremy Hobson; he was at school with me. He's married now and he lives in Grenville Road.'

Hedley said, 'Only the upper crust can afford Grenville Road.'

Lennon nodded. 'I'll say! But the Hobsons have pots of money. Jeremy is on the boards of several companies already. That was it, really – a chance to make contacts. As you know, uncle, you can't get far without contacts these days.'

An hour later, when he was leaving, his aunt slipped three crisp notes into his hand.

CHAPTER FOUR

The Wards' Taxi rounded the corner into Falcon Street. Half-past six and already the sun was shining but Alison had had little sleep on the train and she felt chilled and empty inside. For the twentieth time her mother hoped that Henry had managed all right on his own.

'I do hope he had proper meals.'

Alison said, 'If he ate half you left for him he won't be able to move for a month.'

Her father was looking at the taximeter and searching in his pockets for change. 'I'll bet he's still in bed, fast asleep.'

'Are you very tired, dear?'

'Not really, mum.'

'You don't *have* to go to school, one day isn't going to make all that difference.'

'I'd rather go.'

Remarkably, Henry was at the side-door to receive them. Alison thought he looked a bit wan and her mother fussed over him but it was only when they were upstairs with their baggage that he told them.

'You'll have to know sometime, Yvette is missing.'

'*Missing?*'

'Her mother hasn't seen her since Saturday lunch-time. The police are looking for her.'

'The police!'

Alison's father said, 'I suppose they're bound to take it pretty seriously when a young girl goes missing.'

'But they don't think anything has happened to her, surely?'

75

The novelty of arriving home in the early hours was gone, they were suddenly very tired and deflated.

Henry said, 'There's coffee made and there are eggs in the saucepan . . . '

They drank their coffee but nobody felt like eating and as Henry was persuaded to tell the full story Mrs Ward became increasingly apprehensive. 'You mean the police actually questioned you?'

'Of course.'

'But why? What could you possibly know?'

And so it went on until at half-past seven Kersey arrived. He was very polite and apologized for troubling them so early. 'Really it was Alison I wanted to see. How well did you know Yvette, Alison?'

Alison hesitated and Mrs Ward said, 'They weren't friends—'

'It's best to let Alison speak for herself.' Kind but firm.

'We both caught the same bus to school from the end of the street and sometimes we came back together in the evening so I suppose we saw each other quite often.'

'But as your mother said, you weren't friends – you didn't go out together at weekends, for instance?'

'No.'

'What sort of things did she talk about? Did she tell you about her family or friends? Did she ever mention her father?'

'Well, no . . . '

'As far as you know, has she got many friends?'

It lasted about ten minutes then Kersey began to talk to Alison's parents, skilfully drawing them out about the people in the Court. Mr Ward left the talking to his wife.

According to Mrs Ward they were all nice people; from Willy Goppel, who was really like an uncle to the children, to Geoff Bishop who, whatever people said about him, had always been a gentleman to her. She was sorry for Joan Fiske and for Marty who was a charming and gentle boy. Mr Fiske could sometimes be a bit overbearing but he had business worries. 'It's no joke running any sort of business in these days.' As for the Hedleys, Mrs Ward made them sound like the original Darby and Joan. 'He was an official with the council but he retired at sixty – made redundant when they re-organized his department. Of course he got his pension but he continued to work – several jobs, but finally he went to work in Mr Fiske's office and he only finished there a year back . . . '

Alison and Henry got ready for school which shocked their mother. 'Surely you ought to show some respect . . . '

'Best to let them carry on as usual,' Kersey said. 'We don't know that anything serious has happened to Yvette.'

Alison went off to school with her head in a whirl; she had been less than frank with the policeman, not that she had anything to hide but because what she might have said would have discredited Yvette without doing anybody any good. 'It's not as though I *believed* it,' Alison told herself. 'She made it up to impress me.'

For some reason Yvette had always seemed anxious to impress and, perhaps, shock her. On more than one occasion while they were walking down the street to the bus stop or standing waiting she had treated Alison to alleged revelations about her sex life.'

'Have you ever slept with a man?'

'No.'

'You mean that you're still a virgin?'

'Yes.'

'Good God!' And she had looked at Alison as though she were some strange creature from another world. 'I started two years ago.'

77

'But you were only thirteen!' Alison had not meant to give her encouragement but the words seemed to have been forced from her.

Yvette was complacent. 'I know. It was Geoff Bishop, when he first came to live with my mother. Of course I was a bit simple then and I told mother and she raised hell. But afterwards I got to thinking, "Well, if that's what they want . . ." So now I make them pay.'

'You mean you take money?'

'Of course! What do I get out of it otherwise? There's nothing in it for the woman. It's just dead boring.'

Alison had thought about this and similar talks many times. It could *not* be true. But if it was . . . She was very troubled in her mind.

On his way to police headquarters that morning Wycliffe made a detour to take in Falcon Street. He had never allowed himself to become desk-bound but he sometimes almost regretted the promotion which had taken him 'off the ground'. There was nowhere to park in Falcon Street so he left his car in parallel Church Street and walked through Church Lane with the wall of the churchyard on one side and Paul's Court on the other. He noticed the little iron gate giving pedestrian access to the lane from the Court.

It was half-past eight and Falcon Street was coming alive; the butcher down the street was at work with cleaver and saw, the delicatessen opened its doors as he arrived, and sales girls were waiting outside the mini-market for the manager to unlock. He could not have explained why he had to see all this but he knew that otherwise the people Kersey had described would never be real to him – Natalie Cole, Geoff Bishop, Henry and the Wards, the Fiskes, the Hedleys and Willy Goppel.

A fair girl carrying a briefcase came out of the Court

and set off up the street. That must be Alison. She was followed a minute or two later by a sandy-haired lad on a moped, presumably her brother. Outside the wine-shop a window cleaner started work with bucket and mop. A man, well-dressed and self-important, carrying a briefcase, came through the archway and turned up the street in the direction of the bus-stop. Martin Fiske? One would have expected him to be driving unless he was a keep-fit addict. Bishop – unmistakable – followed a few minutes later, pumping the accelerator pedal of a souped-up Cortina. It was going to be another fine day and the sun was already gaining strength. Wycliffe stood under the pillared portico of the Old Mansion House, now used as offices by a firm of solicitors and an estate agent. He walked as far as Willy Goppel's shop and peered through the glass. The frontage was narrow and the little shop was full of dolls' houses stacked one on top of the other and there was a great variety of miniature furniture displayed on the dusty shelves.

On the stroke of nine the doors of the post office opened and, to Wycliffe's surprise, Kersey came out, seen off by a tall, thin, harassed looking man of middle age. Kersey did not appear in the least surprised to see Wycliffe.

'Morning, sir. I've been having a chat with the Wards, they came back round six this morning. Of course the boy told them what had happened.'

'I think I saw the girl and her brother leaving for school.'

Kersey nodded. 'I got here early to have a word with the girl in particular. She seems a nice kid, sensible and not bitchy. According to her Yvette is a pretty average sort of girl – not academic and thoroughly fed-up with school, but by no means a young tart. Not the sort to do anything really daft.'

Kersey glanced at Willy Goppel's shop. 'I asked Ward

about Goppel and he said he does occasionally go away at the weekends but he's usually back by mid-morning on Monday.'

'Any idea where he goes?'

'Ward doesn't know. He says Goppel is a nice chap but doesn't talk much about himself. He owns a lot of property.' Kersey went on to tell Wycliffe about the incident over Goppel's papers which he had sent to the Home Office. 'I expect you saw it in the reports, sir.'

'If I did, I don't remember it.'

'Well, the theft was several weeks ago, but that wasn't important. The papers came to us only on Thursday, and that was when I talked to Goppel.'

After seeing Martin Fiske leave for work Mrs Hedley allowed a decent interval to elapse before crossing the Court to call on Joan Fiske whom she found in the middle of vacuuming the living-room.

'Never mind, Emmie, it doesn't matter, I can do this any time . . . Could you do with a cup of coffee or is it too early?'

Since the initial breaking of the ice Joan Fiske had been twice more to consult Mrs Hedley but this was the first time the Mountain had come to Mahomet. It seemed that they were becoming friends and already they were on first-name terms.

'Odd, when you come to think of it, after living next door to each other all these years . . .'

Both women went into the kitchen where they could chat while the coffee was brewing.

'They've still not found her.'

Joan Fiske said, 'The police seem to be making a lot of fuss. I mean, the most likely thing is that she's gone off with some boy. She's a real young madam, going around with "Restricted Area" printed across her bosom. In my day she'd have been arrested.'

Mrs Hedley nodded. 'I blame her mother. All the same I can't help feeling that something has happened to the child.'

'You mean . . . ?'

'I've got that *feeling* and I'm seldom wrong.'

Joan Fiske was intrigued. 'I suppose there's no way of finding out what the cards have to say?'

'Of course. You can do a Reading for anybody, they don't have to be present, though it helps.'

'You mean you could do a Reading for the girl?'

Mrs Hedley shook her head. 'No, I draw the line at that, I've never Read for minors but I could do one for her mother.'

'*Really?* You wouldn't care to . . . '

'I'll get the cards.' It was astonishing how much more sprightly Mrs Hedley seemed to become whenever there was something going on which interested her.

By the time she returned Joan Fiske had the living-room habitable and a small table with two chairs placed in a good light. The old lady had not forgotten her black silk square which she placed in the middle of the table.

'I suppose you've no idea when her birthday is?'

'I do, as it happens, I remember when she took out some sort of policy with Martin he said that it was the same as his – that's April the third.'

'So she's Aries, which means the Significator should come from the suit of Clubs. She would chose the Knight.'

'How on earth do you know that?'

'The old lady smiled. 'Never mind. You shuffle for her.'

The cards were laid out and Mrs Hedley meditated on them while Joan Fiske maintained a respectful silence. On more than one occasion Mrs Hedley started to speak then changed her mind. In the end she said, 'I don't like the look of this. If it was anyone else but you I would refuse to Read.'

Joan Fiske said, 'Surely it can't do any harm?'

The old lady pursed her lips. 'No, the harm has already been done. Look at the three cards of the Major Arcana – all reversed, the Empress, Temperance, and Force. You could scarcely have a clearer picture of the woman. Sensuality, an unstable temperament, a complete disregard for others and the implication that self-indulgence – *physical* self-indulgence could cost her dear, perhaps *someone who means much to her.*'

Mrs Hedley turned her grey eyes on her disciple to emphasize the point. There was a long interval during which the old lady continued to brood over the Tarot. At one point a fly alighted on her nose and she seemed totally unaware of it.

Joan Fiske ventured, 'What about the other lines?'

It was as though Mrs Hedley had gone into some sort of trance for she turned from the cards with a blank look in her eyes. 'What?'

'The other lines.'

'Oh, it's the same story. I've never come across a first Reading like it. Look! The two of Cups reversed, the Knave of Swords and the five of Money – sex again, and jealousy this time – and greed. But a dark, secretive child is involved as a source of bad news. *A dark secretive child – a source of bad news . . .*' Mrs Hedley stared at her companion with disturbing intensity.

'But that doesn't necessarily mean that Yvette . . .'

The old lady shook her head. 'No, it doesn't but look at this in the next line. It begins with the nine of Swords – danger, a serious illness, or *news of a death . . .*'

Suddenly she swept the cards into a heap. 'I don't want to go on with this!' She remained motionless for a full minute, her long, bony fingers spread over the jumbled cards, then she turned with a twisted smile which was half apologetic, 'Sometimes the cards get the better of me.'

Joan Fiske was impressed. 'It's astonishing! I would never have believed it if I hadn't seen it with my own eyes.'

Wycliffe and Kersey were still on the pavement outside the Dolls' House shop. Wycliffe said, 'I shall be at headquarters all day, keep in touch and let me know when Goppel gets back.'

Kersey was surprised by the importance which Wycliffe seemed to attach to the toy-maker. He glanced at his watch, 'Well, he shouldn't be long, it's ten o'clock already.'

Wycliffe was on the point of turning up Church Lane when there was a shout and a man in overalls came running along the pavement towards them. 'You're the police, aren't you?'

The man was middle-aged, flushed and breathless. 'I've found the girl . . . She's lying between my shed and the wall . . . She's half naked and she's dead.'

Kersey took him by the arm and walked him back to the entrance of the churchyard. 'Who are you?'

'Me? I'm the sexton. My name's Couch – Jim Couch.' He wiped his forehead with the back of his hand. 'Christ, I had a shock when I saw her! I look after the church and the graveyard and I dump all my grass cuttings, prunings and so forth on a heap between my shed and the wall. I went there with a barrow-load and there she was . . . '

There was a little brick-built toolshed with a space of four or five feet between it and the wall of the churchyard adjacent to Church Lane. Yvette's slight, pale body was lying sprawled on a mound of rubbish. She wore her jeans but she was naked to the waist. She had been strangled.

There was no point in disturbing the body.

Within half-an-hour the churchyard was over-run by

83

police and their ancillaries; a large area was being roped off and a canvas screen erected. There were uniformed men at the gates and a van was on its way with a temporary coffin. Sergeant Smith, photographer to Wycliffe's squad, arrived and started taking photographs, first of the body, then of the immediate neighbourhood. Detectives were going over the ground looking for whatever they could find. Dr Franks, the pathologist, was expected at any moment.

Detective Inspector Scales was in charge and Wycliffe told him to ask the vicar to allow the use of the church hall as an incident post until an incident-van arrived.

Church Lane was closed and a small crowd began to collect in Falcon Street though they were constantly moved on.

It was fairly obvious that Yvette's body had been pushed over the wall and it interested Wycliffe to see that this had been done at a point immediately opposite the little iron gate which led into Paul's Court.

'It looks as though we may have to look very near home.'

Kersey nodded.

'We'd better tell the mother, there are enough people here.'

Natalie came to the door wearing a housecoat and looking as though she had not slept. 'Ah, it's you. Any . . .?' She broke off. 'I can see from your faces, you don't have to tell me, she's dead.'

They followed her into the living-room where she poured herself a whisky. 'What about you?'

'Not now.'

'Where was she found?'

'In the churchyard.'

'Had she been . . . '

'It doesn't look like it.'

'How did she die?'

84

'She was strangled.'

There was no point in mincing words with Natalie, all her life she had rubbed shoulders with violence.

'Poor little devil! When can I see her?'

'I'll take you along in about an hour.'

She nodded. 'I'd better get dressed.'

'Are you all right?'

'I'm not going to faint or cut my throat if that's what you mean.'

'We'll be back.'

Out in the courtyard Marty was walking round and round the oak tree.

Wycliffe glanced at his watch. 'It's gone eleven, you'd better see if your friend Goppel is back yet.'

'You think he might have killed the kid and scarpered?'

'No, but it's a possibility.'

Kersey left Wycliffe standing under the tree. Marty stopped his orbiting and looked at him, ' 'vette gone?'

'Yes, Marty.'

'Gone away?'

'Yes.'

Marty nodded his head slowly. He made a curious gesture with his hands as though trying to communicate something then, finding the effort too great, gave up.

Kersey came back. 'Nobody home.'

They walked back to the churchyard where things were quietening down. Yvette's body had been removed. Franks, the baby-faced pathologist, was on the point of leaving. Wycliffe and he had worked together so often that there was no ceremony between them.

'What did you make of her?'

Franks shrugged. 'I'll tell you more this afternoon but I'd guess that she's been dead for more than twenty-four hours. The scratches on her arms and breasts are almost certainly postmortem injuries –

85

probably caused by the twigs of the bushes and the stonework of the wall.'

Franks ran his hand through thinning sandy hair. 'Odd case, isn't it? I mean, what was the motive? It's unlikely that she's been raped. Some weirdo, that's for sure. A bosom fetish or something. It takes all sorts.'

Franks himself was a notorious philanderer; at fifty plus he was still notching up conquests at a rate which kept him in the Casanova class. 'Can't understand deviants myself; it's as though you could improve on nature.'

Wycliffe, who had had a puritanical upbringing, disapproved of this kind of talk. 'Yes, well, let me know as soon as you can. I've arranged for her mother to see her at about noon. Is that all right?'

'That should be okay. See you!' Franks went to his parked car which looked more like a weapon than a means of transport, the engine roared out decibels and he was gone.

'He must be trying hard to prove something to somebody,' Kersey said.

Inspector Scales had established a temporary base in the church hall and he came over to Wycliffe. 'Her bag was under her body.'

There it was on one of the tables, the contents spread out beside it. They included a purse, lipstick, handkerchief, a key, a sachet of aspirin tablets, a small bag of sweets and a medicine bottle full of some clear liquid bearing a chemist's label with Saturday's date. There was also a dog-eared piece of paper on which somebody had written a prescription.

'Camphor, aether, aspirin, liquor ammoniæ, benzoic acid, oil of anise . . . Some sort of 'flu mixture?'

Scales nodded. 'That's what I thought but we can check with the chemist.'

The purse contained a five-pound note, four singles and some loose change.

At a little before mid-day Wycliffe picked Natalie up in his new Granada. She was wearing her blue dress with white facings and she carried a matching handbag. She wore little make-up and anyone might have taken her for an ordinary suburban housewife . . . '

Wycliffe drove through the city centre and out on the other side of town. The mortuary was attached to the pathology department of the city hospital. They waited in a bare little room like a doctor's waiting room and after five minutes they were fetched by a white-coated attendant.

Yvette's body lay on a trolley covered by a sheet. At a sign from Wycliffe the attendant lifted the edge of the sheet, exposing the slightly discoloured features of the dead girl. Natalie stared at the face briefly then, taking the edge of the sheet, she whisked it clear, uncovering the naked body. The attendant looked scandalized.

'Is this how she was found?'

'No, she was wearing her jeans, socks and sandals; they have been sent to forensic.'

'What about the scratches?'

'She was scratched by the bushes.'

The attendant looked from one to the other in astonishment at this calm exchange. He moved to replace the sheet but she stopped him with a gesture and pointed to the girl's hand nearest her. 'Why have they cut her nails?'

Wycliffe looked at the attendant who shook his head.

'She must have cut them herself.'

Natalie turned to him with a curious expression which had in it a certain pride. 'Like that? Never! Yvette was proud of her nails; she wasn't fussy about the rest of

87

her appearance but she never neglected her nails. She had nice hands and she knew it.'

The attendant replaced the sheet.

Natalie said, 'Do you want me any more?'

'Just a couple of questions and your signature on a form.'

She followed Wycliffe into the waiting-room. 'Well?'

'Her handbag was found near her and apart from the usual things there was a full bottle of medicine – influenza mixture. I wondered if you had any idea who it was for?'

'Not for her, anyway. She would never take any medicine apart from the occasional aspirin.'

'So you can't help us there. The other question concerned any trinkets or jewellery she might have been wearing – necklace, rings, bracelets?'

'Only her watch, she always wore that.'

'What sort of watch?'

'Just an ordinary wrist watch, nothing expensive. It had a bracelet made up of lucky charms – you know the sort of thing.'

Natalie signed the form which the clerk had prepared for her.

'Now, I'll take you home.'

'No, drop me off at La Cass, it's better to be working.'

Wycliffe dropped her outside the club. In all the ordeal not a single tear, not a word of sentiment, just a hint of pride when she mentioned the girl's nails. And yet Wycliffe felt sure that Natalie was grieving, silently and without demonstration, as an animal grieves.

Back in Falcon Street they had succeeded in manoeuvring one of the big blue incident-vans through the gates of the churchyard to be parked on the gravel. These vans offered limited office accommodation and provided radio and telephone links.

As Wycliffe got out of his car he was accosted by two

reporters, the first of many. 'Nothing to say at the moment, you know as much as I do.'

Inspector Scales was already installed in the van and he was on the telephone to the chemist whose label appeared on Yvette's bottle of medicine.

'Mr Martin? ... I'm enquiring about a bottle of medicine – influenza mixture, I think it is – dispensed by you sometime on Saturday ... No, there's nothing wrong with it as far as I know, we merely want to know when it was dispensed and who for ...'

The conversation continued for a while then Scales replaced the receiver.

'He says the prescription was brought in by a young girl on Saturday evening and that she waited for it to be made up. She told him that it was for somebody with 'flu. Apparently quite a few people have their own prescriptions for their ailments and insist on them being made up even when there is an identical proprietary medicine available off the shelf.'

'Did he say what time she was in his shop?'

'At about half-past five.'

Another piece in the jigsaw of Yvette's movements on Saturday afternoon and evening.

'Is Kersey about?'

'No, I think he's taking his meal break but he shouldn't be long. Incidentally, Willy Goppel hasn't turned up yet.'

It was odd about Goppel.

The police had finished their main task in the church-yard but three men were engaged in a systematic search for anything which might have been missed and they were joined by a couple of press photographers. A TV van was cruising down Falcon Street, looking for somewhere to park.

Scales said, 'I hope this isn't going to be one of those.'

Wycliffe knew what he meant. A couple of potentially

sensational cases will pass by scarcely noticed by the press then, for no apparent reason, one hits the headlines and stays there throughout the investigation with almost as many pressmen as policemen on the ground.

Wycliffe tried to focus his ideas. Yvette might have been attacked in Church Lane or even in the churchyard but it seemed at least as likely that she had been killed in a nearby house. No prizes for guessing which. Her mother would have arrived home at about three when Yvette had been alone in the house with Bishop for several hours . . .

A quick and easy solution? After all, murder is more often than not a domestic crime.

When Kersey returned from his meal break Wycliffe aired his thoughts and the sergeant agreed. He was sent to talk to Bishop.

Fenton Street was as different from Falcon Street as two streets can be. A quite unnecessarily wide road cut through a random assortment of dreary concrete blockhouses with an occasional gap where a starved and anaemic tree struggled half-heartedly for survival – the planners' concession to 'the environment'. Bishop's Car Mart and Vehicle Hire Service had a forecourt full of old bangers and a huge, asbestos-roofed shed with a concrete façade painted a bilious shade of green and lettered in red.

Kersey and his colleagues had been taking an interest in Bishop for more than a year – since each of three break-ins on the industrial estate had employed one of his hired vans, later to be found abandoned on the motorway.

'You can't expect me to know whether a client who hires a van is a crook, Mr Kersey. I mean, once I'm satisfied that he has a licence to drive the class of vehicle concerned and he's paid his deposit . . . '

There was also some question about insurance write-offs turning up in new and beguiling fancy dress.

Kersey made his way among the hardware to the office which consisted of two rooms, one for the receptionist and an inner one for Bishop. The receptionist was nowhere to be seen and Kersey went through. Bishop was seated at a roll-topped desk tapping his teeth with a ball-point while he studied a battered loose-leaf ledger. He swivelled round in his chair.

'Mr Kersey! Have a pew. Evelyn's gone to spend a penny.'

Kersey continued to stand. 'I suppose you've heard about Yvette?'

Bishop registered grave concern. 'I have. Natalie rang me; she's pretty cut up, poor girl. Well, it's natural, isn't it? I mean, I feel pretty rough about it myself. I know I'm not her father but I've lived in the same house for some time now. She was a good kid.'

Kersey found himself staring at a calendar picture of a nude girl who by suitable contortion had contrived to get her breasts and buttocks in the same picture and still look pleased about it.

'When did you last see Yvette?'

Bishop fiddled with the ends of his bandit moustache. 'I suppose I saw her some time on Saturday but I can't remember for sure. I mean, you don't take much notice of somebody living in the same house.'

Purely as a matter of tactics Kersey stared at him as though in disbelief and it worked; Bishop put his pen on the desk with great deliberation. 'You're quite right, Mr Kersey, Yvette looked in here to see me on Saturday afternoon. It had gone out of my mind.'

'What time?'

'Time?' He screwed up his features. 'Fourish? A bit later, perhaps. I can't say exactly.'

'What did she want?'

'Oh, she often looks in here when she's passing.'

'What did she want?'

Bishop shrugged: 'If you must know she wanted a part-time job. We open seven days a week and she wanted to work here Saturdays and Sundays.'

'Did you agree?'

'No. For two reasons. First, Natalie wouldn't have gone for it and second, I haven't much use for a girl about the place weekends. I mean it's when the chaps come to buy cars and a girl of fifteen can't be expected to flog bangers.' Bishop tried hard to look and sound reasonable.

'Why did she want the job?'

'Why do any of us? You know how it is with youngsters these days, Mr Kersey; where we used to think in terms of a few bob they think in fivers.'

'What did you say to her?'

'Well, what could I say? I told her it was no dice.'

'How did she take it?'

'She was disappointed but I chatted her up a bit and when she left she was laughing. After all, I'm the only one who can talk to her something like a father.'

Kersey looked at him solemnly. 'You should take up social work; you're wasted flogging bangers to mugs.' He lit a cigarette and settled in his chair. 'Did you ever give her money?'

'Money? No, Natalie wouldn't have stood for it.'

Bishop sat waiting for more questions and when none came he began to fidget. 'If that's all you want to ask me, Mr Kersey . . . '

'What time did you get home Saturday night?'

The question took him momentarily off balance. 'Saturday? Oh, it must have been half-eleven or thereabouts.'

'Was Yvette home?'

Bishop glowered. 'I don't like that, Mr Kersey, you know bloody well she wasn't. Of course, I didn't know it at the time, I thought she'd be in bed as usual.'

'Where did you spend Saturday evening?'

92

'Actually, in the local boozer with a few of the lads –
The Sportsman's in Falcon Street.'

'So you didn't take your car.'

'No, I walked.'

'Did you notice anything unusual on your way home
– hear anything, see anything?'

'Bishop shook his head. 'No, I didn't. Nothing;
between you and me I was pretty far gone.'

Naturally the Wards at the post office had heard the
news almost at once, now customers stood about the
shop, mostly in silence but occasionally exchanging a
few words in low voices as if in church. Falcon Street
was old-fashioned enough to mourn its dead.

Mr Hedley was sent to buy stamps and to find out
what had happened. When he returned his wife was in
the kitchen preparing their mid-day meal.

'Well?'

'They've found her.'

'Alive?'

'No, the sexton, Jim Couch, found her; she was lying
on a pile of rubbish behind his shed, strangled.'

Mrs Hedley softened, 'Poor child.'

Hedley sighed. 'Apparently the body was pushed
over the wall.'

Mrs Hedley left her preparations for the meal and
went across to tell Joan Fiske who looked at her with
something approaching awe.

'You *knew*!'

The old lady shook her head. 'No, I merely *felt*, but
the cards knew.' After a moment she went on, 'Her
body was pushed over the wall right opposite the gate
from our Court.'

Mrs Fiske clasped her hands. 'Oh, my God! You mean
that it was somebody from the Court!'

Mrs Hedley looked round as though she feared being

93

overheard and lowered her voice. 'I'll tell you something but I don't want it repeated; you understand?'

'Of course.'

'It's something my husband said he saw. You know he goes out on our verandah at all times of the day and night – he's old and he gets restless . . . '

'Yes, I often see him there.'

'Well, he was out there late on Saturday night and he says he saw somebody behaving very strangely – very strangely indeed. He said he thought this person came out of Willy Goppel's but he might equally have come through the gate.'

'But who . . . ?'

The old lady shook her head. 'I'm saying no more! You'll have to work it out for yourself. But just think – who in this Court would be likely to assault a fifteen-year-old girl? And who would have the best chance with this particular girl?'

'But shouldn't Mr Hedley tell the police?'

'No! That's what he wants to do, but do you think they would take any notice of an old man? And if they did, could they act on it? It is not as though he saw this man doing anything actually incriminating. And what would happen if this person got to hear that we were making accusations? I wouldn't feel safe in my bed – two old people living alone.'

Joan Fiske was scared herself, 'Yes, I hadn't thought. Of course, if Mr Hedley hasn't got any actual evidence . . . ' She shivered. 'Really, I wish you hadn't told me; I'm nervous enough as it is.'

To Marty it seemed a very long time since he had seen Mr Goppy's cat and he felt uneasy. Any interruption in the even tenor of his life disturbed him and made him feel vaguely restless and unhappy. Several times that morning he had leaned on the rail of Mr Goppy's yard and called softly, 'Fritzy! Fritzy!' But nothing had happened. Now that he had had his lunch he tried again. 'Fritzy!' But the cat did not come and he did not hear the familiar, tentative little cry with which Fritzy sometimes greeted him. He became increasingly concerned and it occurred to him that he had not seen Mr Goppy for a long time either. Perhaps they had gone away together – gone away like Yvette . . . He did not like it when people went away.

Greatly daring he raised the latch of Mr Goppy's gate and entered the yard. He looked back anxiously to make sure that he was unobserved and then advanced to peer through the glass panel of Mr Goppy's back door. He could not see anything very clearly but he thought there was somebody inside moving, then he realized that he was seeing his own reflection in the glass. It amused him and he tried several exaggerated movements which made him chuckle. But he did not forget the cat. Once or twice in the past he had crept into the workshop very quietly when Mr Goppy was at work on his little house and Mr Goppy had not been in the least angry. He would stand watching until he became bored and then say politely, 'I got to go now, Mr Goppy.'

Very gently he turned the door-knob and to his surprise the door opened. He knew that if Mr Goppy was away it should have been locked so he felt relieved. He called again in a voice scarcely above a whisper, 'Fritzy!' But the only response came from the animals in their cages, scuffling and scratching and squeaking. He had forgotten about them and for a moment he was frightened, then he remembered and went over to look at them. He stood for some time by the cages, his hands caressing the wire mesh. He liked the guinea-pigs but he was a little afraid of the lizards so he tried not to see them or only looked at them out of the corner of his eye.

A slight creaking noise startled him and he called out, 'Mr Goppy!' But no-one answered and after a little while he plucked up courage and worked his way round the central bench to the door at the far end of the workshop where he had never been before. With great boldness he opened the door and found himself in a little room at the bottom of a flight of stairs, but what interested him was yet another glass door through which he could see into the shop. He was delighted to be able to look through to the street and see the cars going by, but then came another of those disturbing creaks and it seemed much closer. He looked up the stairs and at first he could not make out what it was he saw, something was hanging over the stairs, swinging very gently; it seemed large and shapeless in the dim light and he was intrigued. At the same time he realized that it was this swinging object which made the occasional creaking noise and he felt reassured. Then, abruptly, as though his eyes had come suddenly into sharp focus, he saw what it was, it was Mr Goppy. Mr Goppy with a blue string round his neck, hanging like a balloon. Marty stood for a long time, wide-eyed, fascinated, then all at once he was overcome by a nameless terror and he fled. He blundered through the workshop and the yard and raced across the Court, up the verandah steps and through the house to the kitchen where his mother was washing dishes.

'What on earth . . . ?'

But Marty was beyond words, he merely tugged at her arm and pointed wildly.

Wycliffe met them by Willy Goppel's little gate, Mrs Fiske, pale and scared, Marty in a state of intense excitement.

'I think something must have happened in there.'

96

CHAPTER FIVE

Wycliffe looked up the stairwell and saw a man's body suspended by a blue cord from the top landing. He could make out the stockinged feet, dark trousers and light fawn jacket. The body oscillated slowly on the suspending cord as it was disturbed by draughts. He climbed the stairs to the first landing where his face was level with that of the hanging man. Wycliffe was seeing Willy Goppel for the first time and Willy was dead; there was nothing to be done. His features were livid, his lips blue, his eyes bulged slightly and the tip of his tongue protruded from his mouth. The blue, nylon cord was anchored to the newel post of the banisters on the top landing.

He heard a cat crying and opened one of the doors off the landing. A marmalade cat ran out of the room and padded quickly downstairs with one frightened backward glance. Wycliffe returned to the workshop; the key of the back-door was on the inside so he took it, let himself out and locked the door behind him.

At the incident post Scales was on duty and Kersey had just returned from interviewing Bishop.

'Goppel is dead; it looks as though he hanged himself.'

Kersey said, 'So he didn't scarper.'

Scales asked, 'Has this anything to do with the girl?'

'God knows! But we must assume that it has. *If* she was killed in Goppel's house there might be something to give us a lead and it will be too late to think of that when the whole place has been trampled over.'

Half-an-hour later Willy's house was a scene of ordered chaos with numbers of large men and one woman each intent on a specific task. The one woman was Lucy Crabbe – the first fully operational woman detective to be attached to Wycliffe's squad.

Wycliffe had briefed them before letting them loose. 'You may think this is a lot of fuss about a suicide but it's possible that Yvette Cole was murdered in this house and if she was there is sure to be some evidence of the fact. It's your job to find it, not to trample it out of existence. Don't move round more than you have to, keep to the sides of stairs and corridors and think twice before you touch anything.'

Dr Franks arrived, breezy as ever. 'Business is looking up! What are you calling this? Suicide or murder? I've never come across murder by hanging but I expect it's been done. This will delay my report on the girl. Can't be in two places at once – not on the money they pay me.'

It is impossible to document and record a whole house in the detail necessary to ensure that nothing has been missed. Which surfaces to fingerprint? Which to ignore? From where does one take dust samples and where does one stop taking them? At best it is a hit-and-miss business but after years of experience a good jack develops something of a sixth sense which gives him slightly better odds than chance in getting it right.

Wycliffe remained in the workshop where, presumably, Willy had spent most of his working hours. He marvelled at the dolls' house which might now never be completed. It seemed to be a model of a late Georgian town house with, as far as Wycliffe could judge, every detail represented accurately to scale. In theory he was attracted to model making, he had something of the peep-show mentality, but he knew that in fact he would want a more practical reward for such expenditure of time, skill and patience.

At the end of the workshop, nearest the shop, there were a few shelves with books, and a high desk of the kind once favoured by schoolteachers. The books were all concerned with the architecture of the Georgian, Regency and Victorian periods and, propped against the desk, there was a portfolio of drawings, sketches and plans, evidently Willy's own work.

The desk contained a couple of ledgers in which he kept simple accounts of his dolls' house business; there was a bundle of receipts, a clip of unpaid bills, a few letters from suppliers, cheque book, paying-in book and a folder of bank statements. Flicking through the pages of a desk diary Wycliffe came across a loose sheet of notes written in a careful though spidery hand. It was a list of firms – small firms engaged in retail trade in the city: City Butchers Limited, The Elite Printing and Stationery Company, Excelsior Furnishings Limited . . . About a dozen altogether. Against all but three of the entries was the abbreviated name of an insurance company: Eagle, Sun, Legal, Phoenix . . . with either a tick or a cross. Probably Willy had been trying to get cheaper cover for his properties and had compared notes with other owners.

In addition to all this there were three files of correspondence, one each for Crowther and Grant, solicitors; Cassells and White, estate agents; and The Martin Fiske Business Accountancy Service.

He heard Kersey's voice on the stairs. 'Come up here, sir. Take a look at this . . .'

Wycliffe went upstairs. Willy's body had been removed to a stretcher and was about to be carried downstairs to the waiting mortuary van. Wycliffe followed Kersey into the living-room which was one of the unspoiled rooms of the old house, still with its moulded cornices, ornamental ceiling, carved architraves and marble mantelpiece. Willy's ancient three-piece suite was lost in one corner and most of the rest of the floor space was occupied by trestle tables on which there was a scale model of the whole Court, the houses, the garages, the yards and the gardens – even the oak tree, all convincingly portrayed. But beyond all this there were figures, carved in wood and meticulously painted; they were disposed outside the houses to which they belonged. The Ward family was immediately recognizable; Mr and Mrs Hedley, tall, lean and slightly stooping, brooded over the scene from their verandah; the Fiskes were there with Marty, his head twisted a little on one side in characteristic pose; Natalie, a slim, black-haired siren, was sunbathing – in her bikini. Bishop lounged against the doorpost, unmistakable with his broad shoulders and piratical countenance; and in Yvette Willy had caught the languid posture of bored youth to perfection. Willy's own figure, bent over his sink-gardens, was vaguely defined; enigmatic.

Kersey said, 'This thing is a bit kinky, don't you think? There's something *Alice Through the Looking-Glass* about it, all innocently childish on the surface but underneath, spooky and a bit sinister.' He screwed his face into a grimace, searching for words. 'It's childish all right, but it's the childishness of an adult. When you remember that Willy didn't have to make a living out of dolls' houses and you think of those sink-gardens, then this . . .'

'Go on.'

Kersey was cautious. 'All I'm saying is that it's easy to imagine a man like Willy becoming attracted to young girls – or boys, for that matter. After all, look at Lewis Carroll – or Barrie. Often there's no harm in it but when a lonely man starts fantasising over kids, it's dangerous; there's a risk. Don't you agree?'

'In general, yes. In this case I can't see Yvette as Alice – Lolita, perhaps, but too old for either. However, what

100

you're suggesting is that Goppel murdered the girl and then, in a fit of remorse, hanged himself.'

'It's possible.'

Wycliffe prodded his cheek with the stem of his unlit pipe. 'It's certainly tempting to link Yvette's murder with Goppel's suicide but just imagine for a moment that we didn't have a murder on our hands. Suppose Yvette was still alive and we found Willy like this. With your previous knowledge of his troubles, what would you say?'

'Suicide because of the business with his papers. That would be the reasonable explanation in the circumstances.'

'But Yvette being murdered makes it less so?'

Kersey was dogged. 'I think the two must be linked.'

Wycliffe said, 'You're probably right but we've got to be sure. I want to know who stole Willy's papers and why they were sent to you. There's not much to go on but it seems that whoever did it must have had a grudge against Willy and sufficient acquaintance with the Mallet Street nick to know that you are a D.S. there.'

Kersey grinned. 'And that still leaves it as wide open as a Scotsman's kilt but I'll have a go.'

'Good! By the way, didn't you say Goppel had a son?'

'That's right, he lives with a chap called Toby Lennon – the Hedley's nephew – in Telfer Street, behind the pannier market.'

'He'll have to be told but I'll see to that.'

Willy's living-room was clean but depressingly drab and shabby. He had done his household chores conscientiously but without enthusiasm or much imagination. The old-fashioned fire grate was filled with red crêpe paper for the summer and there was a small electric fire for chilly evenings. The chairs were drawn up, one on each side of the fireplace, and there was an empty whisky glass on the hearth-rug by each chair. A bottle of whisky, half-full, stood in the fender.

'Looks as though he had company,' Wycliffe spoke to Fowler, the detective constable who was searching the living-room.

'Looks like it, sir. With any luck we shall get prints off the glasses.'

Willy Goppel's body was in the van and Franks, the pathologist, came over to Wycliffe.

'Who are you sending?'

A police officer should be present at any post-mortem where there are possible criminal implications.

Wycliffe hesitated. 'I'll send Scales along. I want all the clothing sent to forensic and I want you to look out for scratches and abrasions which might have been caused immediately before death.'

'Why, for God's sake?'

'If he murdered the girl, isn't it likely that she fought back?'

Franks nodded. 'Point taken. Well, if all murderers had the sense to hang themselves it would save the tax-payers a lot of money and put a few lawyers out of work. I'd be all for that.'

Wycliffe was greatly puzzled. He agreed with Kersey that it would be stretching coincidence rather far to suppose that the murder and the suicide were not connected. On the other hand there were difficulties in the theory that Willy had murdered the girl then hanged himself in remorse. Allowing for the fact that lonely, middle-aged men may brood on nubile girls there was little evidence of a sexual motive for the crime. More than that, if Willy had killed her he had gone some way towards covering his tracks – by disposing of the body – before being overwhelmed by guilt.

But in Wycliffe's view the most telling point was a simple one. He had seen the girl and he had seen Willy. In a struggle it was likely that the man might have got the

102

upper hand but not before Yvette had made her mark on him and had time to scream the house down.

Brooding, Wycliffe went upstairs to the top landing where the nylon cord was still secured to the base of the newel post. Sergeant Smith, who doubled as the squad's photographer and finger-print man, was taking flash pictures of everything in sight. He was a middle-aged, dyspeptic misogynist. Wycliffe was tempted to ask him if he had fantasies about teen-aged girls.

'A lot of fuss about a suicide, isn't it, sir?'

Wycliffe muttered something non-committal. It was best to ignore Smith's leading questions.

'A clove-hitch round the newel post,' Smith said, 'and a running noose on the other end. About ten feet of cord altogether.' He stood looking down the stairwell. 'If he went over the banisters he would have had a free fall of eight feet – more than he'd have got from the hangman in the old days. I wonder the jerk didn't dislodge the newel post.'

Wycliffe shook his head. 'He certainly didn't go over from here. His head went into the noose on the landing below.'

Smith looked at him with curiosity. 'How can you know that?'

'You as good as said it yourself. Goppel died of asphyxia – you saw his head and neck. In judicial hanging, with a drop of six feet, death was never due to asphyxia – always to the extension and severance of the spinal cord.'

'You mean that he came up here to fix the rope then went calmly down to the next landing and put his head in the noose, hoisting himself over the banisters – is that it?'

'I've no idea how calm he was but quite apart from the evidence, you know as well as I do that suicides by

103

hanging rarely allow any drop.' As he spoke Wycliffe was looking over the banisters down to the next landing. 'That rail down there doesn't appear to have been dusted for prints.'

'No sir, it hasn't, I didn't think—'

'Then do it now; that's where his head went into the noose. Look for smears as well as prints and for any fibres which might have caught in the joints of the woodwork. Examine the uprights to see if there are any signs of fresh scuffing.'

There were two bedrooms on the top floor, Willy's and another which must have been his son's and was still furnished as a single room. Willy's bedroom could hardly have changed since he shared it with his wife; the furniture was old-fashioned and shabby, the carpet and curtains were faded and whatever pattern there had been on the wallpaper had almost disappeared.

As Wycliffe came into the room D.C. Crabbe was turning over the bedclothes. 'I've just started in here, sir.'

'Don't let me disturb you.'

D.C. Crabbe was an extremely efficient and determined young woman and Wycliffe was sure that she would climb to somewhere near the top or know the reason why. No quarter asked; none given. In her presence it was dangerous even to think of sex.

On the wall over the bed there was a framed photograph of a younger Willy seated next to a thin, frail looking woman with a baby on her lap. Willy had a moustache at that time and he carried more weight; he sat confidently, legs apart, looking at the baby in his wife's arms with a proud smile.

'Was the bed unmade when you came in?'

'No, I disturbed the bedclothes just in case—'

The news that Willy Goppel had hanged himself spread to one or two reporters who lingered in the neighbourhood in the hope of fresh scraps of information on the murder of Yvette, and when Wycliffe arrived back at the incident post others had arrived. Not that suicide by the little German would have had much of a news rating but a possible link with the murder made it a different matter.

'Are you treating this man's death as in any way connected with the murder of Yvette Cole?'

Wycliffe conducted his press conference from the steps of the incident-van.

'We have to consider every possibility but at the moment there is no firm evidence of a connection.'

'Goppel was an elderly bachelor, living alone, spending his time making dolls' houses – don't you think—?'

'Mr Goppel was not a bachelor, he was a widower.'

'All the same, a man in his position might be expected to become sexually frustrated and . . . '

'I am not a psychologist, gentlemen.'

'Do you know yet whether the girl was raped?'

'She was not. There is nothing to suggest that she was sexually assaulted.'

A very little man, wily and persistent, whom Wycliffe knew of old, tried a different line. 'I suppose this will change the nature of your inquiry, superintendent?'

'No, we shall carry on as before.'

'In the expectation of making an arrest?'

'All policemen work in the expectation of an arrest when a crime has been committed.'

'But you can't arrest a dead man.'

'I must admit that I have never tried.'

There was a laugh from the other reporters.

Hedley came in from one of his routine visits to the verandah. 'The police are in Goppel's house. Something must have happened there.'

'What's that?'

105

Hedley was saved from having to repeat himself by the arrival of Mrs Fiske, so excited that she did not wait for the door to be opened but came in after ringing the bell once.

'Willy Goppel has hanged himself.'

Mrs Hedley looked at her for a moment as though she did not understand, then she said, 'Why? Why did he do that?'

'Well, he must have killed Yvette then hanged himself; they reckon he's been dead since Saturday.'

Mrs Hedley had never seen Joan Fiske so animated, it was almost as though she had been drinking. Mrs Hedley turned to her husband. 'Did you hear that?'

'Of course I heard it but I don't believe it. Willy Goppel wouldn't hurt a fly.'

His wife laughed shortly. 'Not a fly perhaps, but a young girl is a different matter. All men are alike when it comes to sex.'

'But why should he kill her? She used to help him with his animals.'

'Are you purposely stupid? I suppose he tried to rape her and she made a fuss . . . '

Hedley was trying to light a fresh cigarette but his hand trembled. 'I suppose it's possible but I can hardly believe it.'

Mrs Fiske said, 'Oh, it's true all right, I'm so *relieved*.'

The old man looked at her with a gleam of antagonism. 'Why should you be relieved?'

'Because it's all over! It was dreadful having that hanging over us, simply dreadful, and it might have gone on for weeks!'

Mrs Hedley gave Joan Fiske a knowing look. 'Well, at least we can forget about you know who . . . '

Mr Hedley talked but the others took no notice. 'If that's what happened, I suppose it's for the best. If Willy hadn't killed himself they would have put him in prison

106

and he couldn't have stood that. He was like me, he needed his freedom . . . '

Of all the people in the Court Willy's cat adopted the Hedleys and after some preliminary skirmishing Mrs Hedley accepted him.

Telfer Street was narrow and dingy and smitten with planning blight. The blank wall of the market, decorated with spray-painted slogans, formed one side of the street and a row of seedy shops with decaying fronts the other. Most of the rooms over the shops were let as flats and the whole was scheduled for demolition when the spirit moved those in high places and the money-tree bloomed again.

Wycliffe enquired from a little Irishman in a second-hand shop for Goppel.

'Goppel, is it? I've never heard of any Goppel round here.'

'He lives with a chap called Lennon.'

'Ah! Toby Lennon, to be sure! You're looking for the pansy-boy. I can't say I've heard his name before. Their flat is the top of number fifteen.'

Number fifteen was a shop whose windows were entirely covered by posters advertising every kind of event from all-in wrestling to a meeting of the Parousia Society in preparation for the Second Coming. There was a passage at the side leading to a dark, uncarpeted staircase. Wycliffe climbed three flights to a landing with two doors on one of which the name 'Lennon' had been written with a felt pen. He knocked, and after an interval knocked again. There was a sound of move-ment and the door was opened by a slight, fair young man who stood looking at him in a vague uncompre-hending way. Wycliffe introduced himself.

'Mr Goppel?'

'That's right.'

'May I come in?'

He followed the young man into a shabby, dusty living-room which smelled of mice and decaying food. Goppel was quickly recovering his self-possession and Wycliffe, who had suspected drugs, decided that he had merely been asleep.

'I've got some bad news for you, Mr Goppel.'

'Bad news? Not about Toby?' His voice was slightly higher pitched than is usual in a man and taken with his slim figure and almost feminine features it was inevitable that he should be labelled a queer whether he was one or not.

'Your father.'

'Is he dead?'

'Yes.'

'How did it happen?'

'He was found hanged in his house.'

'*Hanged*? You mean he committed suicide?'

'It looks like it. Have you any idea why he might have taken his own life?'

'Good God, no! He was all right when I saw him last.'

'When was that?'

'A week ago or a bit more, perhaps.'

'Did he mention that some papers and money had been stolen from his workshop?'

'No, he didn't say anything like that.'

'When did you leave home, Mr Goppel?'

'Just over two years ago.'

'And you came to live with Lennon then?'

'Yes, we've known each other since we were kids. He used to live in the Court, he was an orphan and he was brought up by his aunt, Mrs Hedley.'

'The Coles had come to live in the Court before you left?'

'Oh, yes.'

'So you remember Yvette?'

'Yes. That's the girl who's been murdered.' Two and two made four with an all but audible click. 'You can't think that's anything to do with the old man . . . ? Good God! Is that what you're saying?'

'No, I've no idea whether or not there is any connection between your father's death and the murder of Yvette.'

'But you think there might be?' His concern and distress struck Wycliffe as more or less normal but over and above these natural emotions he seemed inordinately scared so that he watched Wycliffe as a cat watches a strange dog.

'A small point, Mr Goppel, have you any idea where your father spent the occasional week-end away from home?'

'Fishing.'

'Fishing? I saw no tackle in the house.'

'He didn't bring it home; he was friendly with the landlord of the pub at Bickersleigh and he would go to stay there overnight sometimes.'

Wycliffe asked the inevitable questions and received stock answers. 'As far as you know, was anything worrying your father when you last saw him?'

'No, he seemed quite as usual to me.'

When Wycliffe had gone Freddie sat staring at the floor and listening for Pongo's step on the stair. He could not take in the magnitude of what had happened to him or foresee how his life would be affected. Without Pongo he was lost, not knowing what to think or do. But it was an hour before Lennon arrived and by that time Freddie was in a state of great excitement and had to be coaxed into intelligibility.

Joan Fiske was shelling peas for the evening meal. She was almost happy; first because she was relieved of a nagging fear; second, for a reason not so easily explained. It was not that she was vicious or that she wished misfortune on others but when misfortune befell her acquaintances she could not help feeling that some vaguely conceived principle of justice had been vindicated. 'You see!' she told herself, 'you are not the only one who suffers. It happens to others.' And for once she looked forward to her husband coming home so that she could tell him the news and they could discuss it.

When he arrived he went upstairs without a word and by the time he came down she had the soup on the table.

'So they've found Yvette.'

He unfolded his napkin and tucked it in. 'They've found her body, if that's what you mean. Some yobbo she picked up with, I suppose. You could almost say she was asking for it.'

'No.'

'What do you mean – "No"?'

'It was Willy Goppel. He killed her then committed suicide. They found him this afternoon, hanging from his own staircase.'

Fiske paused with his soup spoon half-way to his lips. 'Ah!' He said no more for a moment or two, giving himself time to reflect. He was not a man to express an opinion lightly. 'Well, I can't say I'm altogether surprised. A man living alone, playing with kid's things.' After drinking a little of his soup he added, 'I've always felt that there was something not quite right about Goppel; in some ways he was too good to be true.'

'At any rate they can't come worrying Marty now, can they?'

'Marty? What's it got to do with him?'

Mrs Fiske realized that she had said more than she meant to. 'I don't know, I just thought that being like he is they might . . .'

'Don't be ridiculous!'

110

It was rare that they had a subject of mutual interest to talk about and Mrs Fiske was reluctant to let it go.

'What will they do now? Will there be a trial? They can't try a dead man, surely?'

'Of course not! The case will be allowed to drop. We shall hear no more about it.'

But for once Mr Fiske was wrong.

The Wards were having their evening meal, or to be more accurate they were sitting round the table though no one felt like eating. Alison had been crying, Henry was pale and silent.

Mrs Ward said, 'I just don't believe that Willy Goppel was capable of such a dreadful thing. I mean, you two children when you were younger spent half your time in there. You were in there with him more often than you were here with us, what with the shop and one thing and another . . .' She appealed to her husband, 'Do you think he could have done such a terrible thing, Edward?'

Mr Ward shook his head, 'It hardly seems possible.'

Franks sipped very dry sherry and put his glass down on the white, metal desk. 'Apart from the removal of her shirt there is no reason to see this as a sex crime. The girl was, in fact, a virgin. The scratches on her body were caused after death, presumably when she was pushed over the wall of the churchyard.'

Kersey was riding high in the company of a chief-super and a distinguished pathologist, full of bonhomie and chilled lager. 'If the murder and suicide are linked then Goppel must have killed the girl and if the motive was not sex it must have been something else. Perhaps it was Yvette who stole the cigar box from Goppel's desk. She seems to have had a free run of the place and it would account for the money I found in her room.'

111

'Do you think it was Yvette who sent you the papers?' Wycliffe looked at the sergeant with interest.

'It's possible. After all, she might have heard Geoff Bishop and her mother talking about me – they know me well enough.'

'But even if she stole the stuff and sent you the papers to pay off some grudge against Goppel, why did he kill her? The damage was already done.' Wycliffe turned to Franks. 'How exactly did she die? What sort of reconstruction can you make?'

Franks ran a pink hand over his thin hair. 'She died of manual strangulation, facing her attacker who, I feel sure, wore gloves. His thumbs met at some distance above her larynx and the hyoid bone was fractured. A good deal more force was used than was necessary.'

Wycliffe nodded. 'But that is common enough – you are not saying that her attacker was necessarily a strong man?'

'By no means.'

'You have seen Goppel's body, would you say that he was physically capable of having killed her?'

Franks looked puzzled. 'Of course.'

'But if she put up a fight? She was a healthy fifteen-year-old girl, small but wiry.'

'An oldish man of no great physique would have had difficulty.'

'Did you find any scratches or abrasions on Goppel's body?'

'None.'

Wycliffe sipped his beer. 'When her mother saw the body this morning one of her questions was, "Who cut her nails?" If they were cut by her killer it could only have been to make sure they held no tissue or fibres which might incriminate him.'

Franks laughed. 'In your usual roundabout fashion, Charles, you are saying that you don't think Goppel killed the girl.'

Wycliffe did not answer and Kersey said, 'In that case there is no connection between the murder and the suicide and I find that difficult to believe.'

Wycliffe sighed. 'So do I.' He glanced at the white digital clock on Frank's desk. 'It's gone ten, let's think about it again tomorrow.'

Outside it was raining and Kersey said, 'Change in the weather.'

'Where did you leave your car?'

'In Falcon Street, but don't bother, sir, I can catch a bus back.'

'Don't be daft, man.'

'A very decent bloke,' Kersey told his wife. 'The nearest thing I've found to a human being above the rank of inspector.'

'Perhaps this will help you with your promotion.'

'At my age? In any case, I don't know if I want it now.'

'Don't kid yourself, your eyes go green every time you mention it.'

When Wycliffe had dropped Kersey he went into the incident-van for a last look round before going home. Sergeant Bourne had taken over from Scales and a solitary D.C. was doing one-finger exercises on a typewriter.

Bourne was one of the new breed of policemen, weaned on computer print-outs; he was ambitious, a trifle arrogant, and Wycliffe did not like him though he conceded that he was a good officer. Bourne was working at Yvette's little diary.

'Found anything?'

'Nothing world-shaking, sir. The first thing that struck me was these asterisks which occur on consecutive days at intervals. They obviously refer to her periods. As to the initials, there are eight sets and five of these correspond to the names of the boys at her school with whom she was friendly. I got those names from reports of our people who made enquiries. Henry Ward seems to be referred to simply as "H".' Bourne turned the pages. 'The most interesting item is the figures which appear regularly each Sunday during the past twenty weeks – since April. Figures like 5.30, 5.50, 6.10 and so on. At first I thought they referred to times of appointments but some of them are much too precise – here, for example, 5.23. Nobody makes an appointment for 5.23. Not even me.' For once Bourne guyed himself.

'What are they then, money?'

'I think so. Money paid to her each Sunday. Perhaps she was doing a part-time job at week-ends.'

Wycliffe agreed. 'We'll put somebody on it in the morning.'

He got into his car with the intention of driving straight home but his way took him through the city centre, near La Cassandra in King Street. Almost before he realized what he was doing he had parked the car and was walking along the wet, deserted pavements in the direction of the club.

As always on Monday nights the city streets were dead and the flashing lights of La Cassandra were like an oasis in the desert, but inside business was slack. Although he had been in the place only once before, they knew him and he was not asked to show a membership card or to sign the book. The subtle communications system, rivalling ESP, which operates in such places brought Natalie through the curtained door from her office just as he entered the main room. Several customers were sitting at the tables, a few couples were slouching round the floor although the band was not playing. Instead, a slim, gamine-type girl, perched on a stool, was playing an accordion. She wore a sort of leotard which left one breast bare and she played moodily. The dancers seemed to ignore her.

Natalie came across the floor towards him. She was a beautiful woman; you couldn't blame any man for wanting to take her to bed and the wonder was that she had picked an oaf like Bishop for the privilege. The artful simplicity of her white gown and the candour of her dark eyes gave an impression of innocence which scarcely survived two minutes of conversation.

'Any news?'

Wycliffe said, 'I suppose you've heard about Goppel?'

'Yes, but you can't think he murdered Yvette? That funny little man? It's ridiculous!'

It was a novel experience, hearing a mother discussing the very recent murder of her daughter in this objective fashion. But Natalie had been raised in a realistic school.

'I want to talk to you.'

She led him to a table in a corner of the room which was even less well lit than the rest.

'Drink?'

'No, thanks.'

Natalie was keeping an eye on all that was happening, nothing escaped her.

'Where did Yvette get her money? Ninety pounds in the drawer in her bedroom and another ten in her handbag.'

'I've no idea unless she was going with men.'

'She was a virgin. Could she have got it from you without you knowing?'

'No way!'

'Bishop?'

A faint smile. 'Geoff would make Shylock look like a free spender.'

'Is it possible that she had a part-time job? Say on Friday and Saturday evenings?'

Natalie frowned. 'A job? I suppose it's possible. How can I know what she did with herself with me stuck here?'

Wycliffe had been watching the customers round the bar which was better lit than the rest of the room. 'Isn't that Freddie Goppel – third from the left at the bar?'

'Yes.'

'Is he a member?'

'No, but he comes in with the chap next to him who is.'

'The fellow with the black thatch?'

'That's right, Toby Lennon – known as Pongo. He and Goppel share a flat and they're more than a bit . . .' She twisted one finger over the other.

'And the third man, the one with the bandit moustache – is that Bishop?'

She looked at him oddly. 'Haven't you two met?'

'A pleasure in store. Does he spend much time here?'

'He comes in occasionally with Lennon but mostly he'd rather I didn't see what he's up to.'

'Anybody else I should know?'

She pointed to a table near the bar. 'That's Martin Fiske working late.'

A tall, well-made man in his early forties, beginning to go soft; over meticulously turned out; all deodorant and aftershave.

'Who's the girl?'

'You flatter her; she's thirty-four or five. She works in his office and he's set her up in a nice little flat in Parkeston.'

'Does his wife know?'

'If she doesn't she must be the only one.'

The accordionist had stopped playing and the dancers were drifting back to their tables. The girl in the half-leotard put her instrument in its case and tucked it away in a recess, then she crossed the floor to where Natalie was seated with Wycliffe.

'I was due off twenty minutes ago. Where's the group?'

Natalie glanced at her watch. 'They're not coming back – with this lot it's hardly worth it.'

The girl shrugged, totally unselfconscious of her skimpy costume. 'That's not my affair.'

'All right, you'd better go.'

The girl gave Wycliffe a backward glance as she made off to the dressing rooms.

Natalie sighed. 'I shall have to get rid of that little slut; she's too lazy to breathe and she solicits the customers.'

'How did Bishop get on with Yvette?'

'All right, why?'

'No problems?'

'None.' Natalie was fiddling with a glass ashtray, turning it this way and that. 'You don't think much of me as a mother and maybe you're right, but Yvette was difficult; she wouldn't be told. She had no room for me and despite what the books say it's not unusual for kids to take against their parents – especially girls against their mothers. I hated the sight of mine. But I tried to help Yvette, I really did.

'She lived in a fantasy world. You say she was a virgin and I'm not surprised. It fits. She wanted to play with fire and not get burnt. She wouldn't understand that you can't go round sticking out your chest and wiggling your backside and expect the men to say "pretty, pretty" and leave it at that. You have to live in the real world – deliver the goods or not advertise 'em. God knows I've warned her often enough and if she'd listened she wouldn't be where she is now.'

Oddly, in this strange outburst, Wycliffe detected the first sign of real emotion in Natalie. There was a catch in her voice and she had spoken with sincerity. This was her code – not the attitude of every fond mamma to her daughter but there was something to be said for it.

'It's unlikely that this was a sex crime.'

'Of course it was a sex crime, whether she was raped or not. Why else would a fifteen-year-old girl get herself murdered?'

Talking to Natalie was like talking to an experienced colleague in the force.

He sat with his elbows on the table, watching her, giving her time to recover her poise. In the end he said, 'Why don't you go over and have a word with Goppel and his friend?'

She looked at him, surprised and a little scared. 'Talk to them? Why should I?'

'Don't you sometimes have a word with your patrons?'

She stood up reluctantly, suspicious of a trap yet afraid to refuse. 'What do you want me to say?'

'Anything you like. What do you usually say?'

She crossed the room to the bar and joined the party. Lennon was effusive. Wycliffe could not hear what he said but he saw him put one arm round her waist and the other round Goppel, blandly possessive. Natalie glanced back uneasily; Goppel seemed sullen and unresponsive, Bishop looked worried. Wycliffe had seen what he had wanted to see and left.

That night Natalie was home early. By one o'clock business at the club had folded. Bishop was in bed but not asleep.

'What time is it?'

'Coming up for two.'

'What did the law have to say?'

'He wanted to know where Yvette got her money.'

'Well, where did she?'

'I can't think. She was a virgin, Geoff.'

'She must have had a job.'

Natalie had undressed and now she went into the bathroom.

'Did he ask about me?'

'What?'

Bishop repeated his question.

'When he saw you at the bar he wasn't sure who you were.'

'That sounds healthy.'

Natalie came back into the bedroom and sat at her dressing-table brushing her hair. 'Things seem to be running your way at the moment.'

'How do you make that out?'

'If Freddie Goppel comes into his father's property you should be all right. You seem to get on well enough with him.'

'He's a bloody poof.'

'What difference does that make? He's worth keeping in with.'

'Sure! I don't think we'll have any problem with him but I'm not so sure about his stable-mate.'

'Pongo? It's got nothing to do with him.'

Bishop turned over in bed. 'Don't kid yourself, little Freddie won't fart unless he asks Pongo first. That won't change.'

'Then you'll have to watch it with both of them.'

'I do, sweetheart, I do.'

Wycliffe drove home. Home was The Watch House, a former coastguard building of grey stone, solid and four-square. It stood on one of the two promontories which guarded the entrance to the narrows and funnelled all the maritime traffic of the port. The nearest house was a quarter-of-a-mile away and his wife, Helen, with his labouring assistance had turned half-an-acre of rough grass into a garden with rhododendrons, azaleas, camellias and magnolias, all shielded from the salt winds by a phalanx of tamarisk, olearia and senecio. From the road the house showed slightly paler than the darkness and beyond were the navigation lights of the channel and a gliding shape, pin-pointed with lights – a ship of some sort putting to sea.

Wycliffe's claims on life were tentative and his estimate of his entitlement was modest. He attributed what he had and what he was mostly to luck and he was often troubled by the thought that his slice was too large. Helen had no such qualms; she took hold of what was hers with both hands and fashioned it to her liking with infectious enthusiasm. But it was Helen who had grown to love music while Wycliffe found a bitter-sweet escape in the novels of Tolstoy and Balzac, Dickens and Trollope, Sartre and Simenon.

Helen was in the living-room surrounded by gardening books and catalogues, listening to the record player.

'What is it?'

He was being tested. She had taken his musical education in hand.

'Sounds like Mozart.'

'It's Haydn's London Symphony.'

'Oh, well, that's not so bad – if it isn't Mozart it's Haydn and if it isn't Haydn it's Mozart.'

'Nonsense!'

Was it all in the same world?

CHAPTER SIX

Henry Ward could not sleep and at first light he slipped out of bed and crossed the landing to his sister's room. He opened the door and the curtains billowed in the through draught from the window. He could hear the rain driving against the glass but Alison was asleep under the bedclothes, only her hair gleamed dimly in the pale light.

'Alison!'

She shifted her position but did not wake. He tried again and this time he touched her so that she was awake at once, startled. 'Oh, it's you. What's the matter, is something wrong?'

He perched on the edge of her bed. 'I've got to talk to you, Ali. I didn't tell the police the truth about Yvette – at least I didn't tell them everything I knew.'

She sat up in bed, pulling the bedclothes about her and yawning. 'Put on my dressing-gown, you'll freeze sitting there.'

He obeyed with unaccustomed meekness. 'I saw her on Saturday night.' His sister said nothing and he went on: 'When the policeman questioned me on Sunday I had no idea that anything really bad had happened, I thought she'd gone off somewhere to get away from her mother and I'd promised not to say anything.'

'Did she tell you she was going?'

'Well, she said she was going but I didn't think she meant right away.'

'You'd better start at the beginning, Harry, boy.'

'It's difficult. You know when her mother invited me

over for a drink – well, it was like . . . like we thought it might be.'

'You mean she wanted you to go to bed with her?'

'Yes.'

'And did you?'

'Yes.'

'Did Yvette find out?'

'She came in the front door as I was coming downstairs.'

Alison's warm hand searched for his and held it. 'Is that why you wouldn't come with us to London?'

'Yes. I wanted a chance to talk to her alone, to try to explain. I couldn't do it at school, you know what it's like there, and I couldn't risk going to her house. I tried to catch her in the evenings but it was obvious she was avoiding me. Then, on Saturday, when you'd gone to London, I spent most of the day looking for her. In the afternoon, about half-past three, I was in my room when I saw her going out of the Court through the archway. I dived downstairs and out into the street but I missed her –you know what it's like with the market people packing up.'

'So what did you do?'

'Well, I guessed she'd be making for the centre so I hared off up the street to the bus stop and I saw her getting on a bus but I was too far away to catch it. I walked in but of course I didn't know where she would go exactly. I stooged round the coffee bars then hung about waiting for the discos to open thinking she was bound to turn up somewhere like that. Around six I happened to be in Hilary Street – just killing time, walking – when I saw her ahead of me. She went down a flight of steps to a restaurant – a cellar place called The Catacombs. It was closed but there was a notice which said it opened at six-thirty so I hung about.

'It was an expensive place so I didn't like to go in but after it opened, each time somebody did go in, I tried to see through the open door and in the end I spotted her. She was dressed in a red dress with an apron and she was carrying a tray. She was working there as a waitress.'

'You didn't know she had a part-time job?'

'No, did you?'

'No.'

'Well, I thought I would meet her when she finished work and take her home but I couldn't stand there in the street for ever so I plucked up courage, put my head round the door and caught the eye of another waitress. She was a bit shirty but she told me that Yvette finished at ten. I spent the evening in the cinema watching some stupid film and got back to Hilary Street just before ten. She came out about ten minutes past and she was pretty mad to find me there but she calmed down and we walked through the quieter streets until we came to that bit of a garden in Lodge Road where we sat on a seat.

'She was miserable and very bitter about her mother and Bishop but she didn't seem to hold it against me – what had happened, I mean. She said that her mother hated her and wanted to take away everything she had. What had happened with me was the last straw. By this time she was crying and I felt very sorry for her. I tried to say the right things and cheer her up but I didn't manage it.'

'What happened?'

'Nothing, really. When she stopped crying she seemed to get more angry and she kept saying she was going to get even with her mother. I tried to get her to promise not to do anything silly. After all, I felt responsible for her, but all she would say was, "You wait! One of these days I shall just walk out!"'

It was getting lighter and Henry could see a shadowy outline of the dolls' house Willy Goppel had built for Alison. It seemed to belong on the other side of a great gulf and he shivered.

'You're cold!'

'No. Anyway, I told Yvette she must be sensible. With no money and nowhere to go she would just land herself in worse trouble. She said I'd be surprised how much money she had already and that she knew how to get more. She also made me promise that I wouldn't say anything *whatever* happened and she kept on so much that I had to promise.'

'What happened when you finished talking?'

'Well, I wanted to take her home but she wouldn't hear of it; she got almost hysterical when I insisted so I had to let her go.'

There was a break in his voice.

Alison said, 'But you weren't in love with her, were you?'

'No, I suppose not; but I liked her and now . . .'

For a time neither of them spoke and they sat listening to the rain on the window then Henry said, 'What am I going to do, Ali?'

In the strengthening light she could see his drawn, anxious features and the mild impatience she had felt seemed like disloyalty. She squeezed his hand. 'There's only one thing you can do; tell the police, and the sooner the better. Before school this morning.'

'You think so?'

'I'm sure so. I'll tell them at school that you'll be a bit late.'

'They might arrest me.'

'Don't be daft, Henry. Nobody will ever believe you could hurt anybody on purpose, not even a policeman.'

Henry got up, reluctant but resigned. 'I suppose that's the right thing to do.'

'Henry . . .'

He turned back. 'There's something I didn't tell the police about Yvette.'

'You?'

'Yes. Two or three times she talked to me about her sex life and she made out that she was going with men and getting money from them.'

'She was making it up.'

'That's what I thought, but you're quite sure?'

'Yes.' He hesitated for a moment before adding, 'She didn't really like anything like that.'

Kersey gave him a fairly rough passage. After Henry had told his story and been cross-questioned for upwards of half-an-hour, Kersey looked at him with great seriousness. 'So you were the last person to see Yvette alive – as far as we know.'

Henry was startled. 'No, of course not!'

'Then who was?'

'Whoever killed her.'

'And you did not?'

'Me? I've already told you she left me sitting on a seat in Lodge Road and said I wasn't to follow her.'

'We've only your word for that. For all I know you might have travelled back with her on the bus, taken her to the churchyard, tried to make love to her and when she resisted . . . '

Henry went pale. 'That's a terrible thing to say!'

'Why? Somebody killed her.'

'Yes, but I couldn't kill Yvette . . . I couldn't kill anybody. It's horrible! I've told you the truth—'

'But you didn't choose to tell it until you thought you were safe.'

'I don't know what you mean.'

'Until you thought her death was down to Willy Goppel.'

'That's not fair! I didn't tell you on Sunday because I'd promised Yvette and I thought she'd just cleared out. I had no idea that she was . . . that she was dead.'

'But you've known since yesterday.'

'Yes, but—'

Kersey cut him short. 'All I can say is it's lucky for you you weren't in love with Yvette. I hope you've learned something from mother and daughter.'

'I don't understand . . . '

The policeman laughed shortly. 'No, I don't think you do, but try working on it. Anyway, push off now, you can come back this evening and make a formal statement.'

'You mean I can go?'

'If you don't I shall probably kick you, but don't think you're off the hook.'

'At the door Kersey called him back. 'Do you think that Willy Goppel killed her?'

'No, I don't – I can't believe—'

'All right, get out.'

D.C. Dixon had been sitting-in on the interview. 'He could have done it, Sarge.'

'Him? He wouldn't stand on a snail. Anyway, this is no teen-age sex thing.' Kersey sighed, remembering something of what it was like to be seventeen, the poor goof in the middle, neither man nor boy, treading on eggs. 'Well, we know where she was until almost eleven o'clock on Saturday evening; that's something. You'd better check at The Catacombs and ask them if they never listen to the radio, watch TV or read a newspaper.'

'Sarge?'

'Why they haven't been in touch. Not that we can't make a good guess; they've been paying under the odds out of the till – no tax, no insurance, no come-backs.'

Despite the rain and the fact that Marty was miserable because he could not go beyond the verandah, Joan Fiske felt as though a great load had been lifted from her shoulders. Willy Goppel had murdered Yvette and hanged himself. It was incredible but she closed her mind to doubt. Now nobody would be likely to show any interest in the watch which she had hidden amongst her most private possessions in a locked drawer of the little bureau in her bedroom. Relief demanded action and she set about a thorough cleaning of the living-room, pushing the furniture about, dusting and hoovering.

Because of the noise made by the cleaner she did not hear anyone at the front door and she looked up to see Marty standing in the doorway of the living-room with the detective behind him. It was the man Kersey, the policeman who had called on Sunday, the day Yvette was missed.

'I'm in the middle of my work, Sergeant. I thought this whole dreadful business was over.'

The man looked surprised though whether his surprise was genuine or pretended she could not tell.

'What made you think that, Mrs Fiske?'

She felt a stab of renewed fear. 'What made me think it? Didn't Willy Goppel hang himself?'

'So?'

'Well, if he killed Yvette why do you still come pestering us? These people are nothing to do with us, they are just neighbours and we've told you all we know about them . . .' She broke off, conscious that the policeman was watching her with an odd expression. She had reacted too emotionally, she must calm down. 'I'm sorry there's nowhere to sit.' She gestured vaguely at the disordered room.

'It doesn't matter. I came to ask you about a watch, Mrs Fiske.'

'A watch?' It worried her that her question sounded flat and unnatural.

'Yvette was wearing a watch and it's missing.'

'What's that got to do with me?'

Kersey's manner was patient and unhurried. 'When I was here on Sunday, Marty came in asking something about a watch. It struck me at the time that you were

127

anxious to shut him up and get rid of me but I had no idea why until—'

'I don't know what you're talking about!'

He looked at her, not unkindly, 'It's no good, Mrs Fiske. As soon as I mentioned the watch you all but folded on me. I could question Marty, but I don't want to do that. He found it, didn't he?'

She was silent.

'Didn't he?'

'And what if he did? Marty wouldn't hurt a fly!'

Kersey was soothing. 'Nobody is suggesting that Marty hurt anybody, Mrs Fiske, but we've got to have that watch.'

Marty had lost interest and had gone back to the verandah. They could see him through the window, leaning on the rail, staring out at the rain. Joan Fiske left the room without a word to return a minute or two later with the watch, holding it by the bracelet.

'Here, take it! I wish to God I'd never seen the thing; I've hardly had any sleep since it's been in the house.'

'When did he find it?'

'On Sunday morning before you came, he showed it me while he was having his breakfast and I took it off him.'

'You knew who it belonged to?'

'I'd seen her wearing it. I thought she must have lost it in the Court and I was going to give it her back. It was only when you came . . . '

'You should have told me.'

She felt a sudden surge of anger against people who, like this policeman, had no conception what it was like to be watching, shielding, excusing and defending another human being throughout one's waking hours, each day and every day. 'How did I know you would believe that he'd found it? How do I know that you will believe it now? But he's a truthful boy, Mr Kersey; he never lies – *never*.'

Kersey nodded. 'I believe you, Mrs Fiske. So where did he find it?'

'I don't know; I didn't ask him, I wanted him to forget all about the damn thing.'

'Ask him now.'

She hesitated, but not for long. She called the boy in and he stood, looking from his mother to Kersey and back again, like an alert terrier anxious to do what was expected of him.

His mother pointed to the watch which Kersey was holding. 'I want you to tell me where you found it, Marty . . . No, you can't have it, it's not yours. I just want you to tell me exactly where you found it . . . Where did you find it?'

Her voice was quiet, soothing, almost hypnotic – quite different from the harsh tones and staccato sentences in which she carried on normal conversation.

Marty, having reached for the watch and been disappointed, allowed his arms to droop by his sides and stood listlessly.

'Where, Marty? Where?'

In the end, with a movement which signified resignation, he turned and led the way out of the room, down the verandah steps into the rain and across the Court until he reached a point near the steps which led up to Natalie's verandah. There he pointed at the ground and said, simply, 'Watch.'

His mother took him by the hand. 'You are sure, Marty?'

The boy had become indifferent and a trifle sullen but he nodded and repeated, 'Watch.'

Kersey was puzzled. Of course it was possible that the watch had slipped from Yvette's wrist at any time as she was coming out of or going into the house but it seemed unlikely that she would not have missed it at once.

With the watch in a polythene bag, Kersey returned to the incident-van.

'Is the chief in?'

The duty constable nodded. 'Number two, Sarge.'

Kersey found Wycliffe studying reports.

'Got something?'

Kersey slid the watch out of its polythene cover onto a sheet of white paper and explained how he had come by it.

Wycliffe produced a hand-lens and examined the bracelet. 'The catch looks sound enough but one of the little links between the charms has been pulled open leaving a sharp point almost like a hook.' He handed the lens to Kersey. 'There are a couple of fibres caught in the link – they could be wool.'

Kersey examined the bracelet with the lens. 'It might mean something but it's on the cards that Mrs Fiske has been keeping the thing with her winter woollies.'

'Anyway, get it off to forensic and see what they have to say.'

Kersey was leaving when Wycliffe called him back. 'About your interview with the Ward boy, I've seen the memo and I agree this is no teen-age crime but the boy's evidence is important and the sooner you get that statement the better.'

The implied rebuke was not lost on Kersey.

Wycliffe was left to his reports. Rain drummed on the roof of the van and streamed down the windows so that it was impossible to see outside. He skimmed through the forensic examination of Yvette's clothing – fifteen pages on six items – looking for a possible cherry in the cake.

'Dust extracted from the jeans and examined microscopically was found to contain sawdust, animal hairs, traces of bran, fragments of straw . . .'

In other words, at some time on Saturday, Yvette had

probably fed the animals and, perhaps, cleaned out their cages.

Another report, still more bulky, covered a detailed study of Willy's house and its contents, carried out by his own men. Only one point seemed worth making: the whisky glasses in the living-room both carried Willy's prints but one carried those of a stranger as well. The report included a blow-up photograph of the stranger's prints, marked, 'Not known', which meant that whoever he was he had no criminal record.

Wycliffe looked at the growing mass of paper and felt depressed.

Yvette was dead, Goppel was dead, and there seemed to be only two possibilities, one was that the two deaths were unconnected, the other, that Goppel had murdered Yvette then committed suicide. But Wycliffe was not satisfied with either. He could not believe that Paul's Court had been the scene of two unrelated violent deaths in a single week-end. On the other hand it seemed unlikely that a man of Willy's physique had murdered Yvette leaving no sign of a struggle. More than that, despite Kersey's speculation about a possible sinister side to Willy's character, Wycliffe could not see him as a child murderer.

A bizarre idea occurred to him. What if Goppel had been murdered? Murder by hanging, made to look like suicide . . . The difficulties are so great that the mere possibility is usually disregarded. He glanced at his watch. Ten minutes past eleven. He could not expect a report from Franks until mid-afternoon but there was no reason why he should not look in to see how things were going.

Franks had his laboratory in the grounds of the City Hospital on the outskirts of the city and Wycliffe drove there through pouring rain. Car tyres raised plumes of muddy water from the streaming roads and windshield wipers worked overtime. He had difficulty in finding a parking space and when he did it was a couple of hundred yards away from the laboratory so that he arrived wet and feeling rather foolish at this exhibition of unprofessional impatience.

Franks was in his office working on the report with his secretary, surrounded by papers and photographs. Round and chubby, he sat at his desk, immaculate in a pearl-grey suit, striped shirt, mauve tie and with jewelled cuff-links just showing below the sleeves of his jacket.

'You've met Moira. Charles? . . . No? . . . Goodness! How time flies! Moira, this is Detective Chief Superintendent Wycliffe, my conscience. Without his silent disapproval I should be worse than I am. Charles is a rare bird these days, a dyed-in-the-wool puritan. I'm in the middle of dictating my report on your man, Goppel, Charles. Don't go away, Moira, unless you're going to make coffee.'

The girl picked up her notebook and went out smiling.

'I suppose there's no doubt he died from hanging?'

Franks spread his hands in a Gallic gesture. 'He was alive when his head went into the noose, dead when it came out, and he wasn't shot, stabbed, poisoned nor coshed.'

'No unusual features?'

'Unusual? What sort of thing?'

'I'm asking you.'

Franks picked up a coloured photographic enlargement and passed it over. The photograph showed the legs of the dead man from a little below the knees to the feet.

'Notice anything?'

'Nothing out of the ordinary. Post-mortem lividity and ecchymoses of the dependent limbs. Have I got it right?'

'You have, Charles, but look at the legs just above the ankles.'

Wycliffe held the photograph to the light and studied it more closely. 'The pattern seems to be very slightly different in a band round both legs.'

'Good! That's one of your unusual features though what it means I'm not sure.'

'A ligature?'

'It could be but it's too vague to build a lot on. Projecting the negative of that photograph I was just able to see a faint pattern of the man's socks imprinted on the skin in those areas but nowhere else.'

'What about the arms?'

Franks pursed his lips. 'There seems to be something just above the elbows but it's even more vague. However, look at this.' He passed over another photograph, this time in black and white. 'I suppose you could say that to some extent this has been faked. I printed it to emphasize contrast but it shows nothing that wasn't actually there.'

It was a photograph of Goppel's face in front view and it showed clearly the changes which death had brought about but there was something else, a pale area below the nostrils, extending down towards the chin and on both sides round the cheeks.

'A gag?'

The pathologist laughed. 'You said it. I wouldn't dare suggest such a thing in court without more to back it up.'

Wycliffe continued to study the picture. 'I see that, but taking it all together we have to face the possibility that Goppel was bound and gagged before his head was put in the noose.'

'Does that upset your calculations?'

'On the contrary.'

Moira came in with a tray. 'Black or white?'

Franks said, 'Old self-denial takes it black, he says he

133

prefers it that way.' He turned to Wycliffe. 'Murder by hanging, there can't have been many cases.'

Wycliffe sipped his coffee. 'Probably more than we think, we only know about the ones that were caught.' His mind was busy with the fresh evidence, trying to fit it into a pattern. 'One more point – was Goppel in good health before he died?'

Franks frowned. 'It depends what you mean, he was a good insurance risk, likely to live to a ripe old age, but I'd guess he didn't feel too good on the day he died.'

'Why not?'

'There was acute inflammation in the upper respiratory tract and a certain amount of congestion in the lungs. Almost certainly he was running a temperature. I'd say he had a dose of the 'flu which has been going the rounds recently. As you know, 'flu sometimes brings on fits of depression and if he did commit suicide that could have been a contributory factor.'

So Goppel had been bound and gagged before being hanged, which meant that he had been murdered. And at the time he had been suffering from a bout of influenza which would have made it easier for his attacker. Influenza . . . Yvette had been to the chemist with a prescription for an influenza mixture. If she had taken the medicine to Willy on her way home . . .

But how to prove murder? The evidence of the pathologist's photographs would not convince a judge and jury and the only chance of supplementing that evidence depended on the forensic examination of Goppel's clothing. If he had been tied up with some fibrous material – rope or cord, there was a chance that traces might remain, but the photograph suggested a strap and if this had been of leather or plastic there was little hope.

Back at the incident post Wycliffe telephoned the forensic laboratory and was put through to Clive

134

Horton, a scientific assistant with whom he had had dealings in another case. Horton was quiet, self-contained and competent, with the added merit that in court he could stand up to the roughest cross-examination without becoming in the least ruffled. He would repeat the same information over and over again in the most courteous manner possible until defending counsel or the judge tired of the exercise.

'Ah, Mr Wycliffe. I've been working on your man's clothing but I'm afraid I've nothing very helpful to report. Fine sawdust, traces of animal feed, animal hairs – predominantly cat, a few iron filings, wool and polyester fibres . . . '

Wycliffe said, 'I would like you to take another look with the idea in mind that he might have been tied up in some way. There is a suggestion that his legs might have been strapped together above the ankles and if so his arms were probably secured also.'

It was characteristic of Horton that he asked no questions not directly relevant to his work. 'You say that his legs might have been strapped together, presumably you mean strapped rather than tied?'

'Yes, a photograph of the legs shows a vague impression of a constriction about two inches wide just above the ankles.'

'I see. Of course much depends on the material such straps were made of. So far I have only examined samples of dust obtained by shaking out the garments separately in a polythene bag but I will certainly look at likely areas in more detail.'

'What about local creasing?'

'I don't hold out much hope there; the garments are made from materials containing a high proportion of man-made fibres and these are resistant to cold creasing.'

'Will you ring me when you have any further results?'

135

'I will ring you this afternoon.'

In the early afternoon Toby Lennon called on his aunt and uncle. Mr Hedley answered his ring; Mrs Hedley was in the kitchen washing up. For once, piano and radio were silent.

'Oh, it's you, Toby!' Mrs Hedley came out of the kitchen all smiles and kissed him on the forehead. 'What brings you here again so soon?' She reached for his coat. 'Let me take it. You're really *wet*! Why don't you get yourself a little car?'

'There's an obvious answer to that one, aunt.' He sat on the big Victorian sofa where, at this time of day, Mr Hedley should have been taking his nap. 'Freddie has gone to see Crowther at the Old Mansion House about his father's will.'

Mr Hedley hovered. 'How's he taking it?'

'Freddie? Well, he's upset, but he doesn't seem to realize what people are saying.'

'You mean that his father killed Yvette?'

'Yes. Is that what the police think?'

Mrs Hedley said, 'What else can they think? She was in and out of his house all the time, then she's found strangled and he commits suicide.'

Mr Hedley sighed. 'It's hard to credit all the same. I suppose this will make Freddie a rich man?'

'Perhaps; but there's no knowing how his old man left things. You know a bit about the law, uncle; if Freddie doesn't get anything can he contest the will?'

The old man laughed. 'Not a chance! Freddie isn't a dependent – or if he is he shouldn't be. If Goppel left the lot to a cats' home there's nothing Freddie could do about it.'

They were silent for a while; for some reason Mr Hedley's pronouncement seemed to have put a stopper on conversation, then Toby said, 'If the police think Willy killed her I suppose they will drop the case.'

'Bound to. A dead man can't be convicted of anything.'

Mrs Hedley was peering into a small gilt-framed mirror, trying to subdue her straggling hair by a redistribution of pins. 'Well, they hadn't dropped it this morning. That sergeant was with Joan Fiske for half-an hour and afterwards they came out with Marty in the rain and seemed to be searching for something on the ground outside the Coles'.'

'Searching for something, aunt?'

'That's what it looked like. I mentioned it when I was over there just before lunch but she was very tight lipped about it. There's something still going on.' She turned away from the mirror. 'I hope you don't mind, Toby, but I was going to listen to the Bartok string-quartet programme at three o'clock. Don't go away . . . '

Horton kept his promise and telephoned Wycliffe shortly after three. 'I've been over the trousers and jacket again using a vacuum extractor and taking separate samples from different levels on the legs and sleeves. The samples contained varying proportions of much the same materials as before but in three of them I found traces of something new. These were the samples taken from the trousers just above the ankles and immediately above the knees and from the jacket, above the elbows.'

Horton spoke in a dry monotone exactly as he would have given evidence in court. 'The new material is represented by very few fibres and I probably missed them in the earlier sample.'

Wycliffe was patient. 'Have you any idea what the fibres are or where they might have come from?'

'Yes, I have. Luckily I came across similar material in a case a couple of years back. They are cotton fibres, dyed

137

with a greenish brown dye, and I am fairly confident that they came from cotton webbing of the kind once used by the Services for all kinds of slings, belts and straps. Government surplus stores used to be full of the stuff on haversacks, gas-mask carriers, water-bottle holders and goodness knows what.'

Wycliffe was pleased and said so. 'I suppose you've marked on the garments where the samples were taken?'

'Of course. The positions are consistent with the legs having been strapped together above the ankles and above the knees, while the arms appear to have been secured above the elbows. I will let you have my report tomorrow.'

Wycliffe thanked him and rang off.

There could only be one interpretation of the evidence now; Willy Goppel had been murdered by hanging. When and if the case came to court the defence would make a great deal of play with the difficulties of such a murder but Horton and Franks would prove unshakable witnesses, calm, never going beyond the facts, and never using two words where one was sufficient.

But it was premature to rejoice; he now had two murders on his hands instead of one and he was no nearer solving either. Still, truth is its own justification, or so they say.

On his way home that evening Wycliffe's mood was dismally philosophic. Somebody once said that right answers are easier to find than right questions. His questions had been, Who killed Yvette? Why? And why did Willy Goppel commit suicide? These questions had prompted some strange answers that were now irrelevant. The right questions seemed to be, Who killed Willy Goppel, and why?

Progress of a sort.

Yvette had walked off leaving Henry on the seat. She probably arrived back at Falcon Street shortly after eleven and Willy's back door was almost certainly unlocked. Knowing the place as she did, she would not bother to switch on the light in the workshop, enough light came from the stairs. It was easy to imagine her coming quietly through the workshop to the bottom of the stairs. Then, perhaps, she heard a sound. Did she call out? 'It's only me – Yvette!' Perhaps she looked up and saw the swinging body of the hanged man, but she must also have seen someone else – the murderer. Victim and murderer, both taken utterly by surprise, with no going back for either of them.

Did she scream? If she did there was no-one in the Wards' house to hear.

'In practice most murders fall into one of three main categories: domestic or family killings, killings incidental to robbery, and killings by homicidal lunatics.'

In his mind's eye Wycliffe could see the lecturer who had delivered himself of that pearl – on some course or other. And it was true, up to a point.

The man had gone on to say, 'Luckily for you chaps most murders are in the first category – arising out of the joys of family life and, after all, which of us would not cheerfully murder mother-in-law if we thought we could get away with it?' Pause for dutiful titter. Then, 'In such cases there is rarely any doubt about who did the job, it's just a case of finding sufficient evidence to convince a jury.'

Willy's death was certainly not the work of a homicidal lunatic; there was no question of it being a crime of violence committed in the act of robbery. That left domestic and family. Willy's only family seemed to be Freddie and Wycliffe had rarely seen a more improbable candidate for the dock on a double murder charge. Of course, there was Lennon, Freddie's simian friend.

139

Their relationship seemed to be as stable as many marriages so perhaps in these enlightened days Pongo could be looked upon as one of the family.

Motive? In domestic murders the motive is usually irrational – an explosion, a breaking point – but sometimes it is gain, and Willy was a wealthy man.

CHAPTER SEVEN

Wednesday. Yvette was to be buried in the afternoon and Wycliffe was going to the funeral. He had made an overnight statement to the press which, for once, appeared in the papers before it was mentioned on radio or television. *The News*, the city's own daily paper, came out with a headline on its front page:

HANGED MAN IN DOLLS' SHOP: MURDERED – OFFICIAL

Second Murder in Paul's Court

Last night Detective Chief Superintendent Wycliffe disclosed new evidence which makes it almost certain that Willy Goppel, the proprietor of the dolls' shop in Falcon Street, was murdered by hanging. Forensic scientists have been able to show that Mr Goppel was gagged and bound before his head was placed in the noose. It is believed that his bonds were removed after death to create the illusion of suicide.

Murder by hanging is rare in the annals of crime for there are obvious difficulties in persuading an able-bodied adult to place himself in a position to be hung. Cases are on record where the intended victim was either drugged or rendered insensible by a blow before hanging but such treatment would be unlikely to escape the notice of any pathologist.

In the present case the comparatively slight physique

of the victim and the fact that he was suffering from an attack of influenza certainly made the task of his murderer easier than it would otherwise have been.

In a telephone conversation with our reporter, Chief Superintendent Wycliffe mentioned another item of new evidence which may have great significance for both killings. In Yvette's handbag, found near her body, there was a bottle of influenza mixture which she had purchased from a chemist in the city centre on Saturday evening. It is known that Yvette was a frequent visitor to the Dolls' House shop where she helped to look after Goppel's collection of pet animals. The conclusion that she was taking the medicine to her friend is inescapable and it may be that this simple act of kindness cost Yvette her life. However, asked if he was satisfied that both murders had been committed by the same hand, Chief Superintendent Wycliffe said that he could not offer an opinion at this stage.

The report was accompanied by a photograph of a belt with a friction buckle and the caption read: 'A webbing belt as used by the armed services. The police believe that service webbing, easily obtained from government-surplus stores, was used to bind the murdered man.'

Wycliffe was at the incident post by eight-thirty, reading the newspaper report. Scales arrived shortly afterwards, followed a little later by Kersey.

'Sorry I'm late. I got stuck behind an RTA at Millbrook.'

The three men sat on bench seats round a small table to review progress and for the day's briefing. Outside the air was still moist from the night's rain but the sky was clearing, the sun had broken through and mists were rising from the sodden ground in the churchyard.

Wycliffe said, 'Now that we know Goppel was

murdered we must change our thinking. It seems that Yvette's murder was incidental to Goppel's and so we need to know a great deal more about him.'

It was agreed that Kersey should talk to the landlord of the pub at Bickersleigh where Willy had spent the occasional weekend. Scales would go through Willy's papers and see Crowther, his lawyer. Wycliffe said that he would call on Fiske who looked after his accounts. 'And I'll have a word with Natalie. She must have the low-down on a number of people who might interest us. Most of them seem to frequent that club of hers – Bishop, Lennon, young Goppel – and even Fiske. On the night I was there he was having an evening out with his secretary.'

Scales had left and Kersey was leaving when Fowler, the duty constable, came in grinning broadly. 'Visitor for you, Sarge, a Mr Alexander Chatham.'

Kersey looked puzzled then intelligence dawned. 'The Professor! What does he want?'

'He says he's got information concerning the death of his friend, Willy Goppel.'

'Does he now! In that case we'd better have him in.' Kersey looked doubtfully at Wycliffe.

Wycliffe got up. 'I can take a hint, he's all yours.'

The Professor came in wearing a black raincoat and carrying his Homburg, a furled umbrella crooked over his arm.

The Professor had an ambivalent relationship with the police and with Kersey in particular. Several times the sergeant had been on the point of nailing him for dishonest handling or 'fencing' but always the wily old boy managed to slip out from under. Far from bearing any malice, he had several times provided Kersey with useful information. Now he placed his hat and umbrella on a vacant seat and sat in the place Wycliffe had vacated. After fishing in the pocket of his raincoat he came out with a string of medals wrapped in tissue paper which he laid on the table for Kersey's inspection.

'German medals from the second world war, Mr Kersey. As you see, they include the Iron Cross and they belonged to my friend, Willy Goppel.'

'How did you get hold of them?'

'By the merest chance. I bought them in the ordinary way of business; Willy happened to see them on my stall in the Falcon Street market, recognized them, and told me that they had been stolen with other items from his workshop.'

'Go on.'

'I pressed him to take them back but he wouldn't hear of it. He said the medals were of no interest to him but he was concerned about certain papers which had been stolen with them. He enlisted my help to try to find out what had happened to them.'

'So you went to the chap for whom you had fenced the medals and asked him what he had done with the rest of the stuff.'

The old fellow was unperturbed. 'I bought the medals in good faith from a stranger who walked into my shop one afternoon. He said he had had them for a number of years and wondered if they were worth anything. I offered him twenty pounds, paid cash, and he left satisfied.'

'So you couldn't help Goppel?'

'Not so fast, Mr Kersey. I was anxious to do Willy a good turn and now that I knew that the medals had been stolen I simply put the word round. Few transactions are carried out in absolute secrecy as you well know.'

'What happened?'

'To cut a long story short, I found that the medals had already changed hands once before reaching me and that the transaction had taken place in a public

144

house in Tolgate Street called The Fair Maid; you may know it.'

'I do, it's a regular thieves' kitchen.'

'Indeed? I do not frequent the place myself.'

'Is that all?'

'The man who sold them was not an habitué of the place but he had been seen there several times.'

'Does he have a name?'

The Professor hesitated only momentarily. 'Lennon – Pongo Lennon.'

'Lennon!'

'You know him?'

'I know of him.'

'Then you probably know that he shares rooms with Willy Goppel's son, Freddie, and you will understand why I dropped my enquiry at that point.'

Kersey was tapping the table with his ball-point pen. 'Well, I've got to admit, you've done us a good turn there. I shall want you to make a formal statement . . .'

'Don't you want to hear the rest?'

'There's more?'

'A little. On the following Saturday – last Saturday – I expected to see Willy in the market as usual but he did not come and it was evening before I was at liberty to visit him—'

Kersey leaned forward. 'You mean that you were with him on Saturday evening?'

'I was—'

'At what time?'

'I arrived around eight and left just after nine.'

'You realize that you could have been the last person to see him alive?'

'Apart from the killer, that is possible.'

'And you've only now got round to telling us about it?' Kersey's manner was menacing.

'If my friend had committed suicide nothing I had to say was of any importance.'

'But now?'

'If he was murdered, that is a different matter.'

'Tell me what happened on Saturday evening.'

'Not a great deal. Willy was not at all well, it was obvious that he was running a temperature – almost certainly it was influenza. We drank a glass of whisky together and I told him of my enquiries but I had the impression that he was not taking it in. I asked him if there was anything I could do – about the animals, about getting him food or medicine or some assistance.'

'What did he say?'

'He said that everything was taken care of, that the girl from next door had seen to the animals and that she was getting him some medicine from the chemist.'

'He was expecting her?'

'Yes. He told me that she would be looking in later in the evening. When I was leaving he said, "If you don't mind going out by the back door it will save me coming down. I left it unlocked for my little girl when she comes with the medicine."'

Kersey sat looking at the Professor for some time then he said, 'I'm going to put you in with D.C. Fowler and you're going to make that statement.'

Freddie Goppel, in slippers and dressing-gown, slouched across the living-room to the window, threw back the curtains and stared out over the grey roofs. 'Bloody hell!'

He ran his hand through his fair curls; he was pale and hollow-eyed. The room was damp and clammily cold. He crossed to the door, turned the key and went out to the landing where there was a pint-bottle of milk, a newspaper and an official looking letter addressed to him. He took it all inside and opened the letter which was from Crowther, his father's solicitor:

Dear Mr Goppel,
Thank you for calling on me, it is unfortunate that I was engaged at the time but I understand that my clerk was able to give you all the information you required. As your late father's executor I cannot proceed to obtain probate until I have either a death certificate or an equivalent document from the coroner's office. I understand from my clerk that you believe the police to be satisfied that your father took his own life; if this is so there should be little further delay.
May I say how deeply sorry I was to hear the sad news? Your father was a valued client and a near neighbour for many years and it was my pleasure to deal with his affairs personally.
Sincerely yours,
Arthur Crowther.

Freddie dropped the letter on the table and turned to the newspaper. The headline was ironic, a crushing retort to the presumption of the letter: 'Hanged man in Dolls' Shop: Murdered – Official'.
At first he did not take it in, the headline was cryptic; when he did he felt faint and had to hold on to the table for support. The sensation passed and he forced himself to read the whole report though he had to go over each paragraph more than once before he grasped its meaning. When he had finished he slumped into a chair and began to sob. Tears forced their way through his lids and he gave way to weeping.
There was a movement in the bedroom and Lennon came through wearing a brightly patterned dressing-

gown. 'What's the matter, Freddie boy?' He went over and, gentle as a woman, ran his fingers through the curls. 'What's the matter, boy?'

Freddie made no response and Lennon continued to caress him until his eye caught the newspaper headline; his fingers remained in Freddie's hair but they were still.

After a little while he said, 'Well, it doesn't really change anything, Freddie; nothing could bring your old man back.'

Freddie shuddered. 'But it's horrible! To hang him like an executioner!' However, he dried his eyes and blew his nose in a grubby handkerchief then he sat back in his chair, looking up at his companion. 'Pongo . . . '

'Yes, Freddie?'

There was a long hesitation before he said, 'It wasn't you, was it?'

Lennon stiffened. 'What the hell do you mean? Of course it wasn't me! Why should I go for your old man, he never did me any harm.'

Freddie was all but inarticulate. 'Well, you might have thought . . . '

'What might I have thought?'

'Well, I shall probably get his money now and you . . . '

Lennon glowered. 'The young heir bit! Now I've heard every bloody thing! Christ, Freddie, if that's what you think you'd better piss off now!'

Freddie was contrite. He burst into tears again. 'Don't be mad at me, Pongo, I'm confused, I don't know what I'm saying. I'm sorry . . . Truly sorry . . . '

'So you bloody well should be.'

When Mr Hedley returned from the morning shopping he brought the newspaper as usual and after his wife had put away the purchases he spread it on the table and

148

pointed to the headline. 'It says here that Willy Goppel was murdered.'

'Murdered? What are you talking about? How could he be murdered? He hanged himself.'

Hedley merely pointed to the paper and his wife found her spectacles then read every line with close attention. When she had finished she looked up. 'Then somebody else must have killed the girl *and* Willy Goppel!' She returned to the paper and started to read the report again, hardly able to credit what she had read the first time.

Martin Fiske's offices in King Street were situated in a block belonging to one of the big insurance companies and he shared the third floor with a solicitor and an architect. The reception desk was in a room where three typists hammered away at their machines.

Over the telephone Fiske had said, 'I've got a hell of a morning but I could fit you in between eleven-forty-five and noon.'

Wycliffe arrived promptly at eleven-forty-five and was shown in at once. To reach Fiske's office he had to pass through another in which four of five oldish men and a middle-aged woman were at work, and he was shepherded by the young woman who had been Fiske's companion at La Cass.

Fiske sat back in his upholstered swivel chair, behind a clear desk, relaxed and prepared to approach business by way of tangential courtesies.

'I've heard a great deal about you, Superintendent.' He said this in the manner of royalty being gracious.

But Wycliffe got straight to the point. 'You know by now that Goppel was murdered. Obviously his business interests could be important to our investigation. I have come to you to get the broad lines of your relationship with him, but if any detailed investigation of his affairs become necessary it will be in the hands of Inspector Scales.'

It was clear that Fiske was winded by this approach. He spread his white hands and his coat sleeves rode up sufficiently to show the gold links in his shirt cuffs. 'Well, Mr Wycliffe, what can I tell you? We cater for a number of Willy Goppel's in this city – that is to say for people who have business acumen and prosperous businesses but do not like ledgers and are frightened by forms which come in buff envelopes. We are more than accountants, we undertake the routine administration of any business which is not large enough to employ a competent and qualified staff. I don't mind telling you that Goppel's was my largest account.'

He paused and picked an invisible thread from the sleeve of his jacket. 'Willy was a remarkable man. I suppose you know that he married an English wife? . . . She died when his son, Freddie, was six and she left Willy a little property – a few houses scattered about the city and two or three shops in Alton Street – poor class property on the whole. But Willy, by judicious buying and selling, turned this into a little empire which at today's prices might be worth *half-a-million.'*

Fiske paused, as parsons do after mentioning the divinity. 'And all this without employing anybody directly. Crowther looks after the legal side, Cassells and White collect rents and arrange lettings, inventories etcetera, while we keep his accounts, see to his insurances, deal with the tax people and take care of investments. The surprising thing is that it works! Though whether it will continue to work with young Freddie is another matter. Willy had a fantastic grasp of detail, he wrote down very little but he forgot nothing. Fiona, my secretary, called him Mr Memory.'

The windows of Fiske's office reached almost to the

floor and though they were on the third floor, from where they were sitting Wycliffe could look down on passers-by on the opposite side of King Street.

'I suppose it was from here that you saw Yvette on Saturday afternoon?'

Fiske seemed surprised by the change of subject. 'Yes, as a matter of fact it was. Isn't it a dreadful business? To think that little Yvette . . . '

'Will you be going to the funeral this afternoon?'

'Oh, yes. One must. Although we are such an ill-assorted community there is a good deal of the old neighbourliness in Falcon Street. I am going home to lunch today then I shall pick up my wife and we shall go together. As a matter of fact that is why I am so pressed for time this morning.'

'I suppose you can make no suggestion as to who might have had a grudge against Goppel?'

Fiske frowned and studied his finger nails. 'I really can't help you there, Mr Wycliffe. To the best of my knowledge Willy was well liked and he was always scrupulous in his business dealings. I cannot imagine why anybody would want to murder him.'

'No, that seems to be the opinion of all the people who knew him. Incidentally, Mr Fiske, I don't know if Sergeant Kersey has asked you this already, but were you out late on Saturday night? If you were it's possible that you saw someone whose presence meant little to you at the time but might be important in the light of what has happened.'

Fiske shook his head. 'I do understand, Superintendent, but I was not out late on Saturday night.' He chuckled. 'And unlike our neighbour, I do not spend much time on my verandah.'

Wycliffe thanked him and left. Fiske saw him out and somehow managed to convey that the interview had been a waste of his time. One felt that he might enlarge

151

on the theme at the golf club or wherever he met with his peers. 'If that's how they set about a murder inquiry then . . . '

But Wycliffe was not entirely dissatisfied.

Wycliffe and Kersey had a snack lunch with a drink at The Sportsman's in Falcon Street, not far from the entrance to the Court. It was a good local, patronized at mid-day by many of the shopkeepers in the street. The landlord and his wife divided their time between the two bars and the atmosphere was intimate and friendly. The two men sat at one of the tile-topped tables and were able to converse in some privacy. Kersey recounted his interview with the Professor.

Wycliffe said, 'So, as far as we know, he was the last person to see Goppel alive.'

'Yes, but you couldn't take him seriously as a suspect. A spot of dishonest handling is the Professor's limit and he does that as much as anything for devilment.'

Kersey took a mouthful of veal-and-ham pie. 'As I see it, the most significant thing he told us was that Lennon had the medals. If he had the medals he must have had the papers; they were kept in the same old cigar box, and if he had the papers . . . '

But Wycliffe was not to be drawn. 'We'll see what Natalie has to say about the Lennon – Goppel set-up before we make any move.' He changed the subject. 'I suppose you haven't had a chance to get out to Bickersleigh?'

'Not yet, sir. I was going there this afternoon.'

'Good. I'm going to the funeral. We'll meet and see how it looks this evening.'

To Wycliffe's surprise, Yvette's funeral was no hole-in-a-corner affair but a real occasion. He approved, for he believed in ceremony and in the public celebration of private grief. One should be left in no doubt about who

152

it is for whom the bell tolls and the dead should not be flushed away like sewage.

He joined the procession of cars as they formed in Falcon Street. It was an occasion which the whole neighbourhood had come to witness and it was none the worse for the presence of the press and even a television camera. The cemetery was on a slope above the west side of the city and from it one could look away across the docks to the open sea – on this day a silver plain in the sunlight.

They gathered round the grave and from a point a little higher up the slope Wycliffe looked them over. Natalie, discreet in a dark slim-fitting woollen dress; pale and fragile as a Meissen figure. Geoff Bishop by her side, like a bull in the show-ring, on his best behaviour yet wary; his suits were all loud and the best he could manage for the occasion was a black and white check from which he bulged so that it would have been no surprise if the buttons had scattered from his jacket at any moment. Beads of sweat formed on his forehead to trickle down his cheeks and from time to time he wiped them away with a grubby handkerchief. The Wards: Henry with his sister, looking after her with the earnest devotion of a lover. Some girls have to live up to their mothers-in-law; Henry's wife, when he found one, would always suffer in comparison with his sister. Alison seemed unable to take her eyes off the coffin. Perhaps it was her first funeral, perhaps when it came to the point she could not quite believe in mortality – not for the young anyway.

In the second rank Mr and Mrs Hedley, looking as though they were being exposed to the air after a long period of incarceration, grey wraiths who must be thinking of their own final tryst. Then there was Martin Fiske with an expression on his heavy features which suggested that he would have organized the whole thing

153

differently, and his wife Joan – who darted quick, nervous glances about her almost as though she feared being attacked at any moment. Wycliffe wondered who was looking after Marty.

Pongo and Freddie offered their own particular version of the Yin and the Yang . . . Even the Professor was there, the only mourner distinguished by being dressed wholly in black. And there were others, strangers to Wycliffe, one or two of them with a foreign look, probably people from La Cass.

When it was over and the vicar was condoling with the principal mourners, Martin Fiske came over to Wycliffe, blandly importunate, 'Ah, Superintendent! If you are returning to your base in the churchyard, I wonder if you would be good enough to drop my wife off? It would save me having to drive her home and then return to the office. I've lost so much time today already . . . '

'I shall be glad to take Mrs Fiske home.'

'Ah! I knew you would oblige – most kind.'

Joan Fiske stood a yard or two away, passive and resigned, like a parcel awaiting collection.

'Here you are, my dear, the superintendent will take you home.'

She walked with Wycliffe to where his car was parked. He tried to make conversation but at first it was heavy going – until, apparently, the inhibiting effect of her husband's presence had had time to wear off. Then she gossiped freely enough about the Court, about Falcon Street and about her neighbours.

'You must have lived in the Court before young Goppel and the Hedleys' nephew left home . . . '

'Yes, long before. We moved in when the houses were new – at the same time as the Hedleys. That's ten years ago. The place suits us, you see. With Marty as he is

154

it's such a blessing to have the Court, it's secluded and it's *safe* and it's not too far from the city centre.'

'I can see that . . . I gather Lennon was an orphan?'

'His parents were killed in an air crash when he was ten and his aunt brought him up. His father must have been fairly well off for it seems he left money enough to keep Toby and send him to a public school, and when he came of age he had a little nest egg of several thousand pounds. Of course he spent most of it in the first year . . .'

It was obvious that Mrs Fiske rarely had an opportunity for gossip and she revelled in talking to this grave, courteous policeman who listened and nodded and asked questions as though he had a real interest.

'I gather that he doesn't have a regular job?'

'Indeed he doesn't! Work and Toby have never agreed; the nearest he ever came to it was a few years as an all-in wrestler.'

'A *wrestler*?'

She laughed – a rare phenomenon. 'Yes, a wrestler. He was mad on it. During his school holidays he used to spend most of his time at the gym in Wesley Street and when he left school he took it up. Of course, that upset his aunt. I suppose he must have become a professional for he used to appear on the television now and then. That was when he started calling himself Pongo – Pongo the Apeman and he used to come into the ring dressed like Tarzan and letting out blood-curdling yells.'

'What happened? Did he get tired of it.'

'No, I don't think so. I think he hurt somebody badly and he wasn't allowed to wrestle any more. Anyway, he hasn't done a stroke of work since of any sort.'

'And I suppose the Hedleys got fed up with keeping him?'

She denied this with some vigour. 'Oh, no! At least she

155

didn't. I don't think anybody ever asks Mr Hedley's opinion about anything. Mrs Hedley doted on the boy – and still does. If you ask me she still helps to keep him in idleness which is a shame because they can't have a lot.'

She lowered her voice. 'Toby left home because he's *peculiar*.' She would not use the word 'queer'. 'Of course, he couldn't carry on like that at home so he had to find a place of his own. Then it wasn't a great while before Freddie Goppel joined him.'

She broke off as the car turned under the archway into the Court. 'It's very good of you to bring me home like this. What was I saying? Oh, yes, about Freddie – I've never had much of an opinion of Freddie, he's a weak creature at best, but there's no doubt Toby corrupted him and I know his father felt very bitterly about it.'

Wycliffe felt deeply sorry for this neurotic woman, burdened with a retarded son and starved of companionship. When he got out of the car and opened the door for her he tried to say something vaguely consoling. She stood beside him for a moment as though reluctant to break the contact then, as she was turning away, she said abruptly. 'There's a murderer in this Court, Mr Wycliffe; you know that, don't you?'

Wycliffe shook his head, 'No, Mrs Fiske, I don't know.'

She was about to say something further when another car came through the archway. It was Bishop in his Cortina, with Natalie beside him, returning from the funeral. Mrs Fiske watched them while Natalie got out of the car and said a word to Bishop who then drove off again. Natalie went up the steps to her front door and let herself in with a key.

'I expect Mr Kersey told you that Marty found Yvette's watch right by those steps. Don't you think that's odd?'

Before Wycliffe could reply she was moving away

again. 'I must get indoors, I've got a friend keeping an eye on Marty.'

Wycliffe let her go.

After a moment or two he walked across to Natalie's house and rang the bell. He had to wait a little while and when Natalie came to the door she had changed from her mourning dress into a housecoat.

'Oh, I wondered if I was to have a visit.'

'I'm sorry to intrude, I realize it's not the best time . . . '

'No, but I'm not like a normal mother, am I? You'd better come in.'

As he passed her it was obvious that she had already been at the whisky. In the living-room there was a used glass on the drinks table.

'Will you have one?'

'Not now, thanks.'

'Well, what do you want?'

'I want you to tell me about some of the people who use your club. My only excuse for coming to you now is that you probably know them better than most.'

She perched herself on the arm of one of the big chairs. 'I wouldn't quarrel with that. You'd better sit down.' She pulled the skirts of her housecoat round her knees. 'Which ones do you want to know about? Some of them are not so bad, for others I can only think of four-letter words.'

'Freddie Goppel?'

'Freddie? He's a non-starter; he doesn't exist until bat-man pulls the strings.'

'I suppose you mean Lennon?'

She nodded. 'His big, bad friend.'

'Is he bad?'

'I don't know. I think he could be vicious in a tight corner. He's got a big mouth when he's had a few.'

'What about Fiske?'

She looked at him with fresh interest. 'Fiske? You're bringing it a bit near home, aren't you?'

'Do you mind?'

She took a cigarette from a box on the table and lit it. 'No, I don't mind. As a matter of fact Fiske is a client I'd just as soon be without. He's like a dirty minded kid.' She blew a perfect smoke-ring and watched it broaden and rise. 'Let's say I reckon his secretary earns her flat and whatever else she manages to get out of him.'

Wycliffe said, 'You understand I've only one interest in this, to find a killer.'

'So?'

'Coming nearer home still; what about Bishop?'

She did not answer at once and Wycliffe thought that she might take refuge in indignation but she remained calm and matter-of-fact. 'If I thought Geoff had killed Yvette I wouldn't hesitate to say so. He's got a temper and he might do anything when he's really roused but he'd be incapable of planning to kill anybody. Does that tell you what you want to know?'

'Yes, I think it does.' Wycliffe took out his pipe. 'Do you mind?'

'Feel free.'

'One or two more questions. Did Willy Goppel's name ever crop up in conversation at the club – I mean before he died.'

She nodded. 'Sometimes. You see Freddie spends quite a bit of time there and everybody knew his old man had money so there was a bit of leg-pulling.'

'Is that all?'

'No. There was something a week or two back. It was one evening, early, before the customers started to arrive. Toby Lennon was there, without Freddie for once, and he was drinking doubles with Geoff. He'd had several and, as usual, he was convinced he was the life and soul of the party. I think it was Stefan, the barman, who asked Toby where his friend was. I forget what Toby said but the conversation got round to Freddie's father being a German Jew and then there was talk about the Nazis and concentration camps. Toby was well away and he told some ghastly yarn about what they did to Jewish girls in the camps. It made you want to throw up but Toby doesn't like women and he goes for that sort of thing. To change the subject I asked if Freddie's father had been in a camp and somebody said he had.'

'Was that all?'

'No. Toby, without saying a word, took a wad of old papers from his wallet and spread them out on the bar. They were all yellow and practically falling apart and they were printed in German with some ordinary writing and two or three official stamps. When he had everybody watching, Toby said, "Willy Goppel, my children, is an old fraud; he's no more Jew than I am and he's certainly never been in a concentration camp. He was a captain in the German army with a string of medals to prove how good he was." Then he read out a lot of stuff in German which nobody understood.

'Somebody asked him where he got the papers and he made a mystery out of it though it was obvious he must have got them from Freddie. I don't think anybody was all that interested and it fell rather flat. Customers were beginning to arrive so he put the papers away, but just at the end he said to me – you know what his sort are like when they're drunk – "The next time you see Willy Goppel, you say to him 'Guten Morgen Herr Hauptmann' and see how he takes it.'

'He made me repeat it after him once or twice until I had it right. I did it to humour him because I didn't want a scene.'

'Did you try it on Goppel?'

She smiled. 'I did, as a matter of fact. I didn't mean to

but he happened to be standing under the archway one morning while I was in the car, trying to filter the traffic and it just occurred to me.'

'What effect did it have?'

'I don't know; it happened that at that moment I had my chance to move out.'

'You heard no more about these papers of Goppel's?'

She crushed out her cigarette in an ashtray. 'Yes, I did. Pongo – Lennon, that is, came to me next evening and said he'd had his wallet nicked with the papers in it. The fool had taken off his coat and slung it over a chair. I told him that if he'd lost them it was his own fault.'

CHAPTER EIGHT

'Well? How did you get on at Bickersleigh?'

Kersey grimaced. 'Nothing startling but it wasn't altogether a wasted trip and the beer was good. Apparently Willy and the landlord had been friendly since before Willy's wife died and I gather he went there more for companionship than for the fishing.'

It was early on the evening of the funeral and Wycliffe and Kersey were comparing notes in one of the cubicles of the incident-van.

'I got one or two tit-bits. Bishop's property at Fenton Street was leased from Willy and Willy had given him a year's notice of termination.'

'Did you find out why?'

Kersey grinned. 'I did. Willy was going to turn the place into a Disneyland for kids.'

'A *Disneyland*?'

'Well, not on that scale, but a place where the kids could meet the characters from their story books and from TV, in the flesh, so to speak. He had great ideas – all sorts of mechanical models, visits from prominent entertainers and goodness knows what.'

'It would have cost a bit.'

'Apparently that didn't bother him. He was prepared to realize some of his capital to pay for it and in any case he saw it partly as a business proposition. He was going to sell children's books, records and toys and there was to be a small charge for admission to the exhibition area. He realized that he would have to subsidize it but he told Victor – that's the landlord, that he might as well spend his money that way as leave it for Freddie to squander.'

'Interesting. Anything else?'

'Only that he hated Lennon's guts and blamed him for turning Freddie into a queer.'

When Kersey heard from Wycliffe that Lennon had been showing off Willy's papers at La Cass, he was predictably impressed.

'So now we have proof that Lennon had both medals and papers. It seems to me that whoever had possession of those papers and sent them to me, arranged Goppel's faked suicide and murdered Yvette when she caught him at it.'

Wycliffe said nothing and Kersey persisted, 'Don't you agree, sir?'

Wycliffe's answer was indirect. 'Whoever killed Goppel planned the crime very cleverly to look like suicide. The papers were sent to you; naturally you had to confront Goppel with them and take some action, but as soon as you did so you were providing a reason why Willy might become depressed and take his own life. We have already agreed that if it hadn't been for Yvette's murder it's very doubtful whether Goppel's death would have aroused any suspicion of foul play.'

Kersey allowed himself a show of impatience. 'What you are saying, sir, is that Lennon is a clever bloke. He probably is, he had a good education and I've no doubt he's intelligent.'

'But fool enough, apparently, to draw attention in advance to papers he proposed to use in an ingenious murder scheme. Fool enough too, to cash in on those medals and so risk everything for the sake of a few pounds.'

Kersey rubbed his bristly chin. 'As far as showing off the papers is concerned, Lennon was drunk and he made a fool of himself. He must have realized it for you say he was back the next night complaining to Natalie that he'd had his wallet nicked.'

'Perhaps he was telling the truth.'

Kersey's expression made it clear that he was having thoughts which cannot be expressed to a chief superintendent. 'Surely, sir, it's obvious he was trying to cover himself.'

Wycliffe smiled. 'At any rate, I agree that we should talk to him.'

'Shall I have him brought in?'

'No, we'll go and see him, we might get more out of an interview with his friend Goppel looking on.'

Telfer Street was utterly deserted, stoically awaiting the arrival of the demolition men. It was dusk and there was a light in the Irishman's shop. He came to the door as they passed.

'Nice evening, Superintendent. I think your friends are at home, they don't go out until a bit later as a rule.'

They climbed the three flights of stairs in almost total darkness. Kersey knocked on Lennon's door which was opened by the man himself.

'Freddie! You've got visitors.'

'It's you we've come to see, Mr Lennon, but Mr Goppel can stay if you have no objection.'

'Me?' Lennon's surprise was exaggerated. 'What can you possibly want with me?'

They followed him into the living-room where Freddie was in the act of turning off the television. He looked at the two policemen as though they had come to carry him off to execution.

'May we sit down?'

'By all means, gentlemen! This is Liberty Hall. You have a choice of a chesterfield with loose stuffing or an armchair sprung by a sadist.'

163

'I understand that you read and speak German, Mr Lennon?'

'I do, Superintendent. You see before you the product of an expensive public school education.'

Seen at close quarters Lennon was even more hairy and shaggy than Wycliffe remembered. His features, surprisingly pink and youthful, emerged from the undergrowth like geological outcrops in a forest.

'So you were able to read Willy Goppel's papers, and it seems that you did just that to several people at La Cass. On that same evening you coached Natalie to address Goppel as "*Herr Hauptmann*".'

Lennon laughed without much conviction. '*Guten Morgen Herr Hauptmann* – I was pissed, my dear Superintendent. It was a lark.'

'But you had discovered that Goppel was not the person he pretended to be for more than thirty years.'

'So what?' He looked sideways at Freddie who had been following the exchanges with nervous intensity. 'As I said, I was drunk and I did it for a giggle. Who cared after thirty years?'

Freddie seemed on the point of saying something but changed his mind. Kersey took over.

'Why did you send those papers to me if you thought they were of no importance?'

Either Lennon was startled by the question or he put on a good act. 'Send them to you? Why should I do that? To be honest, I'd never even heard of you until a day or two ago. And, in any case, I've no great liking for the genus copper.'

'They were handed in at the Mallet Street nick by somebody last Thursday, addressed to me. We know that you had them so if it wasn't you who handed them in, who was it?'

'A good question, with no answer as far as I'm

concerned. I lost the damn things; more accurately they were nicked along with my wallet.'

'What about the medals?'

'What about what medals? Or, perhaps I should say, What about which medals?'

Wycliffe said, 'We don't want to lay traps for you, Mr Lennon, so I will tell you that last Thursday Mr Goppel told Sergeant Kersey of the theft from his workshop of a cigar-box containing the papers, some war medals and a sum of money. Mr Goppel refused to make a formal complaint so the theft cannot be the subject of a charge. However, you should know that we have evidence that you sold the medals in the bar of The Fair Maid in Tolgate Street and they have since been recovered.' Wycliffe paused and turned to look at Freddie who shrank in his chair. 'Almost certainly Mr Goppel refused to make a complaint because he thought that the box had been taken by his son.'

'I—' Freddie began to speak but choked on his words.

Lennon was sitting on a cane chair which protested at every movement of his massive body. 'I don't get all this. You say that there is no question of a charge, so why all the fuss? A chief super and a detective sergeant chasing a few medals . . . '

Wycliffe's expression did not change. 'We are not interested in the medals or in the papers except in so far as they are linked with the murders.'

Lennon glanced quickly at Freddie and back again to Wycliffe. 'I don't see the connection. What have the papers got to do with the killings?'

'A good deal. Goppel's death was made to look like suicide and the suicide was made credible in advance. The papers were sent to Mr Kersey with a note saying they belonged to Goppel. Naturally he went to see Goppel and as a result the papers were forwarded to the

Home Office. Shortly afterwards Goppel was found hanged. On the face of it the business had preyed on his mind and he had committed suicide.'

For the first time Lennon showed real concern. 'There's been nothing about this in the paper . . . '

'No, but those are the facts. Had it not been for Yvette Cole becoming involved and losing her life in consequence, the verdict on Goppel would almost certainly have been suicide.'

There was a long pause during which Freddie startled everybody by a sudden, almost convulsive movement in which he tucked his legs under his bottom so that he was sitting in his chair Buddha-like.

Wycliffe gave Lennon time to think. Although he behaved like a clown it was clear that he had more than enough intelligence to calculate the score. It did not take him long.

'In the first place I wouldn't have been such a fool as to flash those papers round at La Cass if I intended to use them in some cunning plot – would I?'

'I've no idea. You say yourself that you were drunk.'

Kersey interrupted. 'You say those papers were nicked with your wallet. All right! Where? When? How?'

Lennon took a deep breath. 'As to where and when, it must have been at La Cass on that same evening. All I know is that I had them when I was playing the fool at the bar and I didn't have them when I got back here. My wallet was gone, papers and all.'

'You mean that you were dipped by somebody at the club?'

'I must have been. As I told you, I was a bit far gone and when customers started to arrive Natalie put me at a table near the back. I remember I thought it was bloody hot and I took my jacket off and hung it on the back of my chair.'

'Was anybody with you?'

'Geoff Bishop was told to keep an eye on me, to make sure I didn't disturb the customers or puke on the carpet. Then, Lisa, one of the girls, brought me a cup of black coffee and after that I felt better.'

'Did you tell Natalie about your wallet?'

'I did the next day but she said it was my own fault and there was nothing she could do about it.'

'Are you prepared to put all this in a statement and sign it?'

Lennon ran a hand through his mass of black hair. 'Why not?' He looked from Kersey to Wycliffe, 'Is that all?'

'Not quite. Where were you, say, between Saturday afternoon and the early hours of Sunday morning?'

He took time to consider. 'Well, I was in all Saturday afternoon watching sport on TV. In the evening Freddie and I went to a boozer—'

'Which?'

Lennon grinned. 'The Fair Maid.' He was recovering his nerve. 'We stayed there until round nine then Freddie went home and I toddled along to a party which wasn't Freddie's scene.'

'Where was this party?'

'A place belonging to an old mate of mine in Grenville Road. Chap called Hobson – Jeremy Hobson, number twenty-six.'

'What time did you get there?'

'Half-nine? Thereabouts anyway.'

'And when did you leave?'

He chuckled. 'Good question! It must have been in the early hours of the Sabbath. All I know is I had a thick head next morning.'

'Have you got a car?'

'Where would I get a car? I've got a push-bike and, believe it or not, I rode it back here.'

'One or two more points, Mr Lennon. I would like you to agree to a simple medical inspection.'

167

'What the hell for?'

'I assure you that it's necessary.'

'All right, as long as it's on the National Health.'

'And I want you to allow Mr Kersey to search this flat.'

'Will all this let me off the hook?'

'It will help.'

'Okay, if it amuses you. Anything else?'

'What clothes were you wearing on Saturday night?'

Lennon grinned. 'Well, it wasn't white tie and tails. A pair of M & S slacks and a blazer.'

'We should like to borrow those clothes and the shirt you wore.'

When Wycliffe was leaving Kersey followed him out on to the landing. 'Bloody clown! Do you think he's stringing us along?'

'I've no idea. You know what to do?'

'I think so, sir. Anything special in the flat?'

'Webbing, nylon cord, buckles, fastenings which might have come from Service webbing . . . Your guess is as good as mine.'

'He seems altogether too pleased with himself for my liking.'

Wycliffe said, 'I'll send a car to pick you up here and I'll make an appointment with the police surgeon for say, seven o'clock. If that's not possible I'll get a message to you.'

Back in his car Wycliffe contacted headquarters on the radio and gave the necessary instructions.

He drove back to Falcon Street well aware that he had made little real progress; it seemed unlikely that a case could be made out against Lennon on present evidence. So where did that leave them? Was there a credible alternative? Who wanted Goppel out of the way sufficiently to plan and execute such a hazardous crime? The stack of paper which the enquiry had accumulated carried one clear message: people liked Goppel, at worst they regarded him as eccentric, perhaps a little cracked. There seemed to be only one man with a real grievance – Bishop, but would Bishop murder a man over the renewal of a lease?

However, somebody must have wanted Goppel dead. Wycliffe remembered a Simenon in which Maigret had to keep reminding himself, 'Harry Brown is dead!' Well, Willy Goppel was dead too, and in very odd circumstances.

Kersey was hoping to find answers to three questions: was there anything incriminating in Lennon's squalid little flat? Did he have suggestive scratches on his body? Could his account of how he had spent Saturday night be regarded as an alibi?

Lennon appeared to be completely indifferent to the search of his flat. He sat on the ancient chesterfield reading a magazine while Kersey poked into every murky corner. By contrast, Freddie never let Kersey out of his sight, watching him as though in dread of some imminent catastrophe.

'What are you looking for?'

Kersey said, 'I don't know. Do you?'

'*Me?*'

Lennon was playful. 'Finished already?'

'For the time being.'

'Well, feel free, any time.'

And the medical got them nowhere. When Lennon left the police surgeon he was as jaunty as ever. 'What was the old leech looking for? Did you think I doped? Or spent my nights with poxy women?'

Kersey was not amused. 'Don't pretend to be more stupid than you are.'

Wycliffe had sent young D.C. Dixon with a patrol car to pick him up.

'Are you through, Sarge?'

'Through is the word. But we'll take a look at his alibi which will have more holes in it than a bloody colander.'

Grenville Road was tree-lined with the odd Mercedes, Jaguar or Rover 3.5 left nonchalantly in driveways. Number twenty-six was detached with enough garden to be self-supporting if ever the stock market really dived. It was growing dark, lights were on in many of the houses and there was that late evening stillness when people speak in low voices yet are heard at a distance. Kersey rattled the clapper of a bell on a wrought iron bracket, and the varnished door, studded with iron nails, was opened on a chain; the chain was unhooked when he poked his warrant card through the gap.

'What do you want?' Young and blonde with nothing visible on but a red velvet pinafore dress and a pair of peep-toe sandals.

'Mrs Hobson?'

'Yes.'

'You had a party here on Saturday night?'

'We did. Does that concern the police?'

'Only indirectly. As a matter of routine we have to check a statement made by a witness that he spent a good deal of Saturday evening and night here.'

'Does this person have a name?'

'Toby Lennon.'

'Oh, God! I might have known.' She sighed histrionically. 'What has he done?'

Kersey had the impression that Pongo was not among her top ten party guests. 'Nothing as far as we know.'

'Well, he was here.' She seemed to think that was all that was needed and was about to shut the door again.

'We would like as many details as you can give us and also your husband's recollection.'

Resignation. 'You'd better come in then. Does it take

170

two of you to do this sort of thing? I thought there was supposed to be a shortage of policemen.'

She showed them into a very large lounge where there were zebra-striped settees and armchairs on a pure-white carpet. The walls were creamy white and spotted with Bridget Riley abstracts which made the eyes go funny. 'White,' thought Kersey, 'is in. I must tell Esther.'

'I'll fetch my husband.'

When she had gone, Dixon muttered, 'A bit different from Telfer Street.'

'At home anywhere, our Pongo,' Kersey said.

The blonde returned with husband; perhaps a little older than Lennon, fair and slight, of aristocratic mould and manner. Out of Debrett by the skin of his teeth.

'Molly tells me that you are asking questions about Pongo Lennon. We were at school together.' He seemed to think some explanation of their association was needed. 'Saturday night was a bit of a riot, one of those parties where one evens up the score with a lot of people – pays off one's social debts in one fell swoop, as it were. We must have had upwards of fifty people here at one stage. Pongo arrived between nine and ten – before ten anyway – wouldn't you say, Molly?'

'If you say so.' Molly wasn't interested; seated on the white carpet, showing a great deal of thigh, she played with a cat who matched the carpet so well as to be almost invisible except when one glimpsed the dark nostrils and green eyes.

'Have you any idea how long he stayed?'

'Right through. Pongo never misses free booze if he can help it.'

'But you didn't see him all the time?'

'Not every minute, naturally; but I saw him pretty often and he was certainly among the last to go at about

171

three in the morning. I had to lever him out. Actually I had a pang of conscience. I said to him, "Have you got a car outside?" and he said, "No, old boy, but I've got my bike." Of course he was stoned.'

'Does that square with your recollection, Mrs Hobson?'

'Near enough; he seemed to be about, rather too obtrusively for comfort.'

This drew a mild protest from her husband. 'Molly! He's harmless . . . You have to know how to handle him.'

She smiled, not very pleasantly. 'Unlike you, Jerry, I have no wish to handle him.'

'Perhaps you could let me have the names of two or three other guests who might be more specific in their recollections?'

'Must we, sergeant? I hate the idea of my guests being pestered by this sort of thing.'

Kersey and Dixon left with three names, grudgingly given.

'Willy Goppel must have been quite a character. He had a substantial stake in property – Crowther estimates it as something over four-hundred thousand at present values – but he seems to have had a thing about not letting his right hand know what his left was doing. He spread his work around. Crowther drew up leases and dealt with the legal side generally; Cassells and White collected rents, prepared inventories and found tenants for his properties while Fiske's outfit dealt with his accounts, insurance, investment and tax.'

Wycliffe and Scales were treating themselves to a decent meal in the restaurant opposite Paul's Court which was run by a very fat woman of benevolent aspect. She seemed to have a regular clientele for the atmosphere was chummy and from time to time a little man in a chef's hat put his head through the serving

172

hatch to exchange pleasantries with particular customers. There was not much choice of either food or wine but what there was was good. A diminutive waitress of uncertain age answered to the name of Pearl. She served the tables with assistance from the proprietress when it was needed, but mostly the fat woman presided impressively at the bar and indicated what was to be done by restrained gestures of a plump, many-ringed hand. From time to time she shifted herself to make a royal progress round the tables with an apt word at each.

'Freddie will be a wealthy young man. According to Crowther he gets everything except for a few legacies of four thousand each to the Ward children, Yvette, and the landlord at Bickersleigh.'

The little waitress presented them with the cheese board and they helped themselves.

'No pointers?'

Scales shook his head. 'Nothing very obvious. Bishop has made himself a bit of a pain in the neck to Crowther and the estate agents but they don't take him very seriously. What is odd, neither of them have any idea why Goppel wanted him out.'

Wycliffe told him about the Toyland project.

Scales perched a knob of Stilton on a tiny water biscuit and popped it into his mouth. 'I suppose it takes all sorts but if Freddie knew about this it could be a pointer to him and his pal. But there's another oddity.' He took from his wallet the list of local firms which Wycliffe had seen in Willy's desk.

'I saw that and it didn't mean much to me.'

'Nor to me, but I rang round a few of the firms listed and now I'm not so sure.'

'Could you manage a brandy?'

'Why not? But what are we celebrating?'

Wycliffe grinned. 'Stalemate. But what about that list?'

'Yes, well, I rang City Butchers first and the chap who

runs it told me that Willy had rung him a couple of months back with some yarn about looking for additional insurance cover and could he recommend anybody. The bloke said he did all his insurance through a broker. Willy asked which companies issued the policies and he was told that the business was spread around – vehicles, buildings, employers' and public liability and so on. Willy said that he was only interested in buildings and he was then told that the firm's buildings were insured with the Eagle.'

'So? Sounds straightforward. Willy seems to have been a cautious chap.'

'Yes, but he got nothing useful, it was all too vague – no mention of rates, type of cover – anything anybody would want to know. And it was the same with the other firms on the list I contacted. Not a word about anything useful. In any case that's what brokers are for – to get the best deal for a client.'

Wycliffe shrugged. 'You think there's something in it, John?'

'If there is, I'm damned if I can see what; but it's odd. After all, Willy couldn't have been a novice at this sort of thing.'

They finished their meal and left the restaurant feeling mildy guilty, mildly elated. Outside in Falcon Street it was dusk and street lamps competed with the fading daylight; the air was mild and only a faint breeze disturbed the trees in the churchyard.

Mr Hedley, returning from the verandah to the LSO fortissimo, heard the telephone ringing in the hall. After closing the door into the living-room he answered it but it was some time before he established that it was an incoherent Freddie Goppel at the other end. He understood that Toby was involved with the police.

'For God's sake calm down, Freddie. Has he been

174

arrested?' Mr Hedley was by no means as senile as his wife pretended.

'I don't know. They say they want him to be examined by a doctor and have a blood test—'

'But why? What's he supposed to have done?'

'They seem to think he . . . that he did the murders.'

'Oh, God!' Mr Hedley gave himself a moment. 'Did they accuse him or say anything definite?'

'I don't think so but—'

'Where are you speaking from?'

'The phone box outside the market?'

Mr Hedley's piping, rather plaintive voice became unusually authoritative. 'Right! Now listen, Freddie. Go back to the flat and when Toby comes home tell him to ring. Say to him that if he doesn't his aunt will be frantic . . .'

'But what if he doesn't come back?'

'If he isn't back by eleven you ring again. Got that?'

'Yes, I think so.'

'Good!'

Mrs Hedley was dozing in her chair. Mr Hedley turned off the radio and she opened her eyes. 'What's the matter? Why did you shut it off? I was listening.'

Wycliffe drove home. Helen was in the living-room with the windows open to the night. He kissed her. Her skin was smooth and glowing and he knew that she had been working in the garden until driven indoors by the darkness.

'Have you had a meal?'

'Scales and I pushed the boat out at a place in Falcon Street.'

'Good for you!'

The little crevasse which divided their days had been safely bridged once more.

In bed Wycliffe dozed fitfully, his mind cluttered with

175

the ill-assorted lumber of the day: pictures, fragments of conversation, vague stirrings of the mind which might have crystallized into ideas. It was characteristic of him that his recollections of people were most vivid; sharp as the focused image of a well-made slide. But they were of no use, portraits in a gallery, instant people without past or future; Lennon, Bishop, Natalie, the Fiskes, the Wards, the Hedleys and the gynandrous Freddie. Wycliffe was on the threshold of deeper sleep when he remembered the little slip of paper on which Willy had listed several local firms and their insurers. Scales had said: 'that is what brokers are for, to get the best possible deal for a client . . . After all, Willy was no novice at this kind of thing.'

But Fiske was a broker and Willy's accountant. If Willy wanted advice all he had to do was cross the Court! In his dreamy state this, for some reason, struck him as amusing and he went to sleep smiling.

CHAPTER NINE

According to the police surgeon Lennon's body was whole and without blemish, Kersey's search had discovered nothing incriminating in his flat, but against this Kersey was satisfied that as an alibi the Grenville Road party was a dead duck.

'There's no doubt he arrived there between half-past nine and ten or that he left round three but what he or any of them did in the meantime, God alone knows. It was one of those come-and-go-as-you-please affairs and upwards of fifty people did. Buffet food, help-yourself drinks and the odd spot of fornication upstairs. The thing spread over the whole house and garden. What's more, the Hobson house is only six minutes walk from here if you follow the pedestrian paths, and no more than four on a bike.'

'So,' said Wycliffe, 'Lennon is still a candidate.'

Scales, Kersey and Wycliffe were having their morning conference in the largest of the compartments in the police van.

Scales said, 'If he used his bike to get to and from the Court he would have been fairly conspicuous late at night, it might be worth checking with the lads on the cars.'

Kersey scowled. 'Sitting on their backsides in their cars they see damn all. If Lennon used the paths, only an old-fashioned beat bobby would have had a chance of seeing him.' He stopped and glanced at Wycliffe to see if he had put both feet where angels feared to tread. Cars versus foot-patrols was still a live issue in the force. But Wycliffe was grinning.

'There's no harm in asking the car patrols and, luckily, there are still a few ordinary foot-slogging folk about so why not a house-to-house in the immediate neighbourhood?'

Scales nodded. 'I'll see to it.'

'And John – what about the insurance angle? I think it's worth following up.'

Scales agreed. 'I'm going to visit each of the firms on Willy's list; it's easier to talk man-to-man. After that we can make up our minds whether there's anything in it or not.' He stood up. 'I'll be getting a move on.'

Shortly after Scales had left a constable came in with a package. 'Just delivered from forensic, sir.'

It was Yvette's watch. The brief report which accompanied it was about as informative as one could reasonably expect. Wycliffe read it aloud: ' "The fibres entangled in the bracelet were woollen, of two colours, probably spun together. In which case the garment from which they came would be of a golden-brown colour, it was probably machine knitted, and of good quality. Such wool is commonly made up into jumpers, cardigans, sweaters, etcetera and these are widely sold in the better chain-stores." '

Kersey was unimpressed. 'When we find him we can ask him if he's got a golden-brown etcetera.'

Wycliffe went on: 'There's more. "A link in the bracelet is damaged, leaving a curved fragment of sharply pointed metal almost like a hook. This might easily have caught in a woollen garment of the kind described and, in a laboratory test, the watch, caught in this way, remained attached for fifteen minutes during which time the wearer of the garment was going about his usual laboratory duties." '

'So the guy has a golden-brown pullover or cardigan. I've got one myself.'

The little watch lay on the table between them and for some reason the sight of it stirred Wycliffe to quite unprofessional bitterness and anger.

Mrs Hedley glanced up at the clock. 'It's time you were going, it seems they're there by half-past eight. You must insist on seeing the superintendent.'

'They're bound to ask me why I didn't tell them before. What do I say? That I forgot?'

His wife was contemptuous. 'If you do you might as well not go. Tell them you didn't realize how important it was until you'd talked it over with me.'

When he reached the police van the door was shut and he knocked timidly. A young man opened the door. 'Yes, sir? What can we do for you?'

Hedley told him who he was. 'I would like a word with the superintendent.'

'Mr Hedley from the Court?'

'Yes.'

'Come in.'

Hedley found himself in a little cubicle with a bench seat and a table at which the young man had been working.

'Take a pew, I'll see if the super is free.'

After a very short wait he was taken to a larger room where the superintendent was seated with Sergeant Kersey who recognized him and greeted him in a friendly way.

Mr Hedley found it surprisingly easy to tell his story.

'You say you saw Bishop from your verandah. What time was this?'

'About half-past eleven, I can't say to a few minutes.'

'He was coming out of Goppel's yard?'

Mr Hedley hesitated. 'I'm almost sure he was, but it's just possible he had come through the iron gate from Church Lane.'

The superintendant said, 'It's quite a way from your verandah to Goppel's yard . . . '

'Too far for an old man to see in the dark,' Hedley chuckled. 'You're right there. But there's a light just by the little gate and I could see clearly that it was a man though at that distance I didn't know that it was Bishop.'

'What made you notice the man in particular?'

Hedley considered. 'Well, he was behaving oddly, sort of stealthy, then he ran a few steps until he was hidden from me by the tree. When he came out on the other side of the tree he was walking normally though a bit unsteady, and as he got to his own house I saw that it was Bishop. He let himself in with a key.'

'You are willing to make a statement to that effect, Mr Hedley?'

'Oh, yes; that's what I've come for.'

Hedley looked from one to the other of them, wondering what was coming next. It was Kersey, who said, 'You used to work for the council, Mr Hedley, I believe?'

'Yes. I worked there for forty-three years and finished up as deputy head clerk in the Treasurer's department. Then they started to computerize everything and I was too old to start learning all the new tricks so I took the offer of early retirement.'

'And later you worked in Mr Fiske's office?'

'I did. Four years full-time, three years part-time – three days a week. I packed that in last year.'

Wycliffe said, 'Were you his head clerk?'

The old man shook his head. 'Oh, no, that was Jim Staples – he's still there but I hear that he's retiring shortly.' He chuckled, 'Martin Fiske is clever; he employs oldish men who, for one reason or another,

180

have accepted early retirement, then he doesn't pay them the professional rate for the job. All the same, I don't complain, the money came in handy.'

'Didn't Mr Fiske do Willy Goppel's accounts?'

'Oh, yes. Willy was one of Fiske's clients.'

'I believe the firm dealt with all the administration of the concerns they looked after.'

'Oh, yes, everything. "We do your paper-work" was the motto. Accounting, income tax, V.A.T., insurance, everything – even invoicing and merchants' ledger accounts in some cases.'

'Did you deal with insurance?'

'Not me, personally. Mr Fiske dealt with insurance and investment himself. He was an investment and insurance broker before he had the bright idea of setting up as a wet nurse to the small business man.'

When Hedley had gone Kersey said, 'That was interesting.'

'Very.'

'Bishop is no fool though he puts on an act. While I can't see him murdering the girl for sex I wouldn't put it beyond him to do her in if she happened along when he was dealing with Goppel. I think we should talk to him, sir.'

'So do I.'

Kersey drove the superintendent to Fenton Street. Wycliffe was silent for most of the way, then he said, 'We've been trying to find people who were about at the time we believe Yvette and Goppel to have been murdered but what about the Ward boy? Did you ask him if he saw anybody? If Yvette left him on that seat in Lodge Road I don't suppose he stayed there all night.'

Henry Ward was beginning to look like Kersey's private incubus. 'I'll catch him during the school lunch-break, sir.'

There were no parking spaces in Fenton Street and

Kersey had to chance his arm amongst the hardware on Bishop's forecourt.

Bishop's receptionist, secretary and general factotum – all eye shadow and blonde ringlets – said she would see if Bishop was free but they followed her into the inner office where he was making entries in a dog-eared notebook. Kersey turned to the girl, 'Don't worry, Miss, we're all in the family.'

Bishop said, 'Feel free. I'm having a busy morning, Freddie Goppel and his keeper have just left.'

'What did they want?'

Bishop lit a cigarette. 'I don't know that it's any of your business, Mr Kersey, but there's no secret about it – not on my side. Freddie has had glad tidings from his papa's solicitor and he's anxious to get his hands on some cash so he's offered to sell me the freehold of this place when the will is proved, in return for some hard cash now. Apparently the lawyer is sticky about making any advance until you people have tidied things up.'

'So your worries about the lease are over?'

Bishop raised his eyebrows. 'So you know about that. Well, I don't say my worries are over exactly, it depends on the price, but I expect we shall work something out.'

Kersey said, 'It's an ill wind.'

'What's that supposed to mean?'

'Did Goppel tell you why he wanted your place?'

'No, but Freddie did.' Bishop chuckled. 'Willy must have been going ga-ga; he wanted to turn this place into a sort of amusement palace for kids. According to Freddie he was willing to put all his money into it. Allowing for proper filial affection and all that crap Freddie must feel a bit relieved that papa went when he did.'

Wycliffe intervened. 'You remember the evening at La Cass when Lennon was showing off Goppel's service papers?'

182

Bishop nodded. 'I was there; Pongo was well primed that night.'

'And you saw the papers?'

'I saw something he said belonged to Goppel.'

'You know he lost his wallet and those papers that night?'

'I heard it from Natalie afterwards.'

'But you were with him.'

'Part of the time, yes, but I wasn't watching his bloody wallet. He slung his jacket over the back of his chair and he went off to the toilet at least twice to my knowledge.'

'Did you see him home?'

'Christ, no! He had some black coffee and after that he sobered up a bit. I left him to it.' Bishop jabbed his cigarette into an ashtray.

'What time did you get home on Saturday night?'

'Saturday? I've already told Mr Kersey. I spent the evening in The Sportsman's in Falcon Street and arrived home about half-eleven.'

'Walking?'

'Yes. I've already said that too. What is all this?'

'Did you come into the Court through the archway or through the gate from Church Lane?'

Bishop made an angry movement. 'I'll put all this on bloody tape and you can play it over. I came in through the archway.'

'So you were here in the garage at about four when Yvette called to see you; you drove home, left your car and went out again to the pub – is that right?'

'Yes.'

'Did you drop in to see Willy Goppel on your way home?'

Bishop's brown eyes searched Wycliffe's face for some sign but he encountered only a bland expression-less gaze. 'Why should I drop in on Goppel? We weren't on visiting terms.'

183

'You might have wanted another word with him on the subject of the lease.'

'At that time of night? Anyway, I didn't.'

'Think carefully, Mr Bishop. It's only fair to tell you that you were seen.'

Bishop swivelled round in his chair and glared from Wycliffe to Kersey and back again. 'Are you trying to set me up? Do you think I killed Goppel? Why should I? Do you think I would murder a man over a bloody lease?'

Wycliffe said nothing and Kersey allowed the silence to lengthen uncomfortably before speaking. 'Nobody is trying to set you up but you've got some explaining to do. You were with Lennon at La Cass when he was shooting off his mouth about Goppel's papers, you were with him when he had his wallet nicked, and now we find you paying a late call on Goppel within an hour or so of his death.'

Bishop re-arranged the things on his desk as though playing draughts. 'You bloody coppers have a way of going about your dirty business, I'll say that for you. I'm not sure what sort of a case you could cook up against me but I know I'll bloody soon find out unless I string along. That's the size of it, isn't it?'

'Nobody's threatening you, Bishop.'

Bishop laughed without humour. 'Isn't that what the actress said? All right, I'll tell you what you want to know and I hope to God you'll believe me. It was about half-eleven, as you say. I'd just come through the archway into the Court when I heard a sort of shriek come from Goppel's place. It was cut off short. I'd had quite a lot to drink and I wasn't too sure of myself. I couldn't think what the hell it could be but it certainly sounded as though somebody had hurt themselves bad. Although I was half cut I thought I'd better take a look so I went to Goppel's back door and knocked but there was no answer. I tried the door and it was unlocked so I went in. There was no light in the workshop but there was a light on the stairs so that I could see well enough. The bloody animals were scuffling about like crazy, squeaking and whistling. I shouted, "Are you all right, Goppel?" There was no answer so I shouted again. I thought he might have electrocuted himself or something. I went through the workshop to the bottom of the stairs and I was just going to call again when I saw him. He was hanging from the banisters at the top of the stairs. I reckon it sobered me up a bit. Anyway, it looked as though he'd put his head in the noose on the top landing and just dropped over the banisters. I thought he must have let out that screech as he fell.'

Wycliffe said, 'Was he tied up – bound in any way?'

Bishop shook his head. 'I don't think so except for the rope round his neck.'

'What did you do?'

'Well, first I thought he might not be dead so I went upstairs so that I could see better. He was dead all right; his face looked ghastly.' Bishop lit another cigarette. 'I know I should have called out the bloody marines or something but when you've had as much to do with the fuzz as I have you learn to keep what they call a low profile. Anyway, I was still pretty drunk. There was nothing I could do for the poor bastard and he was sure to be found sooner or later so I just took off for home, a stiff whisky and bed.'

'I suppose you realize now that Goppel must have been dead for some time when you say you found him?'

Bishop nodded. 'Yes, but I didn't think so then.'

'So have you thought any more about that shriek?'

'Of course I've bloody well thought about it and it doesn't make me feel any better to think that it must've been Yvette, poor little sod. The bastard must've been

185

there while I was snooping about and the pity is I didn't snoop a bit more.' He turned to Wycliffe. 'I suppose all this puts me on your little list?'

'Don't worry, Mr Bishop, you were there already. It might help though, in the business of elimination, if you would agree to a simple medical inspection.'

'What for?'

'It seems likely that Yvette struggled with her attacker and she may have scratched him. We would like to make sure that you have no recent unaccounted-for scratches.'

Bishop shrugged. 'Okay.'

'We would also like to borrow the clothing you were wearing on Saturday night. It would help if you would go back to the house with Mr Kersey now and he will collect it.'

'But I've admitted walking through that bloody workshop.'

'I know, and that will be taken into account.'

Bishop glanced at his watch. 'I've got a customer in twenty minutes. How about if I arrange to meet Mr Kersey at the house in an hour?'

'Very well.'

Kersey stood up and opened the door abruptly to be confronted with the blonde receptionist. 'The draught through that keyhole has blown your eyelashes off, love; you look positively naked.'

'Cheeky pig!'

Back in the car, Kersey said, 'So Freddie, and therefore Lennon, knew all about Willy's scheme for a kids' amusement place.'

'It looks like it.' Wycliffe was not in a talkative mood.

I can think of less compelling motives for murder than half-a-million.'

'I suppose so.'

'It keeps Lennon very much in the picture.'

'Yes.' Wycliffe sat back in the passenger seat and lit his pipe. 'Bishop or Lennon, we haven't enough evidence against either of them to bring a charge, let alone secure a committal.'

Traffic in the city centre was at its peak and they were held up in queues at lights which changed from red to green and back again.

'Bishop, if he was telling the truth, heard Yvette cry out. He must have arrived at the very instant of the killer's encounter with her. According to him Goppel's body was not strapped up so the bonds must have been removed before Yvette came on the scene.'

Kersey let in the clutch and the car shot across an intersection to join the end of another slow-moving snake on the other side. 'So?'

'I'm just trying to visualize what happened.' At the next set of lights he added, 'What puzzles me is how the killer managed to get Goppel tied up without a struggle.'

'Goppel was ill.'

'But he couldn't have counted on that.'

'Housebreakers sometimes truss up the occupant.'

'Yes, but when they do, they're usually armed.'

Kersey nodded. 'That's a point worth bearing in mind.'

When the school broke for lunch at half-past twelve Kersey was outside in his car. He asked a lad who looked like a sixth-former if he knew Henry Ward; the lad said that he did and volunteered to fetch him. A few minutes later Henry arrived.

'What do you want?' Henry was a trifle wary and sullen.

'Hop in, I won't keep you long; something I forgot to ask. When Yvette left you on the seat in Lodge Road, did you start for home at once?'

'Within a couple of minutes.'

'Did you catch a bus?'

'I just missed one – very likely the one Yvette caught. I thought it was probably the last for the night so I walked.'

'Once you got to Falcon Street, did you see anyone you knew?'

Henry thought. 'I don't think I saw anybody at all after the square.'

'Any idea what time you got home?'

'I switched on the radio and they were giving the midnight news summary.'

'Did you go straight to bed?'

'Yes.'

'And you are quite sure that you saw nobody in the neighbourhood of Falcon Street?'

'Quite sure.'

'Pity!' Kersey switched on the ignition. 'You'd better go and get your lunch or you won't grow.'

The boy had his hand on the door catch. 'I've just remembered that while I was undressing I happened to look out of the window and I saw Mr Fiske coming home.'

'You mean you saw him drive into the Court?'

'No, he was walking.'

Kersey felt a slight prickling sensation at the back of his neck. 'What time was this?'

'It couldn't have been long after twelve.'

'How was he dressed?'

'I didn't notice – something dark, I think, a mac or coat.'

'Carrying anything?'

Henry giggled. 'Oh yes, he had his briefcase.'

'And that's funny?'

'Oh, it's just a joke in the Court. He has a lady out at Parkeston – somebody from his office – and when he's been there he arrives back late at night, carrying his briefcase and people say, "Fiske working late again," ' He added after a moment, 'Not very funny really.'

'But he couldn't have walked from Parkeston, surely?'

'No, I expect he came by taxi. His car was in dock, somebody backed into him.'

'Did you hear a taxi?'

'No, but I wouldn't have noticed.' He hesitated, still with his hand on the door catch. 'What is all this? What's Fiske done?'

'Nothing – nothing at all. I just wondered if he might have seen anything.'

The telephone rang. Joan Fiske was in the kitchen and she went through to the living-room to answer it.

'This is Martin, I shall be home to lunch. I have to pick up some papers for a client.'

She had no opportunity to reply before he replaced the receiver, but she was used to that. She glanced at the clock, it was a quarter to eleven and he would expect his lunch at one. She and Marty would have made do with fish fingers but he would expect something more than that; she busied herself with calculations – what there was in the freezer, how long it would take to thaw and then cook. In the end she decided on cod fillets with white sauce, steamed carrots and boiled potatoes. They would start with tomato juice and finish with ice-cream.

He arrived promptly at one, ate his meal and even complimented her on it. 'I enjoyed that, the sauce was good.' Then he went upstairs. She heard him in the bathroom and when he came down half-an-hour later he had changed into a light-weight suit which he rarely wore and he carried the inevitable briefcase. He paused in the doorway of the living-room, looking back as though he might have forgotten something.

'Oh, I shall be late home, don't wait up for me.'

There was nothing new in all this, it had happened so often as to become almost a ritual but emotionally she had been on a knife edge since before Yvette's funeral and she had all but made an exhibition of herself in front of the superintendent. Seeing her husband, smug and immaculate, casually informing her of his intention at the very last moment, was too much.

'Don't think you're fooling me, you're going to spend half the night with that slut!' She spoke with such intensity and hatred that her voice was barely recognizable.

Fiske looked at her in utter amazement, then his face closed, losing all expression. 'I have no idea what you are talking about.'

'No? Do you think I haven't known all along about that woman? About the flat in Parkeston? Do you think I don't know why I've got to watch every penny, go short myself or keep Marty short? All so that you can play your dirty games with a little whore who is too selfish to take on a man of her own.'

Fiske came back into the room and closed the door. 'You are out of your mind!'

She was scared of him but she had gone too far to draw back. She laughed hysterically. 'Out of my mind, am I? It would be no wonder with you making me a laughing stock of the neighbourhood and everybody gossiping behind my back. But I wouldn't mind all that if you treated me with a bit of consideration in the home, but all I am is a servant; in fact no servant would stand for being treated as you treat me.'

Her voice was letting her down and soon her hysterical anger would dissolve into a flood of tears but she felt an overwhelming desperate need to empty herself of bitterness which she had secreted like venom over months and years. She sat on the nearest chair because she no longer had the strength to stand. 'With these terrible things that have happened in the Court you go off and leave me alone with a helpless, weak-minded boy when we could both be murdered in our beds.

190

There is a murderer in the Court . . . ' She broke off and looked at him in hatred. 'Sometimes I wonder—'

He had been standing over her, pale but impassive, now – suddenly, his expression changed, he stooped and gripped her by the wrist so that she let out a cry of pain. 'What do you wonder?' His face was close to hers and he forced her to look into his eyes. 'What do you wonder in that twisted little mind of yours? Tell me, I want to know . . .'

She was going to say that she wondered whether he was deliberately trying to drive her into an asylum but now the words would not come, instead she began to sob convulsively and then tears overwhelmed her. He released her arm and stood back, looking down at her. After a little while he went to the door, let himself out and closed it behind him.

In the Court Marty was bouncing a ball on the cobbles. He looked sideways at his father as though half expecting some rebuke but his father strode across to the garages without appearing to notice him.

Wycliffe and Kersey were closeted in the incident-van. It was two-thirty in the afternoon; Thursday – early closing day, all the shops were shut and Falcon Street was deserted. Even the post office was closed. In the church-yard three of four old men shuffled along the gravelled paths, stopping now and then in a patch of sunshine. In the vicarage garden the vicar's little daughter was using her swing. Eek-wok, eek-wok . . .

'I wish to God he'd oil that bloody thing,' Kersey said.

'He probably wouldn't have had a taxi pick him up at the flat.' Wycliffe spoke of Fiske, not the vicar.

Kersey agreed. 'No, I thought of that. I told Dixon and Fowler to enquire about any fares put down in Falcon Street after midnight but I doubt if there will be any.'

The telephone rang. 'Wycliffe.'

It was Scales. 'I won't say too much over the telephone but I think we are on the right track. All the firms on Willy's list with a tick beside them were looked after by Fiske and all of them had been approached by Willy about their insurance position. Two of them have the beginnings of a suspicion what it's all about but I put them off . . . Now, sir, it amounts to this, all the insurance firms concerned have regional offices in the city. If I start raising queries with them it might be difficult to keep our inquiry under cover. On the other hand . . . '

'Carry on, John, just be as discreet as you can.'

Kersey said, 'What about me, sir?'

'You stay here and hold the fort, I think I'll have a word with Natalie.'

Wycliffe strolled down Falcon Street, past the Dolls' House shop which was already acquiring an air of neglect. He turned in at the archway and crossed the Court to Natalie's. The house had a deserted look but after ringing the bell a couple of times he heard somebody stirring and Natalie came to the door. She was wearing a housecoat, her eyes looked puffy with sleep and it was obvious that she had just run a comb through her hair before answering the door.

'I was lying down, you'd better come in.'

He was taken into the white living-room and swallowed up by one of the armchairs.

'Drink?'

'No, thanks.'

'I need something.' She poured a generous helping of gin into a glass and dashed it with lime. She was pale and there were dark rings under her eyes.

'Are you come to tell me or ask me?'

'To ask. That evening when Lennon was drunk and started showing Goppel's papers around – who was there?'

192

She stroked her cheek with the lip of her glass but she made no attempt to deny the incident. 'It's some time ago. It was early evening, before anybody much turns up, and we were round the bar. I know Freddie wasn't there. Of course there was Stefan, the barman, me, the girl who plays the accordion – you remember her.'

'Bishop?'

'Yes, Geoff was there, drinking with Pongo . . . and Martin Fiske.'

'With his girl-friend?'

'No, he was alone. I remember him particularly because I was watching him while Pongo was telling his ghastly yarns about what the Nazis did to Jewish girls in concentration camps. I'm sure Pongo makes those yarns up, he's the sort of queer who has it in for women and he broods on that sort of thing. Fiske was lapping it all up, that man gives me the creeps.'

'What about afterwards? You put Lennon at the back and sent Bishop to keep an eye on him . . . '

She gave him a quick look. 'My! You have been doing your homework.'

'Did you notice who went to that table?'

'You mean, who could have nicked Pongo's wallet. I doubt if anybody did. If Pongo can't draw attention to himself one way he will another.'

'You haven't answered my question.'

She sipped her gin. 'I don't know that I can, I had something better to do than nurse Pongo, but the regulars circulate quite a bit. When I happened to be at the end of the room there were four of them at the table – Freddie had turned up and Fiske was with them. Geoff told me afterwards that he was after more of Pongo's fantasies to help him through his nights.'

She swallowed a mouthful of gin and coughed over it. 'Men!'

CHAPTER TEN

Joan Fiske pushed back the debris of her meal, rested her arms on the dining table, placed her head on her arms, and wept. She wept until her anger had drained away, giving place to self-pity, and her hatred had withered, leaving only emptiness. She found that she could look back on what had happened as though two other people had been involved. Wearily she got up from the table, swept back her hair from her eyes, and looked out of the window. Marty was throwing his ball up into the branches of the tree, over and over again. She went slowly upstairs to the bathroom and bathed her face and eyes in cold water. For a time her mind was almost blank, then she began to recall odd phrases of the tirade she had launched against her husband and they repeated themselves in her mind again and again. But they seemed meaningless, she could not associate them with any intense emotion. What was it all about? Why did it happen like this after months – after years?

She went into her bedroom and sat at the dressing-table, brushing her hair with feeble strokes. What would happen when he came home? Would things go on just as before? Did she want them to?

'Oh, God, I don't know!'

'Forget about your husband and concentrate on yourself ... You lack confidence ... especially in yourself ... you have a great deal of moral courage; you are willing to suffer for what you believe to be right and you have the strength to win through ...' The Tarot. Mrs

Hedley had done her best in difficult circumstances. 'Forget about your husband . . . '

The numbness was wearing off; emotion returned like blood to a chilled limb, bringing pain.

After a while she went downstairs and resumed her normal routine. She cleared away the remains of lunch, washed the dishes and put them away. No evening meal to prepare; she and Marty would have something out of a tin. As she worked, isolated instants of the confrontation presented themselves uninvited to her mind with the clarity of images on a television screen.

'I have no idea what you are talking about.' Amazement, suddenly masked by utter blankness. She could see him plainly, standing in the doorway, half turned towards her. Then he had closed the door and come back into the room. 'You are out of your mind!' More than a figure of speech, for he had always let it be known that Marty's condition arose directly from a history of mental disorder on her side of the family.

He had come to stand over her and she had been scared. She marvelled that she had found the courage and strength to go on. He had towered over her, monumental; and she had known that his expression would be utterly without warmth, lacking even the heat of anger. There was nothing – *nothing* that she could say or do to reach him.

And yet, a moment later, she had looked up into his face, 'Sometimes I wonder—' she had said. That was all. He had gripped her arm painfully, his expression of aloof detachment gone, and in its place – cruelty? No, not cruelty; she had seen his features moulded by cruelty more than once and this was different. Not anger, not hatred, not even contempt – but *fear*.

His face close to hers, forcing her to look into his eyes, 'What do you wonder in that twisted little mind? I want to know.'

But why should he be afraid? It was not possible.

Joan Fiske was not a particularly intelligent woman but she was tenacious, often tediously so, and now she set herself to recall, instant by instant, what exactly had happened before that astounding transformation. She had been speaking of him leaving her alone in the house with only Marty – 'a helpless, weak-minded boy' she had called him, with a sense of betrayal ' . . . we could both be murdered in our beds. *There is a murderer in the Court* . . . ' and then, '*Sometimes I wonder—*'

It was as though she had had a revelation.

'Dear God help me!'

Alison Ward arrived home from school to an empty house. It was Thursday, half-day closing, and Mr and Mrs Ward were visiting relatives in Kingsmeade on the outskirts of the city. Henry was playing cricket in a house match. Alison went to her room and changed her school clothes for jeans and a shirt. It reminded her of Yvette and of Willy Goppel and she felt the tears smarting in her eyes. She was not supposed to be in the house alone – not according to her mother. She had intended to play tennis, then she and Henry would have come home together, but something had gone wrong with the fixtures and the match had been cancelled.

She went down to the living-room with a book and sat on the window-seat with her feet up, reading.

Somebody was ringing the back-door bell, leaning on it apparently, for it never stopped. Perhaps Henry had forgotten his key, but it was too early for Henry. She went downstairs, just a little uneasy, but ashamed of her misgivings. She opened the door to find Mrs Fiske, wildy excited, with Marty behind her.

'I must come in, Alison! You *must* let me in . . . '

'Yes, of course, Mrs Fiske. Come on, Marty . . .' Marty was hanging back.

'Lock the door, Alison – lock it, for God's sake!'

Mrs Fiske was breathing hard and the stairs taxed her but there was nowhere else Alison could take them. She led the way into the living-room, wondering what on earth was wrong and feeling helpless. Mrs Fiske collapsed on the settee.

'Ask your mother—'

'But mother and father are out, Mrs Fiske, they've gone over to Kingsmeade. Is there anything I can do? Would you like a cup of tea?'

Mrs Fiske had her hand to her bosom and her breathing, which had been painfully audible, was subsiding. 'It's my husband . . .'

'Mr Fiske – is he hurt or something?'

She lowered her voice to a dramatic whisper. 'Hurt? He's a murderer!'

'But—'

'I know! He murdered Willy Goppel and he murdered little Yvette.'

Alison, bewildered and frightened as she was, could not help wondering at the blend of horror and triumph with which the frantic woman made her pronouncement. But it seemed to calm her and Alison saw for the first time that she was clutching a much folded piece of newspaper.

'I don't know how I was so blind! He didn't come home until after midnight and he didn't have his car – he only got it back yesterday . . .'

Her words came in short bursts with intervals during which she strove to control her emotion. Marty stood by the window, looking at the floor.

'He wasn't even wearing one of his good suits and I should have known he'd never have gone to her like that – never in a million years.'

Alison perched on the edge of one of the dining chairs, utterly at a loss. Mrs Fiske got up and moved over to the window where she peered down into the Court.

197

'I would have gone to the Hedleys but he knows I sometimes go there and he might . . . Then I thought if I came here, there would be your brother and your father . . .'

'A few days before I had to take Marty to Bristol for his treatment and while I was away he *turned out the box-room!*'

'The box-room?' Alison was mystified.

Mrs Fiske turned from the window. 'Yes. You think I'm mad, Alison, but I'm not. He's never done a hand's turn in the house since I married him and then, suddenly . . . "I've thrown out a lot of old rubbish," he said.'

She moved uncertainly to the table where she unfolded her crumpled piece of newspaper and spread it flat, smoothing it with her long thin hands. 'Look at that – it's from yesterday's paper. See what it says under the picture: "A webbing belt as used by the armed services. The police believe that service webbing, easily obtained from government-surplus stores, was used to bind the murdered man."'

She looked at Alison with great intensity and said, slowly, 'His father was in the regular army and he came to live with us before he died. He had a cupboard full of stuff like that.' After a moment she added with a bitter smile, 'He didn't have to go to any store.'

Alison wished that her parents would come – Henry, anybody . . . Marty shuffled his feet and looked at his mother with pleading eyes. 'Home? Go home?'

Martin Fiske sat at his desk with a client's file open in front of him but he could not concentrate. That lunchtime scene had taken him completely by surprise and at one point he had reacted spontaneously, without proper thought, indeed with no thought at all. A lesson for the future.

Odd, why her melodramatic outburst upset me.

I've taken everything in my stride, even when they found out that Goppel had been murdered . . . *Murder* – so much nonsense talked about murder . . . One is brainwashed into believing that murder is a tremendous act, leaving its mark – the Mark of Cain. Mystical nonsense! But it worried me . . . How would I feel afterwards? What would it be like to have killed a man? Would it be possible to behave normally? Would I feel remorse?

If I had known that I would have to deal with the girl as well I should have drawn back . . . With Goppel I felt nothing – nothing at all. I did what I had planned with as little emotion as I would play a round of golf . . . Finding the old fool asleep made it easier . . .

The girl was different . . . sex . . . her struggles excited me and I was tempted. But for that blundering oaf, Bishop . . . Afterwards I felt as though I really had screwed the little slut . . . I kept her shirt . . . Stupid!

I was obsessed by getting her out of the house – a mistake. Left where she was she would have been down to Goppel . . . They wouldn't have looked any further then . . .

Remorse? A fiction. Killing is making a hole in water . . . That silly, shabby little shop will disappear from the street and there is one sexy young tramp the less . . .

Against that, I am safe.

There are those who hesitate and those who act. Goppel was a fool but he spotted the tip of the iceberg – a few piddling insurance policies allowed to lapse for a time before being renewed with another company.

'I'll give you time to get straightened out, Fiske . . . '

Patronising bastard! No notion of the kind of man he was dealing with.

'Penny for them.' Fiona, standing in the doorway, smiling.

'Sorry, I was day-dreaming.'

'Obviously. The superintendent is back with a sergeant and they want a word.'

'Give me a minute, then show them in.'

The thing is to be on one's guard but to behave normally. A mouthful of brandy . . .

'Ah, do sit down, Superintendent. I'm afraid you've caught me at a bad time, I have an appointment in five minutes.'

The superintendent in the client's chair, he's left his sergeant outside.

'One or two questions, Mr Fiske.'

His manner is different. No apology for calling without an appointment. Not the slightest sign of friendliness . . . Disturbing.

'What questions?' Mistake number one. Better to keep quiet. Look of bored attention.

'Can you remember when you arrived home on Saturday night.'

'Saturday?'

'The night Goppel and Yvette were killed.'

Careful! 'I think I told you that I did not go out on Saturday night.'

'What you said was, that you were not out late.'

'Well?' When in doubt, play for time.

'You were seen in the Court at about midnight.'

A nasty jolt. Of course, it was on the cards; the bloody busy-bodies never sleep.

'A man doesn't want his comings and goings known to everybody.'

'If you are about to say that you spent part of the night at Parkeston, I should tell you that we know your car was out of commission and public transport stops shortly after eleven.'

Think! Keep a clear head. Taxi? Easily checked.

Borrowed car? Ditto . . . Only one possible answer. 'I did not go to Parkeston on Saturday.'

'So what were you doing in the Court at midnight?'

This looks better. An easy laugh. 'I feel such a damn fool! All I was doing was taking a stroll. I couldn't sleep so I got up and dressed and went for a turn round the block.'

'Carrying your briefcase?'

Still not a glimmer of expression; clinically cold. Only way, a flat denial. 'I was certainly not carrying my briefcase.'

The bastard knows how to keep a poker face . . . Where to look? Suddenly it's difficult to know how to hold my head, where to direct my eyes. I'm losing my grip on normal behaviour. My hands are wrong – clasped together on the desk, but too tightly. I can see the whites of my knuckles. Relax! A glance at the clock. 'I hope this isn't going to take too long, Superintendent?' That's better.

'When you went for your stroll, how were you dressed?'

'Dressed?' What the hell is this about? 'Not very elegantly, just a pair of slacks and an old mackintosh.'

'No jacket?'

What in God's name is the man after? 'No jacket, but I really can't see why all this should interest you. In fact, I wore a cardigan.'

'And shirt, pants and socks?'

'Naturally.'

'I would like to see the clothes you wore, Mr Fiske.'

God! I cut her nails. 'Are you making some fantastic accusation against me, Superintendent?'

Still not the slightest change of expression. 'I am asking you to let me see the clothes you wore on Saturday night.'

201

'And if I refuse?'

'You have that right but, of course, the matter would not end there.'

A threat! Christ! My lips are trembling and it's affecting my speech. Ask for a solicitor? An admission of guilt. Better to carry it a bit further first. Try to find out what they know. 'All right, Superintendent, I've nothing to hide but, I warn you, I do not take this intrusion lightly. After I have seen my next client I will go with you and you can inspect my whole wardrobe if you wish.'

'I'm sorry, Mr Fiske, but it will have to be now.'

God! He must be sure of his ground. 'Very well, if you insist; I will ask my secretary to apologize for me.'

'Good!'

The staff watching me as I go through with a policeman in tow. Fiona in the outer office with the typists and the sergeant. She gives me an odd look. She's as stupid as the rest. I tell her to let Staples deal with old Morse when he comes.

Outside, shiny new Ford parked on yellow lines. Beginning to rain; big spots on the pavement. In the back with Wycliffe, the sergeant driving.

'Nice car. Granada, isn't it?'

'Yes.'

'Always a bit heavy on petrol, these Fords, don't you think?'

No answer.

Oh, God, I feel sick! . . . Five o'clock . . . Five o'clock. What does time matter any more? Meaningless! All the time there is . . . The streets slide by . . . already I feel cut off – apart. Raining hard now, the wind-shield wipers sweeping back and forth . . . Shall I ever drive again? Mustn't lose my nerve . . . I read somewhere that three out of four criminals convict themselves . . . I wonder

202

what prison is really like. Do they make allowances for a man's class? They can't just put you in a cell with . . . Oh Christ!

Turning into the Court now. Like a stranger, seeing it for the first time . . . Puddles in the cobbles. Nobody about but somebody is watching; somebody always is. Two men in my garden, one holding a large umbrella . . .

'What are they doing in my garden? Are they police-men?'

'One is, the other is a scientific officer from the forensic laboratory. They are taking samples of ash from your incinerator.'

'But they have no right!'

'You will have ample chance to protest.'

No sign of Joan or the boy . . . Have they taken them away? The door of the house is wide open and there is a policeman on the verandah. Protest.

'This is beyond everything! Searching my house without giving me the opportunity to be there!'

'The door was found open, sir, there was no one about and none of our chaps have been inside.' The policeman on the verandah defending himself.

'You hear that, Mr Fiske?' Wycliffe's voice, level and cold. 'Perhaps you will lead the way.'

No sign of anybody. 'Joan! Marty!' Where the hell can they be?

Old man Hedley watching from his bloody verandah. Upstairs in my bedroom. The wardrobe. 'Here you are. Superintendent . . . '

Mackintosh, trousers, zip-fronted cardigan, shoes . . . 'That's the best I can do. My underclothes and socks have been laundered and I've no idea which they were.' Sounds reasonable and has the advantage of being true. Each item goes into a separate polythene bag.

'Your clothes will go to the forensic laboratories, Mr Fiske, but they will be returned to you.'

Labelled Courtroom exhibits A, B, C . . . They say sex offenders and child murderers are roughed up in prison. But she was fifteen and I didn't rape her . . .

Kersey comes in. 'The small room at the back, is that your study, Mr Fiske? We are going to search it, I think you should be there.'

My own little room. Wycliffe stands by the window, looking down into the yard; Kersey prying and poking into all my things . . . God, how I HATE them!

My little cupboard, my shelves, my books, my filing cabinet, my desk . . . I am ignored. They do not even look at me!

But they find NOTHING. The bastards are slipped up after all.

'I hope that now, Superintendent, you will realize—' God! Kersey is pulling out the drawers of the desk . . .

Kersey was removing the desk drawers and when he had done so he reached into the dusty, cob-webbed recesses behind. He came out with a couple of bulky paper-back novels of the kind which bristle with four-letter words, then a liberally illustrated book on punishment through the ages, another on flagellation and a so-called *Study of Sexual Perversion and Deviant Behaviour*.

Wycliffe looked at the little heap. Frailty thy name is man. But if that were all . . .

Then Kersey, like a conjuror at the climax of his act, produced a package wrapped in newspaper and a gun, an old service revolver. The package was soft and yielding. Without looking at Fiske he removed the wrapping and a springy cotton garment, carelessly folded, lay on the desk. He spread it out – a T-shirt with 'Restricted Area' printed in red across the front. No blood.

'If you insist on writing out a statement for yourself, you should start with the declaration required by Judges' Rules, otherwise it won't count for much.'

Kersey and Fiske sat one on each side of a small table in a bare interview room in the Mallet Street police station. A uniformed constable was posted at the door.

'I'll dictate the formula.'

Fiske picked up the 'Bic' supplied by a benevolent state.

Against Wycliffe's advice Fiske had refused to call a solicitor and had insisted on making a statement which he would write himself. He began to write, apparently calm, pausing now and then over the choice of a word.

During his years in the force Kersey had seen many men driven into that last corner, finally convinced that no amount of lying or twisting will save them from the dock. At that point the professional stops talking and waits for his lawyer. Others react according to temperament. The resigned shrug and say, 'You can't win 'em all!', the optimists sing their little heads off to buy goodwill, others simply deflate. Kersey had expected Fiske to deflate but he bounced.

After the scene in his study he seemed to accept trial and conviction as inevitable and, scared as he undoubtedly was, he was even more concerned to establish that what he had done had required courage, imagination and resource. If he had to go to gaol, everyone would know that it was for a crime cleverly conceived and skilfully executed but dogged by ill-luck. He would be in the books.

'He should have saved it for the newspapers,' Kersey said.

At half-past ten Wycliffe was in one of the little

cubicles of the incident-van, reading a photostat of Fiske's statement – all twelve sheets of it. To begin with it was both legible and coherent but as he turned the pages legibility, coherence and even relevance suffered. Which might do Fiske some good. In the hands of a clever counsel and a pliant psychiatrist it could provide the germ of a plea of diminished responsibility. They wouldn't get away with it but it might temper the mood of judge and jury.

Wycliffe growled to himself, 'Not my affair!'

The telephone rang.

'Wycliffe.'

'It's me.' Helen, his wife. 'Is it all over?'

'All over, I shall be home inside the hour.'

He left the van, feeling deflated. Falcon Street was deserted and it was still drizzling rain. Before going to his car he walked the few steps to Paul's Court, through the archway and into the Court. The wet cobbles gleamed in the lamplight. Willy Goppel's house was in darkness; Natalie was at her club. There were lights in the Wards' and the Fiskes'. As he crossed the Court he was aware of a still figure on the Hedleys' verandah and he could hear, faintly, the sound of a piano. He went up the steps to the Fiskes' front door and rang the bell.

He had arranged for a policewoman to keep Mrs Fiske company until she had made other arrangements or felt able to be left on her own. But it was Mrs Fiske who answered the door and he was immediately aware of a new briskness in her manner.

'Oh, Mr Wycliffe! I'm afraid I sent your young woman away. It was kind of you to arrange it but, as I told Mrs Ward, Marty and I will manage very well on our own.'

'You are sure?'

'Oh yes, quite sure, but thank you for coming.' She stood, holding the door only partly open, 'I don't want

206

to be rude but Marty and I are having a late supper – a little treat for him; he's had such an upsetting day. I'm sure you'll understand . . . '

'Of course! I'll say good-night, then.'

'Good-night, Mr Wycliffe, good-night.'

The door closed before he reached the bottom of the steps.

THE END

WYCLIFFE AND THE BEALES

The Family

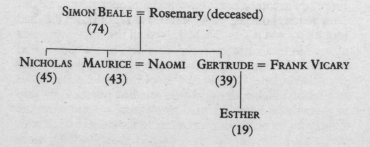

SIMON BEALE = Rosemary (deceased)
(74)

NICHOLAS   MAURICE = NAOMI   GERTRUDE = FRANK VICARY
(45)   (43)   (39)

                                    ESTHER
                                    (19)

Also EDWARD Simon's nephew by marriage
(21)

CHAPTER ONE

Bunny Newcombe must have had a proper first name but
even contemporaries who had been at school with him had
forgotten what it was. He had lived all the forty-four years
of his life in a cottage on the outskirts of the village and
for several months, since the death of his mother, he had
lived there alone. On leaving school Bunny had started out
as a rabbit catcher but myxomatosis had put an early stop
to that and so he had drifted into casual work around the
village and on neighbouring farms. In the weeks and months
following his mother's death he had grown to look more
and more like a tramp, his skin had acquired a smooth
patina of ingrained dirt and he was rarely seen without a
greyish stubble on his chin and upper lip. Recently, too,
he had shown less interest in getting work and this had led
to the belief that his mother must have left him some
money.

Bunny knew and was known to everybody but he had
no close friends; he spent his evenings at the village
pub where he was as much at home as the landlord, and
the last evening of his life was passed like any other.
He sat in his corner near the bar, drank his usual ration
then, at a little before half-past ten, he emptied his final
glass, wiped his lips with the back of his hand, and got
to his feet. He was rarely drunk but by this time of night
he had had enough.

''Night all!'

A chorus of good-nights followed by a general laugh.
Bunny was tolerated; a kind of mascot. He was barely five
feet four in height with the proportions of a barrel.

7

He walked with deliberate, waddling steps to the door and out into the night.

Outside, he paused to accustom himself to the relative darkness and to the fresh, moist moorland air, then he crossed the Green, passed the tall iron gates of Ashill, and turned off to his right down a narrow lane which had the high brick wall of Ashill estate on one side and trees on the other. Although it was a clear night with a half-moon, it was dark under the trees but his steps never faltered and he plodded on like a tired old horse returning to stable.

Bunny rarely indulged in abstract thought and by late evening he was incapable of much organized thinking of any sort; his consciousness was sufficiently engaged with present sensations, with random samples from a rag-bag of memories, and with vague anticipatory longings and resolves. At this present moment he was thinking that he wanted to pee, that it would be a relief to get his boots off and drop into bed, that nobody had ever made a rabbit pie to equal his mother's.

But as a background to these immediate preoccupations his mood was euphoric; Bunny was convinced of a future very different from the past, a feeling which he summed up in the words, 'I'll show the bastards!' And these words he muttered to himself from time to time like a charm.

Another couple of hundred yards and he came to Quarry House, an oddly elegant little house where the Gould sisters lived – twins in their late thirties, who dressed alike and held themselves aloof from the villagers. Bunny, stung by the memory of a recent encounter, muttered again, 'I'll show the bastards!'

From this point he could hear the steady, muffled roar of the waterfall in the grounds of Ashill; a sound which had provided a constant background to his whole life from that very instant when his ears had first opened to the world about him.

Not far from the Goulds' house there was a seat, dating from a time when the parish council had shown a passing interest in the lane. It was too dark to see the seat or anyone

8

on it at all clearly but he could hear whisperings and chucklings. He called out, 'You watch yourself, Nancy Gratton, or you'll need re-bushing before you drag 'im into church!'

A boy's voice came out of the darkness, clear and without rancour, 'Get 'ome you ol' flea-bag an' mind your own business!'

From that point the lane descended more steeply, its surface broken by winter frosts and scoured by rains. A few more yards and, clear of the trees, he could see his own cottage, its whitewashed walls standing out in the moonlight.

He unlatched the gate, which screeched on its hinges, and entered the yard. Small scuffling noises came from rabbit hutches against one wall and he said aloud, 'Goodnight, my beauties!' He lowered the flap on the hen house where the birds had gone to roost, attended to his own needs in an outside privy, then let himself into the cottage by the back door. He passed through a lean-to scullery to the kitchen in almost total darkness but there he struck a match and lit a candle he had left standing on a corner of the table. The scene came to flickering life: the big square table littered with saucepans, dishes, cans, bottles and packets; a dresser with only a few oddments of china left on the shelves; a window with a curtain dragged across it, sagging in the middle.

Bunny had an uncomfortable moment as it occurred to him what his mother would have said and done had she come back to find such squalor. But his mother would never come back – she couldn't; she was dead. Bunny bolstered his ego with another 'I'll show the bastards!' Then he took the candle and, holding it high in front of him, climbed the steep, narrow stairs. As his head came above the level of the upper floor he experienced a vicious jab of stunning pain which shot through his skull; he lost consciousness, staggered, and fell backwards down the stairs. In falling, life deserted the little fat man and there began at once those complex changes which would ultimately restore his body to Mother Earth. Bunny had died in the cottage where he had been born and where he had spent the forty-four years of his relatively untroubled existence.

Another balmy spring day, with Nature propagating in indecent haste. Wycliffe and his wife had spent most of their weekend in the vegetable garden, for this was the year when Helen had made up her mind on self-sufficiency in vegetables and soft fruit. Given a completely free hand she might have acquired an adjoining field and extended her activities to include a goat or two, even a Dexter cow; but he set the limit of animal husbandry at one fastidious and condescending cat who considered that he contributed more than his share to the commonwealth merely by being there.

Now it was Monday morning but Wycliffe found that the feeling of mellow tranquillity lingered, though his hands were scratched and galled. It was the slim file of weekend reports and the little bundle of inter-office memoranda on his desk which seemed unreal. He had difficulty in concentrating his attention; his eyes kept straying to the window where he could glimpse the tops of silver birch trees on the far side of the highway, their leaves breaking out in a greenish haze against the blue of the sky.

It was not long since he had refused to be considered for the post of Deputy Chief Constable, soon to fall vacant. He had no regrets; the job would have cut him off from the kind of police work which gave him most satisfaction, and saddled him with more administration, which he loathed. But the fact remained, he was now at the top of his particular tree, and there he would stay for the rest of his career in the force. There was something definitive and final about the thought which made him vaguely depressed whenever it entered his mind.

Back to reality – reality in the shape of reports of all serious or potentially serious crime in the two counties. A quiet weekend, nothing to get worked up about: a couple of muggings, but against that, the mugger had been caught;

half-a-dozen break-ins, a 'domestic' involving GBH . . .' He turned to his mail but the telephone rang. 'Wycliffe.'

Information Room reporting a 999-call from a member of the public in the village of Washford: 'A chap known as Bunny Newcombe has been found dead in his cottage where he lived alone. The village postman found him; he's been shot through the head. No weapon at the scene.'

'A shot-gun wound?'

'Not according to the postman, who seems to know what he's talking about.'

'You've notified Newton sub-division?'

'Mr Kersey is on his way to Washford now, sir.'

Kersey, newly appointed detective inspector, was beginning his apprenticeship out in the sticks as senior CID officer in a large rural sub-division based on the market town of Newton. After fifteen years as a city 'jack' he was now finding out what it was like to live with straw in his hair.

Half-an-hour later Information Room called again. Kersey had confirmed the report by radio and requested assistance in what he believed to be a murder inquiry.

Wycliffe gave routine instructions; there was no need for him to be involved at this stage but on such a morning the office was poor competition. He called in his personal assistant: 'I shall be in Washford if you want me, Diane.'

Diane looked reproachfully at the unopened mail and at the little pile of inter-departmental memoranda. 'When will you be back?'

'I've no idea!' He said it with the bravado of a rebellious schoolboy.

Washford was twenty miles away in a fold of the southern moor, a village of granite and slate which looked as though it had grown out of the moor itself and, in a sense, it had. The centre of the village was the Green, bordered by the pub, the school, the church, and Ashill – home of the Beale family. A single street bisected the village, known as North Street above, and South Street below, the Green.

Wycliffe drove up South Street from the Newton road and

parked with other cars near the church and under the beeches which fringed the Green. One of the parked vehicles was a police patrol car and there was an officer on radio watch. Opposite the church a smug Regency house with an ironwork balcony was set back behind a high wall and only visible through tall wrought-iron gates.

As Wycliffe got out of his car his first impression was of silence; the village had a *Marie Celeste* air. He had grown up in such a village – not in the West Country, but where the Black Mountains trail their skirts over the Welsh border into Herefordshire, and what he remembered most about his village was this silent stillness. Then he heard the shrill voice of a woman teacher through the open windows of the nearby school; a little later he became aware of the stream which slid swiftly by in its culvert with a continuous ripple of sound, and now and again came the 'ping' of a shop door bell.

The constable on radio watch directed him: 'Down the lane by Ashill, sir. You pass a funny little house on your right; keep on for another couple of hundred yards and you come to a cottage – a tumbled-down sort of place – you'll find Mr Kersey there, sir.'

'Isn't Ashill the Beales' place?'

'That's right, sir. Simon, the old man, lives there with all the family as far as I know.'

Beales' Household Stores, an old-established family business with branches in several towns. A few years back, the firm had taken on a new lease of life with the complete rebuilding of their store in the city centre and the opening of several cash-and-carry depots strategically scattered over the two counties. Wycliffe had met old Simon a couple of times at civic soirées.

Unknowing, Wycliffe followed in the footsteps of Bunny Newcombe. He had the high wall of Ashill gardens on his right and a screen of beeches on his left; the trees arched overhead, filtering the sunlight. He could hear the rippling of the stream close at hand and the more distant sound of a waterfall or mill race. Where the wall came to an end there was a small pink house with white woodwork and dormer windows – like a doll's house – with *Quarry House* on the gate. To that point the lane was well surfaced and maintained, but beyond, it degenerated into a rutted track, fatal to the suspension of any vehicle less robust than a farm tractor. But the while walls of Newcombe's cottage were in sight.

The cottage must certainly have been recorded in the doomsday book of some council official as 'sub-standard' or, more probably, 'unfit for human habitation'. No electricity, no piped water, no proper sanitation, not even a road . . . Its whitewashed walls supported a roof where thatch had been replaced by corrugated asbestos, itself now green with moss. The backyard, with its collection of rural junk, reminded Wycliffe of the backyards of his childhood; a rusting milk-churn, part of a chain-harrow, a broken cartwheel and the inevitable mangle . . . with nettles growing up through it all. There was a sentry-box privy, and a hen-house in which the hens clucked in protest against their confinement; there were hutches where rabbits shuffled and thumped, demanding to be fed . . . Somebody would have to see to the livestock.

Kersey was standing at the door of the cottage with a uniformed constable. A plank on bricks had been laid across the yard to avoid disturbing or effacing traces which the killer had almost certainly not left.

'The local GP has certified death,' Kersey said. 'He didn't have much option. Now we're waiting for the pathologist. This is PC Miller, sir, community officer for the sub-section.'

A constable with several years' service and a soft tongue to turn away wrath; immaculately turned out, shop-window of the force.

'Let's have a look.'

The lean-to with its stone sink and pump, then the kitchen, so dimly lit that he had to wait for his eyes to accommodate; a sickly smell of decaying food and a buzzing of bluebottles; a littered table, a dresser with remnants of crockery on its shelves, a cooking range and a few kitchen chairs. Newcombe's body lay in a heap at the foot of stairs which led to the rooms above. His eyes were open and glazed over; his cap had fallen off and was lying on the floor. He was almost bald and the whiteness of his scalp contrasted oddly with the weather-tan and grime on his forehead and face. The wound of entry was neat and round but the bullet must have torn its way out. A hand-gun, fired at fairly close range. Odd, that! When rural tensions explode into shooting the weapon is almost always a shot-gun. And this little man who looked like a tramp – why would anyone want to shoot him anyway?

Wycliffe had no idea of the trouble he would have, finding an answer to that one. He returned to the backyard, to Kersey and the constable.

'I gather the postman found him?'

Kersey nodded. 'Newcombe didn't have much post but whenever the postman did call he would find him here in the yard, feeding his rabbits. This morning, with the hens still shut up and nobody about he wondered if Bunny had been taken ill, so he opened the door and called out.'

'The door wasn't locked?'

'No, but that doesn't mean much, they don't go in for locking up round here, apparently.'

People hadn't locked their doors in Wycliffe's village either.

'Of course the postman went in and found him.'

Wycliffe turned to the constable. 'Do you know anything of the dead man?'

Miller was flicking whitewash off his uniform with a handkerchief. 'I knew him pretty well, sir. He was the village odd-job man but he hasn't done much lately – not since his mother died. Occasionally he would lend Sammy Pugh a hand in his scrap yard down on the Newton road. Sammy is a rogue; he was nicked for receiving a couple of years back and I wouldn't put it past Newcombe to turn a dishonest penny if he got the chance, but nothing on any scale; nothing organized.'

14

'Yet somebody shot him.'

Wycliffe got a cautious sidelong glance from the constable. 'Yes, somebody did, sir, but I can't think who would want to or why.'

'Any relatives or close friends you know of who should be told?'

Miller eased the strap of his helmet. 'The only relative I know of is an aunt – a Mrs Fretwell, she's the wife of our local builder and undertaker and I think she's his father's sister. As to friends, I don't think he had any; he was a loner.'

Wycliffe said, 'See his aunt and make sure she knows what's happening. Ask her if there are any other relatives.'

A sound of cars further up the lane and a little later Sergeant Smith arrived with his photographic gear and three detectives from Wycliffe's headquarters squad. Dr Franks, the pathologist, followed almost at once.

Franks, bald and shiny as ever, greeted Wycliffe with his usual bonhomie and was taken into the kitchen.

'God! This place stinks. I can't do much with him here, that's for sure.'

He waited while Smith took a series of shots from different angles then made his preliminary examination.

'Not much I can tell you, Charles, that you can't see for yourself. He was shot, probably at a couple of feet, with a hand-gun; the bullet passed through his head carrying with it some of his brains and making a mess on the stairs. He's been dead between twelve and fifteen hours, I should think.'

Franks looked about for somewhere to wash his hands and finding nowhere wiped them on a white linen handkerchief. 'Of course, other features may turn up in the course of the P.M. but who wants other features with a hole in the head?'

Franks retreated into the yard and the sunshine and looked around with acute distaste. 'The amenities of rural life I can do without, Charles. Be a good chap and get him over to me sharpish; I had plans for today.'

15

Kersey said, 'The van is here; the driver managed to back up off the Newton road. I only hope he can get away again without busting his back axle.'

Soon Newcombe's body would be taken away to be subjected to the final indignity of a post mortem. His cottage would be searched from top to bottom; surfaces carrying several months' accumulation of dust would be meticulously examined for prints and, suddenly, a dead match, a cigarette end or a muddy footprint could acquire absurd importance. Detectives would tramp around the village questioning people about Bunny's habits, his foibles and his vices, his friends and his enemies – like journalists ferreting out the private life of a Royal. All this for a little fat man who had been of no importance whatever while he lived.

Sometimes, in a mood of disillusionment, Wycliffe saw the whole routine as macabre. The protection of Society – that was what it was about; not about the little man who never washed and had lived in squalor with only his rabbits and chickens for company. He had no more importance dead than alive except as a pointer to his killer.

Franks said, 'I'll be off then.' He went out of the yard, leaving the gate open, and a minute or two later they heard the roar of his Porsche as the wheels skidded on the rutted surface. The incongruous row died away and Kersey said, 'Are you staying, sir?'

'For the present.' He felt irritable and wondered why; then he realized that he was offended by Frank's boisterous professionalism – really by his total lack of interest in the dead man who, as far as Franks was concerned, was just another carcass to be probed and dissected. Complete detachment; a job of work. But wasn't that the proper, the correct attitude? All the same . . .

Newcombe was carried away on a stretcher, enveloped in a polythene sheet. His body was placed in the van and the van edged off down the lane, bumping over the ground and bouncing on its suspension. Exit Bunny Newcombe; the work could begin. Two men began to search the yard for those unconsidered trifles which are supposed to be the

16

stuff of evidence. Wycliffe stood in the kitchen; he noticed that both drawers of the dresser were open and their contents had been scattered on the floor. Did this mean that someone had searched the place or that Newcombe had become irritated when looking for something he couldn't find?

There was a parlour on the ground floor which Wycliffe had not yet seen; he went in and, to his surprise, found it perfectly habitable – evidently as Bunny's mother had left it, except for dust. The chiffonier, like the dresser in the kitchen, had its drawers open, though their contents had not been tumbled on to the floor. There were photographs on the walls: two sepia prints on glass of seaside scenes in red-plush frames, and a large photograph in a black frame of a plump young man with a Charlie Chaplin moustache. He stood beside a good-looking girl who was seated; she wore a two-piece costume and a high-crowned hat. Bunny's parents?

One picture was missing, though the nail on which it had hung was there, so was the rectangular patch of wall-paper less faded than the rest. Wycliffe found the frame and the broken glass on the floor, apparently kicked aside, but the picture itself was not there. Oddly, the hanging cord was intact so it had not fallen from the wall.

A little window with net curtains looked out on a wilderness which had once been a garden. There were apple trees smothered in blossom, their trunks and boughs encrusted with grey-green lichens, and the grass and nettles were waist high.

Newcombe, it seemed, had been the village jack-of-all-trades. In the past every village had one, just as every village had an idiot; an obliging girl who, for greater convenience, wore no knickers; and a tough guy who had spent a few months in gaol for beating somebody up . . . But such people do not get themselves shot – or, if by some mischance they do, then the weapon is a shot-gun and there is no mystery about it.

Wycliffe returned to the kitchen; this was where

17

Newcombe had squatted since his mother's death; as a tramp squats in a cave, a deserted hut, or under a bridge. He had continued to sleep upstairs, for there were no signs of bed or bedding in the kitchen, but in time he would, no doubt, have contracted his world to the compass of this single room, and the rest of the house would have ceased to have any meaning for him. Wycliffe could not explain this need to encapsulate, to concentrate one's resources and responsibilities, though he could imagine something of the kind happening to him if he were ever left quite alone.

At any rate he was intrigued, and he poked around the smelly, squalid room with more than professional interest.

Finally he climbed the stairs which still bore sinister evidence of the manner of Bunny's end. There were two rooms upstairs, separated by a thin wooden partition, papered over. Here, too, one of the rooms – the front one with a large brass bedstead, was habitable while the other, little more than a cupboard, was just big enough for a single bed. Yet it was here that Newcombe must have slept; the pile of tumbled and grimy bedding testified to that. There were no drawers or cupboards in the smaller room but in the larger one part of the contents of both wardrobe and chest-of-drawers had been turned out in heaps on the floor.

The impression of a search was inescapable but Wycliffe was unconvinced; the evidence had a contrived look, as though someone in a hurry had wanted to convey the idea that a search had been made.

He stood on the little landing, where he could see into both rooms. Bunny's mother, like his own, had had a fondness for framed photographs and there were four or five hanging on the walls of the larger room. One of them could have been of Bunny – a leaner Bunny, at fifteen or sixteen. He was reminded of the empty frame and broken glass on the floor downstairs; that too seemed to have something deliberate and contrived about it. Was he imagining things?

Heavy footsteps on the stairs, and DC Fowler's grey head emerged from the stairwell. 'Is it all right to start up here, sir?' Fowler looked with distaste into the cubby-hole where Newcombe had slept. Wycliffe left him to it and went downstairs, out into the yard. More of his men had arrived and Kersey was briefing them for inquiries in the village. They were being watched by a fair girl in a pink, short-sleeved dress; she was looking over the low wall which separated Newcombe's place from the woods belonging to Ashill.

Wycliffe went over to her. 'Do you want to tell us something?'

She looked at him, her face serenely solemn. 'No.'

'Do you mind telling me who you are?'

'My name is Vicary – Esther Vicary. I live in the house.' She nodded vaguely in the direction of Ashill house. 'Have they ransacked the cottage?'

'Who are *they*?'

'Whoever killed him.'

There was something unreal about the girl; her features and her complexion were perfect yet totally lacking in animation so that one had the impression of a beautiful mask.

'What makes you think the cottage might have been ransacked?'

'I wondered. The villagers pretend to believe that his mother left him a lot of money – you know the sort of thing, hidden under the mattress or up the chimney.'

'You say they pretend to believe – don't they really think she had money?'

'No. They say these things to make it more interesting but somebody might have thought it was true. I can't think of any other reason for killing him.'

She was eighteen or nineteen, older than he had first supposed, self-possessed and cool, yet somehow childish; an odd blend of sophistication and naïvety. She spoke slowly and with a precision of enunciation which matched the perfection of her features but without emphasis and without expression. Helen would probably have spotted that her dress came out of the Laura Ashley stable;

19

Wycliffe thought it had an old-fashioned charm so that she looked like a figure from an Impressionist painting.

He was puzzled by her. 'You knew Newcombe well?'

'I've known him all my life.' Unexpectedly she went on: 'Do you want someone to look after his rabbits and chickens?'

'Will you do it?'

'I don't mind for a day or two; I'll come back this afternoon, when I've changed.'

'Have you ever been inside the cottage?'

'I used to go there quite often when his mother was alive but I haven't been there since. I expect it's in a state now.'

'Do you remember the photographs on the wall in the parlour?'

'Not especially. I know there was a big one of his father and mother. Emily was very proud of it.'

'Emily?'

'That was his mother's name – I used to call her by it because she worked at Ashill and everybody used her first name.'

Wycliffe persisted. 'There were three other photographs on that wall; two were seaside scenes in red-plush frames, the third had an oak frame with a gilt border – do you remember that one?'

'I'm afraid not – why?'

'It's not important.'

She went off and Wycliffe watched her go.

The girl intrigued him; she had the slim asexuality of girls in Egyptian tomb paintings yet he caught himself imagining her nude: small, hard buttocks, slim boyish hips, tiny breasts. . . . Then he felt guilty because a Methodist upbringing still laid claim to his conscience. He could not make her out: sophisticated yet naïve; sexy yet sexless; detached yet apparently concerned . . . enigmatic, that was the word.

Smith brought him back to earth. 'We've found the cartridge-case, sir, and Edwards has dug the bullet out of the lath and plaster at the top of the stairs. Nine-millimetre

Parabellum; a foreigner — Italian, I think.'

Which might tell ballistics something about the gun which fired it. Occasionally scratches on the cartridge-case made by the ejector mechanism will identify the breed of gun. In any case there was a routine response: 'Check the register and bring in any nine-millimetre automatics. Start with this sub-division and see how we go.'

There wouldn't be many; a nine-millimetre is a weapon for professionals — soldiers, policemen and hit-men.

His detectives had finished in the yard so he released the hens who rushed about madly, clucking and pecking, unable to come to terms with their belated freedom. He found an old oil-drum half-full of corn and scattered some for them.

The boundary wall where he had seen and talked to the girl was low in one place with flat stones built in to form a crude stile. He climbed up, standing on the wall; the sound of the waterfall seemed louder, but all he could see was a path disappearing into the trees, oaks and beeches being shouldered out by burgeoning sycamores.

He called to Dixon who was working in the lean-to, 'Tell Mr Kersey I'll see him later,' and dropped down on the other side of the wall. The path was overgrown but easily passable and after following it for a hundred yards he came out of the trees to a clearing which had been planted with rhododendrons and laurels, now running wild. On his left, a scrub-covered slope led down to a large pool, almost a lake, in what had once been a quarry; and ahead of him, from yet higher ground, the waterfall plunged out of a clump of trees to drop thirty feet or more to the pool. Although the volume of water was probably not large, the fall was impressive. A zig-zag path, broken by occasional steps, led up from the clearing to a little pavilion in oriental style which bridged the stream at the point where it plunged over the edge, and there was a verandah which actually projected over the fall. A spot of chinoiserie in landscaping, which looked as though it had been lifted whole from a willow-pattern plate. A folly almost certainly ante-dating the Beales.

He climbed the zig-zag path by the waterfall. From the top the way led on, presumably to the house, but on his left was the faded, red-painted door of the little pavilion. Out of curiosity he tried the handle and the door opened. The building consisted of a single room, furnished with a large table, three or four wicker chairs, a sofa which had once been upholstered in red plush, and a number of cupboards built against one wall. A latticed window and another door opened on to the verandah. A novel summer house.

Dead leaves which must have blown in were scattered on the floor and there was dust everywhere. Faded photographs cut from *Picture Post* were stuck to the walls. He crossed the room and went through the second door to the verandah. It was an odd sensation to look over the low balustrade along the gleaming sheet of water, down to the foaming arc where it hit the surface of the pool. He was startled by the feeling of vertigo which gripped him, quite disproportionate to the drop, and he turned away with a sense of relief. He left the pavilion and continued along the path following the bank of a now placid stream until he came to a high brick wall on his right, ivy-covered, with a tall gate of slatted wood. Through the slats he could see into a well-kept garden with flowering shrubs and grassy paths.

It took him a moment to realize that he was at the back of Quarry House, the pink-and-white dolls' house he had noticed on his way down the lane. He was peering through the gate when a sun-hat emerged from the shrubbery and, beneath it, a woman with a secateurs in her hand.

Wycliffe said, 'Good morning.'

Hesitation. 'Are you a policeman?' She was lean and freckled with reddish hair and, despite the floppy sun-hat, she wore trousers and a mannish jersey. Her manner was abrasive – at least suspicious. Males are unpredictable creatures. Handle with care.

Wycliffe introduced himself.

She mellowed at once. 'Dear me! I had no idea that horrid little man would cause such a stir!' She opened the gate to let him in and, peeling off a gardening glove, held out a

22

thin, aristocratic hand. 'I'm Rose Gould and I live here with my twin sister, Veronica.'

Since daddy died, Wycliffe thought. He said, 'Obviously you know that your neighbour was killed last night; I wonder if either you or your sister heard the shot?'

She went to the back door, which stood open, and called, 'Veronica! Will you come here, please?' Then she turned back to Wycliffe with a shy smile, 'My sister is much better at talking to people than I. More practical.'

The woman who came out of the house was a carbon copy of Rose except that she was not wearing a sun hat. Rose prattled: 'The likeness is remarkable, isn't it? But you can tell us apart because Vee has an old scar just above her right eye.'

'Which you put there,' Veronica had a deeper voice as well as a scar.

'Yes, I know, dear, but not deliberately.' Rose blushed, the colour flooding up over her freckles. 'The superintendent was asking about the shot we heard last night.'

'We don't know that it was a shot; it could have been anything – all we heard was a sharp crack.'

'What time was this?'

Veronica said, 'When we were going to bed – between a quarter to eleven and eleven o'clock.'

'Did you notice anything else yesterday evening? Anyone going up or down the lane, for example?'

'Did we, dear?' Rose looked at Veronica.

Veronica shook her head. 'No, I don't think so. I do remember seeing Newcombe on his way to the public house but there was certainly nothing unusual in that.'

'Why didn't you like him?'

'Did we not?' Veronica was on her dignity.

'Your sister spoke of him as "a horrid little man".'

'Oh, did she! Well, he was. As long as his mother lived she kept control of him; he was reasonably dressed, clean and polite. Though I never liked the man I can't say that he ever gave us cause for complaint.'

'And since?'

Rose was unable to resist cutting in. 'Since, he's behaved abominably. Whenever he passes here, if one of us happens to be in the front garden, he laughs.'

'Laughs?'

'Well, he sneers and calls out in a most unpleasant way. I try not to be out there when he passes. In fact, if it had been left to me, I should have spoken to Constable Miller about him long ago.'

Veronica was contemptuous. 'I don't need Miller to put Newcombe in his place!'

Wycliffe said, 'The path from his cottage to the waterfall doesn't seem to be much used.'

Veronica frowned. 'It shouldn't be used at all; in fact, it shouldn't be there. Newcombe used to treat the woods as though they were his – setting snares and traps – until the family put a stop to it.'

'The family?'

'The Beales.'

'What about the path I came by from the waterfall here – I suppose that leads on to the house?'

He was aware of a sudden slight tension in Veronica's manner; she said in an off-hand way, 'Oh, that's quite different; it's a perfectly legitimate path – private, of course.'

'But where does it go?'

'As you say – to the house.' Brusque.

One of the odd features of police work: one never knows when some innocent probe will touch an exposed nerve and, if it does, whether it has anything to do with the case.

He changed the subject. 'I know the Beales live at Ashill but how many of them are there? Who exactly lives there?' He asked the question in a relaxed, conversational way.

Rose said, 'Oh, there are—'

Veronica cut in, 'They're a very united family. Of course, the fact that they are Roman Catholic helps but it's still quite remarkable to find a family staying together as they have in these days . . . There's Mr Simon, the head of the family; he's a widower; his two sons, one of whom is married and

24

lives there with his wife. Then there is his daughter – Mrs Vicary – she lives there with her husband and *their* daughter, Esther.' She broke off with a little laugh. 'Have I forgotten any of them?'

Rose said, 'Edward—'

'Oh, yes—Edward. He is Mr Simon's nephew by marriage; he's a young man now but he's been there since he was a child – he was orphaned, I think.'

Wycliffe said, 'Quite a family! And, as you say, unusual in these days with them all continuing to live under one roof.'

He thanked the sisters and told them he would send someone to take their statements about the probable time of the shot.

It was absurd for a chief super to be on the ground touting for evidence; his men would visit every house in the village and in neighbouring villages if necessary. With their clip-boards and ball-points they would gather a great mass of mostly useless information which would be typed, photocopied and filed. Eventually he would be presented with a lovely fat file of his own which he could turn over in the privacy of his office or anywhere else he fancied. But he disliked pre-packed, sterilized information almost as much as he disliked pre-packed, sterilized food. It had no taste.

Rose let him out by the garden gate, the way he had come. He continued through the trees, crossed the lawn, walked round the house and out through the tall iron gates without being challenged; as far as he knew, without being seen.

So it was possible that the killer had left Newcombe's cottage by way of the hedge and the footpath through the wood, but why would he want to?

A police incident van had arrived and was parked not far from the gates of Ashill, opposite the church. It would serve as a communication centre and as a base for his men working on the case. The duty officer was DC Potter – the squad's fat boy, known to intimates as The Pot. Potter was settling in, getting organized. On the table there was a duty book

25

and a number of neatly labelled files; on the wall, a two-and-a-half-inch Ordnance map of Washford and district.

Wycliffe looked upon it all with a critical eye and was satisfied.

'Have you had your lunch, Potter?'

'Over at the pub, sir.'

'Any good?'

'I had a chicken curry – very nice, sir, and the beer's good.'

The pub was a 'free house' and not tarted up; no bar stools, no rustic tables, no phoney wrought-iron sconces, horse-brasses or flint-lock pistols; only benches and tables cut in the local saw mill a century ago and polished by generations of backsides and forearms. The room was L-shaped and the smaller leg was separated from the rest by a low rail with a gate and a notice: 'For customers taking meals.'

It was almost two and the few local workers who had been in for a quick drink had gone again leaving only Wycliffe and two old men who were dressed alike in black jackets and caps and grey, baggy trousers. They seemed content to sit, staring into space, exchanging only occasional laconic remarks. Too late for the main dish, Wycliffe ordered a meat pie and a pint.

Harry Blatchford, the landlord, must have been over seventy himself; a large man with a high colour, bald except for a halo of tight grey curls. He had the local brogue but spoke more correctly than most of his customers for he had been a sales-rep for a firm of agricultural merchants before taking over the inn from his parents. A fat, pleasant-faced young woman with a mop of brown hair was busy washing glasses.

'There's nothing much I can tell you, superintendent. Last night was the same as any other. Bunnys at there in his corner from about seven on; he had his usual, then about half-ten, he left. Same as always.'

'But last night somebody was waiting for him at his cottage, with a gun.'

26

'So they tell me, though it beats me why anybody would want to shoot Bunny. They tell me it was a hand-gun?'

'An automatic pistol.'

Blatchford spread his great hands in a gesture of incomprehension. 'As I say, it beats me.'

'Perhaps you would have been a good deal less surprised if it had been a shot-gun?'

Wycliffe received a cunning look. 'I didn't say that, sir; you mustn't put words into my mouth.'

'I gather he wasn't popular with some of the women in the village.'

'Ah! I wouldn't know about that, sir; we don't have much woman talk in here, do we, Dora?'

The fat girl said, 'I couldn't tell you; I never have time to listen.'

Wycliffe was eating his pie at a little table near the bar. He took time to finish it off and sipped his beer.

'You've known Newcombe a long time?'

'All his life. I've always lived here; this pub belonged to my father and his father before him – way back. Of course I knew Bunny's father and mother. His father died youngish – a heart attack when he was out giving a hand in the hayfield one evening. It was the year myxo was so bad with dead and dying rabbits everywhere. Bunny's mother died only this last Christmas – a stroke – popped off just like that. She was a Truscott from Buckfast way – Emily Truscott.' Blatchford chuckled. 'Emily was a strong-minded woman and no mistake! She kept her son on the straight and narrow. I've heard him say in this bar that the old lady would smack his face when he stepped out of line almost up to the day she died.'

'Did he wash then?'

'Had to! She was quite capable of standing him up in the yard starkers and throwing buckets of water over him. And he had to do a day's work. He'd come in here of an evening for a pint but he'd sup up and go. Emily wouldn't have him spending his time and money in here drinking.'

One of the old men who had seemed not to be listening

27

said, 'Bunny liked the women. I mind there were that there maid over to Shipley – '

Blatchford cut him short. 'God, Tom! You're going back a bit; he couldn't 've been more than eighteen or nineteen then.'

Wycliffe said, 'I gather he's got an aunt in the village.'

The landlord folded his huge arms on the counter. 'That's right, sir. Martha Fretwell; she's his father's sister – married to Jim Fretwell, our undertaker. They live up the top of North Street. I reckon Martha had a soft spot for her nephew; he used to drop in there pretty often.'

Wycliffe drained his glass and prepared to leave. 'Newcombe had money to spend, apparently, but he doesn't seem to have earned much lately. Do you think—'

Blatchford laughed. 'You've been listening to tales about Emily's old stocking. She might've left him a few pounds but nothing to write home about. If the old lady had money I don't know where she got it; Bunny's father was a gardener for the Beales and he did a bit of rabbiting on the side; Emily worked at Ashill, too. She was a maid there before she married and afterwards she worked there part-time all the way through up to a couple of years before she died.'

Wycliffe said, 'What's that to do with her having or not having money?'

A broad grin. 'Just that nobody ever made anything working for the Beales. There's a saying in the village – "They wouldn' give 'ee the skin of a rotten tatie." '

Wycliffe thanked him. 'I expect I'll be back.'

'I reckon you will, sir.'

At the door Wycliffe stopped to read an advertisement stuck to the wall, a poster in an antique format announcing Washford Horse and Hiring Fair, to be held on May Day – the following Friday.

The landlord said, 'Have you ever been to our Fair, sir?'

'Never.'

'You don't know what you've missed. Takes you back; a touch of the old nostalgia.'

He made it sound like rheumatism.

CHAPTER TWO

The village drowsed in afternoon sunshine; in school, children were singing *Bobby Shafto*. Wycliffe strolled up the main street in the leisurely fashion of a tourist. On one side a moorland stream slid by in its cobbled channel, bridged outside each front door by a single slab of granite. On the other side of the street, interspersed with the houses, were three or four shops: Samuel Brimblecombe, Tobacconist and Confectioner; Finucane's General Store and Post Office; and a depressing little shop with tins of paint, rolls of faded wallpaper, and few plastic bowls and buckets in the window — Chas. Alford, Household and Domestic. Further up the hill there was a Methodist chapel with an impressive granite façade and another substantial building labelled simply, 'The Institute'.

The windows of the houses had their curtains almost drawn; no sign of life from any of them, though Wycliffe had a feeling that his every movement was observed. He felt a bit like the Lone Ranger entering town, the only one who doesn't know that Billy the Kid is holding up the bank.

At the top of the street the houses gave way to fields which, at no great distance, surrendered to the open moor and finally to the twin tors which, though they were not very high, dominated the horizon.

A discreet board; gold letters on a black ground: Jas. Fretwell, Builder and Undertaker; a double-fronted house, windows and door painted a gleaming black, the panes of glass shining and the curtains almost meeting. Wycliffe decided to call on Martha Fretwell. She was a dumpy little woman, grey-haired with a pink and white complexion any girl might have envied.

Wycliffe learned Bunny's first name from her: 'You've come about our Morley. PC Miller was here this morning to tell me. I couldn't believe my ears! Who could be wicked enough to do such a thing? I mean he's been a foolish boy but he never did anybody any real harm . . .' Her voice was rich and smooth as butter. Although her blue eyes misted over she could not subdue her natural cheerfulness for long. 'Come in, do!'

In the little sitting-room the polished furniture, the framed photographs, the embroidered satin cushions and plastic flowers seemed to be waiting, as a stage-set waits for the actors. Incongruously, there was a roll-top desk against one wall, for this was where the bereaved came to 'make arrangements'.

She put Wycliffe to sit in one of the uncut-moquette armchairs and sat herself on the edge of the other, smoothing the wrinkles from her skirt.

'O' course, I can't deny I been worried about him; he let himself go since Emily died, something terrible . . .' She screwed up her little mouth and lowered her voice. 'He didn't keep himself clean and he took to drinking more than was good for him and more than he could afford. I blame Emily; she ruled the poor fellow with a rod of iron when she was alive and when she went he just didn't know how to cope . . . As I say, I was worried, but I never expected anything like this! My dear life—no!'

'Did he come to see you often?'

'Two or three times a week – he always did, from the time he was a little lad. Then it was my home-made toffee, and I suppose he got into the habit. Lately he's been coming in the morning when I'm about my work but it didn't matter because he was no trouble. He'd just sit there in the kitchen; I'd make him a cup of tea and he'd stay for a quarter of an hour or so. Then, all of a sudden, he'd get up and say, "Well, I must be off, auntie!" And he'd go.'

'Did he have much to say?'

'No, Morley was no talker, but he'd listen to me rattling

on and just put in the odd word now and then.' She smiled and clasped her plump, ringed fingers in her lap.

Outside in the street the sun was shining but in this little parlour with the curtains almost meeting it was difficult to see the pictures on the walls.

'Did you visit his mother when she was alive?'

'Never!' Pursed lips. 'And Emily never set foot inside my house neither.'

'Have you noticed any change in him lately?'

'Change? What sort of change would you be meaning?' She did not wait for an answer but went on, 'I don't know, I'm sure! All I can think of is that he asked me some funny questions I couldn't make head or tail of.'

'What sort of questions?'

'Well, one day he asked me if I had a birth certificate.' She laughed girlishly. 'Well, I told him I had and he wanted to know where I got it. I said mother must've got it when I was born and she gave it to me when I got married.

'Then he wanted to know if somebody didn't have a birth certificate, could they get one, and I told him all you had to do was to go to the register office in Newton and pay them to make one out. He didn't say any more about it that day but two or three days later he wanted to know if you could get somebody else's certificate. My dear life! I was more flummoxed than ever to think what he could be after . . . I told him I didn't know but that I would ask Jim – that's my husband. He said not to do that, it didn't matter.'

'Was there any difficulty over his mother's will?'

Martha laughed. 'Will? I ask you! What would Emily be doing, making a will? She had nothing to leave but that tumbled-down old cottage and a few sticks of furniture, and who would she leave it to but Morley anyway?'

'No money?'

She screwed up her lips, pouting. 'A few pounds maybe; I'd say there most likely was, and that's what Morley's been spending on drink these past few months – but not what you'd call *money*.'

A timber lorry grinding its way up the street in low gear

31

shattered the peace of the whole village. Wycliffe waited until the unseemly racket had subsided.

'Morley's mother worked for the Beales, didn't she?'

For some reason Martha frowned before answering. 'She did; she went into service at Ashill when she was no more than fourteen and she worked there, living in, until she married my brother, Tom. Tom was their gardener. When Morley was born Emily went back there part time and she was at their beck and call one way and another till a year or two before she died. Emily thought the sun rose and set on "the family" as she called them. You'd hardly believe, but she wanted to become a Catholic and have Morley brought up Catholic, but Tom put his foot down; he was born and reared a Wesleyan like all of us and he wasn't having none of that old nonsense!'

Neither the Beales nor Emily rated highly in Martha's charts.

Wycliffe was cautious. 'Your nephew's interest in birth certificates . . . you don't think he could have had doubts about his own parentage?'

An old-fashioned look and a pause to consider how much could or should be said to the pleasant-mannered policeman who looked more like a vicar. 'I don't know, and that's the truth.' Then she added in a burst of frankness, 'I don't know neither whether he had reason. All I can say is mother and father thought our Tom should've had more sense than to marry Emily. As a girl, she was no better than she ought to be.' She smoothed the arm of her chair with the flat of her hand. 'And I don't mind telling you, because nowadays people don't think twice about such things, that it was all fixed up in a hurry because Emily was expecting.'

Wycliffe said casually, 'Simon Beale must have been a young man at that time.'

A shrewd look. 'In his late twenties. Of course his father was alive then; a real martinet he was. He wouldn't stand for no what you might call nonsense.'

'Did Simon have any brothers?'

Her expression did not change. 'No brothers, but two

32

sisters — older than he was and both dead and gone now.'

She came to the door with him and watched as he walked back down the street towards the police caravan by the church.

Three or four women were gossiping with a little red-haired man in a grey overall who stood in the doorway of the shop which sold wallpaper, Chas. Alford, Household and Domestic. They stopped talking as he went by and watched him openly, their attitudes neither friendly nor hostile. He had a feeling that the village was engaged in making up its mind about Bunny Newcombe's death and, when it had, what was said would follow the party line.

Martha Fretwell was shrewd and she had been careful not to contest the notion that Simon Beale might have got Emily pregnant. She was not averse to discrediting the Beales and Emily, even if it made a cuckold of her own brother. To Martha, and probably to the rest of the village, facts were less important than what they wanted to believe.

All the same, Simon was about the right age. But could Bunny have been fool enough to think that even if he was Simon's bastard the fact would appear on his birth certificate? In any case, was it likely that after nearly half a century Simon would settle the affair with a gun?

Kersey was waiting for him in the incident van and they sat in the little interview room, a cubicle two yards square, with a notice on the wall defining the rights of citizens under police interrogation.

Kersey, in the early stages of yet another attempt to kick the smoking habit, felt in his pocket and withdrew his hand with a lost look. He said, 'Smith checked the register for nine-millimetre automatics and there's only one in the sub-division. Property of Nicholas Beale — Simon's eldest, ex-army — a captain. The gun is a Beretta M951, the type issued as a sidearm to the Italian army in the middle fifties. It seems Beale picked it up while serving in Cyprus.'

'It's been sent for tests?'

'No, that's the point. As a matter of fact I went along to Ashill myself out of curiosity. Nicholas was out and I

33

spoke to Simon first, but Nicky turned up while I was there. He wasn't exactly matey but he made no bones about showing me where he kept the gun – a cupboard in his study – but it wasn't there. Nicked, according to him.'

'A break-in?'

'Could be. Certainly the lock of the cupboard had been forced.'

'And the first Beale knew of it was when you asked to see the gun?'

'So he says. I think you should see for yourself, sir. To me it's got a smell.'

'Anything other than the gun missing?'

'About twenty rounds, his service medals, and a few other souvenirs of the army.'

'What sort of chap is he?'

Kersey scratched his stubbly chin. 'Forty-five or six, a bachelor; stiff as a frozen haddock and about as chatty. He's hooked on the Peninsular War and spends his time re-fighting the battles with maps and what-not. The villagers call him "The General" and old Simon, who's used to lording it over people, is wary of Nicky. As a matter of fact, before he turned up I had the impression that Simon was trying to warn me of, or off him. I wondered why.'

'Does Nicholas have anything to do with the business?'

'Seems not. Brother Maurice is managing director and the old man's son-in-law, Frank Vicary, is secretary-accountant or something. Vicary started as a clerk in the office but married Gertrude, Simon's only daughter; now he's the king-pin of the show. Esther – the girl you met – is their daughter and they all live in Ashill with the rest of the clan. One big happy family, though that wasn't the impression I got.'

Kersey himself looked anything but happy, but this was due to continuing self-denial.

He went on: 'Incidentally, Maurice's wife looks a bit like an ageing pro. Out of her element, I fancy. There's also a young man called Edward. I'm not sure where he fits in but he's a painter – canvas, not walls.'

Wycliffe said, 'You must be picking up a fair amount of gossip from the house-to-house reports – what about Simon, any wild oats?'

Kersey's rubbery face wrinkled into a broad grin. 'Well, he's seventy-four, so by this time I should think they'd sprouted or gone mouldy or whatever wild oats do. There's some gossip about him when he was younger but nothing specific.'

'A week or two before he died Newcombe was showing an interest in birth certificates.'

'Whose?'

'He didn't say; his questions to his aunt were general but he brought up the subject more than once. She didn't discount the notion that he might be Simon's by-blow; his mother was a servant at Ashill and she, very conveniently, married the gardener.'

'What would he expect to find out from a birth certificate?'

'I don't know, but I gather he wasn't one of the world's brightest.'

Kersey frowned. 'Would anybody care now? Unless, of course, Newcombe was trying to get money out of the old man. If so, he waited long enough.'

'He may not have known until after his mother died or she might have stopped him from using what he did know.'

Kersey nodded. 'That's a line, sir, certainly. Anyway, The Beales are worth getting to know, if only for the experience.'

Five or six steps took them to the wrought-iron gates of Ashill, which were well preserved, as was the ironwork balcony which ran the length of the first floor (with partitions at intervals to make promiscuity more difficult or more adventurous). The house had round-headed windows and the front was stucco with a moulded cornice – very civilized and refined Regency. The door-bell was answered by a little old woman with a face as brown and wrinkled as a peach-stone, and a waspish manner.

'Police again! You'll have to come in, I suppose, and

35

I'll tell 'em you're here.'

In the hall she hesitated whether to leave them standing or take them into the drawing-room; she decided on the drawing-room. 'In here, then.'

Kersey muttered, 'I was left in the hall.'

Wycliffe spoke to the old woman, 'You must have been here in Emily Newcombe's time.'

He received a baleful glance from her little dark eyes. 'That's as maybe but I don't know anything about that son of hers if that's what you're after.' She shuffled off in her carpet slippers.

The room was dimly lit and sombre; heavy Victorian furniture upholstered in red plush, a grand piano covered with a fringed cloth, over-varnished oil-paintings of Dartmoor in heavy, gilded frames. Above the mantelpiece there was a full-length portrait of a distinguished-looking old gentleman wearing a high collar, a cut-away jacket and tight trousers. Surely Simon's grandfather, the founder of the firm. In his picture, he looked like a tenth earl but in his younger days he must have known what it was to stand under an arcade of buckets and brooms being obsequious to the right people.

The house was silent as a church; not a footstep, not a cough. Kersey whispered, 'It's like a morgue where they aren't quite dead.'

Simon came silently into the room, tall and frail-looking, silvery haired. He held out a thin hand, cold as a fish. 'Ah, Mr Wycliffe; I suppose you've come about this Newcombe business.'

Wycliffe was cool. 'I've come to talk to your son about a missing gun, registered in his name.'

The white eyebrows went up. 'Really? I thought your inspector had dealt with that earlier. However, if it's Nicholas you want to see, you had better come with me.'

They followed the old man along an L-shaped passage to the other side of the house. The interior of Ashill belied the cheerful Regency front it presented to the world: heavy, red carpeting, brown woodwork and bottle-green walls.

36

They were taken to a long room with French windows which could be opened on to the garden but were now closed. Even so, it was an oasis of sunlight in the gloomy house though, the room itself was shabby and threadbare. A couple of armchairs, a sofa, a desk, and bookshelves with the regimented spines of unused books.

Most of the space was taken up with trestle-tables on which the battlefields of the Peninsular War had been reconstructed in a combination of relief maps and coloured blocks and flags to represent fighting units. Vimiero, Rolica, Talavera . . . on to Fuentes, Vitoria and Toulouse, the names of the battles and of the generals involved were repeated on box files stacked on improvised shelves.

Simon said, in a plaintive voice, 'This used to be the library, now my son uses it for his . . . for his work.'

Nicholas was seated at the desk with maps and charts spread out before him. He got up from his chair, tall, sallow-skinned with very dark hair, he had a black moustache so meticulously trimmed that it looked false. Though thin, like his father, Nicholas had a low paunch so that, in profile, he was rather like General de Gaulle. He scarcely acknowledged Simon's introduction and did not invite them to sit down. Father and son stood facing each other for a while as though engaged in some private contest of wills, then Nicholas said, 'I suppose you want to know about my gun; I kept it in that cupboard.'

He pointed to one of two cupboards by the fireplace. 'You will see that the lock has been forced.'

It was true, the woodwork around the lock was bruised though not splintered; the damage was not conspicuous and it was evident that very little effort had been needed to force the flimsy lock.

'When did you first realize that the cupboard had been broken open?'

'When your officer came earlier and asked to see the gun.' Nicholas ignored the fact that Kersey, the officer concerned, was standing within a yard of him.

'Was anything else taken?'

'Apart from the gun and ammunition, my service medals and other souvenirs of army life.'

Nicholas moved with deliberation and his speech was precise. Wycliffe had the impression of an automaton who would go through its prescribed routine without regard to those about him. When Nicholas looked in his direction the brown eyes seemed to focus on some point beyond his head.

'When did you last see the gun?'

'I can't remember. Possibly about three weeks ago when I went to the cupboards for some papers I kept there.'

'Have you at any time seen signs of a forced entry – perhaps through the French windows, or of an intruder having been in this room?'

Simon intervened with a certain animation. 'That is exactly what I've been saying to my son. Someone came in through those windows when they had been left open. It would be quite easy—'

Nicholas answered Wycliffe's question, cutting across his father's words, 'I have never noticed any signs of an intruder.'

'Are the windows often left open?'

'Sometimes, when the weather is hot.'

'Even when there is no-one in the room?'

Nicholas shrugged his shoulders but did not answer.

Wycliffe persisted, 'Do you think it likely that someone came in from the garden when the windows were open, broke open your cupboard and took the gun?'

'The gun is gone.'

'Did many people know that you had a gun and where you kept it?'

'It was not a secret.'

The man seemed remote, indifferent. Surely he must realize the significance of the missing gun?

Wycliffe said, 'There are two cupboards, both locked and, looking round, I see a number of drawers, yet it seems the thief went straight to the cupboard where the gun was, and only to that cupboard – is that so?'

'Apparently.'

38

Wycliffe went to the French windows and put his hand on the lever which operated the opening mechanism. 'May I?'

Beale neither acceded nor refused but merely watched. The catch yielded after an effort and the window ground open reluctantly on rusty hinges. Wycliffe closed it again.

'Have you any idea who might have taken your gun, Captain Beale?'

'None.'

'You realize that we shall have to inquire among members of your family?'

No reply.

Did he actually want to embarrass his father and involve the whole household?

Simon said, 'I think you are drawing an unwarrantable conclusion, Mr Wycliffe.'

Wycliffe turned on him the bland, blank stare which most people found disconcerting, and said, 'I haven't drawn any conclusion, I am making inquiries.' He turned to Nicholas. 'Isn't a Beretta an unusual gun for a British officer?'

'The Beretta was not my service pistol; I carried a Browning like everybody else; the Beretta was a gift from a Greek Cypriot who insisted that I had done him a service.'

It was obvious that no more would be got from Nicholas.

Wycliffe said, 'Mr Kersey will arrange for statements to be taken from you and other members of the household.'

It was Simon who saw them out; they left Nicholas standing by his desk, stroking his moustache, apparently unmoved.

Retired district nurse Ruby Price lived alone on the northern fringe of the village, on the very edge of the moor. Her little house had been built before the First World War by an eccentric Oxford don as a summer retreat. It had three rooms on the ground floor and one above – perched on the rest like a squat tower to command the countryside. Ruby was seventy-five but she had worn well, her hair retained glints of the original gold, she had a healthy tan, her smooth complexion was free of blemishes, and her lean angular body was that of a still active woman. At a quarter to four Ruby was in her upstairs room, sitting in an old wicker chair by the window which looked towards the moor. There was another window in the opposite wall, facing south over the village, so that the room got the sun as well as a moorland view.

On a table at her side was a tray set for afternoon tea; matching china in a floral design, *petits fours* and oolong tea; intimations of gentility. A marmalade cat slept on a cushion at her feet while she listened to a play on the radio. She was hard of hearing and the volume was turned up so that disembodied voices vibrated through the speaker.

Since her arrival there at the age of twenty-four, Ruby had made Washford her own; she had first rented, then bought the little house in which she still lived and after thirty-six years delivering babies, administering enemas, dressing ulcerated legs and rubbing aged, bedridden backs, there was scarcely a door in the village or in neighbouring hamlets at which she went through the formality of knocking. Since her retirement she had assumed the role of maiden aunt to the whole community; she visited the people in their homes, encouraged them to tell her their troubles and confide their secrets, never doubting her welcome. She received few overt snubs, though by some she was regarded as an interfering busybody.

But Ruby was content with herself and, broadly, with her life, though she dreaded the prospect of being forced eventually to endure the unendurable, the brisk professional caring and the ineffable companionship of an old peoples' home.

She reached for a pair of binoculars which had belonged to her sea-captain father, raised them to her eyes and swept the moor: a foreground of tiny stone-walled fields, unchanged since they were plotted by Iron-age Celts; then a rougher terrain of heather and bog, away to the twin tors – one rising smooth and contoured like a woman's breast, the other topped with a rugged castle of Brobdingnagian boulders. Ruby focused on Druid's Rock – a pinnacle of granite about two miles off. Earlier she had seen Edward sketching near the rock but now ponies grazed there. On his way home Edward would call to see her as he always did when he had been out on the moor; a timid, warm-hearted boy, now her only contact with the family – or almost . . . Never mind! They would need her before she needed them.

Edward had given her one of his paintings – a view of the moor in winter from this very window; it hung on the wall above her collection of snapshots of the babies she had brought into the world. With a sigh Ruby put down her binoculars and poured herself another cup of tea, then she closed her eyes. The play was reaching its climax and she settled to listen with greater attention. At that moment she became conscious of a movement close at hand; she opened her eyes again – startled, and in that instant her world was shattered in a single blinding flash.

Instead of going back to the police van, Wycliffe walked in the churchyard – still a good place to get the feel of a village, and here all was as it should have been. The Blatchfords, the Fretwells, the Endacotts, Newcombes and Finucanes were all recorded in moss-covered stone and slate, the credentials of the village.

The church itself, built while Henry Tudor was still trying out his Welsh bottom on the English throne, was undecorated Perpendicular, no nonsense. The church was dedicated to St Dorothea, the martyred young lady who had, post-humously, sent her judge a basket of fruit and flowers from the Elysian Fields. To prove it, there was the basket, carved in stone, above the south porch.

No Beales in the churchyard, no memorial tablets to the family in the church; then he remembered they were Catholics, but the original squires – the Drews – were commemorated through several generations, in stone and brass.

He came out again into the sunshine, thinking of the

41

missing pistol — of the possibilities. Someone who knew about the gun — not family — prowling about the grounds when the French windows were open, had nipped in, picked the right cupboard, opened it and made off with the gun, the ammunition and Nicholas's souvenirs.

Alternatively the intruder, not knowing about the gun, had come upon it by chance while looking for anything worth taking; then presumably he had said, 'Oh goody! Now I can shoot that bastard Newcombe!' Or words to that effect.

Wycliffe growled like a disgruntled bear. The fact was that everything pointed to an inside job — one of the family. But would any of them be stupid enough not to realize that the family would be prime suspects?

And if it was a family affair, a crime arising out of repressed hatreds and jealousies within the Beale household, it was hard to see why an illiterate recluse, living in squalor on the edge of the estate, should be its victim. The victim — that was his starting point. What could Newcombe have had or done or known which made it necessary or worthwhile to kill him?

There was his interest in birth certificates. Generally such documents tell only what people allow to be known, but for some innocents any bit of printed paper carries the seal of ultimate truth.

A young man was coming down the path which cut through the churchyard from the direction of the moor. Slim and dark and pale, with large doe-like eyes, as he drew nearer he moved off the path on to the grass to avoid a possible encounter. He carried, slung over his shoulder, a complicated pack which included a folding easel. After he had passed, Wycliffe was aware of his nervous backward glance and turned to watch him. He passed through the lych gate, crossed the Green and entered through the gates of Ashill.

The young painter Kersey had mentioned. Was he a Beale? Wycliffe had his answer sooner than he expected.

'Good afternoon, Mr Wycliffe.'

He faced round abruptly. One of the Gould twins – no scar, so Rose.

'That was Edward Beale, our local painter; Simon Beale's nephew by marriage. He was orphaned as a young child and Simon adopted him. They say he will make a name for himself in the art world.'

Rose was wearing a floral dress in shades of mauve with a headscarf to match and she had a little spaniel dog on a lead.

'I was taking Jasper for his walk when I saw you . . . I must confess I hoped that we might meet . . . We were speaking of the Beales – such an interesting family I always think. So much enterprise . . .'

Wycliffe smiled. 'I think there is something you want to tell me.'

She coloured like a schoolgirl. 'It's a small thing and my sister feels very strongly that we should not involve ourselves . . .' She smiled up at him, inviting understanding.

'I'm sure that it is a coincidence but the police are always asking people to co-operate . . . It was yesterday – Sunday afternoon, at about this time and I was taking Jasper for his walk, but yesterday we went *down* the lane, towards the Newton road and, of course, we had to pass Newcombe's cottage, both going and coming back. We don't go that way very often, do we Jasper? But we do it sometimes out of *bravado*!' She looked away in embarrassment at the admission. 'It was on our way back, when we were a few yards from the cottage, I heard men's voices. I could not distinguish the words at first but as I drew level with the gate I heard a man say in a fairly aggressive manner, "You've done very well out of this, Newcombe!" '

'Did you see who it was speaking?'

She nodded. 'Yes, I did. It was Mr Vicary, Simon Beale's son-in-law – such a strange looking man . . . He reminds me of those monkeys with wrinkled faces who look like little old men . . . At any rate it was Mr Vicary, and he was talking to Newcombe.'

43

'Did they see you?'

'No, I don't think so. We were very quiet, weren't we, Jasper?'

'Did you hear anything else?'

She coloured. 'Well, I wasn't exactly listening, superintendent . . . I wouldn't like you to think . . . But Mr Vicary's voice *was* raised. When Newcombe spoke it was in his usual rather horrid wheedling tone, like Uriah Heep, I always say, and I didn't hear what he said but Mr Vicary's words were quite clear. He said, "If you adopt that attitude, Newcombe, you are making the biggest mistake of your life!" ' She was looking up at him, half nervous, half excited. 'I don't suppose it's of any importance but you did say . . . In any case, I do hope that you won't find it necessary to mention what I've told you to Veronica. She has a very high regard for "the family" as she calls them.'

Wycliffe thanked her and stooped to speak to Jasper who looked up at him with large, bored, brown eyes.

It was odd to reflect that the Misses Gould existed in the same world as the muggers, rioters and terrorists who made headlines every day. Jane Austen Rules! OK?

Wycliffe returned to the police van and to Kersey. 'I don't suppose you know the superintendent registrar in Newton?'

'As it happens, I've met him: he's a dry old stick called Endacott; looks like a Dickensian lawyer; probably still writes out his certificates with a goose quill.'

'Ring him up and ask if he's had a visit from Newcombe recently – or any inquiries concerning the Beale family.'

Kersey put through the call and spoke to a furry, female voice which said, spitefully pleased, 'We closed for public business at five. If you have any inquiry you should telephone or call after ten o'clock in the morning.'

Kersey grinned. 'Put down your knitting, love, and concentrate. I'm a police officer and I want to speak to Mr Endacott.'

Silence, so that Kersey thought she had hung-up on him,

but quite suddenly there was a bark from the receiver: 'Mr Endacott here, what is it you want?'

'Detective Inspector Kersey' (it rolled nicely off his tongue though still a bit unfamiliar) '—I want to know if you've had an inquiry recently from a Mr Newcombe – Morley Newcombe – a little fat man who probably looked and smelt like a tramp.'

'Any member of the public who pays the appropriate fee—'

'Yes, I know all about that, Mr Endacott, but we are anxious to know about this particular member of the public who happens to have got himself shot.'

The official mind churned almost audibly. 'In that case I suppose I am justified in telling you that a man answering your description did call at the office; I dealt with him myself.'

'When?'

'Last week sometime – I remember, it was market day, so it must have been Wednesday – Wednesday afternoon.'

'What did he want?'

'He wanted to see the entry in the register relating to his birth.'

'Anything else?'

'He requested two other searches and had sight of those entries also.'

'What were they?'

Mr Endacott sighed. 'I suppose I am in order in telling you all this! If you will hold on a moment . . .'

He was back in a couple of minutes. 'The first entry concerned the marriage of Francis Vicary to Gertrude Rosemary Beale, and the second recorded the birth of their child, Esther.'

'Did he ask for certified copies of any of the entries?'

'No.'

'Did he seem satisfied with the information you were able to give him?'

A dry cackle like tearing paper: 'We are not in the business of customer satisfaction, Inspector; we merely

45

make our records available to those entitled to see them.'

'I think you know what I mean. Did he seem surprised or disappointed by the facts as recorded?'

Hesitation. 'I must admit that he seemed disappointed and inclined to blame me for it. He muttered something about having wasted his time – not that I would have supposed that to have much value.'

Kersey thanked the old boy and said that he would send an officer – with the necessary fees – to obtain certified copies of the entries which had interested Newcombe. Then he looked at Wycliffe, 'What do you make of that, sir?'

Wycliffe shook his head. Whichever way they turned they came up against Beales. Means, Opportunity and Motive – the cardinal heads under which suspicion must be justified. Means presented no problem; almost certainly Newcombe had been shot with Nicholas's pistol. Opportunity was equally simple; the footpath from Ashill to Newcombe's yard guaranteed easy and private access. Motive? Well, it looked as though one might be suggesting itself.

Kersey said, 'Surely the whole family can't be in cahoots?'

As often happened, he and Wycliffe were thinking along the same lines.

Simon was alone in the dining-room where the table was set for dinner with eight places. Although the Vicarys had a more or less self-contained flat on the first floor, it had become the custom for the whole family to dine together. Maurice and Frank arrived home from the firm's offices in the city at six-thirty, and dinner was at seven.

Simon poured himself a dry sherry, took it to the window and stood, looking out. A broad lawn on a gentle slope, then woodland with the ground dropping more steeply to the valley below. Through the trees to his left, not yet in full leaf, he could glimpse the icing-sugar pink and white of Quarry House.

He was badly shaken. The shooting of Newcombe,

Nicky's missing gun, the superintendent's questions, interrogation of the whole household — wasn't it obvious what the police thought? He dared not put his own thoughts into words. Had there been an outsider who had come in through the French window? He had tried to lead the superintendent to think so but, in fact, the window was rarely opened and the man had seen that for himself. The alternative . . . the alternative was unthinkable. He shrugged angrily; it was as though Nicholas had deliberately set out to arouse police suspicion, yet he had more reason than . . . But it was dangerous to think like that.

Nicholas and Maurice: Simon felt that he had little cause to be gratified in his sons.

Someone came into the room and he turned sharply, then saw with relief that it was Frank and not one of the others. Childish! But he had come to depend on his son-in-law, and not only in business matters.

Vicary went to the sideboard and poured himself a whisky. He was a little man, dark, with something oddly simian about him; his face was lined and he had small, deeply set eyes, restless and probing. It was strange that there should be such a rapport between two such different men.

Vicary said, 'You've had a bad day.'

They had twice discussed the Newcombe affair on the telephone; now Simon threw up his hands in a half-humorous gesture of despair.

Vicary brought his drink over to the window and the two men stood, side by side. 'What finally happened about Nicky's gun?'

Simon told him of the second police visit and Vicary listened without interrupting, then he said, 'I shouldn't worry too much; the police have to be seen to be doing something. Look at it this way: would anybody in this house be silly enough to draw suspicion on themselves by using a gun kept in the house, and known to the police.'

But Simon was not reassured. 'You may be right, Frank — I hope you are, but I've a feeling . . .' He made a vague gesture with his hands. 'A feeling that Newcombe isn't the real target.'

Vicary said in a dry voice, 'It's Newcombe who is dead.'

Simon sighed. 'I know . . . I know. I'm probably talking nonsense but I wish you hadn't gone to see him on Sunday afternoon. If the police find out you were there and the reason—'

'They won't find out. How can they? And even if they did the business of the pension is a perfectly reasonable explanation.'

'Of course! I'm getting old, Frank. One gets obsessed by an idea . . .' He broke off, then changed the subject. 'Have you been up to the flat since you've been home?'

A wry smile. 'You mean, have I seen Gertrude? I've just come down; she has one of her headaches and she won't be down for dinner.'

The old man nodded. 'I was afraid of that; I saw her earlier and it was obvious . . . I suppose it's understandable, this is bound to affect her, but I wish she would get out more – make some effort. She spends too much time up there brooding; and with Naomi—well, they've nothing in common . . .'

Simon's nephew, Edward, came in. Edward was very thin, very dark, with large brown eyes made more conspicuous by the extreme pallor of his face. 'Oh . . .' He hesitated just inside the door, his manner alert and furtive like some shy nocturnal animal caught in the light. 'I'm sorry, I thought I was late for dinner . . .' He had a streak of green paint across one cheek.

The two men ignored him. Edward looked around uncomfortably then went to sit at the table.

Simon spoke, lowering his voice, 'Have you said any more to Nicky about buying him out?'

Vicary grimaced. 'As I told you, when I first mentioned it he said nothing but I had the impression he was prepared to think it over. Last night I brought up the subject again and he just went over the top. You know that kind of cold fury – it really took my breath away, it was so unexpected.'

'What did he say?'

Vicary shrugged. 'What didn't he say!' He lowered his voice still further, glancing across at Edward. 'First that I had insulted him; second, that I was an interloper, doing my best to take over the firm and the family with it; third, that I had ruined Gertrude's life and that I was turning her into an alcoholic . . .' Vicary smiled a wry smile. 'There was more; none of it pleasant.'

Simon sighed. 'I'm sorry; I had no idea he would take it like that or I wouldn't have suggested it. Now he's got involved with this Gould woman I thought he might be glad to realize his capital and he can't do that outside of the family.'

'Well, he certainly isn't going to sell to me and I've upset him.'

Simon was dismissive. 'I shouldn't let it worry you. He's been the same ever since he was a child – touchy and unpredictable, liable to tantrums.'

A woman's voice came from the hall, strident and minatory: 'I think it was unwise of you, Esther, getting *involved*. Going down there to feed that man's animals! Of course, what you do is no business of mine but we really don't want to get mixed up in this sordid affair! I'm sure your grandfather would agree.'

They came in together: Maurice's wife – Naomi, and Esther. Esther gave no sign that she heeded her aunt, no sign that she had even heard.

Naomi was in her mid-forties; plump and running to fat, and a bottle-blonde. Her cheeks sagged a little on either side of a petulant over-made-up little mouth. She switched on a cluster of lights over the dining table and the room was laid bare in all its shabby late-Victorian pretension. Naomi's fierce little eyes darted around. 'Where's Maurice? Isn't he down yet? And Nicholas – surely it isn't going to be another of those nights!'

There was a move towards the table and Vicary said, 'Gertrude isn't coming down.'

Naomi looked at him, lips pursed. 'So Esther told me.

49

Is there any point in sending something up?'

Vicary said, 'I think not.'

Naomi sat at the foot of the table as Simon took his place at the head; the others arranged themselves, Esther across the table from Edward, Vicary next to Naomi. The old servant wheeled in a heated trolley which she manoeuvred into position on Naomi's right. 'There's more soup if you want it.' She shuffled out, her slippers dragging across the carpet. Naomi started to ladle out the soup and plates passed from hand to hand.

Maurice came in, shorter and stouter than his father and brother and, unlike them, he had a high colour. He sat down, tucking in his napkin, a greedy man. 'I hope I haven't delayed you all; I had a telephone call . . .' He spoke busily as though time pressed. 'Where's Nicky? And Gertrude – isn't Gertie coming down?'

Nobody answered.

He went on: 'This is a bad business! First Newcombe, now this upset over Nicky's gun . . . Who on earth would want to kill the fellow? There must be a madman in the village; there's no other explanation, and to think he must actually have been in this house . . . How else could he have got hold of the gun?'

Nicholas came in and took his seat without a word. He arranged his napkin, rearranged his place-setting to his satisfaction, and accepted the plate of soup Naomi handed him with no more than a slight movement of the lips; but this was normal.

Simon gathered their attention and recited Grace before meals.

They began to eat and there was silence in the whole room except for sounds incidental to the meal.

Simon looked round the table. All was as it would have been on any other night. If tonight they were conscious of any added tension they gave no sign. He thought: We are like actors in a play that has run too long with the same cast. His gaze rested on his nephew, Edward, and he saw the streak of green paint on the boy's face. Simon always thought of Edward as 'the boy' though he must now be twenty-one or two. The child of his wife's much younger sister, Simon had adopted him at the age of eight, in tragic circumstances. He had done so to please his wife. But Edward had been a sickly child and an ailing youth. Now that he was a young man he and Simon were wholly estranged. Though he tried to feel compassion, Simon's attitude was one of contempt. He blamed Naomi, who had had the upbringing of the boy after his wife's death. 'Made him into a sissy! A milksop!'

If Esther had been a boy! But he could hardly bring himself to wish Esther other than she was. He never tired of looking at her. In his private thoughts he called her his Botticelli virgin . . . Was she a virgin? Probably not in the technical sense; few girls of her age were, it seemed. But emotionally – no doubt there. He envied the man who would one day transform the serene countenance . . .

Esther was watching Edward; her eyes steady and intent gave nothing away. What did the look mean? Was it contemptuous? sympathetic? protective? Simon could not guess what their relationship was but he suspected that it might be more intimate than appeared. He was sometimes disturbed by a vision of the boy's thin, pallid body writhing on the naked girl while she lay still and passive, staring at the ceiling with those concealing eyes.

Nicholas watched Esther – not openly, but with quick, shy, surreptitious glances, like an adolescent. Despite his troubles, Simon chuckled to himself. Nicky had never grown up; the business in Germany was proof of that, if proof were needed. Now he played Sir Galahad to the woman down the lane and enticed Esther into the library when he could, to lecture her on his battles.

Edward looked at nobody, he kept his eyes down and plied his spoon; but there was something wrong. Instead of those fastidious, precise movements which often irritated Simon, the boy's hand was trembling so that his soup spilled back into the plate. Suddenly he dropped his spoon with a clatter, got up from his chair, pushing it back so that it

51

toppled over, and made for the door.

Naomi called after him in her most tragic voice: 'Edward!'

What a fool the woman was! Abruptly the mixture of thoughts, fears and emotions which had been troubling Simon crystallized into anger. He shouted: 'For God's sake, woman, leave him alone!'

Naomi looked as though she had been slapped.

Esther stood up. 'I'll go with him.'

'I'm called Gratton — Nancy Gratton — and I work for Mrs Finucane in the shop. She said I ought to come and tell you . . .'

'About what?'

The girl had turned up at the police caravan after leaving work and was talking to Kersey.

'About Sunday night. I was down the lane by Ashill, sitting on the seat with my friend—'

'What time was this?'

'I don't know exactly but we saw Bunny Newcombe on his way home from the pub so it must've been about half-past ten.'

'What happened?'

'Nothing really — he made some silly joke like always and went on down to his cottage.'

Kersey thought she was really a very pretty girl — dark hair and eyes with pale clear skin, but she had never learned how to stand or sit and so she was round shouldered. Kersey nagged his own two daughters about posture like a Victorian governess.

'How far is the seat from the cottage?'

'Not far. Maybe fifty yards or a bit less. The seat is under the trees but the cottage was in the moonlight so we could see it all right.'

'You heard the shot — is that it?'

She nodded. 'Not long after he went in. It was funny — not exactly a bang, more a sort of crack. It sounded as though it came from the cottage but my friend said that was daft. He said it was a poacher in the woods and that shots

52

sounded different at night . . .' She shifted uncomfortably in her seat, glanced at Kersey and away again. 'After all, it didn't seem likely that it came from the cottage, did it?'

'So you didn't do anything about it.'

She shook her head. 'No, and when I heard what had happened I felt awful.'

Kersey said, 'No need: you couldn't have done anything for Newcombe, he was killed instantly. How long did you stay on the seat after the shot?'

'Oh, quite a while; we had a bit of a row.'

'About the shot?'

'Well, it started with that but you know how things go . . .' She smiled a worried smile.

'Could anyone have come out of the cottage into the lane without you seeing them?'

'I'm sure they couldn't have. Apart from anything else that gate makes enough row to wake the dead.'

She had said her piece and Kersey was expecting her to get up and go, but Nancy sat tight, looking uncomfortable, hands gripped between her thighs. Outside a herd of brown cows lumbered past the van on their way from milking, back to pasture.

'There's something else?'

'I saw a light in the cottage *before* Bunny passed us on his way home.'

'A light?'

'Like somebody using a candle or torch – moving around. From the seat you can only see the upstairs and there's only one window that faces up the lane.'

'You saw the light – was that all?'

She was frowning and she hesitated before saying: 'I saw a shadow – I *thought* it was a woman's shadow but I couldn't be sure.'

'How long was this before you saw Newcombe?'

She shrugged. 'Ten minutes? About that.'

'What made you think it was a woman's shadow – try to remember.'

'I've been trying but it doesn't make any difference. I

just thought it was – I said so to my friend. Of course he made a joke about it and said, "Why shouldn't Bunny have a woman like anybody else?" ' She smiled. 'As if any woman would!'

Kersey cross-questioned her for ten minutes without getting any further; the girl was honest; she told what she believed she had seen and she refused to embroider. He said he would send someone to take her statement and that her boy-friend would have to make one as well.

Edward was in his studio-bedroom: a large attic which had once been part of the servants' quarters. An uncurtained dormer window looked out blankly into the night and the room was lit by the yellow light of a naked bulb. There was sisal matting, an easel, an artist's donkey, a table, a superannuated settee and an old armchair. The bedroom component consisted of a single bed and a wardrobe-cupboard.

Canvases were propped face-to-the-wall but one full-length nude – an attenuated Esther – was fastened to the sloping ceiling. Her slimness was exaggerated, diminishing her sex, but the warm flesh tones glowed; a Modigliani version.

Esther and Edward sat side by side on the settee; Esther was turning the pages of a book of reproductions; Edward watched without interest. He was on edge; several times he seemed on the point of speaking but changed his mind, then it came: 'I don't know what to do, Esther.'

'You don't *have* to do anything, Teddy.'

'But when they find her they will know I was her only regular visitor.'

'Perhaps they will, but you visit people because you like them; it doesn't mean that you're likely to . . .'

'The police will know about father.'

'Does that matter? I mean, it would be absurd . . .'

It was all very gentle, words were spoken without emphasis, in sentences which were often incomplete; there was discussion without argument and without urgency; the

54

two of them were like people in someone else's dream.

'They will know that I've been there today.'

'How?'

'Because I must have been seen up on the moor.'

For the first time Esther showed signs of animation. 'You could say that as you were getting near the cottage, on your way home, you saw someone leaving by the back gate.'

He looked at her in surprise. 'Why should I say that?'

She shook her head and did not answer.

'But who should I say I saw?'

'Anybody – a man.'

'But they would want to know what he looked like.'

'You could say that you were too far off to see.'

Edward looked even more worried. 'I don't think they would believe me.'

Esther dropped the book to the floor and turned towards him. 'Don't worry about it now; think it over.'

He slid his hand up under her shirt and caressed her. She remained passive.

'I love your breasts, Esther.'

'They're very small.'

'I love you, Esther.'

'Do you, Teddy?'

CHAPTER THREE

Next morning Wycliffe listened to the seven o'clock news on the radio. Moscow and Washington were counting missiles as kids count conkers; the French were trying to flog us subsidized oven-ready turkeys and long-life milk while refusing our lamb; trade-union leaders warned darkly of strikes and disruptions if their members failed to get the usual quart out of the pint pot. It was the sort of morning which made him want to get off.

But there was nowhere to escape to, even in a pipe-dream. In Alaska they scrambled for gold and oil while the Eskimos drew social security instead of catching seals and building igloos; in darkest Africa they carried Soviet-made machine-guns and had pictures of Castro in their mud huts; in Outer Mongolia they were joining collectives and attending classes in cultural awareness, while up the Amazon they bulldozed forests and doled out influenza and syphilis to under-privileged little Indians who hadn't known what they were missing.

The moon was the last wilderness and that remained unaccessible even in imagination to a middle-aged copper who was fundamentally unadventurous and only wanted people to be reasonable and decent.

Of course it was raining; the weather had changed overnight, and from the windows of the Watch House the estuary looked leaden, like the sky. Inside, for no reason at all, the atmosphere was gloomily tense; one of those mornings.

'What time do I expect you tonight?'

'I've no idea.'

'So you won't expect a meal.'

'I'll ring you after lunch.'

Brittle thread, easily snapped by some pert or hurtful remark, but Helen was worried about him, and came to the door to see him off. She kissed him with a wry smile. 'Remember you've got to last till I get another.'

He squeezed her arm and everything was right again.

He had got to bed late and slept badly, mulling over the day. Some cases hinge on the pathologist's report; others, on what a ballistics expert has to say; sometimes it is highly technical forensic evidence which sets the ball rolling, but in this case the experts had little to offer.

There is not a lot to be said about a shot through the head except that it is usually fatal. (Though Franks had a story about a man who, having shot himself through the temple with a thirty-eight one night, turned up at breakfast next morning.) They had the fatal bullet and the cartridge-case and they knew with reasonable certainty where the gun had come from, but Wycliffe would have been easier in his mind if the gun itself had been recovered.

On reflection, what troubled him most was the passionless cold-bloodedness of the crime. To lie in wait for someone, then to kill them with a single shot through the skull was as near execution as it is possible to get; a calculated economy of effort which he found profoundly disturbing.

The examination of the victim's clothing had told him little beyond the fact that Bunny had worn long-johns and a sleeved woollen vest – both incredibly filthy. He had carried in his pockets seven pounds and sixty-two pence, a few bits of string, a couple of nails and a stub of pencil.

Someone must have worked through the night, for the scene-of-crime report was on his desk. It included a plan of the cottage, all Smith's photographs, and a statement that a complete inventory was under way. Already they had found some money. It seemed that, after all, Emily had 'put something by' – one hundred and forty pounds in fives and singles, contained in an old envelope and tucked under Bunny's mattress. Presumably, this was left of a larger sum he had been living on since his mother's death. It wouldn't have kept him much longer, but if the killer or anyone else had really searched the place it could hardly have been money he was after.

His personal assistant came in with the morning mail. Diane, alias the Ice Maiden, alias the Snow Queen. Diane was like all the 'afters' in TV toilet commercials rolled into one: shampooed, conditioned, deodorized, delicately perfumed and exquisitely packaged. She made him feel uncomfortable so that he wondered if he had shaved properly, if he had soap behind his ears, if he smelled of stale tobacco . . .

'Put them there, Diane.'

She was as impeccable in her work as in her person. She laid down a pile of envelopes, putting one gingerly apart from the rest. It was a straw-coloured envelope addressed in block capitals to 'The Head of Detectives'. The classic format. He opened it with a minimum of handling – not that it mattered. Nobody tangling with the police and having an IQ of eighty-five plus leaves prints any more. The contents were brief and mandatory: *Find out Edwards reel name*. The envelope was postmarked Newton District, which told him very little. The message, like the address, had been written in carefully formed block capitals by someone not very familiar with the business of writing. Although educated people will often pretend to illiteracy when writing anonymous letters this had the appearance of the genuine article. The paper had been roughly torn from a lined exercise book.

Wycliffe received a dozen anonymous letters a week, mostly from nut-cases, some from neighbours-with-a-grievance, the odd one with a useful tip. The problem was to know one from the other.

Edward's real name. Edward – the painter, the doe-eyed young man who had been so self-effacing the previous afternoon when they met in the churchyard. It would be no surprise to hear that he had suffered some traumatic experience in childhood.

Anyway, there seemed to be a conspiracy to put the Beales in the centre of the stage. the question was, how to proceed. He thought of calling on Simon then remembered that Maurice would be in the firm's offices in the city. Whether the anonymous query had any significance or not, it would be an excuse to talk to Maurice whom he had not yet seen.

He sent the note and its envelope up for routine examination and for photocopies to be made, then he put through a call to Beales' Household Stores and asked to speak to Mr Maurice Beale. He was politely interrogated.

'Is it a business or a private matter, sir?'

'Private,'

Mr Wycliffe . . . Would that be Chief Superintendent Wycliffe?'

'It would.'

'One moment, Mr Wycliffe.'

Evidently Maurice was not available to any peasant who happened to have a telephone.

One moment stretched into several then came a high-pitched, slightly irritable voice, not unlike Simon's. 'Mr Wycliffe? You wanted to speak to me?'

'I want to come and see you this morning.'

A pause. 'This morning? I'm afraid I have a very busy morning ahead of me.'

'So have I, Mr Beale, but this is important.'

'I see. Shall we say at ten-thirty, then?'

'Always do your homework!' He said if often enough to earnest young coppers in training and he followed his own precept. He telephoned an accountant friend who sometimes helped him in cases involving finance.

'Beales? I'd say they were riding very comfortably. I doubt if they've even noticed that it's cold outside. . . . Of course, it's a private company – a family concern and in some ways that makes it easier – no beady-eyed share-holders breathing down your neck. . . . About ten years ago Simon had a deed of settlement drawn up; put the capital into a hundred shares and doled them out to the family. As far as I remember he kept about half himself;

I think Nicholas, Gertrude and Gertrude's husband – Vicary – got ten each. Something like that anyway . . . Maurice, as managing director, probably got a few more.'

'And who runs the show – Maurice?'

'Maurice? Maurice couldn't run a stall in a church bazaar. Simon inherited a good business and ran it on sound lines, but the real growth has come in the last few years and it's all down to Frank Vicary. He's a natural – pity he can't take over one of out state-subsidized disaster areas. Strange chap, looks a bit like a monkey I always think. . . .'

Wycliffe thanked him.

'Any time! Love to Helen.'

Beales' Household Stores occupied a prime site in the city centre; four floors of merchandise ranging from tin-racks to power lathes and from nail brushes to complete bathroom and kitchen installations. An assistant escorted Wycliffe to a padded door and a lift which whisked him to the top floor, to a reception desk and a grey-haired lady who told him he was expected, that Mr Beale was engaged but would be free shortly, and would Mr Wycliffe take a seat.

The hub of the Beale empire. A glass partition separated the receptionist from a room full of clerks and typists. Behind her, two doors were labelled respectively, Maurice Beale, Managing director; Frank Vicary, Secretary and Accountant.

At three minutes turned the half-hour Beale came out of his office. 'Mr Wycliffe?' In contrast with his father's spare hardness, Maurice was fleshy and soft and he seemed to be doing his best to smother nervousness with pomposity. 'This way, superintendent.' His office was large, modern, and totally lacking in any trace of individuality. Wycliffe was assigned to a black leather monster of an armchair while Maurice swivelled at his desk and fiddled with a bundle of typescript.

Wycliffe said, 'You know that I am investigating the death of Morley Newcombe and the disappearance of your brother's gun.'

Beale studied his finger nails. 'I really don't see how

I can be of any help, Mr Wycliffe. Of course, as a family, we are very distressed about the whole affair but each of us has been questioned by one of your men and, no doubt, you will see the reports.'

Wycliffe brought out a photostat of the anonymous note and passed it over. Maurice looked at it and became very still, then he said, 'What is it you want from me, superintendent?'

'Simply to ask if you can explain this note which reached me anonymously in the post this morning.'

Maurice decided to be peevish. 'Am I expected to explain the actions of some anonymous person who is clearly out to cause trouble? It seems that our family is a target for someone who is trying to implicate us in the death of this man. First my brother's gun is stolen, now this. . . . Surely you can see that the very idea is absurd. Why would any of us want to harm Newcombe?'

Why, indeed? What had people in offices like this to do with a dirty little fat man who lived with his chickens and rabbits?

Wycliffe said, 'I see your point, Mr Beale, but there must be a straightforward answer to the question in the note and it's surely better for me to come to you for it than look elsewhere. However . . .' He seemed on the point of getting up to go.

Maurice's plump fingers interlocked. 'I'm not so foolish as to refuse an explanation.'

The intercom buzzed and Maurice flicked a button with aggression. 'I am engaged, Miss Marks. Ask Mr Yeo to deal with whatever it is.' He sat back in his chair, swivelling to and fro. 'Rather than have your men ferreting out a garbled version of the facts I had better tell you what this is about and you will see that it can have nothing to do with your case.'

Maurice picked up the photostat and studied it once more. Now that he had decided to talk he was going to extract as much drama as possible from the situation. 'I suppose all families have their skeleton, tucked away . . .' He looked at Wycliffe with a depreciating smile. 'This is ours. Does the name Santos mean anything to you, superintendent? – Eduardo Santos?'

'Not that I recall.'

'I thought you might remember the case: Eduardo Santos, a painter of Spanish extraction, living in Camden, strangled his wife in somewhat bizarre circumstances. The woman he strangled was my aunt – my mother's younger sister; and of course, Edward's mother. Edward was eight at the time and he witnessed the whole horrible business.'

'What happened to Santos?'

'He got a life sentence for murder.'

'Is he still in prison?'

'No, he was released on parole some years ago but there has never been any contact between Edward and his father since, early in his sentence, Santos renounced all claims on his son and the boy was adopted by my father and mother.'

'A tragic affair!'

Maurice nodded with lugubrious emphasis. 'Yes, indeed! Edward was a charming boy and he is a delightful young man, but despite that he has been a great worry to my wife and to me. My mother died seven years ago, but before that she was ill for a long time and so it fell mainly to us to bring Edward up.'

Maurice stared at his clasped hands. 'Through no fault of his own he was a most difficult youngster – his schooldays were a catalogue of illnesses which, according to the doctors, were more of the mind than the body.' He looked at Wycliffe with an owlish expression and grew more confiding: 'I must confess that my father's attitude didn't help. He is a strong man and, although he is very fond of Edward, he has often shown a lack of understanding. . . I'm afraid he has little sympathy for weakness of any kind.'

Maurice lowered his voice. 'During his teens Edward suffered long periods of intense depression and when he was eighteen he attempted suicide on two occasions.'

'How?'

The bald inquiry shocked Maurice but he rallied. 'On

the first occasion he drank weed-killer and on the second, he slashed his wrists.'

Maurice sat back in his chair with a deep sigh. 'Well, Mr Wycliffe, now you know the explanation of your anonymous note. I am sure you will see that it can have nothing to do with the case. After all, a young man who has twice tried to kill himself can hardly be thought of as a danger to others.'

Evidently Maurice had not read the right books. Wycliffe, who had, retained an interest in Edward but was disinclined to see him as a prime suspect without more evidence. For the moment, enough was enough.

He got up to leave. 'Is Mr Vicary in this morning?'

Mild surprise. 'What? No, I'm afraid he's away all day today; he's looking into problems at our Tor Vale depot.'

'Isn't that the one on the Newton road?'

'Yes. Actually it's quite close to Washford.'

Wycliffe was escorted to the lift. 'If I can be of any further help . . .' A soft hand.

Wycliffe drove back to his headquarters and spent an hour coping with rosters, schedules, and inter-departmental queries. He dealt reflexly with the routine bumf, both reassured and irritated by Diane standing over him, watching for any slip.

'The chief wants to know when he can expect your comments on his Emergency Deployment proposals.'

His ball-point ran out, he threw it down and groped for another.

'Here!' Diane's ball-points were like the widow's cruse of oil. She pegged away at him: 'Shall I say that you'll let him have something by the morning?'

He did not answer. It was not that he was wilfully uncooperative but when anything diverted him from a case in which he was deeply involved he exhibited what Kersey called 'the Zombie Syndrome'. It was something more than mere preoccupation; almost as though he had assumed a different identity.

At one-fifteen he went out to lunch at his usual restaurant;

he was served by his usual waitress and surrounded by regulars like himself but for all his awareness he might have been alone. By two o'clock he was on the motorway out of the city.

Visibility was down to fifty yards but vans, coaches juggernauts and cars swished bravely by, firm in their faith in brakes, tyres and St Christopher. Wycliffe had no such faith and he was glad when he reached the turn-off, free to meander in peace.

The road snaked through a narrow wooded valley; mist blotted out everything above ten or fifteen feet but at ground level it was clear. A sign by the road announced, Tor Vale; the valley broadened to make room for a few cottages and the Tor Vale Hotel. A discreet sign pointed into the trees: Tor Vale Cash and Carry Depot. He had decided to call on Vicary. The depot, a barracks of concrete and asbestos, mercifully shielded by trees, was built on three sides of a car-park and dignified only by a four-storey stone building which had once been a flour mill. The way-in led him to a turnstile and a sergeant-major type wearing a security badge.

'Mr Vicary? Straight on through Footwear and Clothing into Gardening, then up the stairs to a door marked Private. Knock on that.'

It worked, producing a plump blonde who said, 'I'll see.'

Two minutes later he was in a large bare office where everything was basic. Vicary was saying to a man in a grey overall with a 'Manager' badge, 'Come back in fifteen minutes.'

Vicary was small, with a boyish figure, but he had a heavily lined face which made him look old as well as somewhat simian. He had a wide mouth and his smile was more like a grimace.

'Ah Mr Wycliffe! I was expecting to hear from you sometime but I hardly thought you would search me out here.'

No voluptuous armchairs, only the bentwood kitchen variety – from stock. They sat down, Vicary on one side of the desk, Wycliffe on the other.

'I've just come from talking to your brother-in-law at the store, he told me I should find you here. I wanted to ask how well you knew Newcombe.'

The grey eyes looked straight at Wycliffe. 'I suppose the short answer is: well enough to know that he was an unpleasant bit of work. While his mother was alive she kept him out of trouble.'

'Trouble which has now got him shot?'

A faint smile. 'I certainly didn't expect that. I regard Newcombe as a layabout, perhaps a small-time crook, but not interesting enough to get himself shot.'

'Did you have much contact with him?'

A canny look; it was not difficult to see why Frank Vicary, clerk, had become Simon Beale's son-in-law and virtual boss of the firm. 'I went to see him on Sunday afternoon as, I suspect, you already know. It will save time and, hopefully, complications if I tell you about it.'

Wycliffe waited while the executive mind switched from stock-control to an orderly recall of the events in question, suitably edited.

'Newcombe's father and mother both worked at Ashill and my father-in-law paid the widow a fairly generous pension. When she died, a few months ago, he allowed the payments to continue as a gesture to the son. It was made clear that this was a temporary arrangement to enable him to get on his feet, and last Sunday I had the job of telling him that it would finish at the end of the month.'

Wycliffe quoted: ' "You've done very well out of this, Newcombe, but there's a limit; all good things come to an end some time." '

Vicary laughed, and his face seemed to split in two; no doubt at school he had acquired an apt nickname. 'You are very well informed, Mr Wycliffe! I certainly said something like that. The man was a sponger and if I'd had my way the cut-off would have come much sooner.'

'I think you went on to say: "If you adopt that attitude, Newcombe, you are making the biggest mistake of your life." '

Did the eyes show a little more concern? If so it was gone in an instant and the explanation came, pat: 'That sounds a bit more suggestive, doesn't it? – in the circumstances. In fact, it was in answer to a remark of Newcombe's which sounded very much like a threat.'

'A threat?'

'It seems absurd, I know, but he really was a most unpleasant creature. He said that if he talked to my father-in-law he thought he would do better.'

'And you saw that as a threat?'

'He meant it as one.'

'But what hold did he think he had over Mr Beale?'

'I haven't the least idea and I didn't inquire.'

Wycliffe said, easily, 'He was obviously not a very intelligent man. A few days before he was killed he went to Newton Register Office and asked to see three entries in the records.'

'Indeed?' Vicary's manner seemed to show only polite interest.

'The first concerned the details of his own birth; the second, your marriage to Gertrude Beale; and the third, the birth of your daughter, Esther.'

Vicary was looking straight at Wycliffe and his expression did not change. He said, simply, 'How very odd! I wonder what he hoped to gain by that?'

Wycliffe said, 'A simple question, Mr Vicary – was he blackmailing you, or hoping to do so?'

A grim smile. 'He certainly wasn't blackmailing me, Mr Wycliffe; I can't answer for what he was hoping to do but if he had any idea of the sort I can't imagine what grounds he thought he had.'

Wycliffe stood up. 'Thank you. I won't take up any more of your time.'

The depot manager was outside the door, waiting to be recalled.

Wycliffe made his way back through Gardening, Clothing and Footwear – passed stacks of consumer goods, waiting to be consumed. Multiply that by tens of thousands. . . It

66

bothered him sometimes; on the other hand he didn't fancy the idea of queuing outside a British version of GUM for the privilege of buying whatever an omniscient state had decided was good for him.

Vicary's story of the pension could be true – it probably was; people like Vicary rarely told outright lies, but it was not the whole truth. He was dealing with a specialist in processing and packaging truth with a deceptive label. And blackmail? It had to be considered.

Washford looked very different from the day before; the moor was obliterated and the village seemed about to dissolve in a moist greyness, half drizzle, half fog. Colours had vanished, leaving a circumscribed landscape in monochrome.

Three or four police cars were parked by the incident van, but the doings of the police were overshadowed by greater activity in the field adjoining the churchyard. Here there were other, more garish caravans: large, box-like trailers and ancient diesels to tow them, and to double as generators when the fun-fair got under way. The fair had come to town and when the fair comes to town, it rains – a law of Nature which Wycliffe had learned as a small boy.

Despite the weather, men were busy erecting stalls and booths, rides and roundabouts. Already the skeletal frameworks of a helter-skelter and a big-wheel reached jaggedly skywards, and other structures were taking shape, not yet identifiable.

The church clock chimed and struck three. From the school came a man's voice, strictly admonishing his class. As Wycliffe was getting out of his car Nicholas came through the gates of Ashill. He wore a shabby raincoat and a fisherman's hat but he stalked along with such a bearing and precision of step that one listened instinctively for bugles and drums. He looked neither to the right nor the left and, if he saw Wycliffe, he gave no sign. He crossed the Green and entered the churchyard by the lychgate.

Kersey was in the police van.

'I was going back to Newton but I heard on the grape-vine that you were on the way, so I waited.'

The movements of senior police officers are monitored with as much care and in as much detail as those of known criminals believed to be on a job.

'There was a message from the coroner's office; it seems the Fretwells are anxious to bury Newcombe on Thursday and the coroner wants to know if we have any objection. I told him to go ahead unless he heard different from you this afternoon.'

'The Fretwells are in a hurry, aren't they?'

Kersey grinned. 'Get him under before the fair so that everybody can enjoy themselves.'

Wycliffe said, 'Anything else?'

Kersey pointed to a stout cardboard box on the table. 'You might like to take a look in there, sir.'

Wycliffe removed the lid and lifted out an official police inventory bag. Underneath were two wads of old 'white' five-pound notes, tightly rolled and secured by a piece of thread; and three linen bags, tubular in form, each with a draw-string top.

'You needn't bother to open them if you don't want to, sir; each of 'em contains sovereigns and half-sovereigns. It's all listed on the tag but the total is sixty sovereigns and eighty half-sovereigns.'

'Where did you find that lot?'

'Smith found it. You remember the old brass bed in Emily's bedroom?'

'I do; my grandparents had one like it.'

'I'll bet theirs didn't have a small fortune stowed away under the knobs.'

'Any idea of what it amounts to in value?'

Kersey shook his head. 'I suppose the fivers carry only their face value and there are a hundred and three of them. I haven't a clue about the gold but it must be quite a packet. I suppose we hold it in the station safe until—'

'For the moment, but notify the legal department and let them handle it; they'll probably contact the Fretwells' lawyer and one way or another, they'll nominate somebody to wind up the estate.'

Wycliffe put the cover back on the box. 'I suppose she bought the gold before the restrictions in the middle sixties.'

Kersey said, 'I wish I'd bought gold in the sixties; the snag was I didn't have any more to buy it with than I have now. Do you think this is what the killer was after?'

'If it was he made a hash of it. In any case it doesn't make sense. Newcombe's movements were known to the whole village and any intruder could have picked his time to make a leisurely search without fear of interruption. In fact, he made sure of being there when Newcombe returned, which seems to clinch it as premeditated murder.'

Kersey agreed. 'That's what it looks like.'

'Any more surprises?'

Kersey shrugged. 'It's got about that the gun which killed him came from Ashill and the house-to-house chaps say the attitudes of the villagers have changed. Yesterday they were chatty, glad to gossip; full of yarns about Newcombe. It seems he had an amorous side, if you can call it that; he used to accost girls and make obscene suggestions. Nobody bothered about it much; all good clean bucolic fun, but at least they told us. Today they've clammed up; all you can get is abuse of the Beales. The feeling against the family is pretty strong and to listen to some you'd think all we had to do was take a Beale and truss him up ready for the pot.'

'Which? Have they any preference?'

'I don't think they're bothered about trifles like that.'

Wycliffe thought he had read the signs the day before but Kersey was having to learn about village ways – in real villages, not suburban dormitories or second-home reservations which are only villages in name.

Kersey said, 'Unless something happens soon I think we and the Beales are in for plenty of stick.'

Wycliffe brought him up to date on his interviews with Maurice and with Vicary.

'You think there could be something in the blackmail angle?'

69

Wycliffe grimaced. 'It's possible I suppose, but these people – Simon, Vicary, even Maurice – they're business people; their job consists in wheeling and dealing, bluff and counter-bluff. If Newcombe was trying to squeeze them on the strength of some family skeleton they'd bamboozle him with tactics and tie him up so tight he'd be afraid to squeak, but I don't think they'd shoot him.'

Kersey sighed. 'Somebody did.'

Wycliffe ticked off points, mentally. 'You've got a statement from the Gratton girl?'

'Yes; it doesn't tell us anything fresh. I don't think there's much in it but I suppose we should try to be sure. If the weather is good enough we could have a re-run tonight – a couple of fellows and a couple of women; put her on the seat and see what she makes of it. At least we might get some idea of what she did see.'

'I agree.'

Wycliffe telephoned his headquarters: 'Telex to the Met: Details of wife-murder: Eduardo Santos in Camden, approximately fourteen years ago. Santos released on parole – details.'

The duty officer brought in an official envelope. 'Just arrived from Newton sub-division, sir.'

He slit open the envelope and spread the contents on the little table for Kersey to see. Copies of two certificates, one recording the marriage of Francis Arthur Vicary to Gertrude Rosemary Beale on January 2nd 1962; the other, the birth of their child, Esther Gertrude, on August 4th in the same year.

Kersey said, 'So what? A seven-month baby? More likely careless premarital sex, but either way, what can we make of it?'

Wycliffe growled. 'I'm damned if I know; the point is, what had Newcombe expected, or hoped for?'

He sat back in his chair, filled his pipe and lit it. Kersey, envious, said, 'I thought you were cutting down.'

'I am; this is only the second today.'

Wycliffe smoked in silence while Kersey turned over the pages of the report file. The church clock chimed a quarter to four and almost at once a bell sounded somewhere in the

70

school. Within a minute, children were tumbling through the gates and fanning out over the Green, interest now focused on the fair.

Wycliffe said, 'Naomi and Maurice have probably been married for twenty years at least.'

'So?'

He seemed about to offer some explanation but changed his mind and said only: 'I think I'll talk to her.'

'Do you want me any more, sir?'

'No.'

'Then I'll get back to the office. My sergeant will think I've gone away to live.'

Wycliffe smiled to himself. Kersey was getting a kick out of his promotion.

'How long have you been married, Mrs Beale?'

Naomi looked at him, unsure whether or not she should treat the question as impertinent; but she answered, 'Twenty-one years. Maurice and I were rather young—'

He cut her short, thinking that she might be more helpful if she was slightly confused. 'So you were here for a long time with Emily Newcombe.'

She amended that promptly: 'Emily worked here for seventeen or eighteen years after my marriage.'

'Part-time?'

'Part-time, full-time – as she wanted it. She and Joyce were as thick as thieves and they worked it to suit themselves. My father-in-law was absurdly indulgent to them – as he still is to Joyce. And that makes for problems in running the house, I can tell you!'

They were in a tiny room hardly more than a cubby-hole, which Naomi called her 'retreat'. It had a writing-table and chair, two armchairs and a shelf stacked with women's magazines; there was no room for more. She had said, 'We shall be more private in here.'

'So you were already established at Ashill when your sister-in-law married Mr Vicary and, of course, when their child was born.'

71

She was clearly puzzled by these remarks, which were not quite questions and seemed inconsequential. After starting a sentence she thought better of it and said nothing.

Wycliffe spoke conversationally, almost dreamily; he had relaxed into his chair and seemed to have all the time in the world. With no particular aim he was offering Naomi a variety of baits, any one of which might draw her into talk.

'I saw your husband this morning and he was telling me about the tragic events which brought Edward to live here and how most of the responsibility for the boy fell upon you.'

'Maurice told you that?' Her sharp little eyes scanned his placid features in surprise. 'Well, it's no more than the simple truth.'

'Of course, your mother-in-law was alive for several years after Edward's arrival. I suppose it was only after her death—'

She cut him short. 'Edward came here when he was eight and he was thirteen when my mother-in-law died, but for those five years she was a virtual invalid; she had a heart condition and we had to be careful not to excite her . . . It was very difficult because I had the responsibility without the authority.' Naomi's cheeks flushed as she recalled her frustrations.

'Your mother-in-law had different ideas about Edward's upbringing?'

Naomi laughed briefly. 'They were Ruby Price's ideas; that's what made it so . . . so galling.'

'Ruby Price?'

'She was the district nurse – a glorified midwife. She's been retired for years now, but she still lives in Washford.'

'She had some influence over your mother-in-law?'

Naomi hesitated, but the chance to unburden some of the accumulated bitterness of years was too much for her; and this man, policeman though he was, had a quiet sympathetic manner which made it easy to talk to him. She said, 'I'd put it strong than that; my mother-in-law was *dominated* by Ruby Price!' The tiny, rather pathetic little mouth trembled. 'Whatever that woman said was right.' She studied the rings on her plump fingers then looked up at him. 'Do you know, all three children – Maurice, Nicholas and Gertrude – were brought into the world by Ruby Price – in this house. Any other woman of her class would have gone into a nursing home and had the best of everything. Even when Gertrude had Esther, it was Ruby Price . . . I said to Gertrude at the time, "If it were me . . . !" '

'But she fell in with her mother's wishes?'

'She—' Naomi stopped herself. 'Well, that's another story.'

'I would have thought that the husband – Mr Vicary would have had something to say.'

Naomi gave an unpleasant little laugh. 'Her husband! You've got to remember that Frank Vicary was very small fry then – scarcely believing in his luck! He wasn't Secretary-Accountant in those days!'

'So that Edward was a teenager before you were in a position to—'

She cut him short. 'Edward, poor boy, was never given a chance. My father-in-law took against him almost from the moment his wife died . . . If I'm truthful, I should say that he was *turned* against the boy.'

'By whom?'

A knowing smile. 'Who do you think? Simon was disappointed at not having a grandson and there was just the possibility that he might have thought of Edward as a substitute . . . Frank Vicary wasn't going to have that!'

'I would have thought Simon Beale a very difficult man to influence.'

'So he is—by anybody other than his famous son-in-law!'

She broke off abruptly, listening to some sound which Wycliffe had missed. Almost at once there was a tap at the door, which opened, and Joyce, their old servant, was standing there. It seemed obvious that Naomi felt she had been caught out.

'What is it, Joyce?' Snappish.

'You haven't said anything about vegetables for tonight.'

CHAPTER FOUR

Mist over the estuary and before he was properly awake Wycliffe could hear the booming of a fog-horn down the coast like the lowing of a cow in labour. The radio promised that the mists would clear, that the sun would break through to give a fine, dry day.

'Take your mack, just in case . . .'

Wycliffe was at his desk by eight, ready for any of his pigeons which might come home to roost. The first was a telex from the Met: 'Eduardo Santos, convicted of wife-murder November sixty-eight. Sentenced life: paroled March seventy-seven. Since lived with sister, Islington. Advise further details or action.'

Another, a report from Ballistics, seemed to clinch the provenance of the gun which had killed Newcombe: 'Scratches on the cartridge-case produced by the ejector mechanism closely resemble those on photographic record of the experimental firing of similar ammunition from a nine-millimetre Beretta M951. The steel, as opposed to the unsatisfactory alloy version of this pistol, was first available in 1955 and was marketed commercially under the trade name: Brigadier . . .'

The file on the case was getting fatter but hardly more enlightening. A middle-aged layabout, a bachelor living alone, had been shot through the head one night with a very professional weapon. This, in a village of a thousand people where crime with a capital C was virtually unknown; a closely knit community where it was soon common knowledge if husband and wife decided on twin beds or a new washing machine. The only outsiders were the Beales, isolated by

74

their money, their religion, their patronage, and the high wall round Ashill. Now it was certain that the gun used by the killer had come from there.

With the ball-point he was holding Wycliffe wrote the word MOTIVE on his scribbling pad and underlined it three times. What had made this middle-aged, verminous yokel a target for the killer?

When Diane arrived he said, 'Find out if Sergeant Willis is in the building and, if he is, ask him to come here.'

Willis worked in the drugs squad but Wycliffe remembered that he was a do-it-yourself fanatic, what used to be called a home handyman, and Beales had a department which was the Mecca of that breed.

Willis was nearing retirement, counting the days, having had his fill of the most depressing and unrewarding job in the force, where the kicks come from both sides, villain and victims. Willis arrived; a massively built man who looked as though he had been hewn from the solid rock and allowed to weather.

'I suppose you are a customer in the DIY department at Beales?'

'Have been for years, sir.'

'Do you deal with anybody in particular? Anybody you prefer to go to?'

A flicker of interest but no questions. 'They're a helpful lot and their prices are competitive, that's why people go there, but there was one chap I used to know especially well. He's retired now – hung up his overall and collected his clock a year ago.'

'He sounds like the chap I'm after.'

'Billy Reynolds? What's he done?'

'Nothing that I know of but I want somebody who can tell me about the firm as it was twenty years ago.'

Willis laughed. 'Billy will do that all right, it's his hobby-horse. He worked there from leaving school.'

'Do you know where he lives?'

'I do, as it happens, sir. As far as I know he's still got the same house in Coronation Terrace out to Havercombe.

75

I can't tell you the number . . .'

Wycliffe would have liked to talk to Billy himself but there are limits.

'Have you got much on at the moment?'

'Nothing that can't wait.'

'You've heard of Frank Vicary?'

'I know he's a director of Beales and that he married the boss's daughter.'

'Good! I want you to go and see Reynolds; find out all you can about Vicary; especially about his early days with the firm and his marriage to Gertrude Beale. It must have caused enough gossip at the time. Tell Reynolds we shall treat what he tells us in confidence.'

Willis said, 'Is it the Washford murder?'

'Yes, and you'd better report direct to me or to Mr Kersey – at Washford.'

Later that evening, when he arrived in Washford, there was more evidence of hardening attitudes in the village. Some creative artist with an aerosol paint can had sprayed the word MURDERERS across the mellow brickwork of the wall in front of Ashill. An old man, presumably their gardener, was trying to get it off with some sort of solvent, and a free-lance photographer of Wycliffe's acquaintance was taking pictures, making sure that the police van was included. So far the press and TV had shown little interest in Washford's murder but anything might trigger them off.

Kersey was in the van, going through house-to-house reports and marking the interesting bits with a red ball-point.

Wycliffe asked him about the Nancy Gratton experiment: 'Did it come off?'

Kersey grinned. 'The girl co-operated and we went through the drill but I doubt if it got us any further. We tried her with two women and two men, in random order, making twenty appearances, with sometimes a hand torch and sometimes a candle. She got the sex right thirteen out of the twenty times. I don't know what the statisticians would make of that but I do know that the seat is a long

76

way from the window and with the dim light of a candle or torch . . .' Kersey screwed up his rubbery features in a grimace. 'I don't think we can rely too much on Nancy.'

Wycliffe said, 'Anything else?'

'Just something in the reports: gossip about old Blatchford, the innkeeper. It seems he's a widower and that his late wife was sister to Joyce, the old girl who works at Ashill. The word is that he now sleeps with Dora, who's less than half his age and not at all bad to look at.' Kersey was mildly envious. 'I'd like to think that at seventy . . . but maybe it's the pub she's after. And speaking of the pub, there's something else. The Blatchfords have been there for generations; they had the place on a lease from the Ashill estate, but when Simon took over he gave them notice to quit. At that time our Blatchford was working as a sales rep for a firm of agricultural merchants and his parents were running the pub. The story goes that he went to Simon and threatened to expose some fiddle over government subsidies on the estate farms. As a result the Blatchfords were allowed to buy their freehold.'

The same sort of tales had circulated endlessly in Wycliffe's village; they were part of the folklore; whether they were true or not scarcely mattered.

Wycliffe was staring out of the window at Ashill. 'That damned wall!'

'The wall? You mean who's been writing on it?'

'I mean the wall; they hide behind it. In a way, the villagers have a point. If the Beales hadn't been who they are we should have gone a long way towards sorting them out by now. But we daren't cut corners; if we do we shall be tripping over lawyers from then on. Before we can tackle any one of them we've got to have a case that hangs together – and that means we've got to have a motive.'

Kersey said, 'You seem sure they've got the answer.'

Wycliffe glanced at him and away again without comment. After a moment he said: 'They don't live their entire lives in there; Maurice and Vicary go to their office; Edward sells his pictures – he must have an agent, a gallery or something. What about the others? What do they do? They must have friends, acquaintances, interests . . . Don't tell me that Nicky, for example, spends all his time cultivating his moustache and playing at soldiers.'

Kersey said, 'You want them filled out; I see that. But it won't be easy to make the kind of inquiries you're after without stirring things.'

'Then let's stir.'

While the two men were talking there had been almost continuous exchanges on the radio next door; occasionally involving the duty officer, whose natural voice sounded oddly out of place amid the bursts of canned speech. It was so ordinary and unremarkable that they had taken no notice but now the duty officer tapped on the door and came in with his message pad.

'Message from PC Miller, sir, on his personal radio. He's at Tower Cottage, Vicarage Road, on house-to-house and he's found a dead woman in an upstairs room. He says she's been shot.'

Wycliffe had an odd feeling; it was as though he had been waiting for this with no real idea of what to expect. He said: 'Presumably Miller knows the woman – what's her name?'

The duty officer glanced at his pad. 'Price – Ruby Price.'

'The midwife?'

The officer looked surprised. 'Well, yes, sir. Miller says she's a retired district nurse.'

'All right. You know what to do. First a GP, then headquarters; they'll notify the coroner and get things organized.'

They looked up Vicarage Road on the map. It branched off from the main street near the top and ran along the upper boundary of the churchyard, above the vicarage; finally it petered out in a lane serving two or three farms. Wycliffe followed Kersey out to his car and they drove up North Street. Vicarage Road began as a double row of terraced houses which were followed by a string of pre-1914 villas in their own gardens; after that, the wall of the churchyard on one side and fields on the other.

Kersey said, 'Have we passed the place?'

But when they came to it Tower Cottage was not easily missed: it looked like a little church which had been domesticated and it stood in a garden behind a privet hedge. A stile on each side of the road marked the line of the footpath to the moor which skirted the grounds of the vicarage on one side and followed the line of the privet hedge on the other.

Miller was waiting for them just inside the gate. 'This way, sir.' He led the way to the back door. 'She never used the front.'

A ginger cat padded about the yard, mewing piteously. Miller said, 'It was up there with her; I had to shut it out.' He pushed open the door, fending off the cat while they entered the kitchen. Music came from somewhere upstairs and Miller said, 'It's her radio – I didn't think I ought to touch anything.'

An electric cooker and refrigerator at least thirty years old, and shelves stacked with preserving jars and bottles; everything gleaming clean but an overall musty smell. Miller pointed to a couple of glass jars popping into their air-locks, 'She makes her own wine.'

Beyond the kitchen, a tiny hall and a staircase – more like a mill-ladder – which led to the upper room. Wycliffe went up alone. At the top of the stairs he was able to look into a large, square room with two windows, one facing the moor and the other looking out over the village. Despite the gloom and drizzle outside the room was bright and cheering. On the radio a choir was singing the hymn, *Ye holy Angels bright*.

The dead woman lay in a heap on the floor by the window which overlooked the moor; her body was partly supported by a wicker chair and she was surrounded by bits of china and a tea-tray which must have been knocked over as she slid from the chair to the floor. She had been shot through the head. Wycliffe did not go into the room. Between him and the dead woman a round, cast-iron stove stood on its iron tray and sent a smoke-pipe up through the ceiling.

79

The tray was littered with paper, some of it burned to ash, some scorched and charred.

Nothing to do but wait for the experts.

'You have been listening to morning service broadcast from the church of St Michael and all Angels . . .' The cultured voice of the woman presenter spoke blindly into the room.

He went downstairs and was joined by Kersey and Miller in the garden, 'How did you find her?'

Miller said, 'She's a Miss Ruby Price, sir. I was on house-to-house – actually, she was the last call on my list. I went to the back door, which was open, and knocked. I know she's a bit deaf and I could hear music coming from somewhere so I called out. After two or three goes I got concerned so I went through the kitchen to the bottom of the stairs and shouted from there. Of course, there was no answer, so I thought I'd better find out if anything was wrong . . .'

'She lived here alone?'

'Most of her life I think, sir. She was the district nurse till she retired and that must have been way back. She was quite a character – well known for miles around.'

Wycliffe had the absurd notion that he was being 'let in' on the plot a stage at a time; only the previous day he had first heard of Ruby Price from Naomi; and probably at that time she was already dead, shot through the head, as Newcombe had been.

The sound of a car stopping came from the road.

'See who it is, Miller.'

Wycliffe walked down the back garden, a series of neatly cultivated, weed-free plots in the black earth: potatoes, broad beans, carrots, parsnips, runner-beans under cloches . . . The bottom end of the garden was given over to fruit trees and here there was a gate opening on to the footpath which led to the moor. At this point the path ran along the edge of a field where sheep were grazing; beyond that other tiny fields, then the open moor, and finally the twin tors on the sky line.

Miller came back with the doctor, a man in his sixties, stout and florid; a physician in need of a spot of self-healing if only by cutting down on the whisky.

He spoke to Kersey: 'You're keeping me busy; two in as many days is a bit much for a village this size.'

Kersey introduced him to Wycliffe. 'Dr Sharpe, Detective Chief Superintendent Wycliffe.'

Wycliffe went upstairs with the doctor and into the room for the first time.

Sharpe went straight to the body and bent over it. 'Poor old Ruby! To finish up like this! What are we dealing with, Mr Wycliffe – a homicidal maniac?' A moment later he went on, 'Well, you don't need me to tell you she's dead. Shot through the head, the same as Newcombe.' He looked at his watch as though it might help him. 'She's been dead a good while; long enough for rigor to come and go . . . She's been there since yesterday at least, possibly before that, but Franks will tell you. After all, he's paid for it.'

Wycliffe switched off the radio; he was looking round the room with curiosity but unwilling to disturb anything until his bloodhounds had sniffed it over. Apart from the cast-iron stove, which reminded him of the one in his classroom when he started school, there was a large work-table, an old treadle sewing-machine, two worn armchairs which did not match, cupboards and bookshelves. The floor was covered with sisal matting strewn with home-made woollen rugs.

'Can you tell me anything about her, doctor?'

The doctor fingered his gingery moustache, which was turning grey. 'Depends what you want to know. I looked in on her now and then for old time's sake; she never needed me professionally, she was tough as old boots. I suppose you know she was our district nurse until she retired ten or twelve years back? She covered the same ground as I do. She must be seventy-four or five now but she very nearly lived off what she grew herself. She was a dedicated vegetarian; she even thought she'd converted her cat till she found he was catching young rabbits and field-mice on the

81

sly, and that was a great disappointment to her.'

'She never married?'

'No. Ruby had very little use for men. She knew her job and she was a worker. When I came here first she was doing her rounds in an old Morgan three-wheeler which she called Boanerges, but before that she had a bike.'

The doctor sighed. 'She and I attended scores of deliveries together in the old days – all winds and weathers, day and night. Of course, that was before the Nye Bevan circus started up, when women still had their babies at home.'

'Did she have many visitors?'

'Very few I'd say; she didn't encourage people to come and see her though that didn't stop her visiting them. She kept in touch with "my mothers and babies", as she called them, though some of the mothers are dead and gone and a few of the babies must be knocking fifty.' He pushed back his fisherman's hat to scratch his thinning hair. 'Come to think of it, she did have one regular visitor – young Beale – Edward. Simon adopted him when he was seven or eight – I think he comes from Simon's wife's side. Ruby was very friendly with Simon's wife, who died a few years back, and she always had a fancy for Edward – Teddy, she called him. He seems a bit of an oddity – he's taken up painting and spends a lot of time on the moor sketching, so whenever he's passing he looks in on Ruby.'

Wycliffe saw the doctor to his car then, from his own car, he radioed instructions for more men and more back-up facilities. Whether they would be of any use was a question but the key principle of modern police work is saturation – cast your net wide and often; collect and collate. Gather enough data and what you are looking for is sure to be there somewhere – if only you can find it. Sometimes it works; just as often the culprit is caught – if at all – because of somebody's hunch or through sheer luck – as with the Yorkshire ripper.

A homicidal maniac the doctor had said, but he was an old-fashioned doctor; we no longer have maniacs, homicidal or otherwise; they have gone the way of idiots, imbeciles and lunatics. Soon criminals will be 'the socially maladjusted' but, for the moment, we do have psychopaths who sometimes take to killing people. At some stage he would have to make up his mind whether he was looking for a 'killer' in the abstract – a psychopath; or a killer with a motive which might be considered rational.

Sergeant Smith arrived with his photographic gear. 'The others are following in the Range Rover, sir.' He went upstairs and began putting Ruby's upper room on film. A few minutes later Franks roared up in his Porsche.

'If it goes on like this, Charles, I shall apply for a full-time appointment. Where is he? Or is it a she this time?'

The room with the two windows was beginning to lose its private character as an extension of the dead woman's individuality, and was becoming a public place.

Franks said, 'Shot like the other. I suppose this one is down to the same gentleman who disposed of Monday's offering? He turned the body over and Smith's camera recorded his every move. 'She's been here for a while, Charles – quite a while, that's for sure.' He stood up, dusting off his trousers. 'Well, shift her when you like; the sooner the better. Is the van here yet?'

It was another quarter of an hour before the mortuary van arrived with two men who removed what was left of Ruby Price on a canvas stretcher.

Wycliffe's own men took over to begin the business of searching and recording. Wycliffe, himself, prowled about, looking vaguely at the things with which Ruby had chosen to surround herself and hoping they might tell him something of the kind of woman she was. The bookshelves first. Apart from nursing manuals and works on obstetrics and midwifery – all somewhat dated – there were books on gardening, on the lives of musicians, on vegetarian diets and cookery, and two whole shelves of detective novels. Then the pictures: part of one wall was covered with snap-shots of babies, framed in sets of six and each labelled with a name and date. The series covered nearly forty years, from the beginning of the thirties to the late sixties. So Ruby had taken her camera on post-natal visits. The Beales were

83

there with the rest: Nicholas, Maurice and Gertrude and, much later, Esther. There were other framed photographs on the walls, two or three of Ruby herself, and one, taken on the lawn at Ashill, showed a younger Simon, sitting next to a fair, frail-looking woman, a faded English rose. No doubt this was Rosemary. They sat in wicker chairs and there was a third, empty chair, and a little table laden with tea things. Presumably Ruby was taking the picture.

On the same wall as the snap-shots of babies there was an oil-painting of the moor in winter, signed E Beale. The tors were streaked with snow, and blue-black clouds against a bleached sky threatened more to come. The foreground was a study in sombre purples and browns, cunningly slashed with white. Not a comfortable painting; no Christmas card snow-scene. Wycliffe told himself it was a competent piece of work, that it conveyed a powerful sense of loneliness. Charlie Wycliffe: art critic. Success for Helen, who had taken in hand his aesthetic development when they married. At that time he had known little that was not inside the covers of police manuals and law books. Now he knew the difference between a Monet and a Manet; he could distinguish between Mozart and Haydn, and had read Dostoevsky.

The first job of the searchers was to find the cartridge case belonging to the bullet which had killed Ruby; after that they would look for the bullet itself, which might be embedded in the woodwork or even in a wall.

On the wall opposite the one with the snap-shots there were three built-in cupboards and the door of one of them stood a little open. Wyclife peered in and saw a cardboard box containing a large number of manilla envelopes, stuffed with papers, all standing on edge in the box as though in a filing drawer. From this cupboard a trail of papers led across the floor to the stove, suggesting that Ruby's filing system had been raided and its contents partly destroyed.

Nothing could be done until Smith had checked all likely surfaces for prints so Wycliffe went downstairs and out to his car.

Outside a group of people had gathered, a dozen or so adults and a couple of children. They stood, silent in the sunshine, looking at nothing, for there was nothing to see except parked cars. Wycliffe had the impression that they were in some way organized, at least that they had a common purpose beyond merely gawping at the comings and goings. There were no shouts, nothing in the nature of a demonstration, but he sensed their antagonism.

So far, press, radio and television had virtually ignored the murder of Bunny Newcombe, but two killings would make them think again. 'Killer loose in Moorland Village.' And it wouldn't be long before someone remembered that this was Baskerville country, though it was hard to imagine a hound operating with a nine-millimetre automatic.

He drove back to the police caravan. He felt reasonably sure that he was not dealing with the doctor's homicidal maniac, nor with the modern equivalent, a psychopath. In these killings there was nothing to suggest that the killer had taken pleasure in his task – that he had achieved any catharsis through violence. There can hardly be a less spectacular way of achieving sudden death than by a shot through the head. But if the killings had some sort of rational motive, what was the link? Again he was back to the Beales.

Franks had said that Ruby had been dead 'quite a while'; exactly how long was important but he would have nothing better to go on until after the post-mortem – if then. In the meantime the obvious thing was to talk to the one member of the Beale family who was known to have kept up contact with the dead woman – Edward.

He parked the car by the police van. On the Green they were stringing rows of flags and fairy lamps between the trees and erecting a wooden platform near the war memorial in preparation for the fair on Friday. The fun-fair was ready for business and due to open that evening.

The church clock chimed and struck three, reminding him that he had had no lunch. Too late now. As he was about to go into the van he saw Esther coming across from Ashill towards him. She was wearing another of her 'Impressionist' frocks, a small flower pattern on a white ground, with plenty of tucks and ruching.

'I've been watching for you.' She looked at him but her face and manner gave no clue as to whether she had come to discuss Newcombe's rabbits or to tell him of some new tragedy.

'My cousin, Edward, has something to tell you.'

Once more he had the feeling that he was playing a role in some drama of which he had not seen the script; it made him uneasy. 'Then why doesn't he come here?'

'He's very upset; I had difficulty enough in getting him to let me come.'

'What's it about?'

'Ruby Price.'

'What about her?'

'You'd better talk to him.'

Wycliffe recalled his encounter with Edward in the church-yard. The young man had struck him as timid – perhaps more than timid – scared; but that was on Monday, two days ago.

'If you are going to talk to him you had better come through our flat, otherwise you will have to face grandfather or Aunt Naomi.' She had the devastating frankness of a child with the poise of an adult and he felt like anything but a high-ranking officer conducting an inquiry.

'All right.'

He followed her through the gates and round the house to an outside staircase which led to the Vicarys' first-floor flat. In the hall, she said, 'Don't make too much noise, I think mother is asleep.'

One of the doors off the hall took them through into the main part of the house, at the end of the first-floor corridor. He followed her, almost the length of the broad corridor, past the head of the staircase, then up a narrow, steep flight of stairs.

'These are the attics where the servants used to sleep when there were proper servants. Edward has the biggest as a studio and bedroom.'

Esther opened one of several doors in the long passage of bare boards. It was a large room with a dormer window facing north and even on this sunny afternoon it was filled with a clear, cold, clinical light. Edward was standing by the window looking like a man in the condemned cell. The room was poorly furnished: a bed, a wardrobe, a worn settee and an old armchair; these, and the tools of his trade: easel, painting table, artist's donkey . . . There were shelves of art books and a number of canvases stacked face to the wall but nothing on show.

'Mr Beale?' Wycliffe held out his hand.

He was given the armchair while Edward and Esther sat side-by-side on the settee and reminded Wycliffe of the babes in the wood.

'You want to tell me something?'

Edward, hollow-eyed and tense, made a couple of false starts before words came properly. 'I know about Ruby Price . . . I wanted to tell you that she and I . . . that I usually call there when I'm up on the moor sketching . . . I'm often up there when the weather is fine enough.'

'Do you call on her every time you go up to the moor?'

'Almost every time.'

'Going or coming back?'

'Usually coming back; in the mornings I like to catch the light.' Edward had both hands tucked under his thighs and he was swaying slightly.

'When did you last call?'

A long silence and Wycliffe repeated the question.

'The day before yesterday — Monday.' The words were only barely audible.

'When you last saw her, was she her usual self?'

'She was dead.' Edward heaved a great sigh as though a burden had fallen from his shoulders.

Esther sat bolt upright, never showing any sign of involvement; in her old-fashioned dress she could have been posing for a photograph.

Wycliffe sounded a note of caution, as much for his own sake as Edward's.

'Remember you are volunteering information.'

'I want to tell you about it.'

'Very well. Did you kill her?'

'No!'

'She was dead when you found her?'

'Yes.'

'When was that?'

'Sometime before five o'clock on Monday afternoon.'

'Not long before I met you in the churchyard?'

He nodded. 'I had just come from there; I was petrified.'

Esther said, 'Tell him what you saw earlier.'

Edward ran his tongue over his lips. 'I spent most of the day sketching around Druid's Rock, which is a couple of miles from Ruby's place, but I could see the cottage from where I was. About four o'clock or a bit later I started to pack up. I happened to glance across at the cottage and I saw smoke coming from the chimney.'

'That surprised you?'

'Yes, it did. It was a hot day and Ruby only used a fire for heating; she did everything else by electricity.'

'Go on.'

'Well, I didn't think a lot about it but I looked over there once or twice and I saw that the smoke soon died away. Then I started out for home and when I was about a quarter of a mile from the cottage I saw someone come out of the garden door and walk off along the footpath towards the village.'

'A man or a woman?'

'Oh, I'm sure it was a man, though I couldn't see him well enough to recognize him.'

'Can you describe what you did see?'

Edward frowned. 'Well, I think he was fairly tall and he had dark trousers, I think, and a jacket or windcheater or something tight at the waist – that was dark too.'

Years of interrogation had made Wycliffe acutely sensitive to changes in the manner of a witness – particularly when he or she stopped telling the truth and started to improvise. He felt sure that Edward had done that now, though he was by no means sure where the improvisation had begun.

'Was there anything familiar about the man you saw?'

'No. Nothing!'

A mysterious stranger, in fact.

'You weren't close enough to describe him very clearly but you are able to say that he was like no-one you know.'

Edward flushed but said nothing.

'What did you do?'

'I didn't do anything. What else could I do? I just walked on till I came to the cottage and let myself in by the garden door as usual. I didn't realize that there was anything wrong.'

'Go on.'

'Well, I went to the back door of the house, which was open, and I called out, "It's me!" There was no answer but I could hear loud music coming from upstairs. I knew that she was a bit deaf so I went up . . . I looked in the room, and there she was . . .' He swallowed hard, then added, 'I could see the wound in her head; I knew she must be dead.'

'Did you touch her?'

He shuddered and shook his head. Edward had not shaved and dark bristles stood out on his sallow skin so that with his hollow cheeks he looked almost corpse-like.

'I panicked . . .'

There would have to be a formal interrogation so Wycliffe was content to let the boy tell his story. 'When you visited Ruby, what did you talk about?'

'All sorts of things; she liked to hear anything and everything about the family and about Ashill.'

'Did she resent the fact that she was not as welcome at Ashill as she had been in the past?'

He frowned. 'Sometimes she said things which made me think she was upset about it.'

'What sort of things?'

Edward hesitated and Wycliffe pressed him, 'Ruby is dead – murdered; you say you didn't kill her. If we are to believe you, you will have to be completely truthful and frank.'

'Well, she would say things like, "They've a lot to thank me for but you'd never think so; I'm treated like a leper!"

and "It's a good thing I'm not one to bear a grudge." '

'Did she know what had happened to your parents?'

'Of course! That was while Aunt Rosemary was still living and she told her everything.'

'Did you mind her knowing?'

'No, she was always pleasant to me. In any case, I don't suppose it could have been very secret: it must have been in the newspapers at the time though I don't remember that.'

'Do you think people in the village connected you with what they might have read in the newspapers about your parents?'

'No, I don't think they did – at least, not until recently . . .'

'What happened recently?'

'I met Bunny Newcombe one afternoon when I was on my way back from the moor – about a fortnight ago, it was. Whenever I met him he used to look at me with a funny sort of grin; when I was young I used to be scared of him. Anyway, this time he said, "Do you ever hear from your father? He must be out now, they only do a few years for a killing these days." '

'Was that all?'

'Yes. I didn't say anything; I just walked on.'

'*Do* you ever hear from your father?'

'No!'

Wycliffe was at a loss to guess at the relationship between Esther and the boy. It was as though, having arranged the interview, she sat-in on it to make sure that her protégé performed properly.

During the questioning Wyclifffe had got up from his seat and was moving about the room, looking at this and that, sometimes standing with his back to the room, staring out of the window at the beech trees on the other side of the Green. At one point he was near a batch of canvases, propped facing the wall. He stooped to pick one up. 'May I look?'

Edward seemed tongue-tied and Esther said, 'Edward doesn't like people looking at his work while he is there.'

He had no reason or right to insist. He said, 'You painted a picture for Ruby Price.'

Edward looked embarrassed. 'I painted the picture and she wanted to buy it so I gave it to her.'

Wycliffe was standing with his hands behind his back, trying to decide on his next move. 'You didn't hear the shot?'

'Shot?' Edward looked startled.

'The shot that killed her; probably the sound would carry across the open moor.'

'I didn't hear anything.'

Edward's position was too serious for anything but a formal approach. Wycliffe said, 'I have to ask you to come to the police station at Newton to answer further questions and to make a formal statement. I will arrange for a car to pick you up at half-past four. In the meantime you can take what advice you see fit.'

Esther said, 'Will he be allowed to leave again?'

'Certainly, if what he has told me is the whole truth.'

Edward seemed to be relieved rather than otherwise.

Esther came with Wycliffe to see him off the premises. At the top of the steps she said to him, 'Will he be in serious trouble for not saying that he found her earlier?'

'No. Failure to report a crime is anti-social but not criminal.'

She stood, her hands resting on the rail, looking down at the cobbled yard and the old stables. She said, 'Edward has a very rough time, you know; it's not only what happened when he was young, it's what happens now.'

'What does happen?'

It was some time before she answered. 'It's the way they treat him . . . Aunt Naomi and Uncle Maurice treat him as though he was still a small boy and not very bright . . . Uncle Nicholas ignores him completely but, of course, he ignores everyone these days . . . Mostly it's my father and grandfather – they treat him as though he wasn't there most of the time; I mean, they don't even speak to him if he comes into the room, but if grandfather does have anything to say it's always something cutting and hurtful.'

'Why?'

She took time to think then turned to him. 'It's difficult to say why. To be "in" with grandfather you have to be exactly what he expects you to be. Edward doesn't come up to specification . . . not by a very long way.'

'Do you?'

She treated the question very seriously. In fact, Wycliffe wondered if this girl ever laughed.

She said, 'I could do very easily if I went in for that sort of thing.'

'Why does your father dislike Edward?'

A pause for thought. 'He despises people who are not interested in money, and he can't use Edward for his own ends.'

'That sounds very harsh.'

'You asked the question.'

She seemed reluctant to let him go and for the first time he sensed that her detachment, her serenity, might be no more than skin-deep.

He tried to leave on a lighter note. 'I hope you are feeding the Newcombe livestock.'

'Yes; it's no problem. I rather like doing it.'

'Don't you have a job or something?'

'A job of sorts; I work mornings – Tuesdays to Saturdays – in a supermarket café in the city.'

'Why not in the family firm with your father?'

She changed the subject. 'Do you have children?'

'They're not children any more; they are older than you – twins, one of each.'

'I suppose they have marvellous jobs.' There was no trace of irony in her tone.

'I think they are both interested in what they do.'

He was puzzled; she seemed in an uneasy, wistful mood. Suddenly she said, 'We are talking as though we were both on the same side,' and with that she left him and went indoors.

Wycliffe was in the little interview cubicle, staring out of the window at the action on the Green – volunteer labour, the men working twice as hard as they would have done for pay. He was brooding on the Beales; it had become almost a way of life for him. What did they *do*? That was not precisely the question he wanted to ask but it was as near as he could get. When Esther had finished playing at being a waitress in the supermarket café did she spend the rest of her time swanning around looking like something out of a Monet poppy field? Vicary – her father – was absorbed in his work, but Wycliffe did not believe in that mythical beast, the Computer Man. How did he unwind – blow off steam? Even Maurice must do something when he tired of the effort of trying to look like a high-powered executive. And Nicholas . . . Nicholas who looked like a man of destiny but had nowhere to go . . . Gertrude, an unknown quantity; Naomi, with her frustrations and spites barely held in check . . . To say nothing of Simon, the ringmaster.

He could not remember a case in which he had been so out of contact with the people concerned; he felt an overwhelming need to *break in*.

'I've seen Billy Reynolds, sir.' Sergeant Willis was standing in the doorway. Perhaps Wycliffe looked blank for he added, 'The chap who used to work in Beales' DIY department.'

Wycliffe nodded. 'Come in.'

Willis seemed to fill the little room with his bulk and his movements were self-consciously restrained. 'He well remembers Vicary joining the firm, sir – he came there as a youngster – seventeen or eighteen, and he must have looked something like he does now for they christened him "The Chimp", but it wasn't long before he showed what he was made of. Simon put him in charge of checking requisitions from the departments and making out order forms but inside six months Vicary had worked out an entirely new system of stock control which remained in use until they went over to computers in their new building.'

Willis grinned. 'I gather that the staff didn't care much for their whizz kid but they had to admit he was something special.'

'How about his marriage to the Beale girl?'

Willis made a wry face. 'It came as a complete surprise

to everybody. Vicary had been with the firm eight or nine years by then and was virtually in charge of accounts—'

'Was he living with his parents?'

'No; as soon as he was able to support himself he moved into a flat with a friend – no queer business, apparently – and the arrangement lasted for several years. After a while, Vicary found a girl he was keen on and was all set to marry, then Bingo! It was all off and in no time at all he was married to the Beale girl.'

'Had she spent much time at the store?'

'Reynolds said he'd never seen her and neither had most of the staff.'

'I don't suppose you know the name of Vicary's old flat-mate?'

'Reynolds did – it's Patterson; he did well for himself too, he's now a partner in Duxbury's – the Blue Chip Garage chain. Lives in Sutton Drive, and you can't do that on social security.'

Wycliffe and Kersey spent two hours with Edward at the Newton police station, during the latter part of which Maurice adopted dramatic postures in the waiting-room. The boy answered their questions without apparent resentment; pale and tense, but lucid and concise. It was obvious that Kersey was surprised and impressed.

One new fact emerged. Asked if he had ever fired a gun, Edward had replied: 'Oh, yes. When I was a boy and Nicholas was on leave, he used to set up a target at the bottom of the garden. I didn't care a lot for it but he said it was up to everyone to prepare to defend the country against anarchy.'

'What did you use, a sporting rifle?'

'Oh, no. We used his automatic; the one that's been stolen.'

It was only much later that Wycliffe and Kersey were to look back and realize that if they had pursued this line of questioning a life might have been saved.

On one point only, Edward's story collapsed: 'This man you saw leaving the cottage when you were on your way back from the moor . . .'

Wycliffe saw the deep flush rise from the boy's neck and suffuse his pale face. 'There was no man, was there? You saw nobody, did you?'

He shook his head.

'Then why did you invent him?'

There was a longish silence before he answered, then he said, 'I thought nobody would believe the truth . . . I thought if I said I saw somebody leaving . . . I thought it would make it all more believable . . .'

Wycliffe was home by a little after seven and he found Helen in the garden.

'There's a lamb casserole in the oven; an apricot crumble to follow, and I've put a bottle of Barsac in the fridge.'

'What's this in aid of? I haven't forgotten an anniversary, have I?'

The garden was reaching its spring peak with magnolias, azaleas and rhododendrons competing for the eye. Through the shrubbery they could glimpse the waters of the estuary, scintillating in the sunlight. The gales and vicious driving rains of winter were forgotten.

'We are lucky.' He was thinking of the Beales.

'Yes.' She was thinking of the little back-to-back terraced house in which she had been brought up. She added, 'I heard on the News about the second murder.'

That accounted for the Barsac.

Helen had laid a table in the window of the living-room, overlooking the garden and the river beyond. They ate a leisurely meal; music by courtesy of M. Claude Debussy. Scrumptious!

Afterwards, while they were having their coffee, he became restless and in the end she said, 'You'd better do it if you feel you must.'

'Do what?'

'Whatever it is.'

He looked up a number in the directory and telephoned. 'Mr Patterson?'

'Speaking.'

'Chief Superintendent Wycliffe. I would like to come and see you this evening if possible.'

'Can you tell me what it's about?' Wary, with a hint of apprehension.

'It's possible you may be able to help us with an inquiry we have on hand. You are not directly concerned.'

'It all sounds very mysterious, superintendent, but I always make a point of being accommodating to the police. Will ten o'clock suit you? Or is that too late?'

'No, ten o'clock suits me.'

'It's the top flat; there is a speak-box in the entrance hall.'

Sutton Drive, overlooking the sea, was one of the most prestigious residential areas in the city; a terrace of tall, mid-Victorian houses, covered with white stucco and looking like a gigantic wedding cake. Built for wealthy Victorian families with no servant problem, they were five storeys high; now they had been furnished with lifts and split up into luxury flats.

Patterson was sturdily built and fair, his tendency to baldness not entirely hidden by a toupee, and he had that carefully groomed, well-preserved look of an ageing bachelor fighting a rearguard action against time.

Wycliffe was shown into a large sitting-room at the very top of the house; the curtains were drawn back and the window looked out to a vast expanse of sea, silvery in the darkness. Erotic Beardsley prints in stainless steel frames hung on white walls; there was a whitish carpet and club-chairs covered with white leather. It was obvious that Patterson provided a temporary roost for any birds of passage who happened along.

Wycliffe got straight to business: 'My inquiries concern the Washford murders. You will understand that we have to cast our net wide and I hope you won't read too much into my questions, which are purely—'

'Routine.' Patterson finished for him.

It was a relief occasionally to deal with someone who habitually sails sufficiently near the wind to know the ropes.

'How can I help you?'

'A number of years ago you shared a flat with Frank Vicary, who is now a director of Beales' Household Stores—'

'And married to the boss's daughter.' Patterson grinned. 'So that's it! I hardly think I shall be able to tell you much, I haven't seen Frankie above twice in twenty years.'

'You quarrelled?'

A canny look. 'No. After sharing a flat with him for five years he walked out on me at less than a week's notice; that's all.'

'He left to get married.'

Patterson was sitting, self-consciously nonchalant, in one of his club chairs. 'As you say, he left to get married.'

'You must have known it was in the offing, surely?'

'I don't think he knew himself.'

'But he must have been seeing the girl; perhaps you didn't share in his social life?'

Wycliffe received a knowing grin. 'We didn't have a scintillating social life; a beer at the local and a couple of girls on lucky weekends was the outside of it. Believe it or not, we were two hard-working guys from pretty dreary backgrounds, determined to beat the system. We worked at our jobs all day and did evening classes and correspondence courses in our spare time. Accountancy, law, business admin and God knows what else. In the end, Frankie got hooked on a girl. She was a pleasant, homely sort of kid, just waiting to turn herself into a good wife and mother. I don't think he was leading her up the garden; he used to talk to me quite seriously about when they were married, though he wasn't in a rush to sign her up. Then, from one day to the next, it was all off; Frankie was to marry the Beale chick.'

Patterson turned to face Wycliffe. 'Lucy – that was the kid's name – was absolutely floored; I don't know what happened to the poor little bastard but I've never seen anybody so winded. It was bloody cruel.'

'Had he ever mentioned the Beale girl before?'

'Never!'

'They had a child seven months later.'

'So I've heard. All I can say, if Frankie seduced his boss's daughter he must have done it in the firm's time. I must admit I was staggered. After all, he wasn't a sex symbol and she, according to all accounts, was a poppet.'

'You've no idea what actually happened?'

Patterson frowned. 'My guess is there was some sort of deal, but why, in the name of God? I mean, what did the Beales get out of it? I know Frankie is a damned good accountant but you don't have to trade in your daughter for a good accountant.'

Patterson broke off and glanced at the gilded sun-ray clock above the fireplace. 'I don't want to be inhospitable but I'm expecting a guest . . .'

Wycliffe felt fairly sure he had got all he was likely to; probably all Patterson had to give, so he got up to go. As he was leaving a blonde girl in a low-cut dress and a fur stole got out of the lift. Patterson was hovering and winked when he caught Wycliffe's eye.

Wycliffe came away feeling that he now had most of the pieces but not the least idea how to put them together. Experience had taught him not to try too hard. Over the hours and days ahead words and phrases recalled, faces and episodes vividly remembered, would present themselves to his mind; patterns would suggest themselves only to be examined and rejected . . . But what if there was another crime?

He drove through the empty city streets, out into the country on the other side, through the lanes which would bring him to the Watch House. For the last mile he could look down on the estuary, shining dimly. A sizeable merchant ship in ballast was slipping downstream with the tide, her superstructure picked out in lights. Sometimes he fancied himself as a skipper on the bridge of such a ship, on her way down channel, bound for Bombay or Colombo; Lagos or Rio . . . He yawned, and the car swerved. Captain MacWhirr was tired.

Helen was in the drawing-room; watching television; the curtains were not drawn and he could still see the lights of his ship as she gathered speed beyond the narrows.

CHAPTER FIVE

Another fine day: the air had a gentle freshness, and the light a glowing quality which belongs to a fine morning in an English spring. But in his office, where it was impossible to open a window and the air was 'conditioned', the atmosphere, as usual, was secondhand, limp and apathetic as flat beer.

'But who am I to be cheerful?' – Wycliffe facing the fact that he had two murders on his hands and was no nearer a solution.

Franks had sent in his preliminary report on the Ruby Price post-mortem, but the only significant passage referred to the time of death: ' . . . some time on Monday, April 27th. It is difficult to support a more precise estimate with firm evidence but my impression is that death probably occurred after midday and before midnight . . .'

This was consistent with Edward's story but it also underlined his vulnerability for, if Franks was right, Edward had been with the dead woman within a short time of her death.

The routine of the day got under way; he signed forms, dealt with queries, dictated letters and memoranda until a few minutes before half-past ten so that even Diane was satisfied.

'Now you've got a press briefing; it's in the car-park for the benefit of the TV people. You've also got a note in the diary of Newcombe's funeral – three o'clock this afternoon, from the Fretwells'.'

Already these names were commonplace in the office, names of people whom Diane had never seen, and never even heard of three days earlier.

The press and television were making up for previous

indifference and there was an impressive gathering on the car-park.

'The man you detained last night, Mr Wycliffe . . .'

'No-one was detained. Mr Edward Beale co-operated with us and made a statement about his visits to the dead woman.'

'Isn't it true that he discovered the body?'

'Yes, that is so.'

'And failed to report it?'

'Mr Beale told me of his discovery yesterday afternoon.'

'Forty-eight hours after the event?'

'That is correct.'

'Are you any nearer an arrest following the interrogation of this young man?'

'No.'

'Is it the case that the weapon which killed Newcombe and the woman, Price, was the property of Captain Nicholas Beale of Ashill?'

'It is true that an automatic pistol belonging to Captain Beale is missing; it is also true that our ballistics expert considers that the bullet which killed Mr Newcombe was fired from such a pistol. As yet I have had no report on this aspect of the second killing.'

'Do you think that the villagers have reason to fear further outrages?'

'I can't answer that; all I can say is that our patrols should help to reassure them.'

'Are you aware of uneasiness among the villagers concerning alleged reluctance on the part of the police to follow certain leads?'

'I can well understand that the villagers are uneasy. As to leads, we shall continue to investigate fully every suspicious circumstance which comes to our notice.'

'Are you looking for a madman or for someone with a real grievance against his victims?'

'I have no information about the murderer's state of mind.'

And so on. The usual charade by which reporters fulfil their sacred duty and some harassed official tries to avoid saying something which could boomerang.

By midday Wycliffe was back in Washford; in the upper room which had shared Ruby's heart with her garden. Three men were at work there; a young man from Forensic was sorting through a quantity of half-burnt paper and even trying to make something of the ash itself. Real Sherlock Holmes stuff this, with forceps and lens. The contents of several of Ruby's envelopes had been reduced to ash or had survived only as charred remains.

The second man in the room was DC Fowler, the oldest member of Wycliffe's squad. He could be relied upon to work away at the most boring job without pause and without complaint, but he was by no means stupid. Now, with glasses on the end of his nose, he was going through the contents of Ruby's other envelopes, those which had not been damaged.

Each envelope had a name on it – the name of one of her 'babies' – and in it was stored, on odd scraps of paper, every bit of information she had been able to gather. All was grist to Ruby's mill, from the winning of a school prize or an attack of measles, to details of love affairs, marriage, job problems, parenthood and, in a few cases, death. It was all there, each envelope a data-bank for a biography and an intimate one at that.

Fowler said, 'Some of this could come in handy to an enterprising village blackmailer – or a poison-pen.'

Was that the explanation of her murder? Was she a blackmailer or, more credibly, a poison-pen writer? If so, where did Newcombe come in? It was hard to imagine them working as a team.

Fowler went on, 'As far as I can see, there's nothing on the Beales.'

Which might mean that Ruby saw the family as out of her range, or it could mean that what concerned the Beales was now part of the charred paper and ash being studied by the boffin from Forensic.

The third man, completing the research team, was new to the squad – a dyed-in-the-wool Cornishman called Curnow, a young man of deceptively gentle speech and manner. He was going through Ruby's diaries – half-a-dozen hard-covered exercise books in which she had noted down a terse record of her days.

'It's not much of a diary, sir, more a list of things she did and of people she visited; when she planted her seeds or bottled her wine or cut back her raspberries. I started with the current book and I'm working back but there's one recent entry you might want to see.'

Curnow handed him the book and pointed to the entry. Written in Ruby's round, schoolgirl hand, it was dated a month earlier, and it read: 'Honoured by a visit from Nicky – the first since dear R died. He took an hour to come to the point, which was that he has found romance – or thinks he has. He is worried that it might be blighted if the lady found out certain things. Her name wasn't mentioned but I've known about it for some time. Poor Nicky! I wonder what R would have made of it?'

For some reason Wycliffe called to mind the well-trodden path through the woods between Ashill and Quarry House about which the forthright Veronica had seemed oddly self-conscious. The idea of the ponderous and repressed Nicky having found romance at forty-six had its ludicrous side, but also a certain pathos, but had it anything to do with the case?

Routine. That blessed word. The uncomfortable truth was that he hadn't the least idea what to do next except plough on with the business of collecting information and hope that significant correlations would emerge. It was orthodox procedure and though he was wary of a surfeit of facts he had to toe the line; in these days a policeman works with one eye on the press and politicians.

Depressed, he went downstairs.

The whole house and garden had been turned upside down and men were tramping around the village again with their ball-points and clip-boards. Statements were being taken, typed, photocopied, and filed. God alone knew how many people were involved . . . And the murderer – what was he doing? A question of more than academic interest. A pathological killer would be at a certain stage of his traumatic cycle; he had achieved release but the initial euphoria would be followed, first by a sense of anti-climax, perhaps a wave of self-disgust, then the germ of a new desire, the growth of a fresh appetite . . . One feature among others which made Wycliffe sceptical of the psycho-path notion was the proximity in time of the two crimes; it was not conclusive but it was suggestive.

But if the killer was a 'rational' being with a credible motive, what would he be doing? It would presumably depend on how far his objective had been achieved. Either way it was a question of two down; how many to go?

He walked along Vicarage Road and down North Street; the sun shone out of a clear blue sky and flags were strung across the street between the houses. Some of the flags were of real bunting, faded and bleached by the celebrations of a century. The murder had not been allowed to cast any blight on the preparations and the whole village wore a cheerful, almost a carnival aspect. On the Green, near the platform, men were erecting a tall and colourful maypole.

Wycliffe went into the pub for a snack lunch and was surprised to find a good crowd of locals as well as men from the fair: the locals wore their best clothes and there was a holiday atmosphere, a good-tempered rowdiness with plenty of laughs. But as Wycliffe approached the bar they fell silent and all eyes turned on him.

The landlord greeted him with an air of amused tolerance. 'Well, sir, what can we do for you?' He pointed to the chalk-board. 'As you see, we've got a bit more on offer today.'

He ordered beer and a helping of cottage pie. The landlord repeated his order in a loud voice to an invisible Dora and turned back to him.

'Shall we be seeing you at the fair tomorrow, sir?'

'I hope so.'

'No arrest yet?'

'No.'

The whole room was listening; even the men from the fair had stopped talking among themselves, realizing that something was up. Dora, red-faced from bending over a hot stove, brought his pie on a heated plate, with a knife and fork wrapped in a paper napkin. He took it with his beer to a vacant place near one of the windows but the hubbub which had greeted him was not resumed. It was as though they waited for a cue and the cue was not long in coming.

Wycliffe had noticed the little red-headed shopkeeper, Chas Alford, at the centre of a small group of men who were plying him with drinks. In the group was another of the tradesmen Wycliffe recognized, the tobacconist and confectioner, Sam Brimblecombe, a stout, florid man who seemed to live with a short-stemmed pipe between his teeth.

Alford cleared his throat and said in a loud cawing voice, intended for the whole company, 'They had young Beale at the nick in Newton last night; kept him there for two hours.'

All eyes now turned on the red-head.

Alfred went on, 'I reckon they don't pull in a chap with his connections unless they got very good reason, but after two hours they let'm go.'

Another of the group, an obvious 'feed' inquired, 'Why would they do that, do you think, Charlie?'

A knowing smile. 'Well, you'd hardly expect me to be what you might call "in" with the police, but I do know something about the way these things work − the way they're *worked*.' He paused, then went on, 'My guess is, Uncle Simon phoned his friend, the chief constable.'

There was an uneasy laugh and several eyes turned on the superintendent, who went on with his meal, apparently oblivious.

But the red-head had not finished. 'Laugh if you like, but what if there's another killing tonight? That wouldn't be very funny, would it? Another innocent man or woman with a bullet through the head. Not funny at all!'

Wycliffe happened to glance across at the landlord and caught the old man watching him with an amused expression. Blatchford was enjoying himself.

Alford went on, 'I believe in looking at a man's *stock*, just like with a horse or a bullock. My father used to say, "Bad blood will out"—'

'And he should know all about that, Charlie!' A voice from another part of the room, which Alford ignored.

'That's not fashionable these days but there's a lot of things that aren't fashionable but is still true. Take this young man we're speaking of, for instance; one or two of us just happen to know his father was sentenced to "life" for murdering his wife. Now, the police know all about that – they should – and if I was they, I'd think about that; I'd think a lot about it. And all we ought to think about it too.'

There was a murmur of approval which sounded genuine.

Encouraged, the little red-head went on: 'But there's more to it than that. You can't just say, "Like father, like son;" you got to have evidence. That's only right. Well, this young man we're talking about, says he found Ruby Price lying dead – shot through the head – a woman we all thought well of, who done a tremendous amount of good for the village and brought most of us into this world. This young man, a regular visitor of Ruby's found her shot, *but he didn't tell anybody.*'

An impressed silence.

'He didn't tell anybody for two days and then only when the police come to question him. Now, we got to ask ourselves, *why* didn't he tell anybody? Why?'

Another pause for dramatic effect but this time it was fatal. A wag spoke up: 'I expect 'e forgot. After all, Charlie, you forget some things – like paying yer bills an' doing yer flies up when there's young girls about.'

There was a great burst of laughter and the little red-head tried to hide his confusion by pretending he had dropped something on the floor. It was not long before conversation returned to normal and then numbers began to thin.

As he was leaving, Wycliffe said to the landlord, 'Charlie Alford – is he the voice of the village?'

'He'd like to think so.'

'They're not taken in?'

Blatchford grinned. 'What do you think?'

'That there was some stage-management.'

Blatchford's grin turned to a chuckle. 'They're a bit like

schoolboys – mischievous; and all the excitement's gone to their heads. Now they've got Bunny's funeral this afternoon and the fair tomorrow.'

'Will many of them be at the funeral?'

'All of 'em! Why do you think they're off work and all dressed up?'

As Wycliffe was turning away the landlord added, 'All the same, sir, don't get it wrong; there's plenty of genuine feeling.'

The procession assembled at the top of North Street, outside the Fretwells, with more than a hundred men walking behind the hearse and a single car for the principal mourners. The coffin was smothered in flowers; more were piled on the hearse and on the roof of the following car. Wycliffe found himself walking next to the innkeeper, who had obviously contrived it. Blatchford, his red face contrasting with his white halo of hair, bulged out of a dark pinstripe suit.

'So Jimmy kept it in the family.'

'Jimmy?'

'Fretwell; that's his hearse, his car and his men driving. It don't seem right to bury your own relative; I thought he would've got a trade price from old Martin the undertaker over to Shotleigh, but trust a Fretwell not to spend a penny if a ha'penny will do.'

The funeral procession seemed out of place under the strings of flags but it was obvious that none of the villagers saw anything incongruous about it; an occasion was an occasion and whether it was sad or gay made little difference. It had been the same in his own village.

The women were at their windows, peering between the curtains, which were nominally drawn. The shops were shut and there was no-one in the street.

Blatchford said, 'In any other circumstances most of 'em would be saying: "A damn good riddance!" '

Wycliffe wondered what the scruffy little fat man himself would have made of it all.

As they approached the Green, Blatchford said, 'You

must've wondered a bit about Charlie Alford. Charlie's got it in for the Beales; he worked in their Newton branch and got the sack for interfering with a girl cashier. After that he set up on his own with money borrowed from his wife's family but he's never made a go of it, he's in debt everywhere and people wonder how he can carry on.' All this *sotto voce* so that his words would not reach the men walking in front or behind. 'Charlie's got a chip on his shoulder the size of a plank.'

They filed into the church, where there was a short service, then they moved to the graveside, with the mourners spreading out over the adjoining graves and paths. The great majority of the men were unknown to Wycliffe. He assumed that the rather pompous fat man, who seemed to be chief mourner, must be Martha's husband – the undertaker himself. Simon was there, standing bare-headed and alone, like a patriarch; and Wycliffe saw Dr Sharpe, looking ominously flushed, constantly fingering his moustache. He caught sight of little Alford and their eyes met for an instant, but Alford looked away quickly. Brimblecombe from the sweet shop, for once without his pipe, stood by a very tall, bony man who Wycliffe knew to be the butcher from the shop on the Green.

When it was over and Wycliffe was leaving the churchyard, still in company with the innkeeper, he said, 'It's time we had a serious talk – without an audience.'

Blatchford turned to look at him. 'I've been thinking so myself; come back with me, Mr Wycliffe, and have a little something.'

They crossed the Green under the strings of flags and coloured lamps. The men of the village were gathering in groups, reluctant to break up and go home. But for the licensing laws there would have been no dilemma. Everybody had a word for the innkeeper and Wycliffe sensed that his own stock had risen through being seen in Blatchford's company.

They went into the inn by the back door, through the over-warm kitchen where Dora was brushing milk on to

107

rows of pasties and pies laid on sheets, ready for the oven.

'Getting ready for tomorrow,' Blatchford said, 'She's got a freezer full of stuff already.'

'Somebody's got to do it,' Dora said.

Wycliffe was taken into the parlour, which overlooked the vegetable garden and the backs of houses in South Street.

'Sit you down, Mr Wycliffe. Light up if you want to; I know you're a pipe smoker. Do you like scrumpy?'

Wycliffe was not partial to the local rough cider, which gave him an acid stomach and a heavy hangover, but he wanted to fall in with the innkeeper's mood.

The old man was all smiles, a little unsure of himself. 'Back in a minute.' He lumbered out of the room and returned with an earthenware jug of cider and two tankards. 'There we are! All nice and cool, straight from the wood.'

Wycliffe was still standing, looking at a large framed photograph of a young woman with small but strong features and a nineteen-thirties hairstyle.

Blatchford said, 'Sarah — my wife. She's been dead ten years come Whitsun.'

'I can see the resemblance.'

'Resemblance?'

'To Joyce at Ashill — weren't they sisters?'

The old man grinned. 'You've been finding out about us, sir!'

The preliminaries had taken three or four minutes by the pendulum wall-clock, which had a prancing horse on the top. Now Blatchford settled his great body into a wing-chair and placed the jug of cider on a table close to his hand.

'Right, Mr Wycliffe.'

Wycliffe said, 'Did your wife get on well with her sister?'

Mild surprise; obviously not the sort of question the innkeeper had expected. 'Get on? They were very close; their parents died young and I think that makes for closeness between the children—'

'And I suppose Emily Newcombe must have been on friendly terms with them both — I mean, working all those years at Ashill with Joyce.'

Blatchford was puzzled. 'They was very friendly, as you say, but—'

'So that one way and another not much could go on at Ashill that you didn't hear about.'

The old man looked put out. 'I know you think I've been holding back, Mr Wycliffe, that's because I don't gossip; a publican's got to be careful – can't afford to let his tongue run away with him, but I can tell you this, sir, if I knew anything about these murders you would hear it soon enough. As to the Beales, whatever my wife thought, I never had a great opinion of the family.' He took a good gulp of cider then wiped his lips with a handkerchief the size of a small tablecloth. 'All the same, I got to admit there's something that's been on my mind a bit.' He fixed Wycliffe with clear candid blue eyes.

'When you was in my bar on Monday you mentioned about Emily having some money laid by and I put you off – I said it was only a yarn, a sort of village joke. Well, since then I've been thinking that maybe there was a bit more to it; in fact, you put me in mind of something Sarah told me . . .' He glanced up at his wife's photograph. 'Sarah had a head for business, which is more than I ever did, and Joyce and Emily used to come to her whenever they had any little problems in the way of business – not that they had many! Anyway, I mind Sarah telling me that Emily was asking her about how to invest a sum of money so that it would be safe.'

The old man chuckled. 'Wouldn't we all like to know the answer to that, sir? Well, you could buy gold then, just like you can now if you got the money, and I remember Sarah said she'd told Emily to buy sovereigns. Sarah had put a bit of her own money in gold about then. Of course, I've no idea whether Emily took her advice.'

'When was this?'

Blatchford shook his head. 'I couldn't put a date on it, Mr Wycliffe, but it must've been in the early sixties. I know it was several years after Emily lost her husband.'

'Any idea of the sum involved?'

109

Another shake of the head. 'No, but Sarah did say she thought it was a fairish amount – enough to make her wonder where it came from, if you understand me, sir.'

'And did she or you find out?'

A shrewd grin. 'No, we didn't, but I will say this, Mr Wycliffe, people in this village don't part with their money without getting value for it.'

'What does that mean?'

Blatchford looked innocently vague. 'Mean? I don't know what it means, sir, it's just a fact.'

Wycliffe was feeling the first effects of the cider he had drunk, a certain mellowness, a sense of relaxed well-being. Blatchford sat bolt upright in his chair; with his bulk he could hardly do otherwise; one large, freckled hand grasped his tankard, the other held on to the arm of the chair. 'Let me top you up, Mr Wycliffe . . . there's plenty more where that came from.'

They were silent for a while. The fair had started up and they could hear the music from across the Green.

When Blatchford spoke again it was in a mood of reminiscence. 'It's hard to believe Bunny's gone . . . Odd sort of chap. He wasn't very bright; I don't think he ever learned to read and write properly but he had a sort of cunning . . .' A deep sigh and a draught of cider. 'And he was clever with animals! I've never seen anything like it. You should've seen him with a little wire-haired terrier bitch he had – talk about tricks!

'And birds – he could charm the birds out of the trees; they'd come and feed out of his hand – out of his mouth!' A chuckle that shook his whole body. 'Animals, birds and women – you'd never believe to see him latterly that, as a youngster, he was a fairish looking chap. The girls used to think so anyway – he never had any problem in that direction. He'd have the pants off 'em before they could remember what it was mother had told 'em. Then there was a bit of bother about some under-age little piece over to Biscombe and from then on Emily did her best to put a stop to his games.' A broad grin. 'I reckon she had her work cut out!'

110

'The funny thing was he never made any friends; there was only one chap he was ever at all matey with and that was Charlie Alford. Bunny used to buy the few bits and pieces he needed for his odd jobs from Charlie's shop.'

The innkeeper sighed once more. 'As I say, Bunny wasn't the brightest but he must've had something. He didn't get shot for nothing and neither did poor old Ruby.' The blue eyes were devoid of any expression. 'It must all tie up, sir, but I'm blowed if I can see how.'

Wycliffe changed the subject. 'Was it generally known in the village that young Edward's father had murdered his mother?'

Blatchford frowned. 'No, it wasn't. Simon's wife's family were sort of outsiders and nobody knew much about 'em.'

'Yet Alford knew.'

'Yes, he did; and he made sure to spread it around but that was recent; how and when he found out I couldn't tell you, sir.'

'Thanks for the cider.' Wycliffe got up to go and Blatchford made no attempt to dissuade him but came with him to the door.

'I hope I haven't wasted your time, sir.'

It was Wycliffe's turn to be enigmatic: 'We shall see, shan't we?'

The sunshine took him by surprise after the dimly-lit parlour, so did the atmosphere of liveliness around the Green. The men had finally gone home after the funeral and it was the turn of the women with young children; they were trailing across the Green to the fairground, giving the youngsters a treat before bed.

Wycliffe crossed the Green to the police van, wondering what to make of the old humbug's erratic powers of recall and more than half convinced that he had said nothing without some definite purpose.

Decoded, Blatchford's message seemed to be that in the early sixties the Beales had presented Emily Newcombe with a substantial sum of money; that Bunny had been, in his younger days, a bucolic Don Juan; and that Charlie

111

Alford might be worth a second look.

In the van Kersey was waiting for him with the man from forensic who, because of his outsize ears, Kersey had christened Dumbo. Dumbo was anxious to get back to his laboratory to work on some of the material and he promised to send his report as soon as possible.

Wycliffe's reaction probably seemed less than enthusiastic; he doubted whether the case would now be solved by anything out of Ruby's envelopes and the cider he had drunk was making him drowsy. When the man from forensic had gone Wycliffe said, 'Anything else?'

Kersey yawned. The sun streamed in through one of the little windows and it was very warm. He turned the pages of his notes. 'Fowler has gone back to write his report on the unburnt stuff in the envelopes but he gave me the gist of what he found. Nothing directly relevant but plenty of material for a blackmailer. There's no doubt Ruby knew all about life in the village, including the seamy side. At first you'd get the impression the place was a sort of Sodom but when you weight it up it's probably no better and no worse than anywhere else. A few kids call the wrong bloke "daddy" and some of 'em have been doing it long enough to have kids of their own. One family seems to specialize in incest as a sort of tradition; the chap who runs the paint shop – Alford – goes around showing himself to young girls, and the butcher, according to his wife, has one or two novel sexual habits. . . .'

Kersey sighed. 'Ruby must have been a remarkable old girl – they *told* her these things and she wrote them all down. You'd think she was doing a Kinsey on Washford and yet, according to Franks, she herself died a virgin.'

Wycliffe said, 'Some people prefer to live by proxy – it's safer. But speaking of Alford, I've a suspicion it was Alford who sent the anonymous note. Get somebody sensible to talk to him. According to Blatchford he was fairly close to Newcombe so there could be something there. They'll have to lean on him a bit.'

Kersey said, 'There's one other thing in the reports. The

112

milkman, Hext, says he saw Newcombe coming away from Ruby's place on Thursday morning. Newcombe was coming out of Ruby's gate, muttering to himself; Hext asked him what was up and Newcombe said: "That bloody old cow in there; that's what's up!" '

Wycliffe said, 'The register office on Wednesday afternoon and the midwife on Thursday morning, it ought to mean something.'

'But what could he have hoped to find out?'

'Whatever it was, it seems Ruby sent him going with a flea in his ear.'

Kersey stretched his arms high above his head and yawned once more. 'Now they're both dead; it doesn't make sense.'

Wycliffe said, 'Nicholas went to see Ruby, and he's not dead.'

Gertrude Vicary dozed in an armchair in the drawing-room of her flat on the first floor of Ashill. She had kicked off her shoes and her stockinged feet were tucked under her body. A low sun flooded the room with light, blinding the television set on which a chat-show was in full cry. Jumbled music from the fairground reached into the room, muted but insistent.

Esther came in; she stood for a moment, gazing down at her mother, then she went to the television and switched it off. The mantel clock chimed; a quarter to seven. Gertrude stirred.

'Oh, it's you.' She glanced at the clock. 'God! I must have been asleep; your father will be here soon.' She stood up, stepped into her shoes, settled her hair and smoothed her frock. She tried to cover a certain confusion with words.

'Have you just come in? Where have you been?'

'I told you I wasn't going out this afternoon.'

'So you did; I'd forgotten.'

A door opened and closed; footsteps in the hall. Although the flat had its own separate entrance and stairs, on his arrival home each evening Vicary always called on his father-in-law, then he would enter the flat through the communicating door.

113

Gertrude stood still, an odd little smile on her lips. 'There he is . . . brief-case in study, glance at the post but don't open . . . cross hall to loo . . . pee . . . wash hands, comb through hair . . . examine features in glass, grimace, displaying own teeth . . . cross hall to drawing-room, "Oh, there you are!" ' She broke off with a puzzled look when the door did not open. 'God! Something must have jammed the works!'

Esther was watching her mother. 'You do hate him, don't you?'

Gertude suddenly looked scared. 'Of course I don't hate your father! Don't be absurd! I was joking.'

At that moment the door did open and Vicary came in. 'Ah! There you are!' He glanced round the room, taking everything in, just as he did when visiting one of the firm's depots, then he went over to his wife and placed a formal kiss on her forehead. It was almost a ritual gesture, as though after an absence, he felt the need to re-establish possession.

'Your father stopped me on the way up; the police are with Nicky at the moment.'

Gertrude became very still. 'Nicky! Why him, for God's sake?'

Vicary seemed to contemplate her concern. 'I have no idea, but your father is very worried.' He allowed this to sink in. 'Of course, it was Nicky's gun and the police are very simple-minded. When you were questioned about the missing pistol, what happened?'

Gertrude frowned. 'What happened? Nothing . . . A young policeman came up here and wrote down my silly answers to his stupid questions.'

'Did you refer to Nicky's past at all?'

'His past? You mean the army business? Of course not!'

Vicary acknowledged his daughter for the first time and said curtly, 'And you, Esther? You were questioned, I think.'

Esther said in a flat voice, entirely devoid of expression, 'I was questioned but I had nothing to tell them.'

'You knew about your uncle's rather tragic experience.'

'I knew about it but it had nothing to do with them or with the missing gun.'

Vicary said, 'I'm very glad you had the sense to see that.' He added after a pause, 'In that case they are probably badgering Nicky because they don't know what else to do!' His eyes returned to his wife; coldly possessive. 'The old man is really rattled; I think we should all three go down to dinner tonight – a gesture.'

Gertrude said, 'Yes, let's make a gesture, by all means.'

'Don't laugh at me, Gertrude!'

'Laugh? What is there to laugh at? Edward was taken to the police station last night; Nicky is being interrogated tonight – I wonder when it will be my turn – or yours.'

He continued to look at her but said nothing.

She became irritable under his eyes and snapped, 'For God's sake don't watch me like that, Frank . . . I haven't been drinking but I shall start at any minute if you go on like this!'

Esther watched her parents with that same quiet gaze that one watches fish in an aquarium tank.

'I have nothing to say.'

Nicholas had used these words two or three times already in response to certain questions. Wycliffe would have preferred the interview to have taken place in the more formal setting of an interview room at the police station but he did not want press reports of a second man 'helping the police with their inquiries' and being allowed to go home afterwards. So Nicholas was facing him and Kersey on his home ground, surrounded by the reconstructed war games of Wellington and Soult, Massena and Beresford.

Kersey was speaking. 'On April tenth you visited Ruby Price at her home and you told her of your association with a lady, not named. You asked Miss Price for a certain assurance – what was that assurance?'

'I have nothing to say.'

'Did she give it you?'

'I have told you; I have nothing to say.'

Nicholas sat motionless in his chair, behind the big desk, his eyes apparently focused on the opposite wall.

Wycliffe intervened. 'You realize that your refusal to co-operate might lead us to think that you had a motive for killing Ruby Price?'

'This is nonsense!'

'Did you visit her on the day she died?'

'No; my only visit was about three weeks ago – you say it was the tenth.'

'She was shot some time on Monday afternoon.'

'So?'

'Where were you at the time? You will remember that when Mr Kersey called you were out, but you came in while he was here.'

'I went for a walk as I often do after lunch.'

'Who is the lady you talked about to Ruby Price?'

Nicholas did not answer and Wycliffe went on, 'Is it one of the Gould sisters?'

Still no reply.

'It would be a simple matter to ask them.'

It worked. Nicholas looked as though the possibility had not occurred to him. 'That would be an abominable thing to do!'

'Which sister?'

'Miss Veronica.' He spoke the name in that special way a boy speaks the name of his first girl. 'I hope that you won't—'

'We shan't interfere in any way with your private life if you are frank with us, Captain Beale. Now will you tell us why you went to see Ruby Price?'

He shook his head. 'I'm sorry; I can only tell you that it has nothing whatever to do with her death.'

Wycliffe tried a different approach. 'We are investigating two murders and it seems they must be linked. Newcombe and Ruby Price were shot with an automatic pistol of nine-millimetre calibre – presumably yours. Can you suggest any connection between the two victims which might help to establish the motive?'

116

'I know of no connection; I find it hard to believe that there was one.'

'We know that your brother-in-law visited Newcombe on the afternoon of the Sunday he was killed, to discuss arrangements about a pension paid—'

There was a sudden change in Nicholas; he flushed and said in a brittle voice, 'I know nothing of my brother-in-law's activities. If his job was to conclude an arrangement with Newcombe I have no doubt that he was successful – he is good at that sort of thing, that is why my father makes use of him.'

The contempt was blistering.

The questions continued but the answers, when they came, were not enlightening. It was gone seven when they left Ashill.

Kersey said, 'He's no fool. Except on the subject of his brother-in-law he gave nothing away that he wasn't forced to. But talk about family solidarity! It seems possible he had some sort of motive for the Price killing; perhaps we should have turned the screw a bit more to find out what it was he's so anxious to keep from his girl-friend.'

'He wouldn't have told us; he's obstinate on principle; the stuff martyrs are made of. It's probably connected in some way with his discharge from the army – a matter of honour. Nicky is strong on honour.'

The fair was doing good business; the whole village seemed to be out and about, streaming across the Green to the field; children dragged along by their parents; young couples, arm-in-arm; raucous youths, aggressively playful, like young steers; groups of giggling girls sending out provocative signals . . . The weather was idyllic; the evening sun still shone and the beeches around the Green cast long shadows.

In the van, Wycliffe slumped into a chair and stretched his legs as far as the chicken-coop accommodation allowed. He yawned, assailed by a great wave of tiredness.

He said, 'Motive, means and opportunity. How many times have we heard that? Well, motive has got us nowhere yet. Means presents no problems – any one of the family, including Nicky of course, could have got hold of the gun. So let's look at opportunity.'

Kersey reached down a file and turned the pages.

'Well, you know already that any one of them could have done the Newcombe killing. Between ten-fifteen and eleven-thirty on Sunday evening, no two of them were together. For a close-knit family they don't seem fond of each other's company.'

'And Ruby Price?'

Kersey frowned. 'That's a different story; it's difficult to get a clear picture. According to Franks, Ruby died on Monday afternoon – that's as near as he's prepared to go and it lets all of 'em in, except Maurice who was in his office as usual, trying to look like a business tycoon. Vicary spent the morning in Newton about a building contract; he had lunch at the Moorview in Bickington and in the afternoon he was at Tor Vale but we can't tie down the times anything like tight enough to let him out. Choosing his route he might easily have passed near Ruby's place without coming into Washford and without losing much time. He could have had an hour at the cottage for all we know.'

'And Nicholas?'

Kersey turned a page. 'Nicky says he went for a walk but as far as he can remember, he didn't meet anybody. Simon and Gertrude say they didn't leave the house, neither did Naomi who was "resting". Monday is Esther's day off because the supermarket doesn't open and she says, after feeding Newcombe's livestock – we checked on that with our chaps there – she returned to the house and spent the rest of the afternoon reading in her room.'

Wycliffe sighed. 'That leaves Edward, who was on the moor, a sitting duck.'

CHAPTER SIX

May morning: a morning of misty sunshine with the promise of a fine warm day to come. Each house had a leafy branch of 'may' secured to the front door and even if these had not been gathered by virgins in the small hours, at least they were there. As to virgins, those who, by reason of their tender age, might be presumed so, were gathered on the Green, dressed in white frocks with green sashes, dancing round the maypole to the music of an accordion. A small crowd of parents, relatives and friends looked on. The coloured ribbons attached to the pole and held by the girls wound round the pole and unwound again as the dancers reversed their steps. The children's voices piped loud and clear:

> 'Little May Rose turn round three times,
> Let us look at you round and round!'

Ten o'clock; the fair people were having their breakfasts; their children sat on the steps of the caravans and their dogs explored the site sniffing unfamiliar scents. The old men of the village, tricked out in their best suits, hung about in small groups, a little at a loose end; but everywhere in the be-flagged streets there was an air of cheerful expectancy. The shops, due to close at eleven, were busy and their doorbells pinged incessantly.

Another police caravan was being moved in beside the first to provide a base for the additional men to be deployed during the fair. Wycliffe had made the arrangements with the uniformed branch; their men would mingle with the crowds, showing the flag, while patrol cars covered the outskirts, keeping an eye on isolated houses and farms. This was mainly a public relations exercise but he thought the villagers deserved some visible evidence of police concern.

But Wycliffe saw and heard all that was going on as one sees and hears a television programme when preoccupied with something else. During a restless night, when it seemed to him that he had scarcely lost consciousness for more than a few minutes, odd phrases had repeated themselves in his mind like one of those irritating jingles which refuses to be forgotten. Now, in the full light of day he realized that he had been striving to marshal the facts and discern some sort of pattern.

He was still trying.

Newcombe at the register office on Wednesday; Newcombe visiting Ruby Price on Thursday; Newcombe in an argument with Frank Vicary on Sunday afternoon and shot on Sunday evening.

Ruby Price shot on Monday.

Nicholas Beale's automatic used for both killings.

These were the more obvious facts but there were others which might have to fit the pattern.

Edward saying nothing of the finding of Ruby's body for two days; Edward inventing a mysterious stranger; Edward's father, a wife-murderer.

Emily Newcombe acquiring a substantial sum of money in the early sixties.

And, unlikely as it seemed, Newcombe with a reputation for a 'way' with the girls.

Facts, and the fancies they gave rise to, chased each other round in his head like the roundabouts at the fair. It was not a new situation; he was used to it, and usually from the mêlée an idea would emerge which could be tried and tested.

He walked across to Ashill and Joyce answered his ring. Without a word she stood aside for him to enter.

'I want to talk to Mr Simon.'

'Then you'd better go across to the maypole.'

'Is he over there?'

120

'Why shouldn't he be? He pays for it being put up every year – or do you think he ought to hide himself because of what they're saying and doing? This morning there was chalk scribblings all over this front door, with your man out there in his van, sleeping most likely. A fat lot of good he is!' Joyce was trembling with indignation. 'You and your lot have started something!'

Wycliffe made the soft answer. 'There have been two murders, remember.'

'You don't give us much chance to forget! Anyway, Bunny Newcombe's not much loss; that boy was never any good to anybody; his poor mother least of all.'

'And Ruby Price?'

Joyce sniffed. 'Well, there's plenty who'll speak well of her.'

'And you?'

'I don't speak about anybody if I can help it but I can't abide busy bodies who aren't satisfied with their own affairs and dabble in other people's.'

'Is that what Ruby did?'

'Well, she interfered in this family. Got a hold on the mistress, poor lady.' Joyce shrugged her thin shoulders. 'Well, all that's over now, but Ruby had a way with her, there's no denying that. People told her their troubles; leastwise, some did; she never got anything out of me.' She broke off abruptly. 'But this is gossip and if it's gossip you want you've come to the wrong place. Are you stopping or going?'

'Is Mrs Vicary at home?'

'It would be an odd thing if she wasn't; she never goes anywhere.'

'Never?'

'Well, she doesn't go out much; perhaps a walk with Mr Nicholas of an evening.'

'Is there something wrong with her?'

'Why should there be? There's nothing wrong with me and I never go out – never!'

'I would like to see Mrs Vicary.'

121

'Then you'd better go round to the outside stairs; they don't like people using the door from the house. Of course, *he* uses it but that's different.'

'Thank you.'

'For what? You got nothing out of me you couldn't've got elsewhere.'

Wycliffe went round to the side of the house where there were steps up to the first floor from the old coach-house yard. The landing at the top of the steps was sheltered by a canopy. He rang the bell and had to wait for some time before the door was opened by a woman in a floral housecoat. She had a mass of auburn hair and the firm but not prominent features which often go with it, but she had escaped freckles. A very attractive woman, looking surprisingly young to have a daughter of nineteen. But there were signs that all was not well; a redness and a moistness about the eyes, and spots of colour on her cheeks not entirely concealed by make-up.

Drink? Almost for certain. Wycliffe wondered what particular sorrows she found it necessary to drown.

'Mrs Vicary? . . . Detective Chief Superintendent Wycliffe.'

She took him into the drawing-room. It was furnished traditionally in subdued colours with fabrics of indeterminate pattern; decoration to match. Just about right for the executive who asks only for a neutral background. One had the impression it might have come in a package deal from somewhere not-quite Harrods. Was it part of Gertrude's problem that she was expected to merge into it?

'Do sit down. You want to talk to me?'

She did not immediately sit down herself, and when she did she sat erect and remained very tense. If he was going to get her to talk he would have to reassure her first.

'I've met your daughter; she is like you.'

She looked surprised. 'Really? I suppose I should be flattered.' But she was anxious. 'What did you want to ask me about?'

'I want your help. I am going to be quite blunt. As you

know, two people have been killed and it seems that the only things they have in common are their connections with this family and the fact that they were both shot with a pistol taken from your brother's room downstairs. We don't want to cause unnecessary pain or embarrassment. It is very easy to find ourselves prying into things about which people are naturally reticent and then misinterpreting their silence. It is much better to be frank with us. Once we are satisfied that whatever it is has no connection with our case it is forgotten.'

Like the March Hare's, it was the best butter and Gertrude responded. 'What is it you want to know?'

'About Ruby Price's connection with your family.'

Wycliffe had expected a sudden relaxation of tension at this seeming anticlimax but there was none. Gertrude remained very wary. She took time to collect her thoughts. 'Well, Ruby was a close friend of my mother's and, as a midwife, she brought us all into the world. It's as simple as that.'

'If you could enlarge a little . . .'

A faint smile. 'It started with my brother, Nicholas, the eldest of the family. He was born prematurely in the middle of a blizzard and Ruby was the only one who could get here. She was young at the time, not much older than mother, and just starting as a district nurse. It was a very difficult birth and mother believed Ruby saved her life and that of the child. Probably it was true; at any rate there grew up between them a close friendship which lasted right up until my mother's death. In fact, Ruby was with mother when she died.'

'Your mother discussed things with her – family matters?'

'Everything!' Gertrude pulled her housecoat over her knees. 'Unless you kept something from mother it was no secret from Ruby.'

'Did she ever make use of your mother's confidences to cause trouble in the family?'

Gertrude frowned. 'Not directly, but she had a lot of

123

influence on mother and we all resented that from time to time.'

On a side table, close to Wycliffe's chair, there was a silver-framed photograph of a young girl – Gertrude, as she had been at eighteen or thereabouts. People must have thought that Vicary, a clerk in her father's firm, had really hit the jackpot; this luscious girl and a stake in Beales' Household Stores. They would have wondered if he had contrived his luck by a spot of judicious seduction, but it was hard to imagine the girl Gertrude had been falling for the little man who was within easy striking distance of being ugly. But sex is a capricious ringmaster.

Wycliffe said, 'Less than three weeks before she died, Ruby was visited by your brother, Nicholas. She noted the visit in her diary. He wanted an assurance that she would not pass on certain information about him to a friend.'

Wycliffe was watching her closely and he saw her relax, she even smiled and inquired, 'A woman friend?'

'Probably Veronica Gould.'

'Poor Nicky! So you know about that. I see now what you've come for but I'm afraid I can't help you.'

Wycliffe persisted. 'What I said earlier, Mrs Vicary, was perfectly true. If we know the reason for your brother's concern and it has nothing to do with our case, there's an end to it. If we are not told we shall poke and pry until we find out.'

She was suddenly bitter. 'Yours must be a very rewarding occupation!'

He did not hold it against her. 'Did your brother complete the full term of his army service?'

'He resigned his commission.'

'Why?'

'Hadn't you better ask him that?'

He risked being blunt. 'He wouldn't tell me if I did. I have the impression that your brother doesn't always act in his own best interest.'

He saw her lips tremble in another smile. 'You are a very

shrewd man, Mr Wycliffe, and I am going to take you at your word — that you will ignore what is not directly concerned with your case. What you say about Nicky is quite true; he is a very obstinate man. In some ways he is very innocent . . .' She searched for an expression. 'I sometimes think that it is a common failing with us Beales — we are emotionally *dumb*. Anyway, enough of that! In a nutshell, Nicky made a fool of himself over a boy — young man, I suppose he was.'

She reached for a box of cigarettes on a side-table. 'Will you smoke?'

'No, thank you.'

She lit one herself and drew on it, deeply. 'Nicky had a desk job with the British garrison in Berlin and he fell for a German youth who worked in the administration. There was a liaison — isn't that the word? It's certainly the word Nicky would have used, with a disapproving twist, if it had happened to anyone else. But, of course, Nicky was trapped. It turned out the boy was a commie plant.'

Gertrude tapped ash from her cigarette into a glass ashtray shaped like a swan. 'I don't know if Nicky had any information which might have been useful to the Russians or to the Democratic Republic — it doesn't seem likely — but if he had, he didn't part with it to the boy. An exhaustive investigation, during which he was suspended from duty, established that much, but it was the investigation coupled with the disgrace which broke Nicky and put him, for a time, in a psychiatric hospital. What made it worse, all this happened shortly before my mother's death and Nicky feels that he shortened her life.'

Wycliffe said, 'Was it at all likely that Ruby Price would have passed any of this on to the Gould sisters?'

'I really don't know. Ruby certainly had no reason to be antagonistic to any of us. Of course, Nicky is a born worrier. All his life he's been convinced that somebody is about to pull the mat out from under him, so he takes precautions and, sometimes, they're a bit ponderous.'

'I can see that you are fond of him.'

She smiled. 'At heart he's a kindly old thing. He was my

big brother when I was a kid and ever since Esther was born he's thought the world of her. Like a lot of others, he's his own worst enemy.' She looked at him in a challenging way. 'Well, I've done what you asked and I hope you'll keep your side of the bargain. I should hate to see Nicky having to go through any part of that again. If he's happy with his battles and his Veronica, let him have them.'

Wycliffe allowed a comfortable silence to drift on for a while then he said, 'I wonder if you can – or will – tell me why Nicholas is so antagonistic towards your husband?'

A faint smile. 'As a fully paid-up member of the clan I suppose I should say that I know of no such antagonism. In fact, of course, we all know about it. It's not surprising really. Nicholas refused to go into the firm because he knew that he would never get on with father and also because he had no inclination for business. He joined the army instead but, as I've told you, his career there ended unpleasantly. On the other hand, my husband – an outsider – seems to be uniformly successful and enjoys my father's complete confidence. Added to that, in Nicky's eyes, I'm still his baby sister . . . I suppose it all amounts to jealousy and sounds a bit absurd but natural all the same.'

Wycliffe nodded.

'It came to a head recently when Frank offered to buy Nicholas's shares in the firm and Nicky chose to be insulted.'

'Thank you for being so open with me; it helps.'

Gertrude had relaxed. Her earlier fears, whatever they had been, had not materialized; now she was expecting Wycliffe to go and, no doubt, she would breathe a great sigh of relief when he did.

But Wycliffe did not go; instead he settled back in his chair and said: 'A week ago yesterday, in the afternoon, Newcombe went to the register office in Newton and asked to see the entry of his birth in the register.'

Gertrude became wary. 'So?'

'Did your husband tell you Newcombe had been to the register office?'

126

'Why should he?'

He noted the evasion.

'Because after seeing the entry which referred to him he asked also for the entries covering your marriage to Mr Vicary and the birth of your daughter.'

'Is it possible for anyone to walk into a register office and see entries referring to other people?'

'Quite possible; Newcombe did so.'

She had herself well in hand and the only detectable change in her was a tensing of her muscles so that she was no longer relaxed in her chair.

'What am I supposed to make of that? I can't imagine what he hoped to gain by it.'

'You can make no suggestion why the entries might have interested him?'

'I cannot. Can you?'

'Just one more question, Mrs Vicary. Do you know of any reason why your family might have paid a substantial sum of money to the Newcombes in the early sixties?'

'I do not!'

And with that he had to be content.

He came out of the house with its oppressive tensions into the sunshine. There was a new warmth in the air; one of those spring days when it would have been good to relax, to grow nostalgic and to be easily amused, but the Beales possessed his thoughts like a toothache.

Gertrude impressed him; she was the most adult of the Beales; at the same time she was a frustrated woman, turning to drink.

'We are emotionally dumb': a graphic image calling to mind the efforts of a deaf mute to communicate – the inarticulate sounds, the despairing gestures, the sullen withdrawal . . . It was tempting to see members of the family as being in different stages of the sequence.

On the Green the crowd had grown; they were crowning the May Queen, a dark, pretty girl, who sat demurely on her throne while the chairman of the parish council, wearing his chain of office, balanced a crown of feathers

127

on her head. A ceremony which had once linked soil fertility with human sex, but now the fields around Washford, like fields everywhere, had their fertility delivered in sacks.

Wycliffe prowled on the fringe of the crowd and reached a place where people were thinner on the ground; then he spotted Simon. It was extraordinary; Simon, standing alone, isolated in the crowd near the platform, with at least a yard of space all about him. There was something almost heroic about the tall, frail old man with the silvery hair; a patriarchal figure. Wycliffe thought the villagers would probably let him be, but when he saw a uniformed policeman standing a little apart, he warned him to keep an eye on the old man.

Washford Fair this year would receive more publicity than at any time in its history; already a TV van had moved in and was parked near the police caravans. Three or four reporters, keeping aloof from the rustic celebrations, sat on a bench outside the pub, settling down to some steady drinking. One of them called to him:

'Anything fresh, Mr Wycliffe?'

'Not a thing.'

'Will you have anything for us today?'

'You tell me. Your guess is as good as mine.'

Wycliffe lunched at the Mill House Hotel on the Newton Road. The pub in the village was so crowded that it was all but impossible to elbow one's way to the bar. At the Mill House business was also brisk with farming families from the district having lunch before going on to the fair. Wycliffe arrived late, when most of the diners had reached dessert, and he watched, fascinated, while plump farmers, their wives and children tucked in to great wedges of Black Forest gâteau loaded with Devonshire cream.

Afterwards he walked back to the village and, for an hour, he behaved like a visitor, looking in on some of the events – a flower show in the church hall, a judo demonstration, a pony gymkhana . . . Village life suited him; the scale was right; an audience of two or three hundred is enough for

128

anything; get into the thousands and you have a mob . . .
Small is beautiful; he agreed with papa Schumacher. He
had read of research which showed that certain rodents
become aggressive if they encounter more than a small
number of their own kind in a day. He could sympathize.

Those who noticed him at all saw a middle-aged man,
rather severely dressed, who looked vaguely like a priest.
He smoked his pipe and watched whatever was going on
with apparent interest, a contemplative interest which more
restless, excitable types might have envied. They could not
have guessed what was going on behind the calm, grey eyes.

The Beales: one of them is a killer. And, a little later:
Is Gertrude the still centre about which it all revolves? Four
days since he had first heard of Newcombe; two days since
the discovery of the second killing . . . What next?

A family with a century of tradition, living in the same
village, in the same house, hedged in by an oppressive
respectability, isolated by religion and class, and uniquely
susceptible to the frustrations, jealousies and repressions
which can nurture thoughts of violence . . . Although the
two victims were not of the family he had no doubt that
this was a family affair . . .

Which of them?

Simon was an old man and frail, but no young muscles
were needed to pull the trigger of a nine-millimetre, and
the crimes betrayed a calculating coldness which was
probably not out of character.

Nicholas: an introvert who had already suffered a
traumatic shock and now seemed destined to go through
life looking over his shoulder and tilting at shadows.

Maurice: pompous and foolish; but sufficiently aware of
his own shortcomings to feel threatened. Often the weak
are the first to turn to violence. And Maurice had a shrewish,
nagging wife.

Edward: son of a wife-murderer; inhibited, striving to
express himself through paint and canvas but still well and
truly knotted. Impossible to guess what went on behind that
timid front.

129

Vicary: according to Patterson he had dropped his girl overnight to marry the boss's daughter. A man who believed in his destiny; others stand back. A blank as far as his emotional life was concerned; no cosy little woman to come home to . . .

That left the women.

Could these crimes be the work of a woman? He saw no reason why they should not. Women have a penchant for direct, practical solutions.

Gertrude: Wycliffe saw her as a passive element, but that was only an impression. She was married to a man with whom she seemed to have nothing in common; she had retreated into herself and was finding what consolation she could in drink; but she was intelligent and shrewd. It was by no means impossible that she had decided to . . . to clear the decks? He was not satisfied with this assessment; there was more, another factor . . . sex. In talking to Gertrude he had sensed . . . he found difficulty in putting it into words, he had been conscious of a powerful yearning, a barely repressed lust . . .

And Esther. With such parents, what might she not be? It was more than possible that her impressive air of calm detachment was a pose. Wycliffe had a daughter of his own and knew from experience that girls dramatize themselves in more subtle ways than boys. Her job in the supermarket had come as a surprise but that too could be part of the role she saw herself as playing.

Which brought him to Naomi; foolish, scheming, nagging Naomi. No killer – certainly not with a firearm.

He sighed. Conning the field is a useful exercise but it took no account of motive. Which of these people had reason to want Newcombe and Ruby Price dead?

His thoughts turned to Newcombe's cottage where, as far as he was concerned, it had all started. It occurred to him that, because she had been murdered, Ruby Price was occupying the centre of the stage, while Emily Newcombe had scarcely been thought about. Yet, if Emily had been alive . . . Ruby had monitored the life of the village

130

with her scraps of paper in envelopes – living vicariously; but Emily had a son and, surely, she would have treasured mementoes of events which affected him . . .

He worked his way back to the police van through the growing crowds. Dixon, as duty officer, was using the slack time to study for his promotion exam. Wycliffe collected and signed for the key of the cottage then walked down the lane beside Ashill, past Quarry House. No-one to be seen anywhere. Only the music from the fairground disturbed the peace. The church clock chimed the three-quarters – a quarter to four.

The cottage looked as he had first seen it, the gate screeched open, but there was no commotion in the hutches and no hens pecked over the weedy yard; the livestock had been removed by the Fretwells that morning.

The key was an old-fashioned latchkey of intricate pattern suggesting a complicated lock, but Wycliffe knew from his childhood that a bit of bent wire worked just as well. He passed through the lean-to scullery into the kitchen and paused while his eyes accustomed themselves to the dim light.

The lapse of time had done nothing to mitigate the squalor or the stench, and there were more flies. He knew from the scene-of-crime inventory that Emily had kept her mementoes in the drawers of the chiffonier in the parlour. He pushed open the plank door which separated the two rooms and, for an instant, he could not believe his eyes; there, standing between him and the window, by the chiffonier, was Joyce; Joyce wearing a long coat of some dark, silky material and a felt hat which must have dated from before the war. A large, shiny handbag with a brass clasp stood on the chiffonier.

Of the two, he was the more disconcerted. She looked at him with her fierce little eyes and waited for him to speak.

He did his best to sound stern. 'What are you doing here?'

'I came to have a look.'

'How did you get in?'

She held up a 'key' of the sort used to open sardine cans.

131

'Why should you want to "look" as you call it?'

Her skin was brown, furrowed by myriads of tiny
wrinkles and she had a thin, whitish moustache; but her
vitality gave her a certain compelling appeal; she could not
be ignored, she could not be wholly disliked.

'I went to school with Emily; I worked with her for more
than fifty years; we started at Ashill in the same week, when
we was fourteen. I should think that gave me the right to
have a look before *she* gets her hands on it all.' Her manner
was both aggressive and defensive.

'She?'

'Martha Fretwell. Martha was a Newcombe and she never
had any room for Emily – thought her precious brother
was too good for a common servant girl; all because, with
his smarmy ways, he'd talked himself into a job as gardener
at Ashill when all he really was, was a rabbit catcher. Too
good for Emily! All they Newcombes was a no-account lot,
and Emily's boy was no different. He was a trial to his
mother and no mistake, but she thought the world of him.
Now she's gone, and see what happened to him!'

Both drawers of the chiffonier were open; one contained
the sort of things to be found in such drawers in thousands
of homes everywhere: letters preserved in their envelopes,
postcards, programmes of local events, a pad of lined writing
paper and a couple of ball-point pens; a few envelopes. The
other drawer held a photograph album, a collection of
cigarette cards in a cardboard box, a couple of board games
and a pack of playing cards.

'What were you looking for?'

'I wasn't looking *for* anything, I was looking at Emily's
photos. Emily was a great one for photos. I remember the
first thing she bought when she'd saved a bit of money was
a camera – one of those box ones. I remember it was called
a 2A Brownie and she said it took bigger pictures.'

Wycliffe hardly knew whether to laugh or be angry. He
said, 'You know you've no right here.'

She bristled. 'I've as much right here as Martha Fretwell – more! I done what I could for Emily when she was

alive – I used to come down here when she was ill and try to keep the place something like. Not Martha! She wouldn't soil her hands for anybody else's benefit. All this—' She pointed to the contents of the drawers, 'Martha won't give it house room but she won't let them have it as would.'

Joyce had dressed for the occasion and she smelt of lavender. She had on a mauve blouse under her coat, caught at the neck with a cameo brooch; she even wore shoes though these made a concession to her bunions by having elastic insertions in the toe caps.

Wycliffe lifted out the photograph album and opened it on top of the chiffonier. Like most of its kind it lacked any labels to the photographs. He turned the pages, stopping now and then for Joyce's comments on the pictures.

'That's the servants at Ashill – Emily got Mr Simon to take that. Of course, he was only a youngster then like we was and his father was still alive. That's Emily and that's me . . .'

A little *gamine*, pert and full of life.

'That's the cook and that's Mrs Endacott, the housekeeper; we was four of us living in then with two daily maids . . . That's Mr Simon and the mistress when they came back from their honeymoon. Don't you think they made a lovely couple? . . . Newcombe with his father . . .'

There were several photographs of the Beales, both as children and growing up, individually and in groups. Sometimes young Newcombe was photographed with the Beale brothers in the woods. Even as teenagers Maurice was the stout one with an expression which seemed to suggest a permanent if vague protest; Nicholas was long and lean and his features expressed nothing at all.

'The Beale brothers seemed to get on well enough with young Newcombe.'

Joyce sniffed. 'Oh, they did. Newcombe and his father saw to that; they knew which side their bread was buttered. They used to take the boys out shooting; they showed them how to set traps and snares, where to find different nests, and sometimes they went on badger hunts. You can't lose if you get boys with that sort of thing.'

One or two of the snap-shots showed Gertrude with her teenaged brothers; a little mop-haired girl in a bib-and-brace overall, clearly determined to be left out of nothing. Wycliffe continued to turn the pages but there were no more pictures of the Beale brothers. Presumably Nicholas had gone into the army and Maurice was starting work with the firm.

On one of the pages near the end of the album there was a blank where a picture had been removed, leaving the 'corners'.

'What happened to that one?'

Joyce shrugged. 'How should I know?'

It had been an idle question but the tone of Joyce's response roused his suspicion.

'I think you do know.'

'I can't stop you thinking.'

He pointed to her handbag. 'Let me see.'

She was about to refuse, but thought better of it. 'All right! I took it because I got a better right to it than Martha Fretwell. She'll burn the lot.'

He held out his hand.

Reluctantly she opened her handbag and took out a print which she laid on the album. 'It's Miss Gertrude at eighteen or thereabouts. She never kept many of her photos and I wanted it to remind me of what she was like before . . . before she was married.'

'She's with Newcombe!'

'Well, I can't help that, can I? I expect that's why Emily took it. I thought I could have him cut off and the rest enlarged. A proper photographer could do that, couldn't he?'

Joyce was uncharacteristically garrulous.

Wycliffe said, 'Yes, I think so,' but he was preoccupied with the snap-shot itself. Gertrude, in a jumper and skirt, stood sideways to the camera, she was smiling at New-combe, lips parted; Newcombe had a rather strained expression on his face while a little bird, its wings blurred by motion too rapid for the film speed, seemed to be feeding from his lips.

Joyce said, 'He could do that sort of thing; he had a way with all sorts of animals. He could bring down most any bird from the trees by imitating its call but 'twasn't because he was fond of them; it was just a knack.'

Wycliffe was not paying her any attention; the snap-shot seemed to fascinate him. If Gertrude had been eighteen at the time, Newcombe would have been twenty-three. He didn't look it. He had filled out since the earlier snaps but he was still not fat, and Wycliffe was reminded of a young bull; earthy and vigorous.

Suddenly a key piece seemed to fall into place; it was all so obvious; the answer had been under his nose from the start. Joyce was aware of the change in him and she stood, waiting; there was no longer any point in her barrage of chatter.

Wycliffe looked at the little old woman with something like awe. 'You know the whole story; you've known it all along; that's why you're here . . .'

She made an irritable movement. 'I've no idea what you're talking about but I can't spend all day hanging about; they have their meal early on fair nights and it's time I was back there.'

He didn't argue. 'One question and you can go.' He pointed to the pale rectangle on the wall where the damaged picture had hung and he showed her the frame. 'What was in that?'

She hesitated, but not for long. 'It was the same photo, but bigger. Emily had it enlarged.' She moved to the door but as she reached it she turned back; she said in a manner that was more cautionary than aggressive: 'You think you've found out something, but you could still get it wrong.'

With that, she went, through the kitchen and the scullery, her steps a little unsure because of the shoes. Wycliffe put the snap-shot in his wallet. He thought that he now knew all that the cottage had to tell him; he was no longer casting about in the dark; he had a motive of sorts and the framework of a case. What remained to be done, he told himself, was routine police work.

135

He let himself out by the back door, closing it by the absurd drop-latch. As he came out into the yard the church clock chimed the half-hour – half-past four; he could hear it plainly above the subdued cacophony from the fairground.

He stood in the yard, looking at the accumulated litter of years, at the moss-grown walls and the nettles. Probably Newcombe would have spent the rest of his life in these surroundings with the place slowly crumbling and decaying before his eyes – and been more or less content. But something had stirred him to uncharacteristic activity and the climax seemed to have been reached on Sunday afternoon, the day of his death, when Rose Gould had passed by with her little dog and overheard Vicary laying down the law: 'You've done very well out of this, Newcombe!' And a little later, 'If you adopt that attitude, Newcombe, you are making the biggest mistake of your life!' And that evening Newcombe had been shot.

On the previous Wednesday he had been at the register office in Newton, and on the Thursday, he was calling on the former midwife. On the day following Newcombe's death the midwife had been killed in the same manner. It had been his job to find out the links between these events and to establish a clear, unambiguous motive for the violence. For the first time he seemed to be making progress.

He decided to walk back through the estate, so he climbed the wall once more and followed the path made by the dead man. He came to the clearing and to Quarry House, which looked deserted in the sunshine though assailed by raucous sounds from the fairground and the incessant roar of the waterfall. Wycliffe climbed the steps to the top, to the little pavilion which bridged the stream at the head of the fall. From the verandah he could see down into the Goulds' garden but there was no-one about. He heard a slight sound behind him and turned sharply; it was Esther. She had come from the house and had been startled to find him there.

'Did you want something?' Her manner was edgy.

'No, I'm on my way back from the cottage. I gather

you are no longer troubled by the livestock.'

She smiled. 'The Fretwells didn't waste time in shifting the rabbits and hens.'

Wycliffe glanced through the window at the little room with its summerhouse atmosphere. 'Do you spend much time down here?'

'No. When we were younger − Edward and I − we used to come down here sometimes; there was a row-boat on the pool and once or twice we went swimming, but it was always very cold.'

He was seeing the girl with new eyes and, not for the first time in his career, he marvelled at the quirky nature of inheritance. But no other explanation was possible.

When he got back to the Green it was crowded with people watching a fancy-dress competition in which the contestants paraded along a raised gangway before a panel of judges. Wycliffe saw the inevitable Walt Disney characters with a little fat boy as Dumbo and two Snow Whites. He had difficulty in working his way through the crowd to the roped-off area where the caravans and police vehicles were parked and when he reached the van he was more relieved than he would have been prepared to admit, to find Kersey there.

Kersey listened and his first reaction was incredulity. 'You mean that girl is his?'

'Yes.'

Kersey needed time to allow the idea to sink in. He reached into his pocket and came out with a packet of cigarettes. He took one out, stroked it between finger and thumb and lit it as though performing a ritual act. 'As the French say on their diarrhoea pills "one in moments of crisis". I must admit the possibility never occurred to me.' He added, after a longish pause, 'Do you think she knows?'

'I've no idea.'

Kersey was thinking aloud. 'If Newcombe had come out into the open it would only have been his word against the others . . . I suppose he was looking for corroboration in a ham-fisted sort of way, and we've now got the same problem . . . There's no way of proving it unless someone talks.'

Wycliffe said, 'This isn't a paternity case, it's murder; but now we have a possible motive, or a complex of motives centred on the girl's parentage.'

Kersey was enjoying the luxury of allowing the smoke to trickle between his lips, watching it rise in thin spirals. He said, 'That motive points straight to Vicary.'

Wycliffe looked dubious. 'It's not that simple. Even allowing that Newcombe was able to persuade Vicary to take him seriously – seriously enough for Vicary to feel threatened and to go for murder – that doesn't explain why Ruby Price was killed.'

'Ruby was the only one outside the family who knew the truth. With Newcombe murdered and the weapon a pistol from Ashill, it wouldn't have taken long to put two and two together . . . Vicary must have seen that risk; he may even have talked to her, sounding her out.'

'He would have had to get a move on. Newcombe was shot on Sunday night, Ruby on Monday afternoon.'

Kersey shrugged. 'Well, he couldn't allow the grass to grow under his feet if he had any doubts, could he?'

'You make him out as a cold-blooded killer.'

'He's an accountant – green ink instead of blood.'

Wycliffe got out his pipe and started to fill it. 'I'll go this far with you: Vicary is our best bet at the moment.'

'So how do we go?'

'With caution; we haven't a shred of proof. When he comes home I'll talk to him.'

Through the little window they could see, over the heads of the crowd, other fancy-dress characters parading along the gangway; a pink panther and an over-fed Snoopy.

Wycliffe got to his feet. 'According to Joyce the family dine early on fair night; Vicary may be home already.' He crossed the little room to the door then turned back, 'I want the house put under observation; the main gates and the entrance in South Street which they use when they're driving.'

'I'll see to it, sir.'

He entered Ashill by the main gates, walked round the house and up the steps to the first-floor flat. He had to wait some time before the door was opened by Gertrude. Gertrude looked flushed, her eyes surrounded by puffiness. She had obviously been sleeping, probably after several drinks, but she did her best to appear normal. 'Was it me you wanted?'

'Your husband.'

'Frank?' She seemed surprised. 'He's not at home; it's Friday.'

'Friday?'

A faint smile. 'Frank doesn't come home on Friday evenings; he goes straight off from the office.'

'Where?'

He must have conveyed a sense of urgency, 'Is there something wrong; has something happened?'

'I simply want to talk to your husband. Where is he likely to be?'

'I've no idea.' She looked blank.

'Your husband goes somewhere every Friday evening, straight from the office, but you've no idea where?'

'That's what I said.' Very curt. She was recovering her poise and beginning to resent his manner.

'What time do you expect him back?'

'He's usually back around midnight.'

'He isn't interested in the fair?'

'It would take more than the fair to change Frank's routine.'

'Thank you.'

He was irritated, almost angry; these people must *know*. Then, when the door had closed behind him he wondered, What did they know? Who knew, and what? Who was suspected, and by whom? It was one thing to build a wall; quite another to have to live behind it. He tried to imagine them sitting down to a meal together.

As a boy he had often walked past the walls of country

houses and looked down tree-lined drives to catch a glimpse of imposing gables. He had thought then that the people on the other side must live story-book lives; lives of dignified leisure, with mutual tolerance filled with innocent pleasures.

On an impulse, perhaps in reaction to a surfeit of Beales, he telephoned his wife: 'You don't feel like coming over to the fair? I have to be here and I shall probably have to stay half the night . . . yes, I had a very good lunch . . . no, you can't bring cars into the village now the fair is on – only residents'; you park somewhere along the Newton road and walk up South Street to the Green. Our caravan is on the Green opposite the church . . . About seven? I'll be there, waiting for you . . . Take care!'

By tradition they dined early at Ashill on fair day and, despite the air of gloomy foreboding which pervaded the house, perhaps because of it, seven of the usual eight places were occupied; only Vicary was absent. The music from the fairground and the cumulative mutterings and shufflings of a great crowd of people reached them as a confused murmur, punctuated by an occasional shout, a raucous laugh, or the cry of a child. There was scarcely any conversation and as soon as the meal of cold meat and salad was over the party broke up.

Gertrude, looking like a woman in a somnambulant trance, went back to the flat. Naomi, with elaborate concern, said, 'Of course, you won't be going out, father, will you?'

The old man turned to look at her and let his gaze linger for a while before saying, 'Why not?'

'I think you would be most unwise, the way things are! With a good deal of drink about the villagers might turn really nasty. I mean, look what . . .' Her words faded under his cold stare.

Esther said, 'Are you coming Edward?'

Naomi pounced. 'Edward! You're not going out, surely?'

Edward looked as though every drop of blood had been drained from his body; he mumbled something incoherent and followed Esther from the room.

140

Naomi sighed. 'Well, *I'm* not going out. I wouldn't feel safe! In fact, I think the police ought to give us more effective protection here.'

Maurice said, 'I shall have to spend an hour or so on our estimates for the next half-year but after that . . .' He turned to his brother. 'What about you, Nicky?'

Nicholas had gone over to the window, where he stood, looking out. 'I shall be going out later.'

'Then let's go together. What about it?' Maurice laughed self-consciously. 'Recapture the days of our youth. Remember fair-night in the old days, Nicky?'

Nicholas said, 'Those days are gone.'

By nine-thirty only the three women were left in the house.

In the big drawing-room downstairs, Naomi sat by an electric fire placed in the large, open grate. She was playing patience on a low table. The heavy red velvet curtains were drawn and two chandeliers blazed with light, but with so little reflection from the walls and furnishings, the room still had a gloomy aspect. Naomi's plump little hands manipulated the cards and her short, tapering fingers hovered like a bird of prey, ready to pounce.

In her own little sitting-room Joyce was watching television; she had kicked off her slippers and her stockinged feet rested on a padded stool.

Gertrude, in the drawing-room of the flat, sat in darkness except for the flicker of the television screen. She had not bothered to draw the curtains and a faintly luminous sky with a silhouette of trees was visible through the window panes. It was impossible to say whether or not she slept; she lay back in her chair, her lips slightly parted, motionless; her lids drooped but were probably not quite closed.

Washford Horse and Hiring Fair was entering its last hours and not a horse had been traded nor a man hired but it had been an enjoyable day and it was not over yet.

As darkness fell a swathe of brilliance cut through the whole village from the top of North Street to the Green;

the stalls which lined the street were selling everything from handbags and sexy nighties to farm boots and overalls. The stall holders came from far afield; some were cockneys who made it their business to follow the country fairs. Two streams of people flowed sluggishly up and down the street, congealing round certain stalls then moving on again. The fun-fair in Church Field was a source of even more brilliant light and more raucous sound, glaring and blaring into the night, while the big-wheel turned majestically, carrying its passengers up, briefly, into the darkness.

The Wycliffes worked their way conscientiously along the stalls.

'Floral pattern, bone-china tea-service – twenty pieces: worth thirty pounds of anybody's money . . . But I'm not asking thirty . . . not twenty . . . not fifteen . . .'

'Knickers, step-ins, scanties, panties, briefs – whatever you call 'em it don't make no difference to me; they all cover the same ground if you get my meaning, an' I bin selling 'em at Washford Fair for fifteen year an' my ol' man before that. The chances are your granny bought 'er passion bafflers from my ol' man an' my God! she needed 'em wiv' 'im about . . .'

'Sheets, ladies! Cotton sheets! None of yer nylon rubbish; none of yer Hong Kong rejects – I'm off'ring you real Egyptian cotton sheets – feel 'em lady! Soft as a baby's bottom . . .'

Helen said, 'We could do with some sheets.'

'But not here; you'll get done.'

'I don't see why; he's handing them around for people to feel.'

'All right; if you like.'

'You go on, I'll pick you up later.'

'In this crowd?'

'We can fix a place.' Helen was not sorry to have a chance to do the stalls at her own pace.

'All right. Let's say by the old organ in the fairground. But watch out for bag snatchers.'

Wycliffe drifted with the crowd, moving towards the

Green: a similar stream moved in the opposite direction; there were bottle-necks but people edged their way through with good humour. He had to admit that he was enjoying himself. He did not want to do or see anything in particular, it was enough to be part of this . . . he searched for a word . . . of this procession, for that is what it seemed to be: all these people, each following their own bent but part of a pattern of movement as regular and symmetrical as if it had been choreographed. Down the street, around the Green, into the fairground, out of the fairground, around the Green, up the street . . .

The police caravans were lit up and, with a number of other police vehicles, had been taped off from the crowd. Wycliffe was borne along past them, past the church-yard with its gloomy yews, and into the fairground. He carried a personal radio so that he could be called if necessary and he had left instructions that he was to be told if Vicary returned.

An old-fashioned fairground organ was playing a Sousa march and canned 'pop' music came from amplifiers in confusing discord, punctuated by banshee wails which accompanied some of the rides. A stall selling candy floss, another nougat. The nougat stall brought back memories; his mother had disapproved of sweets in general but excepted barley sugar and nougat, both of which he disliked, so that fairs were for ever associated in his mind with the chewy, sticky, rather sickly sweetness of nougat.

A shooting gallery, darts and hoop-la, all with elusive prizes which looked much the same as they had done forty years ago; a wrestling booth; a Tunnel of Terror . . . His first visit to a fairground in twenty years and he felt like a time traveller. The chair-o-planes looked more dangerous, and masqueraded under another name; there was a whirling Noah's Ark; dodgems where the lads of the village were giving their aggro a fairly harmless airing; and a devilish contraption which whipped screaming couples round at dizzy speeds in wavering orbits.

Wycliffe stopped to watch and spotted Maurice; Maurice

143

in a tight-fitting, light-weight overcoat which made him look more paunchy than he was. He was gazing at the whirling couples with a lost look.

'Good evening, Mr Beale.'

Maurice started and turned toward him. 'Oh, it's you, superintendent! I don't suppose you've seen my father? I'm just a bit concerned; he's so self-willed and he's not as young as he was . . . I met Esther earlier and she said she'd seen him pottering around the stalls in North Street, but it's hopeless looking for anyone in the crush up there.'

'No, I haven't seen your father, Mr Beale, but are you seriously worried?'

Maurice looked vague. 'Not seriously – no. In fact, I think he is quite capable of looking after himself but my wife . . .'

Maurice was like a fat schoolboy pretending to be grown up and vaguely aware that he was not making a good job of it.

Wycliffe said, 'I wanted to talk to Mr Vicary but I understand he isn't home this evening.'

Maurice frowned. 'My brother-in-law is never at home on Friday evenings.'

'So your sister told me. Do you know where he goes?'

Maurice thought this went beyond the bounds of common politeness and his tone was a rebuke. 'I have no idea.'

'Business or pleasure do you think?'

'Really, superintendent!'

'I'm afraid you will have to get used to the idea that this is a murder inquiry, Mr Beale. I have to ask questions.'

Maurice was about to protest but changed his mind. 'I suppose you must do your job as you think best.'

'So, in your view, business or pleasure?'

'All I can say is that there is no business connected with the firm that would take him away on Friday evenings.'

'Thank you.'

Maurice was unhappy. 'That doesn't mean . . .'

'It doesn't mean what, Mr Beale?'

'That there is anything improper going on. After all, my

144

brother-in-law works very hard, as I do, and he is entitled to some relaxation.'

'Of course!'

Maurice went off with a very formal, 'Goodnight, superintendent,' and Wycliffe made his way through the crowds to the old organ. Once it had been the centre of whirling gondolas or dragons or galloping horses, now it stood alone on its trailer, but it still churned out the same music – marches and dance tunes of the twenties, selections from the early musicals: *Chu-Chin-Chow, The Desert Song* and *Maid of the Mountains* . . .

A gorgeous automaton dressed like a cavaliar, in green embroidered with gold, was perched in front of the gilded pipes, beating time with his baton and turning his head jerkily from side to side. He was flanked by massed trumpets, banks of shining brass, which blared forth whenever the score allowed. Above, a pyramid of bells jerked up and down to provide a tinkling counterpoint, and below, a battery of drums thumped out the rhythm.

Wycliffe glanced at his watch. Half-past ten. Helen arrived a few minutes later with a bulging polythene bag.

'I bought two pairs; they really are good value.'

'What shall we do now?'

Arm-in-arm they toured the fairground and stopped at a stall selling Washford fairings – little cakes filled with whortleberry jam and served hot so that the jam spurted out, burning unwary lips. They ate four between them and tidied up each other's faces afterwards.

Helen said, 'Like when we started. Do you remember Dickie Perk's fish and chips?'

As they left the fairground Wycliffe saw Simon going in through the gates of Ashill. Late return of the prodigal: it was twenty minutes to midnight. Not far off a couple of uniformed men were keeping an eye on the crowd. Wycliffe's man, logging the comings and goings through the main gates of Ashill, did so from the comparative comfort of a cubicle in the police van; his mate, responsible for the South Street entrance, was parked down there in an unmarked Mini.

Wycliffe said to Helen, 'I'll call in at the van to see how things are.'

DC Potter, duty officer, was reading the *Daily Mirror* and slurping instant coffee from a handle-less mug. The radio simmered quietly, coming to life in sporadic exchanges.

'Anything to report?'

Potter tried to look efficient, which was too difficult in the circumstances, and he gave up. 'Yes, sir. Radio message from DC Moss on obo at the South Street entrance: Vicary drove into the yard a few minutes ago.' Potter checked with his report sheet. 'Moss logged his return at 23.45 hours, sir.'

Wycliffe picked up the clip-board and glanced through the entries. The picture seemed clear enough: Maurice and Simon had left Ashill by the main gate within twenty minutes of each other, between eight and half-past. They had returned the same way, Maurice at ten-forty-five, Simon at eleven-forty.

Edward and Esther had left together also by the main gate at seven-fifteen; Edward had arrived back by nine-fifteen, Esther by nine-forty-five. Now, with Vicary accounted for, the books were balanced; all safely tucked up. According to the record, Naomi, Nicholas, Gertrude and Joyce had not ventured out.

Wycliffe hesitated; he had intended to question Vicary immediately on his return but it was almost midnight; unlike some of his colleagues he was reluctant to disrupt a household at night. It could wait until morning.

He rejoined Helen. 'I'm coming with you.' He looked round at the crowds moving to and from the fun-fair across the Green, hemming in the police vehicles. 'It won't be possible to get my car out of this lot for another hour so we'd better use yours. There's only one snag, I shall have to use yours in the morning and get somebody to drive it back . . .'

'Be my guest.'

They walked down South Street, past the wide entrance to Ashill, and a disconsolate copper in his Mini, facing a lonely night. On the Newton road where Helen had left her car there was a line of parked vehicles as far as the eye could see in both directions.

The little engine of Helen's Metro spluttered into life; she made skilful use of the few inches her neighbours had left her and got clean away. By half-past twelve they were home.

'Cocoa?' Helen had great faith in the soporific powers of cocoa.

'I think I'll have a night-cap instead.'

He soon fell asleep but then he dreamed, a disturbing dream in which Simon was accusing him of professional misconduct for failing to fill out certain forms. Very put out, he went to call on Simon and was standing on the doorstep at Ashill, ringing the bell. Although he could hear it ringing insistently inside, no-one came to answer the door.

He was awakened by Helen reaching over him to switch off the alarm clock.

'It can't be that time already!'

'Six-thirty – you set the alarm. Did you have a good sleep?'

'I don't know; I didn't have time to notice.'

Downstairs, he telephoned the incident van at Washford. Potter had gone off duty and been replaced by Dixon.

'Anything to report?'

'Not a thing, sir.'

At a quarter past seven he dialled the Vicarys' number. Vicary would be about. He listened while the brr-brr repeated itself a dozen or so times then a weary childish voice said, simply, 'Yes?'

Esther, prised from sleep.

'This is Superintendent Wycliffe.'

A moment to adjust. 'Has something happened?'

'Not as far as I know; I want to speak to your father.'

'I'll get him . . .'

Lilliputian sounds, then her voice, more anxious, 'His bed hasn't been slept in; he can't have come home last night!'

Wycliffe hesitated. 'You expected him back?'

'I'll ask mother.'

Another interval.

'She says she certainly expected him back!'

'I'll be right over.'

Something adrift; either the man on obo had been seeing things or . . .

No time for more than a cup of coffee. Helen came out to see him off and grumbled when he muffed the gears on her Metro. It was foggy, low clouds blanketed every hill; on the motorway out of the city there was little traffic, only heavy lorries which seemed to be playing tag in the lanes. He arrived in Washford as the church clock chimed the hour – eight o'clock. The grey light was bringing a reluctant village back to life on the morning after; paper and plastic litter everywhere, under the drooping flags. The kitchen-midden mentality.

Dixon came out to his car. 'Mr Maurice has been over, sir, and says would you kindly come to the front door.'

A family reception.

CHAPTER SEVEN

As in his dream Wycliffe found himself standing on the front steps of Ashill, ringing the door-bell; but unlike his dream, the bell was answered almost at once. Maurice came to the door, dressed much as Wycliffe had seen him in the office, not a hair out of place, but a very agitated Maurice.

'I'm glad you've come, superintendent; it's so difficult to know . . .' His voice trailed off.

Wycliffe was taken into the gloomy drawing-room, which in the morning light seemed more sombre than ever. Edward, wearing jeans and a paint-stained shirt, was standing by the fireplace, looking lost. Simon was there in a plum-coloured silk dressing-gown. His thin neck and wrists and his mop of silvery hair gave an impression of an elegant scarecrow. He looked haggard and pale, his eyes seemed to have lost their restless vitality and the gaze he turned on Wycliffe was tired and lifeless.

Simon said, 'Good of you to come, superintendent . . . Perhaps this is a storm in a tea-cup — God knows, I hope so.' He raised his arms and let them fall to his sides in a gesture of helplessness.

Wycliffe felt sorry for the old man and shocked by the change in him, but surely this was over-reaction to the event unless . . .

Simon himself seemed to feel the need to justify his concern. 'I suppose at any time we should be worried, but in view of what has been happening one fears the worst.'

'Do you know where Mr Vicary usually spends his Friday evenings?'

'I have no idea. I gather you put that question to Maurice

last night; did you have any particular reason for asking it then?'

Wycliffe avoided an answer and turned to Maurice, 'When did you last see Mr Vicary?'

Maurice cleared his throat. 'Yesterday afternoon; he came into my office at about five and said that he was leaving. That was quite usual, he always leaves early on Friday.'

'Did he seem worried, or in any way different to usual?'

'No, he was just as he always is.'

Wycliffe returned to the old man. 'Where is your other son, Mr Beale?'

'Nicholas? Oh, he's gone off for one of his morning walks. He often gets up early and goes out.'

'Does he know that his brother-in-law has not come home?'

Simon was dismissive. 'I shouldn't think so for a moment!'

Maurice intervened. 'He does know. I told him.'

Wycliffe remembered that the police log had not recorded Nicholas leaving the estate that morning.

'Has your son-in-law ever before stayed out all night without letting anyone know?'

'Never! It is quite unlike him.'

'Where is Mrs Vicary now?'

'In their flat; my daughter-in-law is with her and, of course, Esther.'

'I would like to talk to her.'

Simon insisted on taking him up to the flat. He led the way upstairs, pausing now and then to recover his breath.

In the Vicarys' drawing-room Wycliffe was surprised to find the lights still on and the curtains drawn, though outside it was broad day.

Gertrude was in her dressing-gown but Naomi was fully dressed and she had taken some opportunity to put on her usual make-up. Esther, in black pants and a white shirt, sat on the hearth-rug looking balletic, but she was pale with dark circles under her eyes.

Wycliffe said, 'I think it would be best for me to talk to Mrs Vicary and Esther alone.'

Simon was looking round the room as though slightly

bemused, probably because he was rarely in this part of the house; people came to Simon, he did not go to them.

Naomi said, 'Come, father, I think we are in the way,' and Simon, with unaccustomed docility, allowed himself to be guided away. At the door Naomi paused. 'I'll be back later, Gertie; after I've got things organized downstairs. Try not to worry; I'm sure it will all come out right.'

Gertrude showed neither interest nor gratitude and when they were gone she turned to Wycliffe, 'I suspect you dislike family conferences as much as I do.'

'In my experience they take a long time to get anywhere.' He went on, 'You told me yesterday you had no idea where your husband went on Friday evenings; is that the truth?'

'Yes it is.' She was on edge, making an effort to control a tendency to jerkiness in her movements.

'And you, Esther – do you know?'

'Me?' She looked surprised. 'I haven't the least idea where he goes.' She got up from the rug, crossed to the window and swept back the curtains, letting in the harsh morning light.

Gertrude said, 'Frank is system personified his whole life runs to a schedule; the only difference between last night and any other Friday was that he didn't come home.' She spoke of her husband with an exaggerated tolerance that was little short of contempt.

'You and your husband do not share a room?'

'No.' She seemed to find the question natural in the circumstances.

'Then you don't know what time he comes home as a general rule?'

'Yes, I do. Often though not always, I am still awake and we exchange a few words. Invariably it is around midnight.'

'So you didn't realize he hadn't returned until I telephoned and spoke to Esther?'

'No, of course not.'

'And, after I telephoned, you raised the alarm downstairs.' He said this in a slightly provocative way, which was not lost on her.

She answered, poker faced, 'In many ways, we are a closely knit family, Mr Wycliffe, and my father likes to be treated as head of the house.'

'Are you seriously concerned about your husband?'

She took her time, then she said, 'Something must have happened to prevent him following his usual routine.' The words were carefully chosen.

Wycliffe went to the window and stood, looking down into the yard and at the roofs of buildings which had been the coach house and stables.

'Have you checked to see if his car is back?'

'How can it be?'

'It would be as well to make sure. If Esther will come down with me . . .'

Without a word Esther went to the door and held it open for him. They went through the hall and down the stairs. Several cars were housed in an open-fronted shed.

Esther said, 'His car *is* there! I don't understand.' She pointed to a dark-blue Rover saloon, neatly parked in its bay.

'Whose are the other cars?'

'The Volvo is grandfather's; the BMW belongs to Uncle Maurice; the Metro is Aunt Naomi's; one of the Minis is mine and the other is Edward's. Mother and Uncle Nicholas don't have cars; they never go anywhere.'

He was no nearer understanding this girl; such an odd blend of reserve and childish candour.

'Do you really have no idea where your father spends Friday evenings?'

She was silent for so long that he thought she had decided not to answer, then she said, 'You think he's got a woman somewhere and you may be right, but that's not what mother thinks – not that she would care.'

'Do you?'

Her answer was sharp. 'It's nothing whatever to do with me!'

He said: 'Tell your mother I shall be back shortly; then I would like to talk to her alone.'

She glanced at her watch. 'I should be at work.'

'Not today; telephone them.'

She didn't argue.

He walked round the house and out through the gates to the van. St Dorothea had withdrawn her protection, it was not actually raining but the air was saturated. Men from the council were sweeping up the litter and feeding it into a truck. The fair was over; Washford was returning to normal for another year – except for the murders.

Kersey arrived. 'I've just heard about Vicary – has he done a bunk?'

'I've no idea. Moss logged him in by the South Street entrance at a quarter to twelve, but Moss is off duty. I want you to get hold of him and find out whether he identified the car, the man, or both. The car is in the yard where he usually keeps it.'

Kersey rubbed his chin which, even first thing in the morning, looked like 'Before' in a razor commercial. 'So he's still somewhere on the estate or he's gone off on foot.'

'Or he's been given a lift or been spirited away by little green men.' Wycliffe was irritable. 'He may be dead for all we know and, by the same token, somebody else could have driven the car back. I doubt if Moss would have noticed. Anyway, get hold of Smith and let him give the car a good going over. As a precaution I think we should organize some sort of search of the estate – say four men, and let them work down through the woods from the back of Quarry House.'

He was delayed in returning to Ashill by the telephone. Crime in the two counties had not come to a halt while he devoted himself to the Washford affair. He spoke to his deputy – John Scales, now chief inspector – and between them they settled a few queries. Afterwards he had Administrator Bellings on the line about some piddling organization problem which could have waited until the Pentecostalists take over the KGB. He thanked God that in three months Bellings would be moving to pastures new.

'I'm going back to Ashill.'

When Gertrude answered his ring she had changed her

153

dressing gown for a housecoat and she had done her hair, but she was not wearing make-up and she looked haggard.

'No news?'

'I'm afraid not. I expect Esther told you that his car is in the yard.'

'She did. I can't begin to understand . . .'

In the hall he said, 'I would like to check to see whether any of his clothes are missing – if he has packed a bag. Will you be able to tell?'

She seemed mildly offended. 'We are married and we do still live in the same house! If you will come with me . . .'

She led the way across the hall. 'This is his bedroom.'

A small, plainly furnished room with a single bed and built-in cupboards. Gertrude slid back the cupboard doors on an adequate but by no means lavish stock of clothes, everything laid out with care. Suits, shirts, socks and tie were all in shades of grey; the man seemed to be obsessed with ideas of cryptic coloration.

Gertrude checked the hangers. 'As far as I can see he's taken nothing with him – only the suit and the raincoat he wore to work yesterday.' She slid open another cupboard, which held a couple of travelling cases and some items of small luggage. 'There's nothing missing from there either.'

Wycliffe glanced over a shelf of books at the head of the bed: novels by C.P. Snow and John Le Carré mixed in with the memoirs of politicians and civil servants. Like the rest of the room it was of almost virginal innocence.

'Does your husband have another room – office or study?'

'He uses the room next to this as an office – do you want to see it?' Her manner was detached, perhaps challenging.

The office was little more than a box-room and spartan in its furnishing: a green metal desk with a filing cabinet and shelves to match. Wycliffe pottered about the room, glancing at the books on the shelves, opening drawers and fingering through files. Two drawers of the three-drawer cabinet were taken up with papers concerning the firm, the third was personal and domestic.

Gertrude stood by the door, watching him. 'You'll find

154

in that drawer a detailed record of my household expenditure over twenty years.'

He turned his attention to the desk and skimmed through the drawers. Nothing to suggest that Vicary was other than industrious, methodical and boring.

'Do you and your husband have a joint banking account on which either of you can draw?'

She smiled. 'That's the theory.'

'You attend board meetings of the firm?'

'Frank holds my proxy.'

Back in the hall she said, 'When you came I was just about to make some coffee – would you like some?'

'Please.'

'Then you'd better come into the kitchen.'

Not a dream kitchen straight from the third floor of Beales' Stores but a fairly homely place; not too clean, but not filthy; not tidy, but not littered.

She busied herself with the percolator and he talked to her back.

'You couldn't make an informed guess about where your husband spends his Friday evenings?'

'I could not.'

'Has he ever stayed away like this before?'

'Never.'

'Do you think it's a woman?'

'I should be very surprised.'

'You don't seem unduly worried.'

'I hope that nothing has happened to him.'

He was sitting on a stool at a plastic-topped table and he felt oddly at home. In a certain way Gertrude was his kind of woman; in other circumstances she might have been another Helen, but she had allowed herself to be packaged young; property of family and firm; a negotiable asset. In her circumstances would Helen have turned to drink and spent her time dozing in front of the television? To be honest he found it difficult to imagine Helen having got herself into Gertrude's position.

She turned and their eyes met; he wondered if she

155

had somehow caught the drift of his thoughts. She was intelligent enough.

She put the percolator on the table, two pottery mugs, milk and sugar. 'Pour your own, how you like it.' She sat down opposite him.

Her housecoat opened as she sat down, showing her breasts but she ignored it. Provocative or indifferent? From his wallet he took out the snap-shot of her with Newcombe and passed it over. She took it, glanced at it and frowned. 'What am I supposed to say to that?'

Her relaxed manner was a façade; little lines of strain showed on her forehead and round her mouth, and her hands were never still.

'I caught Joyce trying to smuggle it out of Newcombe's cottage yesterday. I gather there used to be a framed enlargement on the wall in the parlour but that has been taken away or destroyed.'

She said, 'When my brothers and I were children we spent a lot of time down there. Emily and her husband both worked for us and Morley was the same age as Maurice. He had a wonderful way with animals and it was natural—'

She was over-anxious. Wycliffe interrupted, 'You were no child when that was taken. Eighteen? About that, and your brothers must have been working – Nicholas in the army; Maurice in the firm.'

She was eyeing him closely and Wycliffe noticed that she had not touched her coffee.

'So what?' We didn't just sever relations . . . I still went down to the cottage quite often. Why not? You seem to be trying to make something out of nothing.'

He looked at her, holding her gaze until she looked away, embarrassed, then he said, 'I know about Esther.'

'About Esther?' But her innocence was unconvincing.

'It has taken me too long to see what was fairly obvious. I've no proof now. As Newcombe found, proof is hard to come by, but proof is one thing, certainty another. No doubt we shall get further when we start asking the right questions. . . . But what puzzles me is why two people had to die.

Even if your secret had leaked out at the time it would have been hardly more than a nine-day wonder for the gossips; now, twenty years later, if Newcombe had talked, who would have believed him? Some would have pretended to, but would it have mattered? He realized this himself, otherwise there would have been no point in his clumsy efforts to get corroboration – his visit to the register office and his approach to Ruby Price.'

They faced each other across the table; Gertrude sat motionless, then Wycliffe said, 'Emily kept her bargain for the better part of twenty years but with his mother dead, Newcombe was free to go his own way . . . Did he try to blackmail you or your husband?'

She shook her head but said nothing.

'In my village the father was expected to marry the girl or help to support the child, but in this case both alternatives were unthinkable; the risk here was that the father might assert his rights, so he was compensated – through his mother, of course. Emily was given a substantial cash sum to keep her son quiet and amenable.'

Gertrude spoke quietly. 'Are you trying to humiliate me?' She was tracing little patterns on the table-top in spilt coffee.

'No. I'm sure that you have had more than your share of humiliation but I do intend to get at the truth.'

She looked at him steadily for some time before speaking, then she said, 'I was nineteen at the time – the same age as Esther is now, but there was no real comparison! I had had virtually no contact with boys other than with my brothers and Morley Newcombe. My parents were probably fond of me, but in the same way as they might have been of a pet cat; I was cosseted and protected and forbidden to grow up.' She was staring at her coffee mug, turning it round with the tips of her fingers. 'Well, there came a time when I was ripe for seduction, and I was seduced – by an expert – a natural.'

Wycliffe said, 'Isn't it surprising that your parents, so anxious to protect you, let you associate with Newcombe? I gather that he was already known as a girl chaser.'

She laughed briefly. 'I knew nothing about that and I doubt if my parents did. As far as they were concerned the Newcombes were servants – and therefore *safe*.' She paused and her eyes took on a far away look. 'Ashill was another world then, sometimes I can hardly believe it was real. The uproar when they discovered that I was pregnant! And when they were eventually persuaded that the father was Morley Newcombe!

'Of course, my parents, Ruby Price and the priest went into conference. There could be no question of abortion but, in the end, they worked out the perfect solution; everything for the best. By marrying me, Frank bought his way into the firm and the family; Esther had a reputable father; I became respectable again, and Beales' Stores acquired a first-class business man as a family property.'

After an interval Wycliffe said, 'Does Esther know?'

'I've never told her, but she knows – I'm quite sure of that.'

'Shouldn't you have told her?'

She made an irritable movement. 'Of course I should have told her! But in this family we never talk about anything that matters; we live on the surface and try not to think about what is underneath.'

Unselfconsciously Wycliffe began to fill his pipe as he would have done in his kitchen at home. Gertrude felt the outside of her untouched mug of coffee and, finding it cold, pushed it away.

'I should have divorced him years ago but I am trapped. If I divorced him, what should I have? Can't you see that he is far more necessary to the family than I am? They wouldn't risk losing Frank.'

Wycliffe changed the subject. 'Esther seems a very self-reliant young woman.'

'I suppose one could say that she has to be.'

'And very protective towards Edward.'

'She recognizes another victim.'

'Victim?'

'Of this house – this family!' Her voice trembled, then

158

broke; she slumped down with her arms on the table and her head in her arms and wept. Wycliffe was moved. He got up and went round the table to stand at her side, helpless.

The weeping turned to sobs and the sobs eventually subsided; she lifted her head, her face flushed and creased, her eyes swollen. She made no apology but said with a kind of satisfaction which seemed to invite and acknowledge his complicity, 'That's the first time I've been able to do that in many years.'

The atmosphere in the kitchen had become intimate; time for a middle-aged policeman to make a tactical withdrawal. He said, 'Try not to worry.'

It was a fatuous remark and she smiled up at him, blinking her reddened eyelids. 'I'll be all right.'

She came with him to the door and watched him down the steps. With little sleep and no breakfast he felt cold inside; uneasy too, as one who had come within shouting distance of making a fool of himself.

'I'll keep you informed.'

Had Vicary cleared out? It seemed inconceivable that a man responsible for two murders should be scared off while there was still not a shred of real evidence against him. Incredible too, that he should not have used his car, at least on the first leg of his get-away.

Wycliffe told himself, 'Find out where he spends Friday evenings – in particular, where he spent this one.'

He had asked Gertrude, 'Do you think there is a woman?' and Gertrude had answered, 'I'd be very surprised.' Another time she had said, 'Frank is system personified, his whole life is run to a schedule.' But even if Gertrude saw herself as a sex-starved woman it did not necessarily mean that Vicary was a eunuch. Certainly he was not the sort to complicate his life with any romantic involvement; it was unlikely that he had a Veronica tucked away; more likely there was a business arrangement, efficiently stage-managed, something more subtle than a short-time with a tenner on the mantelpiece though with the same lack of commitment.

But where?

In the yard Sergeant Smith, PC Miller and a little dark man in overalls were standing round Vicary's car.

Smith was at his most dour. 'This is Mr Smerdon who runs the garage on the Newton road, sir. Vicary is one of his customers.'

The little man, who looked like Adolf Hitler and obviously knew it, chipped in. 'He has a charge account for petrol and he's a fanatic about economy. When my chap fills his tank he sets the trip meter back to zero so that he can check the performance.' Smerdon was smoking a tiny black cheroot which wiggled up and down as he spoke.

'When was he last in?'

'Yesterday evening between half-past five and six. My boy was off so I served him myself. I asked him if he was going to the fair and got a dusty answer; he's not a chatty sort of man. What do you think has happened to him, superintendent?'

'I've no more idea than you have.'

Smith cut in. 'The trip meter is reading five-point-two miles and the tank is still as good as full, so he can't have gone far.' Smith turned his morose gaze on PC Miller. 'Miller has a notion about where he might have gone.'

Miller had a cautious man's aversion to sticking his neck out but he had no option. 'It's just that five miles is about the distance from the garage to Biscombe and back here. Biscombe is a little place a couple of miles down the valley.'

'So?'

'Well, sir, it occurred to me that Vicary might be a visitor at Biscombe Manor. I mean, it's possible he spent his Friday evenings there.'

'Why? Is it an hotel or something?'

'No, sir. A few years back it was leased to a chap called Lyne, a retired property dealer from London. He came down here with his wife and daughter; his wife has left him, but his daughter is still there and I hear that she's well in with the horsey set.'

'Why should Vicary go there, do you think?'

Miller frowned. This was getting too specific. 'I don't know that he did, sir, but I've heard that Lyne has several friends among business men who live round here and I thought Vicary might be one of them. I often see cars in Lyne's drive of an evening.'

Wycliffe nodded. 'It sounds promising.' He turned to Smith. 'Did anything about the car strike you as unusual?'

Smith shook his grey head. 'Nothing. There's no sign that anybody drove it but the owner – his prints are everywhere; and there are no indications of any violence. In my view Vicary drove his car home and parked it as usual. What happened after that . . .'

What happened after that was the crunch question.

Wycliffe, on the point of telephoning Biscombe Manor, changed his mind. If, by any chance, the man Lyne was involved in Vicary's disappearance there was an obvious risk in telephoning. He decided to go there himself.

He picked up his car from the Green and drove down South Street to the Newton road. Almost opposite the junction a fingerpost pointed along a narrow lane: Biscombe 2 miles. The lane roughly followed the course of a stream in a gentle switchback, until, topping one rise, he was looking down on a hamlet of a score or so houses. The stream, now almost a river, and moving more sedately, skirted the houses and meandered through the arches of a packhorse bridge which carried the road to the manor house on the opposite hill. The house itself, grey stone and slate, with steep gables, was backed by sombre pines against the high moor. The mists had thinned and a watery sunshine lit the valley in startling contrast with the inky-black clouds lying heavily on the face of the moor. Wycliffe drove through the seemingly deserted village, over the packhorse bridge (maximum width 6 feet) and up the hill to the house. He left his car in the drive and went up the steps of a Victorian Gothic porch to a front door studded with nails and decorated with all the wrought-iron trimmings.

His ring was answered by Lyne himself, a wiry little Cockney who, despite his expensive tweeds, would have looked more at home behind a stall on the Portobello Road.

Wycliffe introduced himself and Lyne's eyes narrowed. 'Chief Super! What's this about then?' He remembered his manners. 'At any rate whatever it is you can tell me better inside.' He led the way into a large drawing-room which looked like a lounge bar in an up-market pub. 'Drink? I've got a nice drop of Scotch sent me by a friend . . .'

Wycliffe excused himself. 'I wanted to ask you if Frank Vicary of Ashill was here last night.'

Lyne looked surprised. 'Frankie? What's he been up to then? In any case, why don't you ask him?'

'Because we can't find him, Mr Lyne. His car is back at Ashill but there's no sign of the man himself.'

'Well I'll be damned!' Lyne poured whisky from a crystal decanter into a matching glass. 'Sure you won't change your mind? I never drink when I'm here alone, but you being here . . .' He chuckled. 'It'd be a pity to pass up the chance.' He sipped the neat spirit. 'Well, Frankie was here last night like every other Friday – but a chief super don't come looking for any Charlie who happens to stay out all night; is this about the Washford murders?'

'That's what I'm trying to find out, Mr Lyne. What does Vicary do when he comes here?'

'Do? He does the same as the rest of us – we play Nap.'

'Nap?'

Lyne laughed. 'It's a good game – English poker. And the way we play it's cut-throat.'

'Big stakes?'

'Far from it! Never more than a few pounds change hands in a night but you'd think we was playing for the Crown Jewels and Frankie is the keenest of the lot.'

'Who else was here last night?'

'The usual Friday night set. Apart from Frankie and me there was Ernie Pemberton, a retired estate agent from Noseworthy, and Billy Norris who used to run a night-club in Torquay – Billy is retired too and lives a

mile or so down the valley – another fish out of water.'
Lyne looked out of the window where the sunlight was still
struggling through the mists in a ready-made watercolour.
'Biggest mistake of my life, coming to a place where there's
nothing to do but die. If it wasn't for my girl I'd flog the
bloody lease and get back to the smoke.'

'What time did Vicary leave?'

'About half-eleven; he never stays late – afraid of missing
the early worm. A keen lad, our Frankie.'

'He comes here every Friday night to play Nap – is that it?'

'What else? A game of cards, a drink or two, and a chat.'

'No women?'

Lyne laughed. 'You think I run a brothel on the side?
It's an idea – liven the place up a bit but I don't think it
would appeal to Frankie. Seriously though, no women.'

'What sort of a chap is Vicary?'

Lyne shook his head. 'That's asking.' He emptied his
glass and put it down. 'I'm no head shrinker.'

'But you know men; you've had to if I've got the measure
of you.'

Lyne grinned. 'You're a persuasive bugger, I'll give you
that. All right! I'd say Frankie is a born fighter who can
never win.'

'A very odd description of a successful business man.'

'You think so? I wouldn't say that. Some people – a lot
maybe – never win if there's nobody there to cheer.'

'You think he needs someone to tell him what a clever
bloke he is?'

Lyne gave him an odd look. 'Why not? We're all human.
Frankie himself doesn't say much but from what I've heard
elsewhere the Beales are a rum crowd. He hits it off with
the old man because he knows how to make the tills sing,
but aside from that . . . one of the brothers is as thick as
two short planks and the other seems to be bonkers. As for
Frankie's wife . . .' Lyne tilted his elbow. 'Like me, she's
too fond of the firewater but from what I hear she don't
wait for visitors.'

'Last night, did he seem much as usual?'

'He was under the weather. I went out with him to his car and we chatted for a minute or two before he drove off. I could tell he was worried about the killings.' Lyne paused then added, 'Last night Frankie was a very worried man.'

Wycliffe thanked him. 'I'll send someone along to take your statement.'

'Any time! I'm always glad of somebody to talk to in this mausoleum. And if, any night, you feel like a game of cards and a drink, you know where to come.'

He stood on the steps and watched Wycliffe drive off.

Wycliffe now knew where Vicary went on Friday evenings and much good it did him. He was still not sure whether he was looking for a fugitive or a victim though it seemed unlikely that a man would spend a social evening with friends before making a bolt for it.

He drove back to Washford and parked on the Green. Kersey was in the van and they brought each other up to date.

'Curnow talked to Charlie Alford — he had to prod him a bit by dangling a charge of exhibitionism. Alford admitted sending you the note — more out of spite against the Beales than anything else. He found out about Edward's father by chance — a relative of his wife in the Met — and he couldn't resist making something of it. Perhaps more important, he told Curnow that not long after his mother died, Newcombe had said, "She had money. I know the old bitch had money and I know where she got it, but I can't bloody well find out what she done with it." And another time, still talking about the money, he said, "Anyway, I reckon there's more where that come from".'

'Anything else?'

'Just that Moss, who was on obo last night in South Street, says the gates were open when Vicary came back and he drove straight in, but a minute or so later he came to shut the gates and Moss saw him quite clearly.'

Wycliffe said, 'You've got a search team out?'

'They've been at it for some time. Perhaps there's something for them to find.'

164

Wycliffe was restless. He left the van and walked through the main gates of Ashill, round the house and across the lawn. The mists had closed in again, clammily damp, though not unpleasant, for the moisture in the air caught and held the tangy smells of the peaty soil and of the plants which grew in it. He needed time to think. It occurred to him that Vicary might have felt the same – coming back from Biscombe he might have felt the need of time to adjust before returning to the claustrophobic atmosphere of Ashill and to the fresh tensions generated by the murders. Wasn't it quite possible that he had taken a midnight stroll in the grounds? Last night at that time it could have been very pleasant – a fine night, moonshine, the glare from the fair, the babel of music and voices, hoots and cries . . . But if he had taken such a stroll, what had happened to him?

There was, of course, another possibility, that Vicary was the killer and, convinced that he had no chance of getting away with it, he had chosen to take his own life. But nothing he had heard of the man suggested that he would give in so easily.

He reached the ivy-covered wall at the back of Quarry House and peered through the slatted gate into the dripping, deserted garden. He made a mental note to find out whether Nicholas had been visiting there the night before. He continued walking through the trees to the little pavilion above the fall and it was as he was descending the zig-zag path that he looked down and saw, by the margin of the pool, four men standing around a body which was sprawled on the ground.

Vicary had been found.

They had found him in the shallow, slack water near the fall, along with a mass of other debris which had been caught up and swept aside by the turbulence. The searchers had dragged the body ashore and now it lay on the muddy shingle, still within reach of the spray from the fall. Wycliffe looked down at the small crumpled figure. Vicary wore a light-grey pinstripe with grey suede shoes, silk shirt and tie to match; all sodden now, so that water seeped from them. His face was devoid of colour but seemed to be smiling, his wide, thin-lipped mouth was widened still further in a sardonic grin.

One of the men said, 'We radioed the van, sir. Mr Kersey is on his way.'

Vicary had not drowned. Like the others he had been shot through the head though the wound of entry was not immediately obvious. It was low down, well behind the ear, a neat hole, as though a pencil had been pressed in. The wound of exit was less discreet, the bullet had blasted its way out of the temporal region on the other side of the skull.

Wycliffe stooped down and felt the oddly flexed limbs to satisfy himself that rigor was still present. As he did so he noticed that the dead man's wallet was on the point of slipping out of the inside breast pocket of his jacket and he picked it up.

A third violent death in less than a week and suicide was out. Apart from the circumstances in which the body had been found, the position of the wound entry made it highly improbable, and the nature of the wound meant that the gun had been discharged at some distance – not far, but outside the practical range of suicide.

Only yesterday he had begun to realize the possible strength of a case against Vicary, now Vicary was dead. He felt a heavy responsibility; almost as though the man had died as a direct result of his suspicion – which was absurd. All the same . . . Joyce had said to him: 'You think you've found out something but you could still get it wrong.' Now her words had a prophetic ring.

Kersey arrived. A master of platitude in moments of high drama, he said, 'This is getting to be a habit!'

'What do you make of it?'

Kersey took his time. 'It seems pretty obvious that he was shot and pushed in the water afterwards.'

Wycliffe said, 'Rigor is still present and the limbs are

166

flexed as you see. I doubt if they set that way while supported in the water.'

'It looks that way to me.'

'But that would mean an interval of several hours between the shooting and the time he went into the water.'

Wycliffe changed the subject. 'We shall have to leave that to Franks. Meantime, we agree that he wasn't shot in the water, so where?'

Kersey ran a hand through his thinning hair and looked at the flotsam trapped in the shallows where the body had been found, then up the gleaming face of the fall. 'I suppose that stuff came from up there by the quick way; perhaps he did too.'

By radio, and for the third time in six days, Wycliffe set in motion the machinery of a murder inquiry.

To make access easier and to avoid having to carry the body up the steep slope by the fall, the four searchers were put to work clearing a way through the shrubbery to the lane, where there was a decaying wooden door which had not been opened for a generation at least.

Wycliffe brooded over the body. It lay on its back as it had been dragged from the water, legs and arms flexed in a bizarre position like a badly trussed turkey, a posture which only made sense if the body was face down. When Vicary was shot he must have collapsed face down, arms and legs somewhat retracted; rigor had set in and, hours later, the now rigid body had been dropped or pushed into the pool. If the shooting had taken place soon after Vicary's return home, the body could have found its way into the water by six or seven in the morning, but not earlier.

Odd!

And there was something else; the fingers of the right hand were set in a holding position though the hand was empty.

'What do you make of that?'

Kersey screwed up his lips. 'Not much; it looks as though he might have been holding something when rigor set in.'

Wycliffe said, 'If I'm not here when Smith comes make

sure he gets a shot of that hand and ask Franks what he makes of it.'

Wycliffe was still holding the dead man's wallet – pig-skin, darkened by immersion. He opened it: several sodden five-pound notes and a couple of singles; driving licence; cheque cards, and a car insurance certificate. In an inside pocket where the water had not penetrated to the same extent he found a folded sheet of writing paper which turned out to be a hand-written letter. The writing was large, round and schoolgirlish and he thought he recognized it before he saw the signature – Ruby Price.

Dear Frank,   Friday.
    I am no longer welcome at the house and, as I never go into the city, I thought it best to write. I am sending this to your office and it is for you to decide whether or not you show it to G. Yesterday I had a visit from N. At first I thought he was drunk because he talked about his rights as a parent! Then he went on to say that now his mother is dead he is determined to have what he claims to be 'his due'. He talked about 'having the law on some people' and said that if it came to that I would have to tell the truth on oath. Of course I know that this is mostly big talk but he is out to make trouble and I think he's shrewd enough to see that he can do it without bringing in the law. He said he was thinking of having a word with G. and then, if necessary, with the girl. I told him what I thought of him in no uncertain terms but I'm worried on behalf of the family and for dear R's sake.

With kind regards,
Ruby Price.

Wycliffe noted that Ruby had not been in any great hurry to pass on news of the visit. He handed the letter to Kersey.

Kersey read it and shook his head. 'It seems a hell of a lot of sweat about an illegitimate kid twenty years after.'

Wycliffe left him to cope with the pathologist and the removal of the body. He climbed the steep path to the pavilion at the head of the fall, opened the red-painted door and stepped inside.

As before the little room looked neglected, dusty and unused; everywhere there were signs of mouldering damp. Between worn and patternless rugs, floorboards were visible and there were narrow gaps through which he could glimpse the racing water below. One wall was taken up with cupboards, there was a large, oblong table, three or four wicker chairs with damp, faded cushions, and a sofa.

He looked for any signs that the shooting had taken place there but found nothing more suggestive than a pale rectangular patch on the floor where it seemed a rug had been removed. One certain change since his last visit, the cupboard doors had been shut, now they stood open. Some of the shelves were stacked with old magazines and books which were losing their spines; others held board games, packs of cards, anonymous boxes of all sizes, a cheap camera, table tennis bats . . . In one of the cupboards a section of the bottom shelf had been removed exposing a cavity in the masonry — the sort of secret hidey-hole children love — and in the cavity he could see the end of a cardboard box which was far too clean to have been there long. He lifted it out and found a smaller, stouter one below it. The smaller box carried a Fiocchi label and contained thirteen nine-millimetre cartridges. The other box was something of a lucky dip — medals, ribbons, regimental cap badges, shoulder flashes . . . Nicholas's souvenirs.

He looked into the cavity again and felt round to make sure but there was no pistol.

It seemed likely that Vicary had been shot in the pavilion and later — much later — his body had been dragged on to the verandah and tumbled over the balustrade. His men would search for the cartridge-case and the bullet, they would crawl over the floor and minutely inspect the verandah and balustrade; they would end up with several little polythene bags neatly labelled, and this would be proof.

He went out on to the verandah. Mist blotted out the valley; moisture condensed on every surface and dripped from the eaves of the little building. Very different from the night before when Vicary had parked his car in the yard and had been cajoled or coerced into trailing across the lawn and through the trees to the pavilion. At that time the fair was lighting up the sky over Ashill, the night was clear and there was a moon.

Wycliffe left the pavilion and walked on through the trees to the back of Quarry House. He let himself into the garden and walked up the path to the back door. Through the window he could see into the kitchen where the two sisters were seated at table, eating their lunch.

It was Veronica who came to the door.

Wycliffe said, 'I would like to talk to you and your sister.'

Veronica stretched her lean, freckled neck like a bird in aggressive display, but something in his manner must have checked her for she stood aside to let him in.

In the kitchen Rose got up from the table with a nervous smile. 'We eat in here at midday, it hardly seems worth carrying everything into the dining-room.'

Veronica said, 'I hardly think the superintendent is interested in our domestic arrangements, Rose.' She stood by the table without inviting him to sit down.

'Last night, at about midnight, Frank Vicary was shot dead in the little house over the fall.'

He cut short the exclamations of shocked concern. 'Presumably you were here last night at that time?'

Veronica said, 'We must have been preparing for bed.'

'You heard nothing – no shot?'

'There was so much noise from the fair it would have been difficult to hear anything; they went on until one o'clock.'

'Before you went to bed, did you go into your back garden at all?'

Rose looked at Veronica, who seemed slightly self-conscious. She said, 'I was in the garden briefly, that was probably a few minutes before midnight.'

On their two plates, lettuce leaves were growing soggy in the liquid which drained from little pink chunks of tinned salmon. If this was typical of Quarry House cuisine, Nicholas was not being wooed through his stomach.

'Was Captain Beale here last night?'

'He was.' Very stiff.

'And you were seeing him off?'

'Captain Beale comes and goes by the back gate because it is obviously more convenient for him. As we like to lock the gate at night, I go down the garden with him.'

'Were you in the garden for any length of time?'

'A few minutes – perhaps six or seven.'

'Before or after Captain Beale left?'

She coloured like a young girl. 'Before.'

'Presumably you were both near the gate?'

'Fairly near.'

'In those few minutes did anything strike you as unusual or odd – did you hear or see anything out of the ordinary? Other than the fair, of course.'

She was all set for a denial but then her expression changed.

Wycliffe said, 'I can see that there was something – what was it?'

She shrugged. 'It was really nothing at all; I don't know why I remembered it. I thought I heard footsteps – somebody hurrying, passing the gate – I had my back to it.'

'And?'

'I happened to mention it to Captain Beale because I know they are concerned about night prowlers on the estate but he said he hadn't noticed anything.'

'Did Captain Beale carry a torch?'

'He always carries one when he comes here in the evening but it wasn't needed last night, with the moon and the lights from the fair it was like day.'

'How was he dressed?'

This was too much for Veronica. 'Really, Mr Wycliffe,

I think you should ask him such a question.'

'But I'm asking you.'

Rose sat as though transfixed; this was not the man she had chatted to so amiably in the churchyard.

'He wore a green cardigan and cavalry twill trousers.'

'No jacket or coat?'

'No.'

'And he carried nothing but a torch?'

'That is correct.'

'Does he usually stay until midnight?'

Veronica flushed but she answered. 'He usually leaves at about half-past ten but last night there was a concert on the radio which we particularly wanted to hear.'

Wycliffe left the sisters to their tinned salmon and, on his way to Ashill, he brooded on oddities. 'If a case has a number of unusual features the chances are they are related.' A truth handed down from on high during his training days and duly recorded in his notebook. Well, there were odd features here. The near coincidence between the time at which Nicholas left his Veronica and the time of the shooting; the fact that he was much later leaving than usual; the fact that though the army souvenirs and ammunition had turned up – more or less exhibited – the pistol was still missing; the fact that Vicary had, apparently, gone to the pavilion instead of to bed; that he had been shot, and hours later tumbled into the pool; that his hand was curiously flexed. And one other fact – that Nicholas was already out when Wycliffe arrived at Ashill that morning.

The links if they existed were too tenuous for a plodding policeman who always had difficulty with sustained logical thought.

He arrived in the coach house yard and climbed the steps to the flat. Gertrude answered the door and took his coat. While they were still in the hall he said, 'I'm afraid it's bad news.'

'Tell me.'

'I'm sorry to say that your husband is dead.'

172

They moved into the drawing-room and she pointed, mechanically, to a chair but they remained standing. She walked over to the window.

Wycliffe said, 'He was shot through the head.'

It was some while before she asked, 'Would he have suffered much pain? He was a child about pain.'

'Death must have been instantaneous.'

The gloom outside seemed to drain what little colour there was from the room, leaving sombre greys, and as Gertrude stood by the window he could only see her form in silhouette.

She spoke in a low voice, her manner reflective. 'It shows how little one can know of another person. I would never have believed him capable . . .'

'Capable of what?'

She turned to face him in apparent surprise. 'Of doing what he must have done and then taking his own life.'

'He didn't kill himself.'

'I thought you said—'

'I said that he had been found shot − shot by someone, murdered like the others.'

She looked at him, wide-eyed, fearful. 'But you found the gun?'

'No.'

She moved to the nearest chair and dropped into it; she seemed profoundly shocked. 'Then it isn't over! I could see yesterday that you thought Frank . . . that you suspected him.' She was twisting her hands together and staring at him with frightened eyes. 'I found it difficult to believe; I didn't think he was capable of such violence, but I *wanted* you to be right − I *wanted* it to be Frank . . . When you told me that he was dead I must confess I thought, "It's over! At least it's over!" '

'Did you?' The words came softly and he was gazing at her with an intensity of which he himself was unaware. He had not intended to speak his question aloud; in fact he had been asking himself whether she was genuinely distressed or whether it was an act.

She said, 'Why are you looking at me like that? Are you

173

trying to frighten me? There's no need. God! I'm frightened enough already. Because it isn't over and you will go on and on until . . .'

There was hysteria in her voice. She reached for a cigarette from a box on the table, lit it, inhaled and blew out a cloud of smoke.

Wycliffe said, speaking very quietly, 'Your husband was shot then, much later, his body was pushed into the pool.'

'In the pool? You found him in the pool? Why are you saying this? You must have a reason, or is it just to torment me?' She was flushed and her hands trembled so that she had difficulty in placing the cigarette between her lips.

'I am telling you what actually happened.'

She was staring at him fixedly but he could see that she had accepted what he said and was trying desperately to fit it in with whatever pattern her thoughts presented. 'But if someone did that to him — I mean, if they shifted his body, he still might have killed himself.'

'No. The position and the nature of the wound rule out suicide.'

She had made a great effort of self-control and when she spoke again her voice was calmer but also harder. 'Have you found out where he went last night?'

'To Biscombe Manor where he spent every Friday evening.'

'Not with a woman.'

'No, he went there to play cards with a few friends.'

She nodded. 'That's more like it!' Suddenly she was aggressive, almost vicious; she crushed out her half-smoked cigarette. 'I knew that there was no woman — he was impotent, that's why he had to be such a big man in the business.'

She was silent for a while, the knuckles of one hand pressed to her lips. 'You're quite sure it couldn't have been suicide? The gun could have been taken from his hand as they put him in the water . . .'

'Suicide is out of the question.'

It was chilly and he felt oddly oppressed in this large,

anonymous room where it was easy to believe that nothing had ever happened which people could look back on with pleasure or warmth. A room that was a mere back-drop for episodes rather than a place where someone had lived.

'When did you last see Newcombe?'

The question took her by surprise and she hesitated. 'See him? I don't know . . . a long time ago.' She added after a pause, 'Over the years I've done my best not to see him.'

'Are you sure that you haven't spoken to him recently?'

She moved irritably. 'What is the good of asking me questions if you don't believe what I say?'

He took Ruby's letter from his pocket and handed it to her. 'I found this in your husband's wallet.'

She took the letter and read it through with obvious anxiety, then she looked at him, 'When did he get this?'

'Presumably at his office on Saturday.'

She was very pale. 'I've never seen it before; I didn't even know of its existence.'

'And you still say that Newcombe hasn't been to see you?'

She seemed deeply preoccupied. 'I've told you!'

'On Sunday your husband went to see Newcombe – what happened then?'

She burst out, 'You ask me? I didn't even know that he'd been until after Newcombe was dead. He told me nothing – nothing ever!'

'And now Newcombe, Ruby Price and your husband have all been murdered.'

She looked at him once more with scared eyes. 'What are you trying to say?'

'Only that I am searching for a motive – a motive strong enough to account for the killing of three people.'

'I—'' She broke off at the sound of the front door opening and of someone in the hall. 'That will be Esther; she hasn't been to work today.'

Esther came in wearing jeans and a denim jacket. Little globules of moisture were trapped in her hair; she looked desperately tired.

'You've been out?'

175

The girl did not answer her mother but spoke to Wycliffe. 'So you've found him.'

Gertrude said, 'Your father's body was found in the pool, he had been shot through the head.'

'I know.' But she continued to address Wycliffe, 'He didn't do it himself?'

'No.'

The girl remained where she was for a moment, irresolute, then she turned in a deliberate way and left the room.

Gertrude said, 'She's off to find Edward; I'm no use to her.'

'Will you break the news to your father?'

'I suppose I must.'

'I'll see myself out.' He felt sure that her need for a stiff drink was all but overwhelming.

Esther had not gone in search of Edward, she was waiting for Wycliffe in the hall. She pushed open one of the doors and beckoned him in. It was her bedroom, a plainly furnished little room, cheerless as a nun's cell.

'Will she be all right?'

Wycliffe preferred not to answer.

'What are you going to do?'

Her tiredness bordered on exhaustion; her movements were slow and the dark rings under her eyes were like bruises.

Again Wycliffe said nothing and she went on, 'It's like a horrible nightmare, like being in a room with the walls closing in . . . I saw your men in the pavilion, is it right that he was shot there?'

I think so.'

'But his body was found in the pool.'

'Yes, we think it was tumbled over the balustrade.'

She put her hand to her mouth in a curiously childish gesture. 'Mother couldn't have done that! She has a back injury – she couldn't possibly . . .'

She looked at him, more frightened than ever, realizing that by her very denial she had brought into the open the stark possibility of her mother's guilt, and now, there it was, pinned out between them like a specimen for inspection.

'Why don't you sit down?'

Obediently she sat on the bottom of her bed, upright and tense.

'How long have you known that Frank Vicary was not your real father?'

She swept back her hair with both hands. 'It's hard to say; it gradually dawned on me that our family wasn't quite right, and when I was a bit older I overheard things. I realized that mother had had a lover before she was married and that I was the result.' She smiled briefly. 'I thought it was romantic until I found out who her lover had been.'

'When was that?'

'I must have been thirteen.'

'Who told you?'

'Ruby Price – with a lot of satisfaction. I know it wasn't long after Granny Beale died, she wouldn't have dared before.'

'You didn't like Ruby?'

She considered the question. 'It was mutual. I wouldn't call her "auntie" and that sort of thing, so she always pretended to forget my name and called me "girl" . . . No, I didn't like her at all. She had a way of talking – always hinting at what she could say if she chose.' She broke off, then added, 'I know Teddy feels differently about her.'

Wycliffe said, 'Last night you went to the fair and you came back at about a quarter to ten; what did you do after that?'

She frowned. 'Nothing really. Mother was in the drawing-room—'

'Did you speak to her?'

'No, the television was on and she was asleep in her chair. I came in here and lay on the bed reading until about half-past eleven, then I decided to make myself something to drink before going to bed properly. I went into the kitchen, but it occurred to me that mother might like something too, so I went to ask her, but she was fast asleep. I switched off the television and left her; that's the best thing to do when she is like that.'

An alibi?

177

CHAPTER EIGHT

Although leaden clouds had rolled down from the moor to engulf the village in a moist gloom, it was still not raining. Wycliffe joined Kersey in the police caravan where young Dixon was duty officer and the two other DCs pecked away at typewriters.

Kersey said, 'I've had a call from Radford of *The News;* it seems his colleagues have pushed off for the weekend and left him holding the baby. He's heard a rumour and I promised him a statement this afternoon but he's not too bothered. His own paper doesn't come out again till Monday and over the weekend, local TV and radio are only interested in balls of different shapes and sizes, kicked, hit, thrown or poked.'

'What's happened down below?'

'Franks has been and gone; he agrees with you – definitely not suicide, an interval of several hours between the shooting and the body going into the water, and he admits that the right hand could have held a gun which was forcibly removed after rigor had set in. They've taken the body away and Smith has gone back to headquarters to work on his stuff. Among other things he's taken fibres from the stone work of the balustrade which might have come from Vicary's clothing.'

'Good! Let's see if we can get something to eat.'

The village seemed to be deserted and the fun-fair, due for a final fling that evening, was shrouded in dripping canvas. But the inn wasn't short of customers though they were anything but lively. They sat in silence, sipping their beer and contemplating the table tops. The two policemen were received with indifference.

But Blatchford was the same as ever. 'They're always like this on the day after. Most of 'em had a skinful last night and they need time to get over it.' He lowered his voice, 'They're saying that Vicary shot himself.'

Wycliffe took refuge in the Irish, 'Are they now!'

'I saw your chaps buzzing around just now and I wondered . . .'

They shared the railed-off part of the bar with a young unisex couple of would-be-walkers who, as they ate, kept an anxious eye on the window and the menacing clouds.

Dora served them with hot pasties and Wycliffe watched with gloomy fascination while Kersey opened his and filled it with tomato ketchup. Afterwards they had treacle pudding with clotted cream, a meal which would not have gained Helen's seal of approval.

At a quarter to two, when they returned to the van, the wind was rising, stirring the limp flags and rustling through the beech trees.

'I want you to put a man in the entrance hall at the house.'

'Am I allowed to ask why?'

Wycliffe was vague. 'It will raise the temperature a bit and he might be useful.'

The church clock was chiming the hour when Wycliffe crossed to the house and let himself in by the front door without ringing the bell. There was no-one about so he hung up his coat and hat in the little cloakroom. As he turned down the L-shaped passage he all but ran into Joyce. She looked at him, startled, but no longer aggressive.

'Mr Simon's been looking for you, he would like to see you in his room – he's in there with Mr Maurice and Miss Gertrude.'

'Where are the others?'

'Mr Nicholas is in the library, Mrs Naomi is upstairs, resting.'

'What about Edward and Esther?'

'They're up in his studio. He usually goes to Torquay on Saturdays where he sells his pictures, but I heard him on the phone putting it off.' She went on, 'They've none

179

of them had any lunch but I took round bowls of soup.'

The little button eyes were fearful. 'When is it all going to end?'

'Soon.'

He went along the passage. Simon's door was partly open and Maurice was speaking on the telephone, his voice high-pitched, domineering and querulous.

'I know quite well that there are problems but you will have to cope . . . Definitely not!' The receiver was replaced with a clatter.

Wycliffe went in and stood just inside the door. Simon was seated at his desk and Maurice, feathers ruffled, stood beside him. Gertrude was seated in a wing chair, her hand-bag in her lap, like a visitor.

The old man passed a thin hand over his white hair. 'This is a great blow, Mr Wycliffe. This morning I was very much afraid, but I hoped . . .'

Maurice said in his most sententious voice, 'It is a great tragedy!'

Simon made a sudden, vicious movement which scattered the papers on his desk. 'Of course it's a tragedy, you fool! How much of a tragedy you'll find out in the coming months, you and your precious wife!'

Maurice flushed and said nothing. Wycliffe could not see Gertrude's reaction as she had her back to him. The burst of temper had taken it out of the old man; spots of colour appeared on his pale cheeks and his hands were trembling. He made am effort at composure. 'I'm sorry, Mr Wycliffe, but what has happened has been a very great shock. I didn't believe it could come to that. There are things I must tell you . . .'

Quite suddenly Wycliffe had had enough of the Beale treatment, as much as he could take. He said, 'I doubt if there is anything you can tell me now, Mr Beale, that would be of use. Earlier it might have been different.' He turned towards the door. 'I must ask you all to remain in the house for the time being.'

It did no good but he felt better.

As he came out of Simon's room he saw Potter's massive bulk stationed in the hall looking useful, like a spare tyre.

Nicholas was seated at his desk, which was littered with maps, photostats of documents, historical journals, and two large, leatherbound volumes with gilded spines. The bowl of soup Joyce had brought stood untouched and congealing amid the rest.

Nicholas's pale features accorded Wycliffe a minimum of acknowledgement and he was left to find a chair for himself and to place it near the desk. As he did so the rain came, lashing against the windows, and across the lawn the trees cowered under a wild sky. Twigs in new leaf were torn off to come bowling across the grass like phantom hoops.

'I suppose you've heard that your brother-in-law's body has been found in the pool?'

Nicholas said nothing but his eyes seemed to assent.

'He was shot in the pavilion at about midnight last night and several hours later his body was dragged out and hoisted over the balustrade.'

Nicholas remained motionless, his large hands clasped lightly together on the desk. His face was expressionless but a persistent tic affected the corner of his mouth.

'Last night you left Quarry House at about midnight and when I arrived here this morning, you had already gone out.' Wycliffe paused for this to sink in then, casually, he said, 'What did you do with the gun? Either you threw it in the pool or you still have it. My guess is that you kept it.'

The two men sat on opposite sides of the desk: Wycliffe, apparently relaxed; Nicholas, despite his superficial calm, drawn and pale, a man near the end of his tether. He remained silent for a long time and Wycliffe made no move to hurry him.

At last he spoke, 'You are quite right; there is no point in prolonging this.' With slow deliberate movements he opened a drawer of his desk, lifted out the pistol and laid it on the desk.

Wycliffe said, 'When did you get it back?'

181

Nicholas's eyes registered alarm. 'It has never been out of my possession. Your experts will tell you that this is the gun used in the three murders and it has never been out of my hands. I take full responsibility for what I have done.'

Wycliffe spoke in a tired voice as though reviewing events whose significance was already in the past. 'Last night, while you were still in the garden at Quarry House, you saw someone hurry by the gate. Miss Gould heard the footsteps but she had her back to the gate and did not see who it was.'

Nicholas would have interrupted but Wycliffe cut him off. 'There is no need to say anything at the moment; let me finish. As I say I am quite sure that you saw and recognized someone and that someone was the killer. I am not sure whether or not you were seen.'

The only perceptible response from Nicholas was a tightening of the jaw muscles; a tic still tugged at one corner of his mouth. Wycliffe went on: 'It was only this morning when you heard that Vicary had not returned and you found his car in the yard that you became worried; you realized the possible significance of what you had seen and you went out to check. You found Vicary's body in the pavilion; he had been shot through the head and, in his right hand, he held your gun – the Beretta. The implication was suicide but you knew too much about firearms to be taken in and you knew that the police would not be either.'

Nicholas could control himself no longer; he burst out, 'This is intolerable! I have volunteered a formal statement at a police station—'

But for once, Wycliffe showed a flash of temper. He slammed the desk with the flat of his hand. 'What you have volunteered to do is to tell me more lies! Since last Monday I have been lied to by every member of your family. Sometimes the lying has had a more or less creditable motive but more often it has been naked self-interest or concern for the Beale image. Not once has anybody shown the slightest concern for the victims – not even for the one who was a member of the family.'

Wycliffe got to his feet and went to the window where

he stood, watching the rain which blotted out the whole landscape.

'When you found your brother-in-law's body your first reaction was to delay its discovery by anyone else. You took your pistol from his hand, dragged the body to the verandah and toppled it over the fall. You thought it would sink in the fresh water and remain submerged for several days. You would have time to think. Fortunately the body was caught by the turbulence and swept into the shallows.'

He stopped speaking but remained looking out of the window with his back to Nicholas. For a time there was only the sound of the rain beating against the windows then Wycliffe said, 'The point is that you were ready if necessary to take the responsibility for three murders. I think there are only two people for whom you might be prepared to do that – your sister and your niece.'

Nicholas reacted angrily. 'My sister and my niece have nothing whatever to do with this! I demand to be taken to a police station where I can make a formal statement – a confession or whatever you like to call it.'

It was at this point that Wycliffe saw Gertrude; Gertrude wearing a green cape and hood with rubber boots, hurrying across the lawn, leaning against the wind and rain.

Ignoring Nicholas, Wycliffe went to the door and called out, 'Potter!'

Potter arrived at the double. Wycliffe pointed to the gun. 'I'm leaving you to get this to Mr Kersey. I want it sent for ballistics tests – you know what to do?'

'Yes, sir.'

Leaving Nicholas without a word, Wycliffe went into the hall, collected his mackintosh and hat from the cloakroom, and let himself out by the front door. A choked drain had caused a huge brown pool to spread over the gravel and he had to make a detour, but he rounded the house and set out across the lawn. Gertrude, of course, was nowhere to be seen but he thought he knew where to find her. The force of the wind abated as he reached the trees, only to increase again as he emerged at the pavilion, exposed to its full force.

He opened the little red door and went in. Gertrude was there standing by the window, staring out at the storm. The torrential rain had swollen the stream and the roar of the fall beneath the little building seemed to threaten its very existence.

Without turning away from the window she said, 'I wanted to come here; I thought it would be my last chance.'

Wycliffe said nothing and she went on: 'I realize that it's all over. When you left this morning I could see that there was no way out.'

A long interval during which the roar of the water and the wind seemed to take possesion of them, then she said, 'I've always loved it here in this weather; you could be in the ark − water roaring underneath and pouring out of the sky; the rest of the world being washed away . . . When we were young we used to spend a lot of time down here. It was a sort of club room refuge from the house . . . If you look in the cupboards you'll find games, packs of cards and stacks of old books and magazines . . . there's a dartboard somewhere and we used to stretch a net across the table and play ping-pong. Maurice became quite an expert . . .'

'Did Newcombe come here?'

'Oh yes, we were thoroughly democratic. He was the wizard of the dartboard.' On the surface she was relaxed but her speech was jerky, the words coming in little bursts.

She turned from the window, back into the room. 'Of course it was later, after Nicholas had joined the army and Maurice was working in the firm, that we used to meet here.'

'You mean you met Newcombe here regularly?'

'Oh yes, it was a real affair, not just a brief encounter.' She smiled. 'It lasted three months, until I discovered that I was pregnant.' She looked down at the threadbare sofa which had once been upholstered in red velvet and patted it. *'La couche d'amour.'*

'Were you in love with him?'

184

She laughed self-consciously. 'What a question from a policeman! It was very romantic – on my side. He was my Noble Savage.' She glanced up at Wycliffe and away again. 'I had a very old fashioned upbringing, Mr Wycliffe – no television, very little radio and lots of more or less improving books. I was going to educate and refine him – do a Pygmalion . . . absurd, wasn't it? A real little peasant, cunning and greedy, with a taste for honey and a way with stupid young girls.'

She stood by the sofa, leaning against the arm. 'Still, at the time I would have married him if they had let me. Who knows? It might have turned out better for both of us. Of course the committee wouldn't hear of it.'

'The committee?'

'That's what we called them – they brought us up – my mother, Ruby Price and the priest.'

'Not your father?'

'Father never interfered in what he called "the domestic department" – that included his children until they were ripe to enter the firm. Of course it only worked with Maurice, but that was the theory.

'I tried to have a real conversation with father once – after they knew I was pregnant, and he said, "My dear girl! I can't possibly talk to you about such things – have a word with your mother or with Ruby Price." This from a man who was going to bed with any woman who would slip off her pants for him . . .'

She was talking compulsively, a flood of words. Abruptly she changed the subject. 'You were with Nicky – poor, dear Nicky . . . When we were talking this morning I couldn't understand. I do now; it's the ink business over again.'

'Ink?'

'Years ago I upset a bottle of red ink over some of father's documents and Nicky took the blame – he's always been like that with me. I think he's the only one of us with any capacity for love.'

She sat on the sofa, her back to the window, and the pale grey light put a faint halo round her auburn hair. An attractive woman in her prime, wife, mother and home-maker – the sort one sees pricing materials in a department store or discussing menus with a friend over coffee, a murderess three times over.

Wycliffe had seated himself in one of the wicker chairs, which creaked with every movement he made. Time to direct the flow. In a conversational way he said, 'It had all gone on for almost twenty years and there was no obvious reason why it shouldn't have gone on indefinitely, but something happened – something tripped the switch and released your pent-up hatred in three killings which were more like executions.'

She made no protest but she got up from the sofa and moved slowly round the room until she reached the cupboards; there, with her back to him, she began to take out odd items and put them back again. She held up a little wooden cat. 'That's Nicky's work – he used to do a lot of carving from odd bits of wood – he made a whole chess set; that must be here somewhere.'

Wycliffe said, 'When did Newcombe come to see you?'

She was silent for a moment or two and she didn't turn round, then she said, 'Saturday it was – Saturday of last week, a week ago today . . . The door-bell rang and I answered it and there he was . . . I hadn't come face to face with him since before Esther was born.'

She turned away from the cupboards and her features creased as though she would weep but she recovered. 'I knew that he had changed, but I was shocked to see him; he was filthy – repellent! I could hardly bear to have him in the flat but it was that or talking to him on the doorstep where he might have been seen.'

'What did he want?'

'In a word – money, but not from me; he wanted to threaten the family through me. He talked a lot about Esther being his child and made vague threats about going to law; he said that Ruby Price would have to back him up . . . But all that wasn't the point . . .'

'What was the point?'

She shivered. 'I can't put it into words; it was partly his manner – intimate, smarmy and menacing . . . he was revolting! He even suggested . . . "For old times' sake," he said. I kept reminding myself that he really was Esther's father and it made me feel sick.

'I got rid of him somehow; I don't know what I said, what I promised, but when he had gone, although he hadn't touched me, I had a bath and I made up my mind to kill him.'

She stopped speaking, her voice had failed her, and it was some time before she could carry on. 'I knew that Nicholas had a pistol. Back in the early seventies Nicholas made up his mind that the country was going over to anarchy and that everybody must learn to defend themselves. He persuaded Maurice, Edward, me, and even little Esther, to learn to shoot. I quite enjoyed it; we used to practise on a target set up at the bottom of the lawn. Well, you know the rest . . . it was so easy, and I didn't feel anything. I certainly didn't feel that I had killed someone.'

'Why did you search the cottage?'

'I didn't; I had a vague idea that by tumbling things about it would look as though someone had been after Emily's money – there's always talk in the village about Emily's money.'

'And the photograph in the parlour?'

She understood at once. 'I don't know – when I saw it it seemed to bring everything back. I snatched it off the wall and smashed it, then I took the photograph home and burnt it.'

The creaking of Wycliffe's chair could be heard above the wind and the dull roar of the water. She reached into some hidden pocket and came out with cigarettes and a little lighter. She lit a cigarette and smoked in silence for a while.

'I didn't sleep much that night – not because I was worried or because I felt any sort of guilt – I was excited. For years I had been hemmed in, stifled, and suddenly I saw how I could be free. It was as though I had been shut up in a room for a long time and suddenly discovered that the door wasn't locked . . . When I came back from the cottage I slipped the gun into one of the drawers in my bedroom. That night I got up to look at it . . .' She broke off, frowning. 'It seems ridiculous, I know, but it was the way a child looks at a favourite teddy bear – a friend, but somehow more than a friend because it had magical powers.' She turned to Wycliffe in sudden doubt, 'You think I'm mad!'

'No.'

'You can't possibly understand.'

'I'm willing to try.'

'I stood looking down at that pistol in the drawer; I touched it – stroked it. I was *comforted* by it.'

Her eyes had taken on an inward look and she allowed her cigarette to smoulder between her fingers. 'I thought a lot about Ruby Price that night. Until then I had always found her rather frightening. Some girls – Catholic girls – get a sort of crush on the Blessed Virgin; I never did; she always seemed to be *watching* and watching with a superior air. It was the same with Ruby Price, but that night I saw her as contemptible – she was nobody – *less* than nobody, for she was a kind of parasite, sucking away at other people's lives . . . I don't remember deciding anything about her.

'It was very odd. At some time in the early afternoon – Monday afternoon – I was walking up through the church-yard with the pistol in my handbag. If someone had asked me where I was going, I should have answered, quite truthfully I think, that I didn't know, that I was out for a walk . . . I took no precautions, I mean I made no effort not to be seen. It was a year or two since I'd been to see Ruby but nothing had changed. The back door was on the latch and Ruby was upstairs with the radio turned up to full volume; it was some sort of play . . . I went in and went up the stairs to her room. I was actually in the room looking at her – she was having tea – before I took the pistol out of my bag; then I walked towards her with it in my hand. She looked up and saw me only when I was two or three feet from her . . .'

She sighed deeply and her eyelids drooped; it looked almost as though she might fall asleep.

Wycliffe said, 'You burned some of her envelopes.'

She made a restless movement and opened her eyes. 'Yes, I did. I took my time, looking around, and I found her *records* – all those envelopes with people's names on them. They disgusted me! To collect information about people like that is not only impertinent, it's indecent. I pushed some of them into the stove and set them alight. I didn't care if it burned the house down.'

'The envelopes you burned were mainly concerned with your family.'

'Probably. I suppose they were the ones which caught my eye but I didn't do it for any special reason . . .'

'You didn't leave any prints – finger-prints.'

'I didn't think about it. I was wearing gloves – I always wear gloves if I go out because my hands are so ugly. "Your worst feature!" Mother used to say.' She held them out. It was true, they were inclined to be red with rather thick, short fingers. 'Mother used to call them "washer-woman's hands".

'I came back without bothering whether I was seen or not; it seemed that nothing could go wrong and I found it very difficult to behave normally so I pretended I had had too much to drink – which I often do.' A sour little smile. 'Of course I was excused from going down to dinner.'

Her cigarette had burned itself down almost to her fingers; she dropped it on the floor and ground it out with her heel, then she looked up abruptly, 'Do they shut you right away? In prison, I mean?'

'It depends on what sort of prison one is sent to.'

'You think they will send me to some sort of prison for psychiatric cases. "Detained at Her Majesty's Pleasure" – isn't that what they used to say? I can't see Her Majesty getting much pleasure out of me.'

'A great deal has to happen before there is a question of sending you anywhere.'

She smiled a bitter little smile. 'You are like father – it's not your department.' She came back to the window and stood, looking out. 'It's a wonderful view on a fine day – right down the valley. If the sun isn't shining in your eyes you can see the sea at Torbay. Mother used to take us there when we were children; she had an old Morris and we used to bundle in . . .'

It was a bizarre situation; he had to remind himself that he was listening to a woman who would spend that night and succeeding nights in a police cell, charged with murder. The tale she was telling, shorn of nostalgic digressions, emasculated and formalized, would appear as a statement, typed by some two-fingered policeman. *I raised the pistol and aimed at her head; I pulled the trigger. At the time I did not think about what I was doing . . .*

'Of course it didn't last – that feeling of excitement – euphoria, I think they call it. That night I woke up in a terrible state. I was scared. There was no way back and I kept saying to myself, "As long as you live; as long as you live . . ." I got out of bed and looked at the pistol lying in my drawer and I almost decided to end it . . . I don't know what stopped me.'

She had her hands clasped tightly together and she was raising and lowering her arms from the elbows.

'I was better next day; almost back to normal.'

She could not stay still; she walked over to the cupboards and stopped by the one with a false bottom. Using her finger nails, she lifted the loose board which one of Wycliffe's men had replaced.

'Of course you found this; I think I left it open. We used to call it Maurice's *Rudery* because he kept in there books we weren't supposed to read and pictures of naked girls . . . It all seemed very wicked . . . I put the things I took from Nicky's cupboard in there – except the pistol. That was how I got Frank to come down here last night, by saying I'd found those things . . .'

She was silent for a long time then, still with her back to him and speaking in a low voice, she said, 'I had to do

190

it . . . What he did to me was despicable, and in all the years of our marriage he gave me nothing . . . nothing! It was his icy coldness; he always looked at me in that speculative way that he looked at a balance sheet or an estimate . . . After Newcombe – after they found him he gradually began to suspect me . . . He said nothing but he watched me – everything I did or said, waiting to catch me out . . .' She drew a deep breath which was almost a sigh. 'Then, on Friday morning – the morning of the Fair, he came into my bedroom when he was getting ready to go to the office. He was wearing only his shirt and trousers, in the middle of dressing, and he stood there at the bottom of my bed, looking at me. I was only half awake at first.

'I don't know how long he stood there, just staring at me; he didn't say anything and I was frightened . . . I knew then that I would have to go through with it.'

She drew her cloak about her and shivered.

The wind had dropped and the rain had eased; in a few minutes they would be able to walk back to the house.

It was dark when he arrived home and Helen was watching the television news, but she fussed over him and insisted on concocting a meal. He joined her in the kitchen and watched her work. Normally he would have prepared the trolley, made the coffee, and been generally useful . . . She had Gertrude's build, Gertrude's colouring – auburn hair without the freckles, and though she was a few years older, she did not look her age.

For days to come he would exist in two worlds, then the Beale images would gradually fade and he would be himself again. Until, with another case, he started to pick up the threads of yet other lives, lives of people of whom he had never heard.

Helen brought him back to earth. 'What happened to my car?'

'Good grief! It's still on the Green at Washford.'

She smiled. 'Never mind; tomorrow is Sunday; we'll drive

191

over, it will be a pleasant trip and if it's fine we can picnic on the moor.'

It was more than a year after the Washford affair when Helen drew his attention to a report in the local paper of the marriage of 'Miss Esther Vicary to her cousin, Mr Edward Beale, both of Ashill, Washford . . . The bride is the granddaughter of Mr Simon Beale, chairman of Beales' Household Stores; the bridegroom is a landscape painter whose work is in increasing demand. The couple are spending their honeymoon touring in France.'

Helen said, 'His father, and her mother; I wonder if they will have children.'

Wycliffe sighed. His feelings were too complex to put into words and all he said was, 'Life owes them something.'

THE END

WYCLIFFE AND THE TANGLED WEB

Readers who are acquainted with Cornwall will probably realise that this story is set in Mevagissey, but those who know Mevagissey must forgive major inaccuracies in topography. These are deliberate as I do not want to imply that the people, the events, or the detailed locations described, have any reality outside the pages of this book.

In particular, and fortunately, the Rules and the Clemos, whose troubles are recounted, are families existing only in my imagination.

W.J.B.

Chapter One

The fair girl looked out of place in a doctor's waiting-room; she seemed to glow with health.

The old man thought so; he watched her, his chin resting on arthritic hands clasped over the knob of his walking stick. He watched her steadily, through bleached, expressionless eyes, remembering other girls with honey-coloured skin, speckled with golden hairs; girls with swelling breasts and cheeks that were smooth and soft with the bloom of youth; girls who were old now — or dead.

The woman thought so too. Her immense bulk, confined in a flowered frock, spread over one of the cane chairs; her shopping bags took up another. Her fat, ringed fingers clutched a leather handbag to her abdomen, and she watched the girl through little piggy eyes.

The girl herself seemed unaware of them; she sat in a shaft of sunlight from a high window, idly turning the pages of a magazine. Now and then she glanced at her wrist-watch and at the excluding door of the consulting-room.

The old man said: 'Doctor's on his holidays.'

The girl said: 'Yes.'

'I reckon it takes the locum a bit longer.'

'Yes.'

'Likely he's a bit more conscientious.' The old man laughed, a senile chuckle.

The woman, feeling that the ice had been broken, said: 'You're Rosie Clemo's girl.' It sounded like an accusation.

'Yes.'

'You buried your granny yesterday.'

'Yes.'

'A big funeral. I was there. Lovely lot of flowers too. Sad! 'Course she was coming on. She must've bin eighty? Eighty-one?'

'She was eighty.'

'A happy release in a way, bedridden like she was. I remember Elinor more'n forty year back, teaching in Sunday school. Your poor mother an' me was in her class.'

It meant nothing to Hilda. Although she had been born and brought up with it, village gossip bored her; it was a background, like the chattering of a radio when one's attention is elsewhere. Especially now.

Through the window of the waiting-room she could see the harbour, the light dancing on the water less than a stone's throw away, yet it was another world, a world from which she was cut off.

One of the boats was in, moored against the fish quay — Peter Scoble. He'd been out wreck-netting and she wondered vaguely why he was back so early. He must be running a trip in the afternoon. These thoughts, like the snippets she read in her magazine, drifted on the surface of her mind while underneath there was a great hollowness of apprehension. On the other side of that door, on a slip of paper . . .

The consulting-room door opened and a scrawny little man in a fisherman's jersey came out, clutching a prescription form. He greeted the others briefly and went out.

A pause that seemed unending, then: 'Miss Hilda Clemo, please!' The doctor, a young man with blond curly hair, and wearing a white coat, stood in the doorway.

The girl followed him into his consulting-room and the door closed behind her.

The woman said: 'Snotty little piece, she is!'

The old man said: 'A good-looker though. I dunno where she got it from. Not from the Clemos, that's for sure. And the Rules is no oil paintings.'

The woman followed her own line. 'I know we shouldn' speak ill of the dead but 'er mother was the same, thought she was a cut

8

above the rest of us — an' all they Rules for that matter. I mind when their father kept a shop in Church Street; you'd think 'e done you a favour just by taking your money.'

The old man said: 'I thought Jimmy Clemo would've married again when 'is wife died. I mean, 'e was still a young man an' that girl was no more'n four or five year old.' He started to cough, then pulled out a grubby handkerchief and spat into it. 'Funny! I always thought they Clemos was a warm lot by nature like.'

The woman was deflected. 'There's Esther.'

'Esther!' Surprise set the old man coughing again. 'You don't think . . . God! I'd sooner go to bed with a bag of ol' bones. Anyways she's gone for religion — Catholic, too.' He chuckled. 'Sensible, I s'pose, looking the way she do.'

For a while silence closed in. The old man stared out of the window with unfocused eyes, and the woman stared at the wall with its notices about smoking, about AIDS, and about inoculations against influenza.

The woman said: 'Jimmy Clemo is making a fortune out o' that caravan site. A gold mine, they say.'

'More in it than farming, that's for sure.'

The woman looked at the closed door. ''E's taking 'is time with 'er.'

'Examining 'er, I dare say. I wouldn' mind being that young doctor!'

'You're a dirty ol' man, Willie Prowse!'

At last the door of the consulting-room opened again. Hilda Clemo came through and, without a look, marched through the room and out by the door to the street.

The white-coated young doctor said: 'Mr Prowse, please!'

The quay loungers were parked in a row on one of the seats; tourists and trippers milled aimlessly about, eating ice-creams and wondering what to do with the day. She spotted Ralph Martin farther along the quay, hesitated, decided not to see him, and turned off into one of the alleys before she reached him.

Her slimness made her look taller than she was, and her suntan appeared deeper because of her straw-coloured hair. She wore jeans and a navy-blue, sleeveless, cotton top, moulded to her body; a white logo on the front carried the words: *M.V. Sea Spray*. She walked with the easy, unhurried stride of a young animal in perfect health.

Expectant mother . . . prenatal . . . midwife . . . labour . . . delivery . . . breast feeding . . . Or, abortion. She had brooded on those words and they had disgusted her. The very thought . . .

She turned inland from the harbour, through the square where most of the shops were, and along a narrow street where cottages opened directly on the road. Strangers turned to look at her, women with a certain envy, men with lust. Locals greeted her, but she did not acknowledge them.

She was remembering her sister's pregnancy and the birth of her nephew: Alice's morning sickness and indigestion; her barrel-like figure and unrelieved peevishness. Though in less than six months from the birth, Alice had gone back to leading the life she had led before, with Esther taking charge of the baby . . . A mother by proxy. But what did Alice's life amount to anyway? I'd rather die than end up like Alice!

'Hi!'

A boy she went to school with, studying the same subjects. In less than a year they should be sitting A–levels together. The boy wanted to stop for a gossip but she brushed him off. To be able to think ahead again to A–levels, without the shadow . . .

Almost from the start she had been sure, and in a curious way she had come to terms with it. She had planned exactly what she would do; how she would first break the news to Alice: 'I'm pregnant.' Alice would tell Esther, Esther would have the job of breaking it to her father. She, herself, would tell Ralph Martin; there would be a session with her brother-in-law, Bertie; another with . . .

She was sometimes troubled by the fact that however desperately she wanted to avoid some threatening prospect, a

10

small voice inside her would whisper: 'But if, in spite of everything, it happens . . .' And the voice seemed to suggest something more than resignation.

In those restless nights she had decided that she could predict their reactions, almost the very words they would use.

Beyond the cottages there were larger houses with gardens; then as the ground began to rise, these gave way to fields on one side, and on the other to a screen of trees. She had left the village behind.

Suddenly she realized that she was smiling.

A break in the trees, and she came to a tall, arched entrance with a suspended sign: 'Tregwythen Leisure and Tourist Park. Camping, Caravanning, Golf, Tennis, and Swimming'. From the entrance, a metalled road curved away between grassy slopes, terraced to accommodate the caravans. The vans were well spaced, with trees and shrubs to mitigate their brash intrusion. On one side of the entrance, reached by a short drive, there was a large, stone-built house with a hipped roof and overhanging eaves; the house where she had been born and where she had lived her life so far. On the other side a building in the style of a Swiss chalet carried a sign: 'Reception, Shop and Café. All enquiries.' Beyond the building there were tables for people who preferred to eat out of doors.

Hilda pushed open a door labelled 'Reception'.

Mid-morning is usually a quiet time in any tourist park and her sister, Alice, was making up accounts. Alice's assistant, a lanky girl of Hilda's age, was entering new arrivals from registration slips.

Alice looked up from her ledger. 'Hullo, kid — bored? Never mind, another fortnight and you'll be back at school.'

'Very funny!'

The two sisters were much alike in features and colouring but, at twenty-eight, Alice was already slipping into matronly slackness, beginning to lose her figure and her looks.

Hilda glanced at the girl. 'Can we . . .?'

Alice said: 'Sharon, be a dear and see if you can find that husband of mine; he should be somewhere on the top site. Ask

11

him what happened to the docket for diesel he had delivered on the twelfth.'

The girl took herself off and Alice said: 'That'll keep her out of the way for a bit; Bertie's cutting the grass behind the toilets. Now, kid, what's your problem?'

'I've just come from the doctor.'

'The doctor? You're not ill?'

'No, pregnant.'

She had said it. The words were out.

'Pregnant! Christ!' It took Alice a while to absorb the news. 'Is it definite?'

'Yes.'

'How long?'

'Eight weeks.'

'You must have been pretty sure you'd put your foot in it.'

'I was.'

'Who is it? Ralph?'

'Yes.'

'You're sure?'

'Of course I'm sure! What do you think I am?'

Alice brushed her indignation aside. 'All right, we won't go into that, but don't come the innocent with me, kid! How long has Ralph Martin . . .?'

'It was the first time.'

'You weren't on the pill?'

'No.'

'And he — '

'We didn't intend to go that far.'

'Famous last words.'

'There's no need to be like that.'

'Perhaps not, but I hope you realize Father will go through the roof. What do you want to do?'

'I told the doctor — the locum — that I wanted an abortion but he was difficult.'

'That can be got over. You'll see Hosking when he comes back from holiday.'

It was all going more smoothly than she had foreseen in her

12

night-time imaginings. Alice was matter-of-fact, prosaic even; so much so that Hilda felt almost cheated.

She was looking out of the window, her back to the office. Across the roadway a young woman sat on the steps of her caravan while her baby, wearing only a nappy, crawled about on the grass. The mother watched with a Mona Lisa smile. Was it conceivable that any woman would actually want to give herself to that?

All the same, she turned back into the room, already growing into the role she had chosen. 'I suppose I could go through with it.' Moving out a pawn.

'And marry Ralph?'

'Yes.'

'The simplest way out — is that it?' Alice was taking her seriously.

'I suppose it could be.'

Alice drew a deep breath. 'Apart from anything else, what would you live on?'

'Ralph is working with his father on the boats.'

'Yes, but Ralph has two brothers, still at school. Charlie Martin manages to make a living for himself and his family but I'd be very surprised if there was enough in it to take on you and the baby. Ralph may want to, and Charlie might agree, but it would mean a thin time all round. For anything more than subsistence you'd be dependent on Father.'

'I'm dependent on him now for everything.'

Alice gave a short laugh. 'You think Father would let you marry Ralph and everything would go on much as it did before?'

'I don't see why not.'

'Then it's time you did. Haven't you noticed how Father looks at you? You're the only one of us who matters: I'm the great disappointment of his life to date; Esther is part of the furniture. As for Bertie . . .'

Alice took a cigarette from a packet on her desk and lit it. 'So it's over to you, kid. As Father sees it, you're going to do brilliantly in your A–levels, then you'll be God's gift to Oxford. A First is a foregone conclusion; then some wonderful job. After

13

that — one day, an acceptable Prince Charming may come along. Of course, for preference, he'll be defective in a vital part of his anatomy.'

Alice exhaled smoke slowly and watched it spiral. 'Do you think he's going to sit back while you put Ralph Martin in place of all that?'

The idea that her father might find her sexually attractive had never occurred to Hilda. It was a new thought, and an intriguing one. For a moment or two it took possession of her mind.

Alice misunderstood her silence. 'Don't worry, kid. It's all in his mind. Men have their fantasies. You happen to be Father's.'

Hilda flicked idly through a little bundle of registration blanks. 'What would you do?'

'About being pregnant? I'd have an abortion. Apart from anything else, seventeen is too young to hand yourself over to a man. You need to learn the not-so-gentle art of self-defence — and I'm not talking about being knocked about physically.'

'Is that what you did before you married Bertie?' She couldn't resist it.

Alice flushed. 'We're not talking about me.'

'Here's Father.'

James Clemo came into the office, his shirt sleeves rolled up, his hands smeared with grease.

'That husband of yours is bloody useless, Alice! The funeral yesterday, half this morning wasted with old Penrose about Granny's will, then I come back here and it's "I can't get the mower to start, Jim!" A ten-year-old boy would be more bloody use! Sometimes I think it's deliberate.'

Alice said: 'Tell him, not me.'

Clemo was stocky, like all the Clemo males before him; his thinning fair hair had a reddish tinge, now tending to grey; his features inclined to fleshiness, and he had a high colour. He went into the toilet cubicle and emerged some minutes later, drying his hands on a paper towel.

He noticed Hilda for the first time. 'Hullo, kid! What are you doing here?'

14

He looked his younger daughter up and down. 'I don't like you wearing that top thing. It's not . . . not suitable.'

Hilda said nothing.

'I suppose you're going out with the *Spray* again this afternoon?' His manner was hostile, almost threatening.

'Yes.'

Clemo rolled up the paper towel, shied it irritably in the direction of a wastepaper basket, and missed. He turned again to Hilda, obviously about to say something more, but changed his mind. He looked at his wrist-watch.

'Twelve o'clock; the bloody morning gone! See you at lunch, and get that thing off, Hilda; I shall be glad when you're back at school.'

Alice watched him go, then she said: 'See what I mean?'

Hilda told herself: It's like the opening scene of a play.

Hilda walked up the drive to the house and around to the back. Esther was in the kitchen preparing lunch and Alice's little boy, Peter, was building his bricks on the window seat. He looked round as Hilda came in, his solemn blue eyes met hers, but he returned at once to his building.

'Anything I can do?'

'You can lay the table.'

Esther was thirty-six but she looked older; her hair was scraped back into a ragged pony-tail, her thin features were ill-assembled, her pinched little nose was red at the tip and her forehead shone. There were unanswered questions about Esther; she had been adopted as a girl of sixteen by Hilda's grandparents and, from then on, treated as one of the family. Why, no one seemed to know.

Gradually, as she grew into womanhood, Esther had taken over the running of the house and, when Hilda's mother died, it was she who had assumed responsibility for the child's upbringing.

Hilda spread a cloth over the pitch-pine table which occupied the middle of the barn-like kitchen. The Clemos had their meals in the kitchen unless there were guests. Though much of their

15

land was rented off, they followed the traditions of their farming ancestry; their house had the appearance of a farmhouse and their ways were the ways of a prosperous farming family.

'What's the matter with you?' Esther spoke over her shoulder. She was straining boiled potatoes at the sink.

'Me? Nothing.'

Esther tipped the potatoes into a dish and slid the dish into the grill compartment to keep warm. 'There's something, my girl, and you might as well tell me first as last.'

It was true that, through the years, Hilda had confided more in Esther than in anyone else, but the idea that she was incapable of keeping a secret from her was one of Esther's illusions.

Six places: knives, forks, spoons, side-plates . . . a special place for Peter: a high cushion, and his own cutlery; his Snoopy mug instead of a glass. Hilda worked mechanically, savouring the thought that by the evening they would all be trying in their different ways to adjust to the idea of her pregnancy.

It was interesting.

'No need to take it out on the china, whatever it is! You've been behaving very queer lately, Hilda, and it's getting worse.' Esther broke off. 'Here's Bertie so we'll talk later.'

Bertie was an obvious intruder into the Clemo clan, dark with sallow skin, and black hair which he allowed to grow long at the back. 'My daughter's married a wog!' — Clemo's comment on his son-in-law.

'Has anyone seen Alice?'

Nobody answered, and Bertie joined his son by the window. 'If you put that one there . . .'

Peter's voice came, shrill: 'No, Daddy! Don't do it; I want to!'

Esther laughed.

James Clemo was eating his meal with scarcely any idea of what was passing his lips. He was uneasy, uncomfortably aware that something was going on behind his back. Was it his fancy? If so, why had the notion come upon him with such force? It had started when he came across Hilda in Reception . . .

Esther had her antennae out too; he could tell by the way she

16

darted glances around the table that he wasn't the only one to sense — to *know*, that something was up.

Alice, too. Out of character, she was trying to make conversation: 'I keep feeling I ought to go upstairs to Granny; it's hard to realize she's gone . . .'

They kept things from him and schemed behind his back, though it was he who gave them the chance to make a decent living. It was his management which kept the act together, and what did he get from any of them?

His gaze fell on Bertie. Bertie — what in hell had persuaded Alice to marry him? Too clever by half — and cunning; you never knew where you were with him. Well, this morning he'd had to listen to a few home truths. But there was no satisfaction in bawling him out, he never answered back. You couldn't have a bloody good row, he just looked at you . . . supercilious. No bite and yet not to be trusted. Did Alice know how little he was to be trusted? Anyway it served her right.

Mother is dead — of old age. That's a stage in a man's life. I'm getting old myself; knocking fifty. And what have I got to look forward to?

Hilda.

His expression softened. The kid seemed very subdued, thoughtful; she scarcely looked up from her plate though she was not eating much. Still wearing that damned sleeveless thing — might as well be topless; defying him. Sex! Youngsters these days are pickled in it from the cradle and it hits them hardest when they most need to concentrate on other things. A–levels in less than a year. He worried about Hilda; too boxed up. He'd no idea what went on in her head. No mother, but how the hell could he be expected to . . .? Alice could do more. Hilda was seeing too much of the Martin boy — probably innocent enough, but you couldn't be sure. He'd have a word with Charlie . . .

That bastard, Bertie, was eyeing Hilda on the sly . . . He wondered if the girl had any idea of the dynamite around her.

Christ! I'm getting morbid!

Saturday afternoon

By two o'clock Hilda was on the quay. *Sea Spray* was berthed by the steps. Charlie Martin, Ralph's father, was there.

'Going out with the boy?'

The words were plain enough but their implication was as vague as his half-smile.

'Yes.'

Charlie Martin was a huge man, shaped like a barrel. A thick, dark moustache just failed to hide his prominent lips and he had little, bright eyes which often said more than his words.

'Father all right?'

'Yes, thank you, Mr Martin.' Faced with Ralph's father she felt uneasy.

'Ralph's down in the launch.'

A board at the top of the steps carried a chalked notice: 'M.V. Sea Spray. 3½ hour cruise. Dodman and Caerhays. Landing at Gorran Haven for Cornish Cream Tea. Leave at 2.15. Tickets from the Boat Office.'

Hilda started down the steps. The *Spray* was a beamy launch, a good sea boat but on the slow side. The engine ticked over; Ralph was aboard, arranging cushions for the comfort of tender bottoms. He looked up, saw her, and no words were needed. 'I didn't know if you'd come . . .'

Ralph was nineteen, five-feet ten and sturdily built. His hair and eyes were dark; the Martins were said to have Spanish blood. Most of the girls in the village were after him but he had eyes only for Hilda. Perhaps she should have felt flattered.

Only a slight, oily swell disturbed the surface of the harbour, just enough to sway the masts of the moored craft, but outside white crests glistened in the sun.

Hilda looked up at the sky. 'What is it? Sou'west?'

'Just about. They'll have a bit of chop going and an easy ride back. They like it that way — gives their teas a chance to settle. We'll do the Dodman and Caerhays on the way out and put in at the Haven fourish.'

The passengers were arriving: middle-aged couples, spinster school teachers in pairs, and some elderly folk who had to be helped aboard. These afternoon cruises were losing out to fishing

18

trips: 'No experience required; all gear provided'. Ralph and his father made three such trips a day in good weather, and this cruise of Ralph's was known as 'the ambulance run'.

At two-fifteen Hilda cast off and Ralph took the launch through the maze of moored craft and out between the heads. Once in the open sea he handed over to Hilda and went aft to chat up his passengers. There was more interest in the girl than in the coastline.

'Is she your sister?'

'No, a friend.'

Beyond Chapel Point they were heading into the wind and the old boat lived up to her name, slapping sheets of spray over the wheelhouse to fall on the passengers. Ralph issued them with plastic cover-alls and found a seaman's jersey for Hilda. She put it on and he joined her at the wheel.

It was from that moment the trip assumed an importance wholly unsuspected by anyone aboard. The young couple stood, side by side, swaying to the motion, the girl's hands rested lightly on the wheel, keeping bow to the sea, so that they rode easily with scarcely any roll. It was obvious that the two were engaged in earnest conversation but nothing could be heard above the hiss of the water and the steady beat of the motor.

A mile or so beyond Chapel Point they were running between a line of vicious-looking rocks and the shore. Two shags, their wings spread in heraldic posture, sunned themselves on adjacent pinnacles, coaxing out cameras and binoculars from under the plastic sheets.

Ralph turned to his passengers. 'The Gwineas Rocks.' He pointed. 'See the bell buoy? And listen . . .'

They listened, and heard the slow, rhythmic clang of the bell, rocked by the waves. Coming across a waste of sea it is one of the most haunting sounds known to man.

'We'll take a closer look coming back.'

A promise never kept.

'The village you can see on the shore is Gorran Haven and that's where we shall put in for tea later. The church on the hill is Gorran church. It's been a day-mark for centuries . . .'

19

Days later Miss Jessup, a schoolteacher from Essex, precise and well preserved, would be asked: 'When did you first observe the young couple to be quarrelling?'

Miss Jessup would purse her lips and quibble over the words: 'I wouldn't say they were quarrelling; it seemed more of a disagreement.'

'And you first noticed they were disagreeing — when?'

'About the time we were passing those rocks, after the boy told us about the bell.'

'Yes, anybody could see they were having an argument. I said as much to the wife and she said "a lovers' tiff". The wife is romantic.' Mr Alec Shipman, a retired builder from Preston.

On the other side of the Dodman they caught the full force of a stiff south-westerly and there were signs of nervousness; the old launch smacked into the occasional rogue wave and rebounded with a jolt; the engine stuttered, then resumed its normal beat. A glimpse of Caerhays Castle seemed to calm all fears; the Nash façade, a Disney castle, peering through trees and fronting the shore. It set the cameras clicking; they went in close and waved to people on the beach.

A broad sweep, and they doubled back. With a following sea it seemed much calmer. As they approached Gorran Haven on the return trip Ralph took the wheel and brought the launch into the little harbour. It was while he was edging alongside that Hilda suddenly jumped the gap and ran up the steps.

At the top she peeled off the jersey he had loaned her and dropped it into the boat. She called back: 'I'm catching the bus home.'

By the time Ralph had berthed she was striding between the holiday-makers on the beach and he still had his passengers to put ashore.

'I felt sorry for the boy — the look on his face!' Mr Shipman, the builder.

Ralph said: 'The café is up on the right; you can't miss it. Just show your boat tickets. We've got an hour.'

The *Sea Spray* was late back and Ralph's father was waiting at the

top of the steps. When the passengers were ashore he said:
'Trouble?'

'Choked feed.'

'Where's Hilda?'

'She's coming back by bus.'

Charlie looked at his son but made no comment.

Chapter Two

Saturday evening

It was left to Esther to break the news of Hilda's pregnancy to her father and he took it badly. He looked bleak and helpless, with none of his usual bluster.

'Why wasn't I told?' Plaintive, rather than aggressive.

He was in the old farm office, next to the kitchen, seated at a roll-topped desk which had belonged to his father and grandfather before him.

Esther was brusque. 'I'm telling you now. Hilda only knew herself this morning; she told Alice just before lunch, and Alice told me this evening.'

'Why didn't Hilda come to me?'

'Would you expect her to?'

'Where is she now?'

'She's not back yet.'

Sitting at his desk, his red face creased in concern, his flimsy half-glasses perched on the end of his nose, he looked both pathetic and slightly ridiculous.

'She should have been in an hour ago.'

'Hilda left the party when they put into the Haven for tea. It seems she had a difference with Ralph and walked out on him.'

Clemo nodded. 'That shows she's still got some sense. I suppose that bloody boy is the father?'

'Yes.'

'I'll break every bone in his body.' But he said it mechanically, without conviction.

'She told Ralph she was catching the bus home but there's only one bus and that got in not long after the *Spray*.'

A new thought occurred to him, triggering fear: 'You don't think she'd do anything daft?'

'Not Hilda. She was talking to Alice quite sensibly about an abortion.'

'Abortion!' The word distressed him.

He reached for the telephone.

'What are you going to do?'

'Phone the police.'

Esther was caustic. 'What will you tell them? "My seventeen-year-old daughter hasn't come home and it's a quarter past seven."'

He glared at her angrily but he did not lift the telephone. 'You're enjoying this!'

'Think what you like.'

He passed a hand over his forehead. 'There's a girl — a school-friend she sometimes spends a weekend with, lives in the Haven . . .'

'Paula Simmonds — yes, you could try.' She leafed through the phone book. 'Here you are; the number is four-two-four-five-three-four. But don't make a fool of yourself. Hilda has probably gone some place where she can think things out.'

He grabbed the telephone and began to dial but fumbled it. 'Here! You do it.'

The usual ritual, then: 'Mrs Simmonds?'

A brief exchange, and Esther replaced the telephone. 'They haven't seen her. In any case Paula is in London, staying with relatives.' She added after a pause: 'If she walked home over the fields I suppose she could have called in at Tregelles.'

Clemo looked doubtful. 'You think she might? Phone and ask — I can't.'

'But you think I can.' Esther was mildly contemptuous but she looked up the number, dialled, and waited. They could hear the rhythmic burr, then a harsh voice said: 'Tregelles Farm.'

'Aunt Jane? It's Esther . . . Hilda was supposed to have been

walking home from the Haven across the fields and she hasn't
turned up. James is worried . . .'

The voice cut across her words: 'I haven't seen her, if that's
what you want to know. I've got trouble enough with your
Auntie Agnes wandering off whenever I take my eyes off her. I
can't watch her day and night. Anyway, I haven't seen Hilda.'
The line went dead as she replaced her telephone.

James said: 'Bitch!' He stood up. 'I'm going to look for her.'

'You'd do better to stay here by the telephone if you're that
worried. Alice and Bertie and I will do it. Bertie can cover the
lanes in the car and Alice and I will walk the footpaths before
dark.'

Clemo hesitated, then gave in. 'You think I'm making a fuss
but I'm worried about the girl, Esther.'

Esther shrugged. 'Hilda isn't the sort to come to much harm;
she knows how to look after herself.'

'She could be frightened to come home.'

'Frightened? Of you? You must be joking!'

By eleven o'clock, and still with no news, James would be put
off no longer; he telephoned the police.

Because so few stations are manned at night he found himself
talking to subdivision. A world away from the days when you
phoned your local bobby, probably called him by his first name
— or you spoke to his wife.

'How old is your daughter, sir?'

'Seventeen.' He said it apologetically. Blast Esther!

'Eleven isn't very late for a young woman to be out these days,
sir. Do you have any particular reason for concern?'

It was too much. James bellowed: 'Yes, I do have a particular
reason!' But he calmed down at once. 'Sorry! I'm a bit on edge.'

A couple of minutes more of the same and the upshot was that
they would send a patrol car. 'Within the next half-hour, sir.
Give the officer all the details . . . But I shouldn't get too
concerned. In the vast majority of instances there is a perfectly
simple explanation.'

Clemo waited on his doorstep. The night was very still and
clear. He could see the lights of the village and, beyond, the

24

faintly luminous sea. A couple of caravanners' cars drove into the site but caravanners generally are early to bed and most of the vans were in darkness. In a few of the tents on the high level, lamps glowed dimly through blue and green and orange canvas. It seemed long but, in fact, it was less than twenty minutes before he saw the blue lights of a police patrol car turning off the road.

One of the two-man crew stayed on radio watch while the other followed Clemo into the drawing-room, a large room, rarely used, and smelling of damp. Alice joined them.

'Constable Baxter — now, sir, about your daughter . . .'

Clemo told his story and the policeman listened; an old hand who had been in the force long enough for the greed and lust and frailty of humans to be all in the day's work. An unmarried girl of seventeen, pregnant — pooh!

'This young man — Ralph Martin — have you spoken to him, sir?'

'I have,' from Alice. 'He's very worried; he's been out on his bike all the evening looking for her.'

'Did he say what they'd quarrelled about?'

'He was upset because Hilda told him she was going to have an abortion. He wanted them to marry and have the baby.'

Constable Baxter made notes. Police notebooks must be a virtually untapped source in the field of literature.

'So there was no question of him denying responsibility?'

Clemo said: 'He's no bloody option! My daughter is a decent girl.'

'Of course, sir! Anyway I shall talk to the lad, but it's as well to have the background clear. The boat put in at the Haven for the passengers to have tea and your daughter left, saying that she would come home by bus.'

'Which she didn't!' Clemo made the point with emphasis. 'I hope you realize you're only getting one side of the story — his.'

'For the moment it's all we can get, but don't worry, young Martin will be questioned and we're not fools.'

'How about searching for her?'

The policeman looked out of the window into the darkness. 'What would be the use, sir? If she still isn't home by first light we shall get busy quick enough. Incidentally, if she was walking home from the Haven, which way would you have expected her to come?'

It was Alice who answered: 'It depends. If she wanted the walk to think things out, she might have come by the coast path, but that's a long way round. The quickest is the field path through Tregelles, my aunt's farm, which adjoins our land just up the valley.'

'Tregelles.' Did the policeman's repetition of the name carry a certain inflection? 'You've been in touch with your aunt?'

'Yes, but she hasn't seen Hilda. During the evening two of us walked the footpaths she might have used and my husband has driven over the lanes.'

The policeman nodded. 'You've done all you could; try not to worry. In the morning we'll start an organized search — if necessary. We'll question people in the Haven who might have seen her; we'll talk to passengers on the trip who might have overheard something, and we'll put out a request for information on the local radio. Of course the coastguard will be alerted and all our officers . . .

'Now, sir, madam, I want a description of Hilda and of the clothes she was wearing, then a recent photograph.'

The black marble clock on the mantelpiece chimed the quarter: a quarter past midnight.

Charlie Martin and his family lived in a little square house set above the level of the harbour. When the police rang his doorbell it was Charlie who threw up the sash of an upstair window.

'What's up?'

'Police.'

'I can see that. What do you want?'

'A word with your son, Ralph.'

No argument. A minute or two later Constable Baxter was admitted to the front room by Charlie who had pulled on a pair of trousers over his pyjamas.

26

'The boy will be down in a minute; he's dead-beat.'

Charlie trusted his bulk to a protesting cane chair.

'Of course it's about the girl. He wanted to stay out all night looking for her but I wouldn't have that. Waste of time!'

Ralph came in looking drawn and tired. He perched himself on a chair next to his father.

'Just one or two questions. You quarrelled with Hilda this afternoon during your boat trip?'

'It was my fault; I was a fool.' His voice was unsteady.

Charlie said: 'Nothing of the kind! The boy didn't want his child — my grandchild — put down like an unwanted kitten.'

'I should have waited until Hilda had had a chance to think things over; it was no place to start talking about it with all those people looking on.'

The walls of the little room were almost covered with framed photographs, the subjects about equally divided between boats and members of the family. Pride of place went to an enlargement of a couple who could only have been Charlie's parents.

'Your quarrel became heated?'

'No, it didn't — '

'Tell me about it.'

The boy told.

'And when you put in to the Haven, Hilda left?'

'Yes.'

'Had she said that was what she was going to do?'

'No! I'd no idea — she was up the steps and away before I berthed and she just said: "I'm going home by bus." I couldn't understand it; I mean, we hadn't really quarrelled — just argued a bit.'

Constable Baxter looked the boy in the eyes. 'And that was the last time you saw her?'

'Yes. By the time I'd tied up and got the passengers off she was nowhere to be seen.'

'When did you first have any idea that Hilda might be pregnant?'

'This afternoon, when she told me.'

'You had no suspicion before then?'

'No.'

'But you must have known that what you were doing might lead to just that.'

Ralph coloured, looked at his father and away again. 'I didn't realize that what happened . . . I mean, I didn't think it could be, well . . . so easy.'

Sunday morning

By Sunday morning there was still no news of the missing girl. Her description had been circulated, the coastguard alerted and, at ten o'clock, the local radio broadcast an appeal for information. In addition, police and volunteers with dogs searched the lanes and footpaths, the hedges and ditches, over the whole neighbourhood. Police made random calls on householders in the hope of gleaning something.

Several people in the Haven knew the girl as a friend of Paula Simmonds, and three of them had seen her on Saturday afternoon. All three agreed that she had been hurrying away from the harbour, alone. This was consistent with her either catching a bus or walking home. The bus driver, questioned, said that he had picked up four passengers in the village, none of them in the least resembling Hilda Clemo.

The inquiry had been upgraded. If the girl (in law, a 'young person' — turned fourteen but not yet eighteen) was later found in a ditch, raped and strangled, officialdom had no wish to be accused of having dragged its feet. But the dilemma is real; the police must think twice before starting a massive hunt for every teenager who chooses to strike out for the bright lights without telling the family. But the feeling was growing that here was something different.

Station staff, bus drivers and taxi drivers at Truro and St Austell were questioned. But did the girl have any money with her? She had been carrying a shoulder-bag but nobody knew what was in it. The whole thing was made more difficult because it was Sunday.

28

Judicious telephoning discovered the whereabouts of some of *Sea Spray*'s passengers. It happened that three of them were staying at the same hotel.

The three were: Miss Jessup, the schoolteacher, and Mr and Mrs Alec Shipman, the retired builder and his wife. They added a little to the sum of police knowledge. Nobody had thought to enquire what Ralph Martin did while his passengers were having their tea. The three disclosed that he had not stayed with his boat; they thought he had gone after the girl.

'Did he go after her at once?'

'No, he couldn't do that; he had to tie up and see us ashore.' Mr Shipman.

'He passed me, almost running, just as I was entering the café.' Miss Jessup. 'And he didn't get back to the boat until some time after we were due to leave.'

'How long after?'

'Well, we were given an hour and we must have been waiting at least another twenty minutes.'

Mrs Shipman agreed. 'All of that. And he wasn't there to help the old people back on the boat. When he did arrive he was panting like he'd been running.' She added, after a pause: 'I must admit I felt sorry for the lad, he looked as though he'd been crying.'

'And when we did get away we went like the clappers.' Mr Shipman with a self-conscious laugh.

On Sunday afternoon Ralph Martin was 'invited' to the subdivisional police station to make a statement. He was taken in a police car. He sat in a gloomy little room with a high window, and a uniformed sergeant who looked like an undertaker wrote out what he said on a form. At the head of the form a declaration, which he was asked to sign, agreed he was making the statement voluntarily, and was aware that what he said might be used in evidence. His hand trembled so much that he could scarcely control the pen.

He was scared but all went smoothly until he came to the bit where Hilda left the boat as he was berthing at the Haven.

29

'When your passengers were ashore did you stay with the boat?'

Hesitation, then: 'No.'

'What did you do?'

'I went after Hilda, trying to catch her up.'

'Why?'

'I wanted to say that I was sorry for upsetting her.' He blushed.

The sergeant wrote: 'I wanted to say that I was sorry.' It seemed absurd, written down like that. Had the grim faced sergeant ever chased a girl to say that he was sorry?

'Did you find her?'

'No.'

'How far did you go?'

'I went to the bus stop but she wasn't there. I thought she might have decided to walk so I went along the coast path a little way — '

'But you didn't find her?'

'No, I didn't.'

'I did not find her' was written on the form.

'Why didn't you tell the officer who questioned you last night that you followed the girl?'

A moment of confusion. 'I didn't want Father to know.'

'That you'd followed her?'

'That I'd left the launch, that I was late getting back with the passengers waiting, and them getting aboard without me being there. I mean, there's insurance, and all that.'

'I did not mention this because I did not want my father to know . . .' It was written down with the rest.

Monday morning

On Monday morning a report on the investigation appeared in the weekend file of incidents on the desk of detective Chief Superintendent Wycliffe, at police headquarters. Somewhere along the line a note had been appended. 'There are aspects of this incident which give reason for concern.' Somebody protecting his rear.

30

Wycliffe told his personal assistant, the unflappable Diane: 'Find out what this is supposed to mean and what they're doing about it.'

The answer came within half an hour. 'The DI is querying possible homicide. The girl is from a stable background and though she's pregnant it's thought unlikely that she would do anything dramatic.'

'Then why couldn't he say so?'

'They're pursuing enquiries.'

'Yes, and I know what that means. What does he think I am? A reporter?'

Diane maintained a discreet silence.

'Ask Mr Scales to come in.'

Diane went out with the haul from the morning's paper-chase. She would hint to John Scales that sir's mood was unpredictable and the word would filter down through the hierarchy. Then an unsolicited cup of strong black coffee.

All because a perfect Sunday, weather-wise, had been frittered away on uninvited guests: 'I hope you don't mind us dropping in like this but it's been such ages . . .'

It was some time before John Scales arrived. He was Wycliffe's deputy, a good administrator who looked more like a bank manager than a policeman. He brought a slim file of reports on the incident so far.

'I've also been in touch by phone. It amounts to this, sir: they seem to have done all that could be done in the way of organised search, using volunteers under supervision. They've covered the ground, including unoccupied buildings, with special attention to the shortest route the girl might have taken. I can show you on the map . . .'

Scales spread a large-scale Ordnance map on the desk. 'Here's the field path; it runs through fields belonging to Tregelles Farm which adjoins the Clemo caravan site and belongs to a relative. Here, where the path enters Clemo land, it passes through woodland and skirts a disused quarry which is flooded. At the moment they've got a frogman making an underwater search there.'

There was a pause while Wycliffe brooded over the map, then Scales went on: 'The local boys are doing pretty well.'

'Perhaps, but I think it's time we took over, John. Get a small team together — Kersey in charge.'

They discussed availability, who was free or could be freed. Balancing one against the other with the fact of leave. Then there was the question of a base.

'A mobile Incident Van to start with, John, and see how we get on.'

Rank allowed Wycliffe to stand aside from *i*-dotting and *t*-crossing. Delegation is the magic word but it had taken him a long time to learn it.

When Scales had gone he opened the file and found a copy of the circulated photograph of the missing girl looking up at him. She was beautiful, not pretty, in the first flush of maturity; certain to be the focus of powerful emotions. At first, one had the impression of an open, smiling face but there was something that disturbed him. Her eyes did not smile with her lips; they gave nothing away; they saw, but allowed nothing to be seen.

Was it possible to read so much into a photograph?

It was becoming increasingly likely that this girl had been murdered and Wycliffe believed in the theory of complementarity between killer and victim. Only in mindless killings does a victim play a purely passive role in the drama of death. Almost always there is some action, accomplished or projected, which prompts the killer to strike. So, get to know the victim as a first priority.

But Wycliffe thought that this girl might prove very difficult to know.

He was late arriving at his usual restaurant for lunch and as he made his way to his favourite table he exchanged nods with other regulars already assembled.

Teague's Eating House, established 1892, had changed little in nearly a century. A long, narrow room like a railway coach, with booths down one side. No music, very little conversation; even the waitresses responded to discreet signals rather than to the spoken word. There he could brood.

'The lamb, today, sir . . .'

A half-pint of Stella Artois, nicely chilled, was placed to his hand. By the time he had drunk this his lamb was ready. No dessert, but a large cup of black coffee.

He paid at the cash desk by the door where a wizened little man put his bill on a spike and transacted money from an open drawer.

'Good day, Mr Wycliffe!'

It had a reassuring air of permanence.

Back at the office he glanced through the memos on his desk. One concerned the missing girl: 'Hilda Clemo: Missing person inquiry. Underwater search of quarry — result negative.' Bloody jargon! Why couldn't they say: 'We didn't find her.' He was irritable and impatient.

'Proposals for the Reorganisation of Night Patrols with special attention to Co-ordination between Crime and Traffic.' A ten- or twelve-page memorandum from the chief's office for circulation to senior staff with a note: 'Comments, please.'

He took a scribbling pad and opened the memorandum at page one: Objectives, numbered one to seven. He stared at the page and passed the next few minutes manicuring his nails with a match stick.

It was a quiet time; serious crime was in temporary recession while the professionals relaxed in the Seychelles or the Bahamas. For a fortnight the sun had shone conscientiously from rising to setting while people watered their gardens and disported themselves in swimming pools, so that the water boards believed themselves conspired against by God and man.

Half the population seemed to be on holiday and Wycliffe kept office hours, doing office work, cosseted and confined in his soundproofed, air-conditioned cell. At five he would deal with his outgoing mail, by six he would be home.

Somehow a blowfly had pioneered the maze of corridors to reach his office and was buzzing, fruitlessly, against the window which was sealed. For a while Wycliffe pursued it, without success, then accepted a truce and returned to his chair. The fly came to settle on his papers.

He reached his decision when his clock showed three minutes past three. A brief tidying operation, a couple of telephone calls, and he confronted Diane in her office.

'I'm going down to see how Kersey is getting on.'

'Now?'

'Now.'

'But what about — '

'I shall be home this evening and here in the morning.' He felt like a schoolboy, a little puffed up by his bravado.

When he arrived in the village the tourists were beginning to drift back to their hotels, their boarding houses, self-catering apartments and camp sites. Most of the day-trippers had already gone home. He found the Incident Van already parked at the western end of the wharf, near the fish quay. Somebody had been busy.

Dixon was duty officer and Kersey was in the larger cubicle being briefed by Detective Inspector Rowse from division. Rowse was young, new to his rank, climbing the ladder and determined not to lose his footing.

Wycliffe cross-questioned him about the inquiry. 'Obviously you've come close to deciding that the girl is dead and that we've probably got a homicide on our hands.'

'It looks that way, sir.'

'In which case we are looking for a body. I gather you've searched the area pretty thoroughly and that you've put frogmen into this quarry. Is there any possibility that the body might have been dumped in the sea?'

Rowse frowned. 'It's not easy to dispose of a body from the shore, sir.'

'I realize that; you need a boat. Is that a problem around here?'

Rowse was cautious, unsure of the extent to which this was a test. 'You have to get the body to the boat, sir, and unless you're a boatman you've got a job to do much along the waterfront here, day or night, without being closely watched. Anyway, as I've just been telling Mr Kersey, a recent development makes the whole idea unlikely. It looks as though the girl was on her way

34

home, by way of the field path through the farm shortly after half-past four on Saturday afternoon.'

'Let's hear it.'

'Just before I left the office on my way here, I had a telephone call from a Mrs Rushton. She lives on the outskirts of Gorran and she says that on Saturday afternoon, at about half-past four, she saw a young man and a girl on the stile near her house. They seemed to be arguing and she had the impression that the young man was very upset. From her descriptions it seems certain that she saw Hilda Clemo and Ralph Martin.'

'But Martin denied seeing the girl after she went ashore.'

'Which makes him a liar.'

Rowse had a positive manner which did not impress Wycliffe who was seldom positive about anything.

'Why didn't your witness come forward earlier?'

'She's an elderly woman, living alone; she'd heard about the missing girl but didn't connect it with the couple she saw until, talking to a neighbour this lunch-time, she mentioned the incident and was persuaded to report it.'

It was all eminently reasonable.

Wycliffe turned to Kersey. 'We'd better send someone to take her statement.'

'I've already done that, sir.' From Rowse.

Wycliffe stared at the young man with a steady expressionless gaze, oddly intimidating. 'I assume you haven't arrested the boy?'

Rowse looked puzzled. 'No, sir. Surely the next step would be to have him in for further questioning?'

'Yes. Well, this stile where the young couple were having their argument, where exactly does it lead?'

'To the footpath across the fields through Tregelles, which is farmed by relatives of the Clemos, past the quarry, and on to the caravan park.'

'Tell me about the girl's family.'

'Her father, James Clemo, is a widower, his wife died when Hilda was four.'

'Married again?'

'No, sir. Then there's Hilda's sister, Alice: twenty-eight or nine, married to Albert Harvey — Bertie to the family. They have a little boy and they live in the house with father and work in the caravan park. A relative, Esther Clemo, looks after the house.

'That's the lot, sir, but perhaps I should mention that James Clemo's mother died last week and was buried on Friday. That is to say the day before Hilda went missing.'

Wycliffe nodded. 'That's clear enough. Now about the people at the farm — Tregelles. You've talked to them, I suppose?'

'Yes, sir, of course. They're called Rule: a widow in her sixties and her son; they're related to the Clemos through Clemo's mother, the old lady who died last week. The son is weak in the head but he seems to manage most of the farm work, though I gather they don't do a lot of real farming; mainly they take in other people's livestock for fattening. There's also an old woman who lives with them, Mrs Rule's sister-in-law.'

'What are they like?'

'The son seems harmless, amiable, and according to the local man he's never been in any trouble. His mother tends to be aggressive. I didn't see the old lady but I gather she's senile. They deny having seen the Clemo girl on Saturday but I got the impression they were holding something back.'

'Any idea what it could be?'

'No, sir, but I intended to look into it if I stayed on the case.'

'I see. Well, as things are, if you've finished handing over to Mr Kersey I expect you'll be anxious to get back to your own desk.'

Rowse left, wondering which foot he had put wrong — and where.

Kersey said: 'He's done very well. You were a bit rough on him, don't you think, sir?'

Wycliffe looked surprised. 'Was I? I admit I get riled by the see-what-a-good-boy-am-I approach. It's unprofessional. There are two kinds of hard-working coppers, the ones who work for the job and the ones who work for promotion.'

The usually phlegmatic Kersey was moved to warmth. 'Don't I know it! I was the first sort and I had to wait until I'd turned forty

36

to make inspector; Rowse has managed it before he's thirty. If I had my time to go over again, I know which I'd be!'

A wry grin. 'Perhaps you're right, but it won't hurt young Rowse to wonder for a bit what more he must do to inherit eternal life.'

The two men had worked together for several years and they understood each other's moods so that much could be said without words.

Kersey lit a cigarette. 'You're worried about this girl, sir, otherwise you wouldn't be here like this. The locals were coping very well. Now, if she turns up bright and smiling in the morning we shall have egg on our faces.'

Wycliffe snapped: 'You think I'd care about that?' Then, more calmly: 'I am worried, Doug. She's been missing for forty-eight hours with no news of any sort. I agree the local lads started well but we need a wider approach. If she's dead, then her body is hidden and may take weeks or months to find. We've got to try another line. Who might her hypothetical attacker have been? I know that sounds wide open, but it looks very much as though she disappeared on her way home, using a little-known field path —and that suggests a local, probably someone she knew.'

'So?'

'So we've got to get to know her, through her family, her school, her friends — and her enemies if she has any. The schools are on holiday but find out which teachers knew her best and try to locate them. And when you talk to the boy try to draw him out. It looks as though he's lied but that doesn't make him a liar. Anyway I can't see this as a boy–girl thing, but he may know something without realising it. Then there's gossip. Cook up some excuse for a house-to-house where it's most likely to be profitable.

'Anyway, who've you got in your team?'

'At the moment, Dixon, Curnow and Shaw. Lucy Lane is winding up the paperwork on her arson case and she could come down in the morning if she's needed. Shaw is fixing accommodation and Curnow has gone to bring in the boy.'

37

Wycliffe said: 'I think Shaw must look for suitable premises for an Incident Room; this tin box isn't going to do us for long.'

Shaw was the squad's collator and administrative officer.

'You think this is going to be a long haul?'

'It looks that way to me.'

A pause, then: 'Are you staying on the case, sir?'

'Me? No, I'm going back tonight. This is your case.'

Kersey grinned but said nothing.

Wycliffe was looking out of the little window, trying to get the feel of the place. On the quay a couple of fishermen squatted, mending their nets, like James and John, the sons of Zebedee, two thousand years ago, except that their nets were orange and green nylon and there was little chance of Jesus happening along.

DC Curnow arrived with Ralph Martin in tow. Curnow was obviously surprised to see his chief. 'The boy, Martin, sir.'

'I'm Chief Superintendent Wycliffe, this is Inspector Kersey. Sit down.'

The boy sat on the upholstered bench, on the other side of the table from the policemen; he sat with bowed head, hands resting on his thighs, near the end of his tether.

Kersey said: 'I've read your statement about what happened on Saturday but we now have evidence that you did not tell the truth. You said that you went after Hilda but that you did not find her.'

Martin gave no sign that he had heard.

'You were seen talking to her by the stile at the beginning of the Tregelles field path.'

The boy raised his head and stared with unfocused eyes out of the window, across the harbour. 'All right, I admit it. I'd already been a bit of the way along the coast path without seeing her so I thought I'd try the fields, though I didn't think she'd go that way.'

'Why not?'

He shook his head. 'I don't know; she would never walk that way with me. I thought it was because she didn't like passing her aunt's place; the families don't get on. Anyway, when I got there, she was sitting on the stile. I asked her what she was doing and she said she wanted a chance to think.'

The boy's arrival at the Incident Van in the charge of a policeman would have been observed all around the harbour; now eyes would be watching to see him leave, either free, or again with a policeman, perhaps in handcuffs.

'And after meeting her like that you still said you thought she'd gone home by bus.'

He made a gesture of helplessness. 'The passengers heard her say what she was going to do. If I said different it would mean I'd seen her.'

'You were afraid to admit seeing her because you knew what had happened.'

'No!' His temper flared but subsided at once. 'I just didn't want to talk about it.'

'You didn't want to talk about it! What did you talk about on the stile?'

'About the baby and what we should do.'

'Together?'

A long pause. 'That was what I wanted.'

'And Hilda?'

Wycliffe saw the boy's expression change from vague distress to dogged obstinacy.

'I'm not going to say any more.' He was near to tears.

'Did she say what she was going to do when you left her?'

'No, but I saw her set out along the field path so it seemed obvious.'

'Were you afraid that she might take her own life?'

'No! . . . She didn't, did she?'

'We don't know that she's dead. Why would anyone want to kill her?'

He brought his hands together, fingers tightly clenched. 'If I knew . . .'

'Yes?'

'Nothing.'

'You realize that you are bound to be a suspect, concerned in her disappearance? You lied to the police on two occasions; perhaps you are lying still. It's possible that you walked along the field path with her, that you quarrelled and that you — '

39

The boy turned to face Wycliffe, his fists clenched. In a harsh voice he said: 'You think that she's dead — that's what you're saying, isn't it?'

'We are saying that we have to look at every possibility, that you are, as far as we know now, the last person to have seen her, and that you are not helping yourself or us by lying or withholding information.'

Martin remained rigid and tense for a little longer then, suddenly, he relaxed, his whole body seemed to sag. 'Think what you like!' And, after a pause, he added: 'And do what you like.'

Kersey said: 'We're not playing games, lad. Don't get the wrong idea. We're trying to make it easy for you but there are other ways. We've got some more questions; you answer them here or you will be taken to the nearest police station and held until you give a satisfactory account of yourself.'

It was strange, this little drama being played out while the evening calm settled over the harbour and village. In the cafés and restaurants along the quay people were browsing over menus. The tide was at flood, but because it was the middle of the neaps, the moored craft rode well below the level of the quays. In some of them men were tinkering with engines or swabbing down the planking. Gulls spaced themselves on railings, on gunnels, and perched on mastheads, beady eyed, and still.

The boy made a gesture of resignation. 'All right, what do you want?'

Wycliffe put the question. 'Hilda is pregnant; is it your child?'

He flushed. 'Of course it's mine. What are you trying to say?'

'I'm asking the questions. How long have you been having sex with her?'

'Not long.' Sullen.

'How long — a month? A year?'

He was massaging his thighs with restless hands. Once or twice he seemed on the point of speaking, then changed his mind. Finally he said: 'It was the first time.'

'Was it the first time she had had sex with anyone?'

He did not answer at once, then he said: 'That's her business.'

'It was; now it's ours too. Answer the question.'

'I think she might have had sex before . . . But she wasn't — I mean she wasn't . . .'

Wycliffe exchanged glances with Kersey then he said: 'I'm going to leave you with Mr Curnow, the officer who brought you here. You will have the chance to make a fresh statement and I suggest that you tell the whole truth this time.'

'Shall I be allowed to go then?'

'Perhaps.'

Chapter Three

Monday evening (continued)

At Tregelles Farm Jane Rule was preparing a meal. Early evening sunlight filtered through the murky window-panes to form a shadowy grid pattern on the opposite wall. Two places were laid on the kitchen table and there was a tray, set with a bowl, a spoon and a slice of bread. A stew simmered on the stove in a saucepan covered with a plate. Little spurts of steam escaped from time to time causing the plate to chatter.

A bare, comfortless room: a slate floor covered in part by fibre matting; yellow painted walls and chocolate-brown woodwork. A black-and-white border collie and a tabby cat slept in amity on the hearth rug; the dog crouched, head on paws, the cat sprawled. An alarm clock on the mantelpiece clicked the moments away between two china dogs.

Jane Rule, gaunt and grey, stood, monumentally still, a ladle in one hand, like an automaton awaiting the signal to go through its routine.

A sound of boots grating on the scraper outside and her son came in: Clifford Rule was built like a heavyweight wrestler but his cheeks were smooth and rosy and he looked out on the world through eyes that were childlike in their innocence, uncritical, accepting whatever they saw. He wore a grey shirt tucked into cord trousers and he smelt of the farmyard.

Neither mother nor son spoke. Clifford went to the sink and washed with a great deal of spluttering. His mother, as though released from her immobility, began to ladle the stew into bowls, including a little for the bowl on the tray.

Clifford, drying himself, watched his mother with interest. 'How long you going to keep doing that?'

His mother snapped: 'Shut up, Clifford! Sit down and have your supper.'

Clifford sat and his mother placed a bowl of stew in front of him. 'You start while I take this up.'

She carried the tray to the stairs which made an angled ascent in one corner of the room. A moment or two later, floorboards creaked overhead and, after a brief interval, she came down again without the tray.

'I told you to start!' She took her place at the table and, in movements which seemed to be synchronized, they crumbled bread on the plastic table covering, picked up their spoons, and began their meal.

'Did you see the police?'

Clifford paused, and thought, his spoon half-way to his lips. 'That was yesterday.'

'They've been back.'

He put down his spoon and turned to his mother with anxious eyes. 'What did they come back for?'

'They wanted to look round.'

'But they looked everywhere yesterday: they had sticks and they poked in all the ditches and in the hedges, they — ' Clifford was becoming excited so that his words came tumbling over each other.

His mother spoke sharply: 'Slow down, boy! All they wanted was to look round the buildings.'

'The buildings.' He looked at his mother, open-mouthed. 'Did they come in the house?'

'Yes.'

He raised his eyes to the ceiling. 'Upstairs?'

'Yes.'

'The dairy?'

'Yes.'

The woman dripped information like a leaking tap. There were long pauses between the questions.

'They didn't — '

43

'No!'

'Did they ask questions?'

'No different to yesterday. Eat your food!'

For several minutes they ate in silence while the shadowy grid pattern crept slowly up the wall and the beam of sunlight was alive with gleaming particles of dust.

'She was here, too. The Innes woman, in her wheelchair.'

'What did she want?' He was anxious again.

'Quizzing about the police. You don't have to worry about her. I can deal with her sort.'

Clifford frowned. 'Mr Innes is good to me.'

'Good to you! Good to you because he gives you half what you're worth when you work for him. I tell you, boy, you'd do better to keep away from that lot!'

When Ralph Martin had been taken into another cubicle, Wycliffe studied the Ordnance map pinned to the wall; he could never begin to come to terms with a case until he had been over the terrain; until, like any naturalist, he had done his fieldwork. To bring in a witness or a suspect for questioning was like caging an animal in order to study it. Something might be learned of behaviour under stress but it is no way to arrive at any understanding of motives, of responses, and of the way the individual fits into the pattern of other lives.

He turned to Kersey. 'These people at the farm — Tregelles — I'm going to take a look at them. I'll drive home later this evening and I'll be in touch in the morning.'

He walked along the quay and through the square, where most of the real shops were, then he followed one of the narrow streets leading away from the harbour. A resurrected villager of a century ago would have had no difficulty in recognising his village, nor in identifying most of the buildings. The transition from fish to tourists (mercifully not complete) had so far been accomplished without wholesale devastation.

He was leaving the village behind as the road began to climb, fields on his left, trees on his right, then the entrance to the caravan park, and an arched sign: 'Tregwythen Leisure and

44

Tourist Park'. Through the arch there was a prospect of terraced slopes with trees and shrubs doing their best to hide the caravans.

He entered the site, passed the shop and reception building on his left, and a drive leading to a dwelling house on his right. A metalled road wound pleasantly, following the valley, with tiered stands for the vans on either side. The sun was still well above the trees but the light was already turning golden, promising one of those summer evenings of infinite calm.

The caravanners were at home, children played on the grass, fathers too; muted radios competed without aggression and, through open doorways, Wycliffe glimpsed women preparing meals on bottled-gas stoves.

The road ended in a footpath where the trees began and there was a perceptible chill as he entered the wood. Sunlight slanted through the branches creating an atmosphere of solemnity and the silence was complete. The path divided into two: a left-hand fork which followed the course of a small stream, and a right-hand one which climbed a gentle slope where trees were sparser and there were outcrops of moss-covered rocks. Wycliffe chose the path by the stream.

Almost at once the path widened into a track and then into a clearing with the stream on one side and a disused quarry on the other. The quarry, gouged and blasted out of the hillside, was now flooded, creating an extensive pool at the foot of cliff-like walls. At the top, thirty or forty feet up, gorse bushes in their second flowering formed a ring of acid yellow against the blue sky and, although the slope was steep, more bushes and even sapling trees had found a root-hold in and on its crevices and ledges.

The surface of the pool was patchily covered with bright green weed; the gaps, where dark water showed, were almost certainly due to the flounderings of the police frogman earlier in the day.

It was a strangely still and sombre place until, suddenly, a flock of chattering starlings flew in to settle on the ledges, then with equal abruptness, as though at a signal, they took off again in a flurry of wings.

Wycliffe continued along the track which rose steadily, leaving the course of the stream and the quarry behind. The trees closed

45

in again but, as he reached the top of the rise, they gave way to low hedges and the track became a lane. He had a view over the whole countryside. Young bullocks and sheep grazed the adjacent fields. To his left, in the middle distance, a wedge of sea cut into the profile of the land, while in all other directions there were rolling fields, the occasional house or farm and, at one point, a church tower.

A farm gate labelled 'Tregelles' and a stile both led directly into a farmyard. A finger-post on the stile pointed 'Footpath to Gorran Haven', so that anyone using the path had to pass through the farmyard. But the lane continued on past the farm and he could see at least two more houses along it before it joined the Gorran road a quarter of a mile away.

If Hilda Clemo had set out along this path from the Haven, how far had she got? Had she reached the farm? The quarry? Or had she, for some reason, followed the lane to its junction with the road?

The farmyard was cluttered with rubbish and straw; a museum-piece tractor and a veteran Morris Minor stood in an open shed. Hens pecked among the cobbles and there were hutches against a sheltered wall where rabbits shuffled and squeaked. A shaggy, black-and-white collie came out of the house, barking and growling by turns, and was followed by a heavily built man, dark, with a ruddy complexion like a burnished apple.

'You want something, mister?'

His manner was in no way aggressive; he spoke softly as though his only wish was to make himself agreeable.

'Isn't this a public footpath to Gorran Haven?'

'People don't come this way much; they mostly go round by the coast path.'

'But Hilda Clemo came this way on Saturday afternoon.'

The dark eyes became fearful. 'If you come from the newspapers I don't know anything, mister.'

'I'm not from the newspapers. I'm Detective Chief Superintendent Wycliffe.' He showed his warrant card. 'Are you Mr Rule?'

46

The man hesitated. 'Yes, that's me.' He was clearly worried, unsure what to say or do. 'The police was here this morning and they was here yesterday.' His mind wrestled with the problem of saying, politely, that there was no point in this further visit. 'They searched everywhere but they didn't find anything . . . I think Hilda must've gone another way.' He nodded in approval, pleased with this idea. 'I think that's what she done.' His manner was almost pleading.

'What other way?'

This was too much for him; he looked back into the house as though in the hope of support but none came and, resigned, he said: 'You best come in and talk to mother.'

Wycliffe followed him into the kitchen. Cold comfort farm. A thin, grey-haired woman was washing dishes at an earthenware sink.

'It's another policeman . . .'

The woman had taken no apparent notice so far; now she turned, wiped her hands on a limp, grubby towel and said: 'This is the third time we've had the police. But we've told all we know, and that's nothing.'

Her voice was harsh and she spoke slowly as one unaccustomed to much conversation.

Her son stood just inside the door. He had taken from his pocket a clasp knife with several blades and he repeatedly opened one of the blades to let it spring back with a loud click.

'If your niece came by the field path on Saturday afternoon she must have come through your yard.'

'Perhaps, but that don't signify. We didn't see her.'

'At about five that afternoon, where were you both?'

Jane Rule stood, immobile, her face expressionless, not a muscle moved; he had rarely seen anyone capable of such statuesque inertia. Even when she spoke, movement seemed confined to her lips. 'Clifford was out in the fields somewhere — '

'I was over to Bassett's — that's a field — mending the gate . . . To keep the sheep in.'

'Near the path?'

'No, the path don't come near Bassett's.'

47

His mother said: 'And I was lying down upstairs before cooking supper. I'm on my feet from six in the morning.'

'But the dog would have barked, surely?'

'The dog was with Clifford.'

'The dog was with me — to keep the sheep in like while I was mending the gate.'

The silence and the stillness which seemed to pervade the whole landscape closed in again, punctuated by the clicks from Clifford's knife, and if it had been left to the Rules it might have continued indefinitely.

'Does your niece pass this way often?'

'If she does, I don't see her. Perhaps now and then.'

'Does she ever call in when she's passing?'

'We're not on terms; we just pass the time of day.'

Clifford said, with obvious regret: 'Hilda used to come here but not now.'

His mother snapped: 'That was a long time ago.'

'What about your sister-in-law? Where was she on Saturday afternoon?'

'Up in her room.'

Clifford tried to join in once more: 'She don't come down much except when she's for going out.'

Jane Rule ignored him: 'Agnes — my sister-in-law — is seventy-seven and she's gone queer in the head; senile, they call it.'

'She thinks she's still a girl,' Clifford said.

'She sits by her window for hours, watching the sea, just watching, waiting for Ernie Pascoe's boat to come in. Ernie was her intended and he was drowned out fishing nearly sixty years ago.'

Jane Rule's grey eyes held his gaze and he was aware of a strange disquiet. A woman ground down by circumstance; she had good features and, at one time, she must have been an attractive woman; now her habitual expression was one of sullen melancholy. Only occasionally the eyes came alive in a momentary flash of resentment. Wycliffe felt sorry for her.

'That's very sad.'

The woman seemed to react to his sympathy. 'The trouble is, although she spends so much time in her room, you can't rely on it. Sometimes she'll creep downstairs and wander off, and we have to go looking for her.'

'So she's all right on her legs?'

'There's nothing wrong with her legs — it's her head.'

The subject seemed to be exhausted and Wycliffe tried another tack. 'This lane which leads out to the road — I see there are other houses along it.'

'A couple.'

'Who lives in them?'

Jane Rule pouted. 'In the first one there's a man and a woman called Innes — that's if they're married. She paints pictures and he's supposed to be some sort of writer.'

'Are they good neighbours?'

A barely perceptible lift of the shoulders but no reply.

'The other house, nearly out to the road, is the Moyles' place. There's a whole tribe of Moyles and the eldest boy works down at the caravan site.' The first time she had volunteered information unasked.

It was depressing: the woman, bleak and sombre, with her feeble-minded son making his pathetic effort at sociability. The woman was resentful and sullen, but wasn't her defensive attitude more than explained by her hard life? A widow with a half-wit son and a demented old woman, struggling to keep the farm going and make ends meet. Of course it was possible that Clifford Rule had raped and murdered the missing girl and that his mother had done, and was doing, all she could to conceal the crime.

'. . . a bit soft in the head but amiable, never caused any trouble' — The local verdict, but Wycliffe, who read psychology more from a sense of duty than conviction, knew that statistically the mentally subnormal male shows a greater proneness to sex crimes than to other forms of criminality.

'Is this farm yours, Mrs Rule?'

'I'm the tenant.'

'And your landlord?'

'I don't see it's your business but I suppose you can find out easy enough; the farm belongs to the Clemos.'

Wycliffe had run out of questions and, still uneasy, took himself off. Clifford and the dog escorted him to the yard but the woman returned to her dishes.

He did not cross the yard to the other stile but decided to follow the lane which would take him past the neighbouring houses to the road.

The first of the Rules' neighbours lived about four hundred yards along the lane in a substantial, large, fairly modern bungalow, surrounded by a field of mown grass. In a corner of the field a clump of ageing pines looked as though they had been lifted from a Japanese print. A grey *deux chevaux* was parked in front of the house.

Wycliffe went to the front door which stood open to a tiled passage. As there was neither bell nor knocker he rapped with his knuckles. No one answered so he knocked louder and a girlish voice called: 'There's someone at the door, Tristan! Will you go, please?'

A brief interval, and a man appeared at the end of the passage: tall, slim, dark, and thirtyish. 'Good evening . . .' Tentative.

'Chief Superintendent Wycliffe . . . Mr Innes?'

'Yes, indeed. I'm glad you've come, Chief Superintendent. I intended to contact someone. Do come in.'

His manner was amiable, flattering in its diffidence; he walked with a slight scholarly stoop and his movements, probably because of his height, were rather slow and self-conscious.

'In here.'

The room which ran the whole depth of the house seemed to be a combination of sitting-room and library. The floor-to-ceiling bookcases, with their moulded cornices, disguised the fact that it was part of a modern bungalow. With a few 'good' pieces of furniture they created an impression of elegance. The over-large window was discreetly cut down to size by brocaded curtains, and the decor was subdued. Indian miniatures hung where there was an exposed wall and the carpet on the floor was Persian, Tree-of-Life design.

Either Innes's writing and lecturing must be very profitable or there were other resources.

'Do sit down . . . This, of course, is about Hilda. Is there any news?' The brown eyes were solemn, concerned.

Wycliffe was momentarily put off his stroke. 'No. Do I understand that you know Hilda?'

A brief smile. 'Yes, indeed. In the past six or seven months we've seen quite a lot of her.'

'How did that come about?'

A slight movement of the long, pale hands. 'As part of my work I travel about the south west, lecturing on aspects of the history of art and it happened that I was invited to Hilda's school. She was sufficiently interested to come here a few days later. It became obvious that she had a quite exceptional intelligence and my wife and I were glad to encourage her.'

Innes's speech was meticulous and unhurried, every syllable received its full value, each phrase and each sentence was followed by a distinct pause so that one could almost see the marks of punctuation. Everything about the man conveyed an impression of deliberation yet Wycliffe sensed that, underneath, there was tension.

'She comes here often?'

A pursing of the lips: 'Once a week? Sometimes more often.'

'Do you give her lessons?'

'Oh dear me, no! Nothing like that. We talk, we listen to music, we read poetry together and we look at and discuss pictures.'

'The three of you?'

A shrewd look. 'Yes, the three of us; my wife is very fond of Hilda. Hilda wants to broaden her horizons and we may be able to help her to do that by offering her understanding companionship and conversation.'

'You said that you were intending to make contact with us.'

'I was. I wanted to tell you just what I've told you now. It happens that I was away yesterday when the police called — in fact, I left home on Saturday evening and only returned this afternoon. I gather that my wife may not have realized how seriously the police regarded Hilda's disappearance — '

51

'So you were at home on Saturday afternoon?'

'Oh, yes. I was due to lecture at a weekend school in Exeter on Sunday, and this morning I had an appointment at the university. I spent Saturday and Sunday nights·with a friend at Tedburn St Mary near Exeter.'

'But you didn't see Hilda at all on Saturday?'

'Yes, I did on Saturday afternoon — '

'Here?'

'No, I was taking the dog for a run across the fields in the direction of Gorran Haven and I met Hilda coming this way. I asked her if she was calling in at our place and she said that she was not; she was on her way home.'

'Your wife didn't mention this to the officer yesterday.'

'She didn't know. I don't suppose it occurred to me to say that I'd met Hilda, there was nothing unusual about the encounter.'

'When did you first hear of her disappearance?'

'Only when I returned home this afternoon.'

'What time did you see her on Saturday?'

He frowned. 'I can't say exactly but it must have been shortly before five.'

'Did she seem her usual self?'

Hesitation. 'I think so. Perhaps a little subdued but Hilda is a moody girl.'

The room faced north and already the light indoors was growing dim; the silence was absolute. Innes sat, his long legs crossed, waiting politely for further questions. Wycliffe was in no hurry; by allowing a silence to become uncomfortable one could provoke questions which were often more informative than answers.

It was only when Wycliffe was beginning to think that he had lost the silent battle that the question came: 'Do you really think that Hilda has come to some harm?'

Wycliffe did not answer directly. 'You must know her at least as well as most people; is it likely that she would walk out on her family, taking nothing with her, and telling no one?'

Innes shook his head. 'No, I must say that it isn't.' After a pause he asked: 'Are you suggesting that something happened to her between here and her home on Saturday afternoon?'

'It's hardly a suggestion. If you saw her near here at five o'clock and she didn't arrive home, it seems a logical inference.'

'Yes, of course. It's just that I find it hard to imagine what could have happened.'

'Do you know that she is pregnant?' Wycliffe put the question with apparent casualness.

'*Pregnant?*'

'Confirmed by her doctor on Saturday morning.'

'Oh, dear! I had no idea. Poor girl! Do you think her pregnancy could have anything to do with her disappearance?'

'Do you?'

Innes looked put out. 'I know nothing of the circumstances but I hardly think Hilda would do anything foolish or dramatic if that is what you mean.'

It seemed that they might be entering upon another lull when there was a sound of rubber wheels in the passage. Innes got to his feet and hurried to open the door to a woman in a wheelchair. She wore a grey smock, heavily spattered with paint. She was so small that at first sight Wycliffe took her for a child.

'I hope I'm not intruding?'

'No, Polly, of course not! Come in and meet Chief Superintendent Wycliffe. He's come about Hilda.' He turned to Wycliffe. 'My wife — as you will see for yourself, she paints.'

Very skilfully she manoeuvred her chair to a convenient position. The chair must have been made specially; it was both narrower and higher than is usual, presumably to give greater mobility and compensate for her own lack of height.

She was looking at Wycliffe with anxious eyes. 'A chief superintendent?'

Innes said: 'Yes, the police are taking Hilda's disappearance very seriously indeed, Polly.' He turned to Wycliffe. 'My wife and I misjudged the situation, we thought that this was no more than a teenage escapade, a consequence, perhaps, of a family row. Young people react so dramatically these days . . .' Then to his wife: 'The fact is, Mr Wycliffe has just told me that Hilda is pregnant.'

'Pregnant! Poor girl!'

Polly Innes was like a perfectly proportioned scale-model of a woman. She must have been less than five feet tall and very slender. Her skin was pale, its paleness accentuated by straight black hair which she wore at shoulder length. Her features had the perfection of a doll's but when her face was caught in the light from the window Wycliffe saw that she looked ill, her eyes were dark ringed and her face was drawn, almost haggard.

Wycliffe said: 'We don't think that Hilda left home of her own accord.'

There was a sharp intake of breath from Polly Innes but she said nothing; she looked from Wycliffe to her husband and back again.

Innes was reflective. 'I was very surprised to hear that Hilda is pregnant. My first reaction was that she is far too intelligent but, of course, that is foolish. Obviously there are times when intelligence is not enough.'

He looked at Wycliffe, perhaps to judge the effect of his remark, but Wycliffe was staring, dreamy eyed, at an Indian miniature which depicted an erotic encounter in a grove of blossoming trees. He was thinking that Polly Innes could have been the model for the woman in the painting.

His interest was not lost on Innes. 'The resemblance is striking, is it not?'

In a strained voice Polly Innes asked: 'Do you know the boy responsible for Hilda's pregnancy?'

Wycliffe shook his head. 'Not with certainty.' He changed the subject: 'In your conversations with her, what were your impressions? Do you see her as a highly intelligent but otherwise average schoolgirl? Or did any particular aspect of her character strike you so that you might tend to think of her as "the girl who . . ."?'

Innes smiled. '"The girl who . . ." I know exactly what you mean; and you have a point. But although we have spent many hours with Hilda I don't feel that I know her any better than I did after her first visit. At that time she allowed us to see something of herself, but what wasn't revealed then has been carefully guarded ever since.'

54

Polly Innes nodded agreement.

Innes went on: 'It was as though she had paid her subscription; a sort of psychological entrance fee, and that was that. I'm no psychologist but Hilda seems to put out feelers anticipating, almost inviting, a hostile response, and when the response is not hostile she becomes suspicious.' He looked at his wife. 'Isn't that so, Polly?'

'Oh, yes, quite so.' Words seem to come with difficulty as from one who is not following the conversation, preoccupied, perhaps by pain.

They talked for a little while longer, or Innes talked, and he agreed to come to the Incident Van to make a formal statement. He saw Wycliffe off at the gate.

The orange sun was low behind the pines creating a dramatic silhouette. At the last moment, as though the admission was somehow being forced from him, Innes said: 'My wife injured her spine in a car accident and she has bad days when she suffers a great deal. This is one of them.'

'I'm very sorry. You are able to leave her in the house alone when you go away?'

'Oh, yes. She feels well enough most of the time and she can get about with crutches, but it is an arduous and somewhat ungainly business so that she is unwilling to meet strangers except in her chair.'

A couple of hundred yards up the lane Wycliffe came to a ramshackle building where the lane joined the road. It was surrounded by an area of rough grass littered with the wrecks of cars and vans. In an open shed a young man, presumably a Moyle, was at work on another vehicle which looked in rather better shape.

Wycliffe was thinking about the Inneses; they left him with a sense of unreality, as though he had been watching a stage performance. The setting, their attitudes, their conversation, reminded him of actors following stage directions and a script. But there are plenty of people who more or less consciously cast themselves in certain roles and surround themselves with the appropriate props, often as a defence against something.

At least he had established that someone had seen the girl after Ralph Martin left her at the stile.

James Clemo lay on his bed, fully dressed, staring at the ceiling. Early evening sunshine flooded the room. A whisky bottle and glass stood, with the alarm clock, on his bedside table. The clock showed ten minutes past six.

The door opened and Esther came in but he gave no sign. She stood looking at him and the lines of her thin, pale face softened.

'Aren't you coming down?'

'No.'

'Alice has just come from the village; she says the police are questioning Ralph Martin again; they've got him in their van on the quay.'

He did not turn towards her but continued to stare at the ceiling. 'They're wasting their time; the boy didn't do it.'

'There's nothing to say that anybody "did it". We don't know that anything has happened to Hilda.'

Clemo made a weary gesture. 'You and I know well enough, Esther.'

Abruptly, he turned away from her and his body was shaken by sobs. For a moment it seemed that she was about to say something but she merely stood over him, her face full of concern, then she picked up the whisky bottle and left the room.

Chapter Four

Wycliffe arrived home in darkness and Helen came out into the drive while he was putting the car away. Their house, a former coastguard station, stood at least two good stone-throws from their nearest neighbour, overlooking the narrows where the river met the sea. Navigation lights twinkled in the channel and, upstream, the sky above the city blazed with a fierce orange glow.

Indoors, Helen said: 'Drink?'

'A small whisky.'

'Worried?' It was unusual for him to drink spirits.

'I suppose I am.'

In the remnant of their day they ate chicken sandwiches while watching a television serial about a poor rich family who, because the husband had thrown up his job, faced hard times, and were forced to sell their yacht. Their teenaged daughter took it badly, but her practically minded, caring brother got a job as a petrol-pump attendant. Granny would have helped but she had invested all her money in half a race horse which had gone lame.

As the credits rolled Wycliffe said: 'I suppose we should be thankful we don't have their problems.'

Helen switched off. 'Don't knock it. The dresses were pretty, so was the music, and you didn't have to think. What more do you want? Anyway, it's early to bed for you. Do you want anything?'

'What about cocoa?'

'You'll only say cocoa isn't what it was.'

'It isn't, but let's try it once more.'

He went to sleep while his mind played tricks, juggling with random fragments of his day. Later in the night he dreamed that he had been awakened by someone calling. In his dream he got out of bed and went to the window. Below him, standing on the grass, he saw Jane and Clifford Rule looking up at him. Although it was dark he could see every detail of their figures and faces. Clifford's features were blank and receptive but Jane was smiling and, for some reason, this angered him. In his dream he banged on the glass and shouted, but his efforts made no sound and the Rules did not move, nor did their expressions change. In his frustration Wycliffe awoke, confused and distressed.

The bedside clock showed two-fifteen. He listened, surprised to hear rain — the first for almost three weeks.

He lay awake, brooding, troubled by his visit to the farm and by his absurd dream. The truth was beginning to dawn on him: that he had been taken in. Jane Rule had been too clever for him — all her talk about her sister-in-law was surely out of character, it had come in response to his sympathy and served to divert his attention from something else. Or so it seemed to him now.

The Rules, mother and son, were recipe suspects, but of what did he suspect them? Were they responsible for Hilda Clemo's disappearance? Perhaps, but it was equally possible that they were attempting a cover-up of something quite different. Women like Jane Rule, shrewd about many things, were often vague about the role of the police, so that in the light of a dodgy tax return or a false claim for an agricultural subsidy any attention from them might seem threatening.

All the same . . .

He decided that he was unlikely to settle down to sleep in a hurry but the next thing he knew it was full daylight, seven o'clock, and Helen was getting up.

'You've been restless.'

'Sorry!'

'It's not your fault. Stay there and I'll bring you your coffee.'

At eight, when the Incident Van would be manned, he telephoned. 'Anything to report?'

'Nothing, sir.'

'Then give me the number of the place where Mr Kersey is staying.'

A minute or two later he was talking to Kersey. 'In the middle of the eggs and bacon?'

'I should be so lucky! I promised Joan to keep to toast and marmalade.'

'I'm coming down; I'll meet you at the van as soon as I can get there. What's the weather like?'

'Drizzle.'

'It's the same here.'

Wycliffe made a second call, this time to his deputy, John Scales, at home.

'Sorry to interrupt your breakfast, John. I want a discreet check on a chap called Tristan Innes . . . Yes, sounds like some character from a novelette, but he's real enough. He's a lecturer and writer on something or other, I'm not quite sure what, but he says he was lecturing at a weekend school in Exeter on Sunday and that he had an appointment at the university on Monday morning. Anything you can find out . . . He's probably a respectable academic so don't stir things . . .'

It was Kersey's first visit to the farm. Misty rain settled out of a leaden sky, the countryside was blotted out, and the prospect dismal. Hens scrabbled in the yard and one came stalking out through the open door of the house as they arrived. Kersey called: 'Anybody home?'

Jane Rule's harsh voice came from somewhere at the back. 'Who is it? What do you want?'

'Police.'

She came, glowering. 'Aren't we ever going to be left in peace?' Then she saw Wycliffe and her manner softened. 'Oh, it's you.'

'Is it all right if we come in?'

59

She withdrew from the doorway. 'If I said no, what difference would it make?'

'Your son is not at home, Mrs Rule?'

'What do you expect? He's got work to do.'

Wycliffe said: 'We want to check all the houses in the neighbourhood to make absolutely sure that the missing girl isn't being hidden — it's routine and we shan't hinder you . . .'

The room had a yeasty smell of warm dough and a pan stood in front of the solid-fuel range, covered by a cloth. On the table there were little heaps of vegetables and a bowl containing rabbit steaks, presumably soaking in salted water.

Jane Rule busied herself, riddling ash from the fire. She turned her head. 'You've got no right to search my house.'

Kersey said: 'You object? Something to hide?'

'I said, you've got no right.'

'It would be simple to get a warrant, but just a quick look round — it won't take more than two or three minutes.'

Kersey was half-way up the creaking stairs as he spoke. The woman dropped her poker and was about to protest but changed her mind. 'The old lady's in the room over this; she's asleep. I don't want her woke up yet; the only peace I get is when she's asleep.'

There were three bedrooms. The first was the son's, a small room overlooking the backyard: a single bed with grey blankets, a battered wardrobe, a chest of drawers, and a pervasive sour smell of unwashed clothing. On the top of the chest there was a veritable menagerie of little animals, carved from wood; and wood chips littered the floor. Wycliffe thought the carvings had vigour.

The second room was larger, a double bed, the furniture in better shape. There was proper bedding, and pictures on the walls — one, a framed photograph of a young couple; the girl was undoubtedly Jane, her features not yet hardened and her body still with its youthful curves. Kersey did a rapid and silent rummage.

In the third bedroom, the old lady's, the furniture was almost elegant, walnut, with maple inlay, and there were pictures on the walls here too — paintings in gilded, swept frames. The double bed was covered with a patchwork quilt of quality and the pillow, placed in the middle, was approximately white.

A small grey head rested on the pillow, the face hidden by the sheet. The old woman's body made a scarcely discernible mound under the clothes. On a bedside table there was a tray with a used cup and saucer and a plate with a few crumbs.

Kersey repeated his search tactics and Wycliffe began to feel foolish. What were they looking for? Hilda Clemo's body in the wardrobe?

They turned to leave, and were confronted by Jane Rule in the doorway. She spoke in a low voice: 'I hope you're satisfied!'

If she had not chanced to bar their way they would have left the room without another glance. As it was, Wycliffe turned and looked back. He was struck by something odd about the figure in the bed. He walked over, and heard Jane Rule catch her breath as he did so. Gently, he lifted the bedclothes and uncovered the head of a dummy, fitted with a grey wig, and a rolled blanket, roughly mounded to represent a human figure.

He turned to the woman, utterly at a loss. He said: 'Your sister-in-law?' He had not intended irony but he could think of nothing else to say.

'I've never hurt anybody in my life. You can say what you like!'

Wycliffe leaned forward in his chair, his arms resting on the kitchen table. 'All right, you've never hurt anybody, so where is your sister-in-law?'

Jane Rule sat, bolt upright, opposite her questioner. She looked him straight in the eyes, betraying not the slightest sign of any nervousness. The little piles of vegetables and the bowl of rabbit steaks were still on the table and the pan of dough still stood in front of the range.

Jane Rule said: 'She wandered off. I told you yesterday the trouble I was having with Agnes.'

'When did she go? This morning, before we arrived?'

She stopped herself from giving a too-ready answer and took time to consider. 'No, she was gone when you was here yesterday.'

'When did she go?'

For once her gaze faltered and she looked vaguely around the poorly lit room. 'Where's he gone? The other one?'

'Mr Kersey is searching your outbuildings.'

'They've done that before — looking for the girl.'

The drizzle had turned to real rain; they could hear it drumming on the corrugated-iron roofs in the yard, and water streamed down the window from a damaged gutter. The stove gave off a humid, drowsy warmth, and the light in the kitchen was dim, steely-grey, obliterating what little colour there might have been.

Wycliffe asked: 'Could we have a light on?'

Without a word she got up and flicked a switch near the door. A naked bulb cast a yellowish glow over the table and failed to reach beyond it.

'I asked you when your sister-in-law "wandered off".'

'Friday — Friday morning it was.'

'And you didn't report her missing?'

'Clifford and me searched for her. She usually made for Drum Point where she used to do her courting when she was a girl — '

'You didn't find her. Why didn't you report it so that a proper search could be made?'

She was less sure of herself now. Her clasped hands made small uneasy movements. 'I thought she would come back and I didn't want the Clemos saying I hadn't looked after her — because I had.'

'She went on Friday morning and it's now Tuesday — that's four days. Are you still expecting her back?'

She looked at him but said nothing.

Wycliffe tried again. 'Your sister-in-law, Agnes, was a sister to Mrs Elinor Clemo who was buried on Friday, is that right?'

'Yes.'

'Isn't it an odd coincidence that she should disappear on the day of her sister's funeral?'

'I think Agnes was upset about Elinor; it was hard to tell whether she understood — whether she took it in that her sister was dead, but she was unsettled.'

'Why did you try to make it look as though she was still in the bed upstairs?'

'In case somebody came.'

Wycliffe was puzzled by the woman; she was by no means stupid but she seemed to reason from her own singular premises. He sat back in his chair. 'I'm sorry, Mrs Rule, but I don't believe much of what you've told me. You would be sensible to — '

They were interrupted by a knock at the door which opened, and Kersey came to stand just inside, out of the rain. The brim of his fisherman's hat dripped on his shoulders and his waterproof dripped on the slate floor. 'Sorry to interrupt; I'm through outside except for a lean-to building at the back which is padlocked.'

Wycliffe turned to the woman: 'Will you let Mr Kersey have the key?'

'He's talking about the old dairy; you don't need a key, you can go through from the scullery. You won't find whatever you're looking for, but you can look; it's all the same to me.'

If anything she seemed relieved by the interruption.

'This way . . .'

They followed her into a damp, cavernous scullery where there was a tap, a trough sink, a fuel bin, an antique wash boiler, and a chest freezer. She opened another plank door and they found themselves in a narrow passage between stacks of furniture, a number of crates, and rolls of carpet; it was like a removals warehouse. The furniture was stored, one piece on another, with layers of felt between. There was little light because the windows were blocked by the furniture and by the crates.

'This all belongs to Agnes. She kept house for her brother. When he died the house was let and she moved in with me and brought the furniture with her. You've seen some of it up in her room.'

'What's in the crates?'

'How should I know? Pictures, china, ornaments, that sort of thing, I suppose. They had a big house. Henry made money — and spent it, gambled away most of it.'

'What happens to all this if your sister-in-law is dead?'

'I suppose that depends on her will — if she made one.'

Wycliffe felt frustrated. But what had he expected? He had set out in search of a missing girl and been side-tracked by this infuriating woman. And yet . . .

Kersey turned to him and shrugged. They filed back into the scullery. It happened that as Wycliffe reached the door the freezer motor cut in, drawing his attention to the battered, rusty chest which must have been among the earliest made. The lid had been fitted, unskilfully, with a brass padlock which looked new.

'What do you keep in there?'

Jane Rule looked at him. 'What would you think? The same as your wife keeps in hers, I suppose.'

'Get the key, please.'

She stood her ground. 'How much more do I have to put up with? You come in here and take over my house — '

'Get the key or we shall break it open.'

She reached behind the freezer and came up with a small steel key which she handed to Wycliffe.

Wycliffe felt strangely reluctant, but he inserted the key in the lock; it turned easily, he removed the padlock, flipped back the hasp, and lifted the lid.

It was like looking down at a crouched burial on some archaeological site. A small, anonymous figure rested on its side, almost filling the chest, knees drawn up almost to the chin. The whole body except the head and hands was swathed in some garment, perhaps a nightdress, now rigid with frost. The flesh, where any could be seen, was grey and appeared to have shrivelled so that the bones were unduly prominent; and the sparse grey hair protruded from the scalp in frozen wisps.

Wycliffe lowered the lid. Jane Rule was standing in the doorway to the kitchen, her back towards them.

'Here's Clifford: I don't want him mixed up in this.'

They heard the front door open and shut, and as they moved into the kitchen Clifford was there, taking off an old trench-coat that was almost waterlogged.

He looked from one to the other with apprehension. 'What's going on?'

His mother said: 'You keep your mouth shut! I'll do the talking.'

Wycliffe trotted out the obligatory warning: 'I have to tell you,

Mrs Rule, and you, Mr Rule, that you do not have to say anything but what you do say may be taken down and used in evidence.'

The four of them were seated round the kitchen table; the clock on the mantelpiece showed five minutes past eleven. The dog and cat were asleep in front of the stove. Jane Rule was once more in complete possession of herself; she sat quite still, her grey eyes on Wycliffe but showing no particular concern.

Clifford, his great body hunched, arms on the table, played with his clasp knife. With total concentration he lifted a blade between finger and thumb, released it, and let it snap back into place. The clicks came with the regularity of a metronome.

Jane Rule said: 'I've said before, I've never hurt anybody, and it's true.'

'Then what happened to your sister-in-law?'

'She died.'

'Of what did she die?'

'She was seventy-seven: people don't live for ever.'

'When did she die?'

A momentary hesitation, then: 'Friday — Friday morning.'

'The day of her sister's funeral.'

The woman said nothing.

'As I've told you, you don't have to answer my questions at this stage. In fact, you might be well advised to get in touch with a solicitor.'

'I don't need a solicitor.'

'Very well. What happened? How did Agnes Rule die?'

She gave the first sign of renewed disquiet, stroking the plastic table covering with the palm of her hand.

'She was sitting in that chair by the stove.' She pointed to a wooden armchair with a slatted back. 'One minute she was all right, then she started coughing, like if something had gone the wrong way — she was always sucking sweets. Then, before I could get to her, she just tumbled out of the chair onto the mat and she was gone. Heart, I suppose it was.'

'You didn't call a doctor?'

'He couldn't have done anything — she was dead.'

Once more Clifford's knife snapped back into place. Without raising his eyes he said: 'She was dead; anybody could see she was dead.'

His mother rounded on him. 'Shut up, Clifford! And put that damned knife away, you're getting on my nerves!'

Like a scolded child Clifford slipped the knife into his pocket and sat, staring at the table.

'Didn't you know, Mrs Rule, that you were under a legal obligation to obtain a certificate stating the cause of death, and to register the death?'

She remained silent.

'Why didn't you?'

She was looking down at the table, not meeting his eyes, then she asked, with unusual diffidence: 'Will they be able to tell?'

'Tell what?'

'What she died of.'

'That depends on the condition of the body and the actual cause of death.'

'What will happen to me?' Her eyes were on her son, for once she was vulnerable; her manner, bleak.

Wycliffe was gentle: 'I shall arrange for you and your son to be taken to St Austell police station where you will be asked further questions and invited to make statements. If you wish, a solicitor may be present during the questioning.'

'What then? Will they let us come home again?'

Wycliffe hesitated then he said: 'It is unlikely that you will be kept overnight. Just one more question: surely your sister-in-law had friends? Did no one visit her?'

Jane was running her fingers over the plastic table covering. 'You don't have friends when you're old. Anyway, nobody's been to see her for a long time — six months, at least.'

'And before that?'

'There was the old lady,' Clifford said. 'She used to come Sundays.'

Jane Rule sighed. 'He's talking about Lily Armitage. She used to come every Sunday but she got arthritis so bad she couldn't get about any more.'

66

'Where does she live?'

'In the village, if she's still there — Albert Place, but I couldn't tell you the number.'

Tuesday morning (continued)

Their police car was parked in the lane, by the entrance to the farmyard which had become a sea of mud.

Wycliffe said: 'Drop me off at the caravan site — at the house. You get back and arrange about the Rules. There's no great rush; they won't run away. Send Curnow with them.'

They had to make a broad circuit to reach the entrance to the caravan site. The rain fell vertically, bouncing off the car, and the roads were deserted. Kersey drove up to the front door and waited until someone answered Wycliffe's ring.

'Yes?'

The woman was painfully thin; her hair, drawn back in a wispy pony-tail, left her face looking strangely naked. She wore a shapeless grey frock which draped rather than clothed her figure.

Wycliffe introduced himself. 'You are . . .?'

'I'm Esther Clemo. You've found Hilda?' Peremptory.

'I'm sorry — no.'

Her features which had been momentarily animated relapsed into a sullen mould. 'They're all out. What do you want?'

'To talk to you.'

She hesitated, then: 'You'd better come in.' Her voice was harsh and her manner abrasive.

He was taken into the drawing-room — a relic of times past: framed family photographs and colour prints of Highland stags on faded flock wallpaper; an open fireplace stuffed with crinkly red paper, and a huge Canton jar of dried grasses in the fender.

Esther stood, her hands clasped against her abdomen, and waited.

'Don't you think we might sit down?'

She shrugged and pointed to a chair, then sat herself on the edge of another.

'I've just come from Tregelles.'

67

'What about it?'

'This morning we found Agnes Rule's body.'

'Her *body*?'

'Yes, she's been dead for some time — several days at least.'

Esther was obviously shocked. Once or twice she was on the point of saying something but changed her mind, then: 'I suppose she wandered off and they didn't find her until too late?' She seemed anxious that this should be the explanation and fearful that it would not.

'It wasn't like that, Miss Clemo. We found Agnes's body in the Rules' freezer.'

A quick glance but otherwise no response; the woman seemed afraid of giving way to any spontaneous reaction. Although she was anxious, distressed, perhaps scared, she retained sufficient self-control to consider her words. Finally, with averted eyes, she asked: 'Are you saying they murdered her?'

'No, I don't know one way or the other, but at the moment it seems that she could well have died a natural death.'

Esther was frowning. 'Then why — ?' But she broke off without completing her sentence.

Bleached light from a tall window filled the room and explored its shabbiness: the threadbare carpet, the worn upholstery, the dusty cornices and discoloured walls.

Esther smoothed the folds of her dress over her bony knees. Wycliffe made an effort to ease the tension. 'I wonder if you would tell me something about the Rules and the Clemos — about the two families and how they are related.'

She looked up at him with suspicious eyes but his expression, mild and receptive, reassured her. 'It's not complicated. James Clemo's mother, Elinor, who died last week, was a Rule. One of her brothers, Gordon, married Jane, his first cousin, and they rented Tregelles from the Clemos.'

'And Agnes was a sister?'

'Yes, there were two girls and two boys. The two boys, Henry and Gordon, are both dead. Agnes kept house for Henry until he died, then she moved in with her sister-in-law at Tregelles.'

68

Esther was relaxing. An attentive listener is better than any amount of diazepam.

Wycliffe allowed a comfortable measure of silence before asking: 'Was there money in the Rule family?'

'Not much. Their father kept a general store in the village; but after the war Henry made money in antiques.'

'What happened to his money?'

'I reckon he gambled away most of it, but Agnes looked after him for nearly forty years, so I suppose what was left came to her.' She broke off. 'You *do* think she was murdered! That's what this is all about!' She was accusing.

'No, I've told you the truth. At the moment I've no reason to think that Agnes was murdered.'

But Esther was unconvinced. 'Anyway it's nothing to do with me — nothing! The Rules are no concern of mine now, thank God!'

'*Now*?'

She flushed, the deep colour spread upwards from her neck to her pale cheeks. 'I used to work for them.'

'Before you came to live here?'

'When I was fifteen. You left school at fifteen then — at least people like me did.'

'You were adopted by the Clemos?'

'That's what it amounted to.'

'The Rules were unkind to you?'

She shifted uneasily. 'There's something queer about that family — they're twisted, all of them!'

'But Elinor Clemo was a Rule before she married, surely?'

A sidelong glance. 'And she took me in so I should be grateful. Is that what you're saying? You can believe me she did it for her own ends. Anyway, it's all over now and that's all I'm going to say. It's my business and it's staying that way.'

'Who were your real parents?'

She shrugged her thin shoulders but did not answer.

'You are worried about Hilda?'

'Of course I'm worried! I brought her up from the age of four — after her mother died.'

'Can you make any suggestion at all as to what might have happened to her?'

She was silent for some time but he saw her eyes redden and fill with tears. In a hoarse voice she said: 'I don't know what could have happened to her; I wish to God I did! All I know is I wish you could find her — alive if possible, but find her! It's not knowing!'

After a pause she added: 'And you should keep the Rules locked up for their own good.'

'What does that mean?'

'Nothing. They aren't safe loose.'

Chapter Five

'Charles! I can't help it if it takes time to thaw her out. As far as I can see there are no external injuries, but even that isn't certain at this stage. Did you read about the trouble the Russians took unfreezing the couple dug out of their permafrost?'

'I'm not interested in the Russians or their permafrost; I want to know how that woman died.'

'Then, my friend, you'll have to wait. What do you expect me to do? Set to with a blowtorch? I need relatively undamaged material. God knows how far putrefaction had gone before the freezing process became effective. I can't afford to risk further tissue breakdown through a too rapid thaw, just because you're in a hurry, Charles.'

But there was a placatory last word: 'Anyway, I'll try to have something for you tomorrow.'

So much for Dr Franks.

The pathologist's call was followed almost at once by one from John Scales: 'About this fellow, Innes, sir. He's quite well known in academic circles as an art historian but he's outside the establishment. He took a fine arts degree, followed by three or four years at the V & A, but after that he dropped out of the academic rat race. Now he tops up his rice bowl by contributing articles to glossy magazines and by lecturing on the extra-mural circuit.'

'Background?'

'Father has a prosperous West End business in Oriental antiques, import–export as well as retail business; lives in St

John's Wood, motor cruiser on the Hamble. There's a rumour that, for some reason, Tristan has been cut off without the proverbial shilling.'

The rain had stopped and the sun was shining; the tiers of little terraced houses on the other side of the harbour were a dazzling patchwork of colour under the inky-blackness of a retreating cloud. The time by the clock on the plywood partition was 15.05, or, in translation, five minutes past three in the afternoon.

Detective Sergeant Lucy Lane had arrived to join the team, and it said something for her tenacity and resource over three years that Wycliffe was glad, even a little relieved, to see her. Still under thirty; dark hair and eyes, and 36-24-36 — a package with no chance of an unruffled reception by the squad. Another forty pounds or an incipient moustache would have helped; as it was she had fended off critics and repelled would-be boarders with hard work and a capacity for stinging repartee.

Wycliffe said: 'Any news of the Rules?'

'Still at subdivision making their statements, with Curnow as nursemaid.'

'I don't want them detained, at least not until we've had a report from Franks.'

Kersey nodded. 'I know, I had a word with Jim Nicolls; they'll be released pending further enquiries.' He hesitated, then went on: 'You don't think you're taking a bit of a chance?'

'We'll see. Find out when they're due to arrive home. We'll have a man keeping obo overnight. There's no one place from where he could see all that might go on, so he'll have to use his wits and move about a bit. Observation only; no interference without radio clearance except in emergency.'

Kersey made a note.

Lucy Lane tried to get the broader picture: 'Do we assume, sir, that there is a connection between the girl's disappearance and the old lady in the freezer?'

Women have a knack of asking the crunch question.

Wycliffe played with a ball-point, making a complex pattern of dots on a scribbling pad, and evading a direct answer. 'On Friday afternoon Elinor Clemo was buried. According to the Rules, her sister, Agnes, had died of heart failure that morning. On Saturday morning, Hilda Clemo — granddaughter to Elinor, and great-niece to Agnes — is told that she's pregnant. That afternoon Hilda disappears, last seen on her way home over the Rules' fields. As a tailpiece, we find Agnes's body in the freezer.'

Kersey grimaced. 'Put like that it seems rather much for one family in two days.'

Lucy Lane said: 'It sounds like the synopsis of a Buñuel film.'

Kersey looked at her, poker-faced. 'What sort of films did he make? Westerns? What we should be asking is whether there's money behind it.'

Wycliffe agreed. 'That's one of the things we have to find out.'

Lucy Lane was wearing that special frown that made her look like a pensive schoolgirl in need of a pen to suck. 'For practical purposes are we assuming that the girl has been murdered?'

Kersey, who treasured a rag-bag of lost causes like real bread, hanging, and paying cash, had never wholly resigned himself to working with women in the serious crimes squad. Traffic, non-violent juveniles, the victim's angle on rape, liaison with social services — all these, and more, he willingly conceded to the woman's sphere, but there were limits, and occasionally the cloven hoof showed.

'With no body, with not a shred of evidence to suggest that she is dead, and with no known motive for anyone to kill her, I find it hard to see how we can assume, even tactically, that she has been murdered.'

Wycliffe was joining his dots together to make a passable drawing of a bird in flight. 'I don't think we should jump to any conclusions until we can see some sort of pattern. All the same, I can't help being pessimistic about the girl. If she intended to leave home, would she have gone off with the boy on a boat trip? Would she have started out in jeans and a sweat-shirt, taking nothing with her? But assuming she had reasons for doing both these things, would she then have left the boat at the Haven and struck out across the fields towards home? We know now that's what she did.

'For the moment we need to follow two lines: get all we can on

73

the girl; on her family, and her associates outside the family. I've a feeling that she used Ralph Martin; that there's someone else in the background who, for some reason, she decided to shield. I want you, Lucy, to get more insight into the family — I'm interested in the son-in-law, Bertie, who seems a bit nebulous so far.'

'You want me to talk to him, sir?'

'I think you should make his acquaintance. And have a word with others employed on the site, try to get their view of the family. There must be quite a few seasonal and part-time workers. Do we have anything on Bertie in Rowse's notes?'

Kersey reached for the file and flipped the pages. 'Not much. He married Alice and came to work here in 1983. Before that he was employed for several years by Lovell and Delbos, the Exeter auctioneers."

'Sounds all right, but make discreet enquiries into background and present activities. Get one of our chaps to pay a call on Lovell and Delbos to find out what his job was and why he left. Meanwhile, Lucy, go and talk to him.

'Incidentally, where was he on Saturday afternoon when the girl disappeared?'

Lucy checked the file of routine interviews. 'He made a statement to one of Inspector Rowse's men . . . Here it is: "On Saturday afternoon I drove the Land Rover to the garage at Highlanes to have the towbar welded . . ."' Lucy scanned the typescript: 'He arrived there at about four and left at five-thirty; he did not stay in the garage the whole time but went for a stroll . . . Saw nobody that he remembers . . . He arrived back at the caravan park at quarter to six and spent some time tinkering in the implements shed . . . Arrived at the house just before seven, in time for the evening meal.'

'And this garage, where is it?'

'On the Gorran road, within half a mile of the farm.'

Wycliffe nodded. 'Wide open. The Rules are the same. Innes admits meeting and talking to the girl at a little before five . . . What about the Moyles? Four sons and no father, that's it, isn't it?'

Again Lucy turned the pages of the file. 'As I remember they were all four off on a trip on Saturday afternoon . . . Yes, here we are — Exeter, stock-car racing. Inspector Rowse checked that out. They didn't get back until nine in the evening.'

Wycliffe nodded. 'Of course there's nothing to say that the girl's assailant, if there was one, is known to us, but everything points that way. I mean, this doesn't look like a pick-up and rape, there's nothing to suggest that she was on the highway. Although it takes up a lot of man-hours we must push on with enquiries among males within as wide a radius as we can manage: "Where were you on Saturday afternoon? Did you see . . .?" Et cetera.'

Kersey said: 'We're doing all we can on those lines, sir.'

'Right! Now, in connection with the old woman's death, I want you to look at the inheritance angle. Granny Clemo, née Rule, died last week, and her sister, Agnes, was already dead or died soon afterwards. There must be a lawyer somewhere in the business. Find out from Alice Harvey, she'll know. We've enough evidence to suggest that there's been at least one serious crime, so you should be able to turn the screw if necessary.'

Kersey said: 'Presumably you're staying on the case now, sir?'

'If I can find somewhere to sleep.'

'There's a vacancy where I am and it's not bad, especially if you're allowed to eat the breakfast.'

'All right, see if you can fix it.'

'You don't look a bit like a cop to me.'

'Your experience is probably limited, Mr Harvey.'

They were at the top end of the caravan park, in a building adjoining the implements shed, where would-be swimmers, tennis players and golfers paid their fees, and collected whatever gear they needed in return for a deposit.

'I'm supposed to be the site manager,' Bertie said. 'In fact, I'm a dogsbody in this place. I do anything from cleaning the loos or cutting the grass, to binding the wounds and consoling the mothers of small brats who fall out of trees or tumble off the climbing-frame. In a crisis I've even been drafted in to chat up the VAT man.' He grinned at her. 'Little friend of all the world: that's me.'

Lucy Lane did not quite know what to make of him. He had charm, and knew it, but she sensed an underlying seriousness which might be worth exploring.

'I want to talk to you about Hilda.'

'About Hilda.' He was immediately solemn. 'Hilda was special.'

'*Was*?'

'You don't imagine that she's still alive, do you?'

'In the absence of evidence to the contrary we have to assume that she is. But perhaps you know something which we don't.'

The dark eyes were on her. 'Now, however you look, you sound just like a policeman, and not a very bright one at that. No, I don't know anything about what has happened to Hilda.'

'All right. You said that she was special; will you enlarge on that?'

'Yes. She was very intelligent, she knew precisely what she wanted, she knew how to use people, and, unlike most young people, she knew better than to let her emotions get in the way.'

'But she was pregnant.'

'That did surprise me. I'll guarantee one thing, that it wasn't the young clodhopper on the boats who got her that way. The seduction of Hilda would have required finesse, a skilful wooing of mind and spirit as well as of the flesh. A task for a man of discretion and experience.'

'Yourself, for example?'

'I take your point; fresher fruit from the same tree. I must confess that I was tempted but, like Hilda, I'm a realist and the situation would have become altogether too messy for my liking.'

'So?'

'So nothing as far as I'm concerned. I can't help you.'

A couple, the man in trunks, the girl in a bikini, came to the window to collect a token for the pool.

Bertie Harvey was a man to be reckoned with. If his position was really one of general dogsbody it was unlikely that he accepted it as meekly as he pretended. He was attractive to women; Lucy Lane was aware of the attraction, though she told herself that he was not — repeat not — a man to be married to. But Alice Clemo had married him.

When he had dealt with his customers she said: 'You've got some very definite opinions about Hilda; presumably you know her well.'

'I've lived in the same house with her for five years and we've talked quite a bit.'

'About what?'

'Oh, cabbages and kings.'

'I see. And whether pigs have wings.'

He smiled. 'A Carroll addict?'

'I'm afraid so.'

'Me too. And Hilda caught it off me.'

Damn the man! 'Getting back to the point: did Hilda confide in you at all?'

'I don't think Hilda confided in anybody. She would talk freely enough for just as long as you remembered the mask.'

'The mask?'

'Doesn't everybody wear one? Of course most people let you have a peek behind now and then — not Hilda; if you even tried, it was end of conversation.'

Lucy Lane felt vulnerable — which was absurd. 'Did you and Hilda discuss anything in particular? I mean, in recent months or weeks did it seem to you that she had anything on her mind that troubled her?'

'Nothing that troubled her particularly; we talked about anything and everything.'

It was leading nowhere; she was bungling a potentially important interview. 'Do you know Jane Rule?'

'The Red Queen.'

'Why do you call her that?'

'Because, poor soul, she's always running to stay where she is. I feel sorry for her, and the Clemos don't help.'

'Do you see others of your acquaintance as Alice characters?'

Harvey laughed. 'Some. My father-in-law, for instance, he's an obvious King of Hearts: officious, a bit bumbling, but really quite likeable.'

'And you, yourself?'

'Oh, I'm the Knave, definitely. I stole the tarts — perhaps that should be singular but then it would sound rude and we should never be rude, should we?' A pause and he went on: 'Of course I could be Humpty Dumpty.'

'Why Humpty Dumpty?'

'Well, poor chap, he was balanced on a wall, wasn't he? And his only way off was to fall.' He was looking at her, not smiling, but with a speculative gaze. 'If it's of any interest, I see you, at this moment, as Alice — not quite sure which side of the looking glass she is.'

Bastard! But she did not say it aloud.

Bertie had more customers, four of them, wanting to play golf, and while he was dealing with them Lucy took stock of the place. The room they were in was provided with racks for storing clubs, racquets, skateboards, and other impedimenta for the various diversions available to the paying customer. There were also displays of sweat-shirts, caps and sunglasses for sale.

A door led off to an office and, beyond that, there was another room which, to Lucy's surprise, was fitted up as a darkroom with shutters to draw across the window, and an array of equipment for processing and enlarging. On a bench, in polythene envelopes, with name-tags and prices attached, were photographs awaiting collection.

'So you're a photographer — also like Lewis Carroll.'

'I enjoy it and it's another way of turning an honest penny.' Bertie was standing in the doorway watching her. 'They come here with two or three hundred quid's worth of camera strapped around their necks, then pay me to take photographs of their kids with my old Praktica that mother gave me when I was eighteen. To coin a phrase: "There's now't so queer as folk!"'

Kersey had no difficulty in running Agnes Rule's lawyer to earth. Everybody knew Hector Penrose who had acted for the Rules and the Clemos through the better part of three generations. Now, officially retired, he lived in a low, white house, high above the village, on the north side of the harbour and overlooking the bay.

Kersey was shown into an untidy room with a bow-window looking, inevitably, over the bay. Sky and sea seemed unnaturally blue after the rain, the gulls whiter, the sun brighter. Penrose was seated at a large desk with several pages from a loose-leaf stamp album spread in front of him. He brandished a hand-lens, waving Kersey to a seat. There was a book-rack of catalogues on the desk, a scattering of philatelic journals, other tools of the trade, and a sleeping tabby cat.

'Inspector Kersey.' The old man looked at him critically. 'Not, I think, of the Cornish Kerseys.'

'I'm told that my people came originally from Suffolk.'

Penrose nodded. 'As I thought. Well, we can't all be of God's chosen.' He chuckled. 'As long as we show proper humility . . .'

'I've been told, sir, that you act for the Rule family.'

'Actually I retired several years ago but a few of my old clients who dislike change have stayed with me. My successors in the practice are tolerant and they do all the chores.'

He examined a couple of loose stamps through his hand-lens and muttered unintelligibly. 'You are not interested in stamps, Mr Kersey? No, of course not — pity! As far as the Rules are concerned I gather that Jane is in some difficulty over the discovery of her sister-in-law's body in her freezer. Obviously I can't comment on that, so what can I do for you?'

He was plump and pink with curly white hair which glistened in the sunlight.

'Some background on the family would be helpful, sir.'

'But you can pick that up from local gossip.'

'More painfully and less reliably, sir.'

The old man laughed. 'Well, there's little enough to tell. John Henry Rule had a general store in the village, worked hard all his life, and made very little. He had two sons: Henry and Gordon — ' He broke off. 'Dear me! I can't make up my mind if this one-cent is from the retouched die or not . . .

'Anyway, Henry went to work for an antique dealer in Plymouth and eventually took over the business. Gordon married your Jane and they rented Tregelles from the Clemos. The two brothers had two sisters: one, Elinor, married a Clemo

79

— it was through her that Gordon got the tenancy at Tregelles. The other sister, Agnes, spent most of her life looking after brother Henry, and when he died she went to live with her sister-in-law at Tregelles. There's the background you asked for, Mr Kersey.'

The lawyer was making a close comparison of the two stamps under a light fitted with some sort of filter. 'The colours are different too . . . If that's carmine, I'm a Dutchman.'

Kersey said: 'Wasn't it Henry who made the money, sir?'

A sidelong glance. 'What money? I said nothing about money. But you're quite right. People who'd lined their pockets in the war and were looking for an inflation-proof investment went in for antiques. Henry found them the right antiques and made a lot of money.'

'What happened to it? The money, I mean.'

Penrose made a derogatory sound. 'I'll have nothing to do with modern stamps — nothing since the last war. Too many damned commemoratives — a racket! Even our lot have cashed in on it.'

'Henry's money, sir — what happened to it?'

'He spent most of it, gambled it away on horses with two wooden legs apiece. When he died everything was left, in trust, to Agnes for life. The house was too big for her, so it was let, and she moved in with Jane at Tregelles.'

'What happens now?'

'Ah! I'm not sure that I can go that far, Mr Kersey.' He was comparing watermarks on his two stamps. 'I remember the excitement there was when they issued special stamps for the Wembley Exhibition of 1924. I was only a boy at the time. And the Postal Union Congress issue of 1929 — marvellous! Now the damn things rain down like confetti.'

'But Agnes Rule is dead, sir.'

'Yes, and in very peculiar circumstances.' He turned away from his stamps with reluctance. 'I suppose it's my duty to assist you. Well, according to the will, if Elinor survived Agnes, everything came to her.'

'And if Agnes survived Elinor?'

'Then the trust was automatically wound up and Agnes became the unconditional legatee.'

'One more question, sir — Agnes's will, if she made one . . .'

The old man sighed. 'In for a penny . . . Agnes did make a will and in it she left everything to Jane.'

'Hence the freezer.'

'I didn't hear that, Inspector.'

Penrose became thoughtful, tapping on the desk with a forceps he happened to be holding, and disturbing the cat. 'Before you jump to any conclusions, Mr Kersey, bear in mind that we are not talking about a large estate — Henry's house is in a part of the city which has gone down hill very badly in recent years; there's some furniture stored at Tregelles, and a small amount of money in shares. Of course when Henry made his will he expected to die a rich man.'

Kersey stood up. 'Thank you very much for your help, sir.'

'You should take up philately, Inspector, it teaches you patience.'

Chapter Six

'Hilda is a brilliant pupil; the astonishing thing is that she rarely displays any apparent interest . . .'

'She takes no part in the corporate life of the school outside the classroom — no games, no drama, no choir . . .'

'Her attitude to the staff is one of indifference . . . Teaching her is unrewarding in the sense that one is treated like a reference book — there is no real contact . . .'

'Her attitude to the boys is mildly contemptuous . . . She became friendly with a girl from Gorran but it didn't last. Hilda is a loner . . .'

'Ralph Martin? Yes, I know him; he was at the school. Not bright, but a pleasant lad . . . I can't believe that Hilda . . . She must be playing with him; she can be very cruel.'

'There must be something which makes her tick but I've never discovered what it is.'

Wycliffe was briefing himself on reports of interviews and on notes made by the interviewing officers. The most illuminating comments on the girl had come from her teachers.

'The girl' — Since the previous afternoon when he had opened the file and seen the face of the missing girl looking up at him she had rarely been out of his mind. He found it impossible to treat the case like any other, it had assumed the aspects of a crusade — not that he had any expectation of finding her alive.

Hilda was dead.

Wycliffe was in a cubby-hole, part of the Incident Van reserved for the officer in charge. Next door, in a larger cubicle, a couple of typewriters were clacking away, contributing to the great edifice of paper which is always the most tangible outcome of any inquiry. Soon he would take over an empty shop premises which Shaw had negotiated. It was on the northern quay, close to the harbour office; the shop, and two rooms over. Luxury! They would be equipped from central stores: the typewriters would be electronic, there would be VDU screens, a computer terminal, and a link with the police communications network. The bureaucracy of crime.

The window of his present cell was fitted with frosted glass, presumably to shield the populace from the spectacle of a police chief sucking the end of his ball-point; but Wycliffe found it claustrophobic and, when he could stand it no longer, he left the van and strolled along the quay like a tourist.

The whole village had a newly washed look after the rain; the air was fresher, perhaps with a hint of autumn; it was the first day of September. With the approach of the school term visitors with children of school age would soon be gone from the streets; for another month there would be coachloads of the middle-aged and elderly to keep the shops and cafés happy, then the village would revert to its quieter more inward-looking way of life — the norm for seven or eight months of the year.

This girl — this pregnant girl . . . Why was he so certain that she was dead? Why was he sure that she had been murdered? Was there any connection between her disappearance and the old woman in the freezer? If only he could marshall the facts and reason from them; but his mind, as always, was a playground for remembered phrases, pictures, ideas, fancies, over which he exercised only a tenuous control. Although he had read Koestler and Storr on creativity, he still had an uncomfortable feeling that the thought processes of intelligent people should be organized in a series of logical deductive steps like a Euclidean proof.

He was on his way to the caravan park to talk to Alice Harvey and he found her alone in Reception. Cars were entering and leaving the site, people were in and out of the shop and café, but Reception was quiet.

'Chief Superintendent Wycliffe . . . You, I believe, are Mrs Harvey, Hilda's sister . . .'

'Have you any news?'

'I'm sorry, no.'

'Do you mind if we talk here? There is no one to relieve me at the moment.'

She found him a chair which she placed by her desk. She was pale, and her eyes were darkened by tiredness. The family resemblance to the girl in the photograph was unmistakable but Alice was putting on weight and already she was beginning to pout. Another neatly packaged bundle of frustrations, product of the Ad-world.

She offered him a cigarette which he refused. 'Do you mind if I do? It keeps me going.' A wan smile, self-conscious. She lit a cigarette with uncertain hands.

He expressed sympathy. 'All this on top of your grand-mother's death.'

Her eyes had a faraway look. 'Yes, we buried Granny on Friday and it seems an age since then.'

'Had she been ill for long?'

'Nearly three months — following a stroke.' She changed the subject abruptly: 'You think Hilda is dead, don't you?'

'Do you think she left home of her own accord?'

'I'm quite sure she didn't!' The words seem to spill out. A moment of hesitation, then: 'Do you still suspect Ralph Martin?'

'Why do you ask?'

She was impatient with evasion and snapped out her reply: 'He's been interviewed three times by the police, hasn't he?'

'Because by his own admission he was among the last to see your sister, and because his account of the circumstances was far from straightforward.'

She looked around for an ashtray and, failing to find one, tapped ash into a potted plant. 'Ralph wouldn't hurt anybody, least of all Hilda.'

'Do you have any idea who might have harmed her?'

She shied away from that. 'Of course not! How could I?'

He said nothing but his steady, brooding gaze disturbed her and, in the end, it was she who broke the silence. In preparation she slid her chair back from the desk and swivelled round as though to confront him. 'I suppose you think Hilda was innocent, with no previous sexual experience?'

'Is that what you believe?'

'I don't think that Ralph Martin was the only one . . . It sounds unfeeling to talk like this now but it could have something to do with whatever happened.' An irritable gesture, then: 'Of course my father wouldn't believe anything of the kind, it would be useless to talk to him.'

She was watching Wycliffe through a haze of cigarette smoke and, after an uneasy pause, she burst out: 'Hilda is a very strange girl, Mr Wycliffe. I can't quite explain, but she seems to treat people as if . . . as if they were white mice, or something . . . Wouldn't it be interesting to try this, or that? I don't think she ever put herself in anyone else's shoes.'

She coloured. 'This must sound dreadful to you but I think you should know.'

'You think she was using Ralph Martin to experiment?'

'I don't know but it seems likely to me.' She turned on her chair. 'Ralph is the sort of boy who lays himself open for it.'

The door opened and James Clemo came in. He stood, looking from one to the other. 'What's going on?' His arms hung loose but his fists were clenched and he pivoted on the balls of his feet in a boxer's stance.

Alice said: 'My father.'

Wycliffe introduced himself. 'I've taken over the investigation into your daughter's disappearance. Let me say — '

'My daughter has been raped and murdered; don't play the word game with me, mister! What will you do with him when you catch him?'

Wycliffe's answer was low key, matter of fact: 'My job is to investigate the circumstances of her disappearance, Mr Clemo. If it turns out that she has been harmed and someone is arrested and charged with an offence, it will be up to the courts to decide what happens after that.'

Clemo was watching the superintendent, his grey eyes un-wavering. 'And if they find him guilty; what will they do with him? Will they hang him?'

Wycliffe's manner did not change. 'I'm sure you know that there is no capital punishment in this country, Mr Clemo.'

Clemo raised his arms. 'So why bother?'

Wycliffe sympathized with the man's despair but said nothing. It was Alice who spoke: 'You're doing no good, father.'

Clemo turned on her in anger but, face to face with his daughter, it seemed that his aggression vanished, leaving him limp and listless. After a while he said in a low voice: 'No, you're quite right, Alice. I'm doing no good at all — and neither is he. Hilda is dead and we're wasting our time.'

He went out as he had come, closing the door behind him.

Alice said: 'You see how things are?' It was a plea.

'Who is Esther? How did she come into the family?'

'Esther?' She was momentarily put off by the abrupt change of subject but she collected her wits. 'Esther was adopted by my grandparents as a girl of sixteen.' A vague gesture. 'Don't ask me why, I don't know; I was only six when she came and it is a subject never talked about. Anyway, when mother died Esther took over the running of the house and she's been doing it ever since. I was fifteen and Hilda was four then.'

'But who is she? Who were her parents?'

A brief hesitation. 'You must ask her that.'

Wycliffe was casting around, trying to trigger any revealing response, and he tried again: 'I understand that Hilda doesn't visit her Rule relations at Tregelles.'

'None of us does. Hilda used to go there until about a year ago when Agnes started to go queer in the head. They seemed to get on, but nobody gets on with Jane. The truth is there's been friction for a long time. Granny persuaded grandfather to let her brother, Gordon, rent Tregelles. That worked more or less until Gordon died, but since then the farm has gone downhill, it's turning into a wilderness and the rent is laughable for these days. Now that Granny's gone I hope father will do something about it.'

These were things Wycliffe understood; his father had been a small-time tenant farmer and he had been brought up in the narrow world of family feuds, squabbles over land, and the conflicting interests of landlord and tenant.

With seeming irrelevance, Alice said: 'You think Agnes was murdered, don't you?'

'I don't think anything. We shan't know until I have the pathologist's report. Jane Rule says she died of a heart attack last Friday morning, the day of your grandmother's funeral.'

'But they didn't send for a doctor, they put her in the freezer!' Alice shuddered and seemed genuinely distressed. 'It's horrible! I can't take it in. Last Friday we seemed to be a family like any other; now — soon, people will read about us in the newspapers and they'll think we are — I don't know — grotesque!' She was trembling.

A young girl came into the office and stood irresolute on seeing Wycliffe. 'I'm sorry I'm a bit late . . .'

Alice regained her control. 'My relief. We can go into the house now if you want to.'

'Yes, I would like to see your sister's room.'

'Her room? Two policemen went through her things yesterday but of course you can see it.'

They walked up the drive together and he followed her into the hall and up the stairs. Everywhere there were signs of neglect: worn carpets, woodwork in need of paint, and the patterns on the wallpapers had merged into a general drabness. A long passage on the first floor divided the house almost into two, with a window at one end and a room at the other. Hilda's was the end room and it came as a pleasant surprise.

The window overlooked a little patch of woodland which separated the house from the road. The room might have belonged to a fairly prosperous young student almost anywhere: light, functional furniture from Habitat; shelves for books, and a music centre . . . The pictures were semi-abstract and vaguely erotic, with a suggestion of improbably entangled limbs. The desk stood beneath the window.

Alice said: 'I expect you know that she's working for her A-levels and the school says she should get an Oxford award.'

'What subjects?'

'English Literature, French, English and European History — a very traditional menu for a bright girl but she chose it herself.'

Wycliffe looked about him; he opened drawers and cupboards at random, picked up books and put them down again. When he looked in the wardrobe Alice said: 'At least she didn't go mad on clothes like most girls.'

The books were largely concerned with her school work but there was a spread of paperbacks, from foreign classics (mainly French) to Le Carré and other writers of intelligent spy fiction. Odd taste for a girl, Wycliffe thought, male chauvinist that he was. Conspicuous among the books because of its twelve hundred pages: *The Works of Lewis Carroll*; Wycliffe picked up the book and opened it. The flyleaf was inscribed: 'To Hilda on her thirteenth birthday with love from the Knave.'

'My husband — Bertie,' Alice said.

He replaced the book. Alice stood as though waiting for some comment or question and when none came, she added: 'He's very fond of Hilda.' Toneless.

'Am I intended to read something into that?'

She looked away. 'Bertie can be very charming when he wants to.'

'It wouldn't be the first time that a husband has been attracted to a young sister-in-law.'

She walked to the window. 'I don't know anything.'

'But you suspect. What, exactly?'

She turned on him, suddenly angry. 'Do you expect me to spell it out? To put all our dirty linen on the line? The fact is I can't really believe that Bertie was having sex with Hilda. He isn't all that interested beyond the titillation stage. If you want it plainer, he's all right with a woman until she takes her pants off.'

He was looking through the records and cassettes all neatly stored in racks and it was as though he had not heard her outburst. 'It looks as though pop has been overtaken by the classical here.'

'What? Oh, yes.' She seemed relieved, perhaps grateful. 'Until a few months ago we were under siege from pop, now it's more likely to be a Bach prelude or a Mozart quintet.'

'What inspired the change?'

'I don't know. Girls go through phases. At about the same time she went over to high fibre and fruit juice.'

Wycliffe was idly turning the pages of one of Hilda's school files. 'Does she support any causes?'

'Causes?'

'Anti-nuclear, anti-pollution, anti-vivisection; save seals, whales, badgers and children.'

Alice smiled. 'Do you know I've never even thought of Hilda in connection with anything of that sort.'

'So she doesn't.'

'No. Hilda reacts to the world only as it directly affects her.'

'Do you know the Inneses at Tregelles Cottage?'

She was becoming accustomed to his abrupt changes of subject. 'They're our tenants. That bungalow was originally built for mother and father when they married but they changed their minds and lived here. Anyway, what about the Inneses?'

'Did you know that Hilda has been a fairly frequent visitor there for several months past?'

'No, I didn't know that. Are you saying that she might have gone there on Saturday afternoon?'

'Innes met her on the field path between the Haven and the farm at about five on Saturday afternoon. She told him she was on her way home. What do you know about him?'

Alice was thoughtful. 'Not a lot. I've heard that his father deals in oriental stuff and that he's got a plush showroom in the West End. Innes is a lecturer and I think he writes articles for up-market magazines. His wife is a cripple.'

'Any scandal?'

'That depends on what you mean by scandal. They owe us money for rent and I hear they're in debt elsewhere. I gather his relations with his father are not all that good.'

Wycliffe said: 'I've seen all I wanted to see here, thank you, but I would like a quick look at the other rooms.'

89

'The other rooms?' She was surprised.

'You object?'

'Why should I? It just seemed odd.'

He led the way into the passage and stopped by the first door.

'That's my room.' She pushed open the door and stood aside. 'You must take it as you find it.' There was a double bed made up for one; a built-in wardrobe, a dressing-table, and a wash-basin. A few books shared a shelf by the bed with a clock–radio. The carpet had not seen a vacuum cleaner for a long time.

He was shown the other bedrooms but only two were of real interest and each of these came as a surprise.

Bertie Harvey slept in a large room with a single bed, more of a study than a bedroom. There was a desk, a filing cabinet, and half of one wall was taken up with bookshelves. The books were about equally divided between nineteenth-century biographies and a specialized collection of works by and about Lewis Carroll, including the mathematical publications under his own name: Charles Dodgson.

Alice said: 'It's an obsession. I think he married me because my name was Alice. He's writing a book called *Alice Now*, and the latest is that he's applied for a place on the next *Mastermind* series on TV with the life and works of Lewis Carroll as his specialist subject.'

'Are the photographs his?'

Wherever there was an available piece of wall there were photographs of children — mainly girls.

'Don't you remember? Lewis Carroll was a pioneer photographer and his subjects were usually young girls. I think Peter was a great disappointment to Bertie. Before Peter was born he used to quote Lewis Carroll: "I like all children except boys." He doesn't say that now but I don't think he's changed.'

Wycliffe hesitated. 'Do you think it's sexual?' It was a stupid question but he wanted to prime the pump.

'I suppose it is, but that doesn't mean that I think Bertie molests little girls. I don't suppose Carroll did either, though there would probably have been less fuss in his day if he had.'

She was looking round the room with a half-smile on her lips. 'In some ways Bertie is still a child himself; that's the trouble . . . Anyway, it's better like this — separate rooms, I mean.'

They crossed the passage. 'This is Esther's.'

The other room he had most wanted to see, and it was unexpected. Immediately opposite the door, on the wall by the window, was a highly ornate plaster statue of the Virgin and, over the bed, a crucifix.

'I can see that you're surprised. She became a Catholic shortly after my mother died — thirteen years ago . . . And you know what they say about converts.'

There was a missal on the bedside table and shelves of religious works, mainly lives of the saints.

He'd had enough to be going on with. His mind had been offered a succession of facts, images, phrases, hints and evasions which he would store away for later rumination. He had been given glimpses of the missing girl in her home, and revealing sketches of her as seen through her sister's eyes. He had seen something of the sombre neglected house, and he had been in the little room which the girl had made her own, as different from the rest of the house as she could contrive.

He had met James Clemo.

'Well, thank you for being so patient and helpful, Mrs Harvey. I shall be back from time to time, but if you want to get in touch don't hesitate to ring the Incident Van on the quay.'

Alice followed him down the stairs. On the front steps she said: 'Don't take too much notice of me. I'm not myself.'

Wycliffe walked back to the Incident Van. He felt frustrated, like a child grasping at soap bubbles. He was sure that the key to much of what had happened lay in the character of the girl, but what he had seen and heard gave him no coherent picture and he was back with her teacher's comment: 'There must be something which makes her tick but I've never discovered what it is.'

In the Incident Van Lucy Lane was typing her report, the only officer on the strength without an addiction to eraser fluid.

'Well?'

91

'I've had a difficult afternoon, sir. I've completely failed to make anything of Harvey.'

'Let's hear it.'

Lucy Lane told her story, and finished: 'He has a certain zany charm which is obviously superficial, but you realize that to bring it off at all requires intelligence. If he's a villain it's going to take us all our time to pin him down.'

'Did you get round to talking to anybody else?'

'I went to see the Moyles. Inspector Rowse left us a list of people employed full-time and part-time in the park. Among them are two of the Moyle family who live not far from the Rules: a girl, Debbie, who works evenings in the shop; and a boy, Jeff, who's a full-time handyman. I caught Debbie at home with her mother.'

Lucy Lane swivelled round on her chair to face him. 'The inside of that house is a revelation! You can't make up your mind whether you're in a kitchen or a run-down motor repair shop. Oily bits and pieces of cars are mixed up with the dirty dishes and the vegetables for tonight's meal. Mrs Moyle, with swollen legs and wearing carpet slippers, pads about doing this and that, serenely content. Debbie is a pretty girl of about twenty-two. Wearing a bra and pants, she was ironing shirts for the boys and those shirts looked clean, though God knows how they managed it.'

Lucy could be relied on to sketch in background and that pleased Wycliffe; it was the next best thing to having been there himself.

'Debbie likes working for the Clemos; the pay is quite good and they get a bonus at the end of the season. James's bark scares nobody and she finds Alice easy to get on with. She's not so sure about Bertie; neither, it seems, are the others. The general complaint about him is that nobody knows where they are with him. He can be very sarcastic and he says things they don't know how to take. I can believe that! He also takes photographs of little girls and, according to Debbie, we all know what that means.'

'Anything on the Rules?'

'I was coming to that, sir. The Rules are definitely unpopular with the Moyles. Mother had a few things to say about them; according to her, they come from bad stock: Jane, Clifford, Agnes, even Granny Clemo who died last week — she was a Rule before she married.'

'Any examples?'

'Oh, yes. Clifford is a half-wit, his father was peculiar — "And look at Jane! There's got to be something wrong with a woman who puts her sister-in-law's body in the freezer, whether she died natural or no!" I couldn't argue with that, and when I pointed out that Jane was only a Rule by marriage, she said that was all I knew; that, in fact, Jane was her husband's first cousin.'

Wycliffe remembered the 'tainted' families from his own childhood. Rustic genetics. 'Anything else?'

'Yes, but I'm not sure whether it means anything. Debbie says that twice in the past few months she's seen Bertie with the site Land Rover down beside the farmhouse, loading pieces of furniture.'

'Jane, selling off Agnes's heirlooms?'

'That's what the Moyles think. It interested me because Bertie professed kindly feelings towards Jane.'

'See what you can find out.'

'Anything else for me, sir?'

'Yes. I've just come from the Clemo's place; I want you to spend some time in Hilda's room, going through everything you can find.'

'Shall I be looking for anything in particular?'

A thin smile. 'Only for the real Hilda Clemo.'

Wycliffe and Kersey lingered over their coffee in the hotel dining-room, feeling pleasantly lethargic.

The hotel was on rising ground, virtually a cliff-top, to the west of the village, overlooking — almost overhanging — the harbour. From the dining-room windows the lights along the waterfront and quays defined the dark pools of the inner and outer harbours, and the lighthouse flashed at the tip of the southern arm.

'I think I shall go for a walk.'

It was a ritual after his evening meal, whenever he was away from home. Kersey knew better than to offer his company. He said: 'I thought of going for a drink at The Seiners later on.'

'I might see you there in about an hour.'

It was a windless night, cloudless too. Wycliffe was on his way down the steep, narrow, and sinuous road to the village; on one side, houses; on the other, a low wall and a long drop.

What Henry Rule had to leave might not have seemed much to his lawyer, but viewed from that kitchen at Tregelles Farm it probably looked very different . . . Fate had been unkind to Jane Rule. With Elinor bedridden, likely to die at any moment, and Agnes seemingly in good physical shape, Jane had good reason to feel secure. But Agnes had stolen a march on her and died first. How long before Elinor, it was impossible to say, though Franks might be able to help there.

A clapped-out Mini with scarcely any lights, whining in second, charged the slope and forced him against the wall. 'Oaf!'

Anyway Jane was equal to the occasion. With Agnes in the freezer she put about the notion that the old lady was in the habit of wandering off, then she simply sat back, waiting for Elinor to die. If anybody called, Agnes was in bed asleep.

If he and Kersey hadn't blundered in when they did, looking for Hilda Clemo, a few days after Elinor's death Jane would have reported Agnes missing. There would have been a search, but nothing found. Agnes would have been added to the list of elderly missing persons, bound to turn up sometime — on a beach, in a ditch, or at the foot of a cliff.

Jane couldn't have kept the body in her freezer indefinitely; in any case she would have had no chance of getting leave to presume death, so with winter on the way, the visitors gone home and few people about, Agnes's body would have been dumped in some ditch — probably somewhere on the farm — and one day, come spring or early summer, Clifford, doing a spot of ditching, would — surprise, surprise! — come across the decaying remains of his Auntie Agnes, too far gone to retain any trace of her stay in the freezer.

It hung together but where did Hilda Clemo come in? Did she come in at all?

Wycliffe had reached the main street of the village where shops and cafés were still doing a lively trade. He was in search of Lily Armitage who had been Agnes Rule's regular Sunday visitor. He came upon a stocky figure wearing overalls and a peaked cap, seated on a window-sill, smoking his pipe.

'Could you tell me where Albert Place is?'

The man removed his pipe from his mouth, looked him up and down, and said: 'Who d'y want?'

'Lily Armitage.'

'Up that street, first turning on your right. Lily lives in the third house.'

Lily Armitage was seventy-eight; she lived with her unmarried daughter in one of a terrace of small cottages opposite a chapel. She was crippled with arthritis but mentally alert, even nimble. At one time she must have been big-boned and upright, now her frame was wasted and deformed though her facial features were still strong and her eyes were a rich brown. She had already heard the news along with everybody else.

'I've known Agnes all my life; we went to school together but when she went to Plymouth to keep house for Henry we lost touch. Of course we exchanged Christmas cards and such like but I didn't see much of her for nearly forty years. Then, when her brother died and she came to live with Jane at the farm, I took up to visit her — I used to go there most Sundays. She was all right then.'

'When was the last time you went to the farm?'

Her daughter had gone into the kitchen to make tea and the old lady called to her: 'How long is it since I stopped going to see Agnes?'

The answer came: 'The last time was in January, in the cold spell.'

'There you are then, it must be seven or eight months ago.' Lily was smoothing the red velvet arm of her chair with a crippled hand in which the veins stood out like cords. 'She'd gone queer, very queer. I know I moan enough about my arthritis but thank

God I've still got my wits! Sometimes Agnes wouldn't know me, once or twice she thought I was her mother . . . She had all sorts of silly notions.'

Wycliffe was seated opposite the old lady in an identical armchair, upholstered in red velvet. There was just space in the little parlour for the two chairs, a settee, and a chiffonier. An electric fire on the hearth made the room uncomfortably warm.

'I suppose Jane couldn't stand it any longer, but it was a terrible thing to do — terrible! And she must've known she'd be found out, surely?'

'Agnes Rule may well have died a natural death, Mrs Armitage. What was her attitude to her sister-in-law? How did they get on?'

'Before or after Agnes went queer?'

'Both.'

Lily shook her head. 'It's hard to say. Two women in the same house usually find it difficult, but as far as I could see they got on all right. Agnes kept herself to herself — I mean she had her own room and I suppose she was paying her way so there was no sort of friction over that . . . Of course Jane isn't the easiest woman to live with . . .'

'And after Agnes got queer in the head?'

'Ah, then she took against Jane. She used to say all sorts of things about her.'

'Such as?'

'Well, silly things — like Jane had ill-wished her, that she was trying to starve her, that she was stealing from her. She'd say: "When she's got everything she'll have me put away."'

'Did you believe any of that?'

Lily was emphatic. 'No!' But she added after a moment: 'Now, of course, you don't know what to think.'

Lily's daughter, a plump, comfortable woman of fifty (who must have taken after her father), brought in a tray with tea, gingerbread biscuits, and floral china on a lace-edged tray-cloth.

'I stopped mother going up there, Mr Wycliffe. It used to upset her too much. Help yourself to milk and sugar if you take it . . .'

'What other things did Agnes complain about?'

96

'She said Jane had changed her room around, that she'd interfered with the pictures — '

'And had she?'

'She'd spring-cleaned the room — not before it was needed, I can tell you! She might have put the furniture and pictures back a bit different.' Lily sighed. 'But Agnes was a long way from normal, Mr Wycliffe.'

Wycliffe held his cup and saucer in one hand and a Cornish gingerbread in the other. The daughter sat on the settee, blandly unobtrusive.

'Was Hilda Clemo ever mentioned in your conversations with Agnes?'

'Hilda! There's another sad thing. You never know what you're going to hear next.'

'Did Agnes talk about her?'

'Hilda used to come and see her, and Agnes was pleased about that because Hilda was a cut above her relatives, if you understand me. But she seemed to take to Agnes. After she went weak in the head Agnes would say: "Jane stopped young Hilda coming to see me." I heard that most every visit, and another time she said: "It'll be all right when Hilda comes; I shall tell her what's going on. She'll understand." '

'Just one more question, Mrs Armitage: do you know who Esther Clemo is? I mean, do you know who her parents were?'

The old lady looked at him in surprise. 'You don't know? Most anybody in the village could have told you about her mother, anyway. Her mother was a Tregenza from over Pentewan way.'

'And her father?'

'I doubt if anybody knew.' A hoarse chuckle. 'Esther came from what they call a one-parent family. They didn't have such things in my day.'

'Not a Clemo?'

A shrewd look. 'I've never heard anything of the sort.'

'I understand Esther worked for a time at Tregelles, then the Clemos adopted her. Why? A girl of sixteen?'

Lily pursed her lips. 'Now that *is* a question and a lot of people have asked it without getting any answer.'

It was almost ten o'clock when Wycliffe joined Kersey in The Seiners for a last drink before climbing the hill back to the hotel and bed.

PC Warren, not in uniform, but wearing jeans and an anorak and carrying a haversack which contained a flask of coffee, a few sandwiches, a torch, and his personal radio, was prepared for a lonely night. A patrol car dropped him just beyond the entrance to the lane leading to Tregelles, and he was left to make his way on foot across the fields to come up on the farmhouse without being seen.

'Have a good kip!' The patrol car drew away.

It was after nine and twilight had all but given way to the advancing night; an orange flush in the sky, way beyond the Dodman, marked the last phase of the contest. He trudged along the margins of three fields where dozy cattle, settled for the night, turned their heads to watch him. There was still light enough for the pine trees behind the Innes place to provide a landmark. He skirted the trees; there were lights in the house and he could hear music. Another field, and he could see in dim outline the block of buildings which formed a square around the farmyard at Tregelles. Here, he came upon the footpath leading to the farm from the Gorran side and, a minute or two later, he was at the gate into the yard itself.

It seemed as good a base as any. He could see the whole front of the house and most of the yard, with plenty of cover nearby if he needed it. There was a light in a downstair room and through the uncurtained window he could see Jane Rule, seated at a table. She was sewing or darning, her right hand rose and fell as she plied her needle. Clifford was not in his field of view.

At a little after ten the light went out and another came on upstairs. Five or ten minutes later the house was in darkness. Vague rustlings, occasional squeaks and thuds and muted squawks came from the rabbits and the hens as they stirred uneasily in sleep. Warren made a cautious reconnaissance round the back of the house. Upstairs a light showed at one window, but was extinguished while he watched. Presumably both the

Rules were in bed. Warren returned to base and drank some of his coffee.

By one o'clock his coffee had run out and, shortly after that, he ate the last of his sandwiches. The night was still and silent, there was no moon, only the stars, but to Warren, his eyes accommodating to the light, it was almost like day. He could hear the sea, a gentle rippling sound as wavelets spread over the beach a mile away. Now and then a motor car sped along the road; once, an aeroplane droned overhead, but that was all.

He made another circuit of the property but this time, as he returned to the yard, a dog in the house started barking. He froze against a dark wall, but nothing happened; the dog, after a few valedictory yelps, settled again. Warren crept back to his base and his granite seat.

He looked at his watch at a little before three and it was then that he noticed an abrupt change. It had turned chilly, he could no longer see the stars and mist seemed to condense out of the air around him. Although there was no wind the mist swirled and eddied; sometimes it seemed to lift, only to close in again almost at once. After what seemed an age he looked at his watch again: ten minutes to four. He got up to restore the circulation in his legs and it was then that he heard what sounded like a distant splash. Somewhere a dog barked, but not for long. Was the splash worth noting? Better put something in the log to show that he'd stayed awake. 'At 03.53 hours I heard what sounded like a splash . . .'

After that he must have dozed, for the next time he looked into the farmyard he was astonished to see a stocky figure, quite motionless, standing in the middle of the yard. It was a man; through the mist and the darkness he could make out very little detail but the man was carrying a gun under his arm — a shotgun, broken at the breech.

Automatically Warren glanced at his watch; it was four thirty-two and there seemed to be a glimmer of light in the eastern sky.

Warren was uncertain what exactly he should do but his mind was made up for him. Abruptly, the man closed the breech of his gun and advanced towards the house. As he moved forward Warren burst through the gate and caught him at the door of the house. 'I am a police officer on surveillance duty; I'm asking you to give an account of yourself.' He was scared and must have sounded breathless.

For the first time he saw the man's face clearly. It was James Clemo from the caravan site. Clemo looked at the young policeman, his expression utterly blank, and said nothing.

'What are you doing here at this time of night, and why are you carrying a gun?'

Clemo still said nothing. The dog in the house started a furious barking. 'Hand over the gun, please, sir.'

A light went on upstairs.

Clemo made no move but he allowed Warren to take the gun from him without resistance. Warren breathed thanks to whatever saints make policemen their special concern, opened the breech, and removed the cartridge. Jane Rule's voice came from the house, shouting to her son and telling the dog to shut up. The door opened and she stood there in her nightgown, joined almost at once by her son.

'What's going on now, for God's sake?'

Chapter Seven

Wednesday morning

Esther woke with a start. Had she been dreaming? She could not remember but she sat up in bed, tense. The house was still and no sound came from the caravan park but she could just hear the distant, rhythmic murmur of the sea. There was no moon but light from the window filled the room with shapes and shadows. It fell obliquely on the statue of the Virgin and she crossed herself. 'Holy Mary, Mother of God . . .'

For days she had been conscious of the approach of evil, now it seemed like a physical presence — in her room. She got out of bed, pulled on a dressing-gown over her nightdress, and worked her feet into her slippers. Still in the darkness she genuflected before the Virgin, then left the room. James's room was next to hers and his door was a little open. She pushed it wider and looked in. She could see the bed, bedclothes thrown back. James was not there. Her lips moved: 'Please, God, don't let him . . .'

She went downstairs and through to the back of the house, to the room next to the kitchen which had been the farm office. So far she had moved about the house silently and in darkness, now she switched on a light. The old clock above James's desk showed twenty minutes past three. The door of the wall cupboard was open and the chain lock which had secured James's shotgun hung loose. The gun had gone.

'Oh God, don't let him!'

She hesitated, then made up her mind. From a cupboard in the back hall she fetched a pair of old shoes which she kept for gardening, and a tweed coat, which she put on over her dressing-gown. There was an electric torch, always kept on a shelf by the back door, and she picked it up as she let herself out.

It was misty, a sea mist that played tricks. The caravans were all in darkness but the site was lit by a number of lamps which glowed through the mist. She ran for the first couple of hundred yards then, panting, slowed to a walking pace. She passed under the trees, out of range of the lamps, and switched on her torch, but the mist threw its light back at her so that she seemed to be walking towards a luminous wall. She found it best to shine the light at her feet where the path was clearly visible but she felt vulnerable — a target. She told herself that this was nonsense and pressed on.

She could hear the stream to her right and gradually vague shapes seemed to differentiate out of the darkness until she could distinguish outlines of trees and an interlacing network of branches against the sky. She stepped out with greater confidence.

For a while, preoccupied with her difficulties, she had almost forgotten her purpose; now its urgency possessed her. The path broadened into a track; she had reached the quarry pool and its surface gleamed very faintly through the mist. There were sounds, tiny sounds, crepitations; and occasional little cracks like the snapping of small twigs. She still could not see more than a foot or two in front of her and she was scared. A small splash in the water close by startled her. A water vole? Although she had lived all her life in the country she knew very little of its wildlife.

'Please, God . . .' She breathed inarticulate prayers.

Suddenly there were loud scraping sounds, followed by dull thuds, then a great splash. It came from the other side of the pool. Birds that had been roosting took to chattering flight.

She stood motionless, paralyzed by fear. 'Holy Mary Mother of God . . .'

But nothing happened, and after a little while, she resumed her way; the track began to rise and the trees closed in on either side as she left the pool behind. At the top of the slope there were no more trees, she was on level ground in open country and, despite the mist, she was able to see where she was going. She felt

102

better. She reached the point where the path from the quarry edge joined the track; now she was skirting the edge of a field; in a short time she would reach the stile and the farmyard. If she didn't find James, what would she do? What *could* she do?

Ahead she could just make out the familiar outlines of the buildings. She was within a few feet of the gate and the stile when there was a commotion in the farmyard followed by a male voice, tense and boyish: 'I am a police officer . . . I'm asking you to give an account of yourself . . .' In surprise: '*Mr Clemo*! What are you doing here at this time of night?' A dog in the house began barking. 'Hand over the gun, please, sir . . .'

Esther was standing by the gate, clutching at the bars for fear she might collapse. She was trembling all over and it seemed that her heart must burst.

Then came Jane Rule's harsh voice calling her son, and a moment or two later: 'What's going on now, for God's sake?'

It was all right!

Her first impulse was to join the others in the farmyard, then she thought what James would say. In any case she couldn't face explanations. When she had sufficient control of her legs she made her way back along the track, and she was about to turn down the slope to the pool when she saw a figure in the mist only a few yards from her.

They had become mutually aware at the same instant and both stood stock still; then Esther, in sheer panic, took to her heels and ran. Once, she tripped and fell, banging her head on a root, but she picked herself up and ran again, blindly it seemed, until at last she emerged from the trees into the caravan park.

Already the sky was beginning to lighten but there was nobody about. She made what haste she could through the park down to the house, and let herself in by the back door. She stood inside, her back pressed against the door. She was panting, her chest felt unbearably constricted, and blood trickled down her temple and over her cheek.

Jeff Moyle was on his way to work at the caravan site. He lived not far from the Rules' farmhouse and regularly took the short

103

cut over their fields and through the trees. Heavy rain the day before had drenched the undergrowth and, although the sun was gathering strength, the mist lingered.

Jeff was seventeen; he had been at school with Hilda Clemo but had left in the fifth form. Now he worked at her father's caravan site and Hilda was still a focus for his erotic fancies, but she had never given him a second look. According to some, others had made it, but that was probably just talk. The Ralph Martin thing had come as a surprise; everybody had taken it for granted that Ralph didn't know what he had it for. Now he was being questioned about Hilda's disappearance; and one or two of Jeff's former mates, still at school, had been tackled by the police. Jeff wondered if his turn would come.

He reached the quarry. Oddly, there was no mist over the water and there were gaps in the green weed which usually covered the surface in summer. On Monday a police frogman had searched the pool for Hilda's body and Jeff shuddered at the thought. A year or two ago he and another boy had gone swimming in the quarry pool for a dare. The water was bitterly cold and, as he emerged, breathless and spluttering, from his first plunge, his face had come into contact with something large and smooth, and hideously clammy, floating just below the surface. For a long moment it had seemed that he could not get away from this nameless thing, and he had panicked, striking out wildly for the shore.

It had turned out to be only a dead dog, hairless from long immersion; but the experience lived on in his dreams.

They must think Hilda was dead.

Was it possible that one of the boys he knew, one of his mates . . .?

He felt scared and quickened his pace. Only self-respect stopped him breaking into a run. But he averted his eyes from the pool. Even so a pale patch, seen out of the corner of his eye, insisted on attention. There, twenty or so yards away, floating almost on the surface, was the naked body of a girl. He stopped and gazed, hypnotized. What he saw could have been beautiful; at that distance the body appeared unharmed, only very white and quite still; yet he was filled with a sense of horror such as he had never known. This was Hilda, the girl of his fantasies, but Hilda had become a thing, like the dog.

He could not have said how long the spell held him but at last he was able to turn away; then he took to his heels and ran.

He arrived at Reception just as Alice, deathly pale, was opening the office to deal with early departures.

The news of James Clemo's arrest reached Wycliffe at seven-thirty, while he was shaving, a time judged by the duty officer to strike a nice balance between unnecessary intrusion and unjustifiable delay. In the event, Kersey had taken the call.

'Our man picked him up in the farmyard at half-past four this morning, with a shotgun under his arm and a cartridge up the spout.'

'Was he violent?'

'Apparently not, but he says he intended to force the Rules to admit what they had done to his daughter.'

Wycliffe was puzzled. Why was Clemo so convinced that the Rules were involved? Was he the sort to go after somebody with a gun on a vague suspicion? He had a good deal to learn about the Clemos and the Rules.

Now, it was eight-fifteen and they were in the hotel dining-room, at a table by the window, poised over the harbour. Sky and sea were blue; there were powder-puff clouds, and gulls soared and swooped over a fishing boat unloading its catch. The little houses across the harbour were stacked in short terraces, one above the other, and the scene had all the ingredients of his childhood vision of 'the seaside'.

Wycliffe was removing the fat from his bacon and laying it on the side of his plate.

Kersey eyed the operation with interest. 'You're leaving the best part. My granny used to say: "Eat up the fat, boy, it's good for you." She lived to be ninety-four.'

Kersey was in a limbo of indecision as far as food was concerned, trapped between the disturbing precepts of his wife, supported by the health freaks, and the consoling old-wives' tales which he dredged up from the past.

105

'Did she smoke?'

'What?'

'Your granny — did she smoke?'

'Good God, no!'

'There you are then.'

His thoughts returning to the case, Wycliffe went on: 'We must talk to Esther. If anybody knows what's going on with Clemo, she does. Incidentally, I was told last night that she worked at the Rules' as a girl of fifteen, before she was taken in by the Clemos.'

'Does that mean anything to us?'

'I've no idea.'

It was a popular time for breakfast, especially among families with children, and there was too much chatter for them to be overheard, but they were aware of being pointed out by the knowledgeable. So, when the manager, with exaggerated discretion, made his way to their table and bent over Wycliffe with a whispered message, all eyes were upon them.

'I'm sorry to disturb you, Chief Superintendent, but there is a telephone call for you . . . You will be quite private in my office . . .'

By nine o'clock Wycliffe was at the quarry with Kersey and Sergeant Fox, the scenes-of-crime officer. Fox was blighted by a non-existent chin, and a nose like Mr Punch. He was good at his job, but his pedantic manner and his self-assurance irritated Wycliffe.

Uniformed men from subdivision stood around, waiting to be useful. One man was paddling over the dark water in an inflatable, towards the body, while Dr Hosking, the police surgeon, stood at the margin, shouting instructions. Hosking was a little red-headed man with freckles and a fiery temper.

'No need to touch her! Just nuzzle the body along in this direction until we can reach it . . .' Then, to the men near him: 'Spread that plastic sheet on the grass, damn you!'

The sun was shining through the trees but the water absorbed much of the light so that the body of the girl seemed strikingly lit by contrast.

One of the constables muttered: 'Poor little bastard!'

The photographer's camera clicked and whirred as the body was eased out of the water to sag limply on the plastic sheeting.

Hilda Clemo. Wycliffe gazed down at all that remained of her; water weeds clung to her pale flesh and tangled with her hair. She had been murdered; he had no need of medical opinion to tell him that. Not that there was any compelling evidence of violence, but how else could she have ended up naked in the quarry pool?

The doctor was speaking to him. 'I thought you had a frogman here on Monday.'

The man who had crewed the inflatable said: 'It was me, sir. She wasn't here then.'

Kersey snapped: 'You'd better be right, lad!'

Hosking was crouching over the body. 'He probably is. She hasn't been in the water long. Franks might give you a better idea but I'd say less than twelve hours.'

Men had been stationed at all the approaches to the quarry; others were questioning people living nearby — the Rules, the Inneses, and the Moyles; also campers and caravanners on the site who had spent the night anywhere near the entrance to the wood. Did they see or hear anything suspicious or unusual? Were they themselves out and about at any time after dark? James Clemo was known to have made his way from his house to the farm during the night, had anyone seen him?

Hosking was carrying on with his job: 'As you see, there are multiple injuries, including limb fractures; most of those injuries were, in my opinion, incurred *post mortem*.'

'Most of them?'

'I'm not a magician, not even a pathologist. You'll have to ask Franks if you want detail.' He looked up at the virtual cliff which was the wall of the quarry. For the most part it was stepped, with ash and sycamore saplings growing on the ledges, but there was one place where the slope was steeper and more or less uniform, broken only by occasional jagged spurs of rock. Hosking pointed: 'My guess is that she was tumbled off there.'

It was the only place where there was a gap in the screen of bushes and sapling trees, around the quarry edge.

'Look at these.' Hosking pointed to marks on the girl's neck on either side of the windpipe, just below the larynx.

Wycliffe said: 'You are not suggesting that she might have been strangled?'

'Hardly, but the marks are interesting.' He had turned his attention to superficial injuries to the face and limbs — abrasions and lacerations — and to patches of slight discoloration on the lower abdomen. Then he parted the fair hair near the crown of the head, exposing a crescent-shaped depression in the skull with a swollen margin. Despite the immersion there were still traces of congealed blood at the roots of the hair.

The photographer was following the doctor's examination with his camera.

Hilda Clemo had become the property of experts.

Wycliffe said: 'What do you make of the head wound?'

'It's not up to me, but I can't find anything else that might have killed her. Anyhow, the sooner you get her to the mortuary and Franks takes over, the better. Isn't the van here yet?'

As he spoke two men arrived with a stretcher and a plastic shell. 'It's easier to carry her to the van than to bring the van up here.'

So, wrapped in a plastic envelope on a makeshift bier, Hilda Clemo was carried away. A sergeant accompanied the body to maintain continuity of evidence.

Hardly known outside her village, this schoolgirl was about to enter the professional ken of dozens, scores, and eventually hundreds of total strangers. Their only interest would be to identify and convict the person responsible for her death and, that done, she would be forgotten. The spotlight would be on her killer and the climax would come in a courtroom melodrama with the killer as the star.

Sometimes it seemed to Wycliffe that it was a very odd machine in which he was a small cog. But how could it be otherwise?

The routine of a murder investigation was under way: a report would go to the coroner; the coroner would issue a warrant for the autopsy in the name of Dr Franks, the pathologist; a policeman, functioning as coroner's officer, would maintain liaison between him and the police. Meanwhile the remains of Hilda Clemo were being put to rest in a refrigerated drawer awaiting the gross indignities that would be inflicted on her in the interests of justice. A procedure which would do neither her nor her family any good at all.

Wycliffe and Kersey walked up the valley, away from the others. Kersey kicked a small branch into the stream, still swollen and turbulent after the rain, and watched it being swirled away.

'So the girl is dead. And it certainly looks like murder. I suppose the Rules are our obvious suspects.'

'But the body must have been pushed into the quarry pool last night. PC Warren thought he heard a splash at a few minutes before four. Are you suggesting that Clifford got out of the house and back in again under Warren's nose? Remember he was with his mother when Warren created a stir in disarming Clemo.'

'Clemo got into the yard without being seen, didn't he? These young coppers are a dozy lot.'

'And the motive for killing the girl in the first place?'

Kersey shrugged. 'Rape. The half-wit attacked and raped her. He seems gentle enough but I suppose he has sexual urges like the rest of us — and no outlet. Of course the cover-up would be Mother's doing. It's significant that the girl's body should turn up this morning. Jane must have thought last night would be their last chance to dispose of it; with Agnes out of the bag, so to speak, she knew that she was in trouble; she must have realized that she was very lucky to have that last chance.'

Wycliffe was sceptical. 'Where was the body when we went over the house yesterday? Remember Rowse claims to have done a thorough job with the outhouses and in the neighbouring fields.'

'He didn't find Agnes, did he?' Kersey said, with a ferocious grin. 'Come to think of it — if the girl had found out about the old lady it could have been a motive for both of them.'

Wycliffe shook his head. After a moment or two he said: 'At

109

least when Franks does his autopsy he should be able to type the embryo against possible candidates for its paternity.'

Wycliffe and Kersey stood close to the spot from where it seemed that Hilda Clemo's nude body had been pushed over the edge, to roll down the slope in hazard of the rocky spurs, and splash into the dark pool below. They were all but surrounded by gorse in brilliant flower and the bees, like the villagers, were busy on the last lap of treadmill before autumn really set in.

A faded notice on a broken post read 'Danger!' And danger there was, for the ground ended abruptly at the quarry edge. Fox pointed to the evidence, which was plain enough. The heavy rain of the previous day had left the immediate approach to the quarry edge soft and muddy. A square groove in the mud, about an inch and a quarter wide, was clearly defined for a distance of nine or ten feet, until it reached the footpath where the ground was compact and stony.

'That groove was made by the iron rim of an old-style wheelbarrow, sir.'

In addition to the wheel mark there were confused impressions; some of them might have been partially obliterated footprints, others could have been made by the body of the girl as it was dragged to the edge. But, superimposed on all this, there were clear and unmistakable footprints.

'Clifford Rule's wellies,' Kersey said.

The patterns in the mud had been photographed; now Fox and his assistant were making plaster casts. Uniformed men were searching the grass and scrub, working away from the quarry edge and along the footpath.

From where he stood, now that he knew the lay-out of the countryside, Wycliffe could identify the farm buildings at Tregelles, the Innes place with its attendant pine trees, and the cottage and ramshackle sheds belonging to the Moyles. He could see the tower of Gorran church away to the west and, to the south, the gleaming horizon of the sea. Somehow it was not a setting for tragedy and yet, in the last few hours, someone had wheeled the naked body of a murdered girl to the quarry and tipped it over the edge like a sack of rubbish.

They walked back along the path for a couple of hundred yards to where it joined the broad track coming up from the stream and the quarry pool.

'You see, sir,' Fox said, 'anyone coming from, say the farm, wheeling the barrow, had a choice. He could take the footpath to the edge of the quarry and tip the body over, or he could go down the track into the valley and ditch it in the pool with less commotion. Our chap chose the earlier option.'

Wycliffe cut him short. 'Where does this one go?' Yet another path which seemed to lead away from the quarry inland, towards the Gorran road.

Fox reluctantly admitted to something less than certainty. 'I'm not sure, sir. The place is like a maze, but from the map I think it goes round the back of the quarry and down to the caravan park that way.'

Wycliffe was reflective. 'We are assuming that, dead or alive, the girl spent three nights and days hidden within a few hundred yards from where we are standing; then, last night, she was brought here already dead, in Fox's hypothetical wheelbarrow.'

Fox nodded. 'It seems obvious, doesn't it, sir?'

Kersey said: 'Well, there they are: the Rules, the Inneses, and the Moyles, the only people within reasonable range. But I wouldn't fancy wheeling a barrow with a girl's body in it along these tracks in the middle of the night.'

Fox said: 'It's very nearly level ground.'

They were interrupted by a shout from one of the uniformed men who had been poking about among nettles and brambles beside the footpath. Wycliffe and Kersey went over with Fox. The constable was holding a little wooden carving of a cow. The form of the creature had been roughed out and detailed carving had begun with the head.

Kersey took the carving from the constable. 'It would be nice to know when he lost it.'

Wycliffe was morose. 'Then you'd better ask him. Get hold of a DC and, starting with the Rules — Anyway, you don't need me to tell you what to do. Get what assistance you need; Lucy Lane is at the house but she should be available shortly.'

He sighed, taking another look around him. 'I'm going back to the van. It's time I put the chief in the picture and I expect to hear from Franks. Shaw is trying to set up an Incident Room on North Quay and I want to see what's happening about that . . .' For a few minutes they discussed organization.

When Wycliffe left he decided to follow the path which Fox thought must lead back to the caravan park by a different route, circling and avoiding the quarry.

It was easy walking, a gentle downward slope between bramble bushes where blackberries were ripening. He walked slowly, feeling guilty because the sun was shining, warm on his skin, and because Hilda Clemo was dead.

Hilda Clemo was dead. But why? Because she was pregnant? What other reason could there be? Unless it was a case of rape, but rapists do not, as a rule, quieten their victims by a blow on the back of the head . . .

In a surprisingly short space of time the scrub gave way to open grassland and a neat notice: 'Tregwythen Leisure Park. Nine-hole Golf Course. Walkers please keep to the path.' A well-made track followed the undulations of the course leading to a long, low building, close to the margins of the wood, and to the first of the caravans. Nearer at hand there were tennis courts and a swimming-pool with a diving-board.

So the quarry edge was approachable from the caravan park by a route which, though longer, was certainly less arduous. In a very few minutes Wycliffe reached the building. It seemed to be an implements store and shop and on the shop door there was a notice: 'Open 11 a.m. until Dusk'. Another hundred yards and he had joined the main road through the park.

Already uniformed men were making the rounds of caravans and tents with clipboards. The atmosphere was subdued; the discovery of the girl's body had cast a pall over the place; this, on top of the gruesome finding of an old woman in a freezer at the farm. Though the sun was shining and it was pleasantly warm there were no children playing out of doors and he could hear no radios. But he was conscious of being watched. He was a link with those sombre events which had taken place only a short distance away, and many of the caravanners had been on the site long enough to have known the girl whose body had been retrieved from the flooded quarry . . .

Wycliffe drove slowly back to the harbour. Even after thirty-odd years in the force he was still profoundly shocked and saddened by murder. He navigated through the square and through one of the narrow alleys which led to the harbour. On the quay he had to squeeze past a fish lorry, his nearside wheels creeping along the quay edge. He saw in his mind's eye a headline in the local paper: 'Police Chief in Harbour Tragedy', and breathed a sigh of relief when he was through.

By bush telegraph or ESP the press had got to hear of the discovery of the girl's body and two reporters were picketing the Incident Van.

'All I can tell you is that the young woman's death is believed to have been due to foul play so this is a murder investigation.'

'A sex crime?'

'I don't know — and that is the truth.'

'Was the body naked?'

'Yes.'

'Badly mutilated?'

'No.'

'The girl has been missing for four days, when did she actually die?'

'I hope the pathologist will tell me that.'

'Was she drowned?'

'I think not but I am not a pathologist.'

'Is it true that a police frogman searched the quarry pool on Monday, and found nothing?'

'Yes.'

'Why didn't he find the body then?'

'Probably because it wasn't there.'

'Yesterday the police found a woman's body in a freezer at Tregelles Farm. Is there a connection?'

113

'I've no idea. I don't know yet how the woman died or when.'

'Died, or was murdered?'

'The post-mortem and the coroner will decide that.'

'Jane Rule and her son are not in custody?'

'No, they are not.'

'Is it true that the son is a half-wit?'

'I'm not a psychologist. And that's all I've got for you at the moment, I'll talk to you again when there's more. Anyway, there's plenty for your imaginations to work on as it is.'

They let him go, in good humour. In the van DC Dixon gave him a little sheaf of memo slips with telephone messages. One was from Franks, the pathologist. It read: 'On my way; be with you before noon.' Dramatic as ever.

Another message was from the Chief Constable asking him to telephone, which he did.

Bertram Oldfield was Wycliffe's chief, also a friend, but the two roles were never allowed to tangle.

'I want you to look in this evening, Charles. Sampson has raised one or two legal quibbles about our submission to the DPP in the Archer–Burrows case. We can do without any cock-ups in that direction so I've arranged for a vetting session here at about half-six.

'Now, just put me in the picture about your case, Charles.'

Wycliffe did so, and answered almost the same questions as the reporters had asked.

'It's an end-of-season gift to the media, Charles, so watch your step. Get your Incident Room organized, have the TV cameras in. Let 'em see the line-up of VDU screens, grim-faced officers pecking away at keyboards, telephones ringing . . . I know how you hate it, so do I, but it helps to convince the public that we're on their side. Look at TV's *Crimewatch* — it even catches villains.'

Wycliffe was old-fashioned; he liked to rely on a few people following clearly defined lines of enquiry rather than on a small army feeding a computer and hoping to press the right keys for the jackpot. He conceded that the computer method might be good for wide-open cases, say the rape and murder of a girl hitcher off a motorway, but the investigation of crime in a small community must be more personal, so much depends on individual contacts and individual assessments.

An expensive throbbing sound announced the arrival of Dr Franks in his Porsche. Although they had worked together for years Wycliffe felt vaguely uncomfortable at each fresh encounter. The two men could hardly have been more different: Franks had an acceptance philosophy; he was at home in the world, and rather liked it, while Wycliffe had an uneasy feeling that he was picking his way, blindfold, across a tight-rope.

'The Chief in?' — Franks in the outside cubicle.

DC Dixon came to announce him with Franks on his heels.

'Charles! I was about to telephone about your frozen old woman when they told me that you had another body for me so I thought I'd come down. A girl, this time, isn't it?'

Franks was a roly-poly man, immaculately turned out, and smelling of aftershave.

'I wanted a word. First about your old lady: she died of a massive cerebral haemorrhage probably triggered by a nasty fit of coughing—there was a good deal of mucus in the air passages. I'd guess that she was swallowing something which went the wrong way; she managed to clear it, but too late.'

'No sign of violence?'

'None; and no indications of poison. She died a natural death.'

'When?'

'What do you mean, when?'

'Time of death.'

Franks looked at him wide-eyed. 'You must be joking! If you asked me for a date I couldn't give it to you, let alone a time. I can say that she was put in the freezer within a very few hours of death.'

'Any signs of internal putrefaction?'

'You don't imagine that with a thing the size of a human body, freezing could be instantaneous?'

'No, I don't, but forensic technicians removed her from the freezer so presumably you were given enough data to balance the rate of putrefaction against the rate of penetration and give me some sort of estimate of how long she was in there.'

Franks grinned. 'You've learned a lot from me in the last fifteen years, Charles. At a guess — and it's no more — I'd say she'd been in the box for two to three weeks.'

'Certainly more than a week?'

'Definitely.'

'And you'll say that in court if necessary?'

'With pleasure.'

'Good! That's all I need. Now about the girl — how long before I get a preliminary report?'

'Seeing she isn't frozen solid, say late this afternoon.'

'Thanks. So, until then . . .'

'Don't be in such a damned hurry, Charles! I came here mainly to tell you that I knew Agnes Rule when she was a young woman. Until this morning, dictating my report, I hadn't really taken any notice of the subject's name. Then I made one or two enquiries to make sure I had the right one.'

'How did you come to know her?'

'When I was a boy my father had a book shop next door to Henry Rule's antiques shop.'

'In Plymouth?'

'Of course, in Queen Mary Street.'

It was the first time Wycliffe had heard Franks mention his family and it came as a mild surprise to realize that he must have had one.

'Henry was a bachelor, living over his shop with his sister, Agnes, to housekeep for him. My people used to invite them out for Sunday lunch — that sort of thing. Later, when Henry decided to show off some of his stock in a domestic setting, he and Agnes moved into a biggish house, Devonport way.'

'I gather he made money.'

'Made it and spent it or gambled it away on the gee-gees. During the war he bought up the salvaged contents of blitzed properties in a big way and, after the war, when people were trying to get started again with everything in short supply, he made a bomb unloading the stuff. It was that and other things that turned father against him.'

'What other things?'

116

'His business methods generally upset father who was very strait-laced. Henry employed "knockers" — characters who toured the countryside persuading impoverished old ladies to part with their valuables at more or less junk prices. It was a lucrative business in those days, the new poor weren't very well versed in the ways of the world. Sometimes it was outright theft and, on at least two occasions, Henry was within a cat's whisker of being done for receiving.'

Franks stood up. 'Well, there it is for what it's worth.'

'Thanks, it could be useful.'

Franks grinned. 'One way and another I spoon-feed you, Charles, and what do you do for me? Now I'm going to take you out to lunch.'

Wycliffe held his peace.

Lucy Lane had arrived at the Clemos shortly after the discovery of Hilda Clemo's body and while Clemo was still detained at St Austell following his arrest in the early hours. Alice, close to hysteria at first, had come to terms with the situation and was finding some relief in the essential routine of the site office. Esther, more than ever resembling a walking corpse, went about her household tasks and looked after the little boy. She had a fresh bruise on her forehead and a bandage on one hand. Lucy had not seen Bertie who was out on the site.

At eleven o'clock Clemo arrived home, released on police bail. He had insisted on being taken first to the mortuary where he had identified his daughter's body.

Lucy and WPC Milly Rees from subdivision were making a detailed search of Hilda's room. Every cupboard, every shelf and every drawer was emptied, its contents examined and put back. At one point Clemo came and stood in the doorway; for a minute or two he watched them with a bewildered expression then, without a word, he went away again.

Milly Rees said: 'Funny girl she must've been.'

'Why funny?'

Milly Rees was a plump, bosomy girl, tailor-made for the modern world, and a little suspicious of those who were not.

'Odd, I mean. It's all so damn dull. A place for everything and all that. Seventeen, she was! If you don't have a good time then, when do you? And clothes — I mean, she didn't have any to speak of. If I open one of my cupboards I got to stand back quick. And I've got part of mother's wardrobe too. I suppose there must be all kinds but it's hard to see where she got her kicks . . . Look at her cassettes — I mean . . . And her books . . . And no make-up that I've seen.'

'She was a very clever girl.'

'God! She'd need to be. Personally I'd rather be dumb and happy.'

Each drawer was turned upside down and inspected before being put back and it was Lucy who scored there.

'Look at this.'

An A4 envelope was pinned to the underside of the bottom drawer of the desk.

Lucy removed the envelope. It was unsealed and she drew out a pencil sketch and a letter on National Gallery headed paper. The sketch was more like a labelled diagram competently done, and showed a road through a village with houses, a couple of horses and carts, a grassy verge, trees and figures. In the bottom left-hand corner there was a copy of a signature with a date: 'C Pissarro 1876'. Labelled arrows indicated colours, and at the top of the sketch, dimensions were given: '18″ x 21‴'. With the statement: 'Painted in oils'.

The letter was dated the previous January and read:

'Dear Miss Clemo,

'I regret that we are unable to offer an opinion about a picture based on the evidence of a sketch or, indeed, on any evidence other than the picture itself. If you are able to bring the picture to London I suggest that you bring it here, or take it to one of the major salerooms where you would get expert advice as to its provenance and probable value. There are also competent people among the fine art auctioneers nearer your home who would help you.

'Your sketch is reminiscent of a number of pictures painted

118

by Pissarro, in the late sixties and in the seventies of the last century, in and around the village of Pontoise. However, I am afraid that means nothing in terms of the genuineness or otherwise of your picture.

'Sincerely, Squiggle, Assistant Curator.'

Milly said: 'What's that all about?'

'I don't know, but I fancy we're going to have to find out.'

It was in the bottom drawer of a small chest, under a collection of winter woollies, that Milly found another envelope, this one contained a dozen or so photographs, mostly of Hilda herself as a little girl, toddler to teenager — just. Milly flicked through them without interest then let out a whistle. 'What about this, then? Full frontal and all.' She held out an enprint of a nude man, facing the camera.

Lucy took it. 'That's Bertie, her brother-in-law.'

'Well, he looks all right to me. Perhaps after all she'd realized there was life before death. But I wonder what big sister would think about it?'

'There's your barrow, sir.' DC Dixon to Kersey.

In Tregelles farmyard, in one of the open sheds, between the old tractor and Jane Rule's Morris Minor, there was a rusty barrow with an iron wheel, spattered in hen droppings.

Kersey said: 'You think so? Try pushing it, lad; it'll make a racket like a tone-deaf drunk playing the "Soldier's Lament" on the bagpipes . . . Go on!'

Dixon wheeled the barrow out of the shed into the yard to a protesting chorus of squeaks and squeals from bearings which had forgotten there was such a thing as grease.

Kersey said: 'I'll bet they heard that in the village. The thing weighs half a ton, anyway.'

'What you want it for?'

Clifford had come out of the house to watch, mildly inquisitive. Kersey looked down at his wellies. 'What were you doing at the quarry this morning?'

119

'I heard some shouting and went over to see what it was about. They was policemen and I think they found Hilda.'

'You didn't stay to find out?'

'I saw two of 'em coming up to where I was so I come back here and told Mother.'

'Did you lose this?' Kersey held out the little cow-carving found near the edge of the quarry.

Clifford looked at it with interest. 'Not then.'

'When?'

He shook his head. 'I dunno.'

Jane Rule came out of the house and crossed the yard. 'What is it now?' She was wearied to the verge of collapse and her face was grey.

'We'd better go inside,' Kersey said.

Once more the Rules sat at their kitchen table faced with two policemen and once more Clifford brought out his clasp knife, but sheepishly, with his eye on his mother.

Kersey said: 'We believe that you have been selling items of furniture belonging to your sister-in-law, Miss Agnes Rule. I have to caution you. You do not have to say anything but what you do say may be taken down and used in evidence.'

Kersey thought: 'What do I care if she flogged the old woman's furniture? This is a bloody charade. Either her precious son raped and killed the girl or he didn't; that's what all this is about.'

Jane Rule said: 'There's no point in denying it; I've no reason to. After Agnes went queer she wouldn't give me any money except her old age pension, which I collected anyway. She had her room, her food, and she was waited on hand and foot — everything I had to do for her. And then she accused me of stealing from her. What do you expect? In any old people's home it would have cost somebody four or five times her pension for what she got.'

'So what did you sell?'

Jane shrugged her thin shoulders. 'A couple of things — a bureau and a table.'

'You sold them through Bertie Harvey?'

'He said he could get a good price.'

'What did he give you?'

'For the bureau I got two hundred, and for the table, one-fifty. That and her pension was all I had to keep her for a year, and the things would've been mine anyway when she died.'

'Only if she'd outlived her sister. Why didn't you go to her lawyer about money?'

'I hate lawyers.'

It was strange. The woman was guilty of concealing a death in a barbarous fashion and with intent to defraud; she was guilty too of disposing of property without the consent of the owner. And yet, Kersey felt sure, all she had done seemed to her logical and reasonable. What struck him as odder still, was that he was half inclined to agree with her.

Chapter Eight

Wednesday afternoon

A crab salad and a bottle of Barsac was the limit set by Wycliffe on the pathologist's hospitality. With it came unsolicited advice: 'You can't change the world, Charles, so why not go with the current? It's too late for poking fingers into dykes; too late to start building a bloody ark. We're all being swept along by the flood, God knows where, but there are still good bits, so make the most of 'em.'

Afterwards Wycliffe felt mellowed, but that was the Barsac. 'Don't forget to phone me as soon as you have anything on the girl. She was pregnant and I'm anxious for you to type the embryo and match it against possible fathers.'

'Rely on me, Charles; I should have something for you by this evening.'

'Then ring me at home.'

The Porsche took off with a screech of tyres, the Franks signature tune.

Wycliffe felt a little like the White Rabbit and wondered why he always let Franks get away with it.

They were now installed in an empty shop premises on the North Quay. DS Shaw, with the help of central stores and a brace of technicians, had established a home from home for displaced coppers. The fascia board over the shop was faded but the sign was still legible: 'Charlie's Whatnot: Knick-knacks and By-gones'. Some clown, in or out of the Force, would make something of that. Anyway it was a definite improvement on the van. On the ground floor there were tables, word processors, and telephones, with accommodation for seven or eight officers. Up the rickety stairs, a room, with its own computer link, had been set aside for the senior officer, and another for interviews. Luxury! There was even a tiny kitchen where Potter, the squad's fat man, was already brewing tea.

The duty officer said: 'There's a Mr Delbos of Exeter trying to contact you, sir. He's left a number and wants you to ring back.'

Delbos . . . The name was familiar but, for a moment, he couldn't place it, then he remembered: Lovell and Delbos, Bertie Harvey's former employers.

'Get him for me, please.'

A suave gentleman, and elderly to judge from his voice. Wycliffe imagined him lean, tanned and military, with a well-trimmed white moustache.

'One of your officers was here this morning enquiring about a former employee of ours; I said that I would telephone you.'

Wycliffe made appropriate noises, and: 'It would be helpful to know whether he left you of his own accord or was dismissed.'

Hesitation. 'He was not dismissed; let us say that he was encouraged to leave.'

'May I ask why?'

'Because he failed to live up to the professional standard of conduct we expect of our employees.'

'In what way?'

Some humming and hawing, then: 'We offer a free valuation service to the public. People can bring things to be valued without obligation. Harvey, in several instances, entered into private arrangements with prospective clients, bypassing the firm.'

'He bought the things himself?'

Hesitation. 'No, he was acting on behalf of certain unscrupulous dealers who use such methods — that is to say, they bribe employees of other firms to act as scouts.'

'Did he specialize in any particular branch of the fine arts trade?'

'We are a smallish firm, Mr Wycliffe, but Harvey was mainly concerned with porcelain and pictures.'

123

Wycliffe found Kersey and Lucy Lane in the upper room. Kersey was depressed, and he looked tired. By afternoon each day he had a growth of dark bristles around his chin which in contrast with his sallow skin made him seem unnaturally pale.

'I've spent the morning trotting about up there: the Rules, the Moyles, the Inneses — isn't she the oddest little thing? And, of course, I've talked to our friend, Bertie Harvey.'

'And?'

'That's just it. Nix! You feel we're missing out all along the line. Fox isn't getting anywhere either. I've had another look at that wheel track of his. I don't think it's a wheel track at all. I made an exactly similar rut with a piece of wood.'

'A plant?'

'I'm sure of it — like the little carving. Somebody's being naughty; too damn clever — like most amateurs.'

'The fact remains that the girl's body was moved, one way or another, to the quarry pool last night. The snag is nobody saw anything, or heard anything except the splash, least of all our dozy wooden-top who must have had a grandstand seat for most that went on.'

Wycliffe said: 'With a plank and a couple of pram wheels you can move almost anything, and without waking the neighbourhood.'

Lucy Lane looked up from sorting reports. 'What about Mrs Innes's wheelchair?'

'I suppose that's possibe,' Wycliffe agreed. 'But we may have things the wrong way round. We're assuming the girl's body was kept in the neighbourhood of the farm; what if it was hidden somewhere on the caravan site?'

Kersey grimaced. 'Bertie?'

'Where was he last night?'

'Tucked up in bed by midnight, according to him. We could check with his wife if that's any use.'

'He doesn't sleep with his wife.'

'Ah! You have inside knowledge, sir. But who in their right mind would hump the body all round the pool, up the slope, and along the top path just to push it over the edge with a splash?'

124

'He wouldn't have to; there's a perfectly good way to the quarry through the golf course. Anyway, what else did you get?'

Kersey reported and Wycliffe listened.

'So Jane Rule admits selling and Bertie Harvey admits handling the sale of a table and bureau?'

'Yes, and there's probably more. No doubt she's technically guilty of dishonest handling or some bloody thing, but it doesn't help us. And Harvey says how was he to know the stuff wasn't Jane's?'

'Get someone to check exactly what the items were, where he sold them, and the prices he got.'

'I've laid that on, sir, but what good will it do us?'

'It's ammunition. What did you make of the Inneses?'

Kersey frowned. 'An odd couple! The mind, as they say, boggles. I couldn't make much of them; people like that are out of my league.' A sly glance at Lucy Lane. 'You need somebody with a bit more of the culture.'

Kersey's banter, never entirely free of malice, rarely missed a chance to knock Lucy's academic background. 'I sometimes think we should have a special squad to deal with witnesses who have more than five 0–levels.'

Wycliffe was used to it. 'It's now GCSEs or something. Anyway, the Inneses heard and saw nothing last night?'

'So they said.'

'Now, Lucy.'

Lucy Lane provided a rapid word picture of the situation at the Clemos. 'To add to the mix, Esther has a nasty cut and bruise on her forehead and she's injured her right hand. She says she fell down in the backyard.'

Lucy made a considerable impression with Hilda's pencil sketch and her letter from the gallery; also with the photograph of a nude Bertie.

'You've had them checked for prints, and photocopied?'

'Yes. There are several sets of prints on the sketch and the letter; only two on the photograph. The prints are being checked out.'

Kersey said: 'What sort of girl would keep a photo of a bloke like that?'

'The other way round would be all right, I suppose?' Lucy Lane, acid.

'More normal, anyhow.'

Wycliffe was impatient. 'Let's forget the battle of the sexes and concentrate on the facts. If there was a sexual relationship between Harvey and the girl — '

'There doesn't seem to be much "if" about it, sir, it seems obvious.'

'Perhaps. Anyway, another interview with Bertie; this time we must be in a position to lean on him a bit. Now the sketch and the letter from the National Gallery . . . Lucy?'

Lucy Lane rarely spoke without reflection, measured by the knitted brow. She turned the pages of her notebook which was unnecessary to her recall. 'Hilda must have had access to a painting, apparently by Pissarro, and wanted to know if it was genuine. She obviously didn't know much about pictures but probably realized that a Pissarro must be worth a lot of money.'

Kersey said: 'How much?'

'From what I've been able to find out, even a smallish oil like the one she sketched — eighteen by twenty-one inches — if well authenticated, would probably fetch two hundred thousand, perhaps more.'

Kersey whistled. 'God! That's money even in these days. Murder is being done for a hell of a lot less. If she was mixed up with some swindle on that scale . . .'

Wycliffe said: 'Hilda was a regular visitor at the farm until Agnes went queer, so it's possible she saw the picture there — the date of the letter fits. But, if so, where is it now?'

Kersey grinned. 'The States? Japan? South Korea? Taiwan?'

'You could be right at that. Now, as to what we do. I want you to find out from Penrose, the lawyer, whether he has an inventory of Henry Rule's stuff stored at the farm. If he has, have it checked by a qualified valuer. Don't mention this hypothetical picture or we shall have the press after us. If there's no inventory, then get one made. It probably won't help but it will show we

126

mean business. If Penrose or the Rules make any difficulty, we want to know how much of Henry Rule's stuff did Jane sell. Has she purged her soul?'

'And then?'

'We'll see. Before we show our hand I want to have all the evidence we can get. With luck, by tomorrow, we should be in a position to tackle Bertie and bring Innes into play. After all, he's supposed to be the art expert.'

Kersey was standing by the window which, because the shop was built in the angle of the sea-wall, gave a clear view along the quay to the wharf. A red-head stood out, her small, thin, angular figure, dressed by Oxfam, aggressively purposeful in contrast with the ambling trippers.

'Ella's coming.'

Ella Bunt, a free-lance crime reporter who rated by-lines over a majority of inside crime stories. For years (and Ella was still in the thirties) Wycliffe had suffered her surprisingly benevolent patronage. She had a soft spot for him or, as he saw it, she thought he was a soft touch.

'See if you can head her off.'

Kersey went downstairs. 'You're too late, Ella. It was all over this morning. No more briefings until the result of the autopsy.'

Ella brushed past him. 'Don't give me that crap, Fido. Where is he?'

She glanced round the room, where two uniformed men and a DC were punching their keyboards as though they were fruit machines, then made for the stairs.

'I've nothing for you until this evening, Ella.'

'But I've got something for you.' She looked at Lucy Lane; a few seconds of critical study. 'I see! The squad's answer to equal opportunity; all nicely packaged. Pity she isn't black, you could have killed two birds . . . What do you let her do?'

Wycliffe was roused. 'Cut that, Ella, or I'll have you put out!'

Ella sat down, unruffled. In winter she wore a sheepskin coat that smelt of goat; in summer the smell was of honest-to-God sweat.

'You've got problems, you're adrift. You don't even know if you've got two cases or one. What possible connection is there between Agnes in the freezer and Hilda in the pool? That's what you're asking yourself.'

'You're going to tell me?'

'No, I've no more idea than you have, but I can give you a tip that may or may not be useful. At least the old woman's case is mixed up with the estate of one Henry Rule, late of the city of Plymouth — right?'

'So?'

She fished out a cigarette from the pocket of her cardigan and lit it. 'Last year I did some work on Henry Rule, among other antique dealers, for a series of articles called "Tricks of the Trade" — an exposé of the antiques racket. To bring in Henry Rule was digging a bit far back. The public, bless 'em, like their victims warm, but that can come expensive if you get it wrong. Henry had the advantage of being a plausible rogue and recently dead.' She broke off and tapped ash on the floor. 'There's a whole lot of his stuff stored at Tregelles — right?'

'His house furniture, I believe. But so far, Ella, you haven't told me anything and I've other things to do.'

Ella blew smoke across the table. 'So have I, my friend. Is Bertie Harvey on your little list?'

'He's the dead girl's brother-in-law.'

'You know anything of his background?'

'Before he married into the Clemo family he worked for a firm of fine art auctioneers in Exeter.'

'Lovell and Delbos. But before that he was with Henry Rule; he worked for Henry from the time he left school at sixteen until he was twenty-one when Henry retired and sold up the business. I ferreted that out when I was doing research for my articles. I came down here to see him then, but he's a canny customer for all his waffle and as there was nothing in it for him he had nothing for me. According to what I've heard he was Henry's protégé and he must have known what went on.'

Ella stood up. 'Well, that's it then! I know you've got nothing now but when you have — Ella expects.'

At the door she turned back. 'By the way, Charlie, I like your signboard. Very apt.'

When she had gone Lucy Lane said: 'Is she reliable?'

'She has to be; she survives on horse-trading. Sometimes I think she ought to be in our business.'

Kersey had shown discretion and stayed downstairs during the visit, now he returned. 'What was it this time?'

'Bertie Harvey worked for Henry Rule for five years before going to Lovell and Delbos.'

Kersey screwed up his features, a sign of cerebration. 'I wonder what that means?' He can't have thrown up his job in Exeter, come down here, and married Alice, all to get an inside view of domestic life at Tregelles.'

'At least we're gathering ammunition for a heart to heart.'

Wednesday evening

When Wycliffe arrived home after his conference at headquarters, dusk was beginning to close over the estuary and the navigation lights twinkled through a thin mist. Helen had spent most of the day working in the garden and her skin was brown and smooth.

'Sherry?'

They took their drinks into the garden and made a tour of inspection in the fading light.

'I took a chance and cut back the elaeagnus pretty hard . . . It was hollow in the middle, so it's kill or cure . . .'

Wycliffe said: 'I'll try to do the grass at the weekend . . . We shall have to be drastic with the water-lily, you can't see the fish.'

'Talking about the weekend, reminds me; Ruth phoned. She's hoping to come home on Friday for a day or two. Will you be free at all?'

Ruth, his daughter. That very morning he had seen the body of another man's daughter lifted from a quarry pool, wrapped in plastic sheeting, and taken away to the mortuary. What had that girl done which Ruth had not? Why was James Clemo spending this summer evening in despair while he strolled in the warm

129

darkness with his wife and planned their weekend? Who or what decides the who? And the when?

'There's a casserole, it seemed the safest thing; I didn't know when to expect you and you don't usually get much in the way of lunch when you are away.'

At nine o'clock they were drinking coffee and watching the television news. Towards the end of the news a picture of the quarry pool flashed on the screen, followed by another of policemen searching the ground near the quarry edge with, inset, a picture of Hilda.

'A lovely girl!' From Helen.

The newscaster read her piece: 'The body of Hilda Clemo, the seventeen-year-old Cornish girl missing since Saturday, was found this morning in a flooded quarry only a few hundred yards from her home at the caravan park run by her family. Police are treating her death as murder. The quarry pool was searched by a police frogman yesterday and the assumption is that the body was placed in the pool during last night.'

The inset picture expanded to take up the whole screen and Hilda Clemo was looking out, smiling her enigmatic smile at the millions of viewers.

'Police are anxious to hear from anyone who saw Hilda or who knows anything of her movements after four o'clock on Saturday afternoon.'

Helen shivered. 'It brings it home! Sometimes I wonder how you can carry on.'

Franks telephoned at the beginning of the weather forecast: 'About your girl, Charles. What a waste! Lovely creature! Well, I can give you a run-down. What do you want to know?'

'When she died, for a start.'

'You've got a one-track mind, Charles. You know perfectly well I can't answer that.'

'The fact that she was alive on Saturday afternoon between four and five should help.'

'It sets an upper limit, but the point is I've no idea of the conditions under which the body was kept before it was put into the water. Putrefaction is at an early stage and its progress would

130

have been slowed down by immersion. Those quarry pools are usually bloody cold and your local chap gave this one seven degrees when they fished her out. Incidentally, I agree with him that she was probably in the water less than twelve hours.'

'So?'

'Well, assuming the body had been kept out of doors in the shade, or in a cool shed of some sort, she could have died on Saturday, shortly after she went missing. On the other hand, if it was exposed to higher temperatures then it could have been Sunday or Monday.'

'What about cause of death?'

'Difficult. Your man — Hosking — favoured the crescent-shaped injury to the skull, almost at the junction of the lambdoid and sagittal sutures; mainly because he couldn't find anything else. Even after immersion there are still signs that the wound bled freely and he concluded that it must have been inflicted before death, and probably killed her. I agree that the wound was inflicted before death though it's an odd fact that *post mortem* injuries in that region can bleed very freely. But, leaving all that aside, in ordinary circumstances I wouldn't have expected such an injury to be fatal.'

'How was it caused?'

'My guess would be that somebody took a swipe at her with a hammer — not a very powerful blow.'

'But it was the result of a deliberate attack?'

'In my opinion, yes; it's not the sort of injury one comes by accidentally.'

'Any ideas about the hammer?'

'Smallish, with a circular, flat striking surface.'

'Now, what are these circumstances which were not ordinary?'

Franks was unusually hesitant. 'All I can say is that if she'd been found within a reasonable time after receiving the blow, and taken to hospital, one would have offered heavy odds in favour of her recovery.'

'So you think she was left to die.'

'That's the size of it.'

'What about the marks on her neck?'

131

'Bruises. They puzzle me; they seem to have been made by somebody's fingers, but they can have played little or no part in her death.'

'And the other injuries?'

'All the significant ones, including the fractures, were incurred *post mortem*, probably when she was tumbled over the quarry edge.'

'Any evidence of sexual intercourse immediately before death?'

'You mean, was she raped? I can't tell you. She was in the water long enough to wash away any direct evidence. There was a certain amount of bruising on the thighs but that's a long way from evidence. I suppose the fact that she was naked suggests a sexual angle.'

'You haven't mentioned her pregnancy.'

'Pregnancy? You were on about it this afternoon, about possible type matching for paternity, but the girl wasn't pregnant.'

Wycliffe felt the ground slipping from under his feet. 'On the morning of the day she went missing she was told by her doctor that she was.'

'Then he was mistaken. She wasn't and never has been.'

'She told her sister — '

'I can't help what she told anybody, Charles; I can only give you the facts. Now, do you want any more?'

Wycliffe was left casting about in a void: 'Don't tell me she was a virgin?'

'No, she'd had a certain amount of sexual experience — limited, I'd say.'

'Anything else?'

'No. I haven't done my microscopy yet so I may have other gems for you, but don't expect much.'

Wycliffe put down the telephone.

The television sound had been switched off but the pictures continued to flit across the screen. Wycliffe looked at them like a man in a dream.

'Franks says she wasn't pregnant and never had been.'

Helen said: 'You forget that all I know about the case is what I've read in the newspapers and heard on the radio. They said nothing about her being pregnant.'

'That's true; only the family knew — or thought they did. It wasn't mentioned in the press briefings to save them unnecessary distress. I wonder what old Hosking knows about it.'

'Hosking?'

'The local GP and police surgeon. She didn't see him, she saw his locum, but there's sure to be a note on her card.'

The red-headed doctor was not pleased to be disturbed. 'This is my private house; my records are at the surgery. What exactly do you want to know?'

'Hilda Clemo visited your locum on the morning of the day she died for the result of a pregnancy test. Later that morning she told her sister that it was positive.'

Hosking was incredulous. 'But that's nonsense! I've seen the report; the girl was no more pregnant than I am.'

'Is it possible that your locum misinformed her?'

'No, it damn well isn't! Young Heath told me about the girl when he was handing over. Said she was coming in again about the missed period that started the scare. Of course she was a strange girl . . .'

'Strange?'

'I've known her literally since birth and I don't know the first thing about her. Her mother died when she was four; I don't suppose that helped. They tell me she was very intelligent but I never got more than "yes" and "no" out of her and felt lucky to get that sometimes.'

Wycliffe settled back in his chair and finished his coffee which had gone cold. 'Why would a girl tell her family she was pregnant when she wasn't, and knew that she wasn't?'

Helen had switched off the television and picked up a book. 'To shock them? To draw attention to herself? To have a weapon against someone?'

'Or out of sheer bloody-mindedness.'

'That's possible too, but it might not be for any of those reasons. I remember when I was a girl trying to imagine what

133

would happen if I kicked over the traces and did this or that. How would the family react? How would my friends? When you're young you think a lot about the impact you have on other people — at least girls do. At the same time you're trying to find out what exactly the rules mean and you're tempted to explore the limits.'

Wycliffe was teasing: 'I knew you when you were seventeen and as my recollection goes you didn't seem anxious to explore any limits then.'

'Just as well, wasn't it? But that didn't stop me wondering what it would have been like if I had.' She said it with a wry grin and for an instant Wycliffe saw again the auburn-haired girl he had fallen in love with, and he was touched by tenderness.

'So Hilda threw a stone into the water just to see where the ripples went?'

'Well, it's possible, isn't it?'

'I suppose so, but whatever her reason for pretending, she disappeared that same day and was found dead — murdered — four days later. Was that because she said she was pregnant? It doesn't seem likely, does it? On the other hand it would surely be too much of a coincidence if the two were totally unconnected.'

'I see what you mean.'

Helen picked up her book, prepared to leave it there. It was unusual for them to discuss his cases in detail; not because of professional scruples, nor because she lacked interest, but because they both recognized the need for a still centre in their lives and that was the role of The Watch House with its half-acre of garden.

He felt restless and ineffective. Too many things had happened in too short a time. He had first heard of Hilda Clemo on Monday morning and it was now only Wednesday evening. His mind was a shifting kaleidoscope of images which defied his efforts to interpret or relate. Two images recurred with monotonous regularity: the old woman's body, shrivelled and grey, petrified in death; and the young girl's, bleached and flaccid, but still retaining the form and semblance of life.

The answer was a book before bed; biography is the best sedative, a dose of proxy living. Wycliffe hoarded his biographies, journals, diaries and published letters, as a hypochondriac hoards his pills; two whole shelves of the big bookcase in the living-room. He pondered his choice, from Shonagon's *Pillow Book* to Liane de Pougy, from Trajan to Tsar Nicholas II; he hesitated over Marie Bashkirtseff but decided that she was for emergencies only.

In the end, with the instinct of a connoisseur, he settled on Pepys. Six pages equal to one Mogadon any day.

Chapter Nine

Thursday morning

Another fine morning. By half-past six Wycliffe was in the kitchen making coffee and toast, pleased with himself for having got so far without disturbing Helen. The radio chattered. Lacking any major crisis or scandal it struggled to breathe life into yesterday's dead bones and arrived, with a certain sense of achievement, at the weather forecast.

'The south-west will start the day fine and dry but a depression will bring rain and gale-force winds to Cornwall early this afternoon, and these conditions will spread rapidly over the whole of southern England to reach London and the south-east by evening.'

He had a ninety-minute drive, a press call at ten, and there were things he wanted to set in train before then.

Helen came downstairs in her dressing-gown.

'Did I wake you?'

'I don't think so. Would you like an egg or something?'

'No, this is fine. There's coffee already made.'

'When shall I see you again?'

'Probably at the weekend.'

'Don't forget Ruth will be home.'

She saw him off. The roads were quiet and he made good time, arriving at the Incident Room by half-past eight. Kersey and Lucy Lane were already in possession. He broke the news.

'I've had Franks's preliminary report: Hilda was not pregnant.'

'You mean — '

'I mean that she was told by the doctor on Saturday morning that her pregnancy test was negative.'

Both Kersey and Lucy Lane took time to digest this.

'She must have had some motive . . .'

'What could she gain?'

'I suppose it could have been sheer bloody-mindedness but it could be that she wanted to score off someone, perhaps to have some sort of lever.'

'Surely not Ralph Martin?'

'I think he was a fall-guy, set up for the family. At the moment, the point I want to make is — no word to the press. It has never been stated that she was pregnant so there is no need to say that she wasn't.

'I want you, Lucy, to tell the family.'

'Do I also tell them that she knew she wasn't pregnant?'

'Yes. They're bound to talk to the doctor at some stage. In any case I think they have a right to know.

'Now, anything else?'

Kersey said: 'Old Penrose has no inventory of Henry Rule's stuff at the farm but he's agreed to one being made. I've passed the job to a valuer in St Austell and he'll be up there this afternoon.'

'Make sure we have somebody there. I want this to be official. I'm seeing Innes this morning, but before that we have the press.'

The press briefing was tricky.

'First, I have to tell you that Agnes Rule, whose body was found in a domestic freezer at Tregelles Farm, appears to have died a natural death; there is no suggestion of foul play.'

'Then why was her body put in the freezer?'

'That is under investigation at the moment. When the investigation is complete, appropriate steps will be taken and you will be told about them.'

Like a politician, he had become practised in hiding behind a mask of words.

'About the girl. Have you had the autopsy report?'

137

'I have had a preliminary report.'

'Was it a sex killing?'

'There is no evidence of the kind of violence usually associated with a sex killing.'

'Was she strangled?'

'No, it seems that the cause of death was a blow to the head.'

'And the motive?'

'If we knew that we should be a good deal nearer finding the killer.'

It went on for half an hour but Wycliffe got away at last and, within minutes, he was driving along the now familiar route out of the village, up the hill past the caravan park and on to the Gorran road. The lane off to Tregelles was unmarked and he almost missed it. The Moyles' place looked derelict and deserted; the car bumped along the rutted lane. He could see the sea, a distant silvery streak under a blue, cloudless sky.

He parked next to the *deux chevaux* in front of the Inneses' house. As before, the door stood wide open. He knocked, but there was no reply. The sleek golden retriever appeared, gave him a disdainful glance, and withdrew. He knocked again and, after an interval, he heard the wheels of Polly Innes's chair. She came into view around the corner of the passage and advanced towards him. She wore the same grey, paint-spattered smock he had seen her in before.

'Oh, Mr Wycliffe! . . . . I've no idea where Tristan can be . . . Tristan!' She raised her voice, tense and petulant.

There was no reply, but the sound of a WC flush came from somewhere in the house.

'Do please come in.'

She manoeuvred her chair to push open the drawing-room door before Wycliffe could do it for her. 'If you will sit down . . . Tristan won't be long.' Then: 'Perhaps you will excuse me, there is something I must do in the studio.'

Wycliffe was left alone in the long room with its dark woodwork, discreet Liberty fabrics, and rows of books with mellowed spines. Blue and white porcelain pots gleamed in odd nooks. All was subdued, muted, except for the gem-like

138

luminosity of the Indian miniatures which, here and there, found a place on the walls.

Footsteps in the passage, and Innes came in. His manner was grave. 'Of course we've heard the news . . . Such a tragedy! Polly is terribly shocked.'

Before he could sit down he was followed by his wife in her wheelchair. She had changed her smock for a jade-green tunic which seemed to emphasize her extreme pallor. Wycliffe thought that she must be a very sick woman.

When they were settled Wycliffe said: 'I understand from the reports that neither of you saw or heard anything unusual during the night of Tuesday/Wednesday?'

'Nothing.'

'Forgive me, but do you share a room?'

Mrs Innes said: 'We share a bed.' The words were spiced with aggression.

'Good!' But Wycliffe did not make it clear what it was that had his approval. 'Then I'll come to the point.' He took from his briefcase the sketch diagram found in Hilda's room. 'I suppose I'm consulting you as an expert witness, but first, have you seen this before?' He handed the sketch to Innes.

Innes studied it for some time then passed it to his wife. 'May I?'

'Have you seen it before?'

'No.'

'I suppose that art historians, like others, have their special period — '

Innes interrupted with a smile. 'Mine is nineteenth-century European painting so I should know something about Pissarro, if that is what you were going to ask.'

'Yes, that sketch was found in Hilda's room pinned to the underside of a desk drawer.'

'How very odd! Do you think it was some sort of exercise? I know that she was becoming interested in pictures, particularly in the work of the Impressionists, but why hide it?'

'This letter was with the sketch; you will see that it is dated last January.'

Polly Innes said: 'That was about the time she started coming

139

here.' She was attempting to join in the conversation but she was tense, on edge.

Innes read the letter. 'How extraordinary!'

'You knew nothing of this?'

'Nothing. As we have told you, Hilda was not a confiding person.'

'Did you discuss Pissarro with her?'

'Not more than any of the other Impressionists. You see, Hilda was by no means knowledgeable about paintings but she was learning fast — as she seemed to do in any field that interested her. She was a remarkable girl which makes it all the more tragic that it should all end like this.'

His wife was looking from him to Wycliffe and back again, obviously under great stress. Abruptly, she said: 'You must excuse me, Mr Wycliffe, I'm sorry . . .'

Innes got up and opened the door for her to pass through. When he had closed it behind her he turned to Wycliffe. 'Polly is having a bad spell and this business has upset her. She was very fond of Hilda.'

When they were settled again he said: 'You think that this sketch and letter might have something to do with her death?'

'I don't know, it seems unlikely, but we have to follow every lead. This is something which Hilda saw fit to hide and that, in itself, gives it importance. Can you offer any comment on the sketch?'

'Only to repeat what the chap at the National said in his letter. Hilda's sketch suggests one of the many paintings made by Pissarro in and around the village of Pontoise where he lived for several years, only interrupted by his taking refuge in England during the Franco–Prussian war. It was, incidentally, in England that he got married.'

'Really?' Wycliffe was attentive and deferential. 'I have heard that from time to time catalogues of the known works of notable painters are compiled, indicating where they were to be found at the time of compilation.'

Innes seemed mildly surprised that Wycliffe should be so well informed.

140

'You are quite right, and at the present time one of the London auction houses is engaged in computerizing a mass of such information which they hope to keep up to date.'

'Indeed! My interest is in any of Pissarro's work which might have been in private hands in the Plymouth area at the outbreak of the last war.'

This very specific statement surprised Innes even more and it was a moment or two before he recovered his poise. 'Then you may be in luck. There is a magnificent, illustrated catalogue, compiled by Pissarro's son, Lucien, and L. Venturi, the critic and art historian: *Camille Pissarro, son art, son oeuvre*. It was published in Paris in 1937. It could be of help. If not, there are other sources.'

After a reflective pause, Innes added: 'If you wish, I will make some enquiries.'

Wycliffe declined the offer. 'Thank you, but no. Now that you have shown me how to set about it I can get the machinery to work and save you the trouble.'

They were interrupted by a scratching at the door; it was pushed open and the retriever padded into the room and settled at his master's feet.

Innes shifted uncomfortably in his chair. 'Your interest arises wholly from Hilda's sketch and her letter to the Gallery?'

'Not wholly.'

There was a lull; it was clear that Innes felt snubbed by Wycliffe's failure to enlarge. He waited for him to resume the conversation — or leave — but Wycliffe gave no sign of doing either, and the silence was beginning to be embarrassing.

Finally Wycliffe asked a question which seemed trivial: 'Are you acquainted with Harvey — Hilda's brother-in-law?'

'I know him as a neighbour; he's been here two or three times and he attended some lectures I gave in St Austell on the precursors of Impressionism.'

'I understand that he worked for a firm of fine art auctioneers in Exeter before he came here.'

Innes was polite. 'Really? He has never mentioned that but

141

it did occur to me that his interest in art generally had a professional bias.'

'Has he ever asked your opinion about a picture, about any *object d'art*, or antique?'

'No.'

'You have had no contact with him of any sort concerning items stored at Tregelles Farm?'

Innes flushed. The atmosphere had changed. He was being interrogated instead of consulted, and he realized that the whole interview might have been a disguised interrogation.

He became brusque. 'I would like you to understand, Mr Wycliffe, that I have never allowed myself to be associated with any commercial transaction involving buying, selling, or even valuing any object of the kind you describe.'

Wycliffe stood up. 'Thank you, Mr Innes — that is what I wanted to hear.'

As he was moving towards the door he turned. 'By the way, I ought to tell you: the autopsy shows that Hilda was not pregnant.'

Innes had got up from his chair and was following Wycliffe from the room but he stopped short. 'Not pregnant? You mean that she was mistaken?'

'Not even that. Hilda was given the result of a pregnancy test on Saturday morning by Hosking's locum. It was negative.'

'But that is incredible! I can scarcely believe that she would have invented such a story. If she knew it was untrue — ' He broke off. 'How very strange!'

Innes followed Wycliffe out. Wycliffe said: 'Do you mind if I leave my car here? I want to call on the Rules and it's hardly worth driving such a short distance.'

'What? No, of course not! Leave it here by all means.'

He stood watching Wycliffe as he walked off down the lane to the farm and his wife, in her wheelchair, joined him.

Once again Wycliffe was affected by the stillness and the silence. He could see over the low hedges, a seemingly deserted countryside and, in the distance, an empty sea. A rabbit, nibbling grass in the middle of the track, scuttled away only when he was within a few feet. Surely the creature was keeping very late or very early hours? Perhaps it hadn't heard about diurnal rhythms.

He let himself into the farmyard and knocked on the open door. Jane Rule's cracked voice called: 'You can come in.'

She was standing over the stove, gently stirring the contents of a large saucepan. She raised a spoonful to her lips and tasted it. The smell was appealing and his taste-buds were tickled. Did they live on soups and stews?

'Smells good.'

'It is good. You cook it slow and never let it boil.' She spooned some into a cup and handed the cup to him. 'Try it.'

Consorting with suspected criminals? Didn't fat-cat lawyers do it every day?

'Mrs Rule, are you telling the Court that the chief superintendent shared your meal with you?'

But he accepted the soup. In part it was in reaction against the atmosphere he had just left.

God knows what was in it but the soup had a wonderfully satisfying taste and substance.

'Anyway, what are you here for now?'

'Several things, but first may I use your telephone? It's long distance but I'll pay for the call.'

She shrugged and nodded towards the telephone which was bracketed to the wall.

He dialled Directory Enquiries, asked for the number of the Courtauld Institute, then dialled.

He had a double purpose: first, to set the business of the pictures in train, and then to see Jane Rule's reaction — if any.

'The Courtauld? . . . May I speak to Mr David Joyce, please? . . . Chief Superintendent Wycliffe . . .'

David Joyce had been called as an expert witness in the Marcella Tate case, just a year ago.

'Mr Joyce . . . Wycliffe . . . You remember?'

Joyce did remember and Wycliffe explained what he wanted. 'Any Pissarros that were in private hands in the neighbourhood

143

of Plymouth during or shortly after the last war . . . Is there a chance? I mean, I hope I'm not asking too much?'

'It's not asking much for me to look up the Pissarro–Venturi catalogue. That came out in '37 and might help. If that doesn't yield, we'll try other possibles. Over the past fifty years we've got together quite a lot of material on the whereabouts of Impressionist works which we try to update. Leave it to me and I'll call you back this afternoon. I may not have anything for you then but at least I should be able to give you the odds.'

Jane Rule was showing no interest. She had gone back to the stove and was lifting dripping anonymous chunks of something from another saucepan into an enamel bowl, while the cat and dog fawned about her legs.

Wycliffe gave Joyce the Incident Room number.

Joyce said: 'What's the weather like down there?'

'Lovely, at the moment.'

'It's the same here, but I'd swap my roofs with chimney pots for your harbour with fishing boats any day.'

Jane had placed the enamel bowl on the floor, and cat and dog were feeding amicably. Now she was standing by the table, motionless. It was as though she could, at will, achieve a state of suspended animation.

Wycliffe took out his wallet and handed her a note. 'That will cover the cost of the call, thank you.'

She said nothing but she crumpled the note into the pocket of her apron.

'I wanted you to know that Hilda was not pregnant.'

'She made it up?'

'Yes.'

'Ah!'

'You don't seem surprised.'

'That girl couldn't resist stirring.'

'Stirring?'

'She looked for trouble, and where she couldn't find it, she made it. James is a fool and he spoilt her, but I feel sorry for him.'

'You feel sorry for James Clemo? But early Wednesday morning he was arrested in your yard with a shotgun.'

144

'Oh, that!' She was laying places on the table for herself and her son. 'With him it's all bluster; he's always been the same, but with the guts he's got he couldn't shoot a rabbit.'

'Why was he so sure that it was your son who assaulted Hilda?'

She was cutting large chunks of bread from a loaf. She said nothing and Wycliffe persisted: 'Mrs Rule, I am reaching a stage where I have to have answers to certain questions. Whether those answers are connected with my investigation or not, I will decide, but I intend to have them. Why was James Clemo convinced that Clifford raped and murdered his daughter?'

Jane looked up at the little clock, ticking away on the mantelpiece. 'He'll be coming in soon for his meal. He's got no watch but he's never more'n ten minutes out.'

'Mrs Rule!'

Her eyes sought his and she seemed to resign herself. 'All right! You know about Esther?'

'I know that she came to work here when she left school, before the Clemos took her in.'

Jane was smoothing the table-top with a skinny hand. 'Six months after she came here she was assaulted and raped.'

'By your son?'

'That's what they said; that's what they got me to agree to.'

'I don't understand.'

'No. Elinor, James's mother, her that they buried last Friday, she arranged it all.' Jane pursed her lips. 'She was a strong-minded woman.'

'But what had she to do with — '

'It was Gordon — my husband, her brother — who did it . . . She was a skinny little thing and though her mother was what she was, Esther was innocent. She'd carry on like we did, she'd strip to the waist to wash at the sink and not think twice about it . . . But she done it once too often. One day when I was out, Gordon took her. It frightened the poor little thing nearly to death, she couldn't speak for hours. I should've known better than to let her carry on like that.

'Anyway, old man Clemo, James's father, was alive then — and if he'd known it was Gordon he'd 've had us off the farm

145

quicker'n you could say knife. Strict chapel he was; we Rules was always church.'

She sighed. 'So the fault was put on Clifford. Gordon could do no wrong where Elinor was concerned, and she had it all worked out. Clifford was weak in the head so it wouldn't hurt him. Esther's mother, who didn't care tuppence anyway, was squared, and the girl was promised a real home as one of the Clemo family if she kept her mouth shut. When you come to think of it the poor lil' toad didn' have much option, did she?'

'And James Clemo doesn't know this?'

She looked him in the eyes. 'After Elinor died last Friday, Esther and me was the only ones living to know it until this minute. They never told Clifford nothing.' There were heavy footsteps in the yard. 'Here he is. Will all this have to come out now?'

'Why should it?'

'Are you going? There's a man coming from the lawyer this afternoon to make a list of Agnes's stuff.'

'I know. I want to look around her room before I go.'

Jane shrugged. 'I only live here.'

The door opened and Clifford came in. 'Oh!'

'Sit down and have your soup. You can dish it up yourself.'

Wycliffe went upstairs to what had been the old lady's room. The curtains were drawn over the small window so the room was almost in darkness. He drew them back. It all looked much the same as it had done when he was there with Kersey. Only the dummy head with its grey wig was missing.

He had come to look at the pictures. There were four oil paintings of different sizes in swept, gilded frames. He was no authority on paintings but they looked to him like 'furnishing pictures', the frames probably more valuable than the paintings. All four bore signatures but he did not recognize any of them.

He went back downstairs. Clifford was eating his meal but Jane was standing, waiting.

'Have you seen all you want to?' She seemed almost reluctant to let him go and followed him out. They stood, looking at the littered yard, the straw, the manure, the pecking hens, the decaying sheds and rusting machinery.

Jane Rule said: 'What will happen to me — about Agnes, I mean?'

'The autopsy showed that she died a natural death.'

'So?'

'You concealed her death in a manner that aggravated the offence. In all the circumstances you'll probably get a suspended sentence, but you must have a lawyer.'

She was silent for a while then she said: 'I shan't last for ever, and what'll happen to him when I'm gone? What will he do?' The questions were rhetorical.

Wycliffe said: 'Has Bertie Harvey ever been in the house — apart from the old dairy?'

'Two or three times, he came to see Agnes with the girl.'

'You mean Hilda?'

'Yes; they two was very thick but it was none of my business.'

'What did they come to see Agnes about?'

'How should I know? It was before she went queer, when she had her own life so to speak. She didn't tell me more'n she had to. Lately I've wondered if she was selling stuff through him — small things.'

'Apart from her visits with Bertie, did Hilda come here often, alone?'

'Often? I dunno about that — once in a month or six weeks maybe.'

'Why did she come? Have you any idea?'

'She didn't come to see me, that's for sure. Once when I went up there for something she seemed to be reading to Agnes, another time she was drawing.'

'*Drawing?*'

'That's what I said. She was doing something with pencil and paper and it wasn't writing.'

'What was she drawing?'

'I never looked to see.'

'And Innes — did he ever come here?'

'He was never in the house to my knowledge but I can't speak for when I was out.'

'Do you go out much?'

'Every Friday I go over to St Austell for my shopping. It's cheaper.'

Wycliffe nodded to the dilapidated Morris Minor. 'You drive over?'

'I don't walk, if that's what you mean; 'tis the best part of eight mile.'

Wycliffe lingered in the sun, as though he too was reluctant to break off contact. It was odd; he felt a perverse admiration for Jane Rule, struggling against the odds, and a kind of kinship. As a boy, living in a remote rural area, he had known other women like Jane, other amiable half-wits like Clifford, other families like the Rules and the Clemos with their loyalties and their feuds, their 'rich' relatives, and their poor dependants.

'Did Agnes show any interest in her pictures?'

'She used to change them sometimes.'

'Change them?'

'With ones that was in store. She was always swapping things around when she was herself. "I think I'll have up that little chest, Jane, this great thing takes up too much room." Clifford and me would've spent half our time humping furniture up and downstairs if she had her way.'

He made up his mind at last and walked back to the car. The Innes place seemed silent and deserted but the *deux chevaux* was still there and the front door was wide open.

Chapter Ten

Thursday afternoon

'Lets go and get some lunch.'

Wycliffe and Kersey walked along the quay and as they reached the wharf the brilliant light was dimmed as clouds building from the south-west obscured the sun.

'Weather's breaking,' Kersey said.

'The Seiners all right with you?'

'Fine.'

A local lad in the Force had commended The Seiners. It was tucked away inconspicuously in an alley and the entrance looked like the way into a private house, so that it was almost emmet-proof. (Emmet = Old English for ant, and modern Cornish for 'summer visitors'.) The landlord's wife was celebrated for her pasties but these had to be ordered in advance so Wycliffe and Kersey had to settle for a helping of the communal beef pie.

Wycliffe ordered a lager for himself and a bitter for Kersey. 'That soup made me thirsty.'

'What soup?'

'Never mind.'

They found a tile-topped table for two in a corner by a window that was little wider than an arrow slit. The locals preferred to huddle around the bar, many of them stood, pasty in hand. There was a hubbub of chat and the occasional burst of laughter, so it was possible to talk, and nobody was interested. Wycliffe brought Kersey up to date.

'You think this picture business might lead somewhere?'

'I've no idea. We are investigating a murder and looking for a

149

motive. Hilda was enquiring about a Pissarro painting and trying to keep her interest in it to herself. Where did she see it? Franks says that Henry Rule made a packet acquiring the contents of blitzed properties during the war, and out of newly impoverished and gullible old ladies afterwards. It seems that some of his acquisitions bordered on theft. It might be useful to find out whether any of Pissarro's works were in Henry's catchment area at the time.'

'Surely he'd have unloaded them long ago?'

'I don't know, pictures in that category are dangerous goods unless you have access to the underground market, and Rule had already burned his fingers once or twice.'

It was beginning to rain. Through the little window Wycliffe could see fat drops making dark splashes on the cobbles. 'Have you ever thrown a stone into a pool and watched the ripples?'

Kersey knew his Wycliffe and was equal to him. 'I think I can remember something of the sort, sir.'

'If you throw in two or three, a few feet apart, you get more fun but it's a bit of a mess where the ripples meet and interact, cancelling or deflecting each other.'

'I must try it sometime. You think someone has been throwing stones into our pool?'

'I'm sure of it. All I'm saying is that we mustn't fall into the trap of looking for one solution to two, or even three problems.'

'You don't think it's time we started turning the screw a bit on the obvious candidates?'

'We're not ready. When we start we must know exactly where we are going.'

Kersey emptied his glass. 'Will you have another?'

'I'd prefer a coffee.'

They had to run the gauntlet of the rain back along the North Quay to the Incident Room. Potter, the fat DC, was duty officer. 'Miss Esther Clemo is upstairs with DS Lane, sir.'

Wycliffe went upstairs. Lucy Lane was sitting at the desk, her back to the window; Esther was perched, bolt upright, on a chair by the desk. She wore a navy-blue gaberdine mackintosh like a schoolgirl's, and a once stylish toque which she must have rescued from a wedding. Her forehead was decorated with sticking plaster and it was obvious that she had a bandage on her gloved right hand.

'Miss Clemo has come to give us some information, sir.'

Esther was uneasy. 'I went to the priest and he told me that it was my duty. I only hope he was right.'

Wycliffe signalled to Lucy Lane to continue and took a chair near the door.

They waited.

'You don't need me to tell you that James made a fool of himself on Tuesday night. I was afraid he might do something silly and when I woke up in the early morning I had a feeling . . . He'd been in such a state that evening — and he'd been drinking. Anyway, I looked in his room and he wasn't there. He wasn't in his office either and his gun was missing, so I went after him.' She broke off with a small gesture.

'You knew, or guessed where he'd gone?'

'I knew all right! Anyway, I went up through the park and through the trees, then as I was passing the quarry pool, I heard a loud splash.' She paused, disturbed by the recollection. 'I couldn't for the life of me make out what it could be. I waited, and almost turned back, but nothing else happened so I went on.

'When I got to the stile into the farmyard I heard a commotion. It was James and the policeman, then Jane Rule joined in so I knew it was all right. I mean he hadn't done anything. I never really thought he would but — ' The blue eyes sought Lucy's in concern. 'James's bark is always worse than his bite but, upset like he was — and, like I said, he'd been drinking — I couldn't be sure . . .'

She brought her hands together against her flat chest. 'First I was for going into the yard with the others and getting him out of it, but I didn't want to make things worse; I know what he is, so I started back. I forgot to say it was very foggy. Anyway, when I reached where the path leads off round the top of the quarry I saw a man standing on the path. He must have been ten yards or so from me.' She shuddered. 'I was frightened, I'm not sure why I was so frightened. I mean, I didn't know then what he'd done, but there it was. I ran down the track and back through the trees . . .' She raised her hand to her forehead. 'That was when I fell down and did this.'

'You're sure it was a man?'

She frowned. 'Yes, but I couldn't tell you why.'

'Was he tall or short, thin or fat?'

'He wasn't fat, but what with the mist and the dark . . . I think he must have been fairly tall.'

'Is that what you came to tell us, Miss Clemo?'

She took a deep breath. 'No, not all. I wish it was.' She was distressed.

Lucy Lane said: 'Take your time, Miss Clemo.'

She nodded. 'When I got back into the house I went up to my room and I noticed that Bertie's door was a bit open. I don't know why, but it made me wonder . . . Anyway, I went into his room . . . He wasn't there, his bed hadn't been slept in.'

Wycliffe spoke for the first time: 'This was yesterday morning, Miss Clemo. You must have seen him since. Have you said anything to him?'

She turned to look at Wycliffe, incredulous. 'There was nothing I could say.'

'No, perhaps not, but has anything about him or his behaviour made you think that he may be aware of your suspicion?'

She made an impatient movement. 'Can you imagine what it's like in that house with everything that's happened since Friday, when we buried Granny Clemo?'

'I'm sorry.'

'We don't look at each other, let alone speak if we can help it.'

The telephone rang. Lucy Lane answered. 'Mr Joyce for you, sir; Courtauld Institute.'

'I'll take it downstairs.' He turned to Esther. 'If you will excuse me . . .'

Joyce said: 'I've got something for you but whether it's what you want is another matter. Have you ever heard of Alleston Manor?'

'I've heard of it but I can't place it at the moment.'

152

'It's somewhere on your patch — on the Tamar, a few miles from Plymouth, I think. Anyway we have a record, dated 1937, of two Pissarros in the possession of the Honourable Mrs Melville-Treece at Alleston Manor. I haven't a clue what happened to them, but we have reproductions which are not too bad for the time.'

'Can you give me titles?'

'Yes. One is *The Village of Pontoise*, and the other, *Fruit Trees at the Hermitage*, both painted in the same year — 1876 — and both oil on canvas.'

'Sizes?'

'The first, eighteen inches by twenty-one; the second, twenty-four inches by twenty-eight.'

'What does the first look like?' Wycliffe was making notes.

'Village street, cottages, larger houses, trees, farm carts and figures. He painted several that were somewhat similar.'

'Sounds promising. Would it be possible to send me a photocopy? Colour doesn't matter at this stage.'

'No problem. I'll put it in the post tonight.'

As a schoolboy studying biology, Wycliffe had shaken samples of soil with water in glass cylinders and watched the turmoil of suspended particles of all sorts and sizes. Then, with a pinch of lime added, in a remarkably short space of time, order would begin to appear out of chaos as the particles settled into beautifully graded layers. Something like that seemed to happen in some of his cases and he felt now that he might just have been handed that pinch of lime.

He went back upstairs.

'Miss Clemo has been telling me — ' Lucy and Esther seemed to have established a rapport.

'I was telling Miss Lane that Bertie was far too familiar with Hilda but I can't believe that he killed her; he always seems to me a weak, not a violent man, but there's no knowing what will happen between a mature man and a girl like Hilda.'

'Like Hilda?'

Esther shook her head. 'She was perverse, there's no denying that, and when a young girl realizes her power over men but she

153

hasn't got the sense to see its dangers — ' She broke off and, to Wycliffe's astonishment, tears were coursing down her pale cheeks. 'I'm sorry . . . I only hope I've done the right thing.'

'You can be sure of that. We have to have all the facts and it's up to us to sort them out.'

'Then I hope you will, for all our sakes.'

'Just one more question, Miss Clemo: the figure you saw through the mist, do you really think it was Bertie?'

She hesitated, frowning. 'I don't know what to say. It could have been but it could have been almost any man. I couldn't see . . .'

Wycliffe said: 'I think we should let it be known that you have been here.'

'But that's just what I don't want! I thought I could come here . . . Father Dole assured me that you wouldn't — '

Wycliffe interrupted: 'I don't want to frighten you, Miss Clemo, but if whoever you saw realizes you have been to the police and made a statement, there will be no point in him taking any steps against you.'

She was agitated. 'You think that he might?'

'We have to make sure that he doesn't. You are willing to make a formal statement?'

She looked at him, weary and frightened. 'I suppose so.'

'If you agree, we will telephone the house and tell them you will be delayed because you are here making a statement.'

She nodded, listless. 'If that's what you think.'

'And one other thing: shouldn't you tell James the truth about what happened years ago when you were at Tregelles?'

She flushed like a girl. 'I've already told him — this morning.' She spoke in little above a whisper. 'He was upset, and he holds it against me.'

'I'm glad you told him. Now Miss Lane will show you to the next room and arrange for someone to take down what you have told us. Afterwards you will be asked to sign it, then we will have you driven back home.

'Would you like a cup of tea — or coffee?'

She nodded. 'Tea, please.'

Lucy took her away, leaving Wycliffe thoughtful. He was often depressed by the sadness he found about him, especially amongst women. In a way Esther and Jane Rule were in the same boat, they belonged to a breed of women who were either unaware of, or disillusioned by their sex, their affection always blunted by its target.

He went downstairs, feeling restless. A mixed bag of DCs and PCs were at the keyboards, nourishing the computer with titbits from the lives of people, some of whom had never heard of Hilda Clemo until she became a news item on the television. Kersey was standing, looking out of the shop window. It had been covered half-way up with brown paper to discourage spectators.

The wind was rising in gusts which swept curtains of rain over the grey sea, over the harbour, and on to the gleaming, grey roofs of the clustered houses. It was no longer a toy-town fishing village for the tourist; in a strange way it seemed to have recovered its identity and its dignity.

Kersey said: 'I've just taken a call from a ward sister at Truro City Hospital. One of her patients thinks he saw Hilda Clemo on Saturday afternoon, near Tregelles. It seems he's a rod-and-line, shore-fishing buff, and he was on his way to his favourite slippery rock near Pabyer Point. Do you think we should send someone down?'

'How did he get himself into hospital?'

'An RTA on Sunday night, his car climbed the hedge and he was badly knocked about; only now able to sit up and take notice.'

'Yes, better get somebody down there. Send Lucy when she's finished upstairs.'

Wycliffe turned to Potter who, as usual, had a mug of tea at his elbow. 'Look in the phone book for Melville-Treece. Could be the Honourable Mrs, but I'm not sure if she's still with us. Last known address, Alleston Manor.'

PC Richards, one of the local lads, spoke up. 'Excuse me, sir, there's a Mrs Melville-Treece, a very old woman, who lives with her daughter up Heligan way, just a couple of miles from the

155

village. Stanley House, it's called. I think she or her family used to have Alleston Manor.'

Potter had found her in the phone book. 'Here we are, sir; "Melville-Treece, the Hon. Mrs M., Stanley House — "'

'See if you can get her on the phone and ask her if she'll see me in the next half-hour.'

It was arranged.

Wycliffe got PC Richards to drive him, a fresh-faced youth who looked as though he should still be at school. Policemen really were getting younger, dammit! 'How long have you been in the Force, Richards?'

'Three years, sir; I'm twenty-two.'

Twenty-two. Wycliffe had been going out with Helen for five years when he was twenty-two, and they were planning to get married.

'Are you married?'

'Hope to be next year, sir.'

Stanley House stood four-square with no nonsense and little charm, built by some hard-headed Cornishman who had made his money out of china clay, or tin, or copper, early in the last century. It fronted on a balustraded terrace and a lawn, surrounded by rhododendron thickets and bounded by a screen of trees. When he stood on his terrace and surveyed his domain he must have felt that he had arrived. Now he and his family had long gone.

'How can I help you, Chief Superintendent?'

The Honourable Mrs Melville-Treece, at eighty-eight, was upright and ambulant, not to say spry. Her voice was a trifle cracked, but she spoke with that incisive and precise enunciation which has become a badge of the Royals.

Wycliffe explained what he wanted, and hoped that the old lady was as indulgent as she was courteous.

'You see, Mr Wycliffe, the old house at Alleston Manor was destroyed by enemy action during the war. It was during one of the night bombing raids on Plymouth. A German bomber being chased, so they said, by night fighters, unloaded its bombs at random and one came down in the yard behind the house. The

156

back of the house was totally destroyed, though the front was untouched. However, architects advised me that any rebuilding would have to be total and that was out of the question. The old house was too big for us anyway.'

She smiled. 'I recall that I was in the small drawing-room with my daughter, Gwendoline, when the bomb dropped and we were listening to the comedian, Tommy Handley, on the wireless.'

Gwendoline, now a plump, matronly woman in her fifties, hovered and smiled but spoke little.

Above the fireplace there was a 'Bloomsbury' portrait of mother and infant daughter.

Wycliffe said: 'The Pissarros — I understand that there were two of them?'

'Yes, indeed, and looking back I realize they were potentially our most valuable possessions from a pecuniary point of view. At the time I did not see them as very important. They had been in the family for many years; my paternal grandfather bought them when he was attached to the embassy in Paris, sometime in the late seventies or early eighties of the last century.'

It was the sort of conversation to be had over cups of China tea in Royal Worcester cups, with Osborne biscuits to nibble. But there was something incongruous about the room; it reminded Wycliffe of a vestry in a Methodist chapel; the furniture, an eclectic assemblage, obviously comprising valued pieces from the old house, now looked as uncomfortable as lots in a saleroom. And the gloom outside was no help; water cascaded down the window-panes, and the light was steely grey.

Mrs Melville-Treece went to a nest of bookshelves and, putting on her spectacles, selected a magazine which she opened and handed to Wycliffe. 'Here is an article published in June 1939. It is really about the old house but the Pissarro pictures are featured there.'

The article was one of a series: 'The Smaller Country Houses of England. Alleston Manor — Number 19.' It referred to the house as 'a perfect example of late eighteenth-century small-scale domestic architecture'. There were photographs of the exterior and of the more important rooms, with colour pictures of some of its contents, including the two Pissarros.

'You may borrow the magazine if you wish.'

It seemed to Wycliffe that one of the pictures might well have been the original of Hilda's sketch.

'Were the pictures destroyed in the bombing?'

'Indeed they were not! The big drawing-room was scarcely damaged. But on the night of the bombing we were advised to move out of the house at once and we went to a cousin of mine. The authorities arranged for a guard on the house and so it remained for, oh, several days, at least. People were rightly more concerned about the carnage in the city. At any rate, when the experts arrived to assess the damage, the Pissarros were missing. The police did what they could but, there again, they had more important things to occupy their time.'

'And you've heard nothing of them since?'

'Nothing, until your visit this afternoon. Do you think it possible that they may be recovered?'

Wycliffe was cautious. 'It seems unlikely; indeed, their connection with my case is, at most, tenuous, and may be non-existent. Just one more question: do you have any recollection of an antiques dealer called Rule? He had his shop in Queen Mary Street.'

Her expression quickened. 'Henry Rule? Of course I remember him! When my husband was alive (my husband was in the RNVR and he was killed in the early months of the war), we did quite a lot of business with Henry. Later, he was a pillar of strength in all the problems arising from our bomb. As a matter of fact it was he who found us this house.'

Mrs Melville-Treece was too well bred to ask questions and Wycliffe did his best to respond to the old lady's courtesy and charm. They parted with expressions of mutual goodwill.

Back in the car Wycliffe compared the magazine reproduction of the Pontoise street scene with a photocopy of Hilda's sketch and decided that she must have had access either to the original picture or to a reproduction.

The young policeman acting as his chauffeur, asked: 'Back to the Incident Room, sir?'

Wycliffe hesitated. 'No, Tregelles Farm. Do you know where it is?'

The wind was still rising and from the top of the hill they were looking out over the bay where a leaden sea was streaked with white.

There was a car already parked in the lane outside Tregelles and Wycliffe remembered the valuer making his inventory. Jane Rule was surprised to see him back so soon but she was almost welcoming. 'What is it now?'

He showed her the two colour reproductions in Mrs Melville-Treece's magazine. 'Have you ever seen a picture like either of these before?'

She opened a drawer of the kitchen table and came out with a pair of spectacles which she put on. They transformed her face, giving it a sudden dignity.

She studied the reproductions then pointed to one of them with her forefinger. 'I've seen that one.'

It was the Pontoise street scene.

'You're sure?'

She nodded. 'I don't take much account of pictures as a rule but I liked that one. It was, well . . . pretty. Agnes had it hanging over her bed for a long time. It was in a nice frame, just like the one in the picture.'

'What happened to it?'

Jane Rule shrugged. 'What's the good of asking me? I told you she was for ever changing things round. It could be out in the old dairy now for all I know.'

'When, approximately, was it hanging in her bedroom?'

She took off her spectacles. 'Before she went queer, anyway. A year ago, perhaps.'

Sounds of furniture being shifted came from the old dairy. 'While I'm here I'll have a word with the valuer.'

Jane tossed her head. 'Three of 'em out there; two to do the work and the other to watch — and one of your lot. You can go through the kitchen if you like.'

159

He did, and noticed the patch on the floor where the freezer had stood. Now it was in the hands of forensic specialists and much good it would do them.

Mr Tresidder, the valuer, was a stocky Cornishman, well laid back, and inclined to be amused by it all. 'There's some decent stuff here; a good thing the place seems to be dry.'

His two assistants were moving furniture about like pieces on a chequers board in order to reach the rest. Nothing could be taken outside because of the rain.

A uniformed policeman looked on.

'Have you been through the pictures?'

A shrug. 'Nothing much there — some of the frames would fetch a bit.'

'No lost Impressionists?'

A polite chuckle. 'Jane should be so lucky! I suppose it all comes to her?'

'I really don't know what will happen to it. Will you show me how the pictures are stored?'

If the valuer wondered at Wycliffe's interest he made no comment. There were two crates with open tops, one for the smaller, and one for the larger pictures. In the crates the frames stood on edge with layers of felt between.

'You can see the list if you want to.' Tresidder removed two sheets from his file and handed them to Wycliffe. 'Edwardian wall-covering, and not very special at that. As I say, he must have bought them for the frames.'

It was 16.45 by the digital clock in the Incident Room, almost exactly five days since Hilda had walked off the *Sea Spray* when Ralph Martin was about to land his passengers for their Cornish cream teas. No pleasure boats had put to sea today; the quays and the harbour were deserted except for those boatmen engaged in moving craft from the outer to the inner harbour in case the gale worsened.

Wycliffe joined Kersey in the upstair room. 'I think we've got as far as we can. Is Lucy back yet?'

'Not yet. Are you intending to make a move now?'

160

'Tomorrow morning. We shall need a scenes-of-crime team standing by and I want our frogman to make another search of the quarry pool — this time for anything that might have been used to transport the body.'

They talked until Lucy Lane arrived back from her interview with the injured man.

'Poor chap, he's pretty badly knocked about; his car climbed the hedge when he swerved to avoid a straying cow.'

'Don't tell us what he had to say.' Kersey, being Kersey.

'It doesn't amount to a lot but it's odd. He was on his way to the cliffs, down the lane to Tregelles and the footpath. As he reached the Innes place he saw Hilda — he knew her by sight — walk up to the front door, which was open. The dog came out, making a fuss of her, and she went in with the dog.'

'He's saying she was alone?'

'Yes.'

'She didn't knock?'

'Not according to him.'

'And the time?'

'He was vague about time but thought it was "about five".'

'Was the *deux chevaux* there?'

'I'm afraid I didn't ask that.'

'Then get on to the ward sister and ask her to ask him.'

It was a lengthy business, with the ward sister feeling that she had something better to do than run errands, but the answer came eventually: 'He says the *deux chevaux* was not there. He was accustomed to seeing it there and noticed that it had gone.'

During the night the gale strengthened and several times Wycliffe was awakened by the buffeting of the wind causing the hotel building to shudder. Towards dawn it eased but, at seven o'clock, when he looked out of his bedroom window, it was still raining, the sky was leaden and the crests on the still turbulent sea were of dazzling white. Waves smashed against the southern breakwater, sending up sheets of spray.

Chapter Eleven

Friday morning

Wycliffe held an early briefing with Kersey, Lucy Lane and Dixon. In their candid moments research scientists admit that the decision to publish is a critical one: have they really got enough data to support their conclusions in the face of criticism? The criminal investigator has a similar difficulty, he has to be sure that, by showing his hand, he will neither offer the criminal a loophole, nor transgress the rules of procedure so that he ends up with egg on his face and an acquittal on technical grounds.

The four, with Kersey driving, made their way to the caravan park. Rain was driven before a strong south-easterly — a grey wind which bleached the colour from land and sea. There would be many more fine, warm days but they would be autumn days; summer had gone for another year.

It was nine o'clock and people were on the move between their tents and caravans and the toilet blocks; some carried umbrellas which were difficult to control, others held sheets of plastic over their heads. The grass and the roadways were littered with leaves and even twigs, torn from the trees.

Wycliffe went to Reception and spoke to the young girl on duty. She was naively helpful, which seemed out of keeping with an excess of lipstick and eye-shadow, and an ethnic hair-do.

'Is Mr Harvey about?'

'Are you . . .?'

'Chief Superintendent Wycliffe.'

162

'I thought so. Bertie's up in his office in the Recreation Centre; I spoke to him on the phone just now.'

'And Mrs Harvey?'

'She phoned too; she's coming across later.' She added, lowering her voice: 'I think she's having trouble with her father. He thought the world of Hilda, you know — spoilt her. Now he's in a terrible state.'

They drove up through the park and found Bertie in his office, next to the room where sports gear was hired to customers. It was Wycliffe's first face-to-face encounter with him.

'Mr Harvey? Mr Albert Harvey?'

'That's me or, if you prefer it, I am he.' A compulsive droll but not looking the part just now; his sallow skin was unnaturally pale and his eyes were dark with tiredness. He was sitting at his desk, back to the window, and there were papers everywhere, but Wycliffe felt sure that he had been sitting brooding when they arrived.

'We want to talk to you, Mr Harvey.'

Harvey looked from Wycliffe to the other three and made some attempt at banter. 'All four of you? I doubt if my seating accommodation will run to it.'

'DS Lane and DC Dixon would like to take a look around the premises.'

A sudden stiffening. 'You mean a search? Have you got a warrant?'

'No, but I'm sure Mr Clemo would give his permission. If you are in doubt you had better ring him.'

'I see; so it doesn't matter what I say.'

Lucy Lane and Wycliffe exchanged glances and she left, with Dixon following.

'They will do the outside premises first.'

Wycliffe was in no hurry. He seemed to be taking stock of the office where the only unusual feature was the collection of framed photographs of children on the walls.

Harvey, still battling, said: 'My shop window.'

'Where were you employed before you came here, Mr Harvey?'

'With a firm of auctioneers in Exeter.'

'Lovell and Delbos, the fine art auctioneers?'

'You know, so why ask?'

'And before that?'

'I suppose you know that too. I worked for Henry Rule at his shop in Queen Mary Street, Plymouth.'

'For how long?'

'From the time I left school until he retired.'

'About five years?'

'About that.'

Kersey said: 'I suppose it was a useful apprenticeship in the crooked side of the business, especially when you came to set up deals on your own account.'

Harvey flushed. 'I don't know what you're talking about!' It was a commendable effort at indignation.

Wycliffe was soothing. 'Anyway, with all that experience you must feel pretty much at home in the world of antiques, particularly in the fine art market.'

'I knew my job.' He was playing with a ball-point, flicking it in and out.

'An odd coincidence that you should come here and marry the great-niece of your first employer.'

Harvey was wary and defensive. 'I came here by chance with a former school-friend when we were having a caravan holiday, touring the coasts of Devon and Cornwall and I happened to meet Alice.'

'When did you discover her connection with Henry Rule?'

'Not for several weeks. I used to come down for the odd weekend now and then and it cropped up in casual conversation. Anyway, why should I have been all that interested?'

'A good question, Mr Harvey, but we'll come to that later.' Wycliffe reached into his brief-case and came out with a photograph of the nude Bertie found in Hilda's room. 'Perhaps you can tell us how Hilda got hold of this?'

Harvey's astonishment was real enough and it was a moment or two before he decided how to cope. Then, with an embarrassed laugh, and man-to-man candour, he said: 'It was a damn silly joke.'

Kersey thrust out his lower lip. 'Funny sort of joke to have with your wife's young sister.'

'You think so? Perhaps you're right. The fact is I was thinking of taking up photography as a full-time occupation.' A bleak look round the little office. 'A chance to get out of this! Anyway, I wanted to try my hand at some nude studies and I asked Hilda to pose for me. She said she would if I let her take one of me first.'

'And did she keep to the bargain?'

'Do women ever? No, she backed out.'

Wycliffe shook his head. 'Ingenious but improbable, Mr Harvey. Good lies are always simple.' He reached again into his brief-case. 'But we'll come back to photographs; let's talk about paintings. Look at this!' He handed over the sketch Hilda had made of the Pissarro painting. 'That is a photocopy; the original was found in Hilda's room. Have you seen it before?'

Harvey looked at the sketch. 'No.'

'Nor this?' A photocopy of the letter from the National Gallery.

Harvey took the letter and glanced through it mechanically. 'No, it's very odd, though.'

'Do you know anything of the circumstances in which Hilda did this?'

'No.'

Wycliffe took back the photocopies and Kersey said: 'Careful, Mr Harvey, there are several prints on the letter and the sketch; now yours are on the photocopies.'

Harvey's hands were clasped in front of him on the desk. He was putting on a good front but the strain was showing. 'Do you think I would have let her do that if she'd asked me first? It's obvious that nobody could give an opinion about a picture from a sketch.'

Wycliffe said: 'I'm not suggesting that she consulted you beforehand, but did she show you the reply?'

He was staring down at the top of his desk, his thin face drawn, his cheeks hollowed by shadows, but he managed a rueful grin.

'In view of everything, I don't have much choice, do I? Yes, she did show me the letter.'

'How did she explain what she had done?'

'She said she had seen a picture like it — an oil painting — and she wanted to know if it was genuine and what it was worth.'

'I wonder where she could have seen it?' Kersey, innocent.

'She wouldn't say, and I told her that without seeing the original I couldn't help her.'

Wycliffe said: 'So after a little persuasion she took you along to Agnes Rule's room to show you the picture hanging on the wall.'

Harvey sat back in his chair. 'Walk into my parlour said the spider to the fly.'

Wycliffe was casual. 'We are not inviting you into any trap, Mr Harvey, there's no need. We know that you made at least two visits to Agnes Rule, with Hilda, at that time. Agnes sometimes changed her pictures around and those removed were stored in the old dairy. When she became senile and Jane Rule began to dispose of items of furniture to pay for the old lady's keep, you had access to that store. Think it over, Mr Harvey.'

There was a long pause. The only sounds came from the seemingly frantic ticking of Harvey's little clock and the beating of the rain against the window. Shimmering through the watery panes Wycliffe could see the diving-board rising above the swimming-pool, a ghostly constructivist sculpture.

Wycliffe was the first to speak. 'We now know precisely which picture we are talking about — the one of which Hilda made the sketch.'

He produced the magazine with the two colour reproductions and got up to lay it, open, on Harvey's desk. 'Both those paintings were in the possession of Mrs Melville-Treece of Alleston Manor when her house was bombed during the Plymouth blitz.'

Harvey looked at the magazine briefly then pushed it away.

Wycliffe went on: 'In the confusion following the air-raid, these pictures were stolen and they've never been seen since. The Melville-Treece family had a lot of dealings with Henry Rule and he played a large part in clearing up immediately after the bombing of the Melville-Treece house. Now it seems that one of those pictures turned up among his effects only to disappear again . . .'

Kersey leaned forward and brought his face close to Harvey's. 'What happened to it, Mr Harvey? Any ideas?'

Harvey was staring at the papers on his desk. In a low voice he said: 'All right! Hilda told me about the picture after she failed to get help from the Gallery and I went to see it with her. I went a couple of times, sounding out the old lady, but she wouldn't consider parting with it.' He broke off, protesting: 'I had a perfect right to try! As far as I knew the picture was hers to do as she liked with.' He looked from one to the other of the two policemen as though seeking some hint of agreement.

Wycliffe said: 'So what happened?'

'Nothing happened as far as I was concerned. The old lady went queer, Hilda stopped going there, and that was that.'

'And you put it clean out of your mind; you didn't even approach Jane during your negotiations over furniture?'

He hesitated. 'I did mention it and she said she had no idea what had happened to the picture. Of course, she was lying.'

'So you checked over the stuff in the old dairy just in case.'

Harvey said nothing.

Dixon came in and stood, waiting. Kersey turned to glare at him. Wycliffe said: 'All right, Dixon, go through.'

Harvey watched the detective go into his darkroom and close the door behind him. 'What's he looking for in there? Don't I have the right to know what he's looking for?'

Wycliffe was smooth. 'I thought you knew already. He's looking for two paintings worth anything up to half a million, but he is also looking for something much more important: for evidence of where Hilda's body was kept for four days; for the clothes she was wearing when she disappeared; for her shoulder-bag, and for anything else that might establish the motive for her killing and help to identify her murderer.'

Harvey leaned forward in his chair, shaken: 'You can't think that I — '

'Why not? Let's suppose that you've been lying to us; let's

167

suppose that the picture has already been hived off through one of the dubious connections you made when you were working for Lovell and Delbos. Or that you have it hidden, waiting for the chance . . . If Hilda found out and threatened you . . .'

'But I've told you the absolute truth!' His voice broke and his features were contorted as though he might burst into tears.

Once again there was an interruption from Dixon; he stood in the doorway of the darkroom like a sentinel and, at a sign from Wycliffe, Kersey joined him. The darkroom door closed behind the two men.

Wycliffe and Harvey were left alone. Harvey waited, not trusting himself to speak. His hands were tightly clenched and there were little beads of sweat on his forehead.

When Wycliffe spoke he had changed the subject and his manner was almost conversational. He had discovered long since that abject fear in a suspect can arouse a latent sadism in the interrogator and he would have no part of it. Choose a new angle. 'Surely, Mr Harvey, you must know that a homosexual relationship between consenting adults is no longer an offence?'

Harvey looked up, startled.

Wycliffe went on: 'Hilda found out about your homosexual relationship. That's what the nude photograph meant, wasn't it?'

Harvey remained silent for a while, then he spoke in a low voice. 'Whatever I say — '

Wycliffe cut in: 'Whatever you say, providing it is the truth, is more likely to help you than otherwise.'

He began fiddling with the papers on his desk. 'All right, yes. She came to me one day with a photograph.' He nodded towards the darkroom. 'She must have found it in there, though God knows when; I never allow anyone to go in there . . .' His voice failed him.

'Was it the photograph I showed you just now?'

He shook his head. 'No, she let me keep the one she brought . . . She said it was the only one but, of course, she lied . . .'

Very quietly, Kersey slipped back into the room and took his seat.

'What, do you think, was her motive?'

Harvey made a vague, tired gesture. 'With Hilda it was always the same. She wanted to *know* . . . She wanted to know everything . . . She couldn't bear to think that people had secrets . . . She wasn't even interested, but if she suspected that anybody was trying to hide something from her she wouldn't rest until, one way or another, she'd found out what it was.'

A kind of petulance was giving him the strength. Wycliffe remembered Alice's words: 'In some ways Bertie is still a child himself.' And here he was complaining as a child complains of his playmate.

'And then? What did she do when she knew?'

He spread his hands. 'Nothing. She just let you know — that she knew. That was enough for her.'

'The photograph she returned, was it also of you?'

He did not answer.

'Perhaps of you, with your partner?' Wycliffe looked at Kersey and Kersey nodded. 'With Innes?'

Harvey flushed, and turned on Kersey in a sudden blaze of temper: 'Yes! You know, don't you? You've been in there gloating with the other one!'

Kersey said nothing and Wycliffe went on: 'The two of you spent some nights here?'

Harvey was still excited. 'Is it any of your business? You said yourself — '

Wycliffe became harsh: 'We are not investigating your sex life, Mr Harvey, but murder; the murder of a young girl for whom you pretended to feel affection. I will decide the questions you are asked and form my judgements according to your answers or your refusal to answer. So, do you spend nights here with Innes?'

He shook his head. 'When we have a night together, it's always in one of the empty vans.'

'What about Tuesday night? The night Hilda's body was pushed into the quarry pool? Your bed hadn't been slept in at five in the morning.'

Fear was returning, and his words were barely audible. 'I was in one of the vans.'

169

'Which?'

'B7 on the far side of the site.'

'With Innes?'

'No, Tristan wasn't with me. We had an arrangement but he wasn't able to keep it.'

'Did you leave the van during the night?'

'No, I did not!'

Wycliffe stood up. 'Very well. After he has finished here, Mr Kersey will ask you to allow his men to search your room at the house, and you will be invited to make a written statement concerning this interview.'

Harvey remained seated, staring at the disorderly array on his desk.

Wycliffe left Kersey and Dixon with Harvey. By arrangement, Lucy Lane was waiting for him in the car. The police radio babbled in staccato bursts.

'Scenes of crime?'

'All laid on, sir.'

Lucy Lane was driving; Wycliffe never did so if there was anyone else to do it for him.

They had to make the broad circuit by road, back through the caravan park, up the hill to the main road.

Wycliffe was silent, apparently morose, but Lucy Lane risked a question. 'Any progress with Bertie, sir?'

'He admits to knowledge of the one picture but to nothing else.'

'Has he involved Innes?'

'Only as his homosexual partner.'

'Oh! I see.' But she did not say what it was that she saw.

Another interval and she tried again: 'Hilda went to the doctor for a pregnancy test. We know that it was negative but she must have had a reason for going.'

'You mean there must have been a man and, if it wasn't the Martin boy, then who was it? I see what you're getting at but the fact that Innes and Harvey have a homosexual relationship doesn't exclude them.'

'No, I suppose not.' And with that she seemed content.

They turned off, down the lane past the Moyles' place. The wind had eased but it was still raining hard. Brown water seeped through the hedges from the fields, flooding the track so that their wheels swished through pools and bumped over hidden ruts. There was no fog, but the south-easterly wind bleached colour and definition from the landscape, propagating a universal, misty gloom.

Lucy Lane parked near the *deux chevaux*. For once the Innes front door was closed.

'Wait for me.' Wycliffe walked up to the front door and knocked. After a moment or two, it was opened by Innes himself.

There had been a subtle change in the man; he looked older and Wycliffe could have sworn that there were grey hairs where there had been none before. His manner had changed too, it was as though the veneer of scholarly urbanity had cracked, revealing a man who was unsure of himself, nervous — perhaps truly afraid.

'Mr Wycliffe . . .'

'One or two points have arisen which I would like to clear up with you and Mrs Innes.'

'Polly is in her studio; I'll fetch her.'

'Not for the moment. If we could talk somewhere in private first . . .'

Innes looked like a man who felt trapped but he made no objection. 'Very well; in here.'

Wycliffe followed him into a small room, obviously his study. The walls were book-lined and there was a desk by the window. On the desk there was a sheaf of lecture notes, heavily annotated in pencil, a carousel from a slide projector, and trays of slides. 'I'm lecturing in Truro on Tuesday to an arts society. One has constantly to revise one's material to present it at different levels . . .'

They sat down. Wycliffe said: 'I've just come from talking to Bertie Harvey, Mr Innes. I know that the two of you have a homosexual relationship. Once I am satisfied that it has nothing to do with either of the crimes under investigation it will be none of my business but, until then . . .'

'*Either* of the crimes, Mr Wycliffe?'

'The theft of two paintings by Pissarro, and the murder of Hilda Clemo.'

Innes's long white fingers beat a little tattoo on his desk. After reflection he said: 'I think you should know that my wife does not object to the relationship. It is not a source of emotional conflict between us.'

'Good!'

Innes looked at Wycliffe, perhaps to decide whether he was being ironic.

It was not lost on Wycliffe that Innes had chosen to talk about his homosexual relationship, rather than the paintings or Hilda Clemo.

'As I told you, Polly suffered her injury in a car accident. I did not tell you that I was driving the car at the time and that the accident was my fault.'

'Did this happen before or after your marriage?'

'Before. One might say that our marriage was a direct consequence of the accident.'

'You mean that it was some sort of accommodation?'

'It was natural that Polly should feel she had some claim on me.'

'I see.'

'In the event it has worked well. What is called a normal sexual relationship between us is not practicable or, from my point of view, desirable . . . Anyway, I am what Polly needs and wants, a caring, affectionate companion.'

'What you are telling me is that you were not sexually attracted to Hilda Clemo.'

'I'm saying that I have never been sexually attracted to women.'

'It is your wife who insists on sharing a bed?'

'Polly prefers it that way.'

The window of the little room looked out on a yard and, beyond, to the pine trees, now desolate against the rainswept sky.

'Does your wife go out alone?'

Innes looked surprised by the question but he answered

172

without hesitation. 'Not alone. She spends Sundays with her mother in Truro but I take her there in the morning and bring her back in the evening. Otherwise I am with her when she is away from home.'

'Did Hilda come here on Sundays?'

'She came here on different days. I've already told you, Mr Wycliffe — '

'Please answer the question.'

'All right, she sometimes came on Sunday afternoons; my wife knew this and had not the slightest objection.'

'Where were you on Tuesday night, Mr Innes?'

'Tuesday night?'

'The night Hilda's body was pushed into the quarry pool.'

'I was here — as usual.'

'It seems that your partner was expecting you.'

Innes studied his fingernails. 'I know. We had an arrangement but I couldn't keep it. Polly was upset and I couldn't leave her in the house alone.'

'So you did not leave the house that night?'

'No, I did not!'

When they stopped speaking Wycliffe was conscious of the silence which seemed to close in like some palpable fluid taking possession of a vacuum. He wondered if he had ever known another place where he had been so conscious of the silences as in this strange countryside between the moors and the sea.

Innes sat motionless and pale in the steely-grey light from the window.

'When you went to Exeter on Saturday, where did you stay?'

He seemed to rouse himself from a reverie. 'Near Exeter with a friend who works at the University.'

'What time did you arrive?'

'Half-past seven or a quarter to eight.'

'And you left here at . . .?'

'I told you, at about half-past five.'

'We can check your arrival time.'

'Why should I lie?'

'When Hilda visited you, was she in the habit of walking into the house without knocking?'

A puzzled look. 'We told her to do that.'

'You were talking to her when you were out with the dog at, as you say, "a little before five"?'

'Yes.'

'A witness who knew Hilda says he saw her go into this house at about five o'clock on Saturday afternoon. The door was open and she went in without knocking.'

A longish pause. 'I suppose she might have decided to look in on Polly while I was still out, got as far as the door, then changed her mind.'

'The witness says the dog came out to greet her; he also says that the *deux chevaux* was not in the drive.'

'Then he was mistaken.'

'When you left, where was your wife?'

'I left her working in the studio.'

Chapter Twelve

Friday morning (continued)

Polly Innes listened with all the concentration she could muster, but all she could hear was the rain on the windows. They must have gone into the drawing-room. No! Now he was alone, he would take the policeman into his study. *But what was he saying*? Her hands gripped the arms of her chair so that her knuckles showed white.

She couldn't work; she couldn't think. At first it seemed that she might come to terms with what had happened, there had been hours when she was able to lose herself in her painting. Now she had only to look at the canvas to know that it was useless to try.

She could not keep her eyes off the floor. It was becoming an obsession. Her studio had been built as a garden-room, with windows down one side and a slatted bench for plants. The floor consisted of uneven slabs of blue slate, strewn with rugs. In winter it was warmed by two large oil-stoves, one at each end.

She was still breathing hard from exertion. She had arranged the rugs, and rearranged them. She had reached down from her wheelchair, straining and tugging to get them into a position where they covered the stains — or where the stains had been, or where she thought the stains had been. She had manoeuvred her chair, she had held her head this way and that to catch every angle, every trick of the light. There were no stains.

There was a blank canvas on the easel, already primed; her painting table was laid out — colours, brushes, palette . . . She had set up an arrangement of Michaelmas daisies, grasses and bramble sprays, to be called *Autumn*. Now they were wilting.

'If only I could paint!' Instead she lay back in her chair, exhausted, staring out of the window at the grey emptiness of the sky and she felt vulnerable, flayed . . .

And the cycle was beginning again as it had done through the nights and days. At first it had been a memory, a recollection, but with each repetition it had become more and more of a living experience — vivid and intense.

'Oh, there you are, Polly!'

She had come in, casual, relaxed, with that supreme indolence of youth.

'Where's Tristan?'

She was wearing jeans and a sleeveless shirt with an absurd logo. At her armpit one could see the curve of her breast. Impudent!

'I wanted to see him . . . Sorry! Am I interrupting your work?'

Only words. She made no move to go; she had no intention of going until it suited her.

'There's something I wanted to tell him.'

As usual she stood, looking at the painting on the easel, damning it with her silence. As though she knew . . . As though she knew *anything*!

'I'd forgotten he was going away for the weekend.'

She was lying.

She sat on the little stool — a milking stool they had found in the house when they took it over. 'My stool' she called it. She sat with her back to the easel, staring out of the window, indifferent. Her hair shone like gold, spiralling away from the crown, a vortex, sinuous, gleaming.

'I'm pregnant, Polly.'

She had walked in and taken possession, treating the place as though it was her own.

'I thought he should know — you too. I haven't quite made up my mind what to do about it . . .'

It was like a target, the centre of the gold . . .

176

The blood seeped slowly through the gold — so very slowly. She had taken an age to fall.

'Why are you so anxious to convince me that you were here at the time you believe Hilda was attacked?'

Innes's gaze seemed fixed on the distant pines. 'I've been trying to tell the truth as I recall it.'

'No!'

'I beg your pardon?' A hackneyed response which came mechanically.

'You are lying. You did not meet Hilda on Saturday afternoon; you had already left by the time she reached here on her way home.'

Innes turned slowly to face Wycliffe. 'What could I possibly gain by lying?'

'You may think that you are shielding someone.'

Before Innes could react there was a crash and a muffled cry. Innes was on his feet in an instant and out of the room with Wycliffe at his heels. Innes pushed open a door at the end of a short passage and Wycliffe had a glimpse of a slate floor with rugs, of Polly's wheelchair on its side, and of Polly herself, clear of the chair, crumpled on the floor, one hand clutching at the corner of an orange rug.

Innes said: 'I knew that chair was unstable when she had it made! I've warned her . . .'

They lifted her, a light burden, and carried her along the passage to her bed. Her eyes were open and she followed their every movement but she did not speak.

Innes made consoling noises and asked her questions but did not press for answers.

Wycliffe said: 'I'll call the doctor.'

Innes looked at him but said nothing.

The bedroom was in the front of the house. Wycliffe went to the window from where he could see his parked car and Lucy Lane waiting. It was only a moment or two before she saw him and joined them in the bedroom.

Wycliffe spoke in a low voice. 'She's fallen out of her chair. I

177

want you to stay with her and note down anything she says. Don't leave Innes alone with her in any circumstances.'

He went to his car and contacted the Incident Room on the radio telephone. 'I want Dr Hosking at the Innes place. If he's out on his rounds, find him and get him here. And tell Sergeant Fox that we are ready for him. Also send a WPC for bedside surveillance and I shall need a couple of uniformed men.'

He sat in the car, waiting and brooding. Rain still billowed in from the sea, slanting out of the sky.

The girl.

It was four days since he had first heard of Hilda Clemo and during that time she had seldom been out of his waking thoughts. Now he knew who had struck the blow from which she had died, and he thought he understood the circumstances in which it had been struck. But who had really killed Hilda Clemo? Her death was part of a pattern which she herself had contrived.

One of her teachers had said: 'She can be very cruel.' Her sister, Alice, had said: 'She seems to treat people as though they were white mice or something . . .'

The white-mice image appealed to him; for them you contrive little hoops, ladders, tread-wheels and seesaws, then you sit back and watch their antics. Experimental, rather than cruel, and less emotional. But white mice are less likely to hit back than human beings.

He heard the police vehicles before he saw them, bouncing down the lane; the scenes-of-crime van and an unmarked police car. They pulled into the gravelled space in front of the house, now becoming congested. Fox got out, followed by his assistant; then, from the car, DC Potter, a WPC, and two uniformed PCs.

Fox came over to Wycliffe.

'Tell them to get back into their vehicles and wait, then come back here.'

When Fox joined him again Wycliffe gave him a briefing. 'The probability is that the crime took place in the studio and Franks thinks there must have been a fair amount of bleeding from the head wound. The floor there is of slate slabs with rugs. That's where you start. If you get a positive reaction to the benzidine

178

test, try to get some idea of the extent of the contamination, then hand over to forensic. Dr Drury will be arriving sometime this afternoon. Apart from that I want you to organize a search of the whole premises.'

'Looking for, sir?'

'Where the body was kept for four days, if not in the studio, the clothes the girl was wearing, the weapon — probably a small hammer normally kept in the studio — and anything which may link the premises with the crime. You can get going at once. I want a uniformed man at the gate and another at the house door. No press.'

The doctor arrived at that moment; the red-headed Hosking, in a battered Ford Escort which looked and sounded as though it was kept going by the sheer will power of its owner.

'What is it now?'

'Mrs Innes has turned over her chair.'

'Is she badly hurt?'

'She doesn't seem to be in any pain and she's conscious, but she either can't or won't speak.'

'Why "won't"? Why wouldn't she want to?'

'Perhaps because she is under police supervision.'

The little doctor stopped as they reached the shelter of the doorway and looked up at Wycliffe in astonishment. 'So that's the way the wind blows! What do you want from me?'

'Obviously that she should receive whatever medical attention she needs, in hospital if necessary.'

'And?'

'I want to know if and when in your opinion she is fit to be questioned.'

'All right! Where is she?'

To Wycliffe's surprise Innes did not stay with his wife while the doctor was with her; he joined Wycliffe in the passage. His manner was nervously aggressive. 'I want to know what is happening.'

They moved toward his study and Innes slumped into his chair as though he no longer had the strength to stand on his feet. His face was grey and a tic affected one side of his mouth. Wycliffe

179

remained standing, as though to underline the changed relationship.

'My men are already at work in the studio. They are looking for evidence that Hilda Clemo met her death there, and that her body was kept there, or elsewhere on these premises until the night of Tuesday/Wednesday, when it was taken to and dumped in the quarry pool.'

Innes turned his head as though about to speak but Wycliffe forestalled him. 'In the first place an examination will be made of the studio floor and of the rugs there. Tests will be made for bloodstains and if these are positive, further tests will be carried out to discover whether the blood is human — and so on. It is impossible on a floor like the one in the studio to remove all traces of a spillage of blood.'

'Why are you telling me this?'

'Because I want you to understand that if Hilda Clemo died here we shall find evidence of the fact. I think you have realized all along that once this house became the subject of an investigation, evidence would be found.'

Innes sat, motionless, staring down at his lecture notes which must now seem as relevant as a papyrus scroll; a man in the process of being cut off from his roots. Wycliffe had to remind himself of the photograph that had looked out at him from the case file on Monday morning, and of the pallid, nude body of the girl he had seen being fished out of the quarry pool on Wednesday.

'What do you want me to do?'

'Nothing for the moment. I will talk to you later, officially. In the meantime you can stay here or you can join your wife in the bedroom if you wish. You will not be allowed to leave the house.'

Wycliffe went into the studio where Fox and his assistant were at work. It was his first chance to take a look at the place. It was also the first time he had seen any of Polly Innes's work. There was not a lot of it; just half a dozen canvases propped against a wall. They were all flower studies; slick, professional — raw material for the printmaker; tailor-made for the walls of people who, reasonably, say they know nothing about art but know what they like.

Already Fox had made three or four chalk marks on the slate slabs and over the crevices between them. They were concentrated in an area not far from an easel which now carried a blank, but ready-primed canvas.

'I've made six tests so far, sir, and four of them have given positive results.' As he spoke, his head raised to see through the lower section of his bifocals, he was dripping benzidine sulphate on floor scrapings placed between filter-papers on a glass sheet. A brief pause, before adding a drop or two of hydrogen peroxide, and the result, almost immediately, was a streaky blue/green colouration.

'That's another positive. It seems to me, sir, that she must have lain here for some time after the blow that gave rise to the bleeding — long enough for it to spread some distance from the source.'

Wycliffe had said to Franks: 'So you think she was left to die,' and Franks had replied: 'That's the size of it.'

Time to bring in the experts. The benzidine test was a hoary old stand-by, easy to do, and reliable enough for blood in general, but non-specific. Although it was unlikely that the Inneses had indulged in orgies with rabbit or chicken blood, one had to be sure. In any case the experts would build up a picture in depth and they would be listened to in court if the occasion arose.

Dr Hosking pushed open the studio door. 'A word . . .'

Wycliffe joined him in the passage.

Hosking said: 'She's asking for you.'

'What did you make of her?'

'I don't know. Physically she seems to have done herself no harm, but I suspect that you're going to be lumbered with the trick cyclists. It's possible she's shrewd enough to be aiming for that.'

'Should she be in hospital?'

'Well, you can't put her in a cell, that's for sure; and I don't imagine you want to keep her here. For one thing the consultant gentlemen won't want to come out here, getting mud splashed all over their BMWs.'

'Will you fix it — hospital, I mean? There will have to be a WPC with her for the time at any rate.'

'I'll see what I can do.'

'Is she fit to make a statement?'

'I've told you she's asking for you. I can't say more than that.'

Polly Innes was lying in the middle of the big bed, making a scarcely discernible mound. Her tiny fingers grasped the edge of the bedclothes holding them so that they covered her mouth and nose; only her large dark eyes and her white forehead could be seen. The mass of her hair was spread over the pillow.

The WPC sitting by her got up as Wycliffe came in.

'No, stay where you are.' Wycliffe brought up a chair on the other side of the bed. The eyes watched his every movement.

'You asked to speak to me, Mrs Innes. I must tell you that you do not have to say anything but what you do say may be taken down in writing and given in evidence. Do you understand that?'

The eyes blinked assent.

The WPC looked her question and he nodded. She opened her notebook.

The woman in the bed lowered the bedclothes just enough to free her lips and, after an interval, she said in a surprisingly strong voice, full of venom: 'She hated me, you know! She wanted to take him away just to hurt me . . . She didn't want him; she didn't want anybody. She was ice-cold!' She turned her head to look at the WPC. 'Is she writing this down?'

'Yes.'

That seemed to please her and she turned back to Wycliffe. 'And he's as bad as her. He married me because it was his fault I'm what I am, and he persuaded me that he was homosexual — he said he couldn't cope with a woman . . . Well, I accepted that, I believed him; but as soon as . . . as soon as she came . . .' Her voice was choked by a dry sob.

Wycliffe said: 'I think you would do better, Mrs Innes, to wait until you are asked to make a statement.'

She was gazing at him with a fierce intensity and her voice was forced and harsh. 'I know it's all over for me now, and I don't

182

care, but somebody has got to listen!' She was holding her tightly clenched fists above the bedclothes and they were trembling. 'She came into my studio, asking for him . . . She sat with her back to me . . . "I'm pregnant, Polly . . . I thought he should know — you too. I haven't quite made up my mind what to do about it . . ."

'She was baiting me! That's what she had come for; she knew perfectly well that he was away . . . What she was really saying was: "This is something between Tristan and me. What do you matter? A cripple! There's nothing you can do about anything!" And she wasn't even pregnant! She was lying!'

The outburst relieved some of the tension, the wild look disappeared from her eyes and when she spoke her voice was subdued, reflective. 'So I hit her. I hit her with the little hammer I use for tacking up drapes . . .'

After another long pause she continued in the same quiet strain. 'I hit her . . .' Her right hand made small movements in the air which seemed to suggest the act. 'I didn't kill her. She didn't die for a long time . . . It was horrible! Her eyes wouldn't close and her mouth was open. She made terrible noises and there was blood . . .

'I couldn't stay in the room with her but all through that night I kept coming back and she still wouldn't die . . . I tried to help her.'

'To help her?'

'Yes. I gripped her throat, but I wasn't strong enough . . . I didn't go to bed that night . . .'

The rain had stopped and the skies were clearing. An ambulance arrived to take Polly Innes to the hospital and Innes came out to see her go. There was a strange moment as he stood looking down at her and she up at him. Neither spoke, there was no kiss, not even a touching of hands, they merely gazed at each other as though in mutual disbelief.

When the ambulance had gone Innes returned to his study and in a few minutes Wycliffe, with Lucy Lane, joined him. As they entered Innes turned his head but said nothing.

183

Wycliffe said: 'This is a formal interview, Mr Innes. I have to tell you that you do not have to say anything but that anything you do say may be taken down in writing and used in evidence.'

Wycliffe placed a chair close to the desk and sat down; Lucy Lane sat near the door, her notebook ready.

'We have evidence to show that Hilda Clemo met her death in this house. We believe that she was attacked by your wife in the studio on Saturday afternoon, after you had left for Exeter. The blow to the back of her skull was not immediately fatal but she was left on the studio floor to die.'

Wycliffe stopped speaking. Innes sat staring out of the window at his pine trees which stood out once more against a sunlit sky. He was quite motionless but a vein in his temple pulsed visibly.

'I think that you returned from your weekend, on Monday, to find Hilda's dead body where she had fallen and where she had lain for two days. How long she took to die is a question that may never be answered. I can understand that you suffered a profound shock. You set about removing the evidence in so far as this was possible but you were faced with the disposal of the body. As I said before, I am sure you realized from the start that your wife's security depended on avoiding any hint of suspicion, for once there was a forensic examination of the studio, evidence was certain to be found.'

The telephone on Innes's desk rang and startled them both. Innes turned, questioning, and Wycliffe nodded. It was some enquiry about a lecture and Innes cut it short. He replaced the telephone with a sigh. 'I'd forgotten there was a world outside.'

Those were the only words he had spoken so far.

Wycliffe was in no hurry to carry on and the silence lasted for a minute, or longer, but Innes gave no sign of impatience or distress. When Wycliffe did resume it was precisely where he had left off.

'There was a limit to how long you could keep the body in the house. It occurred to you that if it was found in the quarry pool — naked — there would be a strong presumption that she had died in consequence of a sexual assault and for that you had a ready-made suspect in Clifford Rule.

'But on Tuesday the Rules were taken in for questioning in connection with a separate offence and, though they returned home that evening, it seemed that they might be arrested at any time. So on Tuesday night — or in the early hours of Wednesday — you transported Hilda's body to the quarry and pushed it over the edge.'

Another prolonged silence was broken at last by Wycliffe: 'I have only one more thing to say to you. On Monday evening I came to talk to you and your wife. That afternoon you must have been working frantically to obliterate the gruesome evidence of your wife's crime. Presumably, by that time, you had shifted Hilda's body to somewhere less conspicuous than the studio floor. Yet despite all this you were able to convey an impression of a calm, cultured existence, only slightly ruffled by the unaccountable disappearance of a young girl whom you had taken under your academic wing. In my opinion that would only have been possible to someone devoid of compassion.'

Lucy Lane's notebook had remained blank throughout the interview, now she looked at Wycliffe in astonishment. Never before had she heard him speak of or to anyone in a tone of such contempt.

Innes gave no sign that he had heard; he turned to Wycliffe and asked in a tired voice: 'What happens to me now?'

'You will be taken to the nearest police station, you will be questioned further and given the opportunity to make a fresh statement about the events of Saturday and what followed.'

'Shall I be allowed bail?'

'You haven't been charged yet.'

'But if I am charged.'

'If you are charged you will probably be bailed to appear at a special court hearing tomorrow.'

By arrangement, Wycliffe and Kersey met in The Seiners shortly after one. Wycliffe was subdued, dispirited.

Kersey said: 'What are you going to have?'

'What? Oh, a sandwich and a glass of lager.'

Kersey went to the bar and came back with a plate of

sandwiches and the drinks. Wycliffe was at the little table by the window. The sun was bringing out the tourists and there was a continual passage through the narrow alleyway, to and from the harbour. Wycliffe was watching them as though they were part of a parade of strange animals.

Kersey made an effort to rouse him. 'Try the beef; plenty of horseradish — the real stuff.'

Wycliffe sipped his lager. 'Polly Innes is in hospital with a WPC at her bedside.'

Kersey nodded. 'I gathered that. Has she made a statement?'

'She rambled on in a highly emotional way for a bit but there's been nothing approaching a formal interrogation, and won't be until the medics say she's fit.'

'And Innes?'

Wycliffe was like a man half asleep; he seemed to need time to digest the simplest question or remark. Now he drank a little more of his beer before replying. 'Lucy Lane and Curnow have taken him to the nick for questioning. I don't think they'll have any trouble in getting a statement.'

Kersey pointed to the sandwiches. 'You're not eating.'

'How did the search go?'

'Clean. Not a thing to implicate Harvey in any deal. Certainly no picture.'

Wycliffe nodded. 'I'm not surprised.'

'You think he's already clear of it — or them?'

'No, I think we're probably looking in the wrong places. Anything else?'

'Our frogman has dredged up a pair of wheels from the quarry pool. They look as though they came from some sort of garden trolley but he can't say whether they were there when he was searching for the body.'

Wycliffe picked up a sandwich. Kersey said: 'That's crab.'

'It doesn't matter.'

There was something that Wycliffe was struggling to put into words, more to clarify his own ideas than for Kersey's benefit, but he spoke his thoughts aloud. 'The girl, Hilda — the victim — by deciding to lie about the result of her pregnancy test

186

accomplished her own death; in doing so she created a murderess, and an accomplice to murder.'

Kersey said: 'It's an odd way to look at it but I suppose it's true.'

They were interrupted by a great burst of laughter from the group around the bar, followed by some horseplay in which a glass was broken.

Wycliffe frowned, but carried on with what he was saying. 'She also changed radically the lives and prospects of others about her — her father, Alice, Esther, Harvey, Jane Rule, and Clifford . . . Think of all that our investigation into Hilda's death has uncovered, affecting these people. Doesn't it strike you as odd, how different the world would have seemed to them today if, between leaving the doctor's surgery and arriving home, last Saturday morning, Hilda had not made up her mind to lie?'

Kersey said: 'Pebbles in the pond, colliding ripples and all that, but I don't see where it leads.'

'In court it will be: A killed B in a fit of jealous rage. C was an accessory after the fact. So put A and C in jail. B has already been tidied away.'

'But how can it be otherwise?'

'I don't know, but it seems a simplistic way of dealing with such a web of relationships, don't you think? The classical Chinese had a theory that justice should attempt to restore the pattern.'

'Perhaps we should hand over to the sociologists.'

Wycliffe looked down at the sandwiches and at his half-empty glass. 'I think I'll settle for a coffee.'

Chapter Thirteen

Friday afternoon

At half-past two Wycliffe drove to the Innes place alone. As he turned off the road, past the Moyles', the scene was serenely peaceful under the afternoon sun: the line of blue sea, the pine trees, the grey slate roof of the Innes house and, beyond, the huddle of buildings that was Tregelles. The surface water had not had time to drain away and he bumped over the hidden ruts and potholes. A uniformed policeman stood at the gate and another by the open front door. The *deux chevaux* was flanked by a police patrol car on one side and the scenes-of-crime van on the other.

'Forensic not arrived yet?'

'Not yet, sir.'

'Press?'

'Haven't seen anything of them either, sir.'

Sergeant Fox came to greet him like a tail-wagging dog with his master's slippers. 'I think we've got this one sewn up, sir. It's extraordinary how people, supposed to be intelligent, can be so stupid when they move outside their own line. I've noticed before — '

Wycliffe cut him short. 'You've found something?'

'I'll show you.'

In the studio, spread out on a table, were several tagged polythene bags each containing a single item in the collection: a small claw-hammer, a grey shoulder-bag, and the various items of a girl's clothing.

Fox lifted the bag which contained a navy-blue sweat-shirt with a white logo. 'See that, sir? The back is caked with blood.'

Wycliffe, troubled, was curt: 'All right! Where did you find all this?'

'You'd scarcely believe it, sir, but the hammer was in that cupboard over there, with other tools; the clothing and the bag were tucked away under bedding in a chest of drawers.'

The contents of the shoulder-bag were displayed separately: a purse, with about five pounds in coins; a small packet of tissues; a few tablets of phenacetin in a tube, and a ball-point pen.

'No engagement book, diary . . . nothing of that sort?'

'No, sir.' Fox added: 'I'm expecting Dr Drury from Forensic at any minute, sir. I suppose you will be here?'

'I may not be. If I'm not, tell him I shall be back shortly.'

Wycliffe was in a strange mood; a mood in which relief was mingled with a consciousness of failure — perhaps not so much failure as inadequacy. Although he had just now been complaining to Kersey about what he called the ABC routine — the linear argument — really that was what criminal investigation was about, it was what he was paid for, to disentangle from the web that single strand which led from victim to culprit. He had tried to take in the whole pattern without success and the pattern was still incomplete.

He left the bungalow on foot and picked his way down the muddy lane towards the farm. With mild surprise he saw that nothing had changed. The hens still pecked between the cobbles and the rabbits still scuffled and thumped in their hutches. He realized with a slight shock that it was little more than twenty-four hours since his last visit.

The door was open and he called: 'Anybody at home?'

Jane Rule came to the door, a wooden spoon in her hand. 'Oh! You better come in.'

The kitchen was pervaded by the smell of stewing blackberries. A preserving pan simmered on the stove.

'Clifford picked some blackberries so I'm putting 'em down for jam.' She stirred the pan with her spoon then turned to face him again. 'Anyway, what do you want now?'

'So they finished the inventory.'

'They finished yesterday evening.'

189

'I know; and they didn't find the picture — the picture that was hanging over Agnes Rule's bed, the one you liked, which Hilda sketched, and Bertie Harvey was called in to inspect.'

She was looking at him with her grey expressionless eyes. 'I don't know what they found; they didn't tell me.'

'Where is it?'

'I don't know what you mean.'

Wycliffe did not raise his voice but there was no mistaking his mood. 'Mrs Rule, I can have men here within a few minutes. If I have to call them they will search every inch of space in this house; it won't be just another inventory. When they have finished in the house they will start on the outside buildings, and they will carry on until they find what they are looking for. When they do, you will be open to a charge — '

She had turned away, and was shifting the pan off the heat. 'I don't want it to boil . . . You better come upstairs.'

He followed her up the stairs to Agnes's bedroom.

'It's behind there.' She pointed to one of the paintings, a heavily varnished rustic scene: *Farmyard with cows and two figures.* 'I thought it would be safer.'

'Safer from whom?'

She shrugged her shoulders.

He lifted the heavy frame off the wall and turned it over on the floor. The Pissarro, still on its stretcher but without the frame, was protected by a sheet of polythene and secured behind the other canvas by a strip of lath, wedged into place. Wycliffe removed the painting and laid it on the bed, reflecting that never before had he handled an art treasure. At close quarters, without a frame, and lying on the bed obliquely lit, it was hard to take it seriously.

'I haven't done anybody any wrong. The frame is under the bed.'

'Does Harvey know the picture is here?'

She looked at him as though the question was a foolish one.

'You thought that even if Clemo laid claim to the stuff in the old dairy he wouldn't feel that he could take away what was actually in the house.'

190

The grey eyes met his, a blank stare.

'And after a while you could try your hand at finding a buyer.'

Saturday afternoon

The major part of the investigation was over. For days to come men would be engaged in supplementary enquiries; there would be weeks of paperwork and many hours spent with police lawyers thrashing out the case to be sent to the Public Prosecutor. But now Wycliffe was at home in his garden. It was hot, and he was sitting on a slatted seat under a cherry tree, sipping an ice-cold drink. The voices of his wife and daughter came to him from somewhere down amongst the rhododendrons. Macavity, the Wycliffe cat, was stalking birds which he would never catch.

James Clemo, Bertie Harvey, Jane Rule, Clifford, Tristan Innes, Polly Innes . . . and Hilda Clemo: all caught in a tangled web to which they had each contributed something. And it had been his job to sort it out.

He looked at his watch; it was five o'clock. One week ago Hilda Clemo had walked up to the Innes front door, the dog had come to greet her, and she had gone in without knocking . . .

ALSO BY W.J. BURLEY

WYCLIFFE AND THE THREE TOED PUSSY

The peace of the village of Kergwyns has been shattered by a bizarre murder. A young woman has been shot. The only things taken from the scene are the shoe and stocking from her left leg . . . exposing her deformed foot.

Wycliffe uncovers evidence of an unhappy woman who routinely manipulated the men in her life. As half the men in the village have been known to visit her, and most have reason to lie about it, finding the murderer will not be easy.

Wycliffe's task is complicated by the discovery of some clues in the form of crossword puzzles left by the victim herself. If Pussy knew she was going to die why did she make no effort to save herself?

Also by W.J. Burley

WYCLIFFE AND HOW TO KILL A CAT

The woman was young and slim, with auburn hair arranged on her pillow. When Superintendent Wycliffe saw her, he could almost believe she was asleep – that is, until he looked at her face. Although she had been killed by strangulation, someone had mutilated her face after she was dead.

As Wycliffe investigates, he finds more questions than answers. Why did a girl with expensive clothing and make-up end up in such a seedy hotel down by the docks? Why was there a thousand pounds hidden near her, beneath a pile of clothng? And why was someone apparently trying to hide her identity?

The more Wycliffe digs, the more he finds there are too many suspects, too many motives – and too many lies . . .

Also by W.J. Burley

WYCLIFFE AND THE GUILT EDGED ALIBI

A river divides the little West Country town of Treen into East and West, with a ferry linking the two. But it isn't just the river which divides the community when a body is discovered by the ferryman . . .

Beautiful Carline Bryce came from the top of the social scale, so when her body is discovered the rumour mill goes into overdrive. Who would want to kill her? Was it a family feud or a lovers' quarrel? A long-hidden resentment or a moment of rage?

As Superintendent Wycliffe picks his way through the clues, he is soon on the trail of a psychotic killer . . . who will not hesitate to strike again.

ALSO BY W.J. BURLEY

WYCLIFFE AND DEATH IN A SALUBRIOUS PLACE

There was no doubt at all that the girl was dead. The front of her skull and her facial bones had been splintered like the cracked shell of an egg. What made it even more shocking was the setting of the murder – an idyllic corner of the Scilly Isles where violent crime was almost unknown.

Angry and distressed, the villagers instinctively turn against the only stranger in their midst, the famous pop star and teenage idol Vince Peters.

But Superintendent Wycliffe is not so sure. Slowly, methodically, he begins to dig beneath the calm surface of the community – and soon uncovers a violent undercurrent of fear and guilt . . .

All Orion/Phoenix titles are available at your local bookshop or from the following address:

Mail Order Department
Littlehampton Book Services
FREEPOST BR535
Worthing, West Sussex, BN13 3BR
telephone 01903 828503, *facsimile* 01903 828802
e-mail MailOrders@lbsltd.co.uk
(Please ensure that you include full postal address details)

Payment can be made either by credit/debit card (Visa, Mastercard, Access and Switch accepted) or by sending a £ Sterling cheque or postal order made payable to *Littlehampton Book Services*.
DO NOT SEND CASH OR CURRENCY

Please add the following to cover postage and packing

UK and BFPO:
£1.50 for the first book, and 50p for each additional book to a maximum of £3.50

Overseas and Eire:
£2.50 for the first book plus £1.00 for the second book and 50p for each additional book ordered

---

BLOCK CAPITALS PLEASE

name of cardholder _____   *delivery address*
                     _____   *(if different from cardholder)*

address of cardholder _____   _____
                        _____   _____
                        _____   _____

              postcode _____   *postcode* _____

☐ I enclose my remittance for £_____

☐ please debit my Mastercard/Visa/Access/Switch (delete as appropriate)

card number ☐☐☐☐☐☐☐☐☐☐☐☐☐☐☐☐☐☐

expiry date ☐☐☐☐   Switch issue no. ☐☐

signature _____

prices and availability are subject to change without notice